DEADSPIN

DEADSPIN

GREGORY MICHAEL MACGREGOR

BANTAM BOOKS
New York   Toronto   London   Sydney   Auckland

DEADSPIN

A Bantam Book/November 1997

Library of Congress Cataloging-in-Publication Data

MacGregor, Gregory Michael.
Deadspin / by Gregory Michael MacGregor.
p.   cm.
ISBN 0-553-10584-1
I. Title.
PS3563.C36812D4   1997
813'.54—dc21   97-9119
CIP

Published simultaneously in the United States and Canada

Bantam Books are published by Bantam Books, a division of Bantam Doubleday Dell Publishing
Group, Inc. Its trademark, consisting of the words "Bantam Books" and the portrayal of a
rooster, is Registered in U.S. Patent and Trademark Office and in other countries. Marca
Registrada. Bantam Books, 1540 Broadway, New York, New York 10036.

PRINTED IN THE UNITED STATES OF AMERICA

BVG   10 9 8 7 6 5 4 3 2 1

In loving memory of my dad, our Chief,
and my personal "Max Devereaux,"
whose spirit inspired his five children to pursue
excellence in all things.

DEADSPIN

CHAPTER 1

LANG SQUINTED AGAINST THE MIDAFTERNOON SUN, releasing a drop of sweat from his brow into his eye. It stung and he reflexively flicked it away. Got to think and think clearly, he told himself. No use worrying now about how he got into this mess. His priority was to assess the situation correctly and quickly, and maximize his chances for getting out of this alive.

He felt the tree trunk against his spine and drew a deep breath to focus his concentration. The Castle, not visible through the woods, was some seventy-five yards directly behind him, twenty-five of dense forest and fifty of open, well-manicured lawn. To his left, maybe twenty yards through thick brush, he estimated that there were three of them. Well-schooled, they didn't speak, but their movement through the woods was not as stealthy as it might have been. More disconcerting was the fact that the last gunfire he had heard, maybe a minute ago now, had come from the right. That meant they had nearly completed a circle around him, methodically squeezing him toward the shooting gallery that was the Castle grounds. His training—and theirs, he remembered—told him that his situation would soon be hopeless. Outnumbered and surrounded, he would be relegated to taking one or two with him before they cut him down. His chances of getting back to the Castle were growing dimmer by the minute. He had to break the circle, and swiftly.

He checked his gun. Firing it only three times since the whole thing started, he had eliminated two pursuers. There were still four left. Ammunition would not be the problem; sheer numbers would.

Before moving—if he could hear them, it figured that they could hear him—he drew a mental route directly through the imaginary circle at its weakest point, where the underbrush was thinnest. Using the points in the circle where he had heard the movement and the gunfire as nine o'clock and three o'clock, he plotted a course through six o'clock, crouched on weary calves and burning quadriceps, then half-sprinted, half-duckwalked toward a small thicket of young Scotch pine. He drew his next breath only after he dropped to his stomach on the pine-needle carpet beneath the trees. If they had heard him, there was no indication yet.

He was sweating profusely in the sweltering humidity. The new fatigues clung to his chest and upper arms, his feet were soggy in the stiff black boots. Dust from the forest floor, which had seen no rain in weeks, had turned to mud on him. His face, under a day and a half's growth, was smeared and streaked. He concentrated on being still, silent, invisible, meticulously regulating his breathing.

The ground beneath the pines was becoming comfortable for a body unaccustomed to being hunted, when suddenly a boot appeared not two feet in front of his face. He flinched in anticipation of the shot to the back of his head. It didn't come. Given a split-second reprieve, he brought his gun up without moving his head and fired where he guessed the upper torso of his pursuer would be. The crack of the gun was followed by the snap of the missile hitting home, then the surprised gasp of his pursuer. The man's knees landed next to Lang's ear, while the rest of his six-foot frame brought down a new Scotch pine. Remholt, thought Lang. "Sorry," he whispered to the fallen enemy. Three down and three to go.

Movement to his left suggested that they had seen or heard his kill. Ahead of him on the other side of the thicket was a large gray rock, cloaked in the underbrush, that would serve well as a blind if he could get behind it without being shot. Never mind that his every movement now was *away* from his objective; he was resigned to the fact that his only hope was to eliminate all the hunters and then worry about getting to the Castle. He was reasonably sure the remaining three would be in front of him once he got behind the rock. Slowly, quietly, he inched, snakelike, toward the rock. He was vaguely aware, off in the distant valley below, of the call of a great Canadian goose. Abruptly there was a gunshot behind him, followed instantly by a small explosion in the pine needles beside his right cheek. Instinctively, he rolled away from the impact, onto his back, and fired upward at about a forty-five degree angle. Looking into the sun as it filtered through the branches, he could see nothing. He fired again, into what he thought was a silhouette. "Aaahh!" came the scream of anguish as the fourth pursuer was eliminated. Lang didn't wait for him to fall, but scrambled behind the rock.

Now, thought Lang, he was getting on top of the situation. With only two hunters left and the rock between him and them, he felt, for the first time, that the odds had begun to shift. He drew a deep breath to collect his thoughts. Over a small notch in the top of the rock he had an unimpeded view of the forest for nearly twenty feet in front of him. Behind him, however . . . a sudden crack sounded as one of the others broke a dried twig. He whirled around to see what was happening and looked directly into the gun barrel held by Blades, the tall one with the odd teardrop-shaped scar on his cheek. Before he could react, Blades, smiling triumphantly, fired twice, striking Lang in the throat and the chest. Shocked, Lang looked down in amazement to see the deep crimson liquid released by Blades ooze down his neck and saturate his fatigues. After a moment, still stinging from the impact, he noticed that the fluid had an oddly iridescent quality to it. He had heard about this but hadn't expected to see it so vividly himself.

"Dead meat, Lang." Blades laughed.

"End of the game," added Ohlmeyer, the other survivor, as he came around the rock.

From a little distance away, Remholt called, "Did you guys nail that son of a bitch?"

"Not before I blew your ass away, Rembo," shouted Lang, rising to his feet. Then to Blades, "That stings."

"I wouldn't know," said Blades, shouldering his gun. Lang raised his own and fired twice into Blades's midsection.

"Hey!" Blades shouted in protest, "you can't do that after you're hit!"

"So sue me," replied Lang.

"Asshole," muttered Blades as he surveyed the damage to his new fatigues caused by Lang's aquamarine-colored paint pellets. Ohlmeyer fingered a silver whistle hung around his neck. "Ready to phone this one in?" he asked. Two or three of the others agreed and Ohlmeyer blew two long blasts on the whistle. With that all the players started back to the staging area on the west side of the Castle.

The MacNaughton Family Castle sat atop Afton Mountain, at the crest of the Blue Ridge Mountains, where the Blue Ridge Parkway meets the Skyline Drive. According to local history, the massive medieval structure was dismantled, stone by stone, in its native northern Scotland, shipped by the MacNaughton Steel family to the mountains of central Virginia, and there laboriously reassembled. Surrounded by a huge field of carefully tended lawns resting just over the mountain's eastern shoulder, it commanded a spectacular view of the vast green valley east of the Blue Ridge. The sprawling estate on which it sat also encompassed thick virgin forests of magnificent silver maple, mountain ash, birch, and Scotch pine, mixed in with lush mountain laurels and azaleas. In spring and fall the natural beauty of the spot was overpowering. Even now, in early summer, it was a truly arresting sight.

Christopher Lang downshifted the rented red Mustang GT as he climbed the switchback that led to the Castle. In mid-June there was still sunlight washing over the top of the mountain, though the cocktail hour was well under way. It warmed the old gray building, giving it an open, friendly glow that it probably never enjoyed while sheltering its lords and ladies in its native Scotland.

Since finishing the war game—a lot more fun than he'd thought it would be—Lang had returned to his room at the Boar's Head Inn, showered, placed four calls, and reviewed the deposition transcript of an expert witness he would cross-examine next week in Los Angeles. The three calls to witnesses had gone well; all were thoroughly prepared for trial.

The fourth call had not gone so well. After the predictable but vitally important mini-conversations with each of his three children—three daily reports, three problems of the day, three pretty good solutions of the day, and three awful jokes of the day—he had spoken with Ro. Three years ago, when she had announced that their lives had grown irredeemably apart, one of his few lucid thoughts had been that, at least, the incessant fighting would stop.

The fights had never seemed to be about anything, certainly never anything important, and yet the sense that damage was being done, accumulated, was undeniable. But the fighting, it turned out, had merely been postponed. The divorce had been civilized enough; it wasn't in their nature to air private differences in public, and the one thing each of them had always conceded the other was an unwavering devotion to their children. The process had unfolded with an unnatural civility, the better to shield the children from the trauma. The artificiality of that time had since given way to a relentless procession of disputes involving everything and nothing at all. It was as if, denied the release of telling Lang loudly and publicly to go straight to hell with his career, his ambition, his preoccupation with perfection, Ro was determined to have the proper measure of satisfaction extracted not by sword, but by pinprick. And the more she seemed committed to doing so, the greater was Lang's willingness to wade into the melee with her. It had become a chronic source of aggravation for them both and, ironically enough, well after the divorce, had begun to take its toll on the kids.

A familiar parade of thoughts marched through Lang's mind as he labored his way up the winding road: We've got to sit down and talk this thing out once and for all, find a way out of the destructiveness at work here; but that will have to wait until I can focus, until the *Severstone* and *Fulton* trials are wrapped up; no, that's not a good idea, because not long ago it was wait until after the institute presentation, before that the *Calder* trial and the *Peterson* investigation; is there something going on with my priorities? Am I avoiding the confrontation because I can't win it, or am I really so shackled to my job that I can consistently justify postponing my greater responsibilities? But that can't be entirely true because I'm a good father, not all that available to them, but I know the value of quality time. . . . As always the circle raced around itself too fast, closed too tight, and finished with a deafening ringing inside his head.

The narrow road shrank to a single ten-foot lane of blacktop as it reached the Castle's massive stone entrance. Inside the estate the driveway split into a large circle, designed for one-way traffic. Lang swung the Mustang to the right and climbed the gentle slope for nearly a quarter mile toward the imposing Castle. In front of the main entrance a valet took the car and Lang, in his perfectly tailored tuxedo, bounded up the steps into the Great Hall.

The Great Hall and the Banquet Room adjacent to it overflowed with lawyers and judges from all over the country. The Uni-

versity of Virginia School of Law's annual Trial and Appellate
Advocacy Institute had grown in prominence each year and was
now regarded as one of the most prestigious professional events of
the year, attracting the best and best-known in the legal profession.
As a graduate of the law school, Lang had long aspired to participate. Now, two weeks shy of his forty-seventh birthday, he was
about to accept the award for delivering the week's most telling
closing argument from the hands of the chief justice of the United
States.

On his way to the bar, at least a dozen people stopped him to
offer congratulations on his closing argument. He thanked each in
turn, surprised at the reaction he was getting from total strangers.
Taking his vodka tonic from the bartender in the corner of the Great
Hall, it struck Lang that there was an important message in the fact
that he could formulate, polish, and deliver an hour-long, emotionally charged yet logical summation in a purely hypothetical case he
had had virtually no time to master, but could not bring sufficient
time, reason, and sensitivity to his own marriage to have saved it.
Unfortunately, he had little clue as to what that message was.

"Chris! Chris Lang!" Lang turned to the sea of black jackets
and white shirts punctuated by a spray of evening gowns in the latest
summer hues. "Lang!" A tall, slightly gangly figure in black and
white emerged from the crowd under the brooding MacNaughton
tartan that draped the far wall. As he approached, Lang finally recognized the man.

"Jad? Jad Piersall? My God! You haven't changed a bit!"

Jared "Jad" Piersall reached Lang, right hand extended. "It
hasn't really been that long, has it, Chris?" Piersall said as they
shook hands.

"Maybe fifteen or twenty years isn't long to a man of your age,
Mr. Piersall," Lang replied, "but to a youth like me, it's been a
lifetime."

Piersall smiled at Lang's modest attempt at humor. He was five
or six years older than Lang, having been part of that sizable contin-
gent of the class who had served in the military between college and
law school. This evening, however, standing in the dusky light with
a scotch in his left hand, he looked tired and drawn, much older
than Lang knew him to be.

"Have you been here all week?" asked Lang.

"Unfortunately not. I just popped down from D.C. this afternoon," Piersall replied, taking a good pull from his drink. "I understand I missed all the good stuff."

"If you mean the war games this afternoon, we had a lot of fun."

Piersall shook his head. "No, not that. I mean the summation from hell you delivered yesterday. It's all anybody's talked about since I walked in. I always knew you had quite a bit of the evangelist in you."

Lang reddened slightly. "Oh, that. Well, thanks. It was a juicy hypothetical that cried out for some drama. I really couldn't resist."

"Well, I hear you blew the other guys away," Piersall said, with more than a little pride. "Not surprising, though. I understand you were the only UVA man in the contest. To me, that doesn't sound like a contest."

"Don't tell that to the chief justice. He's Stanford."

"Hell, Chris, I heard he all but applauded when you finished," said Piersall.

"I don't know about that," Lang replied. "But he did seem a lot more impressed than he did when I argued the *Riverside County* case before him in real life."

"I read about that," said Piersall, turning back to the room and surveying the crowd. "At least Sandra Day O'Connor liked you in the *Riverside* appeal. Your arguments ended up in the best dissenting opinion she's written yet." As he polished off his drink, the lights in the massive chandelier dimmed twice. "Time to eat. Mind if I join you?" he asked.

"That would be great. I'm meeting a couple of people. Do you remember Laura Carey and Phil Demarco?"

"Laura Carey?" A smile broke across Piersall's face. "Laura, I remember. Not Phil, though. But I'd like to meet him."

"Good." Lang smiled, too, at the idea that anyone could have forgotten Laura Carey.

"Hang on for a second while I grab a refill," Piersall said. He stepped over to the bar and ordered. While waiting, Lang scanned the crowd as it moved toward the Banquet Room. He caught sight of Laura and Phil heading into the dining room and gestured that he would meet them inside. He reflected back on what he knew about Piersall from law school. They hadn't been that close. Both were Ivy League undergrads, but Piersall was part of a small group of Yalies who believed in a hierarchy of excellence in which Yale men from the right families occupied the top rung and a guy from a middle-class Midwestern family who had been tickled just to get into Dartmouth ranked considerably lower. Like most of the guys in the class, Piersall had arrived in Charlottesville a ready reveler, a frequent and raucous visitor to the beer-stained mansions of Fraternity Row. But Piersall's outlook had taken a sudden, tragic turn at the beginning of their third year. His older brother, an Air Force captain, had been shot down and lost over North Vietnam, one of the last casualties of the war. Details had been sketchy and the rumors around the school had him flying some sort of covert operation. The change in Piersall was dramatic. The garrulous partygoer turned sullen and withdrawn, his face and demeanor permanently transformed by an angry seriousness. He became deeply involved in a militant local Vietnam veterans' group and distanced himself from most of his friends. The last thing Lang remembered about Piersall was that he had turned down a promising Wall Street job and gone *back* into the service after graduation.

Piersall returned and they fell in with the crowd drifting into the Banquet Room. "So, Jad, what's been keeping you busy all these years?"

"I did a stretch at Sheehan and Johnson. A few years that felt like a lot more. Then I hooked up with Bell, Bolton, and Verhoeven. Been there for twelve years. It's a small shop."

"What kind of work do you do?"

"Government work, mostly. Various agencies."

"Contracts, or what?" Lang asked, a little absently. He really wasn't focused on what Piersall was saying, caught up instead in studying his face, trying to discern which of the two Piersall personalities that he had observed in law school had survived.

"Some," Piersall answered vaguely, gulping again from his scotch. "Other things, too."

Sensing Piersall's reluctance, Lang changed topics. "If I remember my alumni update correctly, you got married since I last saw you."

"Five years ago," said Piersall, nodding. "The amazing Susan Dahlquist. She's a lawyer with the FCC."

"Is she here?" asked Lang.

"No, she's traveling. Business in Canada. British Columbia." He checked his watch. "Probably just finishing lunch at Whistler Mountain," said Piersall wistfully. Lang couldn't tell if it was because he missed her, or envied her.

They found their table and renewed old acquaintances. As usual, Laura's striking good looks, tireless effervescence, and musical Texas accent dominated the gathering. After the salads were served, Piersall turned to Lang. "How's Ro?" he asked.

Lang hesitated. He noticed Laura shift almost imperceptibly in her chair. "Looks like you've kept up with my career better than my family life. We split up."

"Oh, I know that," said Piersall matter-of-factly. "But you see her, don't you? I mean, with the kids . . ."

Lang was slightly taken aback. "Sure, sure, I see her," he managed to respond. "I guess she's doing okay. She's a good person. But let's put it this way: I imagine she does better when I'm not around."

The speeches were stuffy but brief, with the chief justice the stuffiest and least brief. Lang accepted his award to warm applause and spoke only for a moment, drawing unexpectedly hearty laughter for his remark, "It seems entirely backward to receive an award for giving a speech. Perhaps it would be more fitting if I thanked you by making a movie."

As they filed out of the Castle, Piersall cornered Lang. "I just had a thought. I don't know why it didn't come to me before." He looked around quickly at the others who were moving toward the front entrance. "This will only take a minute."

Piersall maneuvered Lang into a corner of the Great Hall, under the billowing MacNaughton tartan, largely out of earshot of anyone else. "Have you done any aviation law?"

Lang thought for a moment. "Disasters? Design defects? That sort of thing?" A prodigiously busy trial lawyer, Lang had never lost his taste for new and interesting challenges. Besides, as Devereaux and Brace's senior litigator he was expected to produce a lot of new business.

"Not exactly. We have a client, an English company, that thinks it has a claim on an experimental airplane designed out in California. I haven't really looked into it but one of my partners thinks they may have something," said Piersall. "On the surface it appears to be a good breach of contract claim. I'd like to have them sit down with you and find out what you think."

"I don't see why not. But, I've never handled a technical aviation lawsuit," said Lang, somewhat apologetically.

"Maybe not," replied Piersall. "But you're the best damned trial lawyer I know, and I don't think there's a case you can't try and win."

"I appreciate your confidence—"

"It's just a statement of fact," Piersall said, more than a hint of the old steeliness in his voice. Lang realized that Piersall, despite belt after belt of hard liquor, was chillingly sober. "Look, Chris," he said, the warmth returning as quickly as it had fled. "I've got to get back tonight. My client will call you." He started for the door, where the crowd had thinned considerably.

"Fine, Jad," said Lang, thrown off balance by the sudden fluctuations in Piersall. "Who's going to call?"

They were outside and Piersall had handed his claim check to the valet. "Clive Andrews of Pegasus Technologies," he answered. His car, a large maroon Mercedes, was deposited at the curb. Lang walked him to the driver's side.

"And just for the record," Lang said, "who is the defendant in this aviation case?"

As he climbed in, Piersall said, over his shoulder, "Ah, but that's the best part. None other than Arrow Dynamics." He closed the door and opened his window.

Lang exhaled audibly. "Oh, really?" he mused aloud. "The big leagues, eh?"

"Don't get any bigger, Chris," Piersall said. "But you're the big leagues, too. For that matter, so is Arrow's lawyer, Gentry Hickman. I see it as a 'clash of the titans.' Got to run. Keep in touch." Lang watched him drive off.

Arrow Dynamics meant one thing and one thing only, thought Lang: Russell Lindstrom. It was the first of his many successful companies and, though he had little to do with it anymore, the public would always associate it with the giant swashbuckling businessman who created it. Lang's mind swarmed with the possibilities as he watched Piersall's red taillights grow smaller in the night. The prospect of a career-maker of a lawsuit suddenly loomed before him.

Laura Carey walked up behind him. "Don't you be a stranger, now, Chris," she said warmly. As Lang turned around, she presented her cheek for him to kiss. He did so, but without conviction. She looked past him, down the drive. "Jad Piersall seems to be doing okay, don't you think?"

"I guess," he replied with a shrug. "Still a little odd, I think."

"Who wouldn't be?" She hesitated, watching Lang's face in the darkness. Over the years she had grown familiar with his moodiness and the intensity from which it sprang. It never failed to sting her, however, when he turned inward, shutting her out.

He seemed to sense her thoughts. "Would you like to find some place in town for a cup of coffee or a nightcap? Poe's is gone but I'm sure there must be a Starbucks near the grounds."

She smiled. "Love to, darlin', but I've got an early flight back to Houston. Thanks just the same." They embraced. She regarded him with concern. "You okay, Christopher?"

"Yeah, Laura. I'm fine. Just a little distracted." Their cars were delivered. "Good night. Have a safe trip back and I'll call you next week."

"Good." She squeezed his hand. "And make your next trip to Houston real soon, okay?"

He smiled. They got into their rented cars and drove off into the balmy Virginia night.

CHAPTER 2

THE HONORABLE CARLOS ESPINOSA, A HANDSOME man, graying at fifty-seven, peered down over his reading glasses at the two lawyers standing at counsel table. The suddenly silent courtroom still rang from the echo of their heated exchange. The judge was clearly turning the matter over in his mind. A normally decisive man known for reaching quick, if often erroneous, judgments, he had just heard nearly three-quarters of an hour's argument from two powerhouse advocates. At last, he spoke.

"I'm sorry, Mr. Phelps, but I find Mr. Lang persuasive on this point. And I must admit, that's a little surprising even to me."

Lang couldn't resist the slightest of smiles. Espinosa was notorious for sticking to his tentative rulings on motion matters, even in the face of compelling arguments. To have turned him around against no less an adversary than Aubrey Phelps was nothing short of remarkable. Out of the corner of his eye, he could see—and maybe feel—that Phelps's red face was glowing with suppressed rage.

Judge Espinosa had risen to leave the bench. He chuckled

good-naturedly. "Don't rest on your laurels, Mr. Lang. It's early in this war to start counting your winnings."

Lang's smile broadened just enough to acknowledge the gentle chiding. "Warfare it is, Your Honor," he responded. "I understand all too well."

The judge disappeared into his chambers. Phelps flipped his briefcase shut and wordlessly left the courtroom. As always. Lang put his papers in order, his smile opening into a small chuckle. The evidence he would now be able to exclude in his upcoming trial would virtually eliminate the risk of massive punitive damages against his insurance-carrier client. There would be rejoicing this evening back in East Lansing. Suddenly, a voice called to him from behind.

Lang turned to see two men standing directly behind the railing that separated the counsel table from the gallery.

"Mr. Lang, I'm Graham Ellerby and this is Clive Andrews," said the taller of the two, extending his right hand. His accent sounded more Scottish than English. "We thoroughly enjoyed watching you work."

"Thank you, Mr. Ellerby. Mr. Andrews," Lang said, shaking their hands. "It's only a status conference but we had some points to score."

"Well, you seemed to do that, all right," Ellerby said. "I hope you don't mind our coming to see you in court unannounced."

"Not at all," replied Lang, hefting his oversized litigation bag. "I've been expecting a call from you since I spoke with Jad Piersall in Virginia."

"Ah, then you know who we are," said Andrews. This time Lang was sure the speaker was English.

"Well, not really. Jad didn't tell me much about you, but I recognized your name. Other than that, all I know is that you may have a bone to pick with one of Russell Lindstrom's companies."

"Does that bother you?" asked Ellerby.

"Bother me?"

"Well, we all know how powerful and mysterious Mr. Lindstrom is," Ellerby explained.

"Mr. Ellerby," said Lang evenly, "I don't know what Jad told you about me, but I try cases. Some against big companies, some against governments. If the case is interesting and the client's got a position I can defend, I put everything I have into it. And I really don't give a damn who's on the other side."

Ellerby and Andrews exchanged looks. "Right," said Ellerby. "Where and when can we talk?"

"I've got some time now," Lang lied, checking his watch. It was already five-fifteen and he had nearly four hours of work planned for the evening. "Can I treat you to some of Uncle Sam's coffee?"

"Fine," said Andrews, a little dubiously. Perhaps he'd sampled the coffee here before, thought Lang.

Two hours later, Lang climbed into his Porsche Carrera 911 and punched the speed dial for the office on the cellular phone. His secretary answered the line as if it were the middle of the workday.

"Hi, Alex," he said, uncradling the handset and giving up on the hands-free feature as a concession to the combination of freeway noise and the scream of the Porsche. After an update of the calls he'd missed, he laid out the plan for the evening. An unfortunate young associate would be working on a second draft of a critical document late into the night. He looked at his watch. "And, Alex, tell Rick we'll have to go over his brief. Have him meet me in the thirty-fifth-floor conference room at nine o'clock."

"Tomorrow morning?" asked Alex.

Lang laughed. "Nice try. That's P.M., as in tonight. Is Amy still there?"

"I doubt it, Chris. She said something about Hollywood Bowl tickets with her husband. But I'll check." He was placed on hold. While he waited, Lang reflected on his meeting with the Pegasus people. He had taken an immediate liking to Graham Ellerby. The Scotsman was warm and charming, and a fountain of information he was intent on sharing. Time would tell as to Clive Andrews, the cooler, more reserved partner. But both were people he could work with, fight for.

And what a fight. They had bought the rights to an experimental airplane, a genuine Russell Lindstrom design, built and tested by the man himself. And it didn't fly. "Fell out of the bloody sky," Andrews had said. "Like a flipping seed pod." Somebody didn't do the tests right. Or missed something.

Alex was back. "She's gone, about twenty minutes ago. But she said you could reach her for a while on the cell phone."

Lang said good-bye and punched in Amy Quinn's number.

"Hello," said a tinny female voice, followed by the sound of the handset falling to the floor, then after a moment, "Hello?"

"Good hands, Amy." Lang laughed.

"Hello to you, too, Chris," she answered.

"Where are you?"

"Hollywood Freeway, in the traffic pattern for the Bowl. You're not going to make me come back, are you? Did those bastards in *Severstone* give *ex parte* notice or something?" There was a touch of panic in her voice, suffused with violent anger. Lang loved litigators.

"Nothing like that. And no, you don't have to come back until tomorrow. I wouldn't do that to Bill. I just had an impromptu meeting with two guys from Pegasus Technologies."

"Shit, Chris!" More anger. "You told me that was going to be my case. Why did you meet them without me?"

"Couldn't be helped. They ambushed me at the *Fulton* status conference. Don't worry. You're the associate on the case. I've got some fascinating background on it, though."

"Tell me—quick. I'm in the parking lot and I see Bill's 'Vette."

"The airplane was a genuine Lindstrom design—drawn, built from the ground up, and tested by the old man himself."

"No way. He doesn't do that himself. Hold on. I've got to get Bill's attention." Weeks earlier, when Lang had first returned to his office from Virginia, he had asked Amy, his best young associate, to research Russell Lindstrom thoroughly. She had read no fewer than 126 articles and press releases on the Internet spanning thirty years in the life of the celebrated and very private Lindstrom. The picture that emerged was a cross between Renaissance man and Superman: a general among captains of industry who had climbed to international prominence as an innovative designer of secret military aircraft, then suddenly, at the pinnacle of his success, had turned on the "military-industrial complex" and moved decisively into information, environmentally sensitive energy alternatives, and economics. Hardly an article or release had failed to include a reference to the fact that Lindstrom had handed Arrow Dynamics off to his underlings in the late 1960s and had gone into these other areas of endeavor. Nothing in any of the articles suggested that Lindstrom ever had tested any aircraft himself.

Amy was back on the line. Lang said, "Anyway, Andrews and his partner are pretty sure Lindstrom did it and they seem savvy enough."

"Don't they *know*? Didn't Arrow Dynamics build the prototype for them?"

"No. They bought the company with the rights to the plane in place. And get this: They bought the company from the estate of Nigel Daultry."

"Nigel who?"

"Nigel Daultry. Ever hear of Daultry Motor Car? Daultry-Philips-Grindelwald? The man who invented zero-emissions passenger-car engines?"

"Can't place him," replied Amy.

Lang kept trying. "The America's Cup? You know, the yacht race a while back in Hawaii?"

"I know what the American Cup is," replied an indignant Amy, out of the car now and headed up the hill toward her husband.

Lang shook his head. "*America's,* not American. Anyway, he's the guy from New Zealand who caused all that fuss—"

"The road race in Italy!" shouted Amy. "I remember now. Wasn't he killed in a crash?"

"Very good, Amy. I'm impressed. It was in the Italian Grand Prix in Milan a few years back. Anyway, it was his company that hired Lindstrom's company to design this airplane. The whole project was already done when the Pegasus Technologies guys bought the company. Then they hired some aviation people, took the plans, the prototype, and the test report, and built the first production model. Then, guess what?" He paused. She listened. "The son of a bitch fell out of the sky."

"Crashed?" Lang heard Bill's voice say hello. Amy continued. "No shit, it really crashed?"

"No. No crash. The test pilot who flew it for them was a real pro and he got it under control, but only after eight revolutions. They claim they have a real stomach pump of a videotape, from two angles."

"That sounds like pretty graphic jury material," she replied. "Bill says hello, by the way."

"Tell him hi for me. Just one last thing. After the production plane went into a flat spin, they told Arrow about it and Arrow tried to fix it. But they couldn't. Six months of intensive testing and refitting and they couldn't get it to stay up in the sky."

"Something doesn't sound right," Amy said.

"I know. Well, there's a hell of a lot more, but I'll tell you tomorrow. How's eight sharp?"

"Just great," Amy answered. "Maybe I'll just head there straight from the concert."

"Okay. Eight-thirty."

. . .

An ancient eight-millimeter film, aging poorly, flickered on the warped and cracked movie screen in the darkened room. The images, in smeary bluish tones, blurred and jerked across the screen. The only sound in the room was the clicking of the projector and the roar of the fan that kept the lightbulb from overheating.

Up on the screen, an unmarked troop carrier, a bulky forerunner of the C-130, dropped precariously from the sky above a remote landing strip, hung awkwardly for a moment, then fell to a hard, graceless landing. Dust rose beneath its wheels against the afternoon sky and a low range of mountains thick with foliage. As the airplane taxied toward the camera, a half dozen or so men, bare-chested caucasians in military-fatigue trousers, scurried from the foreground to meet it.

After an abrupt and amateurish cut, the film resumed, now shot from closer to the plane, off its port side, the image still blurred and indistinct. The door under the wing was now open and more men in fatigues were scrambling out onto the hard-packed dirt of the runway. A tall figure, with blond or maybe gray hair, appeared in the doorway. The distance and the condition of the film made it impossible to identify him. The projector stopped and froze the murky image on the screen.

Jad Piersall, his left hand on the freeze-frame dial of the Bell and Howell and his right cradling a cold drink, sat transfixed before the frozen image. At length, he mumbled, "Dien Bien fucking Phu. You know it and I know it." He threw back the rest of his drink and poured another. The telephone rang. Tossing in a couple of ice cubes, he answered, "Yeah?"

"Do I hear a government-issue eight-millimeter projector in the background?" asked the voice at the other end.

"Hey! Colonel!" he answered, forcing brightness into a voice heavy with drink. "Yeah. I'm watching it. Again."

"Wallowing in frustration never got anybody anywhere, Jad," replied the other man.

"I realize that, Shep. It's just so goddamned clear to me," Piersall responded, biting off the last few words. "It's obviously Lindstrom. In the North. Summertime. July, maybe August. Has to be '72, '73 at the latest. I know that airstrip. Hell, it wasn't even there before '71. You've seen the recon photos. And you know as well as I do that the radar deflector is right there in the troop carrier. And *I* know that's how they tracked Robbie's jet."

"I guess if we could prove all that, Lindstrom would be history and we wouldn't need the sideshow. But you of all people should know where we stand without proof. The day Barlow was killed was the day his film and all the other things in his locker became worthless. Anything based on it is no more than pure speculation. Even the part about the radar deflector. And your brother."

"But come on, Colonel. Why else would he be there, with mercenaries, on enemy ground, at the end of the war?" Out of a rising alcoholic fog, he was becoming belligerent.

"We don't *know* they're mercenaries," Colonel Easley gently chided. "It's a logical deduction from what we can see, but we can't prove it. Which brings us to Plan B. How do our prospects look there?"

Piersall squirmed slightly in his chair. "I'm not sure. Probably pissing up a rope but that might be the only way to get close to him without his guard getting in the way. Anyway, I think we have the right man there."

"That's a start, Jad."

"I sure as hell hope so. One of these days it's going to be too late."

A muted bell rang and the highly polished brass elevator doors opened with a whisper. A willowy brunette stepped out, wearing a taupe silk suit and carrying an oversized leather portfolio under her arm. The brass-and-granite logo on the far wall announced that she had reached the penthouse headquarters of Beau Rivage Limited. Her four-inch heels clacked authoritatively as she strode over the marble of the richly appointed lobby toward the receptionist. Even in an office accustomed to beautiful women fashionably dressed, more than one set of eyes followed her to the center of the room.

"Good morning, Ms. Lang," said the strawberry-blond receptionist, her huge blue eyes underscored by her magazine-cover smile. "Welcome to Seattle. Did you have a nice flight?"

"Very nice, thank you, Susanne," the woman replied cheerily as she shifted the portfolio to the other arm. "I have a ten o'clock meeting with Mr. Stingley."

"I know. I'll let them know you're here." The receptionist beamed once again. "Won't you have a seat?"

"Thank you." While the receptionist called Stingley's secretary, Ro found a deep black leather chair, situated in a set around a large green granite coffee table. On the end table at her elbow was a white ceramic coffee decanter with cups and saucers.

Ro stirred her coffee, taking in the stunning panoramic view of the Puget Sound through the floor-to-ceiling windows behind the reception desk. She had visited corporate headquarters a handful of times in the year or so she had worked for the magazine, and each time she felt more at home in these elegant surroundings. No doubt that was due in large part to the charm and warmth of the man who had discovered her, the publisher himself, David Stingley. He was a gracious man, far more so than his reputation would have suggested, and every time she dealt with him he managed to make her feel more important to his operation than she knew she was. It was a good feeling, indeed.

Before she finished her coffee, Stingley's secretary arrived to escort her. Ro's casual air as she hefted her portfolio belied the excitement she felt. In keeping with his flair for intrigue, Stingley had been evasive about the purpose of the meeting when he had called to ask her to come to Seattle. Although it was likely that it had something to do with her Gettysburg project, he had managed to create enough uncertainty that she had thought of nothing else for the past day and a half. She did a subtle breathing exercise to try to expel the butterflies as they walked down the thickly carpeted hallway.

The secretary stopped before a huge black double door and knocked. She paused a second, then swept into the office. "Mr. Stingley, Ms. Lang is here."

Stingley stood behind a huge desk situated diagonally in the mammoth corner office, speaking into a high-tech headset he wore over his perfectly coiffed gray mane. Ro was surprised that the ready smile she had come to expect was absent today, replaced by a grimness about his eyes and mouth. He motioned for Ro to take a chair, then turned his back to continue his conversation in privacy. While he spoke quietly into the clear straw that functioned as the mouthpiece of his headgear, another man, seated in front of the desk, rose to greet her. He was muscular-looking, dressed casually in khaki, and had a youthful, handsome face framed by a full red beard and longish light brown hair.

"Mark Fassero," the man said.

She shook his hand and returned the greeting. It was common for Stingley to have others attend their business or production meetings, but Ro had never seen this man before.

"I'm here for a special assignment," Fassero explained, reading the question on her face. "I think I'll let David explain it. I learned a long time ago not to steal the boss's thunder."

Before she could reply, Stingley ended the phone call. "Hello, Ro," he said, slipping the headset off, somehow leaving his hair undisturbed. He came around the desk to extend his large, perfectly manicured right hand. As she took it, Ro noticed a heavy gold bracelet partially visible under the crisply starched French cuff of his blue-and-white-striped shirt.

"Great to see you again," Stingley said in his richest baritone. The smile was returning, but it was somewhat forced, hardly the short-range laser she was used to. For the first time, it occurred to Ro that the purpose of the meeting might be less pleasant than she had assumed.

"That goes for me, too, David," she replied. "I love the chance to come here."

"I see you've already met Mark Fassero." He cast a look at the other man that Ro was sure was significant; she just had no idea why.

"I haven't said anything, David," Fassero said, with a gentle laugh that was intended to take the defensive edge off the remark. Ro was becoming uncomfortably nervous.

Stingley said nothing in reply, then turned to Ro. "It's your Gettysburg piece. It's terrific. Your proposal really connected with me, on a very emotional level."

Ro could feel a cool sense of relief coursing through her, followed quickly by the delightful heat of excitement.

"Fact is," he continued, "I feel it has cover potential."

"David, that's fantastic!" she managed to reply. Furiously, she tried to grasp the magnitude of what he was saying. She had had a splendid run at *Beau Rivage,* better than anyone could have expected on the basis of her previous work. After all, just five years ago she got her first professional job for a neighborhood newspaper in the West Valley, shooting the kids in costume at a Halloween parade. Her work at *Beau Rivage* had been good, very good, but nothing that would have suggested a shot at the cover, the most coveted of all plums at one of the most highly regarded magazines in the country.

"Well, it's good. Very good," he replied. "So good that I've decided to exercise my prerogative as CEO." He looked briefly at Fassero. "We're not going with our usual team approach on this one. No brainstorming sessions. I'm giving the go-ahead and you'll report directly to me."

Ro tried hard to focus on Stingley's words but lost him in a rush of wind through her ears. This was it. A sentimental, almost manipulative piece on a 130-year-old war—a piece she liked, to be sure, but an ordinary piece by her reckoning—was about to be her break-out work. Stingley was still talking.

"Mark is a veteran. Literally and figuratively. He's worked with us before, done some terrific work elsewhere, too." He paused again to look at Fassero, who nodded slightly. "Cover assignments always get a project coordinator and he'll be yours for this one."

Ro turned to Fassero. "That's great. I don't know what to say."

"What's to say? You have a great idea. Maybe I can help you pull it together."

"Thank you very much," she replied, vaguely noting that the guy had a great smile.

"I'm very impressed with your concept of the battle as seen through the eyes of the soldiers. And your descriptions of those men whose lives you researched—" He took her proposal from Stingley's desk. It was clipped open and marked with a half dozen sticker notes. "How did you come up with the idea?" he asked as he thumbed through it.

It occurred to her that her new "assistant" seemed surprisingly at ease in the boss's office. She guessed that, despite Fassero's youth, they had probably worked together over the years. "Well, I don't really know," she replied, honestly. "The truth is my daughter was doing a report on the turning point of the Civil War and wanted to look at some photographs. So we went to the library and found this Mathew Brady volume and then I found a couple of contemporary accounts of the battle from soldiers who actually fought there, who knew these boys were real people. Anyway, right after that I went on an assignment back to Washington and—"

"The Cherry Blossom Festival for the *Times*," Fassero interrupted. Ro was impressed that the man had obviously done his homework. She smiled.

"Yes. And I took a two-day side trip to the battlefield and there the idea just came together. I think coming from the Vietnam Memorial had a lot to do with my frame of mind when I shot the proofs." She shrugged, signaling that her explanation was as complete as she could make it.

"It's great," he said softly. "I can't wait to get started."

"That goes for me, too," she said.

"Good," said Stingley. He started to say more, but Fassero stepped in.

"I'll take care of everything," he said. "Setting up the schedule, transportation, equipment, communications."

Somewhere in the back of Ro's mind, it registered that Fassero had remarkably few qualms about treading on Stingley's prerogatives. She checked the older man for a reaction, but he said only, "I've got you on a rather tight schedule. Do you think the December issue is too soon?"

"No," she said. Then, with less conviction, "I don't think so."

"Not at all," interjected Mark. "December's fine. In fact, it's pretty exciting, don't you think?"

"You have no idea," she replied.

CHAPTER 3

LANG STOOD BEHIND HIS DESK FACING THE HUGE window that was the east wall of his office. It was a rare day, he thought, when the summer smog permitted a glimpse of the famed Hollywood sign on the hills west of Griffith Park from his thirty-fifth-floor Century City office. Today wasn't one of those days.

"Chris? Did you hear me?" Amy asked, her voice suddenly intruding on his brief reverie.

"Yeah," he said, turning around. "Sorry. Must be those late nights." She was seated at the glass conference table near the far wall of the sprawling, richly appointed office, bobbing in a sea of law books, document clips, deposition transcripts, and yellow legal pads.

"Yeah, right. Another late night reading depo summaries?" For a long time now Lang's moribund social life had been a point of discussion between them. Over two years after his divorce and feeling a total failure for the experience, Lang had gone through the motions of two brief relationships and was beginning to resign himself to permanent solitude. Amy, whose motto might have been "Quit Wasting Time," had found herself in a profoundly rewarding marriage and was sure that everyone else could have one, too, if he just approached it with the right attitude. But, since all the attitude in the world wouldn't do you any good without the right partner, she had learned to become a dedicated matchmaker. Although Lang appreciated her enthusiasm and her efforts, he had not found any of her choices particularly appealing.

"No. Cubs game. On tape. Took them sixteen innings to lose to the Pirates this time."

"You wasted precious sleep time to watch a tape of a baseball game? You could have gotten the score off the radio. That's what Bill does. Sixteen innings? Jesus, what's that, about five hours?"

"Close. But I watch in fast forward. Took me fifty-nine minutes."

Amy shook her head in mild disgust. "Mr. Excitement. Baseball on tape till the sun comes up. Never mind. Let's get back to this stuff. I was saying that Rachel has all the documents they produced on the computer and they are cross-indexed in the usual way. I think we're beginning to see order creep into the horror show that Lindstrom's company dumped on us."

"Good. Somewhere in that blizzard of paper is the smoking gun that's going to make our case against him and his company."

"His company, maybe. But not him. The bad news is that we ran a word scan on the entire database once Rachel got it loaded and Lindstrom's name's not in there. Not a mention of the man in fifteen thousand pages. Not one."

Lang's concentration was returning. Well, not fully. As a trial lawyer he had long since learned to operate on several mental tracks at one time. It was an essential skill in a business that required you simultaneously to listen to a witness's answer, frame the next question, observe the jury, keep track of the judge, and anticipate your adversary's cross-examination, all the while plotting how best to lead the witness into a trap that you knew was already laid in the pages of his very own sworn deposition transcript. While Amy was talking, he had been pondering just how it was that the Cubs, in a lucrative market in a great city that could afford to attract talented, big-name free agents, consistently finished behind smaller-market teams that annually lost their biggest stars to wealthier teams and drew no one.

"Can't be. Graham Ellerby is certain that Lindstrom designed the prototype, structured the test plan, flew some of the tests, and wrote the final draft of the engineering report. It's just not possible that his name isn't in there somewhere."

Amy shook her head. "I'm afraid not. Remember, Ellerby wasn't there at the time. Anyway, he's clearly mistaken. Don't worry, though, there's still probably a good breach-of-contract case against Arrow in here. Maybe even fraud. If there is, we'll find it."

Lang turned back toward the window. Damn, he thought. Without Lindstrom, the case would become just another case, maybe a good one, but not the case Lang thought he had. The telephone rang and Lang punched the speaker button. "Yes?" he said.

"John Carrick is here," announced Alex.

Lang looked at his watch. It was precisely two o'clock. "Punctual, isn't he?"

Amy gathered up her notes and documents for the meeting. Lang hefted his massive working file and followed her out the door, down the thickly carpeted corridor toward the main lobby.

"You know, Chris," Amy said, "this plan of yours to work on the Pegasus case no more than three hours a day while you're preparing for the *Fulton* trial may work for you, but it leaves me in the dark a lot."

He turned to her with a quizzical look on his face. "*You're* working on it full time, aren't you? I don't see the problem."

"Yes, I am," she answered, slight exasperation in her voice. "More than full time, in fact. And I'm on top of the discovery plan, the database, the chain of title issues, and a lot of other things. But, for example, you go out and retain this aviation expert, then expect me to help frame his assignment and create the package he will work from and I know absolutely nothing about the man, or what you really want from him or how he will fit into the final trial plan or—"

"Hold on, Amy. Calm down," Lang interrupted, stopping in front of the main reception desk under the stately brass placard that read simply Devereaux and Brace. "Let's have a little patience. The trial won't be for another year or so. Our case will evolve dramatically, probably change direction a couple of times, before we're ready to seat a jury. And it will change almost as many times while the trial is in progress. You know that. You don't have to have all the answers today. You don't even have to know all the questions, but you seem like you're pretty close."

He started down the sweeping staircase that connected the thirty-fourth and thirty-fifth floors, now walking beside her. They had been through this conversation many times before during her six years with the firm. Lang recognized much of himself in her consuming need to know everything there was to know about a case, to have all the answers lined up, to be prepared as early as possible for all eventualities. But he knew that those characteristics were also a prescription for professional frustration and personal unhappiness. The job they did, complete with its flashy six- and, yes, for some, seven-figure incomes, was a pressure cooker that drove more than an occasional lawyer to drugs or alcohol abuse, destroying careers, families, and whole lives along the way. The only way to avoid those pitfalls was to recognize them and try to keep it all in perspective.

"Look, Amy. Don't worry," Lang said softly. "You *are* on top of this stuff and I know it. I have the utmost confidence in you and I am willing to risk my professional reputation on your talent. In fact, that's exactly what I've done in every case we've handled together since you got here. I don't think it's asking too much for you to have a fraction of the same confidence in your skills that I do."

She seemed mollified. I'm becoming her Max Devereaux, thought Lang, and he liked the notion very much. As they reached the conference room on the thirty-fourth floor, he resolved to pay his mentor a visit. Though he spoke to Max at least weekly, he hadn't visited him in months, hardly admirable since Max treated him like the son he had never had.

John Carrick was an aviation expert straight out of central casting. Fifty-six years old, tall, athletic, and handsome, he was a retired Air Force colonel with a Ph.D. in aeronautical engineering and an M.B.A. He had been an astronaut during the waning days of the Apollo program, serving as backup to the last Americans to walk on the moon. After Stanford Business School he became a private consultant, working with a number of aerospace firms. He was a seasoned expert witness who had also testified before Congress. Married to the same woman for twenty-four years, he had three college-age sons, two at service academies. On paper, he was the ideal weapon to attack a fortified adversary like Arrow Dynamics.

Lang shook hands with Carrick, then introduced Amy. "We're delighted to meet you, Colonel. And even more pleased that we may have a chance to work with you. You have no idea how relieved we were to find out you had never worked for Arrow Dynamics."

I have no idea, either, thought Amy, since I'm hearing all this for the very first time. Involuntarily she rubbed her palms together. They were perspiring.

"Chris, please call me John," said Carrick in what Lang thought had to be called his astronaut voice. "I'm past all that

'Colonel' stuff now. Besides, it makes me sound like I fry chicken or run a third-world country."

"Fair enough, John," replied Chris, laughing at Carrick's references. "But I warn you that when we get to court, you'll be 'Colonel' all over again in front of our jury. And no one will mistake you for anything less than what you are." Carrick smiled. Amy guessed he'd heard all this before.

Lang ran Carrick through a quick overview of the case and where it now stood. When he reached the end of his succinct summary, he said, "That's where we are for the moment. This afternoon, I just want to pick your brain a bit about some of the more technical aspects of the case."

"That's fine with me, Chris. I hope you don't expect definitive answers at this point."

Lang caught a sideways glance from Amy and the hint of a smile. To Carrick he said, "Not at all. I'm sure in your experience you've seen that a lawsuit, especially one of this magnitude, isn't built overnight. It can't be. Patience and persistence are the keys to this type of enterprise. What we don't know, we'll find out."

Lang outlined what he had already learned from Ellerby and Andrews. The sleek experimental model designated XRL-22 by Arrow Dynamics was nicknamed StormTree. It was the brainchild of famed New Zealand race-car designer and driver Nigel Daultry and Russell Lindstrom. The idea was for Lindstrom to design and test a prototype of a lightweight recreational airplane that could easily be flown by the most amateur of pilots. Although it was to be the ultimate toy for the successful man who had everything, it would also be a serious airplane, combining state-of-the-art materials and equipment that could feasibly be incorporated into a light aircraft. It would be constructed of the most advanced lightweight, superstrong graphite epoxy composite known and would employ the latest in aerodynamics under development at Arrow. The power plant would be a superlight version of the "Mini Indy" engine then being refined by Daultry-Philips-Grindelwald and it would employ a number of Daultry's other technological advances then under development in his various companies worldwide. Once the plane was designed and tested, Daultry was to provide a coordinated international marketing effort. The proceeds from the distribution were to be split between Arrow Dynamics and Daultry Research PLC.

Arrow Dynamics built and tested the prototype and pronounced it a successful design. In fact, its final engineering report had concluded that the aircraft had easily exceeded all of its expectations. It referred to the StormTree as a "superb aircraft" that was a "joy to fly," "responsive and friendly," "safe, even for the most inexperienced of pilots."

Lang concluded his summary with a description of Pegasus Technologies' near-disastrous flight testing of the production prototype they called the Peregrine.

"You say a flat spin?" asked Carrick, furrowing his brow.

"That's right. A flat spin," replied Lang. "How significant is that?"

"Very. You see, many airplanes spin. Most are meant to, when commanded by the pilot. But the aircraft you describe has two distinctions, both of which are very dangerous. The first is that it would apparently spin without the pilot trying or wanting to do so. That's bad. But, once it does, its spin mode is flat, meaning that the aircraft spins at an attitude that is absolutely parallel to the ground. And that takes bad to much worse. Pilots call the flat spin the dead spin, and for very good reason. It is virtually unrecoverable."

"I don't follow," responded Lang. Amy was furiously taking notes.

Carrick used his hands to explain. "Look. This is an aircraft in a typical spin mode. See how the nose is down? There is almost always a slight nose-down attitude in a spin. By throttling the engine up, or even using the raw force of gravity, a pilot can capitalize on this attitude to drive the aircraft downward."

"Straight to the ground?" asked a slightly incredulous Lang.

"Yes, Chris." Carrick smiled. "Toward the ground, but not into the ground. Once the aircraft is moving forward relative to the angle of the wind, even straight down, it reestablishes aerodynamic flight. It is flying again, not a spinning brick.

"In the case of a flat spin, or dead spin, however, there is no downward inclination, not even a slight one. Powering up will do no more than accelerate the rate of spin. Unless the pilot can create a downward angle by manipulating controls that are almost by definition useless in that mode, he's going to lose the aircraft. And he'd better have an ejection charge and a parachute."

The impact of Carrick's words hung heavily in the silence of the room. After a moment Lang dug a fifteen-page document out of his working file, opened it to a place tabbed with a sticker note, and handed it to Carrick. "This is a copy of the Arrow-Daultry contract. Section G, here." He pointed. "This is the testing requirement section. Take a look at it for a minute, if you would." Carrick read the section with great care.

"Now, John. Based on what you're looking at, would you say the contract provided for any spin testing?"

"Certainly, that's exactly what Section G-5 is for. 'Resistant to departure and spin per MS 92121.' 'Departure' means any uncommanded motion by the aircraft. 'Spin' means spin in the sense that we are talking about."

"Uncommanded motion?" Lang asked.

"Something the aircraft does that the pilot doesn't intend. It means the aircraft has left aerodynamic flight and is ballistic. We were just talking in terms of spin. But the aircraft can depart controlled flight without actually spinning. That's not as bad, but it isn't good, either. Anything an aircraft does that the pilot doesn't intend it to do creates an inherently dangerous condition."

"Now, if this aircraft hadn't been tested for departure or spin resistance, would that be bad?" Lang asked.

"Very," replied the astronaut. "Especially when you consider that its spin mode was the most dangerous one there is. But not only that. I'm not an attorney, but this contract is very specific that departure and spin resistance and recoverability must be tested."

"In your opinion, could the prototype have been tested for departure and spin resistance, passed the tests, and still be susceptible to unintended spinning?"

"No way. Not with this language. That's what I can't figure out," said Carrick, a puzzled look on his face.

"What do you mean?"

"Well, you said this was to be a recreational aircraft, right?"

"Yeah?"

"Why would anyone put a military specification for departure and spin testing into a contract for the design and manufacture of a recreational aircraft?"

"What do you mean, John?" asked Lang, now puzzled himself.

"MS 92121. That is the universal military specification for the departure and spin classification of military aircraft. Warplanes."

The main dining room of L'Escoffier in the Beverly Hilton was not full by any means. Not a problem, thought Congressman Henry Gillingham, Perrier and lime in hand, as he surveyed the room. What counts here, he reminded himself, is quality, not quantity. From his station just to the left of the head table, Gillingham half-listened to two women from the Altadena Republican Women's Club while observing clusters of three and four well-dressed individuals circulating in a slow and uneven waltz around the floor. Black-vested, black-tied waiters of various nationalities pedaled smoothly through the crowd with trays full of champagne flutes and hot hors d'oeuvres. The conversation was decidedly political. A sixtyish woman wearing a slightly too snug maroon cocktail dress was working over a similarly attired contemporary.

". . . absolutely no idea what he's saying on any issue whatsoever," she chirped.

"Until one of his mistresses puts the thought in his head, you mean," added her companion, fairly cackling at the cleverness of her barb. She slugged hard at her champagne flute.

"Now, ladies," Gillingham's ponderous baritone chided gently. "The issues are the important thing, not the personalities."

"*Character* and leadership *are* the issues, Henry," shot back Maroon Cocktail Dress. Gillingham smiled broadly. That's the way to think, ladies. That's exactly what we need.

Off in a darker corner of the dimly lit room, a youngish-looking blond man with a bright political smile, deep tan, and sharply carved dimples whose badge identified him as Dick Banfield held the elbow of an attractive blond woman in a navy business suit. "More and more our polls are telling us the same story. The mood of the country is right for a whole new breed of man in the White House. I wouldn't announce this tonight in this room, but it doesn't even matter, quite frankly, if he's a Republican or a Democrat. He's just got to come from the right place. Just so happens that my man is a Republican." His grip was firm and the attitude of the woman's body suggested the mildest tug away from his grasp.

"So what makes your guy the right man?"

"Think about it," he replied, loosening his hold, while maneuvering for a better look at her badge and the ample bosom behind it. "The country's fed up with professional politicians. Right, Ms. Morain? Carole?"

"And?"

Having found her badge, bosom, and cleavage, he lost his focus for the moment. "Don't you see?" he fumbled. The look on her very pretty face told him she did not. After a short pause, phrases from a speech he had written winked on in his mind and he recovered. "It's a very basic concept, really. Politicians have run this country for a long time. In fact, we've been run by the so-called professionals for more than a half century. And what's their collective legacy?"

"I think you're going to tell me," she said around a plump shrimp she had just popped into her mouth.

He ignored her acerbic tone. "Our politicians lack the most basic sense of *business judgment*. Never having had to withstand the crucible of the marketplace—"

He was interrupted by the speaker. "Good evening, ladies and gentlemen. I'm Henry Gillingham," said the congressman. Around sustained applause, surprisingly robust from the small crowd, he introduced the main event of the evening. He was well known to this constituency and they responded enthusiastically, just as he and the other party chiefs had calculated.

"I've asked you to come here tonight to join me in launching a rare and wonderful adventure, a crusade, you might say, that I think presents our first real hope in a generation to regain control of our destiny and restore order to our future."

Gillingham rolled easily into his stock introduction, painting the liberal spendthrift opposition in cascading shades of purple, setting the stage for the candidate *Time* had already christened the Great Right Hope.

"Over the years as I've watched this country struggle, I've always had the feeling that we could do better. We had to do better. That a nation of two hundred and thirty million descendants of Thomas Jefferson, Abraham Lincoln, and Benjamin Franklin could just once come up with a candidate of vision, decision, wisdom, and guts."

Carole Morain turned to Banfield. "Guts?" she repeated.

He shrugged. "I don't write for Henry Gillingham," he explained. Gillingham was a good choice, Banfield decided as he watched and listened to the veteran politician reach the crossroads where good sense tells him to shut up before he loses the congregation but his heart won't let him forget that he's a politician. To Banfield's relief, he went with his head.

"And so, my fellow Americans, my fellow *Republicans*, without further ado, let me introduce to you the one man who can lead us back to greatness, a great American patriot and a great friend of mine, Russell Lindstrom!"

Applause fairly shook the room as a tall, handsome man of poise and presence rose from the head table to join Gillingham at the rostrum. His jaw was square and defiant, his eyes a steely blue, his thick mat of hair, in several shades of gray and white, perfectly but conservatively cut and combed. He filled his exquisitely tailored navy pin-striped suit with the sinewy bulk of an athlete not far past his prime. His smile was bright, yet genuine, as he pumped Gillingham's hand to the strong and steady applause of the moneyed

Republicans in the room. He was quite simply the very picture of Henry Gillingham's vision of America doing better. As he turned to wave at the crowd, the cheering intensified.

Out on the floor, Banfield, the speechwriter whose work was about to get another public forum, beamed his largest smile. "There's the man I work for," he told Carole Morain, nodding proudly toward the head table.

Lindstrom held up his hands to preside over the reluctant abatement of applause. Clearly, this small, wealthy crowd had come to see this man. And before he had uttered a word, they were sure they liked what they saw.

"Please," Lindstrom intoned, his voice oddly gentle, but resonant with power. With that single word he assumed complete command over the room. He quietly thanked the crowd and urged them to please quiet down and let him speak. For over a full minute.

"Thank you all so much for that very warm reception. And thank you, Congressman, for your kind words. If we had 534 more lawmakers like you in Washington I could go about the business of making new and better products and forget all about the Oval Office." More applause, while he paused for effect. "But, we don't and I can't." Louder applause, another strategic pause. "And I won't." Thunderous applause.

"As you know, I have decided to run for president and I'll be seeking the Republican nomination next year." Still louder applause. "And you know, with friends like you, I believe I'm going to get it!" A crescendo.

When the applause slackened, he continued, seamlessly shifting into his prepared remarks. Prepared, yes, thought Banfield, but not canned in the hands of this remarkable man, and certainly not stale. A veteran of numerous regional political campaigns—cynical exercises for the most part, he had to admit, where his gift for special operations that were now called dirty tricks had been his principal contribution—Banfield was feeling a thrill tonight he had seldom if ever felt before. It was like grasping a high-tension line. And he wasn't alone. Lindstrom was building an astonishing rapport with the audience in a matter of minutes.

And tonight was not an isolated incident, Banfield reminded himself. He had just been through this in Dallas, Phoenix, and Denver, all within the past ten days. This man was a force of nature, brilliant, charismatic, and learned, yet strong, avuncular, and solid. As Banfield listened to Lindstrom tell the now-familiar story of his father farming the dusty, played-out soil of Oklahoma while sto-ically burying one child after another, he tried hard, once again, to get a reading on just what it was that this man had. Despite his own ego, he doubted that it was merely the text he had written for him, the simple, clear story of a smart kid from a dirt-poor family who rose to become one of the wealthiest, most successful businessmen on the planet. Possibly, it really *was* the message, that America could use a good, stiff dose of the kind of business savvy that could pull a ruined company right out of the depths of bankruptcy, that a busi-nessman could make a huge profit, verging on the hundreds of millions, by making an *oil company* synonymous with ecological responsibility. Still another possibility, of course, was that it might just be the man himself, tall, virile, handsome, the very image of the American entrepreneur that John Wayne, Gary Cooper, and, yes, Ronald Reagan, had encouraged the nation to hope for, to pray for. However you looked at it and whatever it was, for Banfield it was like a dream, the nearest he'd ever been to a certain ride to the top of the world. If only, as Lindstrom himself had cautioned him, they didn't hang a nail on the little things.

Up on the podium, Lindstrom was moving quickly through an understated account of his Korean War record, a stunning chronicle of personal valor. After that, he would cover, with equal modesty, his triumphs with the spy planes he designed at the Skunkworks and his spectacular successes in business and industry, and then he would wrap it up. The speech was long, excessively so by five-thousand-dollar-a-plate fund-raiser standards. But, by God, thought Banfield, I'll keep him talking as long as they keep panting for it. He watched for yawning, wristwatch glancing, clinking glasses, brows-ing through the handout—the classic signs of the ebbing tide of interest. And he saw none.

Lindstrom moved to the climax. ". . . a mighty and majestic nation of tough and intelligent men and women has been driven to the brink of bankruptcy. But, like a great company foundering on the seas of commerce, there are assets that can be marshaled, re-sources that can be tapped, strategies that can be devised and exe-cuted. And I believe I—we—can make a difference and with God's help we can recapture a far better America than the one we have today."

The room once more erupted, the staid Republican crowd hooting and whistling. Not a man or woman there that night failed to grasp the thrill of what they had been there to observe and share.

None doubted that they had witnessed the renewal of a political party, the emergence of a giant destined for greatness, and the rekindling of the best that the American spirit can offer.

The feeling of kinship that swept the room, however, failed to touch one tall man standing in the very back, where the light was dimmest. A forced smile on his face, a stale scotch in his hand, Jad Piersall observed the events of that evening with a deepening sense of dread.

The long black Lincoln nosed its way confidently through the narrow, bustling streets of Georgetown. The thick air, redolent of midsummer in the nation's capital, hung heavily about the car's exhaust as the driver swung through a sharp curve and accelerated down a brick lane. Here the noonday crowds of diners and shoppers were nowhere to be seen, a dim and fading sound in the distance. Smoothly the Town Car came to a stop near the end of the short lane, in front of the portico of an old colonial red-brick building. On the faded blue canopy that ran from the front door to the curb were the words The Roan.

Jad Piersall, heavy black briefcase in his right hand, slid silently out of the backseat and hustled up the steps to the front door. Reflexively he ducked his head under the canopy, though he had a good half a foot to spare. With a faint chirp of its tires, the sedan sped off and disappeared around the corner as Piersall went inside.

While Piersall's eyes adjusted to the darkness of the restaurant, a middle-aged hostess in authentic colonial dress met him. "Mr. Piersall," she said with the faintest Carolina accent. "We haven't seen you in ages."

"How are you, Sally?" asked Piersall, still squinting at the colonial decor through the darkness. "Are the rest of them here yet?"

"Mr. Piersall," she replied, in mocking reproach. "You know these old men better than that. They were here an hour ago. But don't fret. You're right on time and they're real anxious to see you."

"Thanks, Sal," he said, patting her affectionately on the shoulder as he walked past and climbed the stairs to the private room on the second floor.

The colonial hunt motif was carried out on the second floor of the old building with the same attention to authenticity as on the first, although very few of The Roan's patrons were privileged to see it. The light up here was better and Piersall could see each of the others' faces clearly, even through the smoke of a half dozen cigars and cigarettes, as he entered the dining room. "Here's our boy now! Hello, Jad!" boomed General Winfield Scott Hendricks, USMC, retired, as Piersall headed for the only empty seat around the large oval table.

"Good afternoon, General," replied Piersall with obvious respect. He nodded to the other men at the table. "Gentlemen. Hope I'm not late."

"Not at all, son," said Hendricks, looking at his watch. "Right on time with typical military precision, which I guess we can credit as much to the airlines and our driver as to your Army training." This brought laughter from all around the table. Piersall took the opportunity to turn to the man next to him. "Colonel," he said softly, nodding and smiling at his one-time commanding officer with genuine affection. The smile was returned with a quick pat on his knee.

Piersall ordered a scotch from the young colonial waitress, and Hendricks, his bearing still that of a man who had headed the nation's military-intelligence operations for nearly a decade, easily assumed control of the meeting. "Jad, we've already taken the liberty of starting the meeting in your absence and have disposed of the formalities." He checked his carefully printed notes. "We've already taken limited action on that House subcommittee issue and got an update from Professor Sikorski on the Iraqi missile-launcher snafu. Do you want us to recapitulate for you?"

Piersall recognized the offer as the hollow courtesy it was. Besides, the truth of the matter was that, while the rest of the Fortress's agenda was certainly important, all he really cared about was the Lindstrom issue. He declined.

"Good," replied Hendricks, obviously pleased that Piersall was sharp enough to know the protocol without being told. He paused a moment to allow the waitress to complete her duties and leave the room, closing the door as she did. "Well, then, let's get right down to the business that is dearest to your heart. Can you brief us on where we stand?"

"Certainly, General."

For an hour and a half Piersall told the six old men who called themselves the Fortress every relevant detail of his efforts on their behalf. He began by updating them on his trace of each movement made by Russell Lindstrom, his many companies, and their numerous spin-offs and affiliates. Referring to data he summoned from the files of his laptop, he took them through the details of key transactions of the last quarter. The deals he recounted represented an astonishing array of virtually every type of mainstream commerce being conducted in the world. Diamonds bought in South Africa, sold in Brazil. Paper mills in Oregon purchased through land leases, then converted at staggering expense to increase product output, while cutting pollutant by-products by ninety percent. A fading commuter airline in the Midwest recapitalized out of bankruptcy with the pension-plan funds of its own unions, resulting in both a stable company and a spectacular advertising campaign. Piersall estimated the net profit to all affiliated entities for the quarter at just over eleven billion dollars.

Piersall concluded with an ominous report of the fund-raiser in Los Angeles the previous night. As he finished, Clayton Hasselrig, the burly former deputy director of the CIA, asked, "Excuse me, Jad. But why does the son of a bitch need a *fund-raiser* if he's got so much money?"

"Good question, Mr. Director. And, as a matter of fact, I asked that very question of one of his speechwriters at the reception."

General Hendricks sat up suddenly. "He didn't know who you were, did he, Jad?"

"No, General, he didn't. I think I managed to fit into the crowd pretty well. Besides, he was so intent on impressing one of the few women under fifty in the room, I doubt that he gave me more than a passing thought. Anyway, I asked him your question, almost verbatim. He asked me what I thought the American public would make of a candidate who was too rich for fund-raisers and couldn't be bothered to court the party regulars on their own turf. I took that to mean that the whole process was more a public-relations strategy than anything else. Besides, I have to tell you, it worked. They loved him from the moment he stood up. It was frightening."

"You bet your ass it's frightening," agreed General Hendricks. "That son-of-a-bitch turncoat has always been bad news and he's about to become a lot worse."

"There's a long way to go, General," reassured former National Security Advisor Leon Sikorski in his thick Eastern European accent. "I've lived through many presidential campaigns. A good crowd this early, months before the primaries even begin, means nothing in the final analysis. The media will love him at first, then they will challenge him, then dissect every meaningless piece of information about him, then savage him. Perhaps, then, even lose interest in him. The truth is he's too good a potential president to get nominated."

"Good?" shouted Admiral Larry Crispin, former superintendent of the U.S. Naval Academy. "As president? That fucking traitor?" Sikorski waved him off but the fiery admiral wasn't finished. "Do I have to remind you that this is the man whose radar deflector took out a prototype stealth fighter in 'Nam as early as '73? Or that a complete book of his DELPHAR command and control encryption codes turned up in Iran in '78? Or that he—"

"Sold electronics components illegally to the Contras while we were still officially supporting the Sandinistas in Nicaragua," Hendricks finished, a note of disgust in his voice. "We all know the charges, Larry, just as well as you do. And if the man weren't a goddamned master at covering his tracks with layer after layer of subordinates and a web of deniability mechanisms, we wouldn't be going through these gyrations. We all agree that there would be damned few things worse for the country, for our security, than for that snake to get in the White House. What Leon is saying is that he's too strong *not* to get driven off by the pain-in-the-ass media long before he gets the prize."

"I'm not so sure of that, General," offered Colonel Shepard Easley, shifting in the chair next to Piersall's as he spoke.

The others, long accustomed to giving great weight to the observations of this heavily decorated former Special Forces commander, turned their attention to him now. It had been on his recommendation that the small group had expanded its ranks once in the quarter century of its existence, adding the able lawyer with a military-intelligence background, Jared Piersall, five years ago.

"In my view, we have never had a candidate for president in this country more skilled at handling the dynamics of the press and the media than Lindstrom. Clinton was undeniably smooth but not credible. And Reagan was an actor, damn good at delivering a scripted speech. Of course, Kennedy was very accomplished at—"

"Burying the peep," interjected Chris Panotti, former chairman of the House Armed Services Committee, punctuating the remark with a graphic hand gesture. As usual, he got a roomful of laughter for his efforts.

Easley laughed appreciatively, then continued. "That, too. But, in addition, he was good at the other type of give-and-take, the one with the White House press corps. But Lindstrom. Lindstrom is entirely different. He can deliver a speech with Reagan or Clinton—and charm the press with JFK. And he's effective as hell on his feet. But his real genius here may be his ability to manipulate the press from within. Don't forget. He knows that business, too. He's run newspapers. He's bought and sold news agencies. He's had a hand in a national news weekly."

"Is there any fucking thing this guy hasn't done, been, owned, run, or recapitalized?" lamented Crispin disgustedly.

"Don't get discouraged, Larry," soothed Easley. "I'm not saying he's invincible. Far from it. *We* know what we're dealing with here. The trick is to make sure everyone else finds out, too. I just don't want to underestimate Lucifer himself."

"Amen," Hasselrig added.

"And, besides," Easley said, "we still have Jad here with our ace in the hole."

"That's right, Shep." General Hendricks smiled around the glow of his fat, soggy cigar as he turned to face Piersall. "Tell us where our little insurance policy stands, Jad."

CHAPTER 4

AT PRECISELY NOON, LANG WALKED BRISKLY PAST THE
security guards, metal detectors, and X-ray equipment that cluttered
the Main Street entrance to the United States Courthouse in Los
Angeles. The morning, the first of a trial expected to last more than
a month, had gone well for Consolidated Michigan and for Lang:
three motions argued and two won, the more important two. Aubrey Phelps was bright crimson by the time Judge Espinosa recessed
for lunch. Lang bounded down the short flight of stairs and out
the heavy glass doors. And headlong into ninety-four-degree heat
and uncharacteristic eighty-percent humidity. Staggered for the
moment, he thought vaguely about another summer under the influence of El Niño, the mysterious tropical weather phenomenon
that, to him at least, made a strong case for the theory of global
warming.

Like the typical Angeleno he had become, he patiently waited
for the signal before crossing the street. He was already deeply
engaged on all levels in the trial and resented the interruption to his
concentration. But Amy had called him in the car this morning

and insisted that John Carrick needed to talk to him right away. Although she had explained the near-mystical need Lang had to maintain his focus during trial, Carrick had been adamant. When Lang had remarked that he wished that Carrick would become more comfortable dealing with Amy, she had jumped on the suggestion with savagery.

"So do I!" she had exclaimed. "It's frustrating. I mean, I told him, 'Look, John, I'm the second chair on the case.' But, I don't think it's got anything to do with being your subordinate. This problem—whatever it is—is in the technical area of the case and I think he's got a gender problem there. You know, the goddamned military, Operation Tailhook and all that shit. Too bad one of his sons wasn't a girl."

Lang smiled as he crossed the street, remembering how the birth of his own Jennifer had opened his mind in areas he hadn't even known were closed. As he reached the other side of the street, the smell of frying grease slowly overtook the fumes of the MTA buses that lumbered down Main Street. He scanned the half dozen fast-food places that were clumped in the north end of the plaza, looking for a sign of John Carrick or Amy Quinn. Satisfied that they were not yet there, he ordered a salad and an iced tea from the Italian place and found a seat under an umbrella in a prominent location in the plaza. At 12:17, he glimpsed Amy's fashionably cut head of blond hair. She had emerged from the door to the parking garage and moved directly toward him. John Carrick followed in lockstep. It occurred to Lang that they made a perfect couple for a fitness video.

"Hello, John," said Lang as they reached him. To Amy he nodded and smiled his familiar smile. She narrowed her eyes slightly in response.

"Hi, Chris," replied John, the easy professional air that had characterized him on his three previous meetings with Lang decidedly absent. Lang, with only one hour before he was to move back into the ring in Judge Espinosa's court, dispensed with the amenities.

"Amy told me you needed to talk."

"I do. I know you're really pressed for time, but I felt this couldn't wait until Saturday. And I mean no offense to Amy, but I think you're going to have to make an important decision here pretty quickly and I thought you might need more than just the raw input from me."

If he was trying to pacify Amy, Lang could see that he had

failed. She was still smoldering under her professional mask. "Go ahead, John. What's the problem?" Lang asked.

"Okay. We've already talked about your approach to Arrow's having failed to test the plane properly. Without any indication that they kept an engineering log of any kind other than loose-leaf flight cards, they can say just about anything they want about what they did or didn't do. And of course, I can tell the jury that the mere failure to keep records of that kind constitutes negligence in the testing regime, in and of itself. But then they're going to say they tested the prototype for departure and spin resistance and it was resistant to both."

Lang involuntarily glanced at his watch. "And we're going to show that the production aircraft we built on the basis of the proto-type, the one Pegasus Technologies called the Peregrine and sank millions of British pounds into, spun out of the sky and would have crashed to the ground but for the superhuman skills and efforts of our finest test pilot. This was the direct result of Arrow's inadequate tests, false engineering report, and failure to report the tendency to spin. So what's the problem?"

"I can see you are in your trial mode today, Chris," said Carrick. He glanced toward Amy, apparently for help, but she was far from ready to respond to him. "Look. This is the problem I see. The aircraft that Pegasus Technologies spun was the Peregrine, *their* production version of the prototype."

"Which was not only based entirely on the information provided by Arrow Dynamics, but was, in fact, identical to Arrow's prototype." Lang was beginning to sound impatient.

"That's just the problem, Chris. There are two different planes. The prototype, the StormTree, is not the Peregrine."

"Why is that material, John? Isn't the Peregrine meticulously based on the aerodynamic principles and design configuration of the StormTree?"

"Absolutely."

"And the Peregrine spun?"

"Undoubtedly."

"In fact, as an expert without peer, you are going to testify that the Peregrine was highly susceptible to both departure and spin, are you not?"

"Most certainly."

"And that the spin mode most common to that aircraft is the deadly 'flat-spin' mode, the 'dead spin,' as it were, which is virtually unrecoverable?"

"You are absolutely right again."

"The Peregrine spun. Ergo, as we lawyers like to say, the StormTree must have spun. So, John, tell us. What's the problem?"

"Weight," replied Carrick.

"For what? I've got to go back into trial here in twelve minutes."

"Not 'wait.' 'Weight.' As in avoirdupois."

Now Amy waded in. "He means the airplane's weight in pounds."

Carrick nodded. "Yes. But not airplane. *Airplanes.* The two planes are geometrically identical. Their aerodynamics are indistinguishable. The schematics are a perfect overlay. But they do not have the same weight."

Lang barked, "What are you talking about? We went over the specs in minute detail in my office on your first visit. They both weigh, what is it, Amy? Eight hundred—"

"Eight hundred seventeen pounds, unloaded," she recited from memory. "But you're not listening, Chris. Listen to what he's trying to tell you."

Carrick continued. "The StormTree, the prototype tested by Arrow Dynamics, weighed 817 pounds unloaded, exactly as specified. I've confirmed that with Grover Young, the fellow who's storing the aircraft down there in Florida. The Peregrine, the production aircraft built by Ellerby and Andrews, on the other hand, weighs 1,147 pounds, unloaded. I just got that information from an old buddy of mine in England."

Lang was losing his temper. "Old buddy? In England? What are you talking about, John?"

"Look, Chris. When I did the math on that Peregrine spin, some of the figures just didn't come out right. Things like moments of inertia and mass response time. I thought my calcs were wrong, so I called Graham Ellerby. When I couldn't reach either him or Clive Andrews, I talked to the fellow in charge of their factory in—"

Amy stepped into the pause. "Sheffield."

"Right. Anyway, I told him who I was and what we were doing and he confirmed that the Peregrine was sitting right there in the middle of the floor under a tarp. I got a buddy of mine, Jack Brubeck, an Air Force major who's stationed over there at Lakenheath, to go up and weigh it. They have an aviation scale right there in the factory. Anyway, Brubeck weighed it three times and came up with the same figure each time. And I've got to tell you, my calculations fit perfectly with the weight of 1,147 pounds."

Lang was crestfallen. Amy was perplexed. "I still don't understand," she said. "If the two planes are geometrically and aerodynamically identical, what difference does the weight make? Don't all of your arguments still make sense?"

Carrick responded, "They do, Amy. I will still testify the same way, but—"

Amy finished the thought. "But if you're asked about the weight differential, you'll have to admit that that factor *could* affect departure and spin resistance."

"Exactly."

Lang, his head back, gaze skyward, spoke. "It also means we're going to have to fly the StormTree ourselves and see if it has the same tendency to spin as the Peregrine that the Brits produced." Carrick nodded gravely in agreement. "Tell me this, John: Will it spin?"

"I guarantee it. I don't think you'd want to be on board."

"That dangerous?"

"Absolutely. Could lose the plane. Maybe even the pilot."

"Jesus," Lang replied. He paused thoughtfully. "Assuming our client is game, do you have any ideas about who we could get to fly this mission?"

"I've got a few possibilities. With your permission I'll make some calls."

Lang nodded. "Okay. When I call Graham and Clive maybe they'll let me in on why they gave us bad specs for their production plane."

The house was dark as Lang's Porsche roared up the street and into the driveway. The outside lights, regulated by a photosensitive cell, burned brightly for the benefit of would-be burglars, but the inside lights that he maintained on timers had yet to be adjusted for the shorter days of August and would not come on for another forty minutes. Since this was the first day this month he had come home before eleven o'clock, he hadn't noticed the problem before. As the garage door came up he made a mental note to reset the timers before he went to bed. He noted briefly that the gardeners had been there and the large front yard looked particularly well-maintained. For some reason he suddenly thought back to his youth outside Rockford, where he and his brothers had cut the grass, and the grass of several neighbors, for a tidy summer income, and the notion of a "gardener" was as foreign as the men he now paid handsomely to do it for him.

As always, the empty house had a sterile quality, which lately he had grown to dislike intensely. Odd that he, known throughout his considerable circle of friends and professional acquaintances as a stickler for neatness and order, would find himself longing for the clutter of toys and the cacophony of unruly children. The house had begun to resemble a museum where his kids came to visit on occasion, like students on a field trip. Not for the first time he lamented his trial calendar, which had forced the cancellation of their last four weekend visits.

He passed through the kitchen he hadn't used, even on weekends, in nearly two months. In the main foyer, the light of his answering machine announced that two calls had been recorded during the day. He punched the button to harvest them.

Andrea's unmistakable voice lit up the darkened hallway. "Hi, Dad. I know you're not home because it's only four-thirty and you're never home at four-thirty, but I didn't want to bother you at the office for anything so silly as telling you how much I love you and I forgive you for the fight with Mom about Jack's broken arm. It wasn't anybody's fault but Jack's. He's a klutz. I've been telling you that for years. But what is *with* you guys, anyway? Do you have to litigate with Mom all the time? Sorry, Daddy, I know you're thinking that's Mom's propaganda and I'm sure it is and I don't want to do that to you. I just wish you guys would get along a little bit. God, we love both of you but Mom's gotten to be pretty hard to take every time she has to deal with you and we're afraid you guys'll just stop trying to work with each other—and us—at all. Sorry, I know, it's the 'worst-case scenario' you always warn me about. Anyway—dumb message—I love you and I want everything to be, if not like it used to be—fat chance—as good as it can. At least Mom's really excited about this new *Beau Rivage* assignment—she's so obsessive. But it is *the* magazine! Anyway, I love you so much. Mom, too! G'bye. Oh, wait, this is Andrea." The short beep signaled the end of the message to Lang, who hung for a long moment midway between laughter and tears.

The second message was dead air for about twenty seconds, which Lang guessed indicated some sort of minor malfunction of the machine. He reset it and climbed the stairs of the new, perfectly decorated mock-Tudor tract house he called home.

Twenty minutes later, clad in pajamas and robe, he switched on the VCR and the television in the sitting room off his bedroom. Suddenly he was overtaken by a deadly combination of exhaustion and sheer loneliness. It occurred to him that, surrounded as he was from morning to night with partners, associates, witnesses, judges, juries, clients, and opposing lawyers, he was desperately lonesome. He regretted that he had erased Andrea's rambling but poignant message. A severe bout of self-pity threatened to overwhelm him.

No way, he thought. He willed the demons of solitude back into their cells and took a long drink from the plastic Evian bottle he had pulled from the refrigerator dutifully stocked by Mrs. Bruton yesterday morning. At last, venerable Wrigley Field, drenched in the sunshine of earlier in the day, sprang forth from the television screen in the corner. And just like that he was in the midst of thirty-five thousand of his dearest friends.

Lang dutifully listened to the thirty-second setup for the pitching matchups, the injuries, and the all-important wind information, then kicked the VCR into fast forward. Twenty minutes later, with the hated Dodgers ahead, 7–5 (the wind was blowing out today), the phone rang. Lang hit the pause and answered.

"Hi, Chris, it's Amy," said a tired Amy Quinn.

"Hi, Amy. What's going on?"

"Me. I'm going on, and not too well in spite of all the coffee I've been drinking. What are you doing home at such a sensible hour during trial?"

"Espinosa is dark until noon tomorrow so I thought I'd sneak home for a halfway normal evening."

"So, you watching a baseball game on tape?"

Lang smiled. "Guilty."

Amy was philosophical. "Whatever it takes. To me, it just seems like pretty much the last thing I could imagine doing with the gift of half a day."

"To each his own," Lang conceded.

"Anyhow, I didn't just call to critique your perversions. I sent a fax to Clive Andrews when John and I got back to the office this afternoon because it was about nine-thirty in England. I figured we'd have some answers by return fax when I got to the office tomorrow."

"Just out of curiosity, how did you handle the questions?" He restarted the tape, with the mute button on.

"Nothing subtle or clever, I'm afraid. I just gave him a paragraph synopsis of John's discovery and the implications for the case, our recommendation that we should fly the StormTree, and asked him for his best guess regarding the miscommunication about the weight specs for the Peregrine."

Lang was impressed. "Well, that was diplomatic."

"I think this case is getting weird, though. Before I left the office, I got a fax answer, about seven forty-five."

"That's three forty-five in the morning," Lang calculated. The Dodgers scored another run on a two-base error.

"I know. But it's only two forty-five tomorrow afternoon in Sydney, where the answer came from."

"What?"

"That's right, the answer came from Sydney even though my fax was received in London long after the Pegasus Technologies offices were closed."

"Well, those guys are globe-trotters, you know."

"No. It's not that. The answer didn't come from Clive or Graham."

"Who, then?"

"Whom," Amy corrected. Before Lang could express his annoyance, she continued. "Jared C. Piersall, Esq."

"Jad?" Lang was genuinely confused. "How did Jad get into that loop so fast? And what is he doing in the loop?" The whole business suddenly made Lang uneasy.

"I don't know, Chris, but there is something about this case that doesn't ring true."

"I know what you mean. But it's not as if we've never represented flakes before. What did Piersall's reply say?"

"Nothing, really. Just a quick acknowledgment of receipt of my letter and instructions to proceed to hire a test pilot."

"How did he couch the instruction to proceed?"

"That was also odd. He says, let's see, '. . . read your letter . . . considered available information . . . risk analysis.' Here it is: 'Our best assessment at this time is to follow your recommendation and proceed to hire a qualified test pilot.' Period."

" 'Our' assessment, huh?"

"You got it."

"Well, go ahead and get Carrick started on it in the morning and we'll see where it goes. I'm beginning to wonder if Lindstrom is the only player in the game who's pulled a fast one."

"I know what you mean. *If* Lindstrom has pulled a fast one."

"Don't worry. He has. And we're going to hang him with it."

"You're the boss. I've got to get some sleep. Good luck tomorrow."

"Thanks. And good night, Amy."

.   .   .

The perspiration poured down Lang's forehead and temples. His chest and arms, swollen from months of strenuous manual labor, glistened in the scorching late-afternoon sun. The oversized lawn mower he pushed was particularly unwieldy today as it gnawed and choked away at the thick mat of overgrown grass. The vibration of the monstrous machine was becoming intolerable and extremely dangerous. Desperately he looked around for someone to help him, but everyone else on the job was fully occupied fighting his own runaway. The accelerating motion made it more and more difficult to see, much less control, the cutting head of the mower. Just as it slipped from his exhausted hands, he lost his footing and fell. As he tried to scramble back to his feet, he realized that he was in his bed in his pitch-black room—and still shaking violently. His whole bed was bucking and pitching, the walls of his room torquing grotesquely. The floor seemed to be alive, breathing in rolling convulsions that threatened to catapult him, bed and all, straight into the rippling ceiling. The realization that he was riding through a very violent earthquake came to him just as the motion stopped. Home-security and auto alarms punctuated the suburban night. Shaken, literally, by the quake and its brutal awakening, he half-walked, half-crawled to the back window. Below, in the dim light of a street lamp still swaying wildly, he could see his pool, Lake Michigan in a gale, whitecaps snapping across it, water sloshing madly onto the decking on all sides. He clicked on the radio on the nightstand.

". . . a major earthquake felt as far north as Santa Cruz and as far south as Hermosillo, Mexico. Scientists at Cal Tech have not yet determined the quake's epicenter and magnitude . . ."

Lang went to the bedroom in the front of the second floor. From that window, things looked relatively normal. Lights all along the street told him that the power was still on throughout the neighborhood and all of his neighbors were up trying to assess how well they had weathered the quake. He picked up the telephone on the table under the window and punched the speed-dial button labeled Ro. As he did, a car across the street suddenly started up and drove away, without putting its lights on. Lang checked the Regulator clock on the far wall. It was 3:47.

CHAPTER 5

RO CRANED HER NECK TO SEE PAST THE WING TO THE vast, empty ground thirty-five thousand feet below. Far to the north, a mountain range of thick, creamy clouds, a spectacular meringue, hung weightlessly in the ether. Above, the sun burned hot and bright in the blue. Everything around her was serenity and contentment. She was alone, comfortably ensconced in the front cabin of a jumbo jet, blissfully beyond the reach of children, teachers, editors, and associates. Her kids were on their way to spend some time with her parents. The long, tough weeks of research that made her feel more like a student who'd lost the point of her studies than an artist with a vision to fulfill were finally behind her. She was traveling first class on someone else's tab, all the while being paid by one of the world's glossiest magazines to do a cover piece that would be seen in every corner of the world. She was basking in the glow of putting the long-overdue exclamation point on the new person she had aspired to be when she had decided to end her marriage. Things couldn't get much better.

It was characteristic of Ro Lang, however, that even in this moment of supreme contentment, a faint dark shadow, barely perceptible, hovered on the periphery. Like a new filling, it would not be ignored. Despite her bravado with friends about how the *Beau Rivage* cover was "the next logical step" in her career, the fact was that it represented both a quantum leap from where she had been and the biggest challenge of her professional life. Doubts that had always lurked about the margins of her self-image had lately begun to make frontal assaults on what confidence she had built up over the years. Put bluntly, she wasn't sure she could pull it off. David and Mark needed a photographer to create a powerful visual statement that would form the centerpiece of an issue of a magazine sold in every civilized corner of the world and what they had hired, thought Ro, was a divorced mother of three who liked to take pictures.

Negative thoughts, Chris would say, and, damn him, he'd be right. Anger flashed at the very thought of him. The passion that had once been the envy of her sorority sisters was fully spent, a cold, bitter resentment left in its place. That bitterness, of course, was all the harsher for the sweetness he had once brought to her life. Chris Lang was the man who had taught her to challenge the barriers she had grown up to accept, to push back her personal frontiers. It was the cruelest irony of her life that he would come to redefine those limits by his sheer domination of their lives.

Even now he evoked anger in her. After consecutive weekends too numerous to count when he could not take the kids because of his crushing trial schedule, he had been furious when she told him that she had to go to the East Coast for three weeks and, if he could not keep the kids, she would leave them with her housekeeper. She had been logical, coolly ticking off the reasons it made sense: School was out until Labor Day; the housekeeper, though new, was highly recommended and extremely capable; and Chris's all-important Consolidated Michigan trial—this year's "trial of the century"—had him occupied fifteen hours a day. Of course, he had no good answer, but made a hell of a summation out of it anyway. He focused on Alma Garcia, the housekeeper. What did they know about her? Where did she come from? How could they trust her with the kids?

She had done her best to reassure him, providing him with the references she had been given, complete with the numbers of the women Alma had worked for, women she herself had interviewed at length over the phone. "Besides," she had pointed out, "this woman came recommended by the people *I* work for." In the end, Chris had been only partially mollified and they had reached a compromise: ten days in Pittsburgh with Ro's parents, then the balance of the time at home with Alma in charge. Ro knew that Chris would do everything in his power to get to her house every day while the kids were in the care of "this stranger."

"Enough about Chris," she heard herself say, through slightly clenched teeth. She shook her head, marveling at the hold he still had over her life. She picked up her book from the empty seat beside her. Mark had booked the flight from LAX to Dulles for both of them but had called Tuesday to tell her that something had come up and he would meet her there. She had been oddly relieved at the news. He was still something of a stranger, after all, and the areas of their common interest were limited. There was the difference in their ages, for one thing—a good ten years, she guessed. In her experience, younger men tended to lack substance and bearing. They were inclined to dwell on superficial things like appearance and status—theirs as well as yours—and meaningful conversation about anything that wasn't on television or an integral part of the job—theirs, not yours—was next to impossible.

To be honest, though, Mark did not really seem to fit that cynical stereotype. He was a serious and mature young man whose interests, at least based on their brief time together, were varied. Besides, it was no ordinary younger man who would have not only suggested that she needed a full-time housekeeper, but dipped into the resources of *Beau Rivage* to find her one. And a good one, at that. No, she realized, her discomfort about being with Mark for four hours had little to do with his boring or disappointing her. It was fear. But it was more than the fear of exposure that had accompanied her through each difficult challenge of her life. Her feelings about Mark were more complicated than that. He had consistently made her feel very good about herself and her ideas during their project meetings. He was an attentive listener, nonjudgmental and open. Not once had he given her the sense—and here the contrast to Chris was graphic—that her ideas were any less valid than his own or anyone else's.

And therein lay the problem, she decided. Mark was a nice guy, bright and sensitive. And very good-looking. But the stirrings of attraction she had begun to feel for this man were a double-edged threat to her well-being. On the one hand, he was unlikely to have a similar interest in her. After all, younger men rarely did, and there would be no reason to expect this impressive young man, apparently without the baggage of commitment, to have any genuine interest in her, with her ex-husband, house in the suburbs, and three kids.

On the other hand, if, by some remarkable long shot, they did share a mutual interest, Ro could only see a thorny tangle of complications, touching every area of her life, personal and professional, that would threaten much of what passed for stability and security in her life. Better to leave the whole area unexplored, intriguing though it was as a theater of fantasy. Such were the rewards of mature judgment, she concluded gloomily, and turned back to watch the cloud mountains racing by.

At the terminal building, she scanned for Mark Fassero among the dozens of unfamiliar faces meeting the flight from Los Angeles. At last she heard her name called from the back of a large knot of craning necks and saw a hand wave above the heads. Mark threaded his way through the crowd gracefully, a broad smile on his face. His beard looked redder than she remembered it, but the way it set off the brilliance of his even white teeth was familiar.

"Hi, Ro," he said as he reached her, shaking her hand warmly. "Did you have a good flight?"

"Very nice, thank you," she said, returning his smile. "There really isn't much that can happen on a seven forty-seven from L.A. to D.C."

"Hopefully not. How do you feel about little airplanes?" They had fallen in with the crowd moving toward the baggage claim.

"All right, I guess. Why do you ask?"

"Well, by rental car, we're a good three hours or more from Gettysburg. On the other hand, we're a forty-five-minute hop in a Piper Cherokee."

Ro did not break stride, but swallowed hard, hoping Mark would not notice. If he did, it didn't show.

"Sure," Ro answered bravely, deciding not to tell him she couldn't even ride the teacups at Disneyland.

Twenty minutes later, Mark was standing at the counter of an outfit called AppalachianAir, filling out forms for the trip to Gettysburg. Ro sat in a cheap red molded-plastic chair, careful not to catch the fabric of her blousy shirt in the jagged rip in the backrest. Her luggage sat next to her where Mark had placed it. Gradually, she was calming herself about the prospect of flying in a small airplane. Thousands of people do it, probably millions, she told herself, and most of them not only survive, they love it. She cursed that part of her nature that tended to focus on the risk of new experiences and not the exhilaration. But she could do it, she told herself. This was a new era in her life, a great time for new beginnings, a personal Renaissance. Mark came back.

"All set?"

"Absolutely," she replied, perhaps a little too bubbly.

"The Cherokee is out on the flight line, not far, but they'll drive us out there because of the bags."

A brief ride in a beat-up Ford station wagon left them next to a small airplane on the flight line. Ro was shocked at its size. It seemed smaller than a minivan. And it had a flimsy look to it that was disconcerting. She pressed her hand furtively against the side of the plane and the metal skin dimpled easily, springing back when she released the pressure. She tried hard to swallow her apprehension while Mark and the driver quickly loaded the bags behind the rear seats. It looked as if it would accommodate four. Mark carefully examined a clipboard with the other man while she situated herself in the right front seat. Once or twice she had to fight back a fleeting sense of claustrophobia, which she did by looking straight out the windshield. It crossed her mind that there was something vaguely paradoxical about being claustrophobic in a space separated from the vastness of the sky by only a flimsy metal skin with a large window. It was a lot like the terror of being trapped in a soap bubble.

Mark finished and climbed into the left front seat next to Ro. He quickly strapped himself in.

"What are you doing?" she asked.

"What do you mean? I'm flying us up to Gettysburg."

"*You?*" she asked, unable to hide her shock.

"Yes," he replied, with mild indignation. It immediately softened. "Oh, I'm sorry. You didn't know I could fly. Well, I can. And I'm very good at it." He flipped a series of toggle switches and set dials while he spoke, as if to validate his familiarity with the process. "Tens of thousands of hours flying airplanes, everything from these little guys right up to C-130 transports, every type of aircraft you can imagine, civilian, military, you name it. And I only fly airplanes that are certified safe beyond any doubt."

She was clearly unnerved now. The facade she had carefully maintained since a small airplane was first mentioned, began to crumble, and she sat mute.

"Would you rather we drove? We've pretty much lost any real shot at surveying the grounds in the daylight today, anyway, and I really don't mind the drive in the dark if you don't."

Suddenly Ro realized that she was on the brink of becoming an impediment to the most important job of her life. She fought back the panic rising in her stomach. Still, she said nothing.

Mark sensed her inner struggle. "Look, Ro. I know you're not entirely comfortable with this small plane and until this minute you didn't even know I could fly one. You have every right to be a little uneasy. It will be no big deal to get a rental car and drive the three and a half hours up to Gettysburg."

"No," she blurted, not having any warning that she would. "I'm okay, Mark. I've just never flown in a little airplane before. I trust you. I really do." She had no idea why she had said this but felt better somehow when she did. He smiled that stunning smile and took her hand in his. It felt very natural.

"Good. You're okay, Ro Lang. You're really okay." He removed his hand but the sensation of it lingered on in hers. He turned to the task of final check for takeoff and clearance from the tower. She braced herself for the epic psychological battle sure to be waged within her over the next hour or so.

Operating well out from the main terminal and its heavy commercial traffic, they got immediate clearance, taxied only briefly, and were airborne. Ro's hands locked onto the armrests with a death grip as the first sensation of flight rolled over her. She guessed she now knew what it felt like to ride a kite. There had seemed to be little wind on the ground, but as they climbed, the Cherokee rocked slowly from side to side. Once or twice the plane's ascent was interrupted by mild turbulence and Ro thought the plane was headed down. Her grip tightened, to the extent that was possible.

"Relax, Ro," said Mark in his easily confident way. "This is all very typical, a smooth flight, actually. We're not in that behemoth that brought you in from L.A., so we're much more sensitive to the forces of flight, thrust, lift, and drag. It's a little like driving a good sports car after riding in a Greyhound bus. You're just feeling the road under the wheels. Believe me, it's a more honest sensation and puts you in far better contact with the flight environment." He looked over to see if his words were doing any good.

Looking straight ahead, she said stiffly, "It's all right, Mark. I'm doing fine. This is an entirely new experience and I'm feeling my way. You don't have to worry about me." She managed a smile, still looking straight ahead.

Mark laughed. "You don't strike me as the kind of person who needs to be worried about. However—" He reached behind his seat and drew a silver flask from his duffel bag. "I know a thing or two about first flights. Why don't you have a slug of this?" He offered her the flask.

She turned to him gingerly, as if their chances of staying aloft depended on her watching the space directly in front of them, and noticed that *he* wasn't even looking where they were flying. But he was smiling, and his confidence in the aircraft, and especially in himself, was reassuring. The flask looked good to her. She took it.

"I hope you won't think less of me for taking this," she said, unscrewing the cap.

He was rummaging in the duffel bag again. "Of course not, Ro. If that were the case I would never have offered it to you in the first place."

She slugged hard at the flask, twice. As she turned to see his reaction, she realized he was holding a cup out to her. She blushed violently. He laughed and handed her the cup. "I hope you won't be offended if I don't join you until we land. I'd like to hang on to my FAA license."

She filled the cup and sipped steadily from it. A sense of well-being gradually displaced the urge to panic. Shortly before they landed she even caught herself remarking on the magnificence of the late-afternoon sun on the rolling Pennsylvania—Maryland?—countryside.

After he got clearance to land from the tiny tower, he said, "I'll bet you're going to love the flight back down to Dulles. And hate the jumbo jet to the coast. You know, once you've turned the country roads in a Porsche, an eighteen-wheeler's just no fun anymore."

Ro smiled and thought, I wish you hadn't brought up Porsches.

Ro opened one eye to survey her surroundings. The heavy blackout drapes over the window admitted very little light, making it difficult for her to get her bearings. She squinted at the ancient alarm clock on the nightstand, but the light behind the dial was dim. It could be either 6:25 or 5:35. Her mouth felt like fabric and tasted awful. Her head ached. The room—a motel room near the Gettysburg Battlefield, she remembered now—had a vaguely musty odor to it, not overpowering, but strong enough to remind Ro that she was in the humid East.

She slowly stirred, very gingerly starting to rise. A powerful shot to the side of her head stopped her immediately. At first she actually thought something had hit her. The realization slowly dawned on her that the headache she had sensed when she had first opened her eyes was the handcar out in front of the freight train. With a sudden sense of panic, the enormity of her predicament took shape. She was at Gettysburg for her first day of work in the field on her *Beau Rivage* cover story, with a project coordinator yet, and she was spectacularly hungover.

She crawled to the side of the queen-sized bed, where she got a better look at the clock; it was *8:28.* She stopped and closed her eyes for a moment. She had no recollection of staggering to her room, stumbling out of her clothes. Nothing. But there was no time now to reconstruct the event. She had to get into some semblance of order as fast as possible. After a moment, she grabbed three Tylenol tablets from the bottle in her purse and washed them down with a long gulp of water from a pitcher on the nightstand. The water, she noticed, tasted remarkably sweet, the first remotely pleasant sensation of the morning. Again she rested for a moment, savoring the water and collecting her thoughts. She became aware of the air-conditioning unit that had been blasting away from under the window since she woke up. Slowly she made her way to the window.

"Jesus," she heard herself say. Could this please be a dream? An awful, truly shitty dream? Then, she remembered the little airplane and the comfort she had taken—and needed!—from Mark's silver flask. That tiny airplane had bounced and jounced her silly, pitching and rolling merrily over the buffeting currents and cross-currents. And all the while Mark had calmly explained the forces of aerodynamic flight as if she were a graduate student in a lab course. Thank God for the silver flask!

But what a price she was paying now. Slowly, she pulled back the drapes. She squinted against the brilliant sun sparkling over the vast, dewy expanse of well-manicured lawn that fell away from the window to the highway below. Off in the distance a large truck rumbled by. The shower, she thought. The shower is the place to start. She had no idea how much time she had before Mark would come by, raring to get the project off to a flying start. Not flying, she decided as she reached the bathroom. Definitely not flying.

Despite her urge to rush, the hot shower was too good to leave and she luxuriated in its heat and power a full twenty minutes. While she was drying there was a sharp knock at the door. She froze. Even under the best of circumstances she was twenty to thirty minutes away from being presentable. Today, she felt as if it would be hours. She considered not answering the door. She could tell him later that she had been in the shower. Another knock.

"Miss? Miss Lang? It's the front desk. I have a message."

Wrapped in her towel, she tiptoed gingerly to the door and opened it a slight crack. "Yes?"

Outside, in the brilliant sun and sweltering humidity of the morning, was a large black woman, carrying a huge tray draped with a white linen napkin. "Morning, Miss Lang. How are you today?"

"Fine, thank you," Ro replied, uncertainly.

The woman smiled warmly. "Mr. Fassero sent this for you. Said you probably be needin' it right after we hear you in the shower. He said he had to take care of somethin' that come up this mornin' and he was sorry but he'd see you after lunch."

Relieved beyond words at the reprieve she had just been given, Ro opened the door wide to let the woman in. She placed the tray on the desk and turned to leave. Ro suddenly remembered to tip her but the woman waved her off. "Thank you, ma'am, but Mr. Fassero already took care of everything. And he said to get you anything you want. You just ring the front desk, you hear?" Again she flashed the friendliest of smiles, then swept from the room.

The door closed with an inadvertent thunder that echoed violently in Ro's head. She removed the linen napkin from the tray. Beneath it were coffee, sugar and milk, a croissant, a small package of Special K, an assortment of fruits and juices, three packets of vitamins, a small bottle of Maalox, and a large pitcher of ice water. She smiled faintly and set about trying to pull herself together.

Eleven o'clock found Ro sitting cross-legged in the center of the motel room bed, her notebooks, journals, maps, sketches, and photos spread all around the room in anticipation of her photographic tour of the battlefield at Gettysburg. She was certain that the adrenaline running through her in anticipation of the adventure ahead was having a salutary effect on her healing powers. She had finished the croissant and twice called for refills of the sweet ice water and was beginning to sense the first stirrings of genuine hunger. Finally she felt ready to see Mark and tackle the day's challenge. And she knew exactly how she would approach it. She rose to stretch and walked over to the window. The air conditioner had labored continuously since she first awoke, effectively masking the overpowering humidity that was unleashed each time the door had opened.

Outside, a family of four was loading its station wagon for the trip home. At least, Mom and Dad were loading the wagon. Junior and Sis were too busy chasing each other around the deserted parking lot to do much good. Suddenly, Ro remembered that she hadn't called her own kids yet. Not that they'd expected her to. She lifted the phone to speak to the front desk—the room phone had no dial or keypad—and had them place the call.

In a moment her mother's voice was on the line. She sounded bubbly with pleasure. "Where have you been? I've been expecting your call since early last evening."

"Sorry, Mom. We got in late last night and I've been in a meeting all morning." Lying to her mother had never felt comfortable to Ro, but her sense of the greater good and the shorter story occasionally made it a palatable option. "How are my three bundles of joy?"

"By now, they're probably eating hot dogs and watching batting practice at the stadium. After that fiasco at the airport, I'm just glad they're all here in one piece."

The kids had gotten bumped from their flight and the agent had arranged to put them on a later one, with another airline. The relief Ro felt that the whole thing had worked out with nothing more than her parents sitting an extra three hours at the airport was tainted by a strong sense of guilt. Where had their mother been when these three children were being shuffled back and forth by strangers at a cold, impersonal airport? Off pursuing her career, she thought darkly. A rich tale for their father's consumption, no doubt. Damn! Her headache threatened to renew itself.

Her mother's view of the situation was rosier. "All's well that ends well, as your dad said." Ro was not fully mollified and the woman who raised her could tell. "Now don't you go getting upset over something that's over and done, Rochelle. You've raised them to be smart, reliable children and they were fine, believe me. Jack thought the whole thing was pretty neat, actually."

Ro smiled at the image of Jack's enthusiasm for all things new. "He would. How's Dad?"

As Ruth Deyton brought her only daughter up to date on Pete Deyton's health, and then moved on to the doings of the Dormont Garden Club, Ro caught sight of someone going through the door into the front office of the motel. Her first thought was that it might have been Mark. After a few minutes, the man came out and went around the back of the office. Again, she caught only a glimpse of him but this time she was sure it was Mark. Her mother was nearing a breaking point in her narrative.

"Mom. Mom, sorry to interrupt. But I've got to go. My associate is back."

"Oh, you professional women, always on the go. What's he like, anyway, Rochelle, this man who's an assistant to my little girl?"

"Stop it, Mom." Ro laughed. Her mother was firmly planted in the past and it was a running joke between them. "He's my associate, not assistant. Actually, he's the project coordinator. And he's a nice guy. Very pleasant. Charming."

"Well, why don't you bring him here on the way home? You could pick up the kids."

"Hold it. Slow down, Mom. He's ten years younger than I am and our relationship is purely professional."

"All right, all right, if you say so. Professional. But young is okay. You're young. And you look a good ten years younger than your age. He'd be delighted to have someone like you."

"Enough, Mom. I've already had one who was delighted to have someone like me. Not so good."

"That's because you expect too much. You think two imperfect people are going to put their lives together and it's going to come out perfect. You ought to know that's not how it works. But it's what you expect or you just give up on it."

"Mom, please. I have to go. He'll be here any second. And you know I don't want to talk about my marriage right now."

"Okay, honey. I'm sorry." Over the last three years, Ruth Deyton had never given up hope of a reconciliation; she just had learned to keep it to herself. "Don't worry about the kids now, Ro. They're great. You take care. And have fun."

"Okay, Mom," replied Ro, suddenly weary from the brief call. "Love to Dad."

The oblique reference to Chris had angered her but it had quickly passed, leaving behind a mild sense of apprehension over the inevitable discussion of the kids' flight to Pittsburgh. In a way, she was surprised that her anger had passed so quickly. That's either a sign of progress, she thought, or I'm still too hungover to care. Either way, she returned to her work, expecting Mark to knock at her door any minute. It didn't happen. Nearly an hour and a half later, his knock finally came.

She rose to open the door. "Hi," she said neutrally.

"Hi. How are you? You look pretty good." He was clearly surprised at her condition.

"I feel fine," she replied, affecting nonchalance. "I've been at it for hours and I'm ready to go when you are."

"Great," he said, regaining himself. "How about if we start with lunch?"

"Fine with me," she said, gathering up her equipment. "By the way, thanks for the breakfast tray. It was very thoughtful."

"No problem. Let me give you a hand with that stuff, then we can go over to the restaurant. There's a little place just down the road. The woman at the desk recommends it."

They quickly packed up her cameras and equipment, along with her two most important field journals. "Is everything okay, Mark? I mean, whatever it was that came up this morning."

"Yeah. Fine. Wasn't anything, really. I just had to go over to Philly unexpectedly. Good thing I had rented the Cherokee. Of course, that's probably why David asked me to take care of this for him, in the first place." He laughed easily. "Anyway, I'm sorry about the delay in getting started. I guess David figures as long as I'm working on company business, the interruption is justified. But, I hurried back here as fast as I could. I just arrived this minute." He glanced at his wristwatch, as if for emphasis.

Ro looked quizzically at him for the briefest instant, but he was looking away. She started to mention having seen him at the office earlier but thought better of it.

"All set?" he asked as they finished loading the Jeep he had rented at the airport.

"Let's go," Ro replied, climbing into the passenger's seat. She caught a glimpse of herself in the oversized side-view mirror as she did. She was amazed at how clear-eyed she looked, considering how she still felt. And, she decided, that trip to the Banana Republic in Beverly Hills had been worth the time and the money.

"Now a little greasy lunch at the local burger joint and then who is it? Wilkinson?"

"Okay," she replied, gamely controlling a mild surge of nausea at the image conjured up by the remark. "Lieutenant Stewart K. Wilkinson of the First Pennsylvania Artillery it is."

CHAPTER 6

LANG HURRIED THROUGH THE HALLS OF DEVEREAUX and Brace, a bulky working folder under his left arm and a thick pink memorandum in his right hand. The memo had his undivided attention and more than one passing co-worker mumbled a faint greeting and moved deftly out of his path. His stride gobbled up great chunks of the seamless burgundy carpet that covered the wide, warmly lit corridor. He wore no jacket and his silk tie was loosened at the collar. He was a trial lawyer plainly engaged and operating at full throttle. "Chris," called a voice from a large office as he passed. He stopped and backpedaled to get a look inside. It was Oliver Brace. "In a hurry?" Brace asked.

"What else?" replied Lang warmly. "What's new with you, Oliver?"

Brace was a founding member of the firm, joining the renowned tax lawyer Max Devereaux in 1956 to form a powerful team that had since grown to nearly one hundred lawyers. Now in his early 70s, he had been a formidable mergers-and-acquisitions lawyer years before that term was coined. As the nominal head of the

Partnership Steering Committee, Brace now busied himself almost exclusively with management and administrative concerns, long since having engineered his last corporate reorganization.

"Politics and profits, Chris. I notice you've missed our last few PSC meetings yourself."

"I know," replied Lang, stepping into Brace's doorway. "The crush has been unbelievable. My desk seems to have become to big lawsuits what LAX is to jumbo jets. I can't manage to find much room for firm business these days."

"The wages of success, young man," Brace said, smiling. Immediately it turned to a scowl. "It seems as if partnership meetings are all *I* have time for anymore. I'd give my right arm to do another deal like Consolidated."

It was Lang's turn to smile. "Well, thanks to you the company seems pretty well set from an organizational standpoint. Now if they can only weed out the claims people who make the occasional fifty-million-dollar mistake, they can keep printing money." Lang purposely avoided the issue of Brace's practicing law. Word from his corporate partners was that Brace's skills had declined and he was now considered a major liability in his area, the risky game of corporate securities. In light of the fact that recent court decisions had showed an alarming tendency to stick lawyers with large damage awards for the misdeeds of clients who raise money through the public sale of corporate stock, Lang was not about to challenge the wisdom of his partners. That didn't prevent him from feeling sorry for the venerable old gentleman, who seemed to be constantly fighting against the perception that he had outlived his usefulness. Lang reminded himself not to get old.

"Well, Chris, I know you're swamped. You've been under the gun since you got here. But I'd like you to be at the next meeting if at all possible."

Lang succeeded in suppressing a groan. As the *Fulton* trial picked up speed and the Pegasus case loomed on the near horizon, he had no desire to spend time or energy dealing with partnership politics.

"The tenth?" he asked, as noncommittally as possible.

Brace hadn't gotten to his station in life without knowing something about people. "I know, I know," he said, moving from behind his desk toward Lang. "You really don't have the time or room for the sort of thing we are dealing with these days." He stepped past Lang and discreetly closed his door. "But, Chris, it's important. Your partners are honorable men, I know, but they're not acting honorably, and I think things are about to come to a head."

Lang's interest was piqued. "What's going on, Oliver?" he asked, genuinely interested for the first time during the brief conversation.

"It's about Max. Jerry Zender and Leo Charmey have suddenly hit on the idea that we really don't need Max on an 'of counsel' basis anymore."

"You mean, now that they drove him out of the firm—his firm, your firm—they think we can get along fine without paying him the retainer? The bastards."

"Well, Chris, nothing's ever that simple. And I don't think there's malice intended, but I agree that it pretty much comes out the same however you look at it."

Lang was angry. Two years earlier, the PSC had observed the occasion of Max Devereaux's seventy-fifth birthday and automatic withdrawal from the committee by recommending to the firm's membership that he be placed on retired status and given the ambiguous designation "of counsel." Lang, one of the youngest members of the committee, and Brace, the oldest after Devereaux himself, were shocked at the suggestion. The shock turned to outrage when they discovered that twenty-five of the remaining thirty-two partners agreed. Lang had wanted to go to war, file suit, and do to the insurgents what he was paid to do to his adversaries in court. Brace had been badly shaken by the callousness of the men and women he and Devereaux had largely handpicked over the course of four decades. It had been Devereaux's clear head that had prevailed. He had immediately grasped the significance of the broad support his enemies enjoyed among the partners and the fact that their decision was, as a practical matter, irreversible. He adamantly refused to allow the firm he had built and that bore his name to be sullied in a high-profile circus of a lawsuit. In the end, he had skillfully used the threat of such a lawsuit to negotiate a substantial settlement package providing for the continuation of his one-million-dollar annual salary for five years, with a percentage of the firm's receipts on certain designated clients for the five years thereafter. Although he had been aided and counseled by Lang throughout, he had insisted that the other partners never know of the extent of Lang's involvement on his behalf, for fear that Lang's ability to deal with the partners when his own best interests were involved might be compromised. The fact that Lang had been reelected to the committee was powerful testament to Max's judgment.

"What's the action item for the tenth, Oliver?"

"One of Leo's hotshots in employee benefits thinks he's found a credible way to revoke the agreement with Max and at least save the firm the annual salary over the remaining three years, if not get the first two million back. Jerry Zender is very excited by the prospect, to the point where he told me that the committee would be remiss in its duties to the remaining partners if we didn't do it."

"Let me see if I understand. Charmey's little department grunts have found a technicality in the contract we made with Max where there is a *possible* argument that could undo the deal and Zender feels we're *duty bound* to do that to Max?" Lang's voice rose with emotion as he spoke.

Brace held his hands out in a gesture intended to calm Lang down. "That's basically it, Chris. Now, I have to tell you that, aside from making me a little nervous about what may lie ahead for me, I think that's not only wrong, it's immoral. And I don't want to be part of it."

Lang shook his head disgustedly. "Jesus, Oliver. And they wonder why the world hates lawyers. The scheming, self-serving sons of bitches. I'll be there. I wouldn't miss it. But you and I are only two votes out of seven. We're going to have to do a little groundwork with the other partners before Zender and Charmey bring this to the floor."

Brace looked as though a weight had been lifted from his shoulders. "I know. You're right, of course. I've spoken to Max. He's got some ideas about how to breathe morality back into his former partners. But he says that having you at the PSC meeting will lay the foundation for his plans."

"I hope he's right. I'll have to call him in the next day or two. I've been meaning to do that anyway." Lang looked at his watch. "Hey, Oliver. Sorry. I'm ten minutes late for an important meeting. I'll talk to you about this next week."

"Great." Brace smiled, opening his door again. He clasped the younger man affectionately on the shoulder. "Thanks, Chris. You've got a good heart."

Clive Andrews looked out through the vast expanse of glass that formed the west wall of the conference room on the thirty-fifth floor. Behind him, at the far end of the long polished-marble table, his business associate, Graham Ellerby, was engaged in animated discussion with the aerodynamics expert, John Carrick, and Chris Lang's tenacious young associate, Amy Quinn. Lang's paralegal assistant, Rachel Cruz, moved in and out of the room with files, document clips, and computer disks. Two oversized model airplanes dominated the table in front of them and the large projection television screen on the wall was running a tape of a small aircraft in flight. Andrews sat silently, largely oblivious to the activity behind him, trying hard to see any of the sailboats he was sure were out there in the Pacific Ocean at the far reaches of the horizon. It was fashionable for the English, like most Europeans, to look down their noses at Californians, at Angelenos in particular, with their smog, crowds, third-world immigrants, fast food, and freeways, but Andrews secretly envied these people their sunshine and freedom from suffocating convention and tradition.

Lang reentered the room. "Sorry for the interruption," he apologized. He turned to Amy. "Are we all up to date on the state of the case?"

Before Amy could respond, Ellerby did. "Up to date, indeed," he said with his usual smile. "Amy has covered the nuances of discovery in the federal courts, the pitfalls of sitting for a deposition, and the likelihood that we will all be dead by the time all the paper involved in this case can be read by human eyes."

Now Amy smiled. "You *were* listening. I'm impressed."

"Good," Lang said. "Let's move on, then."

"There is one more thing," said Amy. "Even you aren't aware of it yet, Chris, since I just got Hickman's fax. We're agreed on all depositions but Lindstrom's."

"Figures," observed Lang.

"They take the position that the deposition is for purposes of harassment only, since he had no connection whatsoever with the project. In the motion they have filed for a protective order they argue that you—we—are only trying to harass Lindstrom and grab cheap publicity to create collateral settlement leverage, and they've asked for an order preventing the deposition."

"Harassment and cheap publicity, huh?" said Lang, laughing. "You say it like it's a bad thing. It's the American way, at least in the courtroom."

Amy smiled. "Well, we're going to have to oppose it. And it will be an uphill fight, since the presidential primary season is just around the corner and Lindstrom's already declared his candidacy."

"And so we shall," agreed Lang. He turned toward the television screen. "I understand you and John are becoming experts on the spinning of the Peregrine."

Ellerby was surprised. "Haven't you seen the spin yet, Chris?"

Amy replied, "I told you he's been in trial, Graham."

"Don't worry, Graham," Lang said reassuringly. "There's all the time in the world for me to get up to speed. That's why I have Amy going on this full time and why we have John pulling all the technical aspects together."

"Worry?" answered Ellerby. "I should think I'm not worried. Your associates are first-rate. I'm just surprised that your own curiosity hasn't got the better of you yet. The video of the spin is one remarkable piece of documentation."

"Then let's see it," said Lang. "And get a feel for just what it is that our Mr.—"

"McCluskey," offered Carrick.

"—Mr. McCluskey will be asked to get himself into."

"And out of," added Amy, almost under her breath. She flipped on the VCR and the television controls, deftly cuing the tape and dimming the lights. "Why don't we have Graham narrate this for us, since he shot it?" she suggested.

"Right," Ellerby said as the tape rolled. "The Peregrine had gone through about three weeks of standard evaluation at this point at the airfield up at Doncaster. Nothing terribly challenging, just mapping out the basic power curve, climb rate, cross-wind tolerances, refining the center of gravity, and the like." On the large screen, a nimble little airplane with a futuristic look, all white with blue numerals on its fuselage, cruised gracefully through a brilliant blue sky. It was a perfect replica of the two models now resting on the conference table.

"No envelope expansions of the performance-and-handling characteristics to this point, then?" asked Lang, engrossed in the tape. Again an expression of surprise crossed Ellerby's weathered face but could not be seen in the faint light of the room.

"You've been doing your homework again, Chris," replied Ellerby.

"Those aviation publications you gave me make fascinating bedtime reading, Graham."

"To answer your question, no. We hadn't pushed the aircraft to its limits by any means. Cam MacNeil, the test pilot on the program, was directed to be slightly more aggressive, but not reckless, in taking the aircraft to the edge of its performance envelope. After all, based on the results of the Arrow Dynamics test of the

StormTree prototype, we were absolutely confident of the performance and handling of the plane near stall speed. However, that's where we encountered the problem."

"I'm looking forward to hearing you state that under oath at the trial, Graham. What was the center of gravity for this flight?"

Again, Ellerby was unprepared for Lang's apparent grasp of the technical aspects of the problem. "This flight was at one hundred twenty-seven centimeters, well within the mid-range prescribed in the Arrow Dynamics engineering report."

"Does the fact that the propeller is in the back of the airplane have anything to do with spin tendency and recovery?" Lang asked, his eyes glued to the screen.

Carrick replied this time. "Shouldn't. All things being equal, a canard pusher is just as stable as a standard prop in the high angle of attack."

Lang started to ask about the canard pusher but was interrupted by Ellerby. "At this point, Cam starts the stall progression. If we listen carefully, I think we can hear the radio communications."

Up on the screen, the Peregrine, captured on tape by the "chase plane" flying above and slightly behind its right wing, began to slow considerably relative to the chase plane, and the angle of its nose rose perceptibly. The scratchy sound of the radio could be heard, then the tinny, intermittent radio voice of a Scotsman.

"Starting . . . stall, now. Buffet is normal. Air-speed indicator . . . knots, now thirty-five. Thirty-two. Pitchbuck is . . . typical. Aeronca . . ."

Ellerby interjected. "He's comparing the pitchbuck, the hard up-and-down oscillation at stall speed, with a characteristic of the Aeronca 7AC, a good airplane."

". . . right aileron. Then she rolls off."

The plane clearly rolled off to the left, its nose dropping until it was level, then the roll-off ended and the plane flew straight and level. Three more times, over the span of a good three minutes, the plane stalled, then rolled off, alternating to the left and the right. The radio chatter was calm and unremarkable in each case.

A fifth time, the aircraft approached stall speed and the nose pitched up.

". . . approaching stall again, crossing controls. Nose coming up through . . . Pitchbuck, buffet normal . . . opposing elevator and ailerons . . . I've lost her!"

As the nose came up again for another pass at the stall, with no

other perceptible difference from the previous stalls, the right wing
rose sharply, wrenching the plane over, literally flipping it upside
down. As it rolled grotesquely through to an upright, level attitude,
it began to rotate in a slow, even spin, perfectly parallel to the
ground. Its loss of altitude, captured graphically by the chase plane
flying at a steady altitude, was appalling. Like a leaf, it spun, utterly
flat, straight toward the ground. New voices were heard on the tape.
Ellerby's voice, from the chase plane.

"Christ, Cam! You're in a bloody flat spin!"

MacNeil's voice in reply was chillingly composed. "Right. I've
no oscillation at all. Flat all the way. Altitude at entry . . . ten
thousand feet . . . Backing off throttle . . . Airspeed zero, altitude nine thousand . . . Eighty-five hundred . . ."

"Best get out of there, Cam," said another new voice, possibly
from the ground. On the video, the Peregrine was shrinking rapidly
in size as it plummeted away from the helpless chase plane, straight
toward the green English countryside. The cameraman gamely followed it down.

"Not yet, David. Induce pitch oscillation . . . engine sound
out of phase . . . nose over . . . throttle up . . . altitude six
thousand feet . . . five . . ."

Whatever MacNeil was doing, it plainly had no effect. Amy,
who had now seen the tape a half dozen times, was absently licking
at her lips, her right leg bouncing on the ball of her foot. Lang,
seeing the footage for the first time, was transfixed. Inside that
shrinking toy on the screen, he thought, a man is wrestling gravity
for his very life, and the outward appearance is perversely serene.

Suddenly, after what seemed an eternity, the Peregrine's nose
tilted slightly but unmistakably forward, breaking the hypnotic motion of the flat spin ever so slightly. It seemed to teeter on some
unseen fulcrum for an agonizing moment, the spin still unfolding in
its deceptively slow pirouette. The sound of the engine alternately
rose and fell, with each cycle gradually rising in pitch to a crescendo.
Finally, the aircraft's nose pitched sharply forward and the airplane
literally flew its way out of the spin.

"I'm through it," understated the calm Scot on the radio.
"Altitude loss fifty-seven hundred feet . . . think I'll take her back
to the field . . ."

The tape abruptly cut to a plain blue background. Amy
stopped the VCR and brought the lights up. Somebody in the room
muttered, "Jesus Christ!" Lang noticed that his palms were clammy
and his throat dry.

"There it is, Christopher," exclaimed Ellerby. "The spin of the Peregrine in all her glory."

"Jesus," said Lang softly. "I've got to meet Cam MacNeil."

"When you do, Chris," remarked Andrews, "it'll be an unhappy day. He rode an experimental helicopter down into the Firth of Clyde last May."

"That's why we need another pilot to test the StormTree," added Ellerby. "Your man McCluskey."

"Yes," replied Lang distractedly. "Our man McCluskey." The room fell silent for a long moment. Lang broke it. "Okay," he said, rising to move to the head of the long table. "John, what is the arrangement with Walt McCluskey?"

"Walt McCluskey is ex-Air Force, a former test pilot at Edwards, squadron commander at Wright Patterson, served a stretch at NASA's spin facility at Langley—"

Andrews interrupted. "My God, he's not CIA, is he?"

Carrick laughed. "No. Wrong Langley. He was at Langley Air Force Base in Hampton, Virginia, where NASA does its wind-tunnel testing."

"Too many Tom Clancy novels, eh Clive?" said Lang. Andrews laughed.

Carrick continued. "He retired in '79 and has bounced around a little. A bit of a tough time keeping a job, I guess. For the last seven months he's been the chief pilot for Transforward Corporation, a small electronics outfit up in Salt Lake City. All the reports I've gathered from various sources say that Walt's a solid guy and a pro at the spin regimen. And, yes, he's flown the military specifications for departure and spin that are specified in the contract between Arrow and Daultry's company." He checked his neatly hand-written notes. "Verification-tested the General Dynamics Next Generation Trainer through the entire MS 92121 for the Air Force at Edwards in 1978. And, because of your tight schedule, Chris, he'll be here to meet you at the Camarillo Airport two weeks from Saturday at ten A.M."

"Great," said Chris, rising to signal the end of the meeting. "If we're right and Walt's the right guy, we'll set up a trip back to Winter Haven to fly the StormTree. Well, gentlemen, I'm going to return you all to the capable hands of Amy and get back to other business. I'll see you, John, on the seventh in Camarillo. Clive and Graham, I'll be in touch." He gathered his file for a moment, then added, "By the way, how's Jad doing?"

Ellerby responded, "I don't really know, do you, Clive?"

"Haven't spoken with him in weeks," Andrews offered.

"Hmm," commented Lang ambiguously, meeting Amy's quizzical look without comment. He wrapped up his file. "Got to run."

CHAPTER 7

LANG DOWNSHIFTED AS HE ROUNDED THE BEND ON
Hightower Road and approached the two-story Mediterranean at
21543. As he swung into the driveway a gangly redheaded boy
bounced out of the front door in a baggy short-sleeved shirt and
baggy shorts, a dirty white cast on his right arm. "Dad! Dad! How
ya doing, Dad?"

Lang broke into a wide grin, the likes of which few of his
clients or colleagues even knew he possessed. "Jackie Boy!" he answered and swept the running ten-year-old up in his arms. "Jeez,
you're getting heavy, ace. Or is all the weight in that cast?"

"No chance, Dad," the boy replied, himself all smiles. "It's
space-age material, strong but lightweight." He swung it wildly
over his head to demonstrate the point. "I've been working out,
anyway. I'm going out for the football team next year at Tierra
Rejada."

"Really?" Lang said wryly. "I thought you were a soccer star."

"That's this year, at Willoughby. They have a football team at
middle school, and Coach Neuman says I can probably go out for
placekicker."

"Hey, now that's pretty neat," replied Lang. He glanced at his watch. "Are the girls ready?"

"In a couple of minutes. I'll get the garage door and the keys to the car." He bounded into the house, typically leaving the front door ajar in his wake. Lang followed him in and closed the door.

"Hello?" he called from the front hallway.

"Be right down, Dad," called a girl's voice from somewhere upstairs in the bright, warmly decorated house.

"Ro?" he called out.

"Not home, Daddy," responded a second girl's voice from another part of the upstairs.

Not home at nine o'clock on a Saturday morning? Lang said to himself. Then to the girls upstairs, he called, "I'm going to put my car away and get your mom's out."

Just as he finished doing so, his two daughters emerged from the front door. Jennifer, who looked more mature each time he saw her, even if it was as often as once a week, glided down the walk with the elegance and bearing of a swan. It occurred to Lang that thirteen was supposedly an awkward age but he saw no evidence of it in her carriage. She was, in fact, from her flowing black mane to her dancer's legs, "Little Ro," graceful and demure and thoroughly feminine.

Behind her strode the wiry, compact Andrea, with the red hair and green eyes she shared with her twin brother, likewise an athlete bursting with purpose and drive. Hers was not the flowing kind of grace that Jennifer possessed, but the ripple of kinetic energy. She was shorter than her sister by more than the three years' age difference would suggest, but her shoulders were nearly as broad and her swimmer's torso and arms were well developed.

"Hi, Daddy." Jennifer smiled, underscoring for her father her resemblance to her mother. They embraced by the side of Ro's new four-wheel-drive Oldsmobile, Lang giving her a strong, fatherly kiss on her smooth right cheek. Andrea literally leaped into his arms and buried her head in his chest.

"Oomph!" he exhaled, lifting his little girl high in the air. "I really missed you guys!"

"Me, too!" replied Andrea, not letting go her grip on her dad.

"Jack," called Lang into the house. "Let's go. I have an appointment."

"An appointment?" said the girls, in perfect unison. "You're doing business on a Saturday? That's our day with you," continued Jennifer.

"Not again!" added the little one.

"Business?" chimed in a disappointed Jack as he came back out of the house.

"Well," replied Lang apologetically, "technically it's business. But I know you're going to enjoy it. I have to meet with a test pilot at Camarillo Airport. It's an airplane case. But we've got to get going because I have to meet him at ten." He climbed into the driver's seat while the three kids, apparently placated, settled into the other seats. He ran his hand over the black leather dash of the car. "I like your mom's new car, or vehicle I guess it is. She pick it out herself?"

Jack responded. "We helped. I told her, 'Lose the van, Mom. Let's go for a four-by-four.' "

"Well, you guys did okay. Not really what I'd expect from your mom, but nice."

"She loves to drive it, Daddy," explained Jennifer.

The ride to the airport became a news report. Updates on the new school year, who liked his or her teacher, who had a crush on whom, swimming team and soccer bulletins, filled the car. Lang always appreciated the chance to observe each of his children's distinct personalities as they evolved and matured. Not for the first time, he was struck by how much he enjoyed them as friends, as well as offspring. At last, into a brief and rare silence, he broached the subject that had been on his mind all morning. "So, guys, where's your mom?"

"Out with Mark," replied Jack.

"Again," added Andrea. Jennifer was silent but searched her father's face for a reaction. There was none.

"Mark?" he repeated simply. "Oh, the guy from the magazine?"

"That's the dude," answered Jack.

"He and Mom are finishing up her Gettysburg piece," offered Jennifer. "It's really good, Dad. You should see it."

"Oh, I will, Jen," replied Lang. "I'm sure it's terrific. Your mother's really worked hard on it."

"Day and night," interjected Jack, with what Lang thought for a moment was a snide look at his older sister. He dismissed the notion immediately, reasoning erroneously that a ten-year-old was too young to make such an innuendo.

At the quaint, unpretentious Camarillo Airport, Lang found John Carrick waiting for him with another man. He was perhaps fifty, stocky, with a paunch his ragged bomber jacket did not cover. He wore aviator sunglasses and sported two days' growth of gray beard. A grease-stained baseball cap was jammed down over his brow.

Carrick introduced Walt McCluskey and Lang introduced his kids. McCluskey greeted them all with a firm and friendly handshake. His drawl and speech patterns suggested West Virginia or Tennessee to Lang's ear. Lang immediately sensed in him the same confidence that he had grown accustomed to in Carrick.

"Well, Walt, I'm sure John has told you what we're doing here. We need a pilot, and a good one, for a nasty bit of test-flying."

McCluskey nodded. "Experimental pusher, lightweight composite. Rich man's toy. I've seen the pictures."

"Have you ever flown anything like it before?" Lang asked.

"Not exactly. But, hey, it's experimental. Nobody has." The three men laughed. Jack was under the wing of the nearest airplane. Lang waved him away.

"That's all right," said McCluskey. "That's the one I brought down here. He can't hurt it and I doubt it could hurt him. To answer your question, though, I've flown a number of lightweight composites, like the Long EZ and the Vari-Eze, and I did some of the certification flights on the Aviasud Albatros over in France. Of course, I was in the spin program at Edwards and did the only real-time spinning they did back at Langley."

Lang took an instant liking to McCluskey. He would be a bit rough-hewn for a jury in a federal court in Los Angeles, but he might go over well with the type of jury Lang was likely to see up in San Sebastian. And he had a directness that Lang appreciated in someone he had to rely on. McCluskey was talking about the airplane he had flown down from Salt Lake City.

". . . the company lawyers won't let me do that. Something about insurance or some such thing. I imagine you're familiar with that sort of thing, Chris. Anyway, this little Piper Cub is really just dandy for our purposes today."

"Our purposes?" asked Lang.

"You want to feel a spin for yourself, don't you? I mean, how else you gonna get the experience across to your jury?"

"Well," Lang demurred. "That's really not necessary, Walt. I manage to convey a great many things to a jury that I haven't personally experienced."

McCluskey eyed him dubiously. Jack interjected, "You really going to fly in that airplane, Dad? Neat!"

Carrick stepped in. "It's completely safe, Chris. This Piper Cub is made to spin and recover on command. It's the plane I did spin training in at Travers."

"I'm not concerned about safety, John. I have all the confidence in the world in Walt and his plane. It's just not necessary. I mean the expense and the time. You fellows have places to go, things to do."

Carrick responded, "I cleared the expense of the whole package with Graham. I told him it should include a spin flight and he agreed. And I've set the entire morning aside for this exercise."

"Me, too." McCluskey smiled.

"Neat!" exclaimed Jack. "Wish we could go."

"Afraid not," said Carrick. "Even though spinning in this Cub isn't dangerous, it really wouldn't be a good idea for you kids to go along. I'll stay here with you while your dad goes up with Mr. McCluskey. In fact, we can drive out into the desert where we can get a good view from the ground."

"Great!" exclaimed Jack, his enthusiasm for the entire project growing exponentially with each passing minute. Lang's initial trepidation about the flight—not to mention the spin—took a backseat to his fear of letting his son down.

"Okay, okay," he said, at last. "I'll do it. Let's go, Walt."

Carrick and the children headed for the nearby parking lot. As they piled into Ro's vehicle, none of them noticed the man sitting behind the wheel of the old blue Chevrolet Caprice parked several rows over in the sparsely filled lot. Nor did they notice when he started the engine and followed them out onto the highway at a discreet distance. Meanwhile, in the Piper Cub, McCluskey took Lang over the flight and spin procedures. They advised the tower of their planned acrobatics and got clearance to fly into an area just outside the control radius of the airport. After they gave Carrick a twenty-minute head start, they received tower clearance to taxi and take off.

Lang had flown on many small commuter airplanes but never on anything as small as the classic Piper Cub. He was amazed at the short distance it required for taxi before it was airborne. And, although he knew from his commuter-plane experience that the sense of motion would be more pronounced than in a large aircraft, he was unprepared for the turbulent ride he encountered during climbout. McCluskey read his face.

"Perfectly normal, Chris," he said in his reassuring drawl. "Winds are light but you're still in an aeroplane. You're going to feel the forces with a whole lot more fidelity than you're used to. But there's nothing to be concerned about."

Lang nodded, consciously trying to relax. His neck and shoulders were knotted with tension. He tried breathing deeply and allowed himself to think it was working. The view through the windshield was truly breathtaking, however, on a clear blue day over the southern reaches of the Mojave Desert.

After a long, sustained climb, McCluskey leveled off and advised the tower that he was commencing acrobatics. Lang did not like the sound of the term.

"All buckled in, good buddy?" asked McCluskey, unnecessarily.

"Uh-huh," was the only response Lang could muster. Suddenly, an image of the Colossus roller coaster at Magic Mountain flashed into his head, complete with the mixed sense of dread and duty with which he had boarded it with Jennifer when she was nine. He had hated every second of that goddamned ride, and he was sure that history was about to repeat itself. He wished he had remembered that roller coaster before he got into the airplane.

"Here we go, Chris," McCluskey broke in. He pulled back on the stick, reduced the speed sharply, and threw the rudder left and the ailerons right. Suddenly, Lang felt himself pushed violently upward and to the left. Just as he began to comprehend the upward thrust, he realized that it had become a sharp downward thrust. Strapped tightly into his seat, he was whipping headlong over and over to his left. The horizon in front of the cockpit became a blur, losing all of its meaning in an instant. He had the sensation of pitching over Niagara Falls in a barrel. Just as suddenly as the spin began, it ended, the plane perfectly parallel to the horizon, flying straight and level. His stomach lagged considerably behind the rest of him in regaining equilibrium.

"Shit," Lang whispered when his voice came back to him. "How many revolutions was that?"

"Rotations. Just two," replied an ice-calm McCluskey. "Here we go again, the other way." Once more he pulled back on the stick, cut his airspeed, and applied opposing rudder and aileron inputs. Once more, Lang was in a barrel. This time he was conscious of the whole structure straining, creaking all around him. Abruptly, McCluskey stopped the spin.

"Three rotations," he announced. "So, what do you think? Can you get this sensation across to the jury?"

"I told you I could do that anyway, Walt. The only thing this has done is persuade me to ask the judge to let me drive the jury off a cliff in a cement mixer as demonstrative evidence."

McCluskey laughed hard. "I'll bet you *are* good in court."

"You know this airplane sounds like it's going to come apart when you spin it," Lang observed.

"No chance. But do you have any idea of the torque forces this baby is pulling through that snap-spin maneuver?"

Lang didn't, and didn't ask.

"Of course," McCluskey went on. "These are garden-variety spins. Spirals, really. Not even a close cousin to the flat spin John and you are talking about." He seemed to mull something over for a moment. "You know, the test flights you're interested in are kinda risky." Another pause. "I'm gonna need to charge you higher than my standard test rate." Lang, much more in touch now with the element of danger in the flights, braced for a huge demand. In the dim recesses of his mind he thought to appreciate the business acumen of a man who would take the occasion of his employer's being strapped to a spinning airplane eight thousand feet above the desert floor to negotiate compensation.

"Now, for normal test flights, nothing life-threatening, I charge nothing less than four hundred dollars," McCluskey continued.

"An hour?" asked Lang, who himself got $325 an hour.

McCluskey laughed hard, ending with an unintended snort. "I wish. That's my per diem. You know, by the day." Lang nodded and smiled at the Latin phrase. "For life-threatening, I'm gonna need seven hundred fifty dollars a day." He paused. When he encountered no outrage at this act of piracy, he quickly added, "Plus a ten-thousand-dollar life-insurance policy."

Lang suppressed another smile at the absurdity of a world where a man who stood in a courtroom and talked about things other people had done earned nearly five times as much as a highly trained and specialized technician whose life was on the line.

"I don't think that will be a problem, Walt."

"Good," said McCluskey, visibly relieved. "Let's get back."

On the ground, Lang was shortly rejoined by Carrick and the children, who gushed about the thrill of seeing an airplane spin, not to mention one in which their own dad was a passenger. He arranged to get in touch with Carrick the following week and told McCluskey they would get back to him with details of the trip to

Florida to fly the StormTree. Lang's offer to send him a short contract covering the terms of his engagement was met with a dismissive wave. "You know what we agreed to, Chris. Your word and a handshake are all I need." Shake they did, and everyone was on his way.

On the way back to the parking lot, Carrick caught up with Lang and fell in alongside. "Strange people out here in the desert," he said, squinting off into the bright blue distance.

"Oh?" Lang replied, having no idea what Carrick was talking about. "I don't follow you."

Carrick shrugged, his eyes still out on the horizon. "I don't think it's anything, really. But I could have sworn a guy in a beat-up Chevy followed us out onto Route 16 while we were watching your spin."

Lang caught a vague scent of apprehension in the otherwise steady John Carrick. He stopped and let the kids go on toward the car. "What are you talking about, John?"

"It really is nothing, Chris. But I got a strange feeling seeing that old blue car behind me. I noticed it in the lot before you got here. The guy was just sitting in it."

Lang surveyed the parking lot. It was nearly empty. "Where'd he go?"

"He left us out on 16. I haven't seen him again since. As I say, I'm sure it's nothing, but it made me a little uneasy. Lots of nuts in the desert." Again, he shrugged. They started walking again. "I guess having your kids with me made me feel a little protective."

"I appreciate your concern for the kids, John. But I'm sure it's nothing."

Carrick nodded hastily. "I'm sure you're right. Probably all that military training. When I tested the Next Generation Hermes for Douglas they made us go through a lot of antispook stuff and I guess a little of it stuck. I'm never quite sure who might have his eyes or ears on me." They reached Carrick's car. "Maybe it wouldn't hurt to stay on our toes, though. We're going after some pretty big game in this lawsuit, you know." He did not wait for a reply, but slid in behind the wheel and started the engine. He smiled and waved at Lang through the windshield, then drove off, leaving Lang mystified and a little edgy.

Back on the road, Lang spent the first few minutes looking as much into the rearview mirror as at the road ahead. He saw nothing and gradually his thoughts refocused on his plans for the rest of the day. He checked his watch. "I have about one-fifteen. What do you say we grab a bite at one of these places off the freeway and go for a visit to an old friend?"

"Who?" asked Jennifer.

"Does it matter?" Lang replied. "Besides, I'm not telling. I will submit to a round of Twenty Questions, however."

"Me first!" shouted Andrea, quickly recognizing a favorite, if seldom-played, game.

"Okay. You're first, then Jack, then Jen. But no more shouting."

Andrea could barely contain herself. "Is this friend alive?"

"Good question, Andy," remarked Jennifer, sarcastically. "This isn't regular Twenty Questions. This person is obviously alive or we wouldn't be going to see him. Or her."

"Good logic," said Lang. "The answer is yes and that's your first question. Jack?"

"Is it a man?"

"Yes," answered Lang, somewhat tentatively. "That's two."

"I really don't want to play," said Jennifer. "Your turn again, Andy."

"Wait a minute," said Lang, plainly annoyed. "What's wrong with a little game of Twenty Questions, Jen? Are the old family games suddenly beneath you?" Even as he spoke, Lang knew he was overreacting. Ever since he and Ro had split up he had been constantly on the alert for any sign that the closeness he had shared with his kids before the divorce would disappear. Rationally he knew that there would inevitably come a time when the natural process of maturity would move his children out into what he thought of as their permanent orbit in the family. The trick was to distinguish between the two indistinguishable forces. For the moment, like it or not, he was inclined to be suspicious of any sign that the fabric was weakening.

Jennifer rolled her eyes. "No, Dad," she said with an edge of disgust in her voice. "I'm not above the game. I just don't want to play this time."

Lang wasn't convinced. "Not good enough, Jennifer. This is an official family game on an official family outing. You have no choice but to play."

"Jeez," interjected Jack. "I thought Russia was over."

"Russia is not over, Jack," Lang corrected. "Russia is very much alive. The Soviet Union is over."

"Except in this car," said Jennifer, under her breath.

"Ask your question, Jen," Lang said, somewhat sternly.

"Is it Mr. and Mrs. Devereaux?" she asked.

Lang took his eyes off the road to register his surprise directly into hers. "How did you know?"

"That's who it was the last time you played this game when we were out for a drive," she answered, a mild edge to her tone. She read his disappointment and her tone softened. "That's why I didn't want to play, Dad. It's no fun for the twins when I know the answer."

Lang was relieved that his fears of a family in disintegration remained unfounded for the moment. And he was proud of his eldest child's thoughtfulness. "I'm sorry, Jen. That was very sweet of you."

After a lunch of Mexican food, they drove into Los Angeles to the little Westwood neighborhood where Max and Clarice Devereaux had a charming two-story Tudor on an old and shady street. The sound of lawn mowers and the sweet smell of freshly cut grass punctuated the Langs' drive down the street. For a moment, that pungent aroma carried Lang back to a patch of center-field grass he once patrolled on a ball field at Dartmouth College. It brought a smile to his face as they pulled into the driveway.

Clarice answered the door and was delighted to see the three children, who were the closest to grandchildren she would ever know. The affection was mutual and she and the children exchanged warm hugs and kisses in the crowded foyer of their overstuffed home.

"Christopher, dear," she said to Lang, as they, too, embraced. "Max is in his shop. Where else? He's anxious to see you." Turning to the kids, she said, "Let me guess. You've had lunch but no dessert, right?"

"Right!" came the reply in unison.

"Good. Then I'll have somebody to help me start eating a freshly baked apple-cinnamon pie."

"All right!" exclaimed Jack.

"Sounds great!" offered Andrea.

Jennifer just smiled, earning a warm smile in return from Clarice. She turned to Lang. "Go ahead, Chris. Go see Max. After business, you two can join us."

"Sounds good, Clarice," said Lang, as he headed out the back door. The backyard sloped gently away from a large porch, past lush, well-tended tomato plants, through a small orchard, to a modest building at the rear of the deceptively large property. As he approached, he heard the sound of power tools. The door to the shop was around the rear. He rapped hard on the open door to announce his presence to the man working with the saw.

Max Devereaux cut the power to the saw and swung his goggles up onto his forehead. A huge smile broke out on his broad face.

"Hello, Chris," he boomed with enthusiasm, his Eastern European accent still evident after more than forty years in America. His massive head, imposing and handsome though etched now with deep creases, was ringed with tight white curls, the sparse vestiges of a once-thick blanket of black kinks. The two men, law partners for several years but still much more like father and son, embraced warmly. Lang was disturbed to feel that the strapping, robust man he recalled had grown noticeably thinner, almost frail.

"Max," said Lang simply. He held the embrace just an instant longer than he normally did on the all-too-infrequent occasions when they saw each other.

"You brought your children?" asked Max.

"Oh, yeah. Got the whole brood with me." Lang laughed. "You look good, Max," he lied. "Are you feeling all right?"

Max shrugged. "Aaah. Age has me in its grip, but I'm happy. At peace. And staying busy." He gestured to the shop that surrounded him, a chaotic scene of saws, lathes, drill presses, vises, clamps, electrical wires, and sawdust. "I'm finishing this lingerie chest for Clarice for Christmas. But don't say anything. It's a surprise. What do you think?"

"It's beautiful, Max," replied Lang, running his hand lightly over the perfectly smooth surface of the bare wood. A fine dust collected in the grooves of his fingertips. "How are you going to finish it?"

"Cherry. Like the rest of our bedroom furniture. I have a jewel case—" He motioned to a far corner of the shop. "For her dressing table, but I won't be able to get to it until after the holidays."

"You're a perfectionist at everything you do," said Lang admiringly.

"It's a curse, my son. The same one that's on you."

They talked for well over a half hour about anything and everything, Chris relishing every moment with this kindly genius who was equally comfortable discussing politics, botany, baking, baseball, or law.

Born Miklos Casimir Daviros in Warsaw, Poland, in the early 1920s, he had weathered Hitler's invasion by going underground, had fought tenaciously and courageously, and finally worked his way to France as the war ended. After acquiring a bewildering array of trade skills, he had emigrated to Canada under his adopted French name and thereafter on to the United States. Studies at the University of Chicago and the Harvard Law School had produced one of the most respected tax-law minds the profession had ever known. As a young professor at Columbia, Max had published an avalanche of articles exposing vast areas of the proposed new Internal Revenue Code of 1954 ripe for abuse. As a result, a savvy Ways and Means chairman hastily offered him the job of lead counsel to rewrite the final version of the code. His work was universally hailed as brilliant and the chair of the tax department of the fledgling UCLA Law School followed immediately.

As an accommodation to wealthy entertainers who gravitated to him in the Hollywood glitz of Los Angeles in the late fifties, Max joined with a young corporate lawyer named Oliver Brace to start a small practice in Beverly Hills. The firm prospered and Max quickly grew to prefer the "real" world of the practice to the cloistered halls of academia. He resigned his chair and the firm of Devereaux and Brace rocketed into the prominence it had already attained by the time Christopher Lang interviewed at the office in the late seventies. Max had hired him on the spot and invested a great deal of personal effort in burnishing the young man's considerable talents as a lawyer and promise as a man. The one time Lang had disappointed Max was when he had confessed to his mentor that he wanted to leave tax law to become a litigator. Max was appalled at first—"Litigation is for C students!" he had raged—but later came to respect his decision and, in fact, became very much the proud father as he watched Lang build a first-rate litigation practice for the firm. The two men, a full generation apart, had grown in their respect and affection for each other over the years. Max had paid Lang what the younger man had regarded as the ultimate compliment as his retirement drew near by describing Lang to a roomful of people as "the one man I would trust absolutely to be my own lawyer."

Inevitably the conversation found its way to the Chicago Bears. Chicago was common ground to these men and the football team that carried its standard each year was a passion they shared. Over the years, whenever the Bears' games were carried in Los Angeles, they had spent Sunday mornings together huddled in front of a tube, screaming themselves hoarse at a team that lost nearly as many as it won but always did both with courage and grit. Several years ago, Max had surprised his younger friend by having a satellite dish installed in time for the season opener. Ever since, Lang had come to Max's house whenever possible to watch the game. During the last couple of seasons, however, the combination of Lang's intensely demanding schedule and the fading fortunes of the team had meant that Lang's football visits had become less frequent, a fact he regretted now and determined to rectify this year.

"All right, Max," said Lang, after the strength of the Bears' schedule and the decline of the linebacking corps had been thoroughly exhausted. "Let's talk about Tuesday night's steering-committee meeting. What do we know?"

"Jerry Zender is the problem here. He convinced Leo to find a way out of the deal we made when I left. I don't know what the pretext is; Oliver doesn't know. But it doesn't really matter. This is not about legalities. It's not about interpretations of the contract or the consent mechanism we used or anything else. Hell, Chris, it's not really even about the money. It's about power. Pure and simple. Jerry and his cadre want the satisfaction of squeezing the last ounce of influence I have out of me." He looked away, suddenly saddened. "Of course, I hired Jerry myself. And Oliver trained him with great care and devotion. I don't understand some people."

"Jerry's not so hard to understand, Max. His ego is vast and dangerous. He's been aching to run the firm himself for years. While you were still around, he thought you were old-fashioned, out of step. When you proposed that we go to a steering committee he was caught off-guard. Instead of making him your heir apparent, as he had fancied himself, suddenly you had him boxed in, on a committee where he was one of seven." Lang smiled at the uncanny foresight of this wily man before him. "Since he forced you out, he's told many of the others that you were a loose cannon, made too many rash decisions on your own that he claims hurt the partnership."

Lang's eyes flashed at the thought that the partners would turn on their founder for the very qualities that made him special and made the firm a worthwhile place to work. Max just smiled faintly, thoughtfully regarding his protégé. Lang continued. "You know, Max, you may be gone but you cast a giant shadow from the sidelines. I guess Jerry Zender just can't bear it any longer."

Max's smile brightened. "You always had the keenest judgment about people, Chris. I take back most of the things I ever said about trial lawyers."

Lang laughed. "Exactly what do you have in mind for these greedy little ingrates?"

"Simple game of power. Jerry and Leo are very strong, charismatic partners. You're younger, preoccupied with business outside of the office. They've become the new generation's most visible father figures."

"Ironic, isn't it?" observed Lang. "After all, if it had been up to Jerry, the majority of that generation would never have been brought into the partnership."

"A fact they seem to have overlooked entirely," added Max. "Anyway, Jerry and the gang he speaks for are credited with about seven and a half million dollars in annual revenue among them. And they have influence over another four or five among the other partners, right?"

"And?"

"Well, two years ago, when they threw me out, you and Oliver had about two million in annual billings between you. But now, thanks almost entirely to you, the two of you have nearly six. And I am still rather well thought of by clients who represent another four or so."

"So?" asked Lang. "That still leaves us more than a million short. Assuming this vote goes down by revenue, which it won't."

"You're wrong. Not about the math, but about how it will occur. Certainly, if each side presents its views to the partners and then votes, you're right, everyone will add up the dollars, we will lose, and I will be cut off from my termination benefit. A benefit, incidentally, I don't really need but would like to have for Clarice to fall back on. If, however, the partners hear from you what you really think—"

"And they will, of course, Max. I will stand up for what I think is right. But the votes just aren't there—"

Max held up his hand. "You are overlooking two things. First, your scenario is based on a straight vote. Pay Max his million a year or use Leo's loophole to chop him off and split up that million in additional profits. That won't be how it will happen if they believe it will drive you out of the firm."

Lang shook his head. "I've thought of that, Max. It won't work, though I'd sure as hell do it if I thought it would turn the vote around. If I take my four and a half million elsewhere, that leaves you with no hope of keeping what you have. And they know I'll take Amy, Rick, Jim, and the other associates I use or they'd all lose their jobs. The firm would net the same profit without our salaries, and they'll have your annuity payments to soften the blow."

"That's one view," agreed Max calmly. "Another might be

that you and Oliver leaving together, with all your associates in tow, joined by Howie and Peter, along with the business your old partner Max Devereaux will throw your way from his cronies, would both make a formidable new firm and leave a major revenue vacuum behind you. Not to mention crippling the acquisitions department in a hot corporate market. But aside from the revenue numbers—and I make it a seven- or eight-million-dollar hit to the firm, minimum—this scenario has one other intangible benefit. It's the second thing you are overlooking, Chris. More than half the partners are both young and dependent on others for business. Do you remember that time in your life?"

Lang smiled at the recollection. "I remember insecurity and fear."

"Exactly. The kind of feeling that would have ignited into panic at the very prospect of a breakup of the firm. The kind of quiet terror that blinds you to reality, deafens you to reason. In short, the kind of atmosphere in which a reasonable suggestion that the firm honor its commitments and let everyone go back to work would be regarded as a sign from on high."

Lang smiled broadly. "A thermonuclear war threat, but from the flank, huh? They would expect you to threaten a lawsuit, a risk they have no doubt calculated and provided for. But not a split-up. And one that damned near amounts to a liquidation. It's a litigator's tactic, Max. Straight up from the street. This is not the work of a high-minded tax lawyer. I like it. A lot."

Max also smiled and put an arm around Lang's shoulder. "There's still a little fight left in the old boy, my son."

"One thing I don't understand, Max. Would you really be willing to destroy the firm you built? Two years ago you wouldn't let me bring a lawsuit because you thought it was unseemly."

"Damned right, I would. I gave it birth and I can take it out," said Max with a steeliness in his eyes. "Besides, two years ago, I was young and not so smart as I am today."

They both laughed and started back to the house. As they walked—more slowly than usual, Lang thought—Max, puffing noticeably up the slight grade, asked, "So, Chris, tell me more about this career-maker lawsuit against the dangerous Mr. Lindstrom."

CHAPTER 8

THE BLACK LIMOUSINE SAT SILENTLY AT THE END OF the rain-slicked runway at Hobart Field, just outside of Charlotte. Far from the brightly lit terminal, the car was dark except for the small map light above the front passenger seat. It was trained on the paperback book held in the huge black hands of the driver. He was impeccably dressed in the classic manner, right down to the chauffeur's cap. His large, pleasant face bore no expression as he carefully scanned the pages before him. He glanced at his wristwatch to determine what he could have deduced from his last five time checks: It was 8:37 on the night of the fifth. Ever so faintly the radio played. Not music, but a baseball game, a post-season game. Every few minutes the relative stillness of the big, quiet car's interior was rocked with the booming report of a Lear jet's triumph over the forces of gravity. The driver did not seem to notice.

At 8:43, the driver rechecked his watch and lowered his window. As he looked up into the night sky, he noted briefly that, as predicted, the rainfall had quit entirely and had left only mildly elevated humidity in its wake. After a moment he picked up the approach of a small jet. He lowered the privacy screen between the front and back seats. "Here they come now, Mr. Hickman," he said into the blackness over his shoulder.

"Thanks, Luther," answered Gentry Hickman from the rear compartment. "Not bad considering the lousy weather between here and Bridgeport."

Outside, a sleek, dark blue Gulfstream business jet landed flawlessly, taxied out, and came to a stop not at the terminal but next to the limousine. After its screaming engines were cut, Luther hefted his massive frame out of the car and lumbered toward it. Three people emerged from the door on the jet's side facing the car, the last of whom was Russell Lindstrom. The driver touched his cap respectfully. "Evenin', Mr. Lindstrom," he said. To the others he nodded. "Ms. Calabrese. Mr. Banfield."

Neither Calabrese nor Banfield acknowledged the greeting, but Lindstrom smiled. "Hello, Luther," he said with genuine warmth. Lindstrom, an imposing figure himself, looked up into the giant driver's face and the same fierce, intelligent eyes that had intimidated scores of defensive linemen trying to get past him to the San Francisco Forty-Niners' quarterbacks for more than a dozen years. They shook hands. "Damn, it's good to see you."

"Me, too, Mr. Lindstrom," said Luther, also smiling. "You look pretty good after all your travels."

"You're kind, Luther," Lindstrom replied, putting a hand on Luther's shoulder. "But I feel like horseshit in a hurricane. I hope you didn't mind flying back here with Gentry. I just decided that if I'm going to be doing all this traveling I want to have my regular driver with me as much as possible."

"No sir, I don't mind it at all. That's why I'm on the payroll. Just as soon be driving with you as polishing cars in San Sebastian. And besides, who's going to complain about first-class seats?"

"Good," said Lindstrom as he climbed into the backseat after Calabrese and Banfield. To the man already in the back, he said, "Hello, Gentry. Thanks for making the trip. You didn't talk poor Luther's ear off with all those courthouse war stories, did you?"

Hickman laughed. Luther laughed, too, and interjected, "It wasn't too bad, Mr. Lindstrom. I watched the movie. Headset on all the way." Luther closed the back door and climbed in behind the wheel. "I guess you realize we're running late," he said, over his shoulder. "It's already 8:55 and CableStar's still fifteen minutes from here."

"Don't worry, Luther. Take your time. We telephoned Mr.

Rich from the plane. He knows we're going to be late. He'll fill in with something else until we get there."

"Well," said Luther thoughtfully, "Milo Rich sure knows how to do that. The fresh change you asked for is in the valise."

Lindstrom nodded amiably and thanked his driver as he pushed the button to raise the privacy screen. As Luther drove off the field and into the airport traffic pattern, he turned up the volume of the baseball game.

In the privacy of the rear compartment Lindstrom settled back, sitting next to his campaign manager, Gina Calabrese, and opposite his lawyer, Gentry Hickman, and his chief of staff and speechwriter, Dick Banfield.

"Gentry," Lindstrom began. "You look like a man with more on his mind than keeping me out of legal trouble on Milo Rich's television show."

Hickman smiled and, in a voice once described by Mike Wallace on *Sixty Minutes* as "a Texas baritone marinated in barbecue sauce," he replied, "You're right, Russell. It's that lawsuit out in California. It's a potential problem, legally as well as politically, and I want to be sure you appreciate the risks."

Lindstrom regarded his lawyer silently, while looping his arms out of his suspenders and loosening his tie. " 'Risks'?" he repeated at last. "I don't like the sound of that at all. It's your job to see that there are no risks. And that the lawsuit stays little and as far away from me as possible." He handed his tie to Gina and began to open his white shirt.

"I know that. But it's not going to be as easy as you might think. At least the 'little' part. The 'far away' part looks pretty good long-term. At least within some limits."

Lindstrom frowned as he shook off his shirt and handed it to Gina. "That's awful damned equivocal, Gentry. And it's not what I'm paying you for."

Hickman waved his hand vaguely. "Don't worry. It's nothing we can't handle. But the young fella they got to handle this is real tenacious and every indication is that we'll have a fight on our hands to keep you out of it entirely."

Gina pulled a fresh striped shirt, still folded from the laundry, from the valise on the floor and handed it to Lindstrom. He held on to it for a moment, contemplating Hickman. Hickman moistened his lips reflexively. At last, Lindstrom spoke. "I know. Christopher Stephen Lang, head litigator at Devereaux and Brace, a blue-chip

L.A. firm. Eighty-three percent of his cases either won or settled to the good. He's got an astronaut for an expert. I read the reports. The warriors always fascinate me, even if the wars they wage don't." He turned to Banfield. "Dick, you have a collateral net over him?"

"Standard procedure, Mr. Lindstrom. He's divorced and the kids are young. But we have a full-court press in place all the same."

"Good. I like to have all the information I can get at my disposal," Lindstrom replied unnecessarily. Then turned back to Hickman. "Okay, Gentry, just how am I involved?"

"Well, you are and you aren't—"

"Damn it, Gentry!" Lindstrom's eyes lit up, seeming to drive the darkness from the backseat as they rolled down Interstate 20. "Can't I get a straight answer? How the hell am I involved in the case and how and when are you going to get me out of it? I'm running for goddamned president here!"

"I know, Russell. I know. Now, look. This is the way it is. They've named you as a defendant, personally. Nothing we can do about that as an initial proposition. You know as well as I that anybody who can put up a filing fee can sue anybody they want to. But, of course, there's no evidence whatsoever—not a shred—to link you to their claims, all of which arise out of the design and testing of that microlight airplane the company did for Nigel Daultry in the late eighties."

"So they just named me to add publicity value?"

"More or less."

Lindstrom finished buttoning his shirt and took a fresh tie from Gina. "So get the case against me dismissed. And then beat the 'young fella's' brains out for the company's sake."

"That's my plan, but it won't be quite that quick or easy. They've alleged that you personally tested the plane and falsified the engineering report to hide a dangerous tendency to spin."

For a long moment the car was silent. Lindstrom sat motionless, absently running a finger over the bow of his upper lip. "Alleged?" he repeated. "I assume that can't be proven," he said.

"Not a shred of evidence," Hickman said, very slowly.

Lindstrom nodded emphatically. "Because it's bullshit." He turned toward Gina. "Excuse my French, Gina." She smiled.

Back to Hickman, he said, "I certainly met with Nigel Daultry, of course. And we did kick around the broad outlines of the concept for the plane and the marketing plan before I handed him off to the Arrow boys." He turned back to Gina. "Crazy New Zealander. It's a wonder they have any civilized commerce down there at all. I'm away on business and he and his girlfriend literally drop in, just land their plane on the strip right there on the ranch, and pop in on me right there in my house." He laughed and shook his head.

Hickman continued. "The fact that you met with him or even negotiated the contract doesn't matter for purposes of liability, you understand. The upshot of the complaint has to do with the design, construction, and testing, and there's no evidence that you had anything to do with any of that."

"Then get me out."

"That will require a motion, albeit one we will win. The real problem is not your personal exposure. There just isn't any evidence that will implicate you."

"And now," said Lindstrom, straightening his tie and adjusting his suspenders. "You're going to tell me what it was that required a trip to Charlotte."

"I may not be able to prevent them from taking your deposition. Their allegations, even without proof, may be enough to get them a shot at having you testify under oath. And your personal knowledge of the negotiations may be relevant to the issue of how the contract is interpreted."

"Hmmm," responded Lindstrom, plainly disturbed. "The judge?"

"Schuyler Campbell."

"Who?"

"Schuyler Campbell, out of Idaho, sitting by designation in the San Sebastian branch of the eastern district."

Lindstrom was clearly annoyed that the local federal court in his hometown was being run by an outsider. "Was he appointed by Bush or Clinton?"

"Reagan," replied Hickman. "You're going to have to learn your Republicans, Russell."

"That helps," mused Lindstrom, ignoring Hickman's jab.

Hickman shook his head. "I don't think so. He's beyond influence, although I don't doubt he'll lean our way on the close ones. We have a pending motion to prevent your deposition but Campbell doesn't usually hear oral argument on such motions. We've got a shot but I'm not optimistic. That's why I thought I should let you know about this in person."

"I appreciate it, Gentry," Lindstrom said, suddenly breezy. For him, the subject matter of this conversation was now old business. "I know you'll do the best you can. You always do."

"We won't go down on this one without a fight. I've asked the judge to make them take your deposition on the road, since it will come up during the primary season."

Lindstrom laughed. "That might be fun, after all."

The privacy screen came down. "We're at CableStar, Mr. Lindstrom."

Lindstrom was all smiles. "Great, Luther. Let's go talk to America."

In the studio, behind his desk on the set of *Milo Rich: American Idea Net,* sat the fifty-six-year-old broadcasting legend himself. A tall, handsome, thoughtful journalist who learned his craft under some of the greatest names in American television journalism, Rich not only was one of the most recognizable black men in America, but his was one of the best-known faces in the world. The son of a wealthy Richmond couple, an attorney and a pediatrician, Rich had earned his law degree at Harvard, then headed to New York to pursue a career in broadcasting. When the anchor position he coveted at CBS had gone to another, he walked out on a promising career and took the anchor spot at CNN. When he wanted to move to a current affairs talk program there, he ran into another broadcaster then on track to become an institution. Formation of the fledgling cable network CableStar happened at precisely the right moment for Rich. CableStar put him on the air in a talk-show format and he put them on the broadcast-journalism map. His facile mind and grasp of the language, hitched to a moderately conservative political agenda, made him a favorite of a broad swath of the American mainstream, translating into rising ratings and credibility for the whole network.

Each night he sat, as he did tonight, awash in the heat and glare of the klieg lights, directing the nation's dialogue between its vast sprawling citizenry and the great and near-great figures of the day, all under the watchful eye of television. Five times a week, Rich brought before the CableStar cameras and microphones the most prominent personalities from the worlds of politics, science, the arts, sports, and entertainment for conversation and interrogation, mixing carefully pre-screened telephone inquiries and comments with his own observations and cross-examination of his guests. And, in a telling commentary on the times, most nights, the most famous, enduring, and influential personality on the show was Milo Rich.

Rich wore his trademark white shirt and dark vest, his tie undone at the neck and his shirtsleeves rolled up, the better to get after the business of tackling the various strains of hypocrisy and pomposity that were bound to show up in the course of a ninety-minute show. He chatted amiably, quietly, with a pretty young woman seated as nearly opposite him at his desk as the dictates of television camera angles would allow. A cue from the director, a slight, frenzied-looking man with a clipboard, alerted Rich that they were about to come out of commercial on the live broadcast. As if switched on by one of the team of engineers in the sound booth, Rich snapped out of his casual mode and into the charismatic television personality that had made him a worldwide celebrity.

"Welcome back to the *Idea Net*. On the line is Julio from Puente, California. You're on with Milo Rich and my special guest, Marissa Mathews, acquitted this morning by a New York jury of murder for shooting four subway thugs who tried to rape her. What's your question?"

Julio asked, "How could you plan such a thing? I mean it's obvious that the way you were dressed, riding the subways at night and carrying a gun, someone was going to get it. It's almost like entrapment, don't you think?"

Rich glided in behind the question. "Entrapment doesn't leave you dead, Julio. You may be in trouble but you're still alive. What about that, Marissa? Isn't there a little premeditation going on here?" As he finished the question, Rich looked to the wings, where Lindstrom's party waited. Rich lifted an eyebrow, the one away from the camera, in greeting.

"Not at all," the woman replied. "I was going to a party. I had a right to be dressed in attractive clothes and take the subway. And, as I told the jury, I'd have been crazy to ride the train at night without the gun. In fact, when we talked to them after they came in with their verdict this morning, that's exactly what one of them said to me."

"Now, come on, Marissa," coaxed Rich. "You're wearing a sequined halter top, short white bike shorts, and four-inch patent-leather heels. You're riding through Brooklyn on the IRT at eleven-thirty on a Thursday night. You're maybe in the worst gang-infested part of the city and you've got a thirty-eight in your rhinestone-studded handbag. Weren't you really 'hunting' that night?"

"No, Milo, I was not. I was minding my own business when these punks just came out of nowhere. They insulted me in the most disgusting, degrading way, in the filthiest way you ever heard. But that's New York; I can take that. But then they tried to force me to satisfy their lowest urges. I shot them all right. And with the help of God I shot straight and deadly."

"Boy," muttered Julio, "I hope you never come cruising into California."

Rich proceeded to milk and manipulate his callers, weaving in his own views of violence and vigilantism into the quick and clever repartee. He was brusque and opinionated, but never quite rude and he effortlessly avoided using the questions as a foil. And if the questions were largely predictable, it was Rich's keen insight that brought in fifteen million viewers a week.

It was time to get to the heart of the program. "There you have it, ladies and gentlemen," Rich intoned. "A straight-shooting feminist Bernard Goetz who has received the seal of approval from a jury of her peers. For those of you troubled by this verdict—the civil-liberties people are looking into legal action on behalf of at least two of the victims—take some comfort in knowing that for a while, at least, the streets and subways of our cities may be a wee bit safer, if for all the wrong reasons." He paused, for effect, as long as the cost of live television time would allow. Then he went on. "It's time for a break along the *Idea Net*. When we come back, the most intriguing candidate in the upcoming presidential sweepstakes— maybe the most intriguing candidate in many an election—Russell Lindstrom—will be my guest."

The director signaled that they were clear for commercial and announced that there would be exactly five minutes before they were live again. He handed a sheet of paper to Rich, who patted Marissa on the shoulder with a few words of encouragement, then moved adroitly toward Lindstrom and the man and woman with him.

"Hi," said Rich, smiling broadly with his hand extended. "I'm Milo Rich."

Lindstrom, half a head taller than the host of the program, smiled and shook hands. "Russell Lindstrom, Mr. Rich. It's a plea- sure finally to make your acquaintance. I've been a big fan of yours for years."

"Please. Call me Milo."

"Then call me Russell," replied Lindstrom.

"I'd like that, Russell. Off-camera. When I interview a man who may be president, I never use the familiar form of address. It sounds disrespectful."

Lindstrom smiled. "I understand." The two men exchanged introductions of their associates.

"I'm very sorry that we're late, Milo," said Lindstrom.

Rich waved him off. "No problem. Marissa was a hit, according to our tracking survey. It will cost you a little airtime, though, I'm afraid. We'd figured on you for the full ninety."

"Tracking survey? Already?" asked Lindstrom, genuinely impressed.

"Welcome to television in the twenty-first century, Russell." Rich laughed. "Takes ten operators less than six minutes to get statistically valid numbers." He glanced at the scribbled note his director had handed him. "Sixty-four percent of our viewers liked her. Fifty-nine percent even believed her. Our audience was seven—wow!—percent over our average and we were particularly strong with the male eighteen-to-thirty-five. Not bad for only promo-ing her appearance since six o'clock tonight, when you let us know you would be late."

"I'm impressed," responded Lindstrom.

"Don't be. While the numbers on Marissa Mathews's credibility are solid, it's just as likely you were the draw. We'll know the answer to that one by the time you leave here tonight."

The director nervously broke in. "Milo?"

"Of course," Rich responded. "We need to get you seated and set. You've been through makeup?" Lindstrom nodded. "Let's go."

Just as the two men were seated comfortably at Rich's desk, the director cued the return to live air.

Milo Rich looked into the camera, disdaining both notes and TelePrompTer, and delivered a minute-long introduction of his featured guest. It was flawlessly accurate, vividly detailed, and spoken without a single hesitation. Rich deftly cataloged Lindstrom's hardscrabble youth in Oklahoma, his extraordinary Korean War record, his work as a designer of secret military aircraft, then finished with an account of the man's phenomenal run of business successes.

"And now," Rich said, swiveling ever so slightly toward Lindstrom, "he has set his sights on the Republican presidential nomination next year in Kansas City. Ladies and gentlemen, my very special guest, Russell Lindstrom. Good evening, Mr. Lindstrom, and welcome."

"Thank you, Milo. It's a pleasure to be here. And thank you for your kind words."

"Not at all. Yours is truly a remarkable list of accomplishments."

"It just goes to show you what can happen if you live long enough."

"Let me ask you, Mr. Lindstrom, why president? You've accomplished so much, had so profound an impact on the country, the world, in fact, that some commentators have said, only half in jest, that the presidency would be a step down in power and influence. Why do you want the grief of being president?"

Lindstrom laughed good-naturedly. "That's an interesting way to look at it, Milo. And I understand your point. But I don't see it that way. I see it as a call to service, the highest call there is, and I feel I must do what I can."

Lindstrom moved smoothly into what had already become both his stock stump speech and his political philosophy. In his warm and winning baritone, he spun out his vision of a new and mature American government, disciplined and driven by the principles of an efficient and successful business. He interleaved his message with frequent, colorful examples of companies whose images he had salvaged, businesses whose employees had seized the best within themselves and imbued their companies with their own sense of pride, excellence, and accomplishment. It was a new and even radical vision of government reharnessed by the people and transformed into a tool for achieving greatness.

Rich, a rapt and effective listener, leaned forward. "So you propose something truly new, untried?"

"I do, Milo. I think I bring an entirely new, unique perspective and range of experience to the problems confronting the nation. I've taken over seventeen bankrupt or failing companies during the past nine years and turned every one of them around."

"And what makes you think that experience in saving failing companies makes you more likely to succeed at turning the country around than somebody else?"

Lindstrom was eager to respond and did so, forcefully and persuasively, with his increasingly familiar message: Run the government like a business and excellence will rise to the top. And, according to Lindstrom, there was excellence in every American, if only their leaders were skilled at tapping into it. It was a message that had genuine populist potential, a central fact that was not lost on the canny host. Even as he peppered his distinguished guest with the kind of skeptical questions that had made him a national folk hero, Rich was calculating the ratings bonanza that this remarkable guest would surely net. He could envision a welter of sound bites from his show sprinkled liberally across the major networks for the rest of the next news cycle.

"What you say is undeniably true," offered Rich in response to Lindstrom's principal points. "But, in fairness, it's been said, Mr.

Lindstrom, that the government doesn't work like a company, even a bad one. It isn't profit-driven. It doesn't allow for an autocratic CEO. It is designed to prevent things from getting done unless they suit the majority view, hardly a blueprint for entrepreneurial success."

"You raise a lot of good points, Milo, and I want to address them all because you have identified not the flaw in my approach, but, actually, its unique advantage over anything ever tried in the governing process."

"All right. You'll get your chance and we'll take some calls when we return with my special guest, Russell Lindstrom."

When they were clear, he spoke softly, privately, with Lindstrom. "In all honesty, Russell, isn't this just a campaign gimmick, a way for a phenomenally successful businessman to stand out from the crowd of would-be contenders?"

Lindstrom smiled benignly. "Let's just talk about it on the air, Milo. We don't want our conversation to lose its wonderful spontaneity, do we?"

Rich smiled back. "Touché," he said.

Four days later, in his office with the drapes drawn against the afternoon glare of October in Los Angeles, Chris Lang studied the tape of Rich's program. Meticulously, he rewound the tape until he had listened to Lindstrom's performance often enough to have memorized every question and answer verbatim.

Milo Rich's distinctive voice poured out of the television set: ". . . and I want to thank my special guest, Mr. Russell Lindstrom, for a stimulating conversation about a very intriguing candidacy, a candidacy we are sure to hear much more from over the coming months. . . ."

There was a knock at Lang's door.

"Come in," he called. He hit the pause button, freezing the image of Milo Rich and his very special guest on the screen.

Amy Quinn walked in. "A little dark in here, isn't it?" she asked.

"Old habit. I like to watch television in the dark."

She looked at the screen. "You're still studying the Lindstrom tapes?" Her eyes fell to the box full of more than a dozen videotapes on the floor beside the television cabinet.

"Preparation is the key phase of any trial," he replied, somewhat defensively.

"Isn't 'obsession' more like it? We've been over this at least a dozen times: There's nothing in the evidence to implicate Lindstrom. Not a single mention of his name in thousands of pages of documents. Not in the contract stage, not in the design, not the testing, not in writing the report. It's just as the media has always said, Lindstrom was long gone from the company by the time this deal got started."

"And we always believe the media, don't we?" Lang responded acidly. He leaned forward in his large black leather desk chair for emphasis. "Did it ever occur to you that there has been an effort to cover up Lindstrom's role in Arrow Dynamics, in the StormTree project in particular? That the media knows nothing more than it has been told by a very calculating machine run by Lindstrom?"

"Jesus, Nixon, you're becoming paranoid," Amy retorted, on the verge of genuine anger. "This thing is getting out of hand. Why in God's name would Lindstrom hide what he was doing at Arrow, assuming he was doing anything at all? And why would the media care what he was doing? Your theory presupposes that years ago someone out at Arrow Dynamics had the foresight to doctor records, carefully concealing the involvement of the founder of the company in a small, relatively insignificant development program, to protect Lindstrom from the negative fallout, *political* fallout yet, of a lawsuit that would allege defective design, faulty testing, and fraudulent reporting. Come on, who's going to believe that anyone, even those geniuses up at Arrow Dynamics, are that smart or that . . ." She searched for the word.

"Prescient?" offered Lang.

"Exactly," Amy snapped, in triumph. "Why are you so obsessed with finding a way to pin this all on Lindstrom? We have a pretty good case, assuming the StormTree spins when Walt McCluskey flies it, and Arrow Dynamics has the resources to pay the multi-million-dollar judgment we'll get if we win. Why the fixation on Lindstrom personally?"

"I'm not alone, Amy. Have you noticed how the media are starting to ask hard questions about Mr. Lindstrom's secrets? Questions that go to his character, I might add?"

Amy shrugged. "That's what election-year op ed pieces do. They ask questions, make innuendos, stir up controversy. Besides, whatever the man did in Southeast Asia or the Middle East, crooked or un-American or not, has nothing to do with our case, our theory, or our *evidence*." She bit off the last word for emphasis. "This is not like you, Chris. I've never known you to try to shoehorn a case into a theory that the evidence doesn't support."

"Yeah," responded Lang, obviously deflated by the powerful logic of Amy's words. "I can't totally explain it myself. But I listen to him and I don't trust him, don't believe him."

Amy smiled. "That's the way you always feel about your opponent. You need to dislike, distrust, even hate your adversary in order to hit him with your best shot."

"I know. But this is different. I feel that the whole picture emerging from the documents is artifical, a construct that suggests the true story but masks all the critical facts." He shook his head in frustration.

"So this is a hunch?" Lang did not answer. Amy moved to the corner of Lang's desk and picked up a ceremonial gavel he had received from the competition at Virginia. "It's because of who he is, isn't it?"

Lang silently studied the frozen images of Rich and Lindstrom on the screen.

Amy continued. "I think you just can't believe you are this close to hooking the biggest fish of all, a bona fide running-for-president big fish, and you don't have the facts you need to put him away." Now she shook her head. "Well, the depositions are still ahead and nobody grinds up a deponent like Chris Lang. Maybe you'll get lucky and find something we can go with to get your man. And I still have an awful lot of paper to wade through from the document production. Something could turn up there, even if Lindstrom's name isn't in there anywhere. But, in the meantime, you know better than I that the trial in this case is going to turn on hard, provable facts, and I plan to stick to those in prepping the case."

"I know," said Lang. "And I appreciate it. Don't worry. I haven't gone off the deep end. I'm just very suspicious in this case and, if I'm right, I would hate like hell to let the son of a bitch get away."

"And end up in the White House?"

"That, too."

She turned to leave. Over her shoulder she said, "It's all right, Chris. I think the republic is safe with you patrolling the perimeter."

When the door closed, Lang recued the tape and listened yet one more time to Lindstrom's denial of what Milo Rich referred to as "old unsubstantiated rumors" that he sold a spy plane to North Vietnam in the early seventies, shipped top-secret software to the Iranians in the late seventies, and supplied Nicaraguan Contra mercenaries with military hardware a decade later.

CHAPTER 9

LANG'S HEAD SWAM WITH THE EXPANDING ARRAY OF information he was absorbing in the course of preparing to assume full hands-on control of the lawsuit against Arrow Dynamics. Although he had kept abreast of the larger developments, he had been consumed by the *Fulton* trial and the *Severstone* negotiations and had relied on Amy Quinn to bring the case along. She was, after all, as good a lawyer as he had ever worked with and her talent for analysis and synthesis—critical skills where the facts of a complex case had to be conveyed one lawyer to another without needless duplication of effort—was unparalleled in the firm. As a consequence, she was both the master repository of all important or potentially important facts and their interpreter. For the last three days, they had done nothing but examine every aspect of the case, its theories, possibilities, strengths, and weaknesses. So involved had they gotten in the process that they had ordered both lunch and dinner in the office and had worked until midnight on Friday. Only the call from Max Devereaux to chide him gently for skipping last Sunday's Bears game, again, and to congratulate Lang—again—on the splendid results of their negotiating strategy at the partners' meeting last week had interrupted their immersion in the case against Russell Lindstrom and his company.

Now standing outside the car-rental office at the airport in Orlando, Florida, Lang smiled at the way he and Oliver Brace, with generous help from Howie Spaulding and Peter Weiss, had turned the entire effort to renege on the firm's deal with Max into a crisis about the firm's continuing viability. Jerry Zender, the man who would be managing partner and principal architect both of the ouster of Max Devereaux and of the effort to undo his termination deal, had progressed rapidly during the meeting from self-righteous chief prosecutor to angry proctor to technical nitpicker to a lone voice crying out against a crushing tide of opposition. In the end, the vast majority of partners decided that a collapse of the firm was too high a price to pay for a clever escape from its commitments. Thus was the moral fiber of the good members of Devereaux and Brace reinforced and renewed.

Lang laughed aloud as he recalled that it was this description of the rout of Zender—not the fact that Max's deal and his money were left intact—that had brought the most enthusiastic response from Max when he and Oliver called him after the meeting adjourned at midnight. Max had seemed to take particular satisfaction in the fact that the vote was ultimately unanimous, underscoring the magnitude of Zender's defeat. It was so perfectly Max, thought Lang, that ultimately the money had meant little next to either the principle at stake or the gamesmanship involved. Max's call on Friday morning was to add Clarice's heartfelt gratitude to his own. It occurred to Lang that he had never outgrown the satisfaction he derived from Max's approval. Next Sunday, he promised himself, he would catch the Bears-Steelers game in the Devereauxs' cozy den.

"Wake up, boss. We're out of here," said Amy as she emerged from the rental-car office. "And forget your hairdo, I got us a convertible."

"Well," replied Lang, returning from his reverie. "This *is* Florida. Land of Walt Disney and eternal sunshine." He grabbed his bags and followed her to the parking lot.

Amy drove—"I'll make the arrangements—airlines, hotel, and car rental, but I get to pick the car and drive," she had decreed—and she drove fast. Over the wind in their faces they struggled to have a conversation.

"Are Graham and Walt here yet?" he asked.

Amy shook her head. "Tomorrow," she answered, throwing the Sunbird into fifth gear. "They're flying in from Tallahassee with the experimental permit from the FAA. They're also bringing one of Pegasus's technical people to help with the setup of the plane."

"And Clive isn't coming?"

She shook her head. "In Canada for the weekend. Early skiing at Blackcomb-Whistler, if you please."

"That sounds nice. It's a great resort."

"I wouldn't know," replied Amy.

Lang thought to say something else, but was tired of the battle to be heard over the rushing air and gave up. Neither of them spoke as they roared through the Florida heartland into the gathering evening.

Alone in his room that night, Lang penciled out a number of ideas about the case in general and the impending flight of the StormTree in particular. In spite of, or maybe because of, his prolonged cramming, he was unable to concentrate. His thoughts wandered from Max Devereaux to the future of the firm to his children. But, ultimately, they came back to his relationship with Ro. Despite his resolve of many months to sit her down and talk their situation through, typically, he had still not found the right time. Of course, it wasn't just because of the old standby reasons—his cases, the firm, urgent client needs. A new element had been introduced: Ro's burgeoning career with her camera and her word processor. And her "associate," Mark What's His Name. Several times Lang had called or dropped by only to find her out or unavailable. Once he had actually thought to complain, to suggest that she was not fulfilling her duties to her children with her involvement in the *Beau Rivage* project, but he had rejected the idea as unfair and unworthy. He checked the time: 12:47 A.M. Too late to call, he thought. Then, realizing that it was only 9:47 in Los Angeles, he impulsively picked up the phone and punched in Ro's number.

Andrea answered on the second ring. "Lang residence, Andrea speaking," she intoned in her delightful alto.

"Andrea?" asked Lang. "What are you doing up at this hour?"

"Daddy?" she replied, a brightness in her voice, Lang was sure. Then, a little disgustedly, she added, "It's Saturday night, for goodness' sake. And it's only nine o'clock. Besides, tomorrow we change the clocks back so it's really like eight o'clock."

At the other end of the line Lang smiled. He held out genuine hope that Andrea, perhaps alone among his children, would follow her father into the legal profession. "Is your mother there, sweetheart? I need to talk to her."

"You're in luck. She just got home and she's changing to go out again. I'll take the phone up to her bathroom."

"Thanks, Andy," replied Lang. A quiet gloom descended over him while he waited. Out all day, no doubt, and now going out at ten o'clock at night, he mused darkly.

"Hello," Ro's voice broke into his thoughts. "How are you?"

"Great," he replied. "Yourself?"

"Never better. But a little pressed for time these days."

"Oh," said Lang, as noncommittally as possible.

"Well, this Gettysburg piece I've done has apparently caused quite a stir over at *Beau Rivage*. They had me running around polishing the photos and reworking the text. They tell me it all goes with the cover feature."

Lang's face heated up slightly. "Great," he said without real feeling. "When's it coming out?"

"Newsstands on the twenty-seventh. Monday."

He imagined her standing before the mirror, phone cradled between her cheek and shoulder, hands on her hips for one final assessment before climbing into her dress. "Wow," he said, impressed in spite of the conflicting feelings roiling inside. "Ro, it sounds like you've hit the jackpot."

"Oh, I don't know. I'm trying not to take this whole thing too seriously. But the way it came out of the blue and just exploded is a bit overwhelming. I do find myself giddy at times."

"Have you been getting my messages? I've called a few times."

"I know. And I'm sorry. I have gotten them and there just don't seem to be enough hours in the day. Is everything all right?" Before he could respond, he heard Ro say, "Don't do that, Andrea. They're my best earrings and I don't want to have to hunt for them on the way out the door."

"Everything's okay with me. I'm in Florida, you know."

"Yeah, Jack told me you were going. Something about an airplane case, he said. Here, Andy, give that to me. No, the other one. Thanks."

"Hey, listen, Ro. You sound like this isn't really a good time either."

"I'm sorry, Chris. It really isn't. I was in the art department until seven-thirty and I have to be at a media party, a formal yet, tonight. There are going to be some television types there and a news film crew, I'm told. *Entertainment Tonight,* or some such thing."

Before he could answer, Lang heard some commotion at the

other end of the line. Ro called out, "What is it, Jack?" A pause. "Already? Tell him I'll be down in fifteen minutes. Here, Andy, hand me that dress."

"Sounds like you're out of time," said Lang.

"Just about. What was it you wanted to talk about, anyway?"

"Nothing, really. It's not a big deal. Nothing that can't wait until tomorrow."

"Not tomorrow, Chris. I'm gone all day. Can you call Monday?"

"Sure," he replied. "I'll call Monday. Have a good time at the party. Where is it?"

"I don't know. Some public-relations bigwig's beachhouse in Malibu. I've really got to run. Talk to you Monday."

Before he got the "G'bye" out, she clicked off. He sat motionless on the edge of the bed, holding the dead receiver against his ear. The room around him felt small and remote. Suddenly, he was brimming with dozens of unasked questions about the mundane, everyday lives of his ex-wife and his three beautiful children, four living, breathing human beings who used to be his life but had just been reduced to memories at the other end of a dead phone line. A vaguely familiar, unwelcome feeling settled over him, a powerful sense of loss and regret. He found himself teetering on the precipice of the bottomless sadness he had last felt when he lost his mother and only remaining parent as a college student. This feeling was a pale and distant echo of that awesome devastation, but there was undeniably some kinship between the two. Tears stung his tired eyes. Swiftly, the analytical side of his brain took over and he began to try to determine why he was feeling so bad, so suddenly. Three hours later, when he finally drifted off to sleep, fatigued to the point of exhaustion, he still hadn't figured it out.

An incessant rapping on the thin wood door of his room dragged Lang up from the depths of a heavy sleep. Groggy and a little unsteady, he took in the surroundings of an unfamiliar hotel room. Amy's voice swam to him through the fog.

"Chris? Chris? Are you up yet? Time to go."

Lang fumbled for his watch on the nightstand. Five forty-five. What the hell? Oh, he thought, that's Pacific time. So it's . . . eight forty-five? "Jesus!" he muttered.

"Chris?"

"I'm up, Amy. I'm up," he called out. He stumbled toward the door. Opening it a crack against the bright light of morning, he saw Amy in a tight-fitting tank top and a pair of short shorts.

Tanned and muscular, she looked as if she had just come back from the gym. "I'm up, Amy. I slept in, though. I don't know what happened, how I slept to eight forty-five. You better have breakfast without me while I shower."

"I'll wait," she replied, crinkling her nose for the dual purpose of focusing her thoughts and pulling her sunglasses back up. "Anyway, it's not eight forty-five. It's seven forty-five. We went on standard time last night. Remember? Spring forward, fall back? Call me or knock on my door when you're ready to eat. I'll be looking through some flight reports."

Lang was silent and more than a little sullen through breakfast. Amy, accustomed to the moods of her colleague, stuck to light, noncontroversial topics of conversation, liberally stretched out over long periods of silence. After they finished eating—Lang his waffle and two strips of bacon, Amy her Shredded Wheat, strawberries, and skim milk—Lang remembered what he had wanted to ask the day before on the way to the hotel.

"Do you have that stack of pages with you? You know, the ones that have the entries we don't yet understand?"

"You mean my 'UFO' file? Yeah. It's here in my briefcase." She flipped the case open and retrieved one manila pocket folder from among a half dozen or so. As promised, it bore Amy's neatly printed label, UFO. She handed it to him.

"Jesus, there are still quite a few you and John Carrick haven't fully deciphered."

"That's deceiving. Almost all of them have only one or two minor entries we haven't figured yet. John doesn't think any of them are important but I impressed upon him your passion for understanding every word on every page before we start the trial and he's still working on his set."

Lang sifted through them.

"What are you looking for?" asked Amy at length. "I know that file pretty well. Maybe I can help."

"I'm not sure. I figure that the Arrow employees who worked on the project are going to stick to the party line when we take their depositions. Their loyalty is legendary. I don't expect to make much headway there, although you never know until you try. I guess I was wondering if there's someone who might have been there who doesn't owe a vow of loyalty to Lindstrom or the company."

"The Lindstrom angle again, huh?" Amy laughed agreeably. "You're nothing if not tenacious."

Lang pawed through the file as Amy paid the check and went to the ladies' room. Just as she returned, something caught his eye. "What's this?" he asked. " 'All-hands meeting January seventh, DMC, RTW, SBC, BAM, MOK, ND'?"

"I believe that is a memo from an early meeting shortly after the time the contract was signed. Actually a month and a half after they signed. Contract is dated November twenty-seventh." She closed her eyes, the better to concentrate. "Those present included DMC, chief engineer Doug Chesney; RTW, flight engineer Ray Wollersheim; SBC, project coordinator Steve Castillo; and test pilot Brent Milinsky, that's BAM."

"And the other two, MOK and ND?"

"Can't find a reference to an employee with the initials MOK, but the records aren't particularly well maintained. I figure 'ND' for Nigel Daultry himself."

Lang got up from the table. "Me, too."

"So you think maybe Lindstrom attended the meeting under the surreptitious designation of MOK?" Amy laughed, leading the way out of the coffee shop. Lang noticed that several among the largely good ol' boy clientele in the place lifted their heads from their breakfasts long enough to watch her leave.

Lang pursued the point. "You can't identify this other employee by cross-referencing our database on their documents?"

"No. There's no other reference to him anywhere. If it was a secret designation for Lindstrom he was either only there once or he only used the designation once."

"I wasn't thinking of it as a code for Lindstrom. I was thinking of it as another witness."

In the parking lot, Amy unlocked the Sunbird and climbed in. "And since he only shows up once, you figure maybe he quit or got canned and might talk to us if we can find him?"

"Not exactly, although that's possible. I was thinking, maybe hoping, that it might have been somebody who wasn't with the Arrow operation at all but somebody who was there with Daultry. Now that would be a guy who'd have no reason to protect Lindstrom." Sliding into the passenger seat, he caught a dubious look from Amy around her sunglasses and added, "Or Arrow Dynamics."

"Now there's a thought. Too bad old Nigel bought the farm in Milan. What was he doing racing cars at his age, anyway?"

"He was only fifty-five," observed Lang.

"Still. Fifty-five isn't twenty-five. Anyway, what do you think?"

"I think there's something there. We need to do a little digging into Nigel Daultry and his companies. Maybe we can come up with an employee with the initials MOK."

Amy roared out onto Interstate 4 in the direction of Winter Haven. "Is this possibly a job for the finest LAPD detective ever to moonlight for a law firm?"

Lang smiled for the first time since the phone call to Ro the night before. "Yes. If he has time, Detective William Quinn would be an excellent choice, conflicts of interest notwithstanding."

Amy laughed gleefully, popping the transmission into fourth. "Good! Bill and his hard-working lawyer wife love Devereaux and Brace's pay scale."

"I only use him because he's the best."

"He never disappoints. I'll put him to work as soon as we get back to L.A."

The airport at Winter Haven, like so many in the Sunbelt, was an airstrip from another era. Absent were the pretensions of blinking runway lights, heavily painted taxiway directions, long printed signs of instructions. This was an airfield from the simpler, friendlier days of aviation and the pilots loved it.

On this glorious morning in late October, under a warm, bright sun in a cobalt-blue sky, Amy Quinn and Chris Lang walked along the aging tarmac crosshatched by asphalt sealer from years gone by, past the rusting corrugated hangars that rimmed the field, looking for a familiar face. Under a sign that said Gator Air Taxi, they found it.

"G'morning, Graham," called Lang. Amy waved. Graham Ellerby, standing with Walt McCluskey and two other men in the open hangar door, smiled broadly and returned the greeting. One of the other men turned out to be Bobby Lathrop, an American who worked for Ellerby and Andrews in England. He had been involved with the fabrication of the Peregrine and had come over to help set up the StormTree for the test flight. The other was the owner of Gator Air Taxi, Grover Young, who had stored the Storm-Tree since its last showcase flight in the Sun 'n' Fun air show in Winter Haven three years earlier.

Inside the hangar was the StormTree, brainchild of famed New Zealand engineer and entrepreneur Nigel Daultry and, if one were to believe, as Chris Lang fervently did, aviation and industrial giant Russell Lindstrom. For Lang and Amy, this was their first live look at the wayward offspring. It was sleek and futuristic, a blindingly white fantasy from the dreams of a gifted engineer with a strong romantic streak. Barely eighteen feet long from its gracefully pointed needle nose to the single propeller at its tail—it was a "pusher"—with a wingspan of twenty-two feet, it was a breathtaking sight to behold. Its side-by-side two-place cockpit was wrapped in a darkly tinted dome of Plexiglas that enhanced its futuristic appearance. The ends of the long, elegant wings curled up ever so slightly into tiny winglets, which served both aesthetic and aerodynamic purposes. The tail section, in keeping with the science-fiction/fantasy personality its creator had bestowed upon it, suggested an extruded whale's tail, turned at ninety degrees, with the propeller in its center, and capped off, at the very top, by a simple fragile tail wing.

"God," exclaimed Amy as they took it in. "It's incredible. What a beautiful airplane."

Lang simply observed the aircraft in silence. For all its apparent flimsiness, it had the air of a historic breakthrough. There was an ethereal quality to this machine, as if it were destined to link the gritty earthbound world of hard technology with the mystical realm of the heavens themselves.

As Grover and Bobby walked the plane out of the hangar into the sunlight, Ellerby said to Lang and Amy, "I've just been going over the regimen here with Walt. Bobby and I got here at six this morning to weigh the plane and calculate the center of gravity. We'll start in the forward part of the approved range and nibble at the departure and spin characteristics as we edge back into the aft part of the range. That's where the trouble will be if we are to encounter any, of course."

Lang turned to McCluskey. "Now, Walt, you understand that under no circumstances are you to spin this aircraft. We only need—and want—an expert's assessment we can use in court that this aircraft has a *tendency to depart* and, therefore, *spin*, as has already been documented in the case of the Peregrine. Okay?"

McCluskey nodded emphatically. "You bet. This baby"—he gestured to the parachute he wore on his back—"is just for show on this mission. I've read the reports on both aircraft thoroughly. I think I can determine a departure-and-spin susceptibility from the aerodynamic characteristics of the plane in the high angle of attack without an actual spin. Certainly well enough to verify whether the two aircraft have identical characteristics."

"Great," said Lang. "Just don't spin it. I have no confidence in that plane's ability to recover. At the first sign of departure or spin entry, do what you have to do to back away."

McCluskey laughed. "I read you, General. No acrobatics today."

It took nearly another half hour for everyone to be briefed on his assignment. McCluskey would fly the StormTree alone, in radio contact with both the chase plane and the ground. Grover Young would pilot the chase plane, his own Grumman Cheetah, from which Bobby Lathrop would handle the airborne video camera. On the ground, Ellerby would operate a video camera, as well, while Lang observed and handled the ground-based radio link to both aircraft. Amy turned down Lathrop's offer to ride in the chase plane and decided to stay with Lang and Ellerby.

They were airborne, at last, by ten-forty and stayed with it right through the lunch hour. With the Grumman flying chase above, slightly behind and to the starboard, McCluskey took the Storm-Tree through the most primitive possible version of MS 92121, the Universal Military Departure and Spin Specification required by the contract between Arrow Dynamics and Daultry Research PLC. As called for in the spec, he began with the aircraft configured at its forwardmost center of gravity, the most stable configuration in the high angle of attack, and systematically went through the prescribed control applications: slow to stall speed, pull the stick full aft, left aileron and left rudder; then the same series with right aileron and right rudder. The aircraft dutifully rolled back and forth between banks of sixty degrees to the left then the right. Throughout the regimen the StormTree remained stable and gave no indication that it would depart from controlled flight or spin.

"Why isn't it spinning?" asked a frustrated Amy Quinn.

Ellerby smiled. "Be patient, Amy. This is a delicate operation. Walt has to become acquainted with the plane's nuances, its personality. This is always important when first flying an airplane, but especially so when it's an experimental model you plan to take to the outside of its performance envelope."

Amy frowned, unpersuaded. The test of her patience was only beginning. For the next two days, the process continued, as McCluskey dug deeper and deeper into the nether regions of the StormTree's "personality." Under the watchful eyes of the two video cameras and five witnesses, he took off and landed again and again, each time moving the center of gravity still farther aft and climbing back to a safe altitude to go through the prescribed control applications all over again. And each time, the StormTree responded beautifully, just as the "docile" airplane Arrow Dynamics' report had described as a "joy to fly" was supposed to. And nothing like its offspring, the Peregrine, had.

The "gap" in Lang's case against Arrow Dynamics was threatening to widen into an unbridgeable gulf. No one was more acutely aware of the implications than he: If the StormTree did not show a susceptibility to depart and spin, there was a compelling argument to be made that the demon in the Peregrine was not its relationship to the StormTree, but the extra weight it carried. And, even though Lang did not believe this for one minute—otherwise, he reasoned, when the Peregrine demonstrated a propensity to spin, the Arrow Dynamics engineers hired to correct the problem would have *immediately* identified the additional weight as the culprit, something they *never* did—it would give the jury more reason than it would need to decide for the local hero and against the foreign company that claimed it had lost several million.

By early in the afternoon of the third day, everyone's patience was wearing thin. As Lathrop and Ellerby recomputed the center of gravity for yet another flight, this time at 120.5 centimeters aft of the established baseline, McCluskey and Lang sat opposite each other on rusty oil drums in the mouth of the Gator Air Taxi hangar. Although the humidity was low by Central Florida standards, Lang would have preferred to think this was the reason that he now perspired profusely. He gulped from the bottle of Dr Pepper provided by Grover. A drop of sweat rolled from his eyelid down into his eye.

"Well, Walt," he said. "What do you think?"

McCluskey swigged at his own bottle. "I'm damned if I know, Chris. I've taken that son of a bitch through the regime like a goddamned watchmaker. If she's the other bird's mama, she should be showing me a departure tendency, I believe. Truth is, though, I don't get so much as a twitter out of her."

"Time to give up?"

"Hell, no. We've been nibbling, so far. Nothing more. Your reports, the Pegasus reports, on the Peregrine don't make it sound like they were nibbling to me. That fella MacNeil was pumping that sucker hard when she turned on him. He was doing aggravated control inputs, not little baby-step applications like we've been doing. It's possible that would make a difference."

"Wait a minute," said Lang. "If we move to aggravated inputs in order to show a departure tendency or spin tendency, haven't we lost the battle? Aren't we trying to show that the real vice of the plane designed by Lindstrom was that an amateur pilot, a 'low-time' pilot, in the words of the final engineering report, could get himself unexpectedly in mortal danger in this thing in the ordinary course of routine flying?"

Lathrop and Ellerby had finished their adjustments of the airplane and come over to Lang and McCluskey. Grover and Amy had drifted over, as well, and were listening to the discussion.

Ellerby interjected, "No. They're two entirely different things."

Lang said, "I'm not sure I follow you. And if I don't follow, I'm never going to be able to bring a jury along to the right bottom line."

Ellerby responded, "That's a good point. But it's all right. The Mil Spec runs a graduated regimen to test departure and spin, from gentle control applications to more abrupt ones, all the way up to violent or aggravated ones. Because we're spot on certain this plane will spin, and get to be very hard to recover when it does, Walt has been extremely cautious. The type of pilot who would have acquired and flown this plane would have been nothing of the sort. No careful control applications for him. He would be more likely to cross rudder and aileron applications. And his skill level would have been a microfraction of Walt's.

"But the point is, if it tends to depart or spin even with aggravated controls, we have them two ways. First, they should have picked that up if they really ran the full Mil Spec as they claimed. And, second, because the aircraft would not then be either 'docile' or a 'joy to fly' in anybody's book, we have them in a flat-out lie."

Lang nodded his comprehension. "So, our genteel approach has been out of deference to the dangers we know this plane is hiding, dangers the average user would have no reason even to suspect."

Ellerby replied, "Exactly."

McCluskey broke in. "I'm going to push her just a bit, cross her controls the way I know some ham-fisted amateur would on a low-approach bank turn. I promise you I will back off at the first sign of deterioration."

"If you think it's safe," cautioned Lang.

"Hell, Chris. It's safe, that's why I spent so damn much time climbing to altitude in the son of a bitch. I've got oodles of time to ditch if it comes to that, though I promise to do my best to salvage your plane for evidence."

Up they went again, McCluskey climbing to an altitude of 12,500 feet above Winter Haven for the thirteenth time in three days. Grover Young's chase plane, larger and more powerful, had taken off twenty minutes after McCluskey but achieved its position at about thirteen thousand feet ten minutes sooner.

McCluskey squawked onto the radio. "Okay, I have an altitude of twelve thousand five hundred and am ready to begin the protocol of Mil Spec 92121 at a center of gravity of 120.5 centimeters," he said for the benefit of the growing videotape historical record.

"Video check, chase," said Lang into the radio.

From the Grumman, Bobby Lathrop answered, "Tape running in the chase plane."

"Video check, ground," said Lang.

"Tape rolling on the ground," replied Ellerby from behind his tripod.

"You are clear, StormTree," advised Lang.

"Roger, Control," came the reply from McCluskey and he began the monotonous series of control inputs he had performed on each of the twelve previous efforts. The results were identical.

"Okay, Control," announced McCluskey. "We are moving to a series of gentle inputs of cross controls. Full aft stick, slowing to stall speed. In the high angle of attack. Induce left yaw, with left rudder, right aileron. Whoa! I might be onto something here. This son of a bitch is pitchbucking."

Even from the ground, Lang and Ellerby could detect a flutter in the motion of the aircraft. The chase plane could see it much more clearly, of course. In the StormTree, McCluskey experienced a violent, rapid up-and-down motion. But the aircraft was still within his control.

"Pitchbuck is a constant value," McCluskey reported. Then he neutralized both the rudder and the aileron, immediately restoring stable, straight, and level flight. "Uncrossing controls restores dynamic stability. There was no departure from controlled flight, although I have several loose fillings in my mouth."

Everyone at both remote radio locations laughed, less from McCluskey's sense of humor than the relief they all experienced after the first sign of adversity during the entire project.

McCluskey immediately went on. "I'm going to test this area a little further. I will repeat the procedure, moving through the controls slightly more rapidly and reversing the directions; this time rudder will be right and aileron left."

Even from his position 12,500 feet below the StormTree, Lang could immediately see that something serious was taking place in the sky. McCluskey rolled to a right bank, then flipped over suddenly and violently. Just as the realization came to the observers both above and below the StormTree that it was upside down, it righted itself in relation to the ground, but something was still very wrong. As Lang's mind struggled to grasp what he was observing, McCluskey told him.

"Oh, oh," said McCluskey. "The son of a bitch is into a flat spin."

Ellerby grabbed Lang's arm and pushed him toward the video camera. "Keep shooting!" he hollered. At the same time he snatched the radio from Lang's hand. "Walt, do you have any oscillation in your pitch?"

"Negative," replied McCluskey, fully in control of his emotions if not his aircraft. "This spin is absolutely flat, just like Mac-Neil's."

Ellerby thought furiously. "Can you use power to develop some downward thrust?"

"That's what I'm doing, but I'm telling you this spin is absolutely fucking flat. I have no nose-over to capitalize on."

From Lang's vantage point on the ground the engine whirred like a distant dentist's drill, grinding monotonously back and forth, as the skillful pilot throttled up, then down, methodically applying his years of experience against the spin's grasp. But he could see no change through the viewfinder as he helplessly recorded the inevitable descent of the aircraft. Time stretched out eerily as the tiny white bird floated through the sky, more like a broken child's toy than an airship meant to carry a man into the heavens.

Meanwhile, the radio had become a clearinghouse for advice from every quarter. "Throw your weight against the nose when you power up!" Lathrop shouted.

"Slam the rudder hard left!" suggested Grover.

"Ease off the throttle for a full revolution and see if that does any good," advised Ellerby.

Finally, McCluskey's voice seized the air authoritatively. "Goddammit! I've never seen anything like it. I'm tracking the identical horizon on each rotation." Then, a pause. "Oh, shit! That tears it."

Suddenly, the aircraft went silent. Then, McCluskey's voice. "Engine's quit." Another pause. "Power's gone."

Ellerby responded, "That's okay, you can still sail out of it."

"Not if I can't get this spin to oscillate. It's just dead flat. And I'm at ninety-two hundred feet and losing altitude fast. Engine won't restart."

Lang jumped in, "Punch out of there, Walt. Fuck the airplane, we've got it all on tape. It spins just like the goddamned Peregrine."

"Maybe, but I think it's too early. I'll call you back at forty-five hundred. Man, the torque of these rotations is ferocious on this composite frame!"

Immediately Lathrop broke in from the chase plane, which was diving and circling to stay with the plummeting StormTree. "Get out of there, Walt! That frame will warp on you. Get that goddamned canopy off before it jams!"

At these words, Lang glanced away from the viewfinder of his video camera to see a look of white panic on Ellerby's face.

"He's right, Walt," cried Ellerby, his voice fairly cracking with fear.

"Okay," replied McCluskey calmly. "You talked me into it. I'm getting out."

All eyes were riveted on the spinning airplane, rocketing toward the earth. In a flash, Lang recalled Clive Andrews's description of the Peregrine falling "like a bloody seed pod." But up in the sky, nothing changed. There was no sign of a pilot exiting the aircraft. Only the sickening sight of a spinning plane growing ominously larger to the observers below.

"Goddamn!" shouted McCluskey, still more angry than panicked. "It's jammed all right. The canopy is one hundred percent torqued shut." Over the radio, the others listened, horrified, to the repeated, desperate grunts and gasps of a man trying in vain to snatch back his life from the powerful centrifugal forces at work on the aircraft. He could not do it. But he kept trying with all the strength he could muster until the plane vanished into a fiery flash of light just beyond the horizon from the airfield.

"Jesus Christ!" cried a stunned and shaken Ellerby. Amy turned her head away, ashen, and fought back a sudden wave of nausea. Lang stood, staring at the flaming wreckage, shaking violently. Somewhere on the edges of his field of vision, a handful of people at the airport rushed toward the flames.

CHAPTER 10

RO LANG PLAYED WITH THE CAR RADIO DIAL, scanning from country to oldies to "classic rock" to classical, before switching to AM and settling on an all-news station. Jennifer had picked a bad day to dawdle on the way out of school. Ro had calculated her available time down to the minute and the digital clock on the dash told her she was now running behind. Through the dappled sunlight of late November now splashing across the windshield, she squinted for any sign of her eldest child. Not sure which part of the sprawling "campus" of Tierra Rejada Middle School she would be coming from, Ro decided not to go look for her lest she compound the problem.

I never seem to have enough time for anything these days, thought Ro, as she half-listened to the news of the day on Wall Street. The whirlwind pace had not let up. Completion of photography back in Pennsylvania had turned out to be but the start of the project. Never having done a cover piece before, she had been caught by surprise by the extensive postproduction phase of the project. Proofs, runs, layout options, and repeated rewrites of the text had occupied several five-day, fifty-hour weeks. And, just as postproduction had wound down, the most exhausting phase of all arrived: promotion. But, of course, that was one of the keys to the amazing success of David Stingley's *Beau Rivage*. Less than a half dozen years ago it had been an obscure, "arty" glossy that found its way onto a handful of coffee tables in the living rooms of a few homes on either coast. But since Stingley's arrival, the magazine had, somewhat paradoxically, acquired both cachet and readership, the latter in ever-increasing numbers.

At last, Jennifer Lang, backpack slung heavily over one shoulder, sauntered into view, engaged in an animated chat with a teacher. Ro hit the horn twice to get her attention, then waved to her through the window. Jennifer picked up the signal, said a quick good-bye to her companion, then took off in a gentle lope toward the car. She was out of breath as she tossed her satchel over the front seat.

"Hi, Mom," she said.

"Hi, Jen," replied Ro, checking the mirrors as she wheeled into the quiet street. "Is that one of your teachers? I don't recognize her." Her daughter looked back at her vacantly. "The teacher you were just talking to? She's not familiar."

The light went on in Jennifer's eyes. "Oh, her. She's not a teacher. I think she's just somebody's mom. She was just standing there on the walk when I came out of Mrs. Brampton's class and she sort of started walking when I did."

A gentle alarm, the one every mother has, went off deep within Ro. "Whose mom is she?" she asked.

"I don't know. I mean she looks like a mom. That's all I meant."

Ro had to agree with that assessment. But she thought it better to press a little harder for some insight. These days, you never knew what was lurking out there for your kids to run across. "What did you talk about?"

"I don't know. General stuff."

" 'General stuff' doesn't sound like honors English, Jen. Give it another try."

"Jeez, Mom, don't go all Gestapo on me. She wasn't a drug dealer, if that's what you mean." Jennifer correctly read the reproach on her mother's face. Her tone softened accordingly. "She was just saying some, you know, school-related stuff."

Ro was getting a little exasperated. "Give us a quote here, Jennifer."

"Okay." Jennifer repeated, " 'An honors class in the last period of the day must be pretty tough.' "

"That's it?"

"Just about. The cool weather. How heavy my bag was. That's all I can think of. What's the big deal?"

"No big deal," Ro replied breezily. "We baby boomer moms need to keep an eye on our young, that's all."

Jennifer shrugged. Ro wondered how the world had gotten to a point where a friendly conversation with another student's mother could possibly be cause for concern.

The Century Plaza Hotel in Century City shimmered like an oversized diamond in the cool, crisp Southern California night as Mark Fassero drove around the brightly lit fountain and pulled up to the valet at the main entrance. The man in the beefeater's outfit opened the passenger door and offered his hand to Ro as she deftly negotiated her way out of the low front seat of Mark's white Saab. Although he discreetly averted his eyes, the handsome young man in the costume could not avoid catching a tantalizing glimpse of the beautiful woman's long, well-conditioned legs as the deep slit in the side of her tight-fitting dress opened to allow her to stand. His eyes met hers and they exchanged smiles.

"Nice suit," remarked Ro, with a little laugh.

"Yours does more for you," replied the red-faced young man, who reflected on the benefits of his night job in a glamorous part of town as he watched Ro disappear through the huge front doors of the hotel.

Mark, in the tuxedo Ro had now seen on nearly a half dozen occasions, took her arm in his and escorted her toward the lavishly decorated ballroom where the *Beau Rivage* press reception was to take place. The hotel was bristling with activity, unusual for a Thursday night. The *Beau Rivage* room was festooned with a giant logo of the magazine and huge enlargements of Ro's Gettysburg photos. David Stingley spotted them as they came through the door and immediately swept across the floor to meet them. He greeted Ro with the kiss on the cheek that had become *de rigueur* since the promotion campaign had begun the prior month.

"Ro, you look as wonderful as ever," Stingley said, immaculate as always in his tuxedo. "This is going to be a great night for *Beau Rivage* and for you, my dear," he whispered into her ear, emphasizing the point with a squeeze of her hand. Whatever hidden meaning the comment might have held was lost for the moment on Ro, who just smiled the smile that had become her trademark around the magazine for the last few months.

Mark, standing behind her with a hand lightly resting on the small of her back, smiled and winked at Stingley. Ro excused herself to visit the ladies' room. When she had moved out of earshot, Mark said discreetly to Stingley, "I guess everything's worked out pretty well, after all, David. The woman knows how to take a picture."

Stingley, looking straight ahead, his best smile still in place and aimed out across the room, quietly replied, "I *knew* she was a good photographer." He shook his head very slightly. "You know, you guys act like the fucking mob."

"That's a little melodramatic, don't you think? The tradition of calling in chits from old comrades is as old as warfare itself."

Stingley frowned. "I don't mind doing my part. I just don't like your tactics." With that, he moved off to another part of the room.

When Ro returned, Mark moved in close beside her.

"You know, I think I'm finally getting used to all this," she said, smiling warmly. He smiled his own bright smile from the heart of his warm red beard.

The evening featured what had become staples of the "circuit" Stingley had created for the magazine: sumptuous food and drink, industry small talk, lavish praise liberally bestowed on everyone for everything, and gushing, self-serving statements to the other media representatives who, as Stingley had so shrewdly calculated, could not resist the temptation to add pulp to their own product by the simple expedient of covering another medium. As always, Ro seldom strayed far from Mark's side. The pattern had been established early on, out of sheer necessity, when she was not really sure what to say or how to act. But even as she had grown more comfortable with the ritual of this type of affair, she had shown no inclination to be away from her "associate." While only rarely allowing herself to consider the implications, Ro had gradually come to the realization that she was more than professionally dependent on Mark. And she felt sure that his interest in her now went well beyond his assigned duties. She was still uneasy about where the relationship might go but, for now, under the gentle glow of a glass of fine chardonnay, she allowed herself to feel very good about it.

The evening's highlight was Stingley's announcement of the current sales figures for the December issue. With nearly two weeks of newsstand life left, it had become a very successful issue, a fact that Stingley graciously attributed to Ro's outstanding cover story, despite the fact that she knew the strike that had shut down several other publications probably had more to do with it. It was a good feeling, nonetheless, to be in Stingley's warm and flattering spotlight.

"Great night," Ro purred to Mark an hour and a half later as they stepped out of the warmth of the hotel lobby into the bracing evening air.

"My sentiments, as well," he said back, smiling broadly. "You sure seem comfortable with Stingley's praise."

She laughed. "You know as well as I do that David's a showman. And he likes the *numbers*," she corrected. "My work was along for the ride."

Mark shook his head. "Your work is good, Ro. Let's put it this way: I wouldn't mind having a stake in your future."

"That could be arranged," Ro replied before she realized what she was saying.

"Oh?" he asked.

"Never mind," she said quickly, as he left to take care of the valet.

While she waited for him to return, Ro fought off a shiver. There was a distinct bite in the thin, dry desert air as the temperature dipped into the high 40s.

"Chilly?" asked a voice behind her.

She turned to see a man in a tuxedo who was neither Mark nor anyone else who had been at the party. Her mind, dulled by the chardonnay, raced to make recognition. My God! she thought after a split second that had seemed to last forever.

"Chris!" she said, at last. "What are you doing here?"

"Same as you, by the looks of it," he said, gesturing to their formal evening wear. "But probably not as much fun. It's an ABA function. For the Litigation Section. I gave a speech."

"Oh," she replied. "That's great."

"You?"

"Reception for the magazine. Publicity affair."

"Good for you," he said with genuine warmth. "That cover piece is really fabulous. Damned good." He paused. She smiled awkwardly. Then he asked, "Did you get my messages?"

"Yeah, I did. Thank you for the congratulations. I'm sorry I didn't get back to you. I've been so busy."

Lang realized he hadn't actually seen her in more than three months, so hectic had their schedules been. He was struck by how good she looked. Despite her ultrachic evening gown and formal wrap, there was something about her very reminiscent of the college girl he had romanced back in Virginia when he was in law school.

"Yeah, me too," he managed to say. "What's your dad's expression? Busier than a one-legged man—"

"—in an ass-kicking contest," she finished. "Good old Pete, the master of clichés." They both laughed.

"You look great, Ro," he said.

"You look good yourself."

"You know. Tuxedo. Everybody looks good in a tuxedo," he replied. "A chimp looks good in a tux." He was about to add something else when a man in a red beard appeared behind her and slipped his arm around her shoulders. She flinched involuntarily, a sheepish look on her face.

"Oh," she said, barely regaining her poise. "Chris, this is Mark Fassero, of *Beau Rivage* magazine. Mark, this is my ex-husband, Chris Lang."

Mark smiled and extended his hand. "Pleased to meet you, Chris."

Chris returned the handshake. "Same here. I was just congratulating Ro on the great cover piece in the magazine. I understand that the congratulations go to you, as well."

"Thank you, but I played a small part. The real work and the true genius all came from Ro. She's a very talented lady."

"I know," replied Lang, just a touch of resentment in his tone. He knew he was tired and not particularly prepared for this encounter and resolved to watch his tongue. "I've been a big fan of hers for many years."

"Really?" said Mark, his tone also slightly less than cordial. Mark's car appeared just ahead of Lang's. "Here we are," he said to Ro, sliding his arm down around her waist. To Lang he said, "Nice to meet you."

"My pleasure," replied Lang. "Good night, Ro. I'll call you."

Ro looked slightly apologetic. "Okay. We need to talk about Thanksgiving."

"Fine," said Lang, moving to take his own car from the valet. "I'll try you tomorrow." With that, Mark popped the clutch and roared off.

It was just after eleven when Mark pulled into Ro's driveway. Exhausted, she had slept through most of the ride home. Actually, for a great deal of the way she had pretended to sleep, for some reason not wanting to talk to Mark. The brief encounter with Chris had disturbed her for reasons she couldn't quite define. She had felt guilty but she had no idea why. After all, she was on her own, fully and legally divorced from Chris, perfectly free to act as she chose with neither consent nor approval from him. Yet her brief intimacy with Mark, entirely natural and appropriate in the context of their relationship, had made her oddly uncomfortable in front of Chris. He obviously hadn't liked it much. That troubled her, but worse was the fact that she had allowed his disapproval to intrude on what was otherwise a wonderful evening in Mark's company. She felt deep resentment toward Chris, but equally strong anger at herself. Into the mix, she was tired, slightly drunk, and confused about her remarkable good fortune at *Beau Rivage*. And there was something else. After all the years and all the fights and all the stress, seeing her ex-husband without any prior warning or time to prepare had convinced her of something she had only vaguely suspected: She was not entirely over Chris Lang.

Mark got out and opened the door for her, something, she recalled, that Chris had once been so consistent about before their lives had tumbled off in opposite directions.

At the front door, Ro looked at her watch and asked, "Do you want to come in for a cup of decaf or a Bailey's?"

The glance at her watch made Mark's decision. "No, thanks. I really have to get going. I have an early flight out of LAX tomorrow."

"Oh, right," she replied, unable to disguise the relief she felt. "St. Louis, right?" He nodded. "Mark, I had a great time tonight."

"Me, too, Ro," he said, his customary warmth returning.

"Drive safely, okay?"

"Will do, my dear." He drew her to him and kissed her on the lips. At first, it was a gentle kiss, but he lingered and the kiss grew more passionate. As he pressed harder, she offered no resistance, so he pressed harder still. Their embrace tightened slightly. Despite the chill, Ro could feel a powerful surge of heat radiating from her lips. Suddenly, his tongue, warm and soft, was against her upper lip, gently caressing the bow he found there. Then it was against her straight, white teeth briefly before it met hers. The surge of heat became a firestorm and, dizzy and confused, she was suddenly frightened. She pulled away, out of breath.

"Whew!" she managed to say. "I think I'm a little bit tipsy."

"Are you sure it's from the wine?"

She looked at him. In his tuxedo, tie undone and a white silk scarf draped about his broad shoulders, his handsome face lit with a bright smile, he was very sexy and she was completely under his spell. But she was not foolish and she knew enough not to trust what she was feeling.

"I'm tired and need a good night's sleep," she said, kissing him on his woolly cheek.

He knew the moment had passed. "Don't we both? Good night, Ro."

"Good night," she answered and watched as he walked to his car. She closed the door as his engine started and sighed heavily. In the family room, she found a sleepy Jennifer waiting for a rundown of her mother's evening out.

Not many miles away, Chris Lang sat in his study, tie open and shirt undone at the throat, a tall glass of vodka on the table beside him. In front of him, the television played. No footage of Walt McCluskey's spin or Lindstrom's media machine, this time. Instead, he watched an old videotape of a young family on vacation at Mammoth Mountain, California. Two four-year-olds skied tentatively down a gentle slope toward the camera. At the bottom, a brightly clad seven-year-old girl, so much more assured than her brother and sister on her skis, waited with a lithe woman, mirrored sunglasses pushed up on her raven hair. They smiled and waved at the camera held by the husband and father, unseen and, Lang thought morosely, out of the picture.

CHAPTER 11

BILL QUINN CHECKED THE TIME AS HE WAITED impatiently for the light at the intersection of Olympic Boulevard and Century Park East. Five-seventeen. Although he knew as well as anyone that Chris and Amy would be working late, he prided himself on his punctuality and was not happy that the meeting with his sergeants had run over. Besides, even though Chris Lang was a decent fellow to work for, Amy always seemed particularly critical when Bill worked for the lawyers in her firm. It was as if, thrilled though she was for him to earn the premium fee the firm paid him, she was afraid he might do something inappropriate or blow the assignment, embarrassing her in the process. The fact that no one could recall Bill ever blowing an assignment for anyone, much less for Amy's firm, was apparently of little comfort to his wife.

Meanwhile, in Lang's office, he and Amy pored over the report John Carrick and Graham Ellerby had put together on Walt Mc-Cluskey's disastrous flight. Both Amy and Lang had difficulty accepting the fact that they had witnessed the death of a man, a man they knew, who had died as a consequence of their own litigation strategy. In the world of big-time commercial litigation, huge amounts of money and even the survival of entire companies were frequently at stake but seldom, if ever, did the stakes include a human life. Lang was deeply upset by the loss of this very likable man and he could not help but blame himself for the tragedy.

Amy, with considerable help from Carrick and Ellerby, had tried hard to assuage his guilt, pointing out that every reasonable precaution had been taken and that he had been careful to specify that the test go only far enough to establish a tendency to spin; the decision to push the plane harder had been Walt's alone. The preliminary report of the National Transportation Safety Board, which exonerated all concerned from responsibility in the crash, had concurred. The tragedy had been an accident, nothing more. Lang was not fully satisfied, but had succeeded in getting back to the business at hand despite his lingering misgivings.

Lang read and reread the section of Carrick's report that dealt with the spin entry. It was titled Spin Entry without Warning. "This just about proves our claim that the Arrow people failed to test for departure and spin resistance under the contract, wouldn't you think?"

"I'd say so," agreed Amy. "John says that the whole purpose of the Mil Spec test, or any self-respecting departure test, for that matter, is to discover and identify spin warnings so that pilots— especially the amateur pilots who were expected to fly this plane— would have all the time in the world to get themselves out of the mess. It would certainly be hard for them to argue that they did this test, but found neither a spin warning nor a spin susceptibility when Walt hit it midway through the process."

"Arrow Dynamics' final report doesn't even identify the warning, does it?"

"It's cagey there," she replied, picking up a well-worn copy of the report. "Here it is. Page 27. 'The prototype showed no tendency to depart from controlled flight. Spin entry without warning was not encountered, qualifying the aircraft as resistant to spin, per Mil Spec 92121.' Talk about bullshit techno-speak. What do you suppose that really means?"

"Hard to say. And maybe that was the design—" A knock at the door interrupted him. "Come in," he called.

Bill Quinn's frame filled the door. "Anybody home?" he said.

"Hi, honey," said Amy, brightening perceptibly as she moved to meet him. She reached up to put her arms around him and kissed him on the mouth.

When he freed himself from Amy's embrace, Bill said, "Sorry I'm late, guys." He was a little self-conscious being affectionate with his wife in front of her boss. She, on the other hand, was perfectly comfortable being herself in front of Lang.

"Not at all," replied Lang, not bothering to check his watch. "What's new?" Lang asked Bill.

"Generally, not much. LAPD works me too hard and appreciates me too little," Bill replied, smiling. Though he had shaved this morning, his heavy blue-black beard was already distinctly visible. His white shirt was undone at the neck. His tie—Lang recognized Amy's taste in its bright colors—was loosened. "But I may have found something for you."

"We're all ears, Detective."

Bill opened his briefcase at the glass conference table where he sat next to Amy and pulled out a manila folder crammed with notes from a yellow legal pad and computer printouts. He gratefully accepted the offer of a soft drink. "First, I have a bill from the department for the computer time and paper."

"Naturally," replied Lang agreeably. "Can you get the check issued, Amy?"

She nodded, and made a notation. "I'll have it tomorrow, hon. Is that okay?"

"Great," replied Bill, still consulting his notes. "Okay. Here's the scoop. There is absolutely no record of an Arrow Dynamics employee with the initials MOK. I went back ten years in the payroll tax withholding records."

Amy was slightly alarmed. "Can you do that? Is that legal?"

Bill replied, "Gee, Counselor, I don't know, can you?"

"Stop it, Bill. I'm serious. Aren't there privacy rights involved?"

Lang responded. "Yes, there are. And, yes, it is legal. Under FOI you can get the names, just not the amounts of income or withholding."

To Amy, Bill said, "I told you I'm not going to do anything illegal, okay?"

"Sorry," replied Amy.

"Anyway," continued Bill. "There is also no record of an independent contractor with those initials working for Arrow during the time period you told me to look at, although that information is a lot harder to come by. You get it by cross-referencing taxpayer ID numbers on the business-expense deductions claimed by Arrow.

That, I did only for the six weeks before and after the date of the contract, since you had a date for the meeting attended by MOK."

"Okay," said Lang, mild impatience in his tone.

"Don't worry, Chris. I'm getting there," said Bill.

Lang replied, "I'm not worried, Bill. And I appreciate your thoroughness." Amy beamed.

Bill continued. "Nigel Daultry's company, the one that was involved in the deal with Arrow, was Daultry Research PLC, a British private limited company."

"I thought Daultry was from New Zealand," said Amy.

Bill nodded. "That's right. And he set up most of his businesses in New Zealand. But some of them were British. There were also two that were South African and even one that was Irish. In fact, that's where I finally came up with something I could use. There was no officer, director, or 'senior' employee listed with Daultry Research with the initials MOK. Same for the other British companies. Same result with the New Zealand and the South African companies. That was a tough search. I ended up calling an old acquaintance of mine from Fordham for that. An exchange student who works for Pinkerton's in the diamond mines in Cape Town."

He paused to drink deeply from his Diet Coke. "Ireland wasn't too hard to access, with our network of private resources," he said with a smile toward Amy, who returned it. "And, no, no employee with the initials MOK. But in talking to Uncle Seamus—"

"Uncle *Seamus*?" asked Lang. "You're kidding."

"No," replied Bill, somewhat defensively. "Uncle Seamus Callahan. Is something wrong?"

Lang reddened at the prospect that what seemed terribly funny to him might be lost on, or worse, offensive to, Bill. "No. Not at all. It's just that an investigator named Seamus is a little, ah, I don't know. Comical, I guess."

Apparently not to Bill or Amy. Their faces were blank, the irony, if any there was—and Lang was less sure now than he had been—was lost on them. He decided to forego the effort to explain himself. "Nothing, really. Go on."

Bill and Amy exchanged glances. "Go ahead," she told him.

"Anyway, Seamus says to me, 'Is that MOK or M, O, apostrophe K?' And it hits me. We might be looking at this all wrong. If it's an Irish name that someone just noted as MOK instead of M, O, apostrophe K, we've missed the boat. We might be looking for

someone whose initials are actually MO. Well, I'm thinking, I may
have to go back and do the whole search all over again when Seamus
calls me back this morning—at four-thirty. Seamus is one of the
Callahans who isn't good with the kind of math that time zones
require—"

"Is *that* who that call was?" interjected Amy.

"I told you that this morning, Amy," said Bill.

"Well," she replied. "I'm not too retentive at that hour."

"Anyway," Bill went on. "Seamus calls me this morning and
tells me that the records of the Shannon Constabulary show that
Nigel Daultry's name appears on a routine surveillance report of a
suspected member of the republican underground. You know,
they're required to file these reports even though most of them
sympathize with the republicans. It has to do with receiving their
proper funding."

Again, he drank from his soft drink, this time finishing it with a
flourish. Once more he consulted his notes. "At any rate, Nigel
Daultry was observed in the company of one *Molly O'Keefe* at the
airport in Shannon on October sixteenth of the same year the contract was signed. Molly O'Keefe, born Molly McKinney, was married to Declan O'Keefe, a known soldier in the Sinn Fein, who was
killed by British police during an attempted terrorist bombing of an
armored military truck in Armagh several years ago. Authorities in
Belfast and Londonderry are still interested in questioning her in
connection with various acts of sedition."

"Sedition? Jesus," observed Lang. "This sounds like something out of the 1770s."

"In this country, that would be so," said Bill. "But in Ireland,
these things are happening today. Even as we speak, the British and
Northern Irish authorities are hunting these people down and
dodging pipe bombs in the process."

Once again sensing that he might be inadvertently offending
Bill or Amy in an area where they apparently had strong feelings and
he was woefully ignorant, Lang tried to move back to the topic at
hand. "What else did you learn about Molly O'Keefe, Bill?"

"You know as much as I do, as of right now. She's the only
MOK or M, O, apostrophe K we have any reference to in connection with Nigel Daultry. But I have a couple other ideas I'm trying
out and I think I'll have more by the end of next week. Sorry I don't
have more yet."

"No problem. That's great, really. We certainly didn't give you much to go on. As it is, you needed the luck of the Irish to get what you did."

"That's for sure," agreed Bill. "I'm checking lists of corporate employees and the name we're looking for shows up on a police blotter in Shannon."

"I'll say this," observed Lang. "This case certainly has a lot of interesting angles to it."

"As long as your objective includes throwing a net over Russell Lindstrom, it does," noted Amy. "But if it's just a contract breach against the contracting party, it's really pretty vanilla."

Lang grunted softly at this chiding from Amy. Bill wrapped up some minor details from his investigation and was out of there by six. Amy left, with urging from Lang, at seven-thirty. At ten forty-five, Lang shut off the television, ejected the tape of Russell Lindstrom on *Nightline* from the VCR, and headed for home himself.

A chill mist fell so softly in the night that to any other than a clear, sharp eye, it appeared in the halos of the dim street lamps to be falling upward. From far down the narrow lane that led south toward Limerick came the wail of the bagpipes and the happy, intoxicated sounds of busloads of tourists just winding up an evening's authentic medieval revelry at Bunratty Castle. Constable Seamus Callahan of the Shannon Constabulary turned up the collar of his greatcoat as he crossed the lane from his car to Durty Nelly's Pub. Inside, the sounds were far more subdued—a lone fiddler wound his way through a particularly melancholy rendition of "Molly Malone" near the fireplace—but the quantity of serious drinking was considerably greater. It was warmer in here, to be sure, if no brighter. Several sidelong glances were stolen at the lawman as he moved from the door to the bar.

"What can I do for you?" asked the bartender in the heavy brogue characteristic of that part of County Clare.

"A pint of Guinness, thanks," he replied in the same brogue, surveying the crowd of thirty or so in the pub that Thursday night. When it was delivered, he asked, "Would you be knowin' where I might find my good friend, Michael McDonough?"

The bartender was noncommittal in his expression. "No, I wouldn't."

The constable was undeterred. "Well, now. That's too bad. I need to get in touch with him right away. Matter of the greatest urgency."

"Police business, is it?" the bartender asked casually.

"Business of a private nature. Definitely unofficial."

The bartender frowned. "Unofficial? That seems a bit odd, now, doesn't it?"

"Look," Seamus said evenly. "Michael McDonough's political activities may be of interest to the authorities in Belfast but they're of no concern to me. Personally, I see nothin' wrong with all of Ireland belongin' to the Irish. But that has nothin' to do with why I'm here. I'm tryin' to find someone for an old friend in America and I believe Michael can help me out."

"Wish I knew where he was, Constable," replied the bartender coolly. With that he walked down the bar and turned his attention to another patron.

Twenty minutes later, Seamus finished his second pint and paid his tab. The tip was generous, for which the bartender thanked him.

"If you do see Michael, would you give him my card and ask him to call?" Seamus said, as he shrugged into his greatcoat. The bartender took the card in silence, glancing quickly at it before putting it into the breast pocket of his apron.

Outside, the rain was a little heavier and it was definitely colder. Crossing the road back to his car, Seamus thought he could detect the first fine flakes of an early-December snowfall. The road back to Shannon would become treacherous within the hour.

As he opened the door of his car, a voice behind him spoke. "Lookin' for Michael McDonough, are you?"

Seamus turned slowly, to see a young man standing less than six feet away, his eyes barely visible under his woolen cap, his hands jammed into the pockets of his coat. From experience, Seamus knew to keep his own hands out from his sides, where there was no ambiguity about what they were up to. "That's right, lad," he said. "I've business with him."

"What sort of business would the constabulary have with him that he'd want to know about?" His voice told Seamus he was dealing with a teenager.

"Private matter, son. Not police business."

"Well, I don't think that'd be a good enough answer for him," said the boy.

"Why don't you let him decide for himself?"

"He already has," said another voice, from behind Seamus, on the other side of his car. "I've got a pistol pointed right at your gut if you're of a mind to create a problem for me, Mr. Constable."

"Michael McDonough, I take it," replied Seamus, eyeing the gun in the man's left hand. "I thought you might be around here tonight. Sendin' a boy to deliver your messages now, are you?"

The boy bristled and started toward Seamus. The other man's voice stopped him immediately. "Sean!" he called. "Stop it! We won't be needin' any entanglements with the Shannon police, now will we?" The boy stood frozen less than a yard away from Seamus Callahan. It was not lost on either of them that Seamus had not so much as flinched.

Seamus spoke next. "Mr. McDonough, I mean you no offense. Nor you, lad. Officially, I don't care what you're up to unless you break the local laws in Shannon. Unofficially, I agree with your cause."

"And who says we have a cause, Mr. Constable?"

Seamus waved him off with a gesture. "It's late, Mr. McDonough, and I've neither time nor patience for a game of cat catch mouse. A friend of mine in America is looking for a woman I think you know, to help him in a court case—strictly a civil case—and I'm tryin' to help him out. If you don't know her, fine. If you do and don't want her found, that's fine, too. Either way, I'm in my car in the next few minutes and off to Shannon and I never came to Ennis this cold and dark night."

McDonough stood immobile for a long moment, apparently considering Seamus's words and his credibility. The Underground had long enjoyed the benign neglect of the local law-enforcement authorities in the western counties and it was widely known that the sympathies of most who worked there were firmly with the republicans. Besides, this man had obviously known he was in Durty Nelly's tonight and chose to come in alone and announce his identity as well as his interest in McDonough publicly to the bartender. If his intentions had been hostile, the encounter would surely have unfolded differently.

"Who are you lookin' for, Constable Callahan?" he asked at last.

"Molly O'Keefe."

"Molly O'Keefe," McDonough repeated. "And what makes you think I even know her, much less where she is?"

Seamus shrugged, then turned to get into his car. "As I told you, Mr. McDonough, I'm not here to play games with you. I'm on my own time and my wife and dog are waitin' dinner and a fire for me down an icy road in Shannon."

As Seamus pulled the door shut, McDonough rapped on the

passenger window. Seamus leaned over and wound the window down halfway. "Just what do you want with Molly, Constable?" asked McDonough.

"I told you, Mr. McDonough," said Seamus. He was tired and beginning to sound exasperated. He was also well past the point of wondering whether the effort to help his nephew was worth it. "She may have information about an important court case in the States that might help a friend. No great mystery, I promise you."

"It's just that Molly's a private person, even now that she's, ah, no longer active. I don't think she'd want to talk to you, Mr. Callahan."

Seamus sighed. "Fair enough, Mr. McDonough. I thank you for your time anyway. Good night." He put the small brown Morris in gear. "And I promise you, the secret of your whereabouts is safe with me. As is the fact that you drink in the back room at Durty Nelly's every second Thursday between ten-thirty and two and visit your mother in Killarney the first Sunday of every month." With that he popped the clutch and started down the road to Shannon, leaving a perplexed and troubled Michael McDonough standing in the swirling snow.

Three and a half hours later, Seamus sat in his car along the roadside on the outskirts of the tiny coastal village of Kilmurry, sipping at a leather-bound flask and rubbing his hands together to stave off the chill. He ran the engine intermittently for heat. Just over an inch of snow lay on the ground, giving the surroundings an unusually bright glow in the final moments before daybreak. He could just make out the chimney and rooftop of a farmhouse set back from the highway. To the west, under a heavy woolpack of dark clouds, lay the gray expanse of the Atlantic Ocean. A short swig from the flask took him to the bottom. He opened the door a crack and poured the grounds from his coffee into the snow.

He felt particularly efficient as the west coast of Ireland prepared for its dawn. It's usually that way when Emma's off visiting her sister in Cork, he thought. He was always somehow energized when left on his own to run both his job and the house. It was, in that sense, an ideal time to do a favor for his sister's middle son, even without Bill Quinn's generous offer of a fee for his time. The truth was that he barely remembered what young Bill looked like, except from the pictures. But he was family and that was all that really mattered. Better still, he was family in law enforcement, even if it was in Hollywood, where the crimes those people came up with were unthinkable. Besides, this sort of thing was fun. The fact of the matter was that his duties at the constabulary made little or no demand on the famous Callahan detective skills of which he was so rightly proud. He liked the idea that his work might affect the outcome of an important court case, just like the ones in those American television shows.

Finally, a thin wisp of smoke curled up from the chimney. At this, Seamus started the engine and drove up the road to the narrow lane that served as a driveway, and down to the house. Snow crunched under his feet, his breath billowing in great clouds of steam, as he made his way to the wood steps that led to the front porch of the well-maintained white house trimmed in green. He knocked sharply at the door. After a pause, he knocked again. Off in the distance he heard a voice call out but he could not make out what was said. A full minute went by. At last, the bright, crisp curtain over the window in the front door parted a fraction of an inch, not enough for him to see inside.

From the other side of the door he heard a woman's voice. "Who is it?"

"My name is Seamus Callahan, Mrs. O'Keefe. I just have a couple of things to ask you then I'm on my way. I mean you no harm."

"What are you doin' comin' to call at such an hour as this, Seamus Callahan?"

"If you'll let me in, Mrs. O'Keefe, I'll answer that. It's a wee bit chilly out here."

"You ought to freeze your heart out, knockin' on my door at sunup," came the response.

"I'm sorry. I waited till you lit your fire, after all."

Silence. Then the bolt was undone and the door opened. The woman was shielded behind it as she allowed Seamus to enter. The room was warm and inviting, even at that hour, and the fire on the far wall was already blazing. If he was to be the object of an IRA ambush here, for the moment at least Seamus didn't care. Each succeeding winter he felt older and being up all night on one of the season's coldest nights had numbed him to the dangers he might encounter. Anyway, if they meant him harm, they would have taken action by now. Uninvited, he moved instinctively toward the fire, looking over his shoulder to pick up the woman. The first thing he noticed about her, the first thing anyone had ever noticed about her, was a head of the thickest, shiniest, most luxuriant red hair he had ever seen. She stood with her hands on her hips, a lithe and athletic-looking figure, assessing her visitor.

"I thank you for allowing me inside, Mrs. O'Keefe. I wouldn't have blamed you if you'd have let me stand on your porch all morning."

"It'd do me no good. I've better things to do than keep a vigil on a frozen policeman on the front stoop. What is it you want, Mr. Callahan?"

Seamus was genuinely surprised. "Don't you want to know how I found you?"

She remained behind the door, even after it was closed. She wore a quilted robe over a heavy flannel nightgown. Seamus noticed that, despite the cold, both garments were scooped low in the front, exposing a large, ornate gold crucifix around her neck, framed by her ample cleavage. The belt of her robe accentuated her narrow waist. Huge green eyes beneath high, arching eyebrows dominated the upper half of her broad, unlined face. She had a straight, graceful nose and a wide, expressive mouth. Her pale skin was smooth in the soft firelight.

"Not really," she said in answer to his question. "I'm going to assume that you eavesdropped on the telephone call Michael made to me from Durty Nelly's and probably traced it. And, on the basis of that assumption, I'm going to wonder for the first time since yesterday how in God's name the Underground is still in business with geniuses like McDonough runnin' the show."

Seamus smiled. "Not even close," he lied. "And don't worry about the Underground. There's just too much local law enforcin' to be done to run about doing the work that can best be done by the real professionals in Belfast and London."

This time she smiled. "Can I offer you a cup of coffee or tea, Constable?"

"Pipin' hot tea would be a godsend, ma'am."

Molly walked into the kitchen, which was opened to the front room where he stood. "You might as well take off your coat, Constable, and have a seat. I figure you've done a wee bit of drivin' since midnight."

"Thank you, Mrs. O'Keefe. You're right about that." He removed his coat and sat in the large chair facing the fire, his back toward the kitchen. "Do you mind if I ask, Mrs. O'Keefe, are you here alone?"

"Plannin' to rape me, Constable?" she shot back.

Seamus blushed bright crimson. "Good lord, woman. What would make you say such a thing?"

From the kitchen, she laughed. A bright, sparkling laugh. "Can never be too sure, Mr. Callahan. If you've got such plans, I'd like you to know that I've got several guns about and have no qualms about usin' them."

"Well, madame, rest assured that such a thought would never occur to me. Your safety is guaranteed while in my company."

"We'll see about that," she replied, bringing him a steaming cup of tea. He inhaled its vapor deeply, then drank. She sat down on the couch opposite him. As she did so, her robe parted and her gown rode up, revealing a good section of her long, shapely legs. Seamus, thinking in terms of where she might keep her guns, pointedly looked away from her and into the fire.

"Ah, that's good, Mrs. O'Keefe." He sipped again at the tea. "Thank you very much."

"You're welcome, sir," she said, laughing again, no doubt at his obvious discomfort this time. "Now get on with your business, if you don't mind."

"Certainly. I've had an inquiry from certain parties in America, in Los Angeles, to be precise, about a court case involving a certain airplane. It seems that there is a dispute between the designer and the customer about what the airplane was supposed to do and what it actually did."

"And I'm sure it's all very interesting, Constable, but just how does this involve me?"

"The airplane was designed by a company called Arrow Dynamics."

Her face remained blank. "So?"

"And it was designed for a Mr. Nigel Daultry."

For the briefest instant, more than enough time for a keen observer like Seamus, Molly's face betrayed recognition. Catching herself, she said, "And?"

"My people there think you may have been a witness to some important meetings between Nigel Daultry and the other parties to the contract. They'd like to talk to you about it. Simple as that."

"Well, Constable, I'm sorry you've wasted a lot of petrol and time comin' out to the cliffs. I wasn't there and I witnessed nothing. I don't know a Mr. Daultry or anything about an airplane."

"Come, Mrs. O'Keefe. You may or may not choose to answer questions but you insult me to deny you knew Mr. Daultry. It is a matter of record that you and your late husband, Declan O'Keefe, traveled at least on one occasion to New Zealand to meet with Mr. Daultry. And we have reason to believe that you saw Mr. Daultry after your husband's death, here in Ireland and down there."

For a moment, Seamus thought she would lose her temper. And he suspected that she had quite a temper to lose. Her face flushed, her coral cheeks flaming to scarlet.

After a long moment, she spoke. "I'm not going to deny that I knew Nigel. And I'm not going to throw you out of my house. But, Constable, there are some things that we simply choose not to talk about. Some chapters of our lives are best left closed when they end. So, you see, you have wasted your time and effort, after all." She rose, the anger in her face receding. "You're free to enjoy your tea and have another cup, if you like. But I don't want to talk to you about Nigel and I won't."

"It may mean that Russell Lindstrom will get away with cheating Mr. Daultry out of a great deal of money."

She laughed ironically. "Where Nigel is, I doubt either the money or the principle will matter much to him in the end."

"A man has been killed in that airplane."

"In my world, Constable, death is a tireless worker and a constant companion." Before he could say anything more, she turned and left the room.

Seamus put down the teacup and walked into the kitchen. Molly was busying herself preparing breakfast. "Mrs. O'Keefe," Seamus began, softly. "I realize there's a lot you don't want to talk about. I know what your Declan was doin' when he was killed and I know Nigel Daultry was a good friend to you, before and afterwards. But you don't have to talk about any of that. It's not what they need from you. These people think that Russell Lindstrom designed and built an airplane for Mr. Daultry, an airplane that was either designed or tested improperly. And that he cheated Mr. Daultry or his company by lying about the results of the tests."

"So?"

"There's more at stake here than money. Or principle. Lindstrom claims that he had nothing to do with the whole thing. He says the contract was with a company of his that he had no involvement with at the time, that he had only a brief preliminary meeting with Nigel before the whole project began."

"Then he's a goddamned liar. But what does it matter to me?"

"It matters because it's not right, for one thing." She began to speak, but he waved her off and went on. "I know, principle doesn't matter. But Russell Lindstrom could be the next president of the United States, a lying and cheating fraud."

"Wouldn't be the first time."

"Now, Mrs. O'Keefe. Think about it. You met Russell Lindstrom. You worked with him, or at least Nigel Daultry did."

"So?" she said, again.

"Do you think you could stand by in good conscience, knowing what you know about him and what he did, with all the things you've endured yourself because of the sense of right and wrong you believe in, and allow this crime to go unchallenged, allow this man to profit from his lies?"

This time, she laughed. Not a mocking or derisive laugh, but laughter in which Seamus heard pity and rebuke. "You think I really care about that sort of '*crime*,' Mr. Callahan? And '*lies*'? Where have you been while Ireland's been burnin'?"

He felt his face redden. He reached for one last arrow to shoot. "Don't treat this matter lightly, Mrs. O'Keefe. Your great friend Mr. Daultry obviously considered these matters important and devoted time and energy to the project. Seems that Mr. Lindstrom is fixin' to make him look the fool for his efforts, that's all."

She smiled a kindly smile, having decided the rebuke was too harsh. "Now just how's the man goin' to do that, Constable?"

Seamus shrugged. He returned to the fireside and hefted his coat from the back of the chair. "Seems he's going to sit and tell a jury somethin' like, 'a fool and his money are soon parted' and 'the man couldn't build an airplane any better than he could drive a race car.'"

He immediately sensed that he had overplayed his hand. The woman's cheeks fired and her back arched. "Really now?" was all she managed to say. Seamus nodded, pulling on his coat and watching her very closely. She bit her lip, replaying his words in her mind as she did. Then, she added quietly, "Nigel Daultry was no fool. He was a good and sensible man. But he trusted Lindstrom. Thought he was cut from the same bolt as himself. The kind of man who would make the world a better place." She looked away, out past the curtains hanging over the window on the far wall. "I didn't trust him, though. And I told Nigel so. He just laughed it off. Told me that it was my republican politics that made me so skeptical and cynical. But I knew the son of a bitch couldn't be trusted. I knew."

"Then tell me about it."

CHAPTER 12

MOLLY HESITATED A LONG TIME, STARING INTO THE
bottom of her cup. Seamus wasn't sure what she would do now, but
decided he had said enough. Either she would tell him or she
wouldn't; he sensed that the issue was now completely out of his
hands. He watched quietly while she fixed her eyes on the window,
her focus well beyond the gray morning visible there through the
lace curtain. It was obvious that she was debating the question on
her own terms. He waited, his coat on but unbuttoned.

"It was nearly five years ago," she began at last. "After Londonderry."

"Molly?" Declan called softly. "Molly? It's just another dream, lass.
Another bad dream and another fever got its grip on you."

She looked up dumbly at him. His words were distorted and
distant. She was burning up. Her body ached. The pounding of
train wheels thundered in her head. Londonderry was thousands,
maybe millions, of miles from here. Slowly, it began to come back.

"Molly, dear," he said, still speaking softly lest she sense the
fear he truly felt for her worsening condition. "Just a few miles more

on this godforsaken train and we'll be at Brisbane. Remember? Brian Herlihy will be there. We can rest and get some medicine for your fever." He stroked her hair, matted against her temples in great red ringlets, already growing out from both the black dye and the shearing it had taken at the hand of Mairead Boyne as security for their hasty flight from home.

"Declan? Declan?" she said feebly, her voice cracked and strained from the powerful forces assaulting her body. "Declan, they're here, aren't they? The royals have got us, then, haven't they?"

"No, Molly. No royals. No British at all. They don't even know enough to look for us, sweet Molly. They're back in Derry cleanin' up a mess and straightenin' out the tracks. And maybe thinkin' again a time or two about givin' Ireland back to the Irish."

Even in the haze of her fever, she knew only part of this was true. Australia. Yes, that was right. They were in Australia. Or New Zealand. On the lam. And raising funds among the local Irish. That was right, it seemed to her, and it made sense in a way now. But the British. No. Their resolve to suppress would only be that much stronger. One more freight train was hardly going to end the tyranny.

"What's happenin' to me, Declan?" she asked, shelving larger and less relevant issues for another day, if there was to be one.

"You've asked me this before, Molly. Don't you remember, lass?" he said, smiling at her.

She shook her head faintly.

"All right, then, it's like this. The *Iron Hammer of Ulster* took a death blow from two hundred pounds of explosives planted by an unobtrusive couple ridin' into Derry from down in Omagh—"

She stopped him with a shake of her head. "I remember that part, Declan. Where we blew up the train—"

"Shhh! Quiet, Molly!" he whispered loudly to her, stealing a look around the aging Pullman. Four other passengers, widely scattered through the large car, two reading and two sleeping, took no notice.

"I mean, what's wrong with me?"

"The flu, I believe. Nothin' more, though it's a miserable affliction for sure." His tone betrayed his lack of confidence in the diagnosis, but the nuance was lost on Molly.

As they rode on in what passed for silence on the rickety, rattling train, she considered again the republican protestations of Declan O'Keefe and the many Declan O'Keefes she had known in her thirty-five years. His steady stream of patriotic rhetoric had lost its ring of authenticity. She realized that, though the process had been gradual, her conviction on that point was now absolute. Sadly, she saw it, with blinding clarity, for what it truly was: the futile ranting of a noble race doomed to subjugation and lacking the moral courage or the intellectual honesty to acknowledge the fact. And with that single, massive revelation, she was spent and once more drifted off into oblivion.

The local Irish underground had arranged passage for them from the station out to a small airstrip on the coast for the flight to New Zealand. Brian Herlihy, an old friend who had emigrated from Ballyshannon a few years earlier, drove them on the final leg. He was concerned about an obviously ailing Molly and arranged, despite what he felt was a security risk, to obtain some painkillers for the flight.

Once they were safely underway in Herlihy's dusty Land Cruiser, he turned his attention to his real interest, the blow Declan had dealt the Brits and its potential repercussions. "You know, lad, right after I got your cable yesterday, I got one from Brendan Boyne," said Herlihy. "Encrypted, mind you."

"What did Brendan have to say, then?"

"There's a lot of talk back in Omagh and Derry that the British have identified the perpetrators of the *Iron Hammer* bombing—it's got a media name, now, don't you know?—and they've a lead that the bombers've flown the country."

"Well, now. That doesn't mean much, Brian. 'Flown the country,' indeed. Hardly sounds like they've pinned us down to southeastern Australia, now, does it?"

"Aye, but it'll pay to be careful. Not just here, but over the water, there, as well. They may know you're comin' to New Zealand, after all."

Declan sat up straight. "What makes you think so, Brian?" he asked, his brow deeply furrowed. The one thing he had felt he could count on, traveling halfway around the world, was a little sanctuary.

Herlihy smiled then, and gave Declan the news he knew he was desperate to hear. "Well, for one thing, we've been told that Nigel Daultry's agreed to see you."

Declan's countenance changed instantly. "Daultry's agreed? Are you serious?"

"Agreed only to meet you," Herlihy cautioned. "He knows about your interest in the communications-switching software—in the vaguest possible terms—but he's agreed to a meeting, nothing more than a meeting, mind you. But it's somethin', all right."

Declan was suddenly bursting with questions, his fatigue from the long day falling rapidly away. "What was said to him? Who spoke to him? What did he say?"

"Not so fast, Declan," replied Herlihy, laughing the famous, booming laugh Declan had heard in pubs all across Ireland in times gone by. "I don't know the answers to any of those questions. Paddy O'Hanlon is our contact in New Zealand and he handled the arrangements. Turns out he's an old friend of Daultry's family. All he said to me was that Daultry's intrigued by the audacity of your plan." He started the engine.

"Can O'Hanlon be trusted?"

"Absolutely beyond reproach. He came over in the fifties and still spits when he mentions the Brits."

The 1,200-mile flight from Tweed Heads to Auckland in the ancient DC-3 freighter on which Herlihy had managed to find them room took all night, entirely over water. The medication made the trip bearable for Molly. Declan himself veered back and forth between grave concern for his wife's health and excitement over the upcoming meeting with one of the few men in the world who could make his plan a reality. As day broke over the North Island of New Zealand, the plane bounced to a landing on the west runway at bustling Auckland International Airport.

At the terminal, they were met by a short, trim man in his late fifties, nattily dressed and wearing a snap-brim straw hat. "Paddy O'Hanlon at your service. Mr. Daultry's asked me to fetch you back to Leeward, his estate in Te Puke." Inside five minutes he had the two of them and their luggage loaded into his 1957 Chevrolet station wagon, a yellow one, which O'Hanlon proudly pointed out was in "near-perfect condition." Like most New Zealanders, he drove the narrow roads as if his tailpipe were on fire, hugging the left-hand side of the pavement against the high likelihood that an equally maniacal New Zealander would soon be coming around the next bend and bearing down on him. Fatigued to the point of utter exhaustion, Declan and Molly, her fever now controlled for the better part of twelve hours, sank deep into sleep, oblivious to the thrills of O'Hanlon's ride and a deaf audience for his running narrative of the sights along the way.

.   .   .

Molly O'Keefe stood resting her elbows against the white enameled railing of the great veranda, casually gazing out over the rich green fields to the west. She squinted against the late-afternoon sun, noting with interest that, as May drew to a close down here, the days were, indeed, growing shorter. Still, there was a welcome warmth on the faint breeze escaping through the great crosshatched tree stands planted as windbreaks. It brushed her cheek, carrying a curious but pleasant pungency that she could not quite place. A peculiar chatter from beyond the trees rose and fell with the wind, no doubt the Maori field workers harvesting the major crop of this vast farm in which her host took such obvious pride, kiwifruit.

She felt remarkably well, considering how miserable she had felt not four full days ago. The aches and fever were long since gone and the only vestiges of the virulent Asian flu were a lingering weakness and a general lack of energy. She was clearly on the mend and the grand house of Nigel Daultry with its many servants had proven to be the ideal place for her recuperation.

A young black woman, clad in a perfectly pressed blue-and-white uniform, appeared in the doorway of the house, carrying a tray covered with a lace doily and overflowing with a full-dress tea service. She smiled, a flash of white in her striking black face, and called softly to Molly, "Mr. Nigel wants to know if you would like to take your tea on the veranda today?" Her English was quite good, though she accented the second syllable of her employer's name.

Roused from her reverie, Molly turned to the young Maori housemaid. "Thank you, Rynkah," she replied. "I'd be very happy to take it here." Despite her lifelong republican way of life, and the personal sacrifice that it had always entailed, she found herself strangely adaptable to the opulence that ran easily through Nigel Daultry's home.

Rynkah half-bowed, half-curtseyed, her smile intact and the tray held absolutely still. She laid out the tray and the service with expert precision on a starched linen tablecloth she arranged on the generous white wicker coffee table. She worked quickly and, when finished, disappeared into the great house. Molly sat in one of the wide wicker wing chairs, the one with the view of the mountains to the southwest, and poured herself a steaming cup of tea. From the periphery of her vision she caught a figure clad in khaki striding in her direction. Though his hat was pulled down over the top half of his round, red face, she recognized Paddy.

"Good afternoon, Miss Molly," he called out. "Good to see

you out and about so soon. It would seem that the ministrations of the good Dr. Whitaker are agreein' with you." Despite his decades in New Zealand, his odd accent was still primarily Irish.

"Hello, Paddy," Molly answered agreeably. "I do feel better than I ever thought I would."

O'Hanlon had gained the veranda and bounded up the steps. "Well, don't underestimate the effect of rest on the ails of a body. Or of a safe harbor, eh?" He winked at her with this last statement, drawing a broad smile from her. Paddy had a charming quality that was part stage performer and part leprechaun. The former, at least, he had been. He reminded Molly of her uncle Liam and she had taken to him immediately. He had the same quiet sureness about him that had always been a comfort to her and her cousins growing up in an unpredictable Ballyshannon.

"Nigel in?" he asked.

She nodded. "In the study. With Declan. Join me for some tea?"

Before Paddy could answer, a voice spoke from the doorway. "Certainly he will. As will we, if invited." It was Daultry, followed closely by Molly's husband. Daultry held the door open for the younger man and followed him out onto the veranda.

"Hello, Molly," Daultry said, with the slightest bow. "How are you this afternoon?"

"Very well, Nigel," she replied, using the familiar form of address he had insisted on at their first meeting. At least the first for which she had been lucid. Declan reached her side and, sliding an arm around her waist, kissed her on the cheek. "Whatever it was that had me has been driven off by your Dr. Whitaker."

Daultry smiled and greeted O'Hanlon. In response to Molly, he waved his hand dismissively. "He's a witch doctor, barely the equal of the Maori medicine man, but I keep him around to humor him and because he still plays whist. I think your health is better because you willed yourself well."

Molly laughed. "I don't think so. I did a feeble job on my own till we got here."

"Well," said Daultry. "In any case, I'm glad you got here. Paddy's description of your exploits and your plans intrigued me enough to see you two in the flesh and I'm pleased that it did." He looked over at Declan, who was smiling broadly. Molly was struck by how young, how immature, Declan suddenly looked in the company of these older, worldly-wise men. Especially Daultry. "Your husband and I have been having the most remarkable conversation.

As improbable as the idea sounds, I think there is a way to do what you want to do. It'll take some sophisticated programming and critical timing, a little different from the *Iron Hammer* business, to be honest, but feasible. And we have the hardware and, more importantly, the software to do the job."

Molly listened as Daultry went on to describe his discussion with Declan—Declan's plans, Declan's creativity, and Declan's courage. The more he spoke of Declan, the more conscious she became that he was speaking to her, directly to her, increasingly as if they were the only ones there. At first it made her vaguely uncomfortable. She looked at Paddy and at Declan. If they noticed, they gave no indication. Her discomfort increased, to the point where she actually began to squirm in her seat. This, as well, apparently went unnoticed.

It seemed to her as if Daultry's sky-blue eyes would bore a hole right through her. She felt hot and thought her fever might return. He was articulate, precise, charming, and thoroughly engaging. Though he spoke largely about himself and his life, he made it all seem relevant to the purpose of their visit and he managed to do it in such a way that it was neither egotistical nor boorish. It was, in fact, fascinating. *He* was fascinating, hypnotic. After her initial discomfort over her sense that she and she alone was his intended audience, she found herself drawn to him. It was certainly physical, but it was more than that. Ironically, she realized that he exhibited many of the qualities that had first attracted her to Declan; Declan, the local hero, the brash young warrior, wise and dangerous, brilliant and fearless. Declan, who had somehow diminished over the years just as her own strength and experience had grown. Declan, whose qualities of single-mindedness of purpose and tenacity had come more to resemble narrow-mindedness and pettiness.

But Declan's qualities, Molly realized, even at their height, when seen through the eyes of a young girl who had never left Ballyshannon, who was steeped in the republican catechism, had never approached what she was now seeing in Daultry. Whatever he possessed, it was in no way subtle. And it was working on a level at which she had no prior experience. She was captivated, an unsettling experience.

Daultry was now talking about whether or not he would go any further with Declan's plan. Molly willed herself to stop marveling at the effect he was having on her and concentrate on what he was saying.

"As to my participation, of course, there are other consider-

ations. Though I'm no defender of the British actions in Ireland—
we here wouldn't tolerate that sort of foreign occupation for a
minute—we do enjoy highly satisfactory relations with England,
and my family in particular profits handsomely from our exports to
the U.K. But, since your plan involves only property damage and no
death or injury and because the very idea of throwing British communications and banking transactions into a chaotic babble for the
best part of a business week is irresistible—" The others laughed,
especially Paddy. "I'll do it," Daultry concluded.

Declan leaped to his feet, accidentally flipping his teacup as he
did. "Done!" he exclaimed, swinging madly in the air to catch the
cup before it could crash to the floor. Miraculously, he succeeded.
Molly felt herself physically released, as if from a spell, and stood
oddly outside of herself to observe the scene. The last few moments
had had an undeniably surreal quality to them.

"Easy now, Declan." Daultry laughed, his eyes on Molly. "Tomorrow, you and Paddy can work out the details with my people."
To Declan, he added, "They can also be trusted." To the group, he
said, "For tonight, we have a spectacular feast of prime New Zealand mutton and a half dozen bottles of my best Napa Valley
cabernet."

Saturday-evening dinner was usually a formal affair at Leeward. Although Daultry had offered to relax the custom out of deference to
his guests who, naturally enough, were traveling without evening
clothes, they declined, accepting instead his alternative offer to provide appropriate clothing for them. This was not particularly difficult, since Daultry had taken to keeping a surprisingly generous
selection of tuxedos in the huge armoire he kept in one of the guest
rooms for just such occasions. For Molly, he called in a favor due
him from a neighboring farmer whose wife owned the Rive Gauche
Formalwear Boutique in Te Puke and had a strapless green taffeta
evening gown, sized perfectly by Daultry himself, delivered to her
room at six.

The evening was not unlike the afternoon encounter on the
veranda. To Molly, feeling sleek and beautiful in the borrowed
gown, it seemed as if Daultry were speaking to her, and only her, all
night long. When he commented on the day's most provocative
news story, a German teenager landing a small airplane near the
Kremlin, he actually stopped in midsentence and locked eyes with
her. Once again, it was as if the whole moment were lost on the rest
of the guests. But for her, the moment, and the evening, were

electric. His eyes rarely left her and he was seldom more than an arm's length from her. If anyone thought that odd, there was no indication. Under the influence of the wine, Molly found the attention tolerable, though an undercurrent of anxiety ran steadily through the evening.

On the rare occasion when Daultry chanced to look elsewhere around the room, Molly had an opportunity to observe him. He was certainly handsome—at a shade over six feet tall, he made a dashing figure in his tuxedo. Molly observed that middle age had yet to leave its mark on his physique. He moved with the power and grace of an athlete. His hair, reddish-blond and graying gently at the temples, was thick and wavy. His blue eyes sparkled with wit and intelligence and his tanned face bore the lines of a man who spent time in the sun. A mole on his right cheek gave him a down-to-earth quality that fit his personality perfectly. There was no question that he was a very attractive man. But, she decided, his looks explained only a small part of the overwhelming attraction she felt for him.

Dinner was elegant and sumptuous, the mutton everything Daultry had promised and the cabernet extraordinary. Both the meal and the choice of wine, Daultry explained, were compliments of Gustav, his chef snatched from The Partridge restaurant in San Francisco on a visit three years ago. "A lively and exciting town," he said, looking directly at Molly. "Have you ever been there?"

"We've never been to the States," answered Declan. "And when we leave here it's straight on to New York, not San Francisco."

"Pity," said Daultry, still watching Molly. She sensed his comment had as much to do with Declan's answering the question he addressed to her as with the answer itself.

"But I'm still young," volunteered Molly, a faint smile playing at the corners of her mouth.

"That's the spirit," said Daultry, returning her smile so directly, so intimately, that, wine or no wine, she squirmed again as she had on the veranda. And, as on that earlier occasion, her discomfort was as much over what she was thinking and feeling as anything Daultry said or did. She looked over at Declan, deeply involved in a discussion of partisan politics, and felt more than a twinge of guilt and regret.

Molly stopped and eyed Seamus directly. "Eighteen months later, Declan was killed at Armagh." Absently she fingered the crucifix around her neck.

"I know about it," said Seamus, watching the firelight dance in the ornate surfaces of the icon. "A tragic day."

"Martyred, my Declan was. And set free. But I was neither. The republicans hounded me night and day. 'Your duty,' they said, 'to his memory and Ireland.' " She stopped and held the crucifix out for Seamus to see. "An O'Keefe family treasure," she explained. "From a family that claimed precious few treasures. A gift from my Declan on our wedding day." Again she paused.

Seamus was able to read its abrupt, defiant inscription: The Cause Is Just.

"Perhaps we needn't go into the republican business, Mrs. O'Keefe," Seamus cautioned. "It puts me in somethin' of a position, what with my official responsibilities."

She smiled and shook her head. "Fair enough, Constable. But let's put it this way: The only one who consoled me without marryin' it to a pitch for the Sinn Fein was Nigel."

"Daultry?" Seamus managed to suffuse the word with both surprise and hope.

"Aye. He came here six months later. And I don't mind tellin' you, in half a day's time I knew I would leave here with him."

Molly looked out through a rain-spattered window of a cab sitting in traffic on California Street in San Francisco. She had seen so much in these five weeks, at such a pace, and all from a perspective— affluence—that was foreign to her. Places and times ran together in a hopeless mishmash that defied clear remembering. Sidewalk cafes in Paris. The Grand Opera House in Florence. Or was that also in Paris? The one with the ceiling painted by Chagall? The Italian cliffs towering above the Mediterranean. Or was it the French Riviera? The magnificence of the chateau region in France. The teeming avenues and shops of Manhattan. Phoenix, like a city on another planet, arid, startlingly new and unused. And through it all, there was Nigel. Strong, sweet Nigel, who sat very contentedly next to her now. Nigel, the thoroughly knowledgeable, tirelessly curious tour guide on a journey meant to heal her spirit but which, instead, was inexorably capturing her heart.

She looked at him, the man who had clearly derived far more pleasure than she from whisking through the magnificent women's shops of Paris, Rome, and New York and discovering just the right clothing, jewelry, and accessories for each occasion. And always with a logic and reason to justify the purchase so that she would never feel the object of his largesse. She honestly could not remember knowing a man happier than Nigel was now, in the constant company of a woman with whom he was obviously and hopelessly smitten.

As for herself, she, too, was happy. The face she saw reflected in the taxi window was renewed, revitalized with a glow that spoke of good health in both body and mind. The fear and discomfort that their strong mutual attraction had caused in Te Puke was a dim memory. Where she had fought the feeling there, she was now comfortable allowing it to run its natural course. And its natural course could be called nothing but love, genuine and powerful. Whereas she had spent a great deal of her marriage to Declan searching for stolen moments of solitude and shreds of space for herself, she now found herself genuinely disappointed at each moment they were apart. She smiled now in the deepening twilight at the turn her life had taken.

The cab stopped on a grade in the midst of restaurants and apartment houses, freshly painted and meticulously maintained Victorian confections standing shoulder to shoulder on what they were told was Russian Hill. Nigel paid the fare and they walked through the heavy wood door of the lavender-and-burgundy building right in front of them, past a tiny blue-and-rose hand-lettered sign that read simply, The Partridge.

Inside, Nigel presented himself and they were escorted to a small table on the second-floor loft, in the front, where there was a view of the docks known as the Embarcadero. They could just make out Fisherman's Wharf. Between the restaurant and the wharf, the lights of the city winked through the gathering mist of early evening. Only one other table, the one in the bay window at the far end, was occupied. Although the large party there was obviously having a very festive time, Molly and Nigel had the rest of the place to themselves and, thus, a great deal of privacy. "Well," said Nigel, looking around the loft. "So this is The Partridge. Now we find out if we got their best when we stole Gustav." Molly laughed the gentle, warm laugh that had come to be her signature over the past four or five weeks.

"I love the way you laugh, Molly O'Keefe," he said. "And you can't know how glad I am to be with you to hear it."

"Aye," she responded agreeably. "You're the reason it's there, Nigel. You've brought me a new experience. Happiness. Sustained, sweet happiness. A million miles and more away from politics and bloodshed. I can't tell you how grateful I am."

"You needn't be grateful. You're the reason that I'm the way I am. You make me an entirely different person from the one I used to be. And I don't mind admitting that I like the change."

Just as the waiter came, a loud and somewhat off-key rendition of "Happy Birthday" erupted from the other table. As it finished, one of the men seated there, tall and athletic, rose and came over. In the candlelight, Molly could see that he was very handsome and expensively dressed. He bowed, both a gesture of respect and a matter of practical accommodation to his height under the uneven ceiling of the loft. "Please excuse us," he said in a powerful baritone voice that seemed to vibrate the heavy wood table. "Ma'am," he added, addressing Molly in a slight accent she placed in the American south. His eye lingered for perhaps an instant longer than propriety would have dictated, but Molly put that down to the fact that the man had been drinking. "Please forgive our rude behavior. We're celebrating a very special birthday this evening and we keep forgetting we don't have a private room. I hope we haven't been too much of an intrusion into your dinner."

"Not at all," replied Nigel, with a smile. "It's good to hear friends enjoying one another's company. Our congratulations to the birthday boy or girl." Molly, too, smiled, deciding that absolution from one of them was all that was required.

"Thank you. I'll pass it along. I see that you haven't eaten, yet. May I ask if you've ordered?"

"As a matter of fact we have not," replied Nigel. "Although the John Dory sounded good to me and I think my companion was leaning toward the swordfish."

Molly nodded. "The waiter made it sound wonderful."

"And it is," said the man. "But if I may, the Alaskan salmon is without question the finest dish you will ever eat, in any restaurant in any city in the world. It's not on the menu and they don't mention it as a special but, believe me, it is exquisite."

Nigel laughed. When the man looked inquiringly at him, he explained. "Excuse me. It's just that the man who cooks for me at home used to work here and he's told me about the Alaskan salmon he made here—"

"Gustav? Gustav works for you? You're the New Zealander who shanghaied our Gustav?" Before Nigel could respond, the man turned to the other table and called out, "Doug? Ray? This is the man who stole Gustav." The others made a commotion, two or three of them rising to come over. Nigel and Molly were perplexed, caught somewhere between annoyance, embarrassment, and genuine curiosity. As the others arrived at their small table, the tall man identified each of them, then added, "Meet Mr. Nigel Daultry."

Nigel and Molly were both stunned. Nigel searched his face for recognition, but failed. "Forgive me, sir, but you have the advantage."

"There's my rudeness, again." He thrust out a large, powerful hand. "I'm Russell Lindstrom, Mr. Daultry. And I'm honored to make your acquaintance." They shook, then he extended his hand to Molly. "Russell Lindstrom, ma'am."

"Molly O'Keefe, Mr. Lindstrom," she replied, taking his hand.

"I should have recognized you, Mr. Lindstrom," said Nigel. "I've certainly seen your photograph before. The honor is mine."

Lindstrom waved him away.

"If I may ask," said Nigel, "how is it that you know me?"

"Mr. Daultry, you do yourself a disservice. You are a very famous man. I've known and followed your companies with great interest over the years. Fact is, I was waiting for you to take one of them public so I could buy a piece. But tonight I must tell you that your fame pales in comparison to the infamy you have earned in this very place by pirating away our Gustav."

Everyone laughed at this, Nigel and Molly less vigorously than the others since they weren't entirely sure how serious Lindstrom was. The waiter returned. "Please," said Lindstrom. "We will leave you two in peace to order and enjoy the most magnificent dinner you have had since . . . since leaving home and Gustav." Everyone laughed again. "But I would be honored if you would join us at our table for dessert and a drink."

Molly and Nigel exchanged glances, silently concluding there was no way to decline the invitation gracefully. They ordered— Alaskan salmon—and the others returned to their alcove.

After they had finished, Nigel and Molly joined Lindstrom and the others. The group included two young couples, in addition to Lindstrom. The conversation, which by now was heavily lubricated with the best port and liqueur in the house, was of business and politics, race cars and airplanes, computers and ecology. Molly listened more than talked and found herself fascinated by the stimulating ideas tossed around the table.

Late in the evening, someone—she could not be sure who— began discussing the politics of Nicaragua, the pros and cons of the Sandinista government, and the Contra rebels waging a guerrilla campaign against it.

"Disgraceful." Lindstrom, like Nigel, commanded the full attention of the table each time he spoke. "We Americans like to think of ourselves, for better or worse, as the people who protect democracy everywhere in the world. And yet our own government passes laws that make it a crime to lend a hand to those miserable freedom fighters trying to reclaim their country from the repressive regime we propped up there in the first place."

"What could you do though, Russell, even if it were legal?" asked Nigel. "They're fighting a hit-and-run guerrilla action there against a standing army that gets considerable help from the Soviets and the Cubans."

"You do what you have to do. We could provide them planes, guns, supplies."

"Planes? In a guerrilla war?"

"If they were the right kind, they could do a world of good. Or damage, depending on your perspective."

"Such as?"

"Such as a low-level reconnaissance plane, invisible to radar, capable of delivering a payload of conventional or even tactical ordnance."

Molly noticed that Nigel's eyebrows went up at this remark. "There's such a plane?"

"Not yet. But there could be."

"I'd love to be the man who develops that aircraft."

"Could have done great things for either side in the Falklands, that's for sure," Lindstrom observed.

"I was thinking about the civilian uses. A plane like that would have to be incredibly lightweight, strong. Aerodynamics for low-level maneuverability would have to be extremely finely tuned."

Lindstrom was impressed. "I thought your area of engineering was the racetrack, Nigel."

"Mainly, it is. But, of course, we rely heavily on aerodynamics in racing. The whole advent of the airfoil is pure aerodynamics designed not to keep an object aloft but, to the contrary, to keep it in contact with the racing surface."

Lindstrom nodded. "The real trick isn't the aerodynamics. I've got those figured out. No, the real trick is in the power plant. Quiet enough to carry out close-order reconnaissance work, small enough to fit the configuration of a microlight, but powerful enough to load and deliver the ordnance, at altitude if necessary. Now, that's a tall order."

"I don't think so, Russell. The engine is just a different application of the same technologies I'm developing for the track. In fact, I have a prototype I call the WhisperIndy, a refinement of my racing Mini Indy, which I started using last year, that might work without major modifications."

Molly noticed Lindstrom and one of the men in his party exchanging the briefest of glances. Lindstrom spoke. "Forgive me if I'm dubious, Nigel, but we've run a number of scenarios on just such a theory at our shop down in San Sebastian and we don't think there's a future in that area."

"But you're wrong, Russell," replied Nigel with a smile. "And that's what makes for great teaming arrangements and perfect joint ventures. If you develop the airplane—safe enough for the wealthy playboys with more money than skill—I can deliver the engine."

Their discussion continued, deep into the night, well past the restaurant's normal closing hour. More and more the conversation centered on the feasibility of the aircraft Lindstrom and Nigel were debating. The content grew increasingly technical and, for Molly, less interesting. Still, Nigel was thoroughly engrossed, obviously delighting in the opportunity to compare and assess ideas and information with bright and articulate men like these.

By evening's end, Lindstrom had talked Nigel into a detour on their way to San Diego, a side trip to his ranch in San Sebastian to see if, in Lindstrom's words, "we can't make some business happen out of this promising mess."

The following afternoon, Molly and Nigel landed the orange-and-white Piper Archer they had requisitioned for the trip on the airstrip along the northern edge of Lindstrom's ranch. A new four-wheel-drive vehicle whisked them off to a rambling hacienda on a hilltop at the center of the sprawling ranch. A delicious late lunch had been set up for them by the side of the large Mediterranean-style pool when Lindstrom came out to greet them.

After exchanging a warm greeting, Lindstrom moved straight to business. "So you think you can deliver the engine?"

"I have no doubt about it," Nigel responded. "In fact, I took the liberty of placing some calls before I left San Francisco this morning and I've had some weight calculations performed, as well as some decibel projections. Very feasible with the WhisperIndy."

"Let's take a hypothetical. I design the plane, cutting-edge composite graphite or epoxy, proven aerodynamics for both recon and payload, as well as"—he gestured to Nigel—"your recreational market purposes. You supply the prototype engine as well as the production engines. We share evenly in the development costs and split the revenue upon going to market."

"Well," replied Nigel, smiling. "That's a quick trip to the bottom line. What are we talking about in terms of development costs, net of the engine expense?"

"Hmmm, let's see." Lindstrom pulled a small calculator from his breast pocket, speaking as his fingers flew over the keypad. "Okay. Staff and computer time. Facility overhead. Materials. Engineering. Test-plan design. Licensing. Testing: pilot and ground support, chase and video support. Documentation. Log maintenance. Collateral documentation." He looked up. "That would be critical data for the owner's manual and basic certification program." He turned back to the calculator. "Flight time. Fuel. Insurance. And throw in this for miscellany. I'm sure to have missed something. Let's see. Ballpark of eight and a quarter million dollars, American, give or take."

Nigel was not fazed. "All right. Let's say, then, for the sake of discussion, an even nine million dollars, U.S. The prototype engine, including the two or three modification engines in the evolution of the prototype, all told, and, say, three production engines, with shipping and support, would run about a million and a half, U.S. Call it two million, to be safe."

Lindstrom regarded him carefully, but said nothing.

"So, you will want two and a half million in funding along with my engines for my one-half interest," concluded Nigel.

"That looks about right. What do you think?"

"I think this is pretty damned exciting, Russell." He turned to Molly, whose bemused smile spoke more of the memory of her torrid interlude with Nigel earlier that morning than of this technical coupling of two giant entrepreneurs.

"It's thrilling, Nigel," she managed to say, accurately describing what was really on her mind without dampening Nigel's enthusiasm for the venture. Something in her tone, however, drew a dubious, almost reproachful glance from Lindstrom, but Nigel didn't notice. He was thinking along other lines.

"Russell," he said, "my feeling is that the future for this product is the recreational market. I know you have, ah, shall we say, other applications in mind. That's well and good. But the pilots you expect to fly this aircraft are not the ones I'm after."

"And?" asked Lindstrom, agreeably.

"And I'm concerned that what we may end up with is an airplane perfectly well-suited to the ace pilots who might fly a mis-

sion of the sort you're anticipating but dangerous for the rank amateur whose qualifications in the cockpit will go no further than
having the cash to plunk down for the best toy in the neighborhood."

"And you raise a good point, too, Nigel," replied Lindstrom.
"But there's nothing to worry about. I have designed and tested all
my aircraft over the years to the most exacting military standards—
some drafted by my own people—and the result is always a safe
airplane, even for the low-time pilots you're talking about. You see,
the military have sophisticated missions and the best pilots, but their
vested interest in redundant safety systems is greater than anyone
else's in the world. And the reason for that is obvious: No one has a
greater investment, dollar-wise, in the aircraft, or personnel-wise in
the training of the pilots. Put in its bluntest terms, military airplanes
and pilots just cost too damned much to risk losing them to acci-
dents that can be avoided by safety-conscious design. Trust me, it's
not because they care so much about the planes or the men themselves; it's the money and the heat from the goddamned appropria-
tions committee."

"But what does that translate into for our purposes?"

"I'll give you an example. Most dangerous situation for a pilot?
Loss of control, right?" Nigel nodded in agreement. Lindstrom
continued. "Usually in the approach. Too much altitude, too much
speed. He bleeds a little speed off, maybe with a side-slip if he knows
what he's doing. Drops a little altitude. But this maneuver can be
botched easily, am I right?"

"I've done it myself. And, by the way, you're talking about
exactly what I had in mind."

"Good. Okay, then. What happens? He panics. To dump
speed, he pulls back on the stick, gets the nose up high, cuts his
airspeed to zilch." He demonstrated this nose-high attitude with a
flat and rigid hand. "But he's banking in an approach." He tilted his
hand to demonstrate. "Zap! He's flipped it and got into a spin. At
that altitude, he doesn't even need a flat spin to auger in. He's a
statistic."

"And how do you avoid the very nightmare you've just described?"

"MS 92121."

"Pardon?" asked Nigel, not comprehending.

"Military Specification Number 92121, the universal military
regimen for the testing and validation of all aircraft, from jumbo jets
to fighter planes to recreational lightweights. We build it into every

contract, every design program we do. We require it. That way no design that hasn't been rated and validated leaves our shop. If we stipulate in the contract that it must test out to be departure and spin resistant, that's what we'll have or we won't have performed the contract. Same for ease of recovery from both departure and spin. If we put it in the contract, you get it. Ironclad."

"Then let's put it in the contract," said Nigel, both relieved and enthused over this point.

"Consider it done, my friend," said Lindstrom with a huge smile. "I'll get my people to work on the contract in the morning. In the meantime, let's get inside out of the heat for some dessert."

CHAPTER 13

LANG'S PORSCHE HUMMED ALONG THE NEARLY DE-
serted stretch of U.S. Route 101 north of Santa Barbara on the way
to San Sebastian. A soft blanket of mist hung over the countryside, a
reminder of the ocean, which was now several miles to the west.
Lang liked this kind of weather, the kind that passed for winter
along the central California coast. There had been an unusual
amount of rain already this December and the hills that rolled up
from either side of the road were uncharacteristically green. In the
seat next to him, Amy was also taking in the countryside.

Lang had carefully read the packet that Rachel Cruz had prepared on the trial judge, the Honorable Schuyler Campbell from
Boise, Idaho, including the dry, noncontroversial judicial profile
provided by the ninth circuit on all the judges in the circuit, the four
decisions written by him on discovery matters, the *Boise Citizen
American* article on the "Fisherman Judge," and the excerpts from
the Senate Judiciary Committee's confirmation hearing on his appointment to the federal bench. The packet was a little sterile, so
Lang had called a fellow UVA alumnus practicing in Boise. "Judge
Campbell is a vicious bastard," said the man, a graduate three classes

ahead of Lang. "But, oddly enough, considered to be fair." Apparently, like many judges, Campbell was insecure about commanding his courtroom on the basis of his competency and intellect and compensated for it by bullying those who dared to use his court. For Lang, it meant that a hard case to try would be that much more stressful and unpleasant. The fairness reputation, on the other hand, was a welcome element in a case where the visibility and clout of his adversary were potentially huge factors against the plaintiff.

"So, what do you make of Judge Campbell's order?" Lang asked, breaking the prolonged silence.

"Asking for oral argument on the discovery motions is hardly earthshaking news, even for this guy, I gather. I figure either he's bought Hickman's pitch about how 'Citizen Lindstrom' had nothing to do with the project and he's going to tell you how to conduct yourself from here on in, or he's going to give Hickman the lecture about how no one is above the law and Lindstrom's just going to have to play by the same rules as everyone else."

"No. Mr. Republican Party of Idaho is not about to slap Hickman or Lindstrom around. At best, I read this as initial status conference, a time to lay down the judge's ground rules. At least it gives us a chance to get a line on the judge."

Amy responded, "Maybe we'll get some idea how he'll react to Molly O'Keefe's amazing story." She looked at him sheepishly. "*If* it gets into evidence."

"I didn't say anything," protested Lang, smiling at the recollection of the marathon phone call from Seamus Callahan recounting in scrupulous detail the woman's remarkable saga, none of which would be admissible as evidence unless she was to testify herself.

"But you were thinking it. 'What do you mean, Seamus forgot to nail down her promise to testify?' " she said, mockingly. " 'I thought he was a cop.' "

"I'm not going to get into that again," he said. "What's done is done. Besides, Seamus could just go back and get her to agree to come over to testify, if it came to that. But you know as well as I that with a witness like her, one of us is going to have to go there to meet her in person, get a feel for her jury appeal, credibility. Do a very thorough prep."

Amy laughed. "Why do I have the feeling that you're going to draw that assignment?"

Lang smiled. "Age and seniority, for starters."

"Right. Anyway, Seamus seems pretty sure she's the link that puts Lindstrom and Daultry in the same room, at the same time."

"Negotiating the contract, no less," Lang added. "I would like to know a few more details about the negotiations at Lindstrom's ranch, though. Anyway, I just hope this IRA angle doesn't damage her too much as a witness."

"I don't know. IRA or no IRA, from the way Seamus described her, she sounds like somebody we would want the jury to see."

"Or at least look at," agreed Lang.

"Lecher," she said, shaking her head in mock disgust.

" 'A good trial is pleasing to the eye.' Carlton Overbrook," Lang said, quoting the famous Texas trial lawyer turned author.

The United States Courthouse in San Sebastian, California, was a renovated hotel in the Spanish style that still dominates the California coast. In its earlier incarnation as the Hotel Sierra Madre, it had been a favorite stopover for the Hollywood crowd of the twenties and thirties, more than once serving as a sort of "San Simeon South" for the booze-and-sex orgies made infamous by those legions of contract actors and actresses who had too much time on their hands between making bad pictures. Purchased by the federal government out of bankruptcy in the mid-1970s, it had been renovated in a tasteful, elegant style that made it a favorite venue of lawyers throughout central California.

Judge Campbell's courtroom had once been the Pacific Ballroom and featured a vaulted, oak-coffered ceiling. The wall that separated it from the corridor was lined with French doors covered by plush red drapes. The judge's bench and the church pews that made up the gallery were splendidly detailed in rich honey oak. A stately gray carpet with a fine filigree pattern of red and blue muted all sounds, even the ticking of the massive mahogany grandfather's clock behind the clerk's table. Windows high up on the wall opposite the French doors were also hung with red drapes, but they were generally open to the ocean breeze and the distant sounds of surf, traffic, and the birds that nested in the huge sequoias planted on the west grounds of the courthouse. The bench itself was elevated, and behind the oversized red leather chair occupied by the judge were the American flag and the seal of the United States District Court.

Although it was Judge Campbell's practice to rule on written

motions "on the papers"—without the benefit of oral argument—
there were seven matters on the court's calendar this morning.
Theirs was last on the calendar, a mixed blessing. In exchange for a
long delay before being heard—maybe as long as an hour and a
half—they would get to see the judge in action on six matters ahead
of theirs.

At 9:40, a tall, angular man in a dark blue suit of a faintly
Western cut and black lizard-skin cowboy boots ambled up to the
clerk's desk to examine the court's published calendar and chat a
moment with the clerk. Lang nudged Amy's elbow. When she
looked, he said, "Gentry Hickman."

Amy eyed him for a moment. "Give me a break," she said
snidely. "*Cowboy* boots?"

Lang shrugged. "Don't underestimate him."

Amy scowled. "I won't. I just think we'd kick his ass in a
fashion contest."

Lang laughed. "But he'd kick our ass in an ass-kicking contest.
Are those silver tips?"

"How garish," replied Amy. "I'll bet he wears a fur coat in the
winter."

"He's a country lawyer, Amy, not a football player." This time,
she smiled. Hickman wrapped up his brief conversation with the
clerk and moved to a seat at the far end of the room. He caught
Lang's eye and smiled and bowed to his adversaries, neither of
whom he had ever seen before. To Amy, Lang whispered, "I told
you. He's a lot sharper than he looks."

"I sure as hell hope so."

At precisely 10:00 A.M., Judge Campbell emerged from the
heavy oak door behind the bench. His clerk snapped to his feet and
intoned, "All rise. The United States District Court for the Eastern
District of California, the Honorable Schuyler Campbell presiding,
is now in session." After the judge had climbed into the red chair,
the clerk concluded, "Be seated." The judge was a bear of a
man, well over six feet and two hundred pounds. He appeared to
have more than the beginnings of a paunch under his judicial robe
and his hair, gray and white, had an unruly quality to it, apparently
an unfortunate combination of a bad haircut and an unwieldy cow-
lick. His large, red face was a mass of wrinkles and jowls behind thick
wire-framed glasses.

The clerk called the first case. As the lawyers made their way to
the podium to announce their appearances, the judge teed off.
"Which one of you is Margolis?"

The lawyer on the left took a step forward. "I am, Your Honor."

Campbell peered over his glasses. "This is the United States District Court for the Eastern District of California," he boomed.

"I know, Your—"

The judge fairly leaped from the bench, rising straight up in his chair. "I didn't ask you a question, Counsel!" he bellowed. "You speak when I've asked you to. This is *my* courtroom!

"Now, Mr. Margolis," he continued to a stunned and silent courtroom. "In the Eastern District, we have local rules, a copy of which you may purchase from the clerk. In those rules, you will find a clear and concise statement of everything you need to know in order to practice before this court. Pay particular attention to Rule 3.4, pertaining to the form of papers we will accept in this court. When you do, you will learn that footnotes that are not double-spaced do not conform and will not be read. Then you will know why I have denied your motion without having to read it. Call the next case, Mr. Clerk."

Lang and Amy, along with the twenty or so others in the courtroom cringed in unison. Margolis was stunned. "But, Your Honor, this is a motion for summary judgment in a case for seven hundred thousand dollars in damages—"

The judge appeared to fight back instantaneous rage. "Mr. Margolis, you are not listening. Your motion is denied. With so much at stake, perhaps your client can afford to go out and hire a lawyer capable of reading and following the rules. Call the next case."

As the clerk did so, Lang and Amy exchanged subtle glances. "Jesus H. Christ," whispered Amy. Up in front, Margolis mustered enough presence of mind not to fight the inevitable.

The second case was also a summary judgment, a motion to have the case decided without a trial. After the moving party's lawyer made his appearance and spoke a half dozen words, Campbell interrupted.

"Counsel. Can you tell me where in the record you think it shows that a federal statute is involved in this case?"

"Excuse me, Your Honor?" asked the bewildered lawyer.

The judge was visibly disgusted. "Why are you here? What is the nature of federal jurisdiction?"

"First of all, Your Honor, the other side doesn't contest subject matter jurisdiction; it isn't an issue in the case, much less the motion—"

Campbell flushed a deep scarlet, his eyes widening ominously. "Counsel!" he shouted. "I don't care what you or the other lawyer think. *I* have a question about jurisdiction and *I* want an answer. If I had to depend on the lawyers in here to think of the issues, I'd never get anything right. Now, what's the federal question?"

The lawyer managed to retain his poise despite the question, an utterly irrational one in Lang's view. He patiently explained to Campbell that the controversy involved citizens of two states and an amount in excess of the jurisdictional limit of the federal court, thereby qualifying as a "diversity" jurisdiction case.

As the lawyer finished his explanation, the judge shot back, "I don't see citizens of two states. I see a California plaintiff and a California defendant. No diversity, Counsel. No jurisdiction."

"There must be a mistake, Your Honor. Rochester American is a Delaware corporation with its principal place of business in Minnesota—"

"It is an insurance company and it does business here?" demanded the judge.

"Yes, but for purposes of juris—"

"The case is dismissed for lack of federal jurisdiction. Take it to the state court. Call the next case."

And so it went throughout the morning. In each case, the judge found some reason to verbally abuse one or both lawyers and to act on the issue before him in a peremptory way. Seldom did he address the issues that the lawyers thought they were there to argue. But oddly, thought Lang, what he did was technically defensible, perversely correct. There was a depraved sort of logic to the havoc the judge wrought on the cases on his docket. It occurred to Lang that, apparently, Campbell permitted oral argument only when he himself had a particularly dramatic point to make. Lang wondered what point was to be made on the discovery motion he had come to argue.

At last, a few minutes before noon, the clerk called the *Pegasus Technologies* case. Amy took a seat at counsel table while Lang moved to the microphone on the podium. Gentry Hickman entered from the other side and stood deferentially while Lang announced his name and client for the record. Hickman then followed suit.

"This is a motion to quash a deposition subpoena," said the judge, in the calmest tone Lang had heard him use all morning. "Mr. Hickman, your client, Mr. Lindstrom, is a named defendant in this case. How can he be shielded from the obligation to give testimony at a deposition?"

"Your Honor," drawled Hickman, capturing the sides of the podium in either hand. Lang sat down at counsel table. "Normally, that is the way these things work, naturally. But, Your Honor, this is not a normal case. The claims made by Pegasus Technologies, claims that, I assure you, have no merit whatsoever, are claims against Arrow Dynamics, a company with which Mr. Lindstrom has had virtually no contact in years."

"But, Mr. Hickman, you realize that for purposes of a motion such as yours I must assume that the claims have merit."

Hickman smiled and raised a hand in agreement. "That's certainly true, Your Honor. We have no quarrel with that. At least not as to the company. But the issue on our motion is whether a party, for no more than the price of a filing fee in this court, can use the power of this sovereign court to reach out"—here he shot an arm out dramatically, paused, then clenched his fist—"and snatch a law-abiding, absolutely innocent citizen who's just mindin' his business and haul him into a deposition so's he can go fishin' around for something to make his case out of. I submit, Your Honor, that this deposition is about pressure and leverage since the man who's just mindin' his business also happens to be one of the best-known people in the country, a man who is runnin' for president of the United States." He turned suddenly and pointed accusingly at Lang. "This is about abusin' the discovery rules in order to harass and bother. Rule 26(c) contemplates precisely such a situation in empowering this court to enter a protective order. I submit that this rule has particular application here, where the target of the plaintiff's tactic is a man who, frankly, has more important things to do than sit as a foil to an ambitious lawyer tryin' to squeeze every drop of publicity value out of a threadbare case."

"Let's hear from the other side," said the judge, continuing to speak in a chillingly civil tone.

Lang took the podium. "This is a lawsuit in which we have stated a claim that has not been challenged. That's the threshold test, Your Honor, and we have met it. Mr. Lindstrom is named as a defendant because he negotiated the contract, designed the defective airplane, designed the flight-test program, and wrote some or all of the engineering report, which is alleged to be false and misleading. Whatever he may be running for, Your Honor, he is a defendant and a percipient witness in a lawsuit whose testimony is within my client's rights to obtain. And, to be blunt, it really doesn't matter whether Mr. Lindstrom has 'more important things to do' than testify."

Lang could tell that this last comment, tinged with a dash of sarcasm, had annoyed Campbell. A long pause enveloped the courtroom. At last, the judge spoke. "Well, Counsel, I think Mr. Hickman is right. I think this lawsuit is stitched together for the express purpose of exploiting its tenuous connection to Mr. Lindstrom, a man who very clearly has better things to do than to serve your client's whim."

"Your Honor—" began Lang.

"However," continued Campbell, glaring at Lang. "The complaint has not been challenged and sufficient grounds have not been stated to prevent a party's deposition. So, I rule as follows—"

"Your Honor," interrupted Hickman, obviously sensing that he was about to lose. "Excuse me for interrupting you, but if you are inclined to let the deposition go forward, I would urge you to take into consideration Mr. Lindstrom's terribly busy schedule. He has campaign appearances set for all over the country and can't run down to Hollywood—"

This time Lang, eager to press for the grudging victory he knew was coming, interrupted. "Excuse me, Your Honor, but we are prepared to take the deposition in San Sebastian, Mr. Lindstrom's hometown, in early January when we take the other Arrow Dynamics people's depositions."

"Hold on!" the judge barked at Lang. Then, turning to Hickman, he asked, his civility returning, "Where and when would be convenient to Mr. Lindstrom, Counsel, recognizing that nowhere and never are probably the best answers for a frivolous lawsuit?"

Lang fought back the urge to reply to this gratuitous insult. Hickman made a show of consulting his notes. "February second, Your Honor. Mr. Lindstrom will be in Freeport, Texas, for a campaign appearance. He can make time that day."

"Your Honor, I may need more than a single day," insisted Lang.

"You'll get one day and one day only, sir!" roared the judge. "And I'm instructing you that any attempt to harass Mr. Lindstrom will be dealt with harshly in this court." He turned back to Hickman. "In fact, Counsel, I will make myself available by telephone on that day and if you have any problem with the way Mr. Lang conducts your client's deposition, you may call and I will deal with him on the spot. Is that clear?" He turned his gaze pointedly toward Lang.

"Yes, Your Honor," replied Lang, wisely following the lead of the infamous Margolis from earlier in the day. And with that, the first hearing in the case was over.

Outside in the hallway, Hickman approached Lang and Amy and introduced himself. "Looks like we might be in for a prairie fire of a trial, Mr. Lang."

"Call me Chris, please," Lang replied.

"Sure. It's Gentry, then. You know, I'm tellin' you the truth when I say that Mr. Lindstrom's got nothin' to do with your claim. I sure wish you'd drop him from the suit and let us do battle on the real issues."

"Sorry, Gentry. My evidence says your guy's the one who did the deal. No way I can let him out."

Hickman shook his head and regarded Lang darkly. "You're makin' a big mistake, young fella. A big mistake. I sure hope you got the balls to deal with the consequences."

Amy did a double take. Lang felt his temper flare, but immediately suppressed it. "What's that supposed to mean?" he asked coolly.

"You figure it out, son. This ain't no fucking *L.A. Law* you got yourself into. Better watch your back. And your ass." He moved off down the hall.

"Fuck you, Mr. Hickman," Lang said to his back. Hickman kept moving, raising a hand with a small, dismissive wave over his shoulder. To Amy, Lang said, "Let's get out of here."

From her window on the other side of the country, Ro had a spectacular view of the vast white expanse of Central Park. She could just make out one of the park's several ponds or lakes, frozen over in the December chill, to the delight of dozens of late-afternoon skaters. All around were the lights and trimmings of Christmastime. The familiar music of the season drifted up above the sound of traffic to her tenth-story window.

The Provençal was an old building, but meticulously maintained and thoroughly charming. Ro's thickly carpeted and amply furnished room created a womblike retreat against the frigid outdoors. Nestled under a thick, heavy afghan in a comfortable easy chair in front of the window, she sipped from a steaming cup of tea and felt as good as a mother could three thousand miles from her children the week before Christmas. The antique-style ivory telephone rang.

"Hi," said Mark. "How's your room?"

"Terrific," she replied, still slightly dreamy from the combined effect of the warm afghan and the cheery view.

"Can I come over? We need to go over some scheduling details before the meeting."

"Sure," she answered. "I'll be here."

The trip to New York had come up quickly. Last Tuesday, David Stingley had announced that she had been selected to participate in a PBS program about women in photojournalism, and the taping was in New York in four days. She had to scramble to make it happen. Surprisingly, Chris had a rare soft spot in his schedule and he insisted on taking the kids for the five days of her trip back east. He declined the offer to take Alma along with them. "Of course I can handle them!" he had exclaimed. "Christmas with the kids? How many years has it been? We'll be fine. You go wow 'em on the TV circuit."

She smiled now at his unabashed enthusiasm. She had to concede that there was something undeniably appealing about the man's uncomplicated affection for his children. Her own disappointment over being far from her kids during the week before Christmas was somehow tempered by the thought that Chris was so delighted to have some bonus time with them.

The tea was finished and she was ready to go when Mark knocked at her door. He put his arms around her in what had become their customary greeting but, immediately sensing a stiffness in her, backed off without comment.

"Welcome to New York and the special world of public television," he said.

"I'm really nervous. I know I'm going to say something awfully stupid."

Mark smiled. "I know you're nervous. But you won't say anything stupid. Besides, you have to learn to look at these things the way David does. It's all marketing."

"I know," she replied with a smile of her own. " 'Hype is hype.' "

"They're all in the business of selling something, and right now the product is Ro Lang and *Beau Rivage*. Might as well enjoy the ride for as long as it runs."

"Who is it tonight?" she asked.

Mark consulted the black leather calendar he always carried around. As if he were reading from the Bible, he intoned with mock formality, "Tina Spauldren, senior research associate for WNET, is taking us to dinner at the Yangtze Grille in"—he checked his watch—"an hour and forty-five minutes." He closed the book and set it on the table.

"Yangtze Grille?" repeated Ro, with real enthusiasm. "That's pretty exciting. I've always wanted to go there."

"See and be seen. It's very L.A., for New York. One more piece of evidence that the drift of ideas comes from the left coast these days."

"Spoken like a true provincial, Mark."

"I'll take that as a compliment and be back to collect you in an hour and a half."

"Sounds good." He pulled her tightly to him and kissed her. "Mmmmm," she cooed involuntarily. "You'd better go."

"You seem to say that a lot," he said with a broad smile.

"Only because I mean it." She smiled back.

After her shower, she was once again drawn to the window, where the chill formed a frosty frame on the snowy Christmas scene below, an image almost too perfect to be real. As she toweled her hair, the phone rang again. It was Mark.

"Sorry to bother you, kiddo," he began. "But would you look around real quick and see if I left my appointment book down there?"

"I'm looking right at it, Mark. Right here on the coffee table."

"Thank God. I'd be lost without that thing. I sometimes think I have no existence outside of that book."

"How existential," she teased. "But you needn't worry. I have the book, therefore you am."

"I'll get it when I come by for you. That way, *I'll* know I am, too. See ya later."

She picked up the calendar to put it on the end table near the door so as not to forget it. But her hands were still wet and the book, surprisingly heavy, slipped out of her grip and onto the floor. It fell open to the week in August when they had first gone to Gettysburg. She could not resist the temptation to relive that fascinating time for a brief moment by looking over his entries. On the twentieth, he had recorded merely "Meet R.L. at Dulles. AppAir to Getty." On the twenty-first, his note read "Photos All Day Battlefd." She noted that he hadn't had time to record his trip to Philadelphia that day. Below that, he'd scribbled "Wilkinson." She smiled at their efforts, apparently successful, to recapture the heroic but tragic story of the young man from Massachusetts who had been killed by stray cannonfire from his very own unit. On the twenty-second, he'd written "Caldwell." And so on, for each day of that trip. Nothing particularly revealing, reflected Ro, suddenly realizing that she'd been looking for some secret insight into how he'd felt about her.

Before closing the book, she flipped back a page, to the week before the trip. Two notations caught her eye. The first, the only entry in bold red ink on the page, was a series of letters and numbers that didn't seem related to anything else around it: "USA 1167, USA 1187 STL." The second, written on the space reserved for Friday, August 18, was "A. G. in S. D.: 619-555-1784." There was something vaguely familiar about the number, but it didn't come to her right away. Suddenly, she realized she was violating her companion's privacy and, horrified, slammed the book shut and put it on the end table. Then she went about the business of dressing for her dinner-interview at the Yangtze Grille.

CHAPTER 14

LANG WASN'T SURE WHICH OF SEVERAL ROILING emotions had the strongest grip on him as he geared down and rocketed into the quiet cul-de-sac where he lived. The surprisingly acid encounter with Gentry Hickman, substantially diluted by a thorough strategic analysis of the whole case with Amy, had left Lang with an elevated level of a key ingredient to a successful lawsuit: genuine dislike for the opposition and its lawyer. After dropping Amy off, a general fatigue had rolled in and mingled with doubts over how he would summon the energy to put together a merry Christmas for the kids. Now, as he swung into his driveway, there they were in the gathering dusk: the three most precious people in his world, and a half dozen of their friends, crawling all over the front of his house, stringing lights and hanging wreaths, Christmas carols blaring from a massive boom box on the porch. Suddenly, the day's array of emotions were washed away by the realization that his home would be a *real* home for a few days. He felt a surge of new energy, forged from the afterglow of combat, tinged with the promise of more ferocious encounters to come, and fueled with the rosy prospect of the first happy Christmas since the divorce.

"Hey! Dad's home!" bellowed Jack. "What do ya think?" the boy asked, sweeping a hand toward the work in progress. "I mean, really?"

"It looks great!" Lang replied. "Just right. I'm in the mood for the best Christmas ever." He spotted Jennifer up on a ladder in front of the living-room window, hanging a wreath. "Jen!" he called. "Great job! Just be careful up there, all right?"

She smiled back. "I'm okay, Dad. Is this all okay with you?"

Lang found his kids' doubts about his Christmas spirit frustrating. "Of course it is, honey. I'm pumped for Christmas."

Andrea came barreling toward him through the twilight from somewhere near the garage. "Daddy! Daddy!" she called, then she hit him full force, in her customary way, leaping into his arms and nearly knocking the wind out of him. "Oooh," she said. "You need a shave."

"And hello to you, too, angel," Lang replied, laughing.

"It's the stuff we usually put up at our house. Did we surprise you?" As always, Andrea bubbled with unbridled enthusiasm.

You had to love her, thought Lang, and how he did! He loved them all, suddenly in a huge, boundless way. "You know it, Andy. It really did. And, now, we're going to have the best Christmas ever." He hugged her as hard as he could, then let her down before his back broke.

Lang ordered pizzas and soda for the group and settled back to savor the activity. Later he declined all offers of help and gladly undertook the modest cleanup. Loading the plates and tumblers into the dishwasher, he kept a careful eye on the tiny screen of the television set in the bookshelf above the microwave. Milo Rich had Lindstrom on again, this time outlining his strategy for wiping out a substantial deficit in the polls to the two front-runners. It boiled down to "anything can still happen" but seemed somehow more persuasive coming from Lindstrom.

"Well, now," replied Rich. "Speaking of things that can happen suddenly, there is a report out of San Sebastian, California, today, Mr. Lindstrom, that you and your Arrow Dynamics corporation have been accused of defrauding a customer in the design and testing of an experimental airplane a few years back. Isn't this the very kind of thing that can derail a candidacy? Any truth to these charges?"

Lang, drying his hands, leaned forward to study the tiny figure on the screen. Lindstrom smiled his most avuncular smile and then, calmly, with the slightest hint of condescension, answered. "First, Milo, let me say that there is absolutely nothing to the claim. I was gone years before any part of this project even got started. I played no part in designing this aircraft. In fact, I haven't designed any kind of aircraft for decades." He laughed easily. "And I certainly never tested it. This lawsuit is simply the handiwork of a lawyer with an overactive imagination and an unhappy company from a foreign country that couldn't cut it in the market without the benefit of protectionist laws. And, I might add, it's a darned good argument for the kind of reform of the litigation system I've been talking about. The fact of the matter is I wish I *had* designed this airplane. From what I've heard it sounds like a pretty terrific little airplane. Docile, a joy to fly." He smiled again. "As to the lawsuit itself, Milo, I'm sure that nothing will come of these baseless charges."

" 'Docile,' huh? A 'joy to fly'?" Lang repeated to himself as he muted the sound of the upcoming commercial and grabbed the kitchen phone. He ran a finger down the list of firm home numbers, found the one for his paralegal assistant, Rachel Cruz, and punched it in. "Hello," answered a sleepy, sultry voice.

"Rachel? Hi. Chris," he said. "Did I catch you at a bad time?"

Rachel's voice cleared up perceptibly. "Oh. Hi, Chris. No, not at all. What's up? How'd the hearing go?"

"Not bad," he replied. "We got the depo. We just have to go to Texas to get it. Judge is an asshole, and a mean one."

"Texas? What the heck for?"

"Long story. Look, the reason I called is that Lindstrom was on Milo Rich tonight and I didn't have a tape in. Can you call CableStar tomorrow—"

"I have it. Don't worry."

"What do you mean, you have it?"

"I taped it. I always check the program notes in the paper for the news shows every morning and I tape the ones he's going to be on. You asked me to do it for you in November that one time so I assumed you wanted to stay with it. Anyway, I got it. I'll bring it in tomorrow."

Lang smiled appreciatively and shook his head. "Wow," he said softly. "I'm impressed."

"Good," Rachel said with a warm laugh. "I'll look for a tangible token at my next salary review."

"You won't be disappointed. Thank you, Rachel."

.   .   .

Christmas with the kids had been great, a Christmas like none he could remember. All of them had been gracious and appreciative of their Christmas bounty, but more impressive to Lang was how they clearly derived far greater delight in the gifts they gave than in those they received. He was terribly proud of them, and supremely impressed with the job their mother was doing in raising them. If he had to feel like the outsider, at least there was solace in the way his children were turning out.

Christmas Day dawned cold and blustery. Soon after breakfast Ro arrived to take the kids away. Her trip to New York had been a great hit, as Lang and the kids were well aware, having watched every minute of her national-television debut, many times over. She had looked terrific on the tube, Lang had noted, but on this gray morning the pace of her schedule showed in her face. She looked pale and tired and her hastily applied makeup did a poor job of covering the deep circles that darkened her eyes. Still, her smile, something Lang had almost forgotten in the years since he had lost the capacity to command it from her, was warm and welcome. In the foyer of his home they hugged awkwardly, exchanging greetings as the children raced around, pulling things together for the ride over to Ro's.

"Television looks good on you," he said to her.

"Thanks. They made it pretty easy."

"Nevertheless, you were very impressive. Who would have thought you'd be on national TV?"

"Who'da thunk it?" she said. They stood uncomfortably opposite each other, the venerable old cherry-wood grandfather clock punctuating their silence.

"Want some coffee?" he asked, finally.

"No, thanks. Have to get going. Maybe you can get some rest on a rare off day."

"Not likely. Things are picking up. I've got a mountain to do."

She frowned. "You're not going to work on Christmas Day?"

He shrugged. "No rest for the weary," he lied. He would allow her to condemn him for working too hard but was damned if he would let her pity him his loneliness on this most festive of holidays.

In a matter of moments, the whirlwind that was his children had blown itself out and, in their wake, a heavy, miserable stillness consumed his house. The five-day siege of youth, exuberance, joy, and life at full tilt was abruptly over. He stood in the large, empty foyer and listened hard to the silence, as if hoping it all would return. After a long minute, he picked up the *Times* and a fresh cup of coffee and, still in robe and slippers, shuffled off to the inappropriately named family room to watch one hundred college kids whose names he did not know play a meaningless football game.

The doorbell rang shortly after eleven, while Lang was still working his way through the day's business section, having yet to watch a play of the game. Quickly deciding it was all right for a man to still be in his robe at 11:10 on Christmas morning, he answered the door to find Max and Clarice Devereaux, laden with brightly wrapped packages and dressed in their church clothes.

"We thought you could use the company," explained a smiling Clarice as she slipped past Lang into the house, craning her neck to look for something.

Max followed. "We knew you would need an excuse to get yourself dressed once your children left."

"Are they gone already?" demanded Clarice, huge disappointment on her face. Lang nodded. "That's too bad, Chris," she responded. "We brought their presents."

"I'm sorry you missed them, Clarice. They've gotten to the point where they move pretty much like a well-drilled army."

"We'll have to catch them over at Ro's," offered Clarice as she hung her coat in the hall closet. She took a grocery bag from Max. "I'll whip you boys up some lunch in the kitchen."

Max smiled after her. "Terrific gal, isn't she, Chris?"

"One of the best. Come on in. The Blue-Gray game is really heating up."

"Blue-Gray? Oh, yeah. But at one o'clock . . ."

"One o'clock?"

"The Bears in Houston, my friend. Have you forgotten? Are you working too hard again, my boy genius?"

"I'm no genius, Max, and I'm sure as hell no boy. But I have been hitting the ball pretty hard." He decided to spare both Max and himself any further shop talk and so passed Christmas Day delightfully engrossed in a terrific football game that the Bears needed to win to qualify for the playoffs, and did.

Lang finished off the day by taking his old friends to dinner at a quiet, cozy place nearby, where they sat by the roaring fire and toasted the restaurant's magnificent Christmas tree with a bottle of Bailey's.

"To the best friends a young lawyer ever had," intoned Lang with a raised glass.

Clarice, mixing a dash of Bailey's into her cup of decaf, met his smile with her own. Max said, "To the brilliant trial lawyer who could have been a great tax lawyer."

Lang laughed. "Nah," he said. "Never would have worked. You know how I always said that tax was too boring?" Max nodded. "Well, truth is it wasn't boring. Just too precise, no room for creative latitude."

Max laughed. "I know you know that's not true. The tax-court reports are overflowing with IRS cases caused by too much room for creativity." He shook his head. "I think you chose trial work because it's you. It's bare-knuckle, pure adversarial combat, where you have your enemy right in the room in front of you all the time. It's very difficult, challenging work. And you're the best I know at it."

A surge of powerful emotion overtook Lang. He had never heard Max acknowledge his chosen field before in such terms. "Thank you, Max. You don't know how much that means to me."

Max smiled at him through the soft light of the restaurant. "Yes, I do. I've always known, Chris. Just as I've always known that you are never fully sure of yourself on a tough call unless you run it by me."

"You mean like the first *Severstone* settlement?" Max nodded. "And the *Uzaco* appeal back in '87? I guess I've gone to the well a lot, huh?"

"It's very flattering when a lawyer of your caliber seeks the counsel of an old man like me. Especially when there is no need."

"It's true, Chris," Clarice interjected. "From the very beginning, Max said that your instincts and judgment were flawless."

Max nodded in agreement, drawing another swig from his drink. "You've never needed my counsel, Christopher. But if I had told you that, you might have stopped asking for it." He paused, emotion welling up in his tired, aging eyes. He swallowed hard at the sentimentality that had suddenly caught in his throat. "And then I'd have missed all those great litigation stories you tell." He laughed, only partially successful in his attempt to avert a maudlin conclusion to the evening. "Trial stories are much better than tax stories."

Now it was Lang's turn to try to check an emotional reaction. He could only manage to smile.

As if to change subjects before the season, the years, and the alcohol could reduce them all to tears, Max said, "Speaking of litigation, I've been meaning to talk to you about your Lindstrom case. I got the oddest call the other day from a reporter who wanted to interview *me* about the case."

Lang was suddenly back from the brink of sentimental release. He pulled himself upright in his chair. *"You?"* he asked. "Why?"

Max shrugged, pulling out his wallet to fish for a slip of paper. "Here," he said, handing Lang a phone message. "The name he left was Curt Wallen of the *Bee*. No number, though. Said he'd call again but he hasn't."

Lang looked at the message. "Maybe I should give him a call."

Max shook his head. "I had Louise try. The *Bee* says they have no reporter by that name. If he calls again, I'll have her direct him to you."

"Thanks," replied Lang.

As the Devereaux drove away late that night, the warmth that Lang felt at his good fortune to have found such true and solid friends was tainted by a strong and growing uneasiness. He had the distinct sense that there were forces at work that he could not see or hear, much less anticipate.

The week between Christmas and New Year's is traditionally one of leisure and relaxation, a down time in many businesses. This was often true for the attorneys of Devereaux and Brace, as it was this year for the majority of them. But not for Chris Lang and Amy Quinn. A critical phase of the lawsuit against Arrow Dynamics was about to begin—the depositions of the Arrow Dynamics employees involved in the StormTree project—and there was work to be done.

Rachel Cruz was invaluable in the preparation for depositions of the Arrow Dynamics employees. She had pulled all the pertinent information together and, by week's end, the process was complete, each deposition neatly prepared in its own three-ring binder. On Saturday, New Year's Eve, Lang, Amy, and Rachel met all day to go over the approach they would take to each deponent. Deliberate tactical decisions were made about which areas to go into, and not to go into, with each witness, especially early in the string of depositions, lest a later, more promising deponent be tipped off and therefore prepared with a more cautious answer. Finally, a great deal of time was spent discussing what areas or specific questions to hold for the deposition of Lindstrom himself. The process of "strategizing" a case is far more complex in this regard than is commonly under-stood, and Lang was a firm believer in the principle that proper management of the discovery process invariably yields significant dividends at trial. His track record amply justified his views.

The strategy session ended with an agreement as to who would conduct which depositions. There was a lot of work to be done in a short time.

"Sounds like you guys are going to be busy," noted Rachel.

"What else is new?" commented Lang. "I'm going to call out for some Chinese and dig in to the Chesney outline a little longer. Any takers?"

Amy sank back in her chair and exhaled loudly. "Count me out. Bill and I are going with the Callisons to L'Orange for the New Year's bash and I'd like a little time to get ready. Don't you have plans?"

"Ah, no," Lang replied, a little sheepishly. "I really need to get this stuff all down before my thoughts blow away. Too dangerous out on the freeways, anyway."

"I'm in the same boat, Chris," said Rachel. "I'll stay for a while to give you a hand with Chesney—*if* you order from the Ivory Panda."

"Deal," he answered.

"You guys are welcome to join us, you know," said Amy. "I'll bet we can talk the guard into allowing two more. Especially if you're wearing that red sequined thing you had on at TuJacques, Rachel."

Rachel blushed. Lang smiled and turned to Rachel, clad today in an oversized blue sweatshirt, off one shoulder, over tight black leggings. Her only concession to the office was her high black leather pumps. " 'Red sequined thing'?" Lang said. "What 'red sequined thing'?"

Rachel's rich olive skin darkened further. "Nothing," she said, with a shy smile. "Nothing. Just a dress."

"Right," said Amy, rising from her chair. "Well, it is just about nothing. I guess you could call a small piece of scarlet sequins stretched into a micro-mini tank dress on Rachel's frame nothing. Personally, I got pretty sick of all the guys in the restaurant tripping over their tongues on the way to the salad bar."

"Rachel?" said Lang, in mock surprise. "I had no idea."

"Stop it, you guys," Rachel said good-naturedly. "Are you going to order from the Ivory or aren't you?"

"For the Lady in Red, I guess so," answered Lang. Rachel smiled shyly.

"You guys are nuts," said Amy. "You're going to *work* on New Year's Eve? I'm getting out of here before the contagion spreads."

Later, Lang was back in his office, surrounded by notepads, documents, excerpts from interrogatories, and the Chesney and Wollersheim deposition books prepared by Rachel. The anniversary clock on his desk—a gift brought back by Max and Clarice from their fortieth-anniversary trip to Switzerland—ticked on toward nine o'clock, unnoticed by Lang. He was studying a memo from Max's secretary, Louise, that chronicled her efforts to locate a reporter named Curt Wallen, including calls to all local newspapers and news services. She had had no success. Weird, thought Lang. Why interview Max?

"You know, Chris, I think we blew it." Rachel's voice broke the silence from his doorway. Lang looked up to see her standing by the door, arms crossed in mild defiance, one leg extended in front of her.

"How's that?"

"Working on New Year's Eve when we had the chance to go to *the* nightclub for a big bash."

"I'm sorry. You could have gone."

"Alone? I don't think so. And besides, when you suggested working it really didn't seem like such a bad idea. But now—" she checked the time. "Now, it seems like a bad idea."

"Do you want to go there and try to get in? It's not quite nine yet. I guess we could change—"

"Just about New Year's on the East Coast," she said. "Hey! I have an idea. I'll be right back."

A minute later, she reappeared in his doorway. She held a bottle of pinot noir, a corkscrew, and two plastic stem glasses from the conference room. "Courtesy of the wine basket we got from Uzaco," she explained, holding up the bottle. "Want to toast the New Year in New York?"

Lang was tired of grinding away at the Chesney outline and jumped at the chance for a break. "Good idea, Rachel. No reason why we can't celebrate, just because we missed the party."

He uncorked the bottle and poured out two good-sized glasses. He handed one to her and held out his own. "To the New Year. May it be even better than the last."

"Indeed." They touched glasses and drank.

"Good wine," he said, drinking again.

"Uzaco," she replied, in full explanation of its quality. She, too, drank again from her glass. Looking around, she found a seat on the large plush couch against the far wall. Lang moved to the matching chair next to it.

"Why *are* you working on New Year's Eve instead of partying with your guy?" he asked.

"No guy. I broke up with Derek a couple months ago. What an asshole!" She rolled her eyes. "And I've dated a little since, but no one I could get excited about. No one special."

He regarded her closely as she spoke. Lang had spent enough time in an office to be alert to the dangers of involvement with a co-worker and so, out of nothing nobler than self-preservation, he had developed the habit of never allowing himself to so much as contemplate any of the women he worked with as potential romantic interests. At the moment, however, the combination of fatigue and the pulsing flush of the wine he was drinking with surprising enthusiasm was rapidly eroding his careful fortifications. He found himself not merely looking at, but really *assessing*, Rachel as she sat at the end of the couch, one leg curled underneath her: large black eyes; smooth, tight olive skin; thick midnight-black hair; athlete's, or, more accurately, dancer's body, long and sinewy. As she went on, now talking about the men at her health club whose clumsy come-on lines and dull-witted business chatter left her uninspired, Lang found himself unable to take his eyes off her strong, slender hands. In particular, he was mesmerized by the way she cradled the glass in her bronze left hand, and the way the light glinted off the crimson polish on her perfectly manicured nails each time she raised her glass to her lips. She noticed the look in his eyes and stopped in midsentence.

After a pause that got his eyes off her hands and directly into her own, she asked, "What are you looking at, Chris?" Her smile lit her broad, attractive face brilliantly.

He blushed profusely, shifting uncomfortably in his chair. "Nothing. Nothing. I'm sorry."

"No?" She laughed. "What is it?"

"I don't think I should—"

She leaned slightly toward him, deliberately planting her elbow on the arm of the couch and resting her chin on the heel of her hand. As she did so, the outsized neck of her sweatshirt gapped, affording him an irresistible view of her cleavage. The rapt look on his face told her much about what was happening in his head. She watched him studying her, absently running her thumb and forefinger along the hem that formed the neckline.

"Hmmm," she said, now making a show of examining the contents of her glass. Silence hung heavily in the room.

"You really want to know?" he asked at last.

Again, she flashed that dazzling smile, framed in the high-gloss red of her lips. She nodded brightly.

"It's your hands. I think they are, ah—how shall I put this? They are the sexiest hands I've ever seen. To be honest, I was just sitting here thinking how those hands have the capacity to define sexuality to me at this moment."

"At this moment? As the New Year hits the Eastern Seaboard?" She regarded him over the top of her glass, through slightly narrowed eyes. "Why, Christopher Lang," she said, her smile returning, to his great relief. "Who ever would have imagined that such dark, dangerous thoughts could be lurking in the midst of all those serious, important legal concepts?"

He blushed harder, not sure whether to try to extricate himself or press on to discover what limits he would meet here. An uncharacteristic caprice seized him for the moment and impelled him forward. "Well, after all, Rachel, contrary to popular belief, I *am* human. And I have my passions." He hesitated, wrestling with a rising tide of desire. Instinctively, he knew that there was danger ahead but the grip of the wine was already strong. He shrugged ambiguously.

"Mmmm," she purred, holding her empty glass out to him. Dutifully, he took the bottle from the table and filled it. "*Now* you've got my attention. What else is going on in your head, I wonder?"

"I don't think you really want to know. Let's just say that I'm not exactly the very proper partner that I'm thought to be."

"Oh, really?" she asked, arching an eyebrow. "This is threatening to become seriously intriguing."

He watched her face closely, suddenly swept up in its physical beauty, as well as the potent sexuality he read there. "Well, for starters, let me confess that I haven't been too efficient this evening."

"And why is that?" she asked, a playfulness in her voice belying the mock seriousness of her expression.

"Truth is, I've been distracted trying to imagine what that 'red sequined thing' might have looked like with you in it."

Now her smile was accompanied by an unmistakable mischievousness playing about the corners of her eyes and mouth. She ran her tongue purposefully along the edge of her teeth. A threshold of sorts had been passed and Lang had no idea where they would go from here. But he found her coquettishness intoxicating, thereby becoming doubly drunk. He was quickly becoming overwhelmed by a powerful, dangerous physical attraction to this lithe, exciting woman. And she showed no signs of reining it in.

"So you don't think I'm the type to wear an elegant evening gown?"

"No, that's not it at all. I just haven't had the pleasure of seeing such a thing and I'm intrigued."

"There's a saying about curiosity and cats, you know."

"Lucky thing I'm not a cat."

"Lucky thing," she repeated. "And lucky I'm not one, either, 'cause curiosity is a two-way street. Come here." She lifted a beckoning finger.

He moved from the chair to the spot beside her on the couch. As he sat down, she arched her back slightly and raised her face to his. Without apparent effort on either's part, their lips were suddenly in contact. Lang felt a jolt of electricity rip through him on circuits well primed by the pinot noir. Rachel's lips were soft and full, excitingly warm and delicious. He hungrily drank in her sensual aroma, a perfume he must have noticed before but of which he had never been so aware. As he bent down closer to her, he felt her breasts, full and round under the bulk of the sweatshirt, rising and falling heavily against his chest. Her arms closed around his waist. The strength of her embrace bore witness to endless hours spent in her health club. He felt her thick, silky hair against his cheek. Meanwhile, he pressed his lips harder to hers. She responded likewise and he felt the sharp edge of a tooth on his upper lip. She bit hard, drawing a warm, salty drop of blood. The sensation aroused him all the more, igniting a rush of passion that surprised him in its intensity.

He pulled her torso up against his, breaking off the savagery of the kiss and looking into her eyes. They sat motionless against each other, their breath coming in brief, frenzied gasps. Rachel's smoldering eyes locked on to his as she slowly opened her mouth and licked the droplet of blood from his upper lip. He gently touched her tongue with his and his eyes closed to a surge of intense pleasure. He trembled with desire as he slid his hands deftly along the contours of her rib cage and settled on either side of her narrow waist. He was acutely aware of the pressure of her breasts against his chest. Slowly, gently, he resumed kissing her, moving now from her lips to her smooth, unlined cheek to the soft, warm flesh beneath her earlobe. She shuddered involuntarily.

"Cold?" he whispered.

"Hardly," she replied hoarsely.

"You're not uncomfortable, are you?" he asked, leaving her to determine whether he meant physically or otherwise.

"I don't think this is about comfort, do you?" she said, with equal ambiguity.

He smiled. "I'm not sure what it's about. All I know is how terrific it feels."

"You know, I have a very comfortable apartment about six blocks from here. Would you have any interest in following me home?"

"Gee. I don't know. I still have a lot of work to do," he teased.

She laughed. He started to stand up. She grabbed his shoulders with both hands and pulled his mouth back down onto hers, kissing him hard once more. "You're not going to lose interest on the way, are you?" she asked softly.

"Only if I die," he managed to reply, his heartbeat still providing most of the sound now reaching his ears.

"I'll make sure you stay alive long enough to do me some good," she said, releasing her grip on him.

Rachel went to her office to get her things. As Lang got his keys from his desk drawer, he noticed the light on his phone indicating a message on his voice mail. He checked his watch: It was 9:47. "Who would call at this hour on New Year's Eve?" he asked aloud. Briefly, he considered retrieving the message later, but decided that he might forget about it until Monday morning. He punched in the code.

After the tone came Clarice Devereaux's voice: "Oh, God, Chris. Where are you? It's Max." The panic in the voice of this strong, capable woman was chilling. "I've never seen him like this. He can't move and he can't talk. I've called the paramedics. He came home from a meeting. And, then, he sat down. In the den. Then—this. I—I need you, Chris. It's, ah, it's now, God, let's see. It's almost nine-fifteen on, it is Saturday? Yes. Saturday night. God, I'm really worried about my Max."

Adrenaline shot through Lang's body and his breath suddenly came in short gasps. His usually sure fingers misdialed twice as he tried to punch in the Devereaux' number. Finally, he got it right but there was no answer. Max and Clarice had never employed an answering machine, so the phone just kept on ringing. He wiped aside a tear as he hung up. Numbly, he headed down the hall to find Rachel, contemplating the unimaginable void that the loss of Max Devereaux would create in the world. Especially his world.

CHAPTER 15

THE FIRST NINE DAYS OF CHRIS LANG'S NEW YEAR were a blur, a spinning, oscillating collage of intensive-care nurses and doctors, hushed hallway conferences, green- and blue-clad technicians, rambling philosophical and theological apologies for the various unacceptable faces of death, and a string of small, unrealistic hopes first raised then immediately dashed, punctuated by an occasional, wholly irrelevant yet perversely important report from Amy Quinn from the deposition battlefield, all against the backdrop of a long and emotional bedside vigil.

His good friend and surrogate father, Max Devereaux, never regained consciousness following what the chief resident called a massive bilateral stroke. On New Year's morning, however, when Lang first walked into the small, hardware-crowded room to see Max, under an oxygen mask and living off an IV, the old man had suddenly opened his eyes wide and, with a look that, to Lang, was a combination of the anguish of Moby Dick and the fury of the bull lining up to charge, wept for several minutes. In the contradictory logic that sometimes drives the practice of medicine, this was at first seen by the chief neurosurgeon as "an encouraging sign." It proved to be nothing of the sort, of course, as the ongoing analysis of the continuous stream of data eventually confirmed a "terminal scenario."

Lang fought the inevitable with every ounce of will he could muster. So accustomed was he to confronting impossible odds in his business and, by dint of tireless creativity and tenacity, overcoming those odds, that, as a purely intellectual matter, he could not accept that there was nothing to be done.

"Let me ask you this," he began, after the chief neurosurgeon, Charles Devlin, carefully, if clinically, explained to him the physics of a blood clot lodged at the junction of the principal vein at the base of the brain stem. "It sounds like you could go in there surgically—laser surgery, microsurgery, whatever—and get the damned thing out, restore the flow of blood."

Dr. Devlin shook his head. "There are limits to what medicine can do. What you are talking about isn't viable."

"Let me put it this way: What would you do if this were the president of the United States, Doctor?" Lang's voice was cracking with fatigue and frustration.

"I don't mean to be flip, Mr. Lang," replied Devlin. "But I'd swear the vice president in."

Deep into the week, at the urging of Lang, who simply could not shake the effects of that powerful encounter with Max, the medical team placed Max under an increasingly heavy morphine blanket to dull his senses and ease what pain he might be feeling. For the balance of the seemingly endless vigil, the venerable old giant of a man appeared to sleep comfortably and peacefully, belying the ferocity with which his mortal being raged against the power of the inevitable. The net effect of all this, however, was that, for the rest of his life, Lang would never forget that singular moment of Max's anguish and fury, just as he would never be able to divine its true meaning, though he would lose long days from time to time trying.

At times, Clarice seemed to Lang to deal with the hospital ordeal better than he did, showing particular strength of character to the numerous well-wishers who, not knowing what to say, nonetheless came to visit. Lang, for his part, found himself largely under his own blanket of fog. The surreal existence of life in the tiny hospital room assumed the security of a womb and he grew increasingly reluctant to leave it. By the time the end came, it was Clarice whose role it was to comfort and Lang's to feel the massive impact of bereavement.

Ro arrived on the fourth day. Lang was surprised at what a comfort she was, both to Clarice and to him. Somewhere in the deep recesses of his consciousness he marveled at how his Ro had grown in grace and poise. This situation, precisely the kind that Lang would have expected to have threatened and upset her terribly, did not seem to stress her visibly. She was devastated, naturally, by the realization that Max, a favorite of hers since they had joined his firm, was irretrievably lost to them all as friend and counselor. Nonetheless, she handled the strain with a quiet strength that moved Lang in a curious way. Not surprisingly, Lang's grief over the impending loss of the man who had been his father throughout his adulthood became suffused with a renewed melancholy over the demise of his marriage and the loss of intimacy with his wife. He felt himself doubly bereft.

As the days passed, Lang grudgingly came to terms with the only outcome there could possibly be to his vigil. Still, when he returned from the hospital cafeteria, where he had forced down yet another tasteless, unwanted meal, he was utterly unprepared to find a priest at Max's side. Summoning all his depleted strength, he began to shake, actively suppressing the urge to rush into the room. Though every instinct told him to do something, anything, to try to drive back the priest's Latin incantations, he stood in the doorway, fists clenched in wordless frustration and despair.

Ro had been standing in the corner of the room and she was suddenly at Lang's side. "Chris," she said, gently but firmly. She put her arms around him. "Chris. I'm so sorry. He's gone."

"I know," he whispered hoarsely. "I know." He went limply into Ro's arms, sobbing quietly into her shoulder. She squeezed his upper arm and whispered to him, trying to comfort him. The priest, through it all, continued his ministrations. Lang found a chair in the corner. In the adjacent seat sat a dewy-eyed, immobile Clarice, staring blankly at the ashen face of her lifelong partner, now lifeless on the bed. Absently, she put a hand on Lang's knee and pressed gently.

"He had a good life, Chris," she said softly. "We all had a good life and he was a big part of the reason."

Clarice convinced Lang that it was all right for him to leave her that night and that she and her sister, who had arrived from Montreal the day before, would be fine on their own at her house that night. Thus released from his duties, he suddenly found himself standing outside the hospital door in a gathering January mist as dusk rolled over Los Angeles. Suspended somewhere between abject grief and utter fatigue, he stood there a long time, unsure of where he'd left his car or even how he'd gotten to the hospital that day—or was it yesterday?

Just then Ro pulled up to the curb in front of Lang. For a second or two he did not seem to recognize her.

"Chris," she called as she rolled down the window. "What are you doing out here? Are you okay?"

He focused on her face. A light of recognition clicked on. "Ro!" he said. "Ro, what are *you* doing here? I thought you'd gone home."

"I did. But I'm back. Get in. You're getting soaked."

He got in the passenger seat, his body aching as if from a brutal physical beating.

"Are you okay?" she repeated gently.

"Yeah, Ro. I'm a big boy. I just didn't think it could hurt so bad." He fought back another wave of tears.

She put a strong but gentle hand on his dampened cheek. "I know, sweetheart. I'm so sorry."

He could only nod and swallow hard in response, tears rolling down his unshaven cheeks.

"Look," she said, command in her tone. "You don't look like you're in any shape to drive tonight. How about spending the night in the spare room? I'll bring you back tomorrow for your car."

He resisted the reflex to decline the offer. To his surprise, he said, "Okay. That would be nice. I don't think I can be alone tonight."

"Neither do I," she said, throwing the car into gear and roaring off down the rainslicked driveway and into the street.

Lang felt as bad as he could ever remember feeling. His marathon vigil of the past week and a half was suddenly over and he had neither adequate strength nor clear enough vision to determine his next move. Now, as he sat heaped in the right seat of Ro's car, every fiber of his being ached with despair and exhaustion. If ever he were inclined toward a total mental and physical breakdown, he thought, this was going to be it. But, somehow, the sight of Ro, appearing through the literal and figurative gloom, out of nowhere, had buoyed his spirits, sparking the faintest flame of hope that there would come a new day, a return to all that was normal and hopeful and positive in his life. Even as this sense settled over him, he knew it was more likely than not the folly of a desperate, irrational man, but he embraced it anyway, needing to bask in its false warmth. It was, after all, all he really had.

It was raining harder and very dark when they reached Ro's house. As she pulled her car into the garage, it occurred to Lang that he had nothing to sleep in, no toilet articles, no change of clothes.

"Maybe you should just take me home, after all, Ro," he said as he got out of the car. "It's only another fifteen minutes and I feel much better than I did at Cedars."

She waved him off and grabbed his hand, pulling him toward the door to the kitchen. "Don't be silly. We'll manage for one night. So maybe you'll sleep in the buff. Wouldn't be the first time." He started to reply, but she cut him off. "Besides, nobody's going to see you in the guest room."

Both of them had missed dinner, but neither had much appetite. Nevertheless, a glass of cold milk and a handful of Andrea's Girl Scout cookies sounded good to them both. The kids were already in bed, but made the pilgrimage downstairs, one at a time, to welcome and console their father. Lang was surprised that none of them commented on his being there or his spending the night. Jack touched him perhaps most of all when he followed a shake of the hand and a kiss on his cheek by burying his head into Lang's chest and saying, "Don't you just wish it was all a dream and you could wake up with everything still okay, after all?"

Lang and Ro sat together in the living room by the fire until well after midnight. Exhausted though he was, Lang knew he could not sleep. Ro simply could not leave him in that condition, so there they sat, side by side on the couch, sipping cream sherry and staring into the fire. When Ro got up to refill their glasses, Lang himself rose to stretch. Through the curtains he could see that the rain was coming down heavier, in perfect harmony with his mood. On the end table in front of the window he found a small frame of two family photographs, relics from nearly a half dozen years ago when the kids were small and he and Ro were still smiling between bickering sessions. The one on top was the five of them, dressed in their church clothes and posing under a trellis covered with pink and lavender roses and carnations in full bloom. The one on the bottom, from the preceding summer, he thought, showed all of them on the white porch swing of the vast veranda of the Grand Manan Inn on an island off the coast of Maine, the site of what Lang remembered as their best family vacation ever. Suddenly, he was struck by the strange mixture of emotions he was experiencing. Certainly his grief over Max's death was overwhelming, looming large over everything else. But in the shadows of that massive sense of loss was a smaller, older, more chronic sense of remoteness, emptiness. Despondency crouched in the corner, ready to pounce. Lang consoled himself with the thought that pure exhaustion would soon take over.

He was still holding the framed photographs, still feeling their effect, when Ro returned with two more glasses of sherry. "They've really grown, haven't they?" she said, as neutrally as possible.

"Like weeds," he replied, trying to mirror her tone.

"Wasn't that trip to Grand Manan fabulous? I think it was our best vacation ever."

"It really was," he agreed. "Spectacular place at the end of the summer. You know, this other one was taken by Max," he said, indicating the top photo.

"I remember," she said. "In their backyard on Easter Sunday."

"How's this for pathetic? Do you know what I remember from that day?"

"I bet I do. The fight we had on the way over."

"Right after church," he said, shaking his head in wonder at how things had gotten so far off track between them. "I was—"

"Let's not talk about it, Chris," she said firmly.

He looked at her inquiringly for a moment, then shrugged. "Okay. But you're the one who always says we should talk about these things."

She moved back to the couch. "Not these things. Not the past."

"What, then? The future?" His tone was mildly biting.

She did not pick up the bait. "Not really. I just think maybe we're past the time when talking about these things will do us any good."

"Maybe." He rejoined her on the couch and drank deeply from his glass. They both looked into the dancing flames as if there were answers there. After a long silence, Lang said, "Is it my imagination or have we had fewer conflicts between us lately?"

She seemed to tense slightly. "I don't know. Maybe. We've both been busy. Our lives have probably moved far enough apart to reduce some of the tension."

"Maybe," he repeated, without conviction. Another moment went by. "You know, I never meant to hurt you, Ro. Nothing I ever did, none of the neglect that you felt, none of the pressure I put on you, was intended to hurt."

She continued to stare into the fire, turning over his words in her head. These were easy words to say, she thought, but there was little that mere words could do now to erase years of behavior. She sipped her drink, saying nothing.

He turned to her. "You never thought I intended to hurt you, did you?"

She met his eyes with her own. "We were young. You weren't a bad guy. You were just ambitious, so damned ambitious, driven." She shook her head at the intensity of the recollection. "You occupied all the space in our lives. There wasn't any room for me to be me. I didn't like being reduced to a mere reflection of you." She looked away, into the fire. "There were times when I actually wished, no, I *prayed* that once, just once, you would turn down a new case or a new assignment. But that wasn't you. Each new case was an affirmation of your self-worth and you took them on with relish, whether you had the time to handle them or not."

He watched her closely, moved as never before by the depth of her hurt and silenced by the clarity with which she articulated it.

She shrugged. "Ultimately, I had started to settle for the tiny space your drive and ambition left for me and I couldn't let that happen. Pete and Ruth Deyton raised me to be more than that. *I* wanted something more. I was vulnerable, Chris, and you hurt me, whether you meant to or not." She was surprised at how clinically she stated the fact. She felt no anger, only the regret of opportunities lost.

He nodded slightly, not in agreement, but at least to indicate that he understood her point. "I guess I never knew."

"Well, you have no excuse for that. You're a smart guy, as bright as anybody I ever met. You can cut through the most complex legal issues like a laser. I've seen you do it. But in some ways, Chris, you're dense. It's as if you spend most of your time asleep at the wheel where real life's involved."

Her words stung him and he felt like an overmatched boxer several rounds past the point where they should have stopped the fight. Still, in a perverse way, he knew the discussion had value. It was, he realized with irony, the very discussion he had been promising himself they would have for months.

The discussion continued, not as a light, euphemistic rehash of the things that had bothered and divided them, but a gritty, an-

guished excursion into the most painful regions of their failed relationship, the very ones they had studiously avoided for years.
Alternately, they raised their voices, challenged recollections and
interpretations, wept and embraced, defended themselves and, surprisingly, exchanged heartfelt apologies. Hour after hour they
talked, finishing the bottle of sherry and dipping deep into another.

At long last, Ro went sleepily off to make up the spare room.
By now, the fire was reduced to a handful of glowing embers, its
heat long since a memory from what seemed to Lang an earlier age.
He knelt before the hearth and tried to coax out a last spark with the
poker. Although few, if any, questions could be considered resolved,
a bewildering number had been aired. Somehow, he had begun to
see their marriage from her point of view. In fact, he saw their
relationship with a new clarity, as if he were examining it for the first
time, from a distance, as he would a new case being presented by a
prospective client. He *had* suffocated her, casting her without thinking into what could only be considered a secondary, supporting role
in his life. And in his effort to encourage her to improve on the lot
to which he had unthinkingly consigned her, he had come across as
critical, judgmental. It was not what he had intended but it was the
natural consequence of living his life the way he had intended it.
Legally, he thought wryly, it amounts to the same thing. With that
realization, he reached the point of utter fatigue. Without warning,
the great leonine head of Max Devereaux, his face contorted in what
would forever be its state of rage and torment, materialized out of
the dying fire and consumed Lang with the despair of things that
cannot be undone. He wept uncontrollably for a long time, until Ro
finally returned and cradled him, on the floor, in front of the ghost
of their fire.

They dozed off where they were, arm in arm on the floor, and
slept until nearly dawn. Ro awakened to find the room lit by only
the small corner lamp. She looked at the sleeping face of the man
who had been her husband and partner for so many years. He
looked tired as he slept on, snoring rhythmically, finding peace for
the first time in weeks. He was finally beginning to show his age, she
thought. She could count more than a few gray strands sprinkled
through his thick head of hair and there was a distinct puffiness to
his eyes. Unmistakable lines were etched along the corners of those
eyes. Still, he was, and had always been, a handsome man. And,
sleeping as he was now, in a state of total exhaustion, there was
nothing hard or menacing about him. For the man she once considered the most oppressively overbearing human being she had ever

known, he looked as vulnerable as a child. Perhaps, as she had begun to suspect as they had talked, he had mellowed. And perhaps she herself had grown tougher. She smiled and went back to the spare room to get a pillow and a quilt. In a moment, she returned and carefully propped his head on the pillow and covered him with the heavy blue down coverlet. When she was satisfied that she had made him comfortable, she looked again at his face and then, on an impulse, bent over him and kissed him sweetly on the forehead. She turned out the lamp and went to bed, never knowing that Lang had opened his eyes after the kiss and smiled weakly to himself. Despite the unspeakable sadness of his last day with his beloved Max, and the terrible catharsis of his long dialogue with Ro, that tiny smile was still on his face as he drifted back off to sleep.

Amy Quinn wrapped up test pilot Brent Milinsky's deposition at five minutes past six on Friday, thus ending a marathon four days and thirty-seven hours of depositions in San Sebastian. The coastal weather was cold and damp, so she and Rachel Cruz reluctantly made the drive back to Los Angeles with the top up. There was little conversation on the way, the two of them preferring instead the soothing melodies of Amy's rhythm-and-blues tapes. Rachel quietly passed the time listening to the music and watching the road ahead, musing about where things might have gone between her and Chris if fate had not intervened in the final hours of the old year. On balance, she told herself, they were probably both better off this way.

Amy's thoughts focused on the case she was building. When she had received Rachel's call on New Year's Day to tell her about Max Devereaux's stroke, she had immediately realized that, since Lang was to take the bulk of the depositions, she would need an agreement from Gentry Hickman to postpone them until Max's health stabilized. She had succeeded only in reaching his voice mail in Oklahoma City on the holiday, and when he called her back the following day—just a day before the depositions were to begin—he was very flowery and proper but had refused her request. He had politely invited her to ask the judge to change the schedule. Amy knew, as did Hickman, that the likelihood of her getting any such relief from Campbell—especially on such short notice—was remote. She pressed her case with Hickman, but he proved intractable. In the end, the best she could do was to move all the first-week depositions to the second week and cancel the series originally scheduled for the second week.

The four depositions had been virtually identical in substance and tone. Their answers were pat, minimal, and utterly consistent with one another. Amy had never before encountered such remarkable identity in the stories told by more than one witness. It was this studied consistency that convinced her, for the first time in the case, that Lang might well be right: These guys were hiding something. Whether it had anything to do with Lindstrom, as Lang was convinced, was a matter of sheer speculation.

Still, her efforts had established a number of points. The witnesses admitted that Arrow Dynamics had not tested the prototype StormTree for departure and spin under the military spin specification or any specification, for that matter. Their position was that they weren't required to do so under the contract. While Amy was aware that Molly O'Keefe had told Uncle Seamus otherwise, there was always the possibility that her recollection would be discounted as that of a layperson who was not directly involved in the transaction.

Arrow did not maintain an engineering log on every project, and the StormTree was one where they hadn't. Nobody could really tell Amy how they went about deciding which projects should have a log and which should not. On the StormTree, they used only "flight cards" to record data, loose-leaf five-by-eight filing cards that were not kept after the project ended. This was potentially useful since John Carrick would testify that the mere failure to maintain such a log was tantamount to negligence. Although video footage was taken of some of the test flights, none of it was kept, and the tapes were subsequently reused. Nobody could recall if any of the departure tests had been taped.

As for the Peregrine, the aircraft built by Pegasus, although Brent Milinsky testified flatly that it was "an entirely different aircraft" weighing several hundred pounds more and having numerous different features, he did admit that the Peregrine was "geometrically similar to the StormTree." Helpful, reflected Amy, but not as good as it needs to be, according to Carrick. Milinsky also testified about Arrow's effort to determine why the Peregrine tended to spin and, like the rest of the team that gave up on the project, he had no explanation for that tendency. "I don't know," he testified with a shrug. "Just one of those things, I guess." Somewhere in all this information is a key to this thing, she thought. Maybe even the answer to where Lindstrom might fit into this orchestrated story; I just can't think hard enough right now to find it.

Then, as she sped toward Los Angeles through the thickening gloom and a rising tide of fatigue, Amy made a determined effort to disengage the analytical part of her brain that was struggling to crack the riddle and cast the rest adrift to the music. She met with only limited success.

On Saturday morning, they buried Max Devereaux. Dozens of celebrities had been eulogized over the years from the pulpit of the Church of the Good Shepherd in Beverly Hills, but few had drawn the size and stature of the congregation that came to pay their last respects to Max. From the attorney general of the United States to the governor of California and the heads of the major studios, on down to the kids from the East Los Angeles job retraining facility founded by Max, the mourners filled the church and spilled out into the adjacent streets.

At the request of the widow, Chris Lang delivered the eulogy. Although he had argued numerous important and difficult cases before the United States Supreme Court and the California Supreme Court and had tried scores of cases he never made a public appearance that was as difficult for him. Not that it was hard to say something about Max, or hard to find words to describe the man. He had merely to look within his heart and read his own feelings. The hard part was to stand before those hundreds of Max's friends and talk about the man around the pain in his heart. But, after the first minute or so, Lang realized that he was speaking directly to Max and that made it easier.

As he helped Clarice out of the limousine at the cemetery afterward, Ro and the kids approached. His delicate grip on his emotions was lost in an instant at the sight of his children and their mother, eyes red and swollen, picking their way along the grassy path through the grave markers.

"Nice job," whispered Ro as she hugged him. "Max would have been proud."

"Don't cry, Daddy," said Andrea, squeezing her father around his waist. "Mr. Devereaux's gone to heaven. I'm sure of it."

"I know, Andy," he managed to say, squeezing Jack and Jennifer in turn.

It was while he stood at Clarice's side and Father McDowell prayed over the casket being lowered into the ground that Lang noticed Russell Lindstrom in the crowd. He found the moment doubly disturbing since Lindstrom appeared to have been watching him. Lindstrom's smile seemed warm and friendly, but Lang found it jarringly inappropriate and offensively intimate. It went right through him, leaving a profound uneasiness in its wake.

As he escorted Clarice back to the limousine, Lindstrom approached. "Chris," he said, extending his right hand. Lang shook it instinctively. Too stunned for the moment to respond to this brazen gesture, Lang stood in silence while Lindstrom turned to Clarice. "Mrs. Devereaux. Russell Lindstrom. I'm so very sorry. Unfortunately, I did not have the good fortune to know your husband well, but, like everyone else, I knew enough of him to be deeply saddened by his loss. Godspeed, my dear." He took her hand briefly. She nodded mechanically and slid into the car. As Lang closed the door after her, Lindstrom shook his head sadly. "These are difficult times, aren't they, Chris?" The comment infuriated Lang but he wasn't sure exactly why. Before he could reply, Lindstrom, touching his brow in an abbreviated farewell gesture, melted back into the crowd and disappeared.

CHAPTER 16

CONCENTRATION HAD BECOME AN OVERWHELMING chore for Lang over the past three weeks. He grew morbidly introspective, feeling the loss of his friend and mentor as he had never felt a loss before. As so often happens with an event that triggers depression, it made everything else that was wanting in his life look all the more bleak. It was ironic at best that his most valued source of wisdom and counsel on all things difficult and troubling would be unavailable to him as he attempted to deal with a new and devastating hole in his life.

As but one consequence of the powerful malaise afflicting him, the fine details of his most important pending case, in many ways the most important of his career, were reduced to trivia and banality during the painfully tedious process of preparing for a terribly technical trial. Frequently, an increasingly impatient Amy Quinn had watched his eyes glaze over as she laid out the open issues, unexplored areas, and rapidly changing landscape of the case.

"Chris!" Amy barked at last. Lang's head snapped up from his doodling in the notebook before him. "You're not listening to me."

"Don't yell at me, Amy," Lang said, more hurt than angry. "I'm trying. We'll see how well you concentrate after you bury me 'neath the green, green grass of home."

"Don't try to manipulate me, Chris. We have a hell of a case for contract breach against Arrow Dynamics. I just don't want to dilute it by aiming too high and missing. There is *no* meaningful evidence to tie Lindstrom to this case other than his early conversations with Daultry. Since they predate the contract and the testing of the airplane they'll only go so far. Even if Molly testifies, her testimony will have no corroboration from anyone else. And it flies directly in the face of the testimony of that gang up in San Sebastian. It's possible but, in my view, unlikely that the situation will change with Lindstrom's deposition. If the jury focuses on a fraud case against Lindstrom and doesn't see it because, say, there is no evidence to support it, they may wash us out altogether, contract case and all, just through their sheer stupidity."

"Now, there's a ringing endorsement of the jury system," he remarked dryly.

"Like you don't agree. 'Twelve citizens, more or less, sharing a half a heart and a third of a brain between paychecks from the federal government,' " she said, quoting Lang.

"That's unfair. I said that at the bottom of post-trial depression. Even I'm not that cynical."

She looked at him skeptically. "Whatever. The point is that I strongly disagree with the emphasis you are placing on this case. I think it's ill-advised and dangerous."

"Since when did you graduate from ace assistant to moral conscience of the legal team?" He bit the words off with a cutting edge.

Amy was clearly hurt by the barb. "Look," she said, swallowing back the sting of his words. "That's the way you trained me. To think critically and see issues from both my side and the other side. And you know I'm pretty good at it."

His look softened. "Sorry," he said. "Been through a lot lately."

She pursed her lips and nodded, though she continued to feel that his curt treatment of her was not warranted. It was late and they were both exhausted.

"Amy," he said, his tone genuinely conciliatory. "Let's just go over these key areas one more time, for clarity's sake, then we'll call it a night."

"Okay. At least you can call it a night. I have to go over Dean's brief in the Uzaco motion before tomorrow. Where do you want to start?"

They agreed that the contract case was fairly straightforward: Arrow failed to deliver the airplane it promised to design, build, and deliver. That part of the case was hardly a slam dunk, but it was fairly simple.

"And the fraud case?" he asked.

Amy shrugged. "Against the company, it's simply that they knowingly falsified the report, in essence doing two things."

Lang continued the thought for her: "First, concealing their discovery of what must have been an obvious tendency to spin, and second, deliberately doctoring the results of the testing to make the StormTree sound like the airplane bargained for in the contract instead of the death trap that it was."

"Great theory. Only problem with it is that we have no evidence that the StormTree did, in fact, demonstrate the instability that we know it had, and no evidence that the airplane did not fly exactly the way they represented it did."

"But," Lang replied hastily, "the jury could infer the truth from the testing history of the Peregrine and, for Christ's sake, we have a dead test pilot on our hands from flying the StormTree. I think the jury could conclude that all was not right with the airplane."

Amy shook her head. "Look, we've discussed that. Walt had to push the airplane for three days to get it to spin. Even John admits that it's possible that they reached the conclusion about its spin susceptibility innocently—incorrectly, mind you—but not fraudulently, before they got that far. That's a breach of the contract but not a deliberate act of fraudulent concealment or misrepresentation. And, you will recall, we don't have any records that contradict their testimony that during testing the StormTree neither exhibited any spin tendency nor, for that matter, was anything but a 'joy to fly.' To the contrary, all the testing data they have turned over supports their contention that the airplane did exactly what they said it did in the final engineering report."

"But the military specs?"

"They admit that they did not run the Mil Spec test itself, but their argument is that they were only supposed to test the airplane's spin and departure resistance to the point where they were reasonably satisfied that the StormTree was resistant in both categories, which they claim they did and which all the documentation supports."

"But they did not run the whole Mil Spec regimen?" Lang asked, with a hint of the tone that generally characterized his cross-examination style.

"Absolutely not. Their understanding was that the customer knew that the reference to the Mil Spec in the contract was only a means of providing definitions for the terms 'departure-resistant' and 'spin-resistant' as used in the contract. As you know, the last three pages of the Mil Spec do define certain terms, and those two are among them."

"Yeah," agreed Lang dubiously. "A forty-four-page specification that has the most detailed testing regimen ever devised for spinning an airplane, and they claim that it was in the contract for definitional purposes only. Molly O'Keefe will say something very different, though."

"Yes, and no," responded Amy. Lang's look immediately challenged her statement. "Don't get me wrong, but Molly's not a technical person and all she heard was what Lindstrom and Daultry said sitting by the pool."

Lang waved dismissively. "I'll take my chances with her testimony." He paused to reset his focus. "I guess I don't have to ask you about the fraud case against Lindstrom personally."

"Zero case, from where I sit," she replied. "Unless you shake his story or find a damned good witness to impeach his credibility, the closest we have is a couple of preliminary discussions with Daultry, then he moves out of the picture. Nothing suggests he flew the plane, discovered its tendency to spin, wrote, edited, or approved the final engineering report. *Nada*."

"Of course, we have yet to hear from Lindstrom himself. And maybe Molly O'Keefe will surprise us, come to testify and hang a lot more on Russell Lindstrom."

"Possibly," replied Amy without conviction. "Then there's always Santa, the Easter Bunny, and the Tooth Fairy. All I know is that they are going to have Lindstrom and everybody else who was on their side of the contract testify, and we won't have Nigel Daultry take the stand to say otherwise."

"Hmm," he grunted, getting up from his chair. "An uplifting thought to sleep on. But if it were easy, we wouldn't earn these ungodly sums."

"Nor develop these ungodly ulcers."

"Stress is absolutely necessary for every living organism to

achieve its fullest potential. I'm gone. Good luck with Mr. Silver-
berg's brief."

She rolled her eyes and headed back to her own office.

"Good night, Soon," droned a bone-tired Amy Quinn as she
dragged her way across the darkened lobby of Devereaux and Brace
toward the elevator door. Just as she reached the button she banged
her knee roughly on the edge of the big, heavy litigation bag she
carried in her right hand, opening a wide run in her nylons. "Shit!"
she said under her breath.

The Korean cleaning lady polishing the brass lamp in the corner looked up, smiled her perpetual smile, and nodded deeply
toward her twice. "Good night, Miss Amy," she called after the
lawyer. "See you tomorrow."

"You probably will," replied Amy, again under her breath, as
she picked at the ruin that her stockings had just become. "Well,
there goes another seven-fifty down the drain."

She stepped into the empty elevator and checked her watch. It
was 10:57. "Got to get me a life," she said to herself as she punched
the button and headed down toward the parking garage. Dean Sil-
verberg, she thought, you are not up to the standards of Devereaux
and Brace and I predict you will not see the next annual salary
adjustment. Rewriting the young associate's brief had been a major
task, one Amy vowed not to repeat.

There wasn't a soul around when the door opened onto the
level where she kept her car. The only sound she heard was a steady
buzz from one of the fluorescent lights in the ceiling. She'd been
working like this for six years and was still not comfortable with the
emptiness of the garage late at night.

The walk from the elevator to her car was always the worst
part. Her footsteps echoed loudly on the concrete floor of the cavernous garage as she covered the fifty or so yards to her black-on-
black BMW. Out of force of habit, she scanned the area steadily
from side to side, sweeping the emptiness for the unexpected late-
night attacker who is the nightmare of every woman in every big
city in the country. Fortunately, there wasn't another car parked on
the entire level, thankfully limiting potential hiding places for a
mugger/rapist. Satisfied that the place was utterly empty, she allowed herself to look her car over. Seeing it under the glare of the
harsh fluorescents made her feel guilty that she had allowed it to get
so dirty. Bill, who had persuaded her to buy the used convertible in
the first place so he could completely refurbish it, invariably washed

it Saturday mornings, but he had been to a department seminar this past weekend and he hadn't gotten to it. Since he flatly forbade the use of a car wash on his masterpiece for any reason whatsoever, her only option would have been to wash it herself. Fat chance, she thought, the way Captain Bligh ran her around on his various cases. Suddenly her heart seized and she froze right where she stood, twenty feet from her car. Looming up out of the fog of her tired brain came the realization that something was terribly wrong. Quickly she searched her mind and there it was: The time for filing for an extension on the appellee's brief in the *Severstone* appeal had lapsed on the twenty-second! She checked her watch: Today was the twenty-second!

"Fuck!" she shouted and turned on her heel and raced back to the elevator. "Goddammit!" she added, only slightly less loudly. "How the hell am I supposed to keep all these goddamned balls in the air? Goddammit, Chris! What do you think I'm made of?" She got back into the elevator and headed back up to double-check the date. But everything inside her, which was now thoroughly flooded with the acid rush of adrenaline that all litigators know only too well, told her she had blown it. Quickly, she recalculated: The appellant's brief had been filed on the twenty-third of last month, meaning that the thirtieth day, the last one to seek an extension, was the twenty-second. Today. The ride upstairs was then consumed by the kind of panic-driven creativity lawyers specialize in. Could she still get an extension *ex parte*? She wasn't certain but strongly suspected that an extension of the briefing schedule was not specifically delineated as an order she could get without a full-blown motion with two weeks' notice. Would the appellant stipulate to a continuance? No way, she thought. Not that pompous, whining snake, whom she had practically called a crook and a cheat in open court. Was there any room to argue "excusable neglect," the lawyer's last resort because it is both an unseemly submission of oneself to the naked mercy of the court and an engraved invitation to the client to sue for malpractice if it doesn't work? Not really. "I'm overworked and was too busy, Your Honor" just wouldn't cut it.

In a cold building with the heat off for the night, great beads of perspiration nonetheless stood out on her forehead as she raced from the elevator to her office. Furiously, with a combination of sinking heart and the underdog's last gasp of unwarranted optimism, she grabbed her calendar from her desk drawer and flung it open. *Severstone* was nowhere to be found on the twenty-second. How about the twenty-first? No. The twentieth? She flipped for-

ward. February 3! Of course! Oh, thank you, God! The court had
granted the other side an extension, not of the standard thirty days,
but of forty-five when the court itself had requested briefing on the
jury-fees issue that wasn't part of the original notice! How could she
have forgotten? Never mind, she told herself, just enjoy the moment. Amazing, she thought, what can pass for a victory in the odd,
medieval world of litigation. She sank into her chair and let the
adrenaline rush play out. Briefly she toyed with the idea of dictating
the motion right then and there but decided to settle for leaving
herself a huge reminder on a legal pad in the middle of her desk:
"SEVERSTONE!!! You have ten days!!!"

A minute later, she was back in the elevator on her way down
to her car, this time wide awake and full of energy. "Better than a
trip to the gym," she said to herself.

Downstairs, she stepped lightly, breezily, from the elevator,
oblivious this time to the noise of the lights, the clacking of her
heels, and the layer of dust on her Beemer. She all but floated across
the floor to her car. But as she pulled out her key, she heard a car
door open behind her. Wheeling around, she saw, against the far
wall, in a darkened spot under a burned-out fluorescent light, an old
blue car that she was certain had not been there fifteen minutes
earlier. As she squinted into the darkness to get a better look, the
car's driver-side door closed. She could not see if anyone had gotten
out. From where she stood, the windshield seemed to be coated
with a black film, making it impossible to see inside, as well. A chill
ran up her spine as she fumbled to get the key in the lock. Now, all
her senses were alert for the sight or sound of an attacker. "Where is
that goddamned security guard, anyway?" she muttered as she fiddled with her keys. They slipped from her hand and fell to the floor.
She tried to pick them up while looking back toward the blue car,
but only succeeded in pushing them under the car. Now, feeling
very vulnerable, she got down on her knees to fish the keys out from
under the car, making a matching run in the other knee of her
pantyhose. Still she heard no sound, saw nothing. Her heart rate
was definitely climbing as she finally grabbed the keys and unlocked
the door. Inside, she quickly relocked the doors and started the
engine. Still she neither heard nor saw anyone. Quickly she slipped
the car into gear and drove away from her parking space, her eyes
watching the old blue car in the rearview mirror.

As she pulled out into the night, it occurred to her that there
was no way a car should have been able to get into the garage at that
hour unless it had a tenant's pass. And, yes, the building was large

and the tenants numerous, but most of them parked in the same space each day and she knew just about all the cars in her section of that level. And, besides, the cars parked there tended to be Mercedes, Cadillacs, BMW's, Porsches, Lexuses, and the like, all late models. If that old blue car had belonged to a tenant, she surely would have noticed it before. Nervously she checked her rearview mirror again. Santa Monica Boulevard was virtually deserted at this hour. There was no sign of the car behind her.

As she hit the freeway, she began to feel more relaxed. The traffic was light for Los Angeles, and she quickly hit seventy-five miles an hour. Quite possibly, she had let her imagination run away with her. The car probably belonged to one of the building's many cleaning-crew workers. No doubt one of them had gotten hold of a tenant's card key. And, she reasoned further, it was certainly possible that a cleaning crew for some floor or other came on at eleven o'clock, just about the time she had gone back upstairs. And if there had been someone in the car, it probably meant nothing more than a last cigarette before the shift started or, at worst, a quick joint to make the toilets and sinks a little more tolerable. I've got to get a better handle on my emotions, she told herself. Between *Severstone* and the Phantom of the Parking Garage, I'm going to be a basket case any day now.

At last, she moved over into the right lane and headed down her off-ramp. As she sat at the light at the bottom of the ramp, she looked in her mirror again. Just leaving the freeway and headed down the ramp behind her was a car that she felt sure was the blue car! Now she really was panicked. Although the light was still red, there was no traffic on the cross street, so she punched the accelerator and shot through the intersection. To her relief, the other car stopped at the light and remained at the intersection.

Her palms were beginning to sweat. But still, she was not even sure it was the same car. She was terribly upset by the prospect of being pursued, however, and she was still a good twelve to fifteen minutes from home, much of it through narrow, dimly lit streets. She picked up her phone and punched in the short code for home. It rang three times, then Bill said, "Hello. You've reached Bill and Amy. We can't come to the—"

She hung up. Where *is* he, she wondered. Then, she remembered that he, too, was working late tonight. She punched in the short code for his car phone. He answered right away.

"Hello?"

"Bill!" she said. "Thank God."

"What are you doing, Amy, checking up on me?" He laughed.

"No, Bill. Listen. I'm being followed. I'm really scared."

"All right, honey. Don't panic. Where are you?"

"I'm on Manhattan Beach Boulevard, just past Aviation."

"Okay. Where's the other guy?"

"I don't know."

"What do you mean you don't know? I thought he was following you."

"He *is* following me, Bill!" she shouted. "When I got off the freeway, I ran the light and he stayed there."

"You ran the light? Jesus, Amy. How do you know he's following you? I mean, every time I get off the freeway there's another car behind me. And if I were to run the light at the end of the ramp, chances are he would stay there, too."

"Goddammit, Bill. This guy's following me." She checked the mirror again. Nothing. "He has an old blue car that wasn't in the garage when I came down to get in my car, and then when I came back down after I checked my calendar, he was there. Then he was right behind me on the freeway ten or twelve miles from the building. He's following me, for Christ's sake!"

Bill knew that his wife was not given either to panic or flights of fancy. There was a real chance that she was in some jeopardy. "Okay, okay," he said. "Calm down. I'm just transitioning from the Harbor to the San Diego. I'll be there in a couple of minutes. Don't go home. Just drive in very large squares, say five or six blocks at a time. And don't speed. You can go through lights and stop signs if it's safe."

"He's here! He's behind me again, Bill." She saw headlights in her mirror that looked like they could be the same car. Still, she was not quite sure.

Bill, already cruising at eighty in his Corvette, punched the accelerator and took it up to ninety-five. "Okay, okay. It's all right. Has he done anything other than follow you?"

"What do you mean? No, not really."

"Has he said anything to you?"

"No."

"What's he look like?"

"I don't know. I haven't seen him." She glided through a red light. The other car—it was definitely blue, and old and beat-up—stopped at the light. "He didn't go through the light. But he's staying with me."

"How far back?"

"I don't know," she snapped impatiently. "Maybe a half a block, now. The light just changed."

"Just stop and see what happens."

"What? Are you nuts?"

"No, Amy. Really. Just stop and see what he does." He decided not to tell her that if the guy had wanted to hurt her, he would have already done it by now.

She slowed from the forty-five she had been doing to less than ten. The other car turned off onto a side street. "He's gone," she said. "I slowed down to nothing and he turned off."

"Maybe it wasn't the same car."

"Maybe."

"And maybe you weren't followed at all."

"Hell, Bill. I don't know."

"Look, I'm getting off the freeway now. Don't go home. Just go down to Sepulveda, then turn right and head up to Marine. Take another right on Aviation and just go in that circle until I catch up with you."

"Okay. I'm sorry about this, honey."

"It's okay, sweetheart. But I don't think I'm going to call in any backup just yet. Let's just stay on the line to be sure."

She did as he had instructed, driving right at the speed limit. It was now nearly midnight and the streets were almost empty, except for the part of the loop she was driving that ran along Sepulveda Boulevard, a main artery through the beach communities. She and Bill chatted about nothing, just to keep the connection open. She did not see the blue car again.

"Okay," Bill said finally. "I'm coming up Sepulveda now. When you get to Sepulveda this time, go straight toward home and I'll turn left and fall in behind you."

He reached the intersection first, but the left-turn lane had a red arrow. The traffic headed west on Manhattan Beach—where Amy would be—had the light. She waved to him and said hello over the phone as she went through the intersection. Just as he waved back, he spotted the pursuer two cars behind her. He noted that it was a somewhat battered 1976 Chevrolet Caprice with California plates. He recorded the number mentally. Behind the wheel was a black male, approximately thirty, wearing sunglasses. Vaguely he wondered if she really was being followed and, if so, whether it could possibly have anything to do with his investigation of gunrunning in the East L.A. gangs. As the old wreck of a car passed through the intersection, he noticed that it had a telephone antenna on the rear window. His suspicions aroused, he checked the cross traffic and ran the light. He held his position three cars behind the Chevy and followed him.

Into the phone, he said, "Okay, Amy. I think I've spotted your man. But don't worry. I'm right behind him. Just keep going down all the way to Highland, then turn left down the beach. I want to get a good look at this guy."

Amy was not nearly as upset now, with Bill behind her. She could not see the blue car in her mirror since there was another vehicle, a truck, between them. She did as Bill had instructed and got into the left-turn lane at Highland Avenue. The truck kept going straight so she had a clear view of the blue car. It slowed to a crawl, as if the driver were reluctant to get too close. There was at least one car behind it but she could not see if it was Bill. She got the green arrow and turned. The blue car reacted slowly, just beating the light. The car right behind it didn't make it, though, nor did either the one behind that or Bill. In her rearview mirror, Amy saw that only the blue car was now following her.

"Bill?" she said into the phone. There was silence. She had entered a dead zone in the cellular grid and lost her connection. Suddenly she felt alone and frightened. Still, the blue car kept a fair distance behind her. She kept at the speed limit and the blue car did the same, trailing her by about a long half-block. When she stopped at a red light, it did the same, maintaining the same distance. Then, suddenly, it turned off and was gone. Her phone rang.

"Bill?" she answered.

"Yeah. What's happening, Amy?"

"I'm not sure. I started down Highland and when it turned into Hermosa, he turned off again."

"Which way?"

"Left, I think. Onto Longfellow. Or maybe one of those other little streets."

"I think you're right. I think he's gone. Do a U-turn and come on back up here. I'll meet you and we'll drive up to the house together."

"Okay." She was suddenly exhausted beyond all description, as she whipped the BMW around its tight little turning radius, right in the middle of Hermosa Beach's main drag, and headed back up the street toward home.

Meanwhile, Bill also made a U-turn and pulled over to the right-hand curb on Highland to wait for Amy. Suddenly, up ahead, about a block away, the Chevy came out onto Highland and headed north, away from him. He threw the Corvette into gear and closed on the old car rapidly. A moment later, the driver must have spotted him, since the Chevy suddenly lurched forward and started to accelerate rapidly. But even on its best day, a day long since gone, the Caprice had never been a match for the muscle of Detroit's only true sports car. Bill raced along the narrow, deserted stretch of Highland Avenue, rapidly closing on the clumsy Chevy. Anticipating the inevitable conclusion of a footrace with the Corvette, the Chevy suddenly veered to the left, then shot off to the right, into one of the scores of tiny residential side streets that crisscross the South Bay. Here, space was scarce, with less than two feet of clearance on either side of the big, old car as it careened between two lines of parked cars. Bill spun the wheel as he downshifted into the turn to follow, then rocketed down the narrow, dimly lit street in pursuit. The large taillights of the Chevy were clearly visible up ahead as he once again began to close the distance.

But the other driver was good. He turned again, this time, impossibly, into an even narrower backstreet. The clearance diminished to nothing but, incredibly, he avoided contact with any of the dozens of vehicles parked in tight along either side of the street. Again, Bill followed, though his speed suffered from the sheer risk of a collision. The Chevy, traveling upward of sixty on a street designed for less than ten miles an hour, was beginning to pull away now. Quickly, Bill ran through his options as he mentally reviewed the map of the area. This part of the city was laced with tiny cul-de-sacs such that the slightest miscalculation could lead either of them into a blind alley that, one way or the other, would end the pursuit. He thought about calling for police backup, either from the LAPD or, more properly, from the Manhattan Beach Police, but dismissed it, since the guy had really done nothing to this point other than speed. Besides, he didn't want the hassle of interagency paperwork if he could get a good look at this guy without it.

Losing ground rapidly, Bill decided to gamble. He broke off the pursuit and turned off onto a short, narrow lane. At the end, he whipped out onto Valley, a superhighway compared to the tiny walk streets he'd just been on. He revved the 'Vette and reached seventy miles an hour before he rapidly downshifted, standing it on its nose to make a sharp right onto yet another backstreet. In a moment, he emerged onto Poinsettia and, precisely as he'd hoped, just down the block was the Chevy. He shut off his lights and waited at the nearly blind intersection. The driver did not expect him and surely did not see him as he came up Poinsettia. Suddenly Bill, counting more on the other driver's skill than was really prudent, whipped out into Poinsettia and pulled right alongside the Chevy. He got a great look at the man's startled face, wide-open mouth and all, as he drove abreast of him in the opposite lane through the widest stretch of Poinsettia. Up ahead, Bill knew, the street would curve and narrow sharply, right where an old warehouse sat so close to the road that it would have violated the code had it not been built in the early forties. As they rounded the bend and bore down on the warehouse, Bill gambled and pulled slightly ahead of the Chevy, then veered toward it. The other driver's reflexive response to avoid a collision forced him to screech to a full stop, just inches separating his car from Bill's on the left and from the old brick warehouse on the right.

Bill was out of the car in a flash, his service thirty-eight-caliber revolver drawn and ready. "Out of the car with your hands up!" he commanded. "This is LAPD."

He had no spotlight on his car and the dimness of the light along this stretch of the street made it difficult to see the man clearly, much less make out his features. Slowly the man opened the door and climbed out of the car. One of his hands was partially up, the other down.

"Hands up, I said!" Bill shouted, as the man came free of the huge Chevy car door.

"All right, man. All right. Why are you hassling me, anyway? Gonna beat me up? I don't have no video camera."

"Save it, punk. You were speeding, driving recklessly, endangering others." He moved forward, carefully, his revolver held tightly in both hands in front of him. Still, the man's right hand was not up.

"I said raise your hands!" shouted Bill, knowing full well that he could do nothing if the man failed to comply, since he had not brought in backup. He could fire only if he perceived a genuine lethal threat—

Suddenly, the man jerked up his right hand and, without taking aim, fired a handgun of some sort at Bill. Instantly, almost before he heard the strange popping sound, Bill felt a powerful impact to his chest and, oddly, a second to his thigh. Then, the realization hit him that he had been hit with a monstrous electric shock, from a taser gun of some sort, that sent him into furious convulsions. He had no control of his arms, legs, or, for that matter, any muscular function as he writhed on the pavement. He was so overwhelmed with the pain caused by the charge, he did not even see the other man get back into the car and drive away. Eventually, he stopped twitching and lay there motionless in the quiet of the street.

A good fifteen minutes passed as he phased in and out of consciousness from the high voltage ordeal. His mind cleared before his body was ready to try standing. He reached for the dart in his chest but could not find it. Neither could he find the dart that he had felt hit his leg. Slowly he opened his jacket and his shirt and, with considerable effort, looked down to survey the damage caused by the dart. Incredibly, there was nothing there but a round purple mark, already fading to reddish pink around the edges, of about an inch and a half in diameter. There was no dart and there did not appear to be a puncture of the type that Bill knew was characteristic of the standard taser. Looking around at the pavement he saw neither darts nor the wires that connect the darts to the battery pack.

Finally, he struggled to his feet, just as a man in his bathrobe and slippers approached. "What's going on?" he asked suspiciously.

Still very unstable in all his joints, Bill realized he must have appeared drunk to the man. "Detective William Quinn, Los Angeles Police Department," he explained, pulling his shield from his breast pocket. "Everything's all right here, sir. I was investigating a crime here."

"Investigating?" the man said, moving closer. "Looks like you were victiming a crime."

Bill managed to laugh. "I guess you could say that."

"You need to call someone?"

"No, thanks," Bill replied. "I'll call from the car."

The man eyed the Corvette suspiciously. "Nice police cruiser," he said. "What happened to all the budget cuts?"

Bill grimaced and thanked the man for his concern. Then he fell heavily into the driver's seat of his car and placed a call to Amy, then one to the station to run a check on the license number.

CHAPTER 17

LANG ATE UP GREAT STRETCHES OF THE CORRIDOR
with an exaggerated stride as he made his way through the terminal
of Houston's Intercontinental Airport. It was late. The flight had
been delayed nearly two and a half hours on the ground in Los
Angeles and he still had to drive down to the industrial town of
Freeport on the gulf in time for Lindstrom's deposition, set for 9:30
the next morning. Naturally, he beat his luggage to the baggage
claim and sat down to program his cellular phone to roam.

He was not looking forward to the call he needed to make.
Laura Carey had been a good friend since law school and they
remained close. In fact, after his divorce, he had begun to call her on
a regular basis. But the pairing had been a classic of miscommunication: He had thought he wanted a serious relationship while she had
looked on him as a good and worthy friend needing a boost out of
an emotional trough. It was a tribute to Laura that she had straightened the situation out between them without damage to their underlying friendship. All the more reason he now dreaded telling her
that events had conspired to cheat them out of a few hours together

while he was in Houston. He was sure that she would not be content with a rain check.

"This is Laura Carey," Laura's melodic Southern accent sang into his ear. Her voice had always had the ring of fine crystal to Lang. He smiled involuntarily.

"Laurie darlin'," he drawled back.

"Christopher Lang! At last!" she said, bubbling instantly. "Where have you been? It's nearly five o'clock."

"Well, we were late out of L.A."

"You're here now, aren't you?" she asked suspiciously.

"I'm here, all right, at Intercontinental. Waiting for my luggage."

"Luggage? Chris, don't you know by now not to check anything—"

Lang laughed. "I know, I know. I had to bring a lot of documents with me and it was easier to check my suitcase—"

"So what time you coming over?"

"Well, that's what I want to talk to you about. I can't. I have to get down to Freeport tonight, because the depo is at nine-thirty in the morning. I had thought I could catch an earlier plane out of LAX but—"

"Wait. You mean to tell me, darlin', that you're sittin' at the airport here in town and you're going to be driving right by my place on your way down to the gulf and you're not even going to stop by and see me?"

Her tone was unquestionably hurt, and maybe a little bit angry. He checked his watch just as the red light on the giant luggage carousel flashed and the conveyor began to turn. Over the whooping of the siren, he said, "Look, Laura. I'm sorry, honey."

"Hold on," she said, covering the mouthpiece. Lang could hear the muffled noises of a conversation being carried on in her office. After a moment, she came back on the line. "Okay. Here's the deal. Did you bring your workout clothes?"

"Huh?"

"You brought your workout clothes, didn't you, sweetie?"

"Well, yeah, as a matter of fact I did."

"Good. There's no way I can get through the god-awful northbound 59 traffic to pick you up, so you go outside and grab a cab. That'll get you here by six or six-thirty. I'll reserve a court at the club for seven. You still play racquetball, don't you?"

"Look, Laura. You're not listening."

"Do you or don't you, Chris? 'Cause I plan to kick your butt."

"Of course I still—"

"Good. Afterward, you can take me to dinner at Zapata. It's new and it's *great*. Then, if you're good and if you've played well, but not quite well enough to win, and if you've bought me a really great, very expensive Tex-Mex right-side-of-the-menu dinner, you can spend the night here."

Lang was becoming exasperated. "Laurie, you're not—"

"*You're* not listening, darlin'. I got this thing all figured out. You were going to rent a car from Intercontinental, then drive down to Freeport tonight, right?"

"Right."

"Because it's a two-hour drive, right?"

"Right."

"And that means you're already completely prepared for the deposition and you don't have any more work to do before it starts, right?"

"Right."

"So if I can get you a ride on a private plane that'll put you in Freeport no later than eight-forty-five tomorrow morning, you got no problem, right?"

Lang smiled. "Right."

"Well, what are you waiting for? Grab your suitcase and get your butt in a cab, sweet cakes. I'll be home and dressed when you get there. Bye."

"Bye," he answered, as she clicked off. He laughed aloud and headed for the baggage carousel.

From the rear seat of AlphaMedics Corporation's Mooney MSE, Lang quietly watched the Gulf of Mexico grow larger on the far horizon. The pilot, Joe Bill Atkins, had settled into silence behind the mirrored lenses of his aviator's sunglasses a few minutes out of Houston's Hobby Airport and hadn't said a word since. Forty minutes later they were approaching a small private airstrip in the flatlands south of Lake Jackson. Lang checked his watch: 6:27 in the morning. Of course, that was Pacific time, since he never reset his watch on these quick jaunts into hostile time zones. That meant he had just over an hour before the deposition would start in the boardroom of Bloomington-Gate Chemical, on the water in Freeport.

Lang couldn't help smiling at the whirlwind twelve hours he had just spent with the incomparable Laura Carey. Their evening had gone precisely as she had planned. At 6:23 his cab had dropped him at the gate of her condo where Laura, already in her eye-popping spandex racquetball togs, had met him in her Ferrari—her gift from her father, "Judge" Carey, who had never sat on the bench, to ease the pain of her last birthday—and they stepped onto the court at the club at 6:59. One hour and one minute later, they headed for her place to shower for dinner to celebrate her 15–12, 14–16, 15–10 victory. Dinner at the new and predictably trendy Zapata had been all she had said, spectacularly opulent Tex-Mex cuisine that was exquisitely prepared and delicious. The crowd, Lang noted, could only be called Tex-Mex chic and the platinum-headed lawyer on his arm fit in perfectly.

They had talked straight through dinner, with Lang's principal contributions seldom exceeding the very occasional "Uh-huh" or "Right" or "And?" Yet, as always, he had enjoyed himself immensely with this irresistibly charming and fiercely intelligent woman. She was fascinated with the Lindstrom case, which she illustrated by talking about it more than Lang did. He was amazed at how little information she required to grasp the key issues.

"That is one son of a bitch rattler in the tall grass, Christopher. Stay the hell clear of his dangerous black-hearted self. He's a fraud and a dangerous one at that. He knew goddamned good and well that plane wouldn't fly and he tried to pull a fast one."

"Well, I think so, but so far the evidence just isn't there."

"Of course it's not. Who do you think you're dealing with? Businessmen and politicians, especially the ones down here, are a breed apart, my friend. I know what I'm talking about. My daddy and my daddy's daddy are old hands at this business, cut from that Sam Rayburn, Lyndon Johnson bolt of cloth and, hell, Oklahoma's just Texas-Lite anyway. My Lord, Chris, these are the guys who killed Kennedy, for God's sake."

"So you think he really could have managed to purge his name from all those records?"

"Purge? No, I don't think purge. I think he knew right from the get-go to keep his name out of the project. Whole thing was probably a cover for something illegal."

Lang laughed. "That would probably be the assessment of my star witness. She apparently thinks the aircraft was intended for covert military applications. But, then again, she's got a shadowy past of her own in the dark recesses of Irish politics."

"Doesn't sound too crazy to me."

Lang shook his head and looked at Laura through his half-empty bottle of beer. "Nah, I don't think much of Lindstrom but I have a hard time buying the argument that the man is a criminal, or a traitor. At worst, he probably cut some corners and tried to hide his tracks. Just like most business clients. I believe his political aspirations came later."

Laura smiled and shook her head. "You know, Chris, for all your success, you're really not that different from the clueless bumpkin who sat down next to me in Henderson's contracts class that first day, are you? Haven't those years in the L.A. shark tank taught you anything, darlin'?"

He laughed. "You're a real cynic, Laura."

"Could be. But I'm just about always right. And I'm right about this guy. Don't take a word he says for truth tomorrow. And watch your back."

"My back? God, you're melodramatic when you're drunk."

She shook her head. "And a blind dog ain't worth snot on a hunt, sweet cakes. Don't you realize what's at stake for him? He's spent his whole life building for a run at the biggest brass ring there is and suddenly along comes Mr. Strait Laces with a briefcase full of trouble. Fraud? Don't you realize what that charge can do to his whole freaking plan if you can make it stick?"

Lang said nothing but took a long swig from his Corona.

"Look at it this way. Just imagine you're an intruder in his home, late at night, where his wife and kids are sleeping. And he's got a gun in the nightstand drawer. That's who he is and that's who he thinks you are."

He laughed again and shook his head. "You're really something."

"And *you* better be careful," she said, suddenly chillingly sober.

At the little airstrip, there was a car ready to take him to the chemical plant, just as Laura had promised. At 9:03 he reached the main gate of the Bloomington-Gate Chemical Corporation. In a dingy Gulf Coast industrial town of oil-stained corrugated metal buildings and rusty cyclone fencing, where the smell of sulfur and crude oil competed for attention, the Bloomington-Gate factory looked as if it had just been built. The glossy two-tone green concrete-block main building rose stolidly above the rust and grease of Freeport like a freshly iced cake of stupendous proportion. Along with its two nearly identical companion buildings, it sat in the midst of a lush green park of a campus that was alive with the first flowers of spring in southeast Texas.

A uniformed security guard who was more a Marine than a

rent-a-cop met Lang's car and telephoned ahead to confirm his appointment. "You may go right in, Mr. Lang," the polite and handsome young man said to Lang. To the driver, he cautioned, "Please stay on Campus Drive, sir, and follow the signs to the Administration Building. You'll see it on the left, about a quarter of a mile inside. Please do not leave the main drive. Your clearances are only good to the Administration Building and expire at seventeen hundred hours."

Lang's driver, a good old boy from Lubbock, rolled his eyes and saluted the guard. "Well, shee-it, Mr. Lang," he said to Lang as he drove away from the kiosk. "I guess we musta stumbled onto Quantico or some shit."

Lang laughed, though he found the snap and sparkle of the place impressive. Along the winding drive lined with small fledgling elm trees, all neatly trimmed and shaped, they passed at least a half dozen landscaping crews. If it seemed like wasteful excess, Lang knew from his research that the company was supremely profitable, had an exemplary ecological record during Lindstrom's four years of ownership, and was the darling of the market analysts. Whatever you might think of the guy, Lang mused, there was no denying Lindstrom's Midas touch with the companies he bought.

Finally, Lang was deposited in front of the Administration Building, a simple but extremely well-maintained office building of four stories, surrounded by small orchards, hedge-lined paths, and flower gardens. Inside, he was met at a reception desk by a smiling young woman whose badge identified her as Tara Braden.

"Good morning, Mr. Lang," she said, a cool efficiency right behind her smile. "Welcome to the Bloomington-Gate Chemical Corporation. I'm Tara. If you would please sign the register, I'll issue you a visitor's pass and let Mr. Hickman know you're here."

Lang thanked her and signed the register. When he was done, she handed him a clear acrylic badge, into which a machine of some sort had carved "Christopher S. Lang, Devereaux and Brace." He had never seen anything like it. "Just clip this to your lapel or your breast pocket. You'll need to wear it where it can be seen at all times when you are in the building. The slot on the side is for the access ports you will find on the doors. It's programmed to give you access to all the places where you are permitted to go, which include—" She looked down to check the computer screen in front of her. "Well, actually, I'm afraid it's limited to the men's room." She added apologetically, "It's a minimum-clearance pass."

"At least it'll get me into all the best places," he said, with only a slight hint of sarcasm.

She smiled, apparently unsure of the protocol for an attempt at humor by a visitor, then picked up a phone. "Mr. Lang to see Mr. Hickman," she said. To Lang, she said, "Please have a seat. Mr. Hickman will be right with you."

A treat, to be sure, thought Lang, as he found a place on the large, contemporary couch. In a moment Gentry Hickman appeared at the top of the stairway. Looking down over the banister he called out, "Chris? Hello. How are you?" His tone was cordial, almost cheery, a far cry from the darkly threatening exchange that had ended their only previous meeting, out in San Sebastian.

"Mr. Hickman," Lang replied coolly as he rose from the couch and hefted his bulky litigation bag.

"We're upstairs today, Chris," continued Hickman, very much the host here on home turf. "In the boardroom." He moved to the edge of the stairs to meet Lang coming up. He extended a hand and shook firmly. "It's kind of an odd arrangement," he said, gesturing to an elevator door on the far wall, at the other end of a small mezzanine area. "Crazy way the building was designed way back when. The elevator only goes to the second floor." He pushed the button and the door slid open. Inside, he pushed the button labeled Boardroom.

"Good trip down?" Hickman asked.

"Fine," said Lang, his game-face very much in place for the pending encounter.

As the elevator door opened into a lobby area much like the one on the second floor, Hickman said, "Mr. Lindstrom isn't here just yet."

Lang checked his watch. It was 9:31.

Hickman laughed. "Now, you're not going to get technical on me, are you, Chris? He's a busy man and he'll be here. You can wait in the boardroom."

The practical, almost spartan personality of the physical plant he had seen so far was left at the double doors to the boardroom. A huge onyx-topped table dominated the vast room, which seemed to occupy close to half of the top floor of the building. Nearly three dozen enormous high-backed plush leather chairs mounted on smooth, quiet casters surrounded the oval-shaped table. Massive flower arrangements sat on each of the many sideboards and cabinets that ringed the room's perimeter. Three of the four walls were entirely of glass, affording a breathtaking view of the Gulf of Mexico which, at this hour, sparkled and glittered in the morning sun. Sound was effectively deadened by a luxurious gray-and-green plush carpet. Two of the sideboards were piled high with an extensive assortment of muffins, rolls, croissants, bagels, and sweet rolls. Huge silver coffee urns stood ready to serve.

"Expecting a large crowd?" asked Lang.

"Not really. Just the two of us and the stenographer."

"And the witness."

"And the witness," Hickman repeated, nodding. "And the house counsel for Arrow Dynamics. And one of my associates. And a reporter from the *Wall Street Journal*."

"Excuse me?" Lang asked dubiously.

"Sarah Layton of the *Journal*. Just to be sure our side of the story gets told accurately."

"This is a deposition in a lawsuit, Mr. Hickman, not a campaign appearance."

"You'd be surprised, Chris," Hickman replied with an easy laugh.

"In any event, we will exercise our right under the federal rules to limit attendance. You, your colleague, house counsel, and the witness."

"And the stenographer."

"And the stenographer," repeated Lang. He liked this man less as each minute passed and he was reasonably sure it wasn't lost on Hickman.

Two other men appeared in the doorway of the room. Hickman greeted them. "Hello, fellows. Christopher Lang, this is J. D. Royster, general counsel for Arrow Dynamics. And this is Randy Overbrook of my office."

The men exchanged perfunctory handshakes. Royster, a dour-looking man of about fifty, eyed Lang with open hostility. Overbrook, tall and handsome, and perhaps half Royster's age, was poised and confident, a very sure young warrior.

"Overbrook, huh?" Lang asked. "Any relation to Carlton Overbrook?"

Overbrook smiled easily. "You mean of *Trial by Ordeal* fame? Yeah, you could say that. He's my daddy."

"That's quite a famous father you have, Mr. Overbrook," said Lang, trying hard to calculate the odds that the son of a man whose work he held in such high regard would just happen to be on the other side.

"So they tell me, Mr. Lang."

Hickman broke in. "And his old man's got nothin' on him, as I'm sure you'll see. And, Chris," he added, with a penetrating look at Lang. "He knows every word of that book better than you do."

Lang managed to mask his surprise at Hickman's familiarity with his peculiar fondness for Overbrook's work. Quickly he ran through the possibilities of how that might be but came up blank. Overbrook laughed, timing it so that it was unclear whether it was intended as a response to Hickman's reference to him or a commentary on his dig at Lang. He was a very cool individual, thought Lang, a strong second chair for the flamboyant Hickman. They just may have us in the confidence department, he conceded. Of course, "overconfidence goeth before the reversal on appeal," he reflected, quoting from *Trial by Ordeal*. Meanwhile, he realized that Royster had never stopped glowering at him.

Outside in the lobby, the elevator door opened and two women emerged. The first, a pretty brunette in her late thirties wearing a floral dress and wheeling a bulky computerized stenographic machine on a small dolly, was obviously the court reporter. The other, tall and slightly ungainly in a navy suit, patent-leather flats, and tortoiseshell glasses, carried a rich leather attaché in one hand and had a suede pouch slung over the opposite shoulder. Hickman moved to greet them.

To the stenographer, he said simply, "Go ahead in, darlin', and set up. We'll be ready to go in a jiffy." To the other one, he was more effusive. "Sarah, dear! How are you?" He embraced the woman, a gesture that caused her to stiffen uncomfortably and underscore her awkwardness.

"Gentry," she managed to reply.

Quickly, Hickman went on, "We have a problem here. Mr. Lang, over there, is not going to let the *Wall Street Journal* sit in on the deposition, I'm afraid."

Sarah Layton looked around Hickman to find Lang. "Mr. Lang?"

"It's all right, Sarah," Hickman interjected, putting a hand on the woman's shoulder and turning her gently toward the door. "He's got his rights and we'll have to play along. Mr. Lindstrom and I will cover this business at the press conference outside this afternoon. And you'll get first crack, we promise."

The indignant reporter glared purposefully at Lang, then turned slowly and retreated from the room. Just as Lang began to grasp the likelihood that the whole thing had been staged, since it was inconceivable that Hickman could have expected him to allow a reporter to sit in, the entire room, the entire building, began to vibrate violently. The furniture began to creak and move and the three massive chandeliers over the conference table began to pitch back and forth, tinkling and rattling with increasing intensity. Lang noticed the windows bowing and felt a great sense of pressure. The floor beneath him vibrated with tremendous force. As the blood drained from his face, he contemplated a dive under the great stone table as a leap to safety.

"Ah," said Hickman above the noise. "That would be *Eaglet One,* Mr. Lindstrom's helicopter, landing on our roof." Lang looked hurriedly around to see if anyone had noticed his moment's panic. Hickman, Overbrook, the court reporter, and Royster were all staring at him. And they were all smiling, even Royster.

"You must excuse our friend, Darla," Hickman said to the court reporter. "He's from California."

CHAPTER 18

FULLY COMPOSED, LANG SAT DOWN NEAR THE END OF the huge conference table and spread his papers before him, patiently awaiting the arrival of Russell Lindstrom. The vibrations of the rooftop landing had long since disappeared and it was, by Lang's watch, 10:27, local time. Hickman and his client were certainly making the most of their home-field advantage, he thought ruefully.

Hickman, Overbrook, and Royster had gone across the hall, into another room, immediately after the helicopter arrived. He hadn't seen them since. Lang wondered how much more of this psychological warfare he should tolerate. His options were limited. The standard response to this type of behavior was to make your own statement, on the record, of the particulars of the deposition notice, the time, and the failure of the deponent to show up, and then to terminate the proceedings. This would set the stage for a motion. The judge's attitude at the discovery hearing, however, particularly his deference to Lindstrom's schedule, militated strongly against this line of attack. At a minimum, it would delay the deposition for months and just as likely would necessitate another long-distance trip to some presidential-primary campaign outpost. His other possible alternative, one not normally available, would be to call the judge in his chambers—if, as threatened, he was standing by—and get a ruling on the spot. However, since the judge's threat had been clearly intended to protect Lindstrom from Lang and not vice versa, it was something he would consider only if the delay became truly abusive. He concluded that the prudent course was to wait.

Hickman appeared out of the doorway across the hall. For a moment he seemed surprised that Lang was still there. "Oh," he said, stopping briefly. "Sorry, Chris. We should be ready to go in just a few minutes." He pushed the elevator button.

"Where's the witness?" asked Lang, a definite edge to his tone.

"Be patient, Mr. Lang," replied Hickman, a little testy himself. "He's got a lot of things to take care of and he'll be right up here." With that, he stepped into the open elevator and disappeared.

Somehow, Lang realized, Lindstrom had gotten downstairs from the roof without passing the boardroom. It was 10:47. Repacking and locking his litigation bag so as not to test the ethics of his adversaries, he took the next elevator downstairs.

Outside in a large, tree-shaded patio area just to the right of the front door, Lang saw, and heard, a fairly large knot of people standing around in a loose semicircle. In the center was the tall, stately, silver-haired figure of Russell Lindstrom. To Lang's surprise and amazement, he was holding a press conference! Feeling a hot surge of anger, Lang headed outside to hear what was going on.

". . . plants and factories of this kind. Well, it's the same principle in running a great and asset-rich country like ours, Ray. Yes, many have spoken about it, but I'm the only one who has the experience of having done it." Lindstrom seemed to notice Lang approaching the outer ring of the gathering. He paused for a moment to watch him, then turned his attention back to the crowd around him. "One final question, ladies and gentlemen. I've got important legal business to attend to. Yes? Go ahead, Monica."

Lang recognized NBC's Monica Dallis, the attractive, brutally incisive political field reporter who had made her reputation on a Medicare scandal in Atlanta standing near the front, just outside a ring of large men in dark glasses whom Lang figured for Secret Service. "Mr. Lindstrom," she said in a strong, clear voice. "For years it has been fashionable to champion so-called tort reform, the movement to limit claims that people can make in lawsuits and to restrict lawyers' fees. I haven't heard you take a position on this latter-day Republican saw. Do you have such a position?"

"How's that for timing?" replied Lindstrom, making an effort to look directly at Lang. "Honestly, Chris, I didn't put her up to it." Lang could feel a hot blush spread across his cheeks. He wanted to reply, to slap at Lindstrom with one of a dozen nasty barbs that came to mind, but sensed that there would be no winning such a confrontation, here, in Lindstrom's own arena. In the meantime, every head in the crowd turned toward Lang and several reporters standing near him began to pepper him with questions.

"Come on, folks," Lindstrom called out. "Leave the man alone. He's only doing his job." He smiled at the discomfort that he had created for Lang. Meanwhile, Lang ignored the barrage.

"To answer your question, Monica, I have had the opportunity to experience the inconvenience and expense of unjustified litigation firsthand. You see, after I leave you here today, I'm going to be shut away in a room with a hostile lawyer—at least, a lawyer whose interests are hostile to mine—and he's going to ask me hours of questions about a legal situation I know virtually nothing about and which I did absolutely nothing to cause. Then, I'm going to get a huge bill for legal services from my lawyer for sitting in the room and making sure I'm not taken advantage of. Then, I'm going to have to have my lawyer go into court and maybe sit through a month-long trial, just so I can establish that I had nothing to do with the deal and that the plaintiff has no claim against me or, for that matter, anyone else."

As Lindstrom went on, eloquently extemporizing an answer that, at least for once, was not one he had given before, Lang stood still and quiet, ears burning and face glowing red in the late-morning sun of the Gulf Coast. Lang heard the voices all around him, but succeeded in blocking out most of the words, trying to ignore the collage of faces crowding into his field of vision. Up front, Lindstrom, a gifted and provocative speaker, continued in a profoundly thoughtful denunciation of the civil legal system in general and the claims against him in particular.

When at last he finished his answer, he addressed Lang directly. "No questions from you, Counselor?"

"Mine will have to be answered under oath, Mr. Lindstrom," replied Lang in a strong voice that effectively masked his seething anger. "Inside, away from this circus."

Lindstrom smiled as he held up his hands and shrugged to the somewhat baffled reporters around him. "See what I'm up against?" he said with a rueful smile. The comment drew a light ripple of laughter.

"I have a court order that requires you to sit for a deposition that was scheduled to start nearly two hours ago, Mr. Lindstrom," said Lang. "May we begin now?"

Lindstrom shook his head in mock disgust, his smile still very much in place. "You have no perspective, Mr. Lang. Unfortunately, it's a trait you share with the majority of your profession." To the reporters, he added, "All right. That's it for now. Mustn't slow the wheels of justice. Gina has some handouts for you and, please, just help yourselves to the refreshments." As he walked through the crowd toward the main door, he added over his shoulder, "I'll holler if I need help with this legal lion."

As Lindstrom strode past him toward the building, Lang noticed Monica Dallis coming in his direction. "So you're the high-priced lawyer who's got Russell Lindstrom on the run?" she asked as she reached him.

"I really have nothing to say to the press, Ms. Dallis," he replied. Then, as if to soften the harshness of his words, he added, "I have nothing against journalists. It's just that I have a lawsuit against the man right now. And I don't litigate in the papers."

"I'm on television," she replied coolly.

Despite the growing frustration of the day, Lang smiled. "Nor on television."

"There must be quite a bit you know about the candidate, Mr. Lang. In ways the rest of us don't."

Lang smiled again. "No comment," he replied, turning to follow Lindstrom. The reporter kept her eyes on him until he disappeared into the building.

Lang had always likened building a case through the discovery process, the part involving interrogatories and depositions into the other side's case, to mining diamonds: The process is difficult, time-consuming, and produces only an occasional item of value. "Mountains of dirt," he had once told a temporarily discouraged client, "to secure each tiny gem. But, when you see them at trial, meticulously cut, highly polished, and painstakingly displayed in a jeweler's case lined with black velvet, I promise you that their brilliance will take your breath away."

Now, he wasn't so sure. Lindstrom was a very good witness. Smart and precise. Either very well-prepared or frighteningly bright, or both. Unlike most smart witnesses, he avoided the temptation to try to outthink the lawyer. He listened carefully to each question, gave his own attorney ample opportunity to make an objection, then answered most times with surgical precision. On other occasions, where it was to his advantage, he replied expansively, seldom missing an opportunity to spin the facts his way. Still, he neither replied so quickly that his answers sounded pat nor so slowly that he appeared to be lying. More than once Lang found himself wishing he had clients that were this good.

Not that the deposition had been without conflict. Right from the outset—if 11:51 could be considered the outset of a deposition scheduled to start at 9:30—there had been a dispute. Lindstrom and his three lawyers had been accompanied into the conference room by two hulking men in dark glasses. After Lang objected, Hickman explained that they were agents of the Secret Service assigned by the secretary of the treasury under federal law to protect the person of Mr. Lindstrom as a candidate for president of the United States and their presence was necessary for purposes of national security.

"It's all right, Gentry," Lindstrom had interjected in his most appealing, statesmanlike tone. "I think I'm pretty safe in here. And I doubt that Mr. Lang has a weapon under his suit jacket, though I understand he's a crack shot with a paint-pellet gun. I think we can dispense with the federal officers."

"But Russell," Hickman had protested, while a troubled Lang pondered once more just how much these guys knew about him.

Lindstrom's direct stare bore in on Lang, increasing his discomfort. He had the ability to disarm with the directness of his eyes. "If you feel strongly about the point, Chris, we can send them home."

Lang quickly calculated that there was nothing to be gained by pressing the issue. Better to fight about things that mattered. "It's okay," he said. "They can stay. But I'd appreciate their sitting back away from the table."

"We can do a little better than that, Chris," Lindstrom said in his deep, resonant baritone. "Leon, why don't you go on downstairs and get some good Gulf Coast fresh air. And Matt, you go ahead and sit right outside the door. Keep the bad guys out. Okay, gentlemen?"

Lang had then proceeded to pull out the long, obligatory biographical data, important to Lang in this case since he hoped at some point to find an opportunity to turn Lindstrom's considerable aviation and aerodynamics expertise against him. But the effort was not without cost; Lindstrom was afforded a splendid opportunity to gild his own accomplishments, which he utilized fully. It was during the wrap-up of the biographical information that the first controversy over substance arose.

"Now, Mr. Lindstrom, what types of projects did you personally work on at that Van Nuys facility?" Lang had asked.

Lindstrom turned to Hickman who, taking his cue like a good guard dog, had sat up in his chair and responded. "I'm going to object to that question, Mr. Lang. It calls for privileged information that belongs to the United States government. Sensitive information that the witness cannot disclose."

Lang was disgusted with the tactic and took no pains to hide it. "We're talking about projects that he worked on in the fifties and sixties, Mr. Hickman. Surely any security issues are long since moot."

It was Lindstrom who replied. "Actually, that's not true, Chris. Several of those projects involved technologies still very much under the National Security Act. I wish I *could* tell you about them. You'd be fascinated and amazed, I'm sure. But I'd never get clearance from the authorities. Perhaps if you come to work in the federal government one day—I'm sure you could afford to put your salary on hold for a while to give your country the benefit of your talents—if you were to get the proper clearance, I might get such an opportunity."

"At any rate," Hickman said, looking at his watch, "the objection stands. Let's move along, Counsel."

"Well, I'm not persuaded. I'd like the court reporter to note the question for a later motion."

Hickman waved his hand disgustedly. "Fine. Note it and move on."

"When did you first meet Nigel Daultry?" Lang asked, hoping that the abrupt change in subjects might throw Lindstrom off-stride. There was no indication that it did.

"I met Mr. Daultry for the first—and only—time at the end of 1990," replied Lindstrom in the same even-handed tone that had marked the entire session thus far.

"How did you meet?"

"He landed an airplane on my property in San Sebastian."

"So he just landed in your backyard, alone and uninvited?" Lang's tone was intentionally caustic.

"That's how I recall it," Lindstrom replied easily.

"No preliminary conversation of any kind?" Lang goaded him.

Unruffled, Lindstrom laughed his easy press-conference *Night-*

line laugh. "Wacky as it sounds, that's pretty much the way it happened. He said he wanted to talk to me about an idea. He was very intense, very passionate about it. Great men usually are. It was obviously something he'd thought about a great deal. And he had a very appealing plan and strategy. Simple and direct. You know, the simplest ideas are usually the best, Chris."

Lang successfully suppressed a smile. Lindstrom clearly had no idea what Molly O'Keefe had already told Seamus Callahan and it was obvious that he felt confident he had unlimited latitude to manufacture his own version of the facts. Lang now had him in two direct contradictions to Molly's testimony—that Daultry had come alone and that there had been no prior discussion—both of which he would save for the trial. It wasn't the kind of thing that could win a case by itself, but he was sure it was more than Lindstrom ever imagined he would get from the deposition. He continued innocuously, "What was his strategy?"

"Well, it's been a number of years, but as I recall it was to build a light composite airplane, single-engine prop, two-seater, with a lot of fancy bells and whistles to sell to wealthy individuals. He wanted me to design it for him and then split the costs and profit of marketing the finished product."

"And so you designed the airplane?"

Lindstrom laughed easily. "I know you wish that were true, Chris, but I'm afraid you really don't have your facts straight." He turned to Hickman. "Now don't get all upset with me, Gentry. I know you told me not to volunteer anything, but I'm going to try to straighten out Mr. Lang here. I don't see how it will hurt and, who knows, maybe I'll persuade him that there's no real point to keeping me in his little lawyers' confab here."

Lang marveled at the man's temerity. Here he was, committing abject perjury, coolly and confidently inventing one fact after the other, and he was carrying it off with the air of a man relating the details of the ninth inning of last night's game.

Lindstrom's remark to Hickman had the feel of a canned speech to Lang and, since Lindstrom had volunteered freely all day, as long as it had suited his purposes, he wondered if it was a signal of some kind to his lawyer. If so, Hickman's expression betrayed nothing. After a moment, Lindstrom looked from Hickman back to Lang, his good nature brimming over. "Now, exactly what was your question? Could you read it back, Miss Reporter?"

"That won't be necessary, Mr. Lindstrom," said Lang evenly. The question was, 'And you designed the airplane?'"

"Oh, right. I did not design it. Daultry was a great and brilliant man and I was terribly flattered that he wanted to do business with me. I heard him out—who wouldn't?—but I very politely explained to him that my aerodynamics and aviation days were behind me and that I had moved on, into other things. I told him I would put him in touch with my people at my old company—that's Arrow Dynamics—and I would encourage them to work with him on his idea. He's a fascinating—*was* a fascinating man, a true giant in his field. Many fields.

"Anyway, I told him I thought he had a good idea. It was, you know. Surefire winner, I thought. I put him in touch with Doug Chesney at Arrow and that was the end of my involvement. Until I read about Daultry's death at Milan. Then, in subsequent conversations with Doug, I learned that they had gone ahead with the project and had actually finished the testing and validation after his death. Sad day, that was. Sad for the world."

"Have you ever seen the contract?"

"No," Lindstrom replied, very quickly. Then he added, "Wait. Have I seen it? Yes. I haven't read it."

"You've seen it but not read it, is that your testimony?"

"Objection," interjected Hickman. "Asked and answered."

"Nice try, Counsel," said Lang. "But a deposition of a hostile witness is cross-examination and I can ask him the same question as many times as I want." Without waiting for a reply from Hickman, he turned back to Lindstrom. "You can answer the question, sir."

Hickman rose up in his chair. "Objection stands. And I will add that it is argumentative and posed for purposes of harassment."

"You can still answer it, Mr. Lindstrom," said Lang levelly.

Hickman started to speak again but Lindstrom's upraised palm stopped him. "That's what I said, Chris. I saw it, glanced at it, but have never read it."

"Let's look at it." Lang pushed a fifteen-page document across the table toward Hickman and a second copy toward the witness. "Do you recognize it?"

Lindstrom flipped through the document quickly. "According to the title at the top of the front page it's the Experimental-Aircraft Development Contract (XRL-22) between Arrow Dynamics Incorporated and Daultry Research PLC."

"And is this the contract that you glanced at but did not read, according to your earlier testimony?"

"Looks like it, Chris. I didn't read it all the way through just now but it looks like it."

"So now you've glanced at it twice, without reading it, correct?"

Lindstrom smiled a strained, uncomfortable smile, and replied, "That's one way to put it. Yes."

"By the way, what does the designation XRL-22 mean to you?"

"I have no idea but I could guess that XRL-22—"

"Don't guess," interrupted Hickman. "Mr. Lang wants your best recollection of facts, if you have any. None of us needs to speculate, Russell."

Lindstrom shrugged apologetically. Lang continued, "Please turn to Section G on page eleven. It is entitled Testing." He waited until Lindstrom and Hickman found the indicated passage. "Under Section G-5, entitled Departure and Spin, it says, 'Measurement of departure/spin resistance per MS 92121.' Is this section one that you happened to see when you glanced at the contract?"

"Objection," said Hickman matter-of-factly. "That's argumentative. You're harassing the witness."

"Not at all," replied Lang genially. "I'm trying as best I can to use the witness's own words. You can answer, Mr. Lindstrom."

"I don't recall seeing this provision, per se, Counsel. But reading it reminds me of something I had forgotten entirely."

"Let Mr. Lang ask the questions, Mr. Lindstrom," Hickman said. "He's very good at it."

"Are you referring to something that will affect the accuracy of testimony you have already given here today?" asked Lang, ignoring Hickman's interjection.

"In a way."

Lang turned to Hickman. "In that case, Mr. Hickman, I think I'm entitled to hear it."

Hickman frowned. "Off the record, then. I need to confer with my client."

Lang stretched and rocked back in his chair. Hickman motioned to Lindstrom and the two of them went out into the corridor.

There's something significant here, thought Lang. I just wish I knew what the hell it was. He felt as if he were dealing with the case against Lindstrom through a glass-block wall, all of its nuance, texture, and character obscured from his vision. He had no choice but to push on as if he knew where he was going. Twenty minutes later, Hickman and Lindstrom returned.

"Back on the record," Lang said to the reporter. "And please note the time." Hickman looked at Lang darkly but said nothing. "All right, Mr. Lindstrom," said Lang. "Do you need to amplify or correct an earlier answer?"

"Yes. Seeing this provision regarding the military specification jogs my memory that I did speak to Mr. Daultry on one occasion after the time I met with him. Mr. Daultry called me after he had worked out the contract with Arrow Dynamics. He asked me about this section, what it meant, why it was in there."

"When did this conversation take place?"

"I don't recall. Maybe a month or two after we met."

"Let me see if I follow you. In December, you and he talked at your home, where he explained his idea to you about designing an airplane and going in together on the production and marketing, correct?" To himself, Lang was chalking up yet another point of discrepancy between the witness's testimony and Molly O'Keefe's.

"That's right," Lindstrom replied.

"Then you put him in touch with Doug Chesney at Arrow Dynamics and they negotiated the contract with him?"

"Well, I wasn't there, but that's a logical conclusion from the contract they entered into, this one here," replied Lindstrom, picking up and opening the lengthy document on the table before him.

"Then he telephoned you to ask you about a provision of the contract?"

"Yes, he asked me about this particular section, about the military specification."

Lang distinctly heard a small voice in the deep recesses of his mind congratulate him on finally getting Lindstrom to admit to involvement in *something* that happened after the contract was signed. He managed to mask his reaction and followed up with a question he was sure would draw an objection. "Do you know why he asked you about a contract you had nothing to do with preparing or negotiating?"

"Objection. Calls for speculation into the state of mind of Mr. Daultry. And your tone is argumentative."

"My tone?" asked Lang, giving the term a sarcastic twist. "I asked him if he knows. If he doesn't, he can say so. You can answer the question, sir."

Lindstrom looked to Hickman, whose shrug told him to go ahead and respond. "I don't really know."

"What was said when he called you?"

"He asked me if I could tell him what this section meant."

"Meaning just this subsection, G-5?"

Lindstrom shifted slightly in his chair. "Right. G-5."

"And what did you tell him?"

"I told him that it was a standard provision in all of our development contracts." Lindstrom paused and seemed to Lang to be collecting his thoughts more than probing his memory. It was a rare and welcome hint of hesitancy for the witness. At length, Lindstrom continued, "I told him that it was a military specification for measuring stall, departure, and spin susceptibility or resistance. And I told him that we only put it in contracts like this for definitional purposes."

"Definitional purposes?" asked Lang dubiously.

"Yes," replied Lindstrom, a touch of testiness in his tone. "The terms 'stall,' 'departure,' and 'spin,' as well as 'resistant' and 'susceptible,' are defined in that specification and it's easier to refer to it than to write them into the contract."

"You said 'we.' Whom do you mean by 'we'?"

"I'm sorry," replied Lindstrom with a broad smile. Suddenly, any hint of hesitancy Lang might have detected was gone. "Slip of the tongue. I meant Arrow Dynamics."

"How did you know what Arrow Dynamics typically did in its contracts, Mr. Lindstrom?"

"Well, Mr. Lang, I founded the company and was its chief executive and chairman for more than fifteen years. I knew how we did business."

"Did you ever confirm with anyone over at Arrow that your interpretation of the provision was right?"

"Sure. I subsequently spoke to Doug and Steve. Castillo. Maybe Brent Milinsky, as well. They agreed."

"But MS 92121 is a testing specification for the measurement of departure and spin, isn't it?"

"That's right."

"It's not a definitional specification, is it?"

"Well, that's splitting hairs. It has the definitions we wanted right there. That's the point."

"So you told Mr. Daultry that the inclusion of that specification was just to define the terms and did not require Arrow Dynamics to perform its testing regimen?"

"That's right."

"Did that satisfy him?"

"Absolutely. He said he was just curious about it and was perfectly happy with the cross-reference for definitional purposes."

"Did you tell anyone at Arrow about this conversation?"

"I don't recall. I did confirm that interpretation, as I said. But there was no need to trouble the Arrow people about the call. It was inconsequential. I probably didn't."

Lang smiled, fully aware that while Lindstrom's answer dovetailed neatly—too neatly—with the testimony of the people from Arrow Dynamics, it would contrast jarringly with what Lang considered to be the more plausible version of Molly O'Keefe.

Lindstrom noted Lang's smile and narrowed his eyes ever so slightly. He said nothing.

And, in Lang's view, he managed to say next to nothing the rest of the day. Throughout the afternoon, Lang worked hard to suppress his frustration.

"You testified earlier that you were knowledgeable regarding the way Arrow did business. What records did Arrow customarily maintain of its development and test efforts?"

"I'm afraid that I cannot answer that for the time period you are talking about here. My knowledge in that area has to do with a much earlier point in time."

"But you've testified regarding Arrow's business practices at this very 'point in time' earlier today."

"Counsel," said Lindstrom frostily, "I testified about the company's practices as they relate to including the military specification in development contracts. That's something that is not likely to change over the years. That is very different from the company's practices in performing the actual work or, as you have asked it, in documenting or recording the work it does, something that could change from project to project."

Lang was not pleased with the evasiveness of the answer, but said calmly, "Let me ask you this, then. When you ran the company, what kinds of records were kept in development contracts that would reflect the testing activities of the company?"

"Well, let's see. There would be the contract, of course. That's really the checklist. Then there would be a detailed test plan. An aircraft log, showing the number of flights and engine time. Flight cards for each flight. But they would usually be discarded when the final engineering report was prepared. That's about it."

"Would there be any sort of log reflecting pertinent information for each flight?" Lang didn't notice a quick sidelong glance Hickman gave to Lindstrom.

"Possibly. But not usually. In a large, commercial development program, you might. But not this type of project."

.   .   .

Tired and frustrated, Lang tossed his deposition notes back onto the small round Formica table in his tiny hotel room. Having finished with Lindstrom too late to drive back to Houston in time to catch the last plane for Los Angeles, he grabbed a room at the local Holiday Inn. Now, with the remnants of a greasy hamburger and french fries scattered across the table, he replayed the day's testimony over in his mind, absently squeegeeing the condensation from his Coke can with his thumb. On the television, a hockey game played on, without sound. The red LED display on the small nightstand clock read 8:49.

Although Lang was still thoroughly stymied in his efforts to make a case against Lindstrom, there was a ray of hope in the fact that, if Molly O'Keefe was to be believed, Lindstrom was a liar. His credibility could be attacked at trial. Encouraging, yes, but as Amy would no doubt point out, it fell well short of evidence.

He picked up the remote control and scanned through the channels. Milo Rich was hammering on one of the candidates for governor of California. Alex Trebek was trying hard to enliven a game of *Jeopardy!* where the defending champion was drubbing his adversaries by more than $10,000. *Mama's Family* seemed to be on no less than three stations. At least there was no Russell Lindstrom on the tube tonight, thought Lang. Nonetheless, at the top of the hour, the network news update noted that the primary season would begin next week in New Hampshire, where "wealthy industrialist and political neophyte" Lindstrom was expected to finish well behind the front-runners, despite a strong showing last week in the Iowa caucuses.

There was a sharp knock at his door. Lang had no idea who it might be. The possibility of Laura Carey briefly crossed his mind as he moved toward the door. To his chagrin, he caught a reflection of himself in the mirror, noting his faded jeans and torn Tierra Rejada Middle School T-shirt. He opened the door. In the hallway stood two huge men, one white, the other black, wearing dark blue suits. Despite the hour, they wore dark wraparound sunglasses. "Mr. Lang?" said the black man.

"Yes?"

"Agents Robertson and Callero of the United States Secret Service. May we come in?"

"Why?"

"Mr. Lindstrom would like to visit you here and we need to secure the area. Standard procedure."

"Mr. Lindstrom?" Lang repeated. He tried to look down the hall to see who else might be there, but couldn't see past the two men.

"That's right, sir."

"Do you guys have some sort of I.D.?"

They produced shields that looked authentic enough to Lang. It was obvious to him that each carried a gun in a shoulder holster. Since he had nothing of value in the room, he decided there would be no harm in letting them in, since if they wanted to kill him or rob him, they would have little trouble overpowering him anyway. You learn to look at things this way, he thought, when you live in L.A. He stepped back from the door.

Quickly and efficiently they completed a thorough survey of the small room and the adjacent bathroom and exchanged a look that must have meant it was safe. One of them went back out into the hallway and motioned to someone else. Four more men emerged from the dim light of the hallway and entered the room. In the middle was Lindstrom, dressed in a different dark gray suit from the one he had worn to the deposition. There was barely enough room to move with all of them in the tiny space. Lang was feeling decidedly claustrophobic. And he had no idea what was going on.

"Excuse me? What's this all about?" he asked, looking toward Lindstrom through his entourage.

"Hi, Chris," he said with the casual air one would expect from a co-worker at the coffee machine. "Kind of cramped in here, isn't it?" He laughed a hearty, commanding laugh. To the other men, he said, "Please wait for me outside, gentlemen."

A wave of "Yes, sirs," swept the room, and what looked like the offensive line of the Pittsburgh Steelers in Brooks Brothers suits retreated into the hallway. The door closed behind them, leaving only Lang and Lindstrom.

"Nice place you have here, Chris," Lindstrom said with a thin smile. "Mind if I sit down?" Without waiting for an answer he sat gingerly on the edge of the couch.

"I don't mind if you sit down, Mr. Lindstrom. But I can't talk to you. A lawyer can't talk to the opposing party outside the presence of that party's lawyer without the consent of the absent lawyer. It's an ethical requirement."

"Gentry? I don't think I need Gentry's consent to talk to you.

But if it makes you feel better, then I will represent to you that he has given permission."

"That's not the point, Mr.—"

"Let's cut the crap, Chris. You put me through hell today, son. Wrung the sweat out of me in that chair."

"But—"

"One of the worst damned days of my life. You're tenacious, you're bright. A dangerous adversary."

The flattery was a smoke screen for something, Lang knew, but he wasn't sure what. For now, all he knew was that he was definitely off-balance.

"You're wrong, of course, about me and that airplane. That's the God's truth, too. I had nothing to do with it. But I have to admit that you act like a man who doesn't believe that. Worse, you seem like that rare man whose intellect and tenacity equip him to make others believe the way he does, in spite of the evidence."

"Look, Mr. Lindstrom, I appreciate—"

"The point is, Chris, you're everything your sterling reputation would suggest. Maybe better, based on my afternoon in hell with you."

Lang was growing angry. He was obviously the object of a strong-arm attempt to dislodge him from the trail he was sure was genuine and he didn't like it at all. "Mr. Lindstrom," he said, raising his voice and sharpening his tone to avoid being cut off again. "We cannot discuss this case without Mr. Hickman. It's inappropriate and counterproductive. You have your version of the facts and I know what the evidence will show. That's why we're in court."

"Hell, Chris," Lindstrom said, holding up his hand and smiling. "This isn't about the lawsuit. I know we disagree. And I have total confidence in my knowledge of the facts. After all, I was there. Remember? I don't think you know anyone else who was."

Lang successfully fought the urge to blurt out Molly O'Keefe's name. He said nothing, but caught a strange, threatening look in Lindstrom's eye for the briefest moment. Then Lindstrom continued. "This is about you. And duty. And service to your country." He sat back expansively on the cheap plaid couch, taking in Lang, his clothing, the food wrappers and scraps. "You're a terrific lawyer, a tiger with genuine genius up here." He tapped his temple. "The kind of man that has an obligation, an *obligation*, son, to serve your country."

Lang was disgusted. "Enough, Mr. Lindstrom. Now, I think you'd better—"

"You're not hearing me, Chris," Lindstrom said, his powerful voice blowing Lang's away like an unholy gust of wind. "I will need men like you, the very best there are, to put this country right. In the Justice Department, on the federal bench, in the White House itself, in the president's counsel's office. Yours are skills and talents that are as rare as they are vital to the republic."

"Jesus Christ!" Lang blurted. "You're bribing me!"

"What are you talking about, Chris?" replied Lindstrom, his good nature still in place. "I'm presenting you with an opportunity to serve your country at the highest levels, where your powerful arsenal of talents can have real, lasting impact. This has nothing to do with the lawsuit. I will win that, whether you pursue me or not. I don't need to bribe you. I'm offering you a call to the highest service we know, public service at the top. No matter how this silly little lawsuit turns out."

Lang was seething. "Look. Get the fuck out of here, right now, you arrogant son of a bitch."

Lindstrom rose slowly from the couch, to his full height. With one deliberate stride he was nose-to-nose with Lang, and several inches taller. His face reddened slightly and Lang, himself enraged, would later swear he could feel heat rising from Lindstrom's cheeks. "Mr. Lang. You've had your chance. Your ambition is driving your ass to an early grave. You're smart. Lawyer-smart. But you have no idea just how fucking far over your head you are. You're in the ring with pros who know how to play a game you don't even understand, you little shit." With that, he turned slowly and left the room.

CHAPTER 19

"WELL, WHAT DO YOU THINK OF DAVID STINGLEY'S mountain hideaway?" asked Mark, panting from the combination of the altitude and the effort of climbing the icy stairs under the burden of two large duffel bags.

Ro stood in the huge, bright entryway of the massive house. Through the twin floor-to-ceiling windows that bracketed the front door, she was treated to a stunning vista of the snow-covered mountains rising mightily on every side of the shimmering lake. Under the archway to her right, she caught a glimpse of the same view through an immense sheet of glass that was the west wall of the hunting-lodge-scale living room. "It's like a cottage out of a German fairy tale," she replied.

Mark laughed as he puffed past her toward the stairs that led to the second floor. "If fifty-two hundred square feet of tax write-off is your idea of a cottage, I guess."

Indeed, the house was everything Mark had promised, only on a vastly grander scale. Nestled in an enclave of spectacular, sprawling homes loosely scattered over open, rolling fields of snow, just at the edge of the wooded foothills of the eastern shore of Lake Tahoe, the house was clearly inspired by the Alpine chalets and A-frames Ro associated with the Switzerland of Heidi and the Austria of the von Trapp family. Steeply pitched roofs intersected one another in a dizzying display of finely carved woodwork and massive expanses of glass, all hunkered down under a heavy blanket of the purest, whitest snow Ro had ever seen. The late-afternoon sun, pale and distant in the frigid air, sparkled off the crystals in the snow and intensified the fairyland quality of the moment. Across the lake to the west, the pinks and lavenders that would deepen into the reds and purples of the sunset painted an unforgettable masterpiece behind the awesome thrusts of the California mountains. If ever there were a moment in time worthy of freezing for an eternity, thought Ro, this was it. Suddenly, it occurred to her that she could do exactly that, and she scrambled to gather her cameras and tripod.

While Ro set up outside on the second-story balcony, Mark unloaded the Jeep and moved their things into the bedrooms. After he dropped the last bag onto the bed in the corner room he would use—he set Ro up in the mammoth master bedroom, with its Jacuzzi and sauna—he quietly walked back to the front of the house and stood in the living room, below the balcony where Ro was working, strategically out of her line of sight. After a full minute, standing still and silent, watching her shadow on the far wall as she moved about up on the deck, he returned to his room and quietly closed the door. He placed a phone call.

"Hello," answered the voice at the other end of the line.

"It's Mark."

"Hi. What's up?" replied David Stingley's voice.

"Your place looks great."

"Thanks," Stingley replied stiffly.

"You make a lot of money."

"Fuck off, Mark. What do you want?"

Mark laughed. "Straight to business, huh? That military training shows through." He paused but Stingley made no reply. He continued, "Did you get my message?"

"Yeah, I got it."

"Do you have an explanation for a fuck-up of such royal proportions?"

"Listen, Mark. You were in Ops longer than I was. Not everybody is at the top of the class and not every operation comes off without a hitch."

"A *hitch*?" Mark's voice cracked. Reflexively, he looked to the door to be sure he hadn't been heard. "A fucking *hitch* you call it?

Your fresh-assed Special Forces rookie not only gets spotted, he hits a *cop* with a goddamned taser, an Alpha Taser, yet, and you call it a hitch?"

Stingley was uncharacteristically quiet as he absorbed the sting of the other man's insult. He knew it was about to get worse. "I'm afraid there may be more to it than that."

Mark Fassero's shoulders tensed involuntarily. "I'm waiting," he said.

Stingley had been dreading this conversation since he had gotten the report. "There's a remote possibility that Carter may have been compromised."

"What's that supposed to mean?" Mark demanded, his voice taut with suppressed anger.

"Intelligence picked off an aborted contact from, er, Shakespeare," replied Stingley, fumbling for a moment with the secure code for an individual both men knew by another name. Then, he added with a transparent show of optimism, "We can't confirm actual contact, however."

"That's fucking great," replied Mark, biting the words off for emphasis. "And your solution?"

"He was decommissioned within an hour after the intelligence cleared."

"Decommissioned?" asked Mark.

"Not like that," replied Stingley quickly. "I sent him home to sit tight. We've got an eye on him."

"That makes me feel pretty fucking secure," Mark replied acidly, wondering which incompetent had drawn that assignment. He thought about adding something more but decided against it. "I'll be in touch."

Just as the sun was settling into the peaks of the mountains to the west, Mark joined Ro on the balcony, a steaming cup of hot chocolate in each hand. His feet crunched the thin layer of snow on the decking as he moved in close behind her. She continued to shoot a furious stream of pictures, hurrying against the rapidly dissolving scene. He was content just to stand behind her and watch.

"Pretty spectacular, isn't it?" he observed after a moment.

"I can't think of words that could possibly do it justice. It just looks like, like God's work." She took the cup he offered, quietly conceding that her subject had succumbed to the inexorable passage of time. The steaming cocoa was thick and hot against the chill.

He put an arm around her shoulder and drew her to him. She

smiled at him. Even in the fading light, bundled up in ski jacket, scarf, and cap, he was disarmingly handsome, a bold and dashing soldier of fortune who had demonstrated time and again over the months a genuine attraction for her, a steady, persistent emotion that appeared to need little or no encouragement to survive. And the truth was that she really had done very little to encourage him. She felt more than a little guilty about that. Over the past several weeks, she had become strangely ambivalent about her feelings for Mark. Just how comfortable they had grown in each other's company was clear on the course of the long drive up from L.A. The conversation between them had flowed naturally over a wide variety of topics, all with the easy pace and effortlessness that characterize exchanges between two people whose need to impress each other has given way to a genuine interest in what the other thinks. It reminded her of her best days with Chris.

"Hey, it's getting cold out here," he said, slapping his gloved hands together. "How about us pulling your gear together and whipping up some fettuccine Alfredo and Caesar salad?"

"Sounds like a feeding frenzy to me."

"Not really. We'll cut all that rich cholesterol with a bottle of wine. And then, we're going to take a long, brisk, healthy walk. Across the golf course and down to the shore."

"Golf course? What golf course?"

He laughed. "The one right in front of you. That huge field of snow you've been looking at since we got here is a beautiful eighteen-hole golf course."

"Well, I'll be," she said, now looking at the snowfield in the fading light as if seeing it for the first time.

"Things aren't always what they appear, you know."

"I think I heard that someplace," she said, and started to gather up her equipment and take it inside.

After dinner, Mark had renewed his insistence on taking a walk. Ro was tired, from the food, the wine, and the long drive, and wanted to call the kids, but was persuaded that she could do that when they got back. Now, in the swirling steam and warmth of the anteroom of the master bath, she was glad she had. The walk through the heavy snow had been like a trip into a Christmas card, complete with winking colored lights on the sprawling homes that lined the golf course. Through the cloud churned up by the furious bubbling of the Jacuzzi, Ro strained to see herself in the huge mirror over the dressing table. She noted with satisfaction that her face looked youthful and vibrant in the room's recessed lighting. She took a drink from her mug of Irish coffee.

"Okay, Mark," she called out. "I'm ready."

The door opened and Mark, his own mug in hand and wearing a very stylish Hawaiian surfer's swimsuit, stepped into the anteroom. It was the first time she had ever seen him without a shirt. She was surprised by the breadth of his shoulders and the sharp definition of his well-muscled torso. Fully clothed, he had seemed strong but wiry. Now, she realized, he was powerfully built.

As to how he saw her, one look into his eyes told her everything. Although she was more than a little self-conscious standing before him for the first time in a bathing suit, the Irish coffee had given her the courage to accept his suggestion that they share the Jacuzzi, and the look she now saw on his face told her that she had no reason to be shy.

"Mmm, you look great."

His directness embarrassed her, leaving her feeling even more exposed than she was. "Thank you," she replied. "You look pretty terrific in a bathing suit yourself."

"You're beautiful," he said, resting his hands lightly on her shoulders. "And, may I say, very sexy?" His eyes spoke even more graphically than his words.

Her head was suddenly spinning from the potent combination of the whiskey and the steam, and, yes, the primal surge suddenly coursing through her veins. "Why don't we try the hot tub?"

The water *was* hot, at the upper end of comfortable for Ro, but it felt wonderful, instantly purging the physical effects of tension and stress. She felt herself floating on the powerful jets as if on the crest of a great wave, the steamy mist smelling faintly of chlorine reducing the room around her to a dreamy, ethereal plane lacking place or time. Suddenly, she realized that he had taken her hand in his. Deliberately, she left it there, keenly aware of his gentle, solid strength. Her head swam as his face filled her field of vision. His kiss was alive and vibrant, a small window to the passions welling up within them both. Suddenly she was past caution. She allowed herself to drift off on a rising current of desire. Tomorrow was a light year away.

"Could you mute that, Amy?" Lang asked from the bar at the back of his family room. Amy, seated next to Rachel Cruz on the big, comfortable sofa arranged expressly for viewing, complied, leaving the large-screen television playing a commercial without the sound. Lang filled a couple of glasses with crushed ice and diet soda.

"So that's it, Amy?" said Rachel. "You're followed by some thug who tries to electrocute your husband and that's the end of it?"

Amy shrugged. "Not really the end of it. They're following up on the whole thing down at Parker Center, but there's not too much to go on."

"I think the license plate is the creepiest part of the whole thing," said Rachel with a shudder. "How could there *be* a license plate that the state never issued? And how did somebody get their hands on it in the first place?"

"*Who* gets their hands on such a plate," interjected Lang. "That's the real riddle. And that *is* unnerving."

Amy shook her head. "I just assume that part has to do with criminals. I mean, if they outlawed guns, only the criminals would manage to get hold of them. Same principle with a phony license plate, I figure. What gets me is the stun gun. Now *that's* creepy."

"What did they say about that, again?" Lang asked.

"Bill's ballistics guy said that with a regular stun gun, the one they call a taser or taser dart gun, there are darts that are wired to a high-powered battery pack. That's where the charge comes from that disables the assailant. But, there were no darts, no wires with the gun that shot Bill. Only these odd little salt deposits just under the skin at each blast point. And they *dissolved*. They were dissolving right before their eyes. Bill said that within an hour of the attack there wasn't a trace. No sodium, no burns, no lacerations. *Nada*."

"Real *X-Files* stuff, huh?" observed Lang.

Amy nodded. "You think this is the handiwork of Lindstrom, don't you?"

Lang handed Amy her glass. "That's a hard supposition to dismiss, isn't it? But, what about the possible tie-in to Bill's gun-running investigation? Doesn't that make sense?"

Amy shook her head. "I don't think so. This guy was following me to unnerve me, to rattle me. The only contact he had with Bill was when Bill cornered him. If he was involved in the East L.A. gun business, he wouldn't have shot Bill with a ray gun and run off into the night."

"It's on," said Lang, pointing toward the television. Amy hit the mute button.

"Our lead story tonight is the Republican primary in New Hampshire," said the network anchor. "The bellwether early season test of the candidates is less than forty-eight hours away now, and the polls are promising some very interesting results. We have three stories tonight. First, Brandon Kipp with the Gordon campaign in Concord."

The screen cut to a young reporter in a heavy topcoat, standing in swirling snow flurries in front of the statehouse. "The rite of politics in the snows of New Hampshire has hit its final sprint to the primary on Tuesday. Senator Jack Gordon made the traditional rounds in this conservative, tight-lipped New England state, shaking hands at a small downtown Concord diner this morning and greeting workers at an electrical-switch manufacturing plant in Manchester this afternoon. But while opinion polls place the senator well ahead of his chief rival, Richard Manetti, it is opposition from an unexpected quarter that may be more troubling to the Gordon camp. The emergence of billionaire industrialist Russell Lindstrom, with a powerful performance in the Friday debate, was the talk of the Gordon people Sunday even as they tried to downplay Lindstrom's threat."

On the screen appeared a man alighting from a small airplane on a snowy airfield. The reporter continued, "Gordon's normally confident campaign manager, Jim Roundwall, appeared uncharacteristically defensive in discussing Lindstrom with reporters this morning." Roundwall, speaking to a forest of microphones at the airfield, said, "While Senator Gordon has been in this race from the beginning, stating his case on the issues that concern America and talking about his record, Mr. Lindstrom has been running his companies and living high off the land. We don't really know where he stands on the issues and he has no record. I think the electorate knows the difference between a seasoned, tested public servant and someone who thinks the country is just another broken-down company to be salvaged by a quick fix and a public-relations campaign."

The reporter came back on the screen. "But that is precisely where the Gordon campaign may be miscalculating, at least according to the people at the top of Lindstrom's team. David Leveque has the story from Lindstrom headquarters."

The scene shifted to a bus wrapped in a "Lindstrom!" banner in red, white, and blue plowing through snowy city streets. A reporter spoke. "The difference in the Lindstrom campaign since Friday night's debate has been dramatic. A sometimes halting campaign mired in the middle of the pack of Republican challengers suddenly came to life with a stirring debate performance by the candidate. Campaign manager Gina Calabrese was euphoric."

Calabrese appeared on the screen. "I think what the voters finally saw here Friday was a leader, a visionary. This is not just a bright man with an unparalleled record of achievement. He is a creative, dedicated *thinker,* maybe the most incisive, dynamic thinker to seek the presidency since Thomas Jefferson. And I think the public got a rare opportunity to glimpse that quality of the man in the debate."

The reporter came onscreen. "Historical comparisons aside, there appears little doubt that Lindstrom's lifeless campaign has begun to flourish in the hours since Friday's telecast. Predebate polling figures had the political newcomer fifth with an expected return of eight to ten percent, but Sunday's *New York Times*/CBS poll shows that Lindstrom has since moved into a virtual deadlock with Manetti, at about eighteen percent. While that is still well behind Gordon's thirty percent and it is doubtful that Lindstrom will continue to climb fast enough to erase that double-digit lead by Tuesday, there seems good reason to believe that the man who has made corporate rescues one of America's favorite spectator sports may have rescued his own bid for the nomination."

Lang flicked the mute button. "That son of a bitch is for real now."

Rachel observed, "Did you see that debate? He just about blew the other guys off the stage."

"I don't like it," said Amy. "The guy makes my skin crawl."

"I guess any prospect that he might drop out of the race early just went up in smoke, didn't it?" said Lang.

"Don't act like you don't love it, Chris," Amy replied. Lang grinned broadly, saying nothing. Amy continued, "At least maybe I can go on vacation now."

"How's that?" asked Rachel.

Amy looked to Lang. "You don't think our June trial date is going to hold, do you?"

"Good question," replied Lang, stretching. "The primaries will all be over but the convention begins July twenty-third. Assuming Lindstrom stays in the race—"

"We're a lock to get a motion to continue," said Amy, finishing the thought. "And I'll bet Campbell will go for it."

"No doubt," agreed Lang. "That just means we may get to

go to trial against the president of the United States early next year."

"In which case you can bet Lindstrom will revisit the old executive-prerogative arguments that Nixon and Clinton both left on the table."

"Probably," replied Lang. "But I still don't think it applies to acts committed before taking office."

Rachel shrugged her shoulders as if against a sudden chill. "If that guy gets elected president, I think taking him to trial will be the least of our worries."

"Well, at the risk of throwing cold water on your patriotic enthusiasm, Chris, I still don't think much of our case against him. I read that deposition and I think he held up pretty well," said Amy.

Lang frowned. "I didn't nail him the way I had hoped," he conceded.

"He's awfully smooth," said Amy. "It's too bad we three won't be on that jury. Unfortunately, the real jury is going to require evidence."

"We have evidence, Amy," replied Lang defensively. "We have Molly O'Keefe telling a very different story. About when and where Lindstrom met Daultry, the extent of their discussions, whose idea the StormTree was, the importance of the spin characteristics, the role of the Mil Spec. The list goes on."

"But it all comes down to Molly O'Keefe," replied Amy a little hotly. "Alleged IRA terrorist who cannot be brought here by subpoena and cannot be legally compelled to give us a deposition, even if we go to Ireland to take it." Amy softened her tone. "The point is that so far there is no case against Lindstrom unless Molly shows up, testifies to the story she told Seamus, *and* is believed by the jury over Mr. Presidential Candidate."

Lang contemplated her words silently for a long moment. "I hate when you're right," he said at last.

Amy shrugged. "Learned everything I know from you."

"Well, I've got a few more cards to play. In any event, we've come too far to give up on it yet. I'm really going to have to make time to go over there and meet the woman. Could you call Seamus and see if he can set up a meeting with Molly for me? I can clear three days at the end of the week after next."

While he was still talking, Amy had pulled a small notebook out of her briefcase on the coffee table and made a note. "You don't like the deposition idea? I gather she would be amenable."

Lang shook his head. "She might but I'm not. I think it'd be better to have her wait and come for the trial itself. That way there is less opportunity for Lindstrom and Hickman to fire at a stationary target."

Amy nodded. "That's my take on it, too."

CHAPTER 20

EVENING WAS FAST OVERTAKING THE WESTERN counties of Ireland as Seamus Callahan pushed his old but reliable Morris hard along the winding road to Kilmurry. He had hoped to get out here earlier in the afternoon but the constabulary had turned unusually busy toward the end of his shift and there had been no way to leave the station any sooner. Now, despite the slightly longer days of February, he would lose all of his daylight before he reached his destination. The roads were unfamiliar to him out here and, worse, the fine mist of water on the surface was sure to ice up before he could complete his business.

As he methodically worked the hypnotic rhythms of gearbox, clutch, and accelerator along the narrow country road, his thoughts turned to that business. His emotions were mixed as he hurried toward a second encounter with Molly O'Keefe. He had received a call early yesterday morning from Bill Quinn to ask him to visit her again, this time to arrange a meeting between her and the lawyer who was going to try the case against Russell Lindstrom. Unfortunately, there wasn't much they could do with her statement as reported by him and they needed her to agree to go to Los Angeles to testify in person. On one hand, Seamus could hardly wait to see this most unusual woman and drink in the pure pleasure of her company. On the other, he was highly dubious about the prospects of persuading her to agree to the meeting, much less to the trip to the States. He couldn't imagine that the case could mean enough to her to make such a long and exhausting trip worthwhile, let alone wish to expose herself to a courtroom attack on her credibility and possibly worse, in light of old allegations of crimes against the crown. Nonetheless, the favor had been asked and he was honor-bound to give it his best effort.

At last he rounded a vaguely familiar bend and there, dimly outlined against the only portion of the sky with any light left at all, stood the farmhouse where he had met Molly O'Keefe last December. The place was silent, dark, and there was no smoke curling out of the chimney as it had on that earlier morning. The light snow that had fallen two nights ago was undisturbed on the narrow lane leading to the front porch. His heart sank.

There was no answer to his repeated knocks, all executed with proper constabulary force. The turf bricks, stacked near the back door in the old style for use in the fireplace, had not been touched since the recent snowfall. The house was silent, empty. The sensation echoed loudly in Seamus's heart. He checked his watch and pondered his next move.

Seamus sank heavily into the driver's seat of the Morris and switched on the dome light. He flipped open the thick black leather book on the seat next to him. In the dim light thrown by the tiny bulb, he searched back to the entries he had made the previous December. His strong formal hand, in the thick black ink of his prized Mont Blanc fountain pen, filled every page of this notebook/journal/diary he had maintained for as long as he could remember. Under December 3, he found a series of tiny entries, crammed into the lower right-hand corner of the page. "Hmm," he grunted audibly as he ran his forefinger over the linen page, refreshing his recollection. ("Rule One of detective work." He had often been quoted by the many younger constables in the office. "Trust nothing to your memory. Record everything.")

Under his finger was the following entry, "M. McDonough— D. Nell's (Alt. Thurs; 10:30–2:00)—Killarney 1st Sundays." For the first time since his trip to the west had begun, Seamus Callahan smiled. "All right, then, Mr. McDonough. I guess it's back to Durty Nelly's tomorrow night."

.   .   .

The door to Durty Nelly's Pub opened and Seamus Callahan stepped out of the chilly darkness into the dimly lit warmth of Ennis's favorite drinking establishment. A few heads turned to assess the stranger, but that was the extent of the notice he got. He was early for the business he had in mind, so decided to take his dinner there. He headed to a table in the far corner and ordered a Guinness from the waitress to wet his lips after the drive over from Shannon. The bartender, he noted, was not the same one with whom he had spoken on his last visit. But in the opposite corner sat the boy—Sean?—looking him over from behind a folded newspaper.

He drained the Guinness with the businesslike determination of the working man and ordered a plate of Irish stew, not surprisingly, the house specialty. He noticed that the boy had disappeared. He ordered a second pint to cool his throat, wonderfully seared by the steaming richness of the stew.

As he neared the end of his meal, heavily augmented with the rich, thick, dark brown rye bread for which Ennis was justly famous, the boy suddenly appeared before him and slid into the opposite chair.

"Mr. Constable," he said, in greeting.

"Mr. Sean McDonough," replied Seamus, continuing to chew on his gravy-soaked bread. "May I offer you a pint?"

"No," the boy replied tersely. "Michael wants to know why you're here."

"Straight to business, then, is it? Well, all right, young man. I need to find Mrs. O'Keefe again."

From behind him, a voice said, "You found her before on your own, Constable. What's the matter? Losin' your touch?"

Seamus turned to see Michael McDonough pulling a chair up next to him. He had no gun this time and his tone was cautious but not hostile.

Seamus nodded a greeting. "Mr. McDonough, the Elder. Evenin' to you. You're not supposed to be here until ten-thirty."

McDonough ignored the reference to Seamus's intelligence about him. "Why do you need Molly O'Keefe?"

Seamus turned a look of mild disgust toward McDonough. "Haven't we gone through this, Mr. McDonough? I need to see her about the same matter I saw her about in December."

"Then why don't you go out to her place again and see her?"

"Because she's not there, Mr. McDonough. And by the looks o' things, she's not been there for some time."

McDonough shot a quick look to his little brother, who returned it with a perplexed expression of his own. "Shamrock?" whispered the boy.

Michael McDonough looked disapprovingly at his brother. To Seamus, he said, "Not home? Are you sure?"

"I've been out to see her and there's no sign of life there. Has this got anything to do with the Black Shamrock?"

Again, the older McDonough fired an angry look toward his brother. From what Seamus knew, the Black Shamrock was a new offshoot of the Sinn Fein, a far more radical bunch who felt the mainstream revolutionaries in the movement were far too timid in exercising the power of terrorism. There had even been talk that the Shamrock, as they were called, had threatened violence against these older veteran republicans as a means of radicalizing the movement.

"Don't know what you're talking about," Michael said. But Seamus could see that he was clearly troubled. He tried his best, however, to affect nonchalance. "Well, Mr. Constable, I cannot help you. I don't know where she is. Truth is, I've never known her to leave her place without us knowin' about it for the better part of two years. But Molly O'Keefe's an adult, and fully capable of comin' and goin' as she pleases."

"Any ideas?"

McDonough had decided that the conversation was over and he stood up. "Afraid not, Constable. Enjoy your meal." To the boy he said, "Let's go, Sean." With that, they left the pub, leaving Seamus Callahan to chew on his bread and reflect on his options.

Seven hours later and eight time zones to the west, Mark Fassero left his small condo in the Brentwood section of Los Angeles and headed down into the building's security garage. He opened the trunk to his clean white Saab 9000 and quickly checked the contents of a molded aluminum briefcase kept there. A minute later, he roared out into the crisp Southern California evening. Every few minutes he checked the time, alternating between the digital display on the dash and his own analog diver's watch. The radio played the city's only true jazz station, but at a volume that was barely audible.

He traveled north along the 405 Freeway, then east on the 101, following the signs to the Burbank airport. Before reaching it, he turned into a well-lighted lot adjacent to the Rent-A-Wreck lot. He presented himself at the counter and, with a minimum of wasted energy, rented a 1988 Ford Escort. The attendant apologized for the scrape along the driver's side and offered to put him into the '76 Mustang or the '83 Seville, both of which, unlike the Escort, had been washed. Mark smiled and politely declined the offer. In less than fifteen minutes he was back on the road, the aluminum brief-case on the seat beside him.

He got onto the Golden State Freeway and headed north. Driving at a deliberate seventy-two miles an hour, he passed the sign that announced "Pacoima Next 3 Exits." He took the second one and, at the bottom of the ramp, headed south on Laurel Canyon. About a quarter of a mile down, he turned into a narrow street to the right. He was now in the midst of several apartment complexes, the buildings battered and graffiti-stained, well past their peak, if buildings of such cheap construction could ever have been said to have a peak. He slipped the Escort into a narrow alley between two such long apartment buildings. Picking his way through the huge green Dumpsters and assorted debris that cluttered the passage, he leaned forward to study the carports that lined either side of the alley. Under a red numeral 65122, he spotted a battered blue 1976 Chevrolet Caprice, with California license number 434WEP on its old blue-and-gold plates. He pulled the Escort into a Dumpster space on the other side of the alley. He shut off the engine and sat for a moment. It was 10:17 by his wristwatch.

He heard only the sounds typical to that part of the city at that time of the day. A dog barked. Another answered. Tires squealed half a block down the long alley. A domestic quarrel—in Spanish—rose and fell, punctuated by the shattering of something made of glass. Someone under the hood of a '79 Camaro painted fluorescent green throttled the engine up and down by hand. All in all it was a quiet night. There was no gunfire despite a recent spate of racial shootings and bombings between blacks and Mexican gangs living in this area.

Satisfied with the state of the neighborhood, Mark got out of the car and, briefcase in hand, walked over to the Caprice. Casually, he looked through the window on the driver's side. There, visible in this light only to a trained eye that was looking for it, was a slender tungsten filament carefully and tightly strung from the steering wheel to the driver's-side armrest. The owner would have rigged it, then exited from the passenger's side, thus alerting him before he ever got in again that someone had been in the car. It was an elegant safeguard, unnecessary and useless for the type of break-in likely to occur in this neighborhood, but a very sharp precaution for one who knew his most feared enemy would come with a subtler agenda. Before getting to work, Mark noted with approval that the fuel gauge on the dash indicated nearly three-quarters of a tank on board.

Working quickly but calmly, Mark stooped behind the car and removed the license plate from the rear bumper. From the briefcase, he took a battered California plate, number 122ECJ, also of the old blue-and-gold type, and attached it in place of the other one. He did the same with the plate on the front bumper. Then, from the brief-case, he removed a small plain black box, no bigger than a pack of cigarettes, and adjusted a tiny dial on one end. Then he sat on the ground next to the car and carefully reached as far underneath as he could, leaving the box attached to the undercarriage. It was now 10:31.

He got back into the Escort and slowly drove off. Back onto Laurel Canyon, he passed the Silver Filly Bar and Grille and, once again, noted the time. About a mile farther down the road, he pulled into a shopping center. Outside the brightly lit Thrifty Drug Store, he found a public phone.

"Hello," said the voice at the other end, with a decidedly Hispanic accent.

"Mr. Carter?" asked Fassero.

"Who wants to know?" Carter asked suspiciously.

"Major Fassero," Mark replied.

"Yes, sir, Major," replied Carter crisply, the phony accent gone.

"Pretty bad turn of events down there in Manhattan Beach, huh, son?"

"I'm afraid so," replied Carter sheepishly. It was not hot to-night in Pacoima, but he was perspiring.

"Happens to the best of us, Mr. Carter," said Fassero warmly. "I ought to tell you about some of my more glorious fuck-ups sometime." He laughed. So did Carter. "It's a wonder we won the frigging Cold War, that's for sure." More laughter at both ends of the line. "Look," continued Mark. "Procedure requires a debrief and I drew the short straw. Okay with you, son?"

"Sure," responded Carter, as if he had a choice.

"I'm over here at the Silver Filly. How 'bout I buy you a brewski and we shoot the shit?"

"Sure," said Carter. He was oddly relieved. This thing had hung over his head like a latent disease and he was anxious to get the goddamned business behind him. How bad could it be? His record was solid and the screw-up had not done any damage that he could determine. If only the colonel hadn't insisted on sending Major Fassero himself. "When, Major? Right now?"

"No time like the present, I always say. See you in two shakes, soldier?"

"Yes, sir!" snapped Carter. He was out of the house in less than ninety seconds. At the door of his car, he flicked on a penlight to verify that the tungsten thread was still in place. It was and he got in and drove off.

Four minutes later, Mark started the engine of the Escort and headed out of the parking lot. He turned east until he hit San Fernando Road, then headed north. At that same moment, at the intersection of Laurel Canyon and Paxton Street, a blue 1976 Chevrolet Caprice spontaneously exploded, showering the intersection and everything within a hundred feet of it with relatively small pieces of the handiwork of an assembly line in Detroit. Half of a license plate, bearing the letters ECJ, landed in a battered red wagon left by a child on the front stoop of an apartment at the corner. Later, the police would describe the explosion as another senseless gang killing. But, when the bombing incident was not repeated, interest in the matter died out quietly. Since the fragments of the license found matched the one issued to a 1976 Chevrolet Caprice registered in Sacramento, the matter stopped there and no one ever thought to bring it to the attention of Detective William Quinn.

At the very moment the explosion rocked the intersection of Laurel Canyon and Paxton, Mark pulled his Escort into the space where he had parked earlier behind Carter's apartment. He quickly bounded the steps and picked the lock on Carter's door. A second auxiliary lock, recently installed, gave him a little more difficulty and required a special tool but took only an additional forty seconds to open. Inside, a large canvas bag slung over his shoulder, he moved swiftly through the place, which consisted of a bedroom, a bathroom, and the large room that was kitchen, living room, and dining room in one. He snatched up a notepad by the telephone, a set of fatigues hanging in the closet, and another in a bag Carter used for dirty laundry. After his first sweep through the place, he stopped in the middle of the large room and checked his watch. He stroked his unshaven chin thoughtfully and furrowed his brow. He went into the bathroom and checked inside the cabinets under the sink. Nothing there but a couple of spare towels and some toilet-bowl cleaner. He knelt beside the toilet and removed the plumbing access panel set into the wall. There, beneath the junction of the pipes serving the toilet and the sink, was something wrapped in a towel like the ones he had found under the sink. Carefully, he removed it from its hiding place. Setting it gently on the lid of the toilet seat, he unwrapped it, revealing an odd-looking short-length shotgunlike weapon with an unusually heavy hard-plastic stock, known in the Developmental Weapons Division of the United States Army as an Alpha Taser E-45. There was also a plastic bag containing a dozen white cartridges.

Mark wrapped the whole package back up and stuffed it into his canvas bag. Then he replaced the access panel and left the apartment.

The anniversary clock on Lang's desk, barely visible through the forest of Chinese-food cartons and piles of exhibit books, was halfway between nine and ten. To Lang, his tie loosened and his shirtsleeves rolled up, it felt more like midnight.

Amy, ensconced behind the conference table across the room, was reading deposition transcripts while plowing through her Szechuan beef and snow peas. They had sent Rachel and Alex home about an hour ago. The process of preparing for trial had moved into the phase Lang called the Iditarod, a relentless, grueling grind that stretched out into unbroken weeks of long hours, meticulous attention to every conceivable detail, and a near-paranoid preoccupation with what the other side might do with each and every shred of evidence. It was the part of the process that never made its way into popular depictions of trial lawyers' work. It was also the part of the process that separated the best in the business from the rest; without it, the spellbinding opening statements and closing arguments made by lawyers in films and on television would never hold up. Tonight, it also seemed like the part of the process destined to make Lang an old man.

Amy glanced up and caught Lang looking at her. She smiled. "Losing your concentration?"

Lang nodded. "The frustrating thing is that I really do believe the version of the facts that Molly O'Keefe gave Seamus."

"Naturally," said Amy. "That's because you want to believe it." Lang started to protest, but Amy waved him off. "I'm kidding, Chris. Don't be so defensive. I believe her story, too. It's more credible than Lindstrom's and, besides, she has no reason to lie. The problem would seem to be that she may not get to tell her story."

"I know. At least Clive and Graham took Seamus's news pretty well. Jad wasn't happy, though."

"I noticed. No offense, but he sounds like a strange guy."

Lang shrugged. "I'm not offended. I really didn't know him well in school. Different circles, really. Actually, I think you're right, he seemed downright surly about her disappearance. I believe he wants to get Lindstrom even more than Ellerby and Andrews do."

"I think he wants him worse than *you* do and I didn't think that was possible. What was it he said at the end? 'Just don't ever give up'?"

" 'Just keep on digging. You never know what will turn up.' "

Amy nodded. "That's it. Seemed to have a chilling edge to it, though, the way he said it."

"Nah. Just a pep talk from a frustrated client."

"Look, Chris, Molly or no Molly, we have a good, solid contract case for several million dollars against a solvent defendant, substantially more if the judge gives us a little leeway with our lost-profits theory. We have a winning case that you will lay out with your usual gift for logic and clarity. And you will have the pleasure of slapping Russell Lindstrom around. And now, thanks to the judicial council, you will have the pleasure of doing so on court TV."

"Damnedest thing, isn't it?" Lang replied with a smile. They had both been surprised by the sudden reversal of federal-court policy by the Ninth Circuit Judicial Council last week when it had been announced that it would allow cameras in trial courts for the first time, on a limited, pilot basis. For years, cameras had been permitted in most state courts, but the federal courts, insisting that cameras both threatened the fairness of their judicial proceedings and undermined the dignity of their august deliberations, had steadfastly refused to budge on the issue. Then, without fanfare, came the simple announcement of Interim Rule 27(c). That surprise was followed within days by an official minute order from Judge Schuyler Campbell notifying the parties that their case was to be tried under the provisions of Interim Rule 27(c).

"I guess that settles that," Amy had said upon handing Lang the cryptic order that consisted of two terse sentences. "Can I plan my vacation for the summer? With court television coverage *and* the convention right around the corner, there's no way Lindstrom won't go for a continuance now. And get it from Campbell."

"No vacations. And I'm not so sure about the continuance. You know how good Lindstrom is on television. Maybe he'll try to use it as a campaign vehicle."

Amy shook her head. "You think he would allow us to pound him with a fraud claim on court TV day after day while the delegates gather in Kansas City to decide if he could be elected president? Are you crazy? Instead of schmoozing delegates in his hospitality suite at the convention, he'd be sitting there on camera getting raked for weeks!"

Lang had to agree that there was logic to Amy's point. In any event, no vacations were planned, although they anxiously watched the mail for the anticipated motion. None had come yet. And Molly hadn't resurfaced. But there was still time on both fronts, Lang reminded himself. He returned to his labors in silence.

Early the next morning, Russell Lindstrom's impressive entourage paused from its assault on the voters of Michigan for a strategy meeting of its own. Grand Blanc, Michigan, just southeast of Flint, was the headquarters for the Micro Element Information Systems Corporation, the largest and best-known of Lindstrom's information-processing and -delivery companies. It occupied an entire seven-story glass cylinder, rising futuristically from the rolling green hills alongside Interstate 75. The sixth floor of the heavily secured "Micro E" building consisted of the functional equivalent of a television studio, one of nine satellite teleconferencing centers maintained by various Lindstrom companies throughout the United States. Its usual purpose was to provide rapid, real-time video conferencing.

In front of the Micro E building, Lindstrom's long black car came to a halt and Agent Callero bounced out and opened the back door. Lindstrom, in a perfectly tailored dark gray suit and crisply starched white shirt, emerged and was whisked into the building, surrounded by his security escort. In a second car came Dick Banfield and Gina Calabrese.

Lindstrom instructed the Secret Service agents to remain in the main lobby while he went on upstairs. "If your security arrangements were as thorough as mine are here, boys," he explained affably, "the world would never have heard of Lee Harvey Oswald or John Hinckley." They stayed in the lobby as Lindstrom, Banfield, and Calabrese went to the sixth floor.

They were greeted at the door to the video-conference room by Gary Vanderwald, Micro E's director of data transmission. He was a scrawny, balding man with a perpetual film of oil on his sallow complexion, wire-framed glasses crookedly perched on his thin, hatchetlike face, and a persistent tic in his left eye. He was inarticulate and a mumbler, and those who worked with him frequently commented that he had body odor. He also had an IQ of over 190 and had never failed to accomplish a stated objective of the company in less time and for less money than had been budgeted. He was one of Lindstrom's favorite employees.

"Good morning, Mr. Lindstrom," said Vanderwald, his tic in full gallop.

Lindstrom extended his hand. "Hello, Gary. How are you today?"

"Fine, sir," he mumbled. "Uh, thank you."

Lindstrom smiled. "How's Cleopatra doing these days?"

Vanderwald's face lit up, just as it did every time the great man mentioned his dearest companion, a huge, lazy Persian cat. Although Lindstrom asked about the cat every single time he saw him, Vanderwald always seemed to be taken by surprise by the head man's thoughtfulness. "She's fine also," he managed to say.

"No kittens yet, eh?"

Unaccountably, Vanderwald blushed. "Oh, Mr. Lindstrom," he said with an embarrassed grin. It suddenly occurred to Banfield, who had witnessed this exact exchange on several previous occasions, that Vanderwald probably considered himself married to the cat and, therefore, Lindstrom's comment had a naughty quality for him. Then it occurred to him that that was exactly what Lindstrom had intended. With a slight shudder, Banfield forced himself not to think about the whole thing.

"All set for our show?" asked Lindstrom breezily, as they entered the video room.

"Oh, yes," said Vanderwald, into his chin.

The men seated themselves around three sides of a conference table, facing a huge video screen on the far wall. On the screen was the image of another table and chairs, the mirror image of the one in the room, situated so that the illusion was created that the table on the screen was but the other end of the table in the room. Large red letters at the bottom of the screen flashed the words UPLINK ESTABLISHED.

Lindstrom sat at the end of the table facing the screen. He flipped a switch marked Self View on the control panel that was built into the table and immediately the image on the screen was replaced by a live picture of the four of them sitting at their own half-table. He adjusted a dial labeled Zoom and their image grew larger. Satisfied with the picture, he flipped the switch again and the table at the other end of the link appeared.

This time there were people in the other room. At the head of the table was Gentry Hickman. To his left sat his young associate, Randy Overbrook; to his right, J. D. Royster, the dour-faced house counsel for Arrow.

Lindstrom waved. "Good morning, Gentry. Randy. J.D.," he said. "Sorry to be so disoriented, but where the hell are you calling from today?"

Hickman laughed. "We're in Oklahoma City, Russell." There was a split-second delay in the transmission, which was definitely disorienting at first. After a few minutes, however, they were chatting as comfortably as if they really were at the same table.

"What do we need to handle today?" Lindstrom asked, his eyes moving to the huge digital display of the time on the wall above the screen. "And before you tell me, let me confess that I never thought I'd say this, but a lawsuit is starting to feel like a welcome relief from the relentless pressures of the campaign."

Hickman laughed again. "Well, from down here, it looks like you're kicking some real butt out there. And having fun."

"Kicking or getting it kicked?" Lindstrom replied good-naturedly. "Fun, no. That part is all act. But I have to admit it's going better than we expected. So what's up with Christopher Lang's little boil on my behind."

"Strategic call, that's all, Russell. You know that the trial is less than a month before the convention and could last a month. We will try to get you out on a motion but I'm not optimistic. Summary judgments are notoriously hard to obtain."

"Let's assume, just for the sake of argument, mind you, that I don't understand a goddamned word you're saying and let's cut to the chase." There was steel but not yet true annoyance in his tone.

"Do you want to continue, postpone, the trial until after the election? Simple as that."

"Assuming we can't get me out altogether?"

"That's right, assume that we can't."

"If this thing, this campaign, goes the way it looks to be shaping up, I'm going to be pretty darned busy about then."

"That's right."

"Your advice?"

"Continue it. There's nothing to gain. It's a sideshow to the main event and it will only drain you of critical time and energy. And court TV will just be another distrac—"

"Say again," interrupted Lindstrom.

"Excuse me?"

"Court TV. What did you say about court television?"

Hickman looked over at Overbrook, whose smile faded just slightly. Then, into the camera, he said, "I thought we had told you. The ninth circuit has approved experimental telecasting of certain trials. Our case is in the program."

"You mean they're going to televise the trial?" Before Hickman could answer, Lindstrom's mind moved rapidly through the possibilities. "Would any of the major cable networks carry it?" he asked.

"I don't . . ." He hesitated. "I really don't know, Russell."

"Would equal time apply?" asked Lindstrom, referring to the provisions of federal law that require a broadcaster who has given airtime to a political candidate to make equal time available to all other candidates.

"To be honest, I don't know. We'd have to look into it. I don't guess there's a lot of precedent here." Before Hickman's answer was finished, Lindstrom leaned over to say something into Banfield's ear. Hurriedly, the younger man left the room. Lindstrom signaled over to Vanderwald, who was observing the proceedings from a corner of the room off-camera to those at the other end.

"Gary? Can we link up with CableStar through this setup?"

Vanderwald adjusted his glasses nervously and licked his upper lip. His tic had wings again. "Sure. Different transponders, of course," he said, thinking aloud. "Different satellites, but we can send uplink through ours and they can tune to it with our security descramblers."

"How long?"

"Ten minutes. Fifteen, max. We'd have to call them first."

"Dick's doing that. Trying to see if Milo Rich is available."

To the screen, he said, "Look, Gentry. We're going to do a little checking at this end. We will call you back on the system in exactly thirty minutes. That's ten-eighteen your time. And, Gentry, let's have a definitive answer to the equal time question." With that, he rose and left the room.

In fifteen minutes, Milo Rich appeared on the conference-room screen. He wore not a white shirt and vest but a faded red sweatshirt with the word "Gamecocks" in white lettering across the front. His familiar reading glasses were pushed up onto his forehead. He sat at the desk of his *American Idea Net* set.

"Hello, Milo," called out Lindstrom. "Can you hear us?"

"Not only that, Russell, but I can *see* you. I feel like I'm on *Nightline*."

Lindstrom chuckled. "I've got a question for you, Milo. This lawsuit that I'm engaged in out there in California is set to go to trial in June and it doesn't look like we can get it postponed."

"Bad timing," observed Rich.

"Yes, maybe. But I was wondering—if it does go ahead as scheduled, would CableStar televise it?"

Rich sat up in his chair, just a touch of righteousness in the arch of his spine. "Of course we'd cover it, whenever it takes place. And you know we'll give it our best—"

"No, Milo. Not cover it. *Televise* it. Live telecast from the courtroom."

Rich frowned. "Russell, I may be missing something here, but, as you know, I received my training in law and I believe that federal courts do not allow cameras of any kind in the courtroom."

"There's a new rule that allows them on an experimental basis in the federal courts out here in the . . ." He paused and turned to Dick Banfield and Gina Calabrese, who sat to his left.

"Ninth circuit," offered Gina.

"Ninth circuit," finished Lindstrom. "And I was wondering if it would be something that CableStar would be interested in carrying live."

Rich sat up straighter still, his glasses flipping down onto his face. "Gee, Russell," he said, rendered temporarily and uncharacteristically inarticulate by the implications of this revelation. "I'm not the news director here, of course, but I can't imagine that we wouldn't carry it. It could do for us what Simpson did for CNN. I'd certainly push for it. In fact, CNN will probably carry it so we might have to. I'd like to be the on-site correspondent myself. That could be big news." He paused for a moment. "How concerned are you about the outcome?"

"Not very," replied Lindstrom with an easy, warm smile.

Rich nodded, his thoughts already racing far ahead. "Let me get back to you on this, Russell. I'll have an answer by the end of the day."

Lindstrom smiled again and thanked him. It was 11:18. "I've got to run, Milo. I'll look forward to hearing from you."

A minute later, the link to Oklahoma City was reestablished.

"Gentry," said Lindstrom in greeting. "The equal time doctrine?"

"Does not apply, Russell, where the airtime is coverage of a legitimate news event. That's why the incumbent president can get away with murder if he plays events right."

"I don't think we'll need to go so far as murder, Gentry," replied Lindstrom. "But I think this may work out well. Very well, indeed." He paused, then decisively added, "Pending further word from me on the subject, there will be no continuance, okay?"

"It's your call, boss."

CHAPTER 21

THE WIND DROVE THE TORRENTIAL RAIN ALMOST horizontally, across the hood and against the windows of the black Lincoln Town Car as it made its way through the deserted streets of Georgetown. Great chains of lightning danced across the black night sky at regular intervals, punctuated by the artillery fire of thunder. In the rear seat of the car, Jad Piersall could have felt the huge, heavy automobile rock with the sheer force of that powerful southeasterly wind if his concentration hadn't been entirely directed elsewhere. By the dome light, again and again he went over the yellow legal pad on which he had outlined the presentation he would give tonight to the men who called themselves the Fortress. Each time, he found something that had to be changed, often substantially. There just wasn't any good way to do this, he thought as the knot in his stomach tightened yet again. Colonel Easley's words from their afternoon phone call still rang menacingly in his head. "Your operation is all we have, Jad. Don't fuck it up!" It was more than just the uncharacteristically harsh words from his mentor and benefactor. It was the *tone*. Chilling. Threatening. Almost disdainful. Piersall had needed to use the bathroom four times on the plane and would need to use the one at The Roan as soon as he arrived. This was going to be very unpleasant.

The plan had been so perfect, so wonderfully elegant. Track Lindstrom on all fronts, doggedly, with the persistence of an Indian scout—through the press, through television and radio, through every database he could get his hands on. Watch and wait, patiently and meticulously, sifting through the details for a mistake, an opening that could be exploited in the lifelong commitment to destroy the man whose duplicity had brought down Robert Piersall's fighter jet over Da Nang.

Then, years of careful, persistent observation suddenly appeared to bear fruit. There it was, right on the pages of the *Wall Street Journal*. Not a big, splashy article. A blurb, really, buried deep on page 18-C, in the Business Briefs section, but not so small that it could escape his notice. Pegasus Technologies, a small company in England, had announced that it was going out of business. The company had staked its commercial life on a single product, a recreational airplane, an innovative design by the world-renowned experimental-design boutique from California called Arrow Dynamics. Of course, the piece was too small to include a mention of the founder of Arrow. And, besides, he had had little or nothing to do with the company for more than a dozen years, or so the fiction went. But Piersall had known who he was and what this could mean. Suddenly, he was a step closer to his objective and to a measure of retribution for his brother.

The call to the solicitor in London handling the affairs of the company had followed, and the offer to provide important information if they were interested in getting to the bottom of what had cost them their investment. The meeting in the small pub across from the Victoria and Albert Museum that beastly cold, rainy January afternoon. Jad Piersall, looking and sounding more confident than he felt, more informed than he was. Going on instinct, and hope, and more than a little religious fervor. The anticipated reluctance of Clive Andrews to go forward, but the surprise of Graham Ellerby's immediate and obvious interest. The follow-up telephone calls, carefully walking the line between genuine interest and the blind ambition to get Lindstrom that it masked. Finally the offer to bankroll litigation to recover their losses, disguised as an investment in the company, an offer even Andrews could not refuse.

The last piece of the plan was to find the ideal trial lawyer to handle the case. The contract case against the company was not too difficult, of course. And, from Piersall's point of view, it was irrele-

vant. The target was Lindstrom and the objective was to hang a
fraud claim on him personally. Not the equivalent of a criminal
conviction, to be sure, but to an American electorate thoroughly
primed by Watergate and its vast progeny, it would be a heavy
character burden to carry, probably too heavy. From Piersall's perspective, to consign Lindstrom to disgrace, to take from him something he had allowed to become important, vital, would be far more
satisfying than taking the bastard's life. Ironically, the lawyer turned
out to be one he had known for half his life, had watched from afar,
while his star had risen among big-case trial lawyers. Chris Lang, the
cocky, tenacious litigator who had a spectacular record of success
against the toughest, best-financed adversaries in the country. And
he was clean, careful and, above all, ambitious. The perfect weapon
in this highly ritualized arena of combat. In retrospect, he had
seemed to be the strongest link in the chain. But now, even Lang's
prodigious ambition was faltering against the weaknesses in his case.
And the whole fucking thing was about to come crashing down on
Piersall, the Fortress, and the memory of that heroic boy whose
promise had been snuffed out by a high-tech trinket Lindstrom had
traded to the North Vietnamese.

The first floor of The Roan was completely dark and the lights
on the second were barely visible through the driving rain as the car
pulled alongside the curb. As he got out, Piersall was nearly knocked
to the ground by the force of the wind. The door blew out of his
grasp and snapped back hard against its hinges. It took all his
strength to close it. The lash of the bitterly cold rain ripped violently
at his cheek and neck, digging down, inside the fur collar of his
topcoat. A flash of lightning, nearby now, judging from the instantaneous crash of thunder, lit up the street with a ghastly strobe.

The front door of the building was unlocked. There was no
one to greet him as he entered, drenched from the mad dash from
the curb. He heard voices upstairs, barely audible above the tumult
of the storm. Then a shout, and a return shout. The shudder that
went through him had nothing to do with the vicious early-spring
storm raging outside in the night. He stood motionless in the inner
lobby, collecting himself. The pager in his pocket sounded, alerting
him to an incoming message. He checked the readout: It was a
number Clive Andrews was using for urgent messages. Piersall
frowned as the "urgencies" in his life suddenly seemed to mount
up. Clive was just going to have to wait, he thought as he stepped
into the men's room.

General Hendricks had the floor as Piersall entered the second-floor dining room. He looked briefly at Piersall but did not greet him. No one greeted him. The light up here was harsh tonight, giving everything in the room an eerie, malevolent cast. Piersall moved to the lone empty seat at the table. His hands felt cold, stiff, and clammy. Colonel Easley nodded to him ever so slightly as he sat down.

". . . goddamned mess on our hands," Hendricks was saying. "This has been a fucking lifetime project for most of us and, now, we're virtually powerless as the prick closes in on the goddamned White House. And now this, this lawsuit." He gestured toward Piersall with his dying cigar. "We're reduced to this hare-brained, back-door, half-assed attempt to sneak up on him, and it isn't even working."

"For Christ's sake, Win," barked Lawrence Crispin. "What do you want us to do? Shoot the son of a bitch?"

"It's worked before," Hendricks fired back at the admiral. Crispin's response was a disdainful wave and a scowl.

"We're losing our focus," observed Clayton Hasselrig. "Over at Central Intelligence, we became very accomplished at this sort of indirect, covert operation. But it requires patience and meticulous preparation. And putting the right people in the right positions."

Before Piersall could respond, Colonel Easley stepped in. "And it's a matter of how we equip those people, Clay. Now, look, gentlemen, it's late. We've asked Jad here to come all the way from Michigan, on a late flight, to give us some information. I think the least we can do is extend him the courtesy of hearing him out." He turned to the younger man, seated next to him. "Fill us in, will you, Jad?"

For the next forty-five minutes, interminably uncomfortable minutes for Jared Piersall, he laid out all of the critical points the men in the room needed to know about the operation designed to turn a lawsuit for civil fraud into a covert political operation aimed at destroying a presidential campaign. His rigorous military training impelled him to cover everything with meticulous detail, including all of the errors and misjudgments, but his legal training, equally demanding, enabled him to defend his position and his decisions along the way.

When he had finished, there was a long moment of silence in the room. Finally, Easley said, "So, it comes down to this: Is there a fraud case against Lindstrom and can it be won?"

"There is a case, Colonel. It is not yet fully in place. It will depend to a degree on the O'Keefe woman. We're looking for her right now. We'll find her and we'll put assets in place to secure her when we do. There's no doubt in my mind that Chris Lang has the skill and the tenacity to make the case when all of the evidence is in."

General Hendricks pulled his cold, wet cigar out of his mouth. "What's this shit, Jad, about the evidence not being fully in place? Do we have a case or don't we?"

"And," interjected Crispin, pivoting in his chair to face the lawyer, "if you don't have it, what will it take to get it?"

Piersall looked at Easley, but the colonel sat in silence. Piersall said, "There are key items of evidence yet to be uncovered by the trial team. They have to do with exactly what Lindstrom was doing and when, what he knew, and what he did about it."

Hendricks wasn't satisfied. "What the fuck is that supposed to mean?" he stormed. "That sounds like the whole goddamned case, to me. Let's not pussyfoot around this thing, son. Do we have the evidence or not? And how do we get our hands on it if we don't?" The pitch of his voice rose steadily as he spoke.

All eyes were on Piersall. He alone was unaware of the beads of perspiration glistening across his brow. He swallowed hard. "We don't have everything we need yet. I believe there are other pieces of evidence that will strengthen the case. I am confident that we will acquire those pieces in the time remaining."

"Sounds pretty equivocal to me, Jad," said Hasselrig, coolly, without emotion. "I'll be honest with you. We've given you a great deal of leeway and I've always supported your effort. But we're coming down the stretch and I'm hearing more questions than answers. Look, son, this is not a game. The stakes are high. If it came down to killing the son of a bitch, I'm pretty sure we'd have a close vote in this room. We don't even want to think about that. We need to be persuaded that the job can be done your way."

A lightning bolt struck nearby, lighting the room suddenly and starkly, followed immediately by a tremendous explosion of thunder. No one at the table so much as flinched. Piersall licked his lips. "Consider it done, Mr. Director," he managed to say with quiet confidence. "I'll have everything in place well before the trial."

During the uncomfortable silence that ensued, every eye in the room was trained on Piersall. He felt very much alone and under siege. But he was a tough individual, disciplined by the hard lessons of war and service. He was determined to pull this thing together, to move all the necessary assets into place for a successful mission. He sat silently, defiant in his ultimate confidence in himself and his judgment.

At last, Easley stood up. "I've got to get going, gentlemen." To Piersall, he added, "C'mon. I'll give you a lift."

Piersall rose with this cue. "Thank you, Colonel. Appreciate it." He followed Easley out of the room.

Outside, at the head of the stairs, Easley stopped him with a hand on his chest. "I supported you in there, Jad," he said quietly, the warmth he had just exhibited suddenly gone. "But I expect you to deliver for me. If you don't have what you need, we'll get it for you. We don't need a hero and a lost cause."

Piersall stood his ground against the pressure on his chest. "It's under control, Colonel."

"Good," replied Easley, withdrawing his hand. "Because I expect nothing less. Now, let's get out of here."

This is getting to be work, Seamus Callahan realized as he wove his way through the surprisingly heavy traffic on the narrow roads outside of Ballyshannon. He had taken the day off, a Saturday, to follow a hunch and try to find the elusive Molly O'Keefe up near her hometown in the northern part of the republic. But Irish roads being what they were, the drive had consumed nearly half a day already and the effort, which had looked like a good idea in the first light of dawn, was starting to take on the feel of a complete waste of time.

Two more trips up to Kilmurry in the past week had confirmed that Molly had not been to her little home on the cliffs for more than two weeks now, and the prospect that she might not resurface in time to do any good for Bill Quinn's lawyer friends seemed very real. Michael McDonough had not been able to shed any light on her whereabouts, his only real contribution to the enterprise being to give Seamus the sense that her disappearance was unexpected and, possibly, cause for alarm. Seamus did not subscribe to this view; the resourcefulness of the Irish was well documented. If she disappeared, Seamus reasoned, it was likelier than not that she did so because she wanted to, in order to move about more freely. To Seamus, this suggested that she might be headed up north, where the republican issues were harder-edged and the risks to her safety more genuine. All of this, coupled with the fact that her home and a good portion of her family were still up there, made a holiday of sorts in the Ballyshannon vicinity a real possibility.

Seamus glanced down at the open journal on the passenger seat to verify the address. Most of the streets here were narrow and laid out at odd angles, making the going through the heart of the city slow and difficult. At last, he came to the intersection of Old Armagh Road and Kilkenny Farm Lane. The lane, lined with early wild roses and overgrown honeysuckle, was narrow and well hidden from the main road, so that he nearly missed the turn. Its surface had originally been paved with cobblestones, then covered over with asphalt many years later. But both surfaces were cracked and broken now, making for a brutally rough ride that jerked and shook the Morris down to its chassis bolts.

A quarter mile down the lane, past several small, neat cottages maintained with obvious pride despite their modesty, he came to number 43, a white frame bungalow. He pulled the Morris as far to the side of the road as possible and got out. He approached the front gate, where two women stood talking.

"Afternoon, ladies," Seamus said, touching the bill of his cap. The older woman, the one standing outside the gate, eyed him suspiciously. The other, teenaged and very pretty, smiled pleasantly. "Constable Callahan from Shannon," he said affably, flipping out his constable's shield.

The older one glanced at the badge. "What would a constable from Shannon want up here, do you wonder?"

"Would this be the home of Molly O'Keefe, ma'am?" he asked of the younger woman, sidestepping the question of her elder.

"And why would we answer to the likes of you, Mr. Shannon Constable?" replied the older woman, a look of venom in her eye.

Seamus turned to face her directly. "May I assume that you are Mrs. Mairead Boyne, madame?"

Mairead was stunned and it showed.

Seamus took advantage of the space created by her surprise. "I mean Mrs. O'Keefe no harm and I'm not here on any official constabulary business. It's a private matter involving people in America that I need to see her about."

The younger woman spoke. "I'm Deirdre McKinney, Constable," she said with a smile, and extended her hand. Mairead reached out quickly and snatched it away before Seamus could shake it.

"For the love of God, Deirdre, when will you learn to be less trusting?"

"Sound advice," observed Seamus, looking directly at Mairead, "for a happy and well-balanced life."

"For life up here, Constable," retorted Mairead, a fire in her eyes. "If you want it to last very long. Not that you would know."

"Look," said Seamus, suddenly feeling weary. "I've come a long way—"

"For nothin'," snapped Mairead.

Seamus narrowed his eyes slightly. "To talk to Mrs. O'Keefe. I've met with her before and she knows that I'm on the up-and-up."

"Well, now," said Mairead, folding her arms. "Why didn't you say so?"

Seamus frowned slightly at her heavy sarcasm. "Look, Mrs. Boyne. I'm doin' a favor for a friend. Molly—Mrs. O'Keefe—can help him out. Important people are involved and she can help quite a bit, as I understand it. And it'll be no—"

"She's not here," said Mairead simply. "And hasn't been." She turned away and started down the lane. Over her shoulder, she added, "Sorry you wasted the trip, Constable Callahan." Lifting a hand in a wave high over her head, she said, "Good day, Deirdre. Now go back into the house."

Deirdre looked apologetically at Seamus. "I'm really sorry, Constable. But it's the truth. Just like I told the other man who asked."

"Other man?" asked Seamus. "What other man?"

"You know," she replied. "The one with the sad scar on his cheek." She indicated with her index finger. "Molly used to live here—"

"Into the house, Deirdre!" shouted Mairead, continuing down the lane.

Deirdre started toward the house. "But she's gone down to Kilmurry. She hasn't been here for months."

"Do you have any idea—"

"Sorry, Constable," she replied. "I really can't help you. That's just the way Molly is." She disappeared into the house, leaving Seamus to watch down the lane after Mairead Boyne and wonder who the man with the scar might be.

A tall man with an iron-gray crew cut got out of a cab in the middle of a block near Vancouver's waterfront and walked up the street. A five-minute walk found him at the front door of Kay's Fish House.

The restaurant inside was barely brighter than the sidewalk outside. At the hostess's station, he squinted to see into the dining area. Satisfied that what he was looking for wasn't there, he secured a table for two in the back and took the chair against the wall, where he had an unobstructed view across the entire dining room, clear to the front door.

He ordered a glass of water, chilled but with no ice, and sipped from it while he watched the front door. He sat quietly, checking his watch regularly, all the while rotating his glass around the damp circle it created on the cocktail napkin. At exactly eight o'clock, Jad Piersall, carrying a briefcase, entered the restaurant and spoke briefly to the hostess. She pointed to the man in the back.

The man with the crew cut eyed him obliquely from his chair as he approached.

"Mr. Haverstock," said Piersall, managing to suppress his excitement. "Jad Piersall. I believe Clive Andrews explained that I would be taking his place. I'm working with Pegasus's trial counsel."

Haverstock nodded. "He told me I was to talk to you as I would to him."

Piersall smiled and ordered a Dewar's, neat, while Haverstock simply refilled his glass of cold water.

"This is the city's best seafood place," Haverstock said. "Anything on the menu is first-rate."

After they had ordered and Piersall got his second scotch, he turned to the business at hand. "Clive seems to think you may have something very important for me to hear."

"You're interested in sampling the goods, then, are you?" asked Haverstock with a mirthless grin. "We will need to talk about price."

"Later."

Haverstock looked dubious, but said nothing, continuing to rotate his glass on the napkin.

"Okay," said Piersall into the silence. "How about this as a compromise? You give me some background, then we'll agree on a price structure, then you give me the specifics. If and when you deliver, we will pay."

"Background, then price, then specifics, then half the money, then delivery, then the back half."

"Agreed."

"Fair enough," said Haverstock. "Where do you want me to start?"

"How about the beginning? My flight isn't until late tomor-row morning."

Will Haverstock was a flight engineer right out of the Air Force when he landed a job at the mysterious, exciting place called the Skunkworks. The men recognized as the up-and-coming giants of the emerging world of postwar aviation were all there, among them the charismatic Russell Lindstrom. It was nothing less than a pantheon of the latter-day gods of aviation, all huddled in a hot converted Quonset hut on the flight line in Van Nuys, California. Together, they turned dreams and theory into the cold steel and flaming afterburn of aerodynamic reality.

But there was little money and even less security in the academic side of government "spook" work in the fifties. And what made sense for a young guy fresh out of the service was less than adequate for a married man in his mid-twenties with a baby on the way. So, when Lindstrom spun his dream of an alternative enterprise, a private enterprise, where he and the cream of the younger engineers could do for their own account much of what they had learned to do for the government, the vision was irresistible. On a hot, smoggy August morning, Lindstrom and twelve of the brightest, most creative young men ever to toil for the United States Air Force walked out of the Skunkworks, through a rigorous series of exit interviews with the Department of Defense and the Central Intelligence Agency, and set up shop at the airstrip in San Sebastian, California.

From there, it was a dizzying ride to the pinnacle of the world of private aviation. One after another, they conjured up, built and tested some of the most dramatic, innovative aircraft ever to move from the drawing board to the flight line. Ironically, their former employer would become their number one customer and, in effect, for doing the very same work they had previously done for a yeoman's wage, they would all become very rich at the expense of the United States taxpayer.

Arrow Dynamics grew in importance and profitability, but managed to remain small and collegial. Lindstrom was adamant about this, and he succeeded by dint of his clear vision and powerful hand. And his uncanny ability to negotiate with the government. In an era that predated complex government procurement laws, he parlayed that skill into a fortune for his "partners" and a megafortune for himself.

That megafortune ultimately took Lindstrom out of the mainstream operations of Arrow Dynamics and, during the late seventies and early eighties, he was less and less a presence in the company's operations. Instead, he excelled at finding new and different ways to plow his personal wealth back into business ventures that consistently succeeded, and succeeded grandly. Thus, it was no surprise to his colleagues at Arrow when the official announcement came that Lindstrom was stepping down as president of the company and selling his stock back to the other shareholders. All Haverstock knew was that his own bank account never shrank and he always seemed to have plenty of money to do all the things he, his wife, and his three boys wanted to do.

Haverstock, as one of Lindstrom's original "apostles," had enjoyed a certain elevated status among the company's engineers. He assumed responsibilities over key development projects and by the 1980s had become the untitled head of experimental development, the cutting edge of Arrow's business. Thus, every new development program that came to the company went to Haverstock, whose job was to approve the overall plan of the program, make staffing decisions, oversee the design and testing phases, and approve the final engineering report. It was an important function within the company, carrying considerable responsibility, and Haverstock relished it.

But Haverstock's role changed for the worse with the arrival of Brent Milinsky, a brash, cocky fighter jock. Accustomed to brilliant young engineers who came into the company full of awe and respect for this place of reverence, Haverstock was completely unprepared for the swagger of this fresh fighter pilot whose undeniable intellectual gifts were vastly overshadowed by a natural, intuitive affinity for flying airplanes. His clashes with Haverstock, the most authoritative figure on the site, became a staple of everyday existence at "the Hangar," the main building at Arrow's facility. Consistently, test plans, carefully structured by the engineers, meticulously checked and approved by Haverstock, and sanctioned by the FAA, were simply ignored and rewritten in the air by a seat-of-the-pants test pilot. Not only was the practice dangerous and technically illegal, it was the kind of insubordination that Haverstock would not tolerate. Ultimately, he had no choice but to go to Lindstrom, the man who owned no stock and held no office but whose word was still final on every issue that arose.

Lindstrom was in a contemplative mood that Sunday afternoon up at the house. He greeted Haverstock warmly and took him out to the grounds behind the house, overlooking the Mediterranean pool and guest house just at the foot of the magnificent mountains. To Haverstock's annoyance, Lindstrom's recently retained "chief of staff," Richard Banfield, was also there. Haverstock didn't like Banfield and made no pretense to the contrary. He was the first nonengineer Lindstrom had ever brought on board in any capacity and Haverstock found nothing about him to respect or like. Besides, there was something sneaky, underhanded about the man. Normally, however, that didn't matter, since Haverstock's area of operation was limited to Arrow Dynamics, and did not intersect with Banfield's. On this occasion, he did his best to ignore him.

As always, Lindstrom listened attentively. Well aware that Lindstrom himself had handpicked Milinsky, Haverstock trod carefully in making his case. The kid was good, he conceded, and a pilot without peer in the organization. But the rules were there for a reason. There were considerations at stake far beyond the specific flight test involved. At stake was the atmosphere of "disciplined creativity" that Lindstrom himself had made the heart of the enterprise. And there was the undeniable effect on the morale and conduct of the others, who could not help but notice Milinsky's insubordination. He was nearing the point of being out of control, a patently intolerable situation.

At the close of his case, Haverstock waited. He had debated whether to ask for Milinsky's outright dismissal or simply a reprimand, which he feared might do no more than buy time. Ultimately, he did neither, simply telling the story and waiting to see where Lindstrom wanted to go with it. Haverstock thought he detected a tiny smirk on Banfield's face as he concluded, but he couldn't be sure. Meanwhile, Lindstrom drank from his tall, frosted glass of lemonade juiced with a dash of vodka and gazed out over the pool and rolling green lawn beyond to the Sierra Madre Mountains.

"Will," Lindstrom began thoughtfully, "tell me something. Have you ever seen anyone fly a Quixote pusher like Brent?"

Haverstock was thrown a little off-balance by the question. He wondered briefly if Lindstrom had really been listening at all. "I guess not," he managed to say, without conviction.

"You *guess* not? Come on, Will. You've never seen anything like him. Period. Has no fear. I don't mean he suppresses fear, as you and I can do when we have to. I mean he is fearless. Without fear. It doesn't exist for him. Do you have any idea how liberating that can be?" He smiled and shook his head slowly at the wonder of it. "I don't think we can even imagine it."

Banfield nodded in agreement with Lindstrom, which only served to intensify Haverstock's contempt for him. Haverstock sat in silence, watching the reflection of the mountains in the glassy surface of the pool. He had no idea what to say, or what to make of Lindstrom's comments, for that matter. So he said nothing, while Lindstrom, too, sat quietly looking over the water, an oddly bemused expression on his face.

At length, Lindstrom spoke again. "The government is about to move into a whole new technology on a very grand scale. Digital radar imaging. Do you know what that is?"

Haverstock shook his head.

"The projection of false radar images from an array of geosynchronous orbiting satellites. Impossible to tell them from the genuine article without an eyeball confirmation. Do you know what that means?"

Haverstock shrugged. "It'd make combat readiness damned near impossible, I imagine."

"It'd do a hell of a lot more than that," interjected Banfield, incurring a sharp look of resentment from Haverstock.

"It would effectively disable all conventional radar from active engagement in a conventional air war," said Lindstrom, also ignoring Banfield. "For every image projected, the enemy would have to scramble aircraft for visual validation. With no more than two dozen real warplanes, you could have de facto air superiority over any conventional army and air force on the face of the earth. And if your planes could be made to fly low, slow and quiet enough, you could literally pick his pocket without the possibility of a friendly casualty."

"And the U.S. is going to develop this?"

"*We're* going to develop this. Here. In San Sebastian. And you're going to run the program. From the ground up."

Haverstock sat up as the realization of what he was being told hit him. "This is Quicksilver technology, isn't it?"

Lindstrom regarded him, for the first time in a long time, it seemed to Haverstock, once more as the brilliant son. He turned to Banfield. "Damn if he's not the right man for the job. You bet it's Quicksilver," he said to Haverstock. "Our Quicksilver. *Your* Quicksilver. Only it's a brilliant twist on it. It's—"

"The exact inverse!" said Haverstock. "Instead of masking the target, it creates too many false targets to track! Hell, this is better than Star Wars!"

Lindstrom frowned. "Damn it, Will, it's better than that. It's

Star Wars meets *Macbeth.*" He caught Haverstock's quizzical expression. "It's Great Birnam Wood come to Dunsinane Hill."

The light went on in Haverstock's eyes. "Only instead of soldiers carrying tree branches to confuse the enemy, it would be phantom aircraft."

" 'Let every soldier hew him down a bough,' " quoted Lindstrom, " 'and bear't before him. Thereby shall we shadow the numbers of our host and make discovery err in report of us.' "

Once again, as he had been each day since he had met him, Will Haverstock was amazed by the breadth of Russell Lindstrom's knowledge and the casual depth of his intellect. Unfortunately, however, he would look back upon that day as the end of a golden era in his life. And the beginning of a long spiral to desperation. The Digital Radar Imaging program—DiRadImag was its Defense Department acronym—got hung up and severly "descoped" in the Senate Armed Services Committee and, after a short pilot program, lost its funding entirely in the post-Cold War drive to cut the defense budget. In the meantime, Haverstock's place as the head of development had gone to a confident young man named Brent Milinsky.

It was during the waning days of the ill-fated DiRadImag pilot project at Arrow Dynamics that Haverstock, moved over to Building 2 and out of the mainstream operation, nevertheless became aware of a reemergence of Lindstrom on a regular basis at the company. There was an experimental-design project under way that was cloaked in an unusual degree of secrecy. At least once a week, Lindstrom visited the Hangar, where he found himself frequently sequestered for hours behind closed doors with Banfield, Milinsky, and others of the "inner circle." When Haverstock's casual inquiry to Steve Castillo about the project drew the abrupt response that he was not permitted to discuss it with him, he tried to go directly to Lindstrom himself.

But Haverstock was intercepted by Banfield, who politely told him that he was "out of the loop" on the new project and that was that. Repeated calls to Lindstrom were returned only by Banfield, if at all. Within weeks, the funding dried up on DiRadImag, followed by an outright cancellation "for convenience," in the parlance of the United States Air Force. He was suddenly a man without a job. Although it was thought to be temporary, he was pink-slipped three weeks later and asked by Banfield to clean out his office by the end of the day. The only explanation he got for the company's failure to give him the customary two weeks' notice was a shrug from Banfield and something about "national security." Lindstrom's schedule forced him to cancel a meeting Haverstock requested to get some answers. It was never rescheduled. And for Haverstock, the downward spiral never let up. His divorce and bankruptcy followed within two years of his last paycheck from Arrow Dynamics.

Piersall ordered another scotch while he picked at his food. "Do you know what the secret project was?" asked Piersall.

"I believe it was the one your clients' lawsuit is all about."

"How do you figure that?"

"Educated guess. But it's a good one. Superlightweight aircraft. An engine you could barely hear. Off-hours testing. Military spook types up from Central America. Australian guy hanging around the Hangar every now and then." He shrugged to suggest that he had completed his inventory of reasons.

"Australian? New Zealand, maybe?" asked Piersall.

Haverstock shrugged again. "Whatever."

Piersall rolled his eyes, then looked off into the distance. The dining room was now full of quiet late-night diners, but he took no notice. The promise of this potential witness had suddenly dimmed and, with it, his hopes of delivering on his commitments. He rubbed his hands together and flicked his tongue over the bow in his upper lip. "Let me be blunt, Mr. Haverstock. Exactly what *do* you know, personally, about the StormTree project?"

"Personally?" repeated Haverstock. "Zero."

"Shit!" said Piersall. He leaned forward on his elbows and looked down onto the plate of unfinished yellowfin tuna, laboriously trying to collect himself. The feeling that he was being scammed became overpowering.

Haverstock sat quietly across the table. After a long moment, he smiled his mirthless smile again. "Well, maybe zero is a little strong."

"Look, Mr. Haverstock," snapped an irate and frustrated Jad Piersall. "This is no fucking game. I need information—if you have it—evidence that my client can use."

Haverstock narrowed his eyes. "I know it's not a game, Mr. Piersall. But I have to be careful. I have a lot at stake. Besides, we've covered the background now. Before we get to specifics, we need to talk price."

"What are you talking about? What kind of specifics could there be? You've just conceded that you know nothing about my client's case. Why should I pay you anything?"

"You're not listening, Mr. Piersall. True, I wasn't personally involved in the project. But that doesn't mean that I don't have information that can be of value to you."

"What information?"

"Price, first."

Piersall made no effort to conceal his exasperation. "For Christ's sake, Haverstock! How can we talk price when I don't know what you have? Give me an idea, at least."

"No need to get angry, Mr. Piersall," said Haverstock. "But I need a quarter of a million dollars and I need to know if you can pay me that much."

"Look. I can't commit to anything unless I know what we're talking about. If you're asking me whether two hundred and fifty grand is in the ballpark, then yes, for the right evidence, my people can pay that amount. But it has to be good and it has to be admissible. And, frankly, you haven't told me anything that makes me think that we're going to be able to do business on that or any other basis."

Haverstock hesitated, as if to resolve something in his own mind. Apparently satisfied, he moved forward. "All right," he said, a touch triumphantly. "Let me ask you this: Do you have the engineering log?"

"Engineering log?"

"Yes. The record detailing each test flight Arrow conducted on the proof of concept—the prototype—through the course of the program."

"Well, we have the engineering report and the aircraft log, I believe," said Piersall, trying to recall the precise language used in the reports sent to Ellerby and Andrews by Amy Quinn.

Haverstock shook his head. "Not those. The final report is just a summary, the conclusions based on the test program. The aircraft log just shows flight times and hours in service."

"That's right," said Piersall, nodding as his memory was refreshed.

"I'm talking about the book, a notebook, a spiral notebook, actually, where the pilot and engineer for each flight record all of their observations, instrument readings, weather info, that sort of thing."

"I don't think so. The Arrow people testified that they didn't keep any such record."

"Bullshit," spat Haverstock. "They kept it. Or I should say they maintained it. They didn't *keep* it."

"They threw it away?"

"That's what the shredder bin is for."

"But it wasn't shredded?"

"No, sir," replied Haverstock, grinning without smiling. "I have it."

"You *have* it?" Piersall repeated, his voice rising with excitement.

"Sort of a walking-out-the-door insurance policy, salvaged from the jaws of the shredder."

"What does it say?"

"Two hundred and fifty thousand interesting things, Mr. Piersall. One hundred twenty-five of them now and the balance after I let you put the log into evidence."

"All right. I'll get you the first half tomorrow. The rest after you testify."

"Testify?" Haverstock asked, an edge to his voice.

"Yes," said Piersall. "Testify. There's no other way to get a document like that into evidence. Someone has to authenticate it. And there's no way any of the Arrow people will do it."

"Testify, huh? In court?"

"That's the way it works."

Haverstock fell silent for a moment. Piersall broke in. "What does the engineering log say about spin testing?"

"I don't really know," replied Haverstock, still obviously preoccupied with the prospect of testifying. "Haven't really studied it."

"Don't get cute, Mr. Haverstock. I'll pay. If I don't I'll never see the book."

Haverstock considered this point for a moment. "Spin testing is covered."

"What does it say about Lindstrom's involvement?"

"It'll show he was there. That he flew the aircraft, of course."

"Does it show that they discovered the spin problem?"

"It very well might. Probably will."

"Will?"

Haverstock smiled and checked his watch. "Half tomorrow. Half after the evidence gets in." He stood up.

"But—"

"That's all for now. Thanks for dinner." Haverstock headed out of the restaurant into the chilly British Columbia night.

CHAPTER 22

SITTING AT THE KITCHEN TABLE, LINGERING OVER A rare afternoon cup of coffee on a cold and blustery day, Ro was tired and having a hard time focusing on the proofs spread out before her. It was the kind of tired where her legs ached and her feet cramped, where her muscles and joints throbbed the way they did with the first stirrings of the flu. She sincerely hoped that she wasn't about to get sick, and that a day at home and a good night's sleep would fully restore her energy and well-being.

As she paged through her notebook looking for some of the thoughts she had recorded during the shoot up at Lake Tahoe, she came across a notation on the last page, far from the portion where she had made notes, in Jennifer's handwriting: "A.G. in S. D. (619) 555-1784." It was oddly familiar but she couldn't place it. Just then Jennifer was deposited onto the driveway by the car pool.

"Hi, Mom," she said as she breezed into the kitchen.

"Hi, Jen. Good day?"

Jennifer shrugged. "Pretty good," she replied, rationing her words in the fashion of teenagers everywhere.

Ro nodded. "How did you make out on that geometry quiz?"

"A," her daughter responded, managing to use fewer syllables still.

"Good work. I told you an extra half hour with those proofs couldn't hurt. By the way, Jennifer," she said, sliding the notebook across the table to her daughter. "What's this note in my note-book?"

A guilty look spread across her elder daughter's face. "Sorry, Mom. I didn't mean to mess with your business stuff. It's just that I couldn't find anything else to write on when I took the message."

"What message?" asked Ro.

"When Alma called this morning. She wanted to make sure we had her phone number in San Diego while she was gone for the long weekend. And, by the way, she wanted to thank you again for letting her go."

"Okay," Ro replied, suddenly remembering why the notation seemed so familiar. Why, she wondered, with a mild but growing sense of uneasiness, had Mark Fassero recorded Alma Garcia's San Diego phone number in his own diary sometime last fall?

The first light of dawn was barely piercing the heavy cloud cover over Shannon as Seamus eased his Morris into its familiar spot be-hind the constabulary. He was lost in thought about the details of the report he needed to complete for a sentencing hearing sched-uled for the first of the week. Suddenly, his train of thought was interrupted by a voice behind him. "Well, now, Constable Callahan, you certainly are a busy man at the crack of dawn, now aren't you?"

Startled, Seamus banged his head on the door frame, then wheeled around to see Molly O'Keefe standing directly behind him. She smiled the smile he remembered so well.

"Mrs. O'Keefe!" he managed to say. "Don't ever sneak up on an old man like that again!"

She laughed, a happy, carefree sound that, as it did for so many of her countrymen, belied the difficulties of her life. Again, as on the occasion of their first meeting, she affected a pose—hands on her hips, head and shoulders back—in a naked assessment of the man before her. Once more, even in the dimmest possible light, Seamus was struck by the brilliance of her fiery mane and the glow of her lovely face. "A frightened constable, then, is it?" She laughed again. "Saints preserve the God-fearin' folk from down in the county." Her eyes sparkled with mischief in the feeble dawn.

"It's hardly a laughin' matter, Mrs. O'Keefe. You could get hurt startlin' a lawman like that."

"What were you going to do, Constable? Faint on top of me and pin me to the pavement?" Clearly she was having fun at his expense and enjoying herself immensely. Somehow, Seamus didn't really mind all that much. Truth was, he was delighted to see her again, for a number of reasons.

"Where in the name of Mike have you been? I've scoured the county for you, and put in a trip up north, for that matter."

"Have you now? Scoured the county? I hardly think so. A call here and a call there is more like it. You see, Constable, I value my privacy and I had some things to attend to. I'm guessin' you need more information for your friend in California. Is that it, then?"

"It's a little more complicated than that. Can I buy you a hot cup and take a minute of your time?"

She looked dubious for a moment. "I'll not be going into the constabulary, now."

"Casey's," he said, pointing to the small bakery across the street.

"All right, then, for a minute," she said, pulling her shawl tightly around her shoulders and following him.

Inside, they ordered a cup of coffee for him, tea for her. A basket of hot croissants was delivered with the drinks. Molly smiled and raised an eyebrow at the continental touch.

"What is it, then, Constable?"

"The lawyer who's handlin' the case I told you about would like a chance to meet with you."

"That's a mighty long trip to satisfy a man's curiosity, don't you think?" she said, her eyes dancing in a way that told Seamus she was playing with him.

"Well," he replied, squirming slightly. "As I'm sure you've guessed, it's not just idle curiosity at work here, Mrs. O'Keefe. They—we—need you to go to America and testify in their trial against Russell Lindstrom. Just for part of one day, to tell only a part of the story you told me when we spoke at your home."

"Testify? In an American court? I don't think so, Constable. That really is too far to travel, and a little too public. And, remember, I don't really care about who ends up with how much money."

He frowned. "I know. I remember our conversation about money and principle. And liars who profit from their misdeeds. Since the last time we spoke, Mr. Lindstrom has given his side of the story and it differs dramatically from yours."

"Now there's a surprise," she said, taking a croissant. "What's he said?"

He opened his weathered satchel and fished out the bound copy of the Lindstrom deposition transcript that Bill Quinn had sent him. "Plenty," he said. "And nothin' at all."

She stopped in the middle of a drink and looked at him over her cup. "Well, now. There's a promisin' start."

Seamus, though initially disoriented by Molly's sudden appearance, was regaining himself. He was well aware that her decision to testify might hinge entirely on how he put this to her now. He opened up the deposition transcript to the first of several marked passages. "Let me read some of the things our Mr. Lindstrom has said under oath."

She reached out and took the booklet from his hand. "I'll have a look, if you don't mind."

"That's fine," Seamus said. "They've marked the portions they think you may take issue with," he explained.

She opened the booklet and began to read the first indicated passage. After a moment, she asked, "He met with Nigel one time? Why, the bloody lying bastard. We must have visited his place six or seven times in all. Just as I told you."

"Keep readin', Mrs. O'Keefe," urged Seamus.

"He just *landed* in his backyard? Bloody hell! He makes it sound as if Nigel chased him round, beggin' for a crumb of business. Not a word about the dinner up in San Francisco, or the proposition *he* made to Nigel about the airplane in the first place!"

"There's more," said Seamus, concealing his delight that Lindstrom's testimony was having precisely the effect that his people in Los Angeles had hoped.

She read on, sitting progressively straighter in her chair as she went. Her face flushed crimson with anger as she digested Lindstrom's words. "*Nigel's* idea? *Nigel's* idea? To build the fucking airplane? What a bloody lie! That's not how it happened at all. Not even close. How can someone just lie like that? It's a story he's makin' up, a fantasy, Seamus."

"I know it, Molly," replied Seamus, looking around the half-empty restaurant. "Please try to keep your voice down, if you wouldn't mind."

She flashed an indignant look over the page at Seamus but decided her anger was better directed to the printed words in her hand and so returned to the transcript without replying.

" 'I heard him out'!" she quoted. "Bloody *heard him out*? Like Nigel was a bloody kook with a hare-brained scheme? It was Lindstrom's idea! How can he lie about it so casually?" Before Seamus could respond, her eyes lit on the next passage. "He *never read the contract?* He *wrote* the bloody fucking contract. Went through every line of it with Nigel. I don't believe this. I just don't believe this. He makes my Nigel sound like a fool, an insignificant serf comin' to the mighty goddamned Lindstrom with his bleeding hat in his bleeding hand."

She read on, shaking her head and flushing redder every minute. "Nigel called him to ask about the spinning specification? Can he be *serious?* That was the key selling point to their deal. The idea that the airplane would be safe for the amateurs Nigel thought would be his market." She stopped, fuming over the incredible document she held in her hand. " 'Definitional purposes'?" she quoted. "The specification was *not* for definitional purposes, for the love of God. He told Nigel that testing the prototype under that specification would guarantee its safety. That was what made the deal for Nigel. He didn't telephone Lindstrom to ask him about the bloody thing *after* he signed the contract. Without Lindstrom's assurances about that provision, he wouldn't have signed the bleeding thing in the first place!"

Abruptly, she tossed the booklet on the table between them. "When's the bloody trial, Constable Callahan? Tell your lawyer friend I'll be glad to see him. And I'll give his jury a dose of the truth about Mr. Lindstrom. The son of a bitch is goin' to have to deal with the bleedin' facts whether he likes it or not!"

As he hurried across the street to the station, an excited and elated Seamus Callahan tried to calculate the time difference between Shannon and Los Angeles in his head. In the end he was only off by three hours.

Back in Lang's office, the news of Molly's reaction to the deposition transcript had lifted the spirits of the plaintiff's trial team like a drug. The first matter they had dealt with was to schedule Lang's three-day trip to Ireland a week and a half before the trial was to start, the only space he could clear for the time required.

"Now what?" Amy asked, still buoyant over Bill's remarkable good news. "How do we play this to maximum advantage?"

"Okay. Let's think this through," replied Lang, unconsciously rubbing his hands together. "Our pretrial conference order with the witness and exhibit lists is due when? The thirtieth?" She nodded. "What if we leave her off the witness list? We can add her on a supplemental list a day or two before the conference. Give them less time to adjust."

"What are you worried about? They can't get her for a deposition in Ireland."

"I know but I just don't trust these people. The less time they have to react the better."

"I agree with you but I don't agree that we should leave her off the witness list."

He regarded her with curiosity. "And why not?"

"First of all, I don't think you gain much by holding her off the list for two weeks. Secondly, there's a pretty good risk that Campbell will seize on the late designation as grounds for postponing the trial." She stopped to look out Lang's window for a moment. He waited patiently. She continued. "And, thirdly, if you're concerned about bringing her to their attention, it seems to me that holding her name back for a supplemental witness list would defeat the purpose."

He smiled. Her logic, as usual, was powerful. Amy smiled back. "Of course," she continued, "if you want to hold her back until the rebuttal case, that would be the surest way to keep them in the dark."

"I would love to. Except that, without her testimony I don't think we have enough of a case against Lindstrom to get the case past a motion for nonsuit. Let's bury her name in our witness list. Identify her only as M. O'Keefe. In fact, we still have that list of all Arrow employees past and present, don't we? You know, the one Bill put together when we were trying to track down 'MOK'?"

"Naturally. You know I never throw anything out."

"Good. We can put them all down as witnesses for purposes of authenticating those thousands of documents they produced to us. They'll probably end up stipulating to the authenticity of their own documents, of course, but by then we'll have long since had whatever advantage the smoke screen will give us."

"I've got a better idea," said Amy. "I know of no rule that would prevent us from designating her by her maiden name. Do you?"

He smiled again. "Not really."

"It's a little sneaky," said Amy sheepishly. "But I think it'll work."

" 'M. McKinney,' inserted alphabetically in the midst of more than seventy former Arrow Dynamics employees, ought to give them something to puzzle over for a while."

Lang's phone rang and he hit the speaker button. It was his

secretary. "Chris," she said. "You have a visitor in the lobby. No appointment."

He frowned at Amy. "Dammit, Alex," he replied, making no effort to conceal his disgust. "You know how I feel about meeting people without appointments. I can't—"

"It's Ro Lang."

He stopped and exchanged glances with Amy. She raised her eyebrows in silent commentary on the fact that his ex-wife hadn't visited the hallowed halls of Devereaux and Brace since the divorce.

"Chris? You there?" asked Alex.

"I'm here, Alex. I'll go out and get her myself. Thanks." He broke the connection. "I hope everything's okay with the kids," he said to Amy.

"I'm sure. If there were a problem, she'd have called. Probably has a legal question."

"Don't be a smart-ass."

"I'm serious," she protested. Lang frowned and headed out to meet his visitor.

Lang found her seated under the firm nameplate in the lobby on the thirty-fourth floor. Dressed in an elegant silk suit with her hair tied up on her head, she looked very much like a member of the elite Westside clientele that the firm actively cultivated.

"Hi," he said, extending his hand as he strode across the lobby. "You look great."

She rose to take his hand and, to his surprise, turned her cheek toward him to kiss. He did so hesitantly, glancing quickly back over his shoulder to see if the receptionist had been watching. Predictably, the young woman behind the desk appeared to be deeply involved in taking a message from a caller.

"How are you, Chris?"

"Good, Ro. I'm good. You want to come back to the office?"

"Thanks," she replied, to his surprise. He had expected that whatever business she had with him would be brief and would be transacted in the lobby. Instead, she followed him through the great doors and down the hall to his office.

"Everything okay with you?" he asked as they walked past the offices of a half dozen or so lawyers, only one or two of whom, it occurred to Lang, had been with the firm long enough to recognize Ro.

"Yes, thank you. I'm fine."

Ro exchanged brief pleasantries with Alex outside Lang's door, then went in. She took the offered seat on the couch and Lang sat down in the chair opposite.

"Okay, so what's up, Ro?" he asked, genuinely curious.

"I'm not sure, Chris. And I don't even know why I've come to you except that I don't know who else to talk to."

"Well, what do you think's going on?"

"Okay," she replied, drawing a deep breath. "You know Mark Fassero. He's the guy I was with—"

"I know," he interrupted, suddenly annoyed that this unexpected opportunity to spend time with his ex-wife was turning out to be a discussion about her boyfriend. "At the Century Plaza last December. And probably the only subject we didn't deal with the night Max died. I know who he is." He bit off his last words.

Ro appeared hurt by Lang's acerbic tone and paused for a moment. "What's wrong, Chris?"

"Nothing," he said curtly. "Go ahead."

Again she hesitated, apparently reassessing whether talking to Lang was a good idea, after all. Finally she went on. "Anyway, we've gotten pretty close."

"I'll bet." This time his tone was positively belligerent and he immediately regretted it. She looked hurt, as if her face had been slapped. "I'm sorry, Ro. I didn't mean that."

"It's not like that, anyway," she said, surprising herself by how emotional she was suddenly feeling. "We're good friends. Technically, he's my associate, my project coordinator."

"Your next piece is out when?" he asked, eager to erase the effect of his earlier insult.

"Three weeks."

"Right. I'll bet you've been busy."

"I have. But let me tell you about this. And you don't have to patronize me. I forgive your snotty barb and I'm going to forget it. Just listen."

Thoroughly chastened, he did just that as Ro told him of her uneasy feelings about Mark's notation of the housekeeper's telephone number.

"Doesn't sound too ominous," Lang replied, his tone softening the edge his words might otherwise have had. "He has a diary note of your housekeeper's phone number in San Diego? Didn't you say that he helped you find her in the first place?"

"That's true," admitted Ro. "But he didn't have any contact with her. He just got me the name and references through the magazine."

"Maybe he checked her out first. I'm not overly concerned and I don't think you need be."

"Maybe. But that's not all." Then she described the odd incident back in Gettysburg, when she was sure Mark had returned from Philadelphia hours earlier than he had admitted.

Lang shook his head dubiously. "The guy told you a lie. A little white one, it would seem. Probably not the first guy who did so in the history of chasing women. Odds are pretty good that he made a few calls from his room and gave you a chance to get yourself back together. I'm not sure I see where you're going here, Ro."

"Well, I'm not sure either, I guess. Except that it *is* a lie. And there's something else. This morning I had an appointment with Gunther Schell—the accountant?—about my taxes." She gestured to indicate that was the reason she was dressed up.

"Gunther? Right. Downstairs in the building?" He smiled. "Good man. Very solid."

"Yeah, I know. But when we were going over my business-expense receipts, I came across this. I must've misfiled it." She reached into her purse and brought out a credit-card receipt and handed it to Lang.

It was a receipt for three round-trip tickets on USAir from Los Angeles to Pittsburgh from the prior August. Lang looked it over and shrugged. "So?"

"Look at the flight numbers."

" 'USA,' that's USAir, 'Flight number 1167, LAX to PIT via STL,' and 'Flight number 1187, PIT to LAX via STL.' I don't understand."

"In that calendar where I saw Alma's phone number in San Diego, I'm almost certain Mark had written these flight numbers down."

"Almost certain? Forgive me, here, Ro, but I'm not picking this up." Lang was beginning to wonder if his suppositions about Ro's feelings for this Fassero character weren't a little exaggerated, after all.

"What I don't understand is why Mark Fassero would keep track of the flights the kids took from L.A. to Pittsburgh while he and I were in Gettysburg?"

He paused for a long moment, allowing himself to consider, for the first time, whether there might be something here to be concerned about. "I don't know," he said at last. "Maybe it's something you told him and he just was thoughtful enough to write it down for future reference." He was not entirely convinced of this himself, but felt the need to give her an explanation that would comfort her. It didn't work.

She shook her head. "*I* didn't even know those flight numbers. When I left L.A., I thought they were on a different flight. It wasn't until the day after that I found out that their flight had been scratched and they had been put on this flight!"

Lang yawned and stretched, trying vainly to loosen the kinks that had set in over the course of the transatlantic flight from Los Angeles to Shannon. He hadn't touched the bulging briefcase under the seat in front of him for several hours, long since having given up the notion that he could concentrate late at night on an airplane. Outside, the first light of dawn was rising, conspiring with the lingering fog to obscure the few lights burning at this hour on the ground. In moments, the jet touched down and rolled out on the gray tarmac strip cut through the thick green grass.

Lang got through customs swiftly and found himself in the quaint area of the small airport regarded as the grand concourse. A man in his sixties, of medium build, with the unmistakable carriage of command, approached. "Mr. Lang, Constable Seamus Callahan of the Shannon Constabulary."

Lang was mildly disappointed that the man was not quite the leprechaun he had imagined. "Constable," he responded, shaking his hand. "Please call me Chris. I appreciate your meeting me at this unholy hour."

"Not at all, Chris," the older man said warmly. "Matter of fact, we have a bit of drivin' to do, so the early start suits the task." He turned and gestured toward the door to the car park. "And it's Seamus, if it's all right with you."

"Good enough." Lang smiled at the man's wonderfully musical brogue and followed him out into the cool morning.

Seamus pumped away furiously at the clutch and gear shift of the ancient Morris Minor, bucking and chirping over the winding Irish roads. If he had been cramped in the first-class seat aboard the L-1011, Lang felt like freight in the close quarters of the tiny car. But the scene unfolding outside his window was spectacularly diverting: a rich green valley rippling and rolling from horizon to horizon, crosshatched with low stone walls that hugged the contours of the hills like silk thread stitched through a great green quilt. Around each bend, still more of the verdant tapestry opened before them: first, an ancient Celtic cemetery, then a dairy farm that looked like a painting come to life, and, finally, the ruins of a castle whose keystone had been laid three hundred years before the Declaration of Independence was written.

Seamus seemed to read his thoughts. "First trip to our Emerald Island, then, is it, Chris?"

"First time ever," he replied, still drinking in the countryside. "Where I come from we don't have this much history. Or greenery."

Seamus nodded. "Aye. But I hear the streets are paved with gold. Especially out in California."

Lang laughed and caught a look in Seamus's eye that could only have been described as a twinkle. "So they say. But you know there's another, more modern, saying about California. It's the land of the three great plagues: earthquake, fire, and litigation."

Seamus laughed. "From what I can tell from the television, it does seem that you Americans love to sue each other."

"Every chance we get," agreed Lang.

"I'm hopin' that Mrs. O'Keefe can help you out with the one you're takin' to trial next month."

"So am I," said Lang. "So am I."

Seamus knocked again on the front door of the tidy farmhouse in Kilmurry, but it brought no response from within. He tried the door again, and confirmed that it was locked. Lang, standing discreetly on the first step below the porch, could tell the constable was upset.

"Are you sure she said she'd be here on the twenty-sixth?" he asked. "It *is* the twenty-sixth, isn't it?"

"Aye," replied a frustrated Seamus. "The twenty-sixth it is. And a Friday it is. And nine in the morning it is." He strode heavily off the side of the porch and disappeared around the corner of the house. Lang followed.

Seamus tried the back door. It was open. Lang read clear concern on Seamus's face. The constable went in, with Lang right behind. A kettle, still hot to the touch, sat on the stove, but the burners were off. On the kitchen table were dishes from breakfast.

"What do you think, Seamus?" asked Lang, a little apprehensively.

Seamus shrugged. "Mrs. O'Keefe!" he called out. "Are you in here, Mrs. O'Keefe? It's Constable Callahan." There was no reply. He moved to the foot of the stairs and called out again. Still, there was no reply.

Seamus moved off into the front room of the house. "No sign of struggle," he said, more to himself than to Lang. "No indication of foul play."

"Maybe she forgot about our appointment," Lang offered hopefully. He found the talk of foul play slightly melodramatic but said nothing.

"Maybe," Seamus repeated dubiously as he completed his survey of the rooms downstairs. Then, he moved past Lang and up the stairs, calling out again.

In a moment, he returned. "Nothing. And no sign of anything amiss, either. Maybe she did forget."

"Or maybe she's out in the back," suggested Lang. Seamus made no reply but headed out the back door. Lang followed the constable through the thick, high grass that covered the gently sloping rear of the property. The ground was soft underfoot owing to its constant misting from both the sky and the sea. There was no sign of anyone. About fifty yards from the rear door, the land leveled off, then stopped abruptly. A weathered wooden fence ran along the rim of the property, a feeble fortification, it seemed to Lang as he reached it, against the drop of fifty or so feet to the rocks and the pounding surf below. Here the land formed a small promontory, actually extending out above the water. The wind, surprisingly cold for early summer, whipped up off the ocean and snapped at Lang as he stood against the railing. Several yards to the south Seamus had located a rickety wooden staircase, built into the sheer wall of the cliff, that appeared to lead right down to the rocky beach at the water's edge. Before he could begin the descent, they both saw a woman at the base of the stairs.

"Mrs. O'Keefe!" called Seamus, but his words were tossed aside by the thundering surf and the freshening wind.

The woman gave no indication that she heard, even as she mounted the stairs and began the ascent. Seamus headed down to meet her, with Lang right behind.

Even from a distance, Lang could see that the woman was striking. She climbed the stairs with the grace of an athlete and the bearing of a lady. They met at the halfway point and Seamus introduced him.

"Pleasure to meet you, Mr. Lang," she said, shouting against the wind that pushed her remarkable red hair away from her equally remarkable Irish face. "I lost track of the hour. My apologies."

"Not at all," Lang shouted back, shaking her hand. "I appreciate your taking the time to see me."

She invited them to return with her to the house, where she reheated the kettle and offered them tea against the morning chill. After a brief exchange of pleasantries between two people unaccustomed to idle conversation, Molly went straight to the matter at hand. "You know, Mr. Lang, I've told Constable Callahan here just about everything I know about this airplane business."

"I realize that. There were just a few points that I wanted to follow up on."

Molly smiled. "You wanted to see if this face would drive your jury from the courthouse, is that it?"

Lang reddened at the directness of the remark. "Hardly, Mrs. O'Keefe," he said, with some effort. "I like to meet with all of my witnesses before trial and go over their testimony so we can eliminate surprises."

Acutely aware of the general reluctance of this witness, Lang moved briskly through the preparation process, carefully balancing the need for thoroughness against the risk of overstaying his welcome. After reviewing the circumstances surrounding the initial meeting between Nigel Daultry and Russell Lindstrom, Lang focused on their discussions at Lindstrom's ranch.

"So, Nigel Daultry and Lindstrom had a business meeting by the pool?" Lang asked.

"Not really a business meeting," Molly replied. "He had a fine lunch set up on the table by the pool—linen and crystal, it was—but the whole point of it was to get the deal done for the airplane. Lindstrom was very aggressive about it, wanted the deal done that day. I believe he would have done it the night before if they could have worked it out. It was him who insisted we fly down the first thing next morning. Not that Nigel wasn't intrigued, mind you. The aviation business was a whole new field for him and he did love to leave his mark on new places."

As she spoke, Lang listened to the content of her words on one channel, assessing her as a witness on another. The substance of her testimony was as good as Seamus had promised, putting Lindstrom and Daultry in the same place at the same time, tying Lindstrom to the deal in ways clearly at odds with the defendants' carefully concocted story. But it was her presentation that was most compelling. The woman had a natural gift for telling a story, an inherent credibility. And, with it all, Lang, like every man who had ever seen Molly O'Keefe, could scarcely take his eyes off her. He found himself hoping that Gentry Hickman would be foolish enough to tackle her credibility on the stand.

"Why do you think Lindstrom was so interested in this deal, Mrs. O'Keefe?" he asked, anxious to put her version into some kind of a factual context that would make sense to a jury. "I mean, he had plenty of other business interests at the time, and most of them far larger than this one."

She sipped her tea. "Nigel thought it was because he wanted the engine—the quiet one with all the power—for some military use."

"Do you know why Nigel thought so?"

"He mentioned that the level of traffic at that little airfield was high for a ranch in the middle of nowhere. And the airplanes that landed and took off, during just the one day we were there, were old military ones, he said, from Korea and Vietnam." She shrugged. "I think he just had a feeling, nothing terribly tangible to it."

"Did he have any idea how the StormTree might fit into whatever military operation might be going on there?"

She shook her head. "He didn't know and, as he pointed out to me, it really didn't matter. His interest in Lindstrom's operation began and ended with the recreational airplane they were going to design. As long as the plane would fly, and fly safely, he thought he would do very well with it."

"Fly safely, huh?" Lang repeated with more than a tinge of irony in his voice. "And was it in that connection that the two of them discussed spin testing?" he asked.

"Yes," Molly replied, adopting Lang's ironic tone. "Nigel said he was concerned about puttin' a product on the market that was more a weapon than a toy. He told Lindstrom that the customers he was goin' to sell the airplane to probably would have more money than brains. Rank amateurs, is how he put it."

" 'Rank amateurs'?" Seamus repeated, speaking his first words since the interview began.

"That's what he called them," she said to him with a smile of genuine warmth.

"And you returned to California during the project itself?"

"Oh, sure. I believe we made a half dozen trips, all told. We loved California." Then, as if to anticipate the question that had already formed in Lang's mind, she added, "But we only saw Lindstrom there one more time."

"On the last trip, in February of the following year?"

"That's right," Molly answered, a distant look in her eye. "We came up to the ranch again. That's when Lindstrom told Nigel that he had named the project StormTree; 'storm' from Lindstrom and 'tree' from Daultry. Nigel liked it."

"Were you in California for any of the testing of the airplane?"

"Testing? No. They were just about to start testing when we were there in February. That was the last time I had anything to do with the whole business. Then we went on from California to Europe for the Italian race."

"The grand prix at Milan?"

She could only nod in response.

"I'm sorry, Mrs. O'Keefe," Lang said with genuine sympathy. He resisted the urge to reach out and touch her hand. They had talked for the better part of an hour and Lang sensed that it was time to go.

Molly read his thoughts and waved him back into his chair. "It's all right, Mr. Lang. I know the constable has probably prepared you for a bum's rush but you've made quite a journey to see me so you're welcome to your money's worth. Care for more tea?"

Lang thanked her and accepted. He and Seamus exchanged smiles while Molly fetched the tea.

"Well," whispered Seamus. "What do you think?" He could hardly contain his glee, obviously basking in the glow of having discovered such a crucial witness for his new friend from America.

Lang chuckled softly. "An amazing witness, Seamus. An amazing woman."

"Aye," agreed Seamus, unnecessarily. "That she is."

The hour's interview Lang had hoped to extract from this visit stretched into three, culminating with a sumptuous Irish farmer's lunch prepared by their hostess and a stroll on the beach below the cliffs at low tide. Lang's cross-examination, in its most genial form, unlocked a vast treasure house of information from a woman accustomed to discretion and caution. Her life in the tumultuous world of latter-day Irish politics, related casually and without embellishment, made Lang's most lurid cases seem tame in comparison. The list of relatives and close friends lost or destroyed by the "troubles" was long and reached back to her earliest memories. Where Lang could recall only baseball games and family picnics, her formative youth had consisted of one violent episode after the other, each costing a life or a limb to someone important to her. And yet, despite the sadness and tragedy, she had the Irishman's gift for perspective and hope—a belief, tested time and again, that tomorrow held the promise that would justify yesterday. Lang had no trouble understanding Seamus's obvious affection for this unusual woman.

As he bade her farewell in front of her house, he thanked her for her willingness to get involved in his enterprise, one that hardly seemed worthy of her time and effort.

She shook her head. "That Lindstrom is a liar, Mr. Lang. And it won't hurt for someone to know about it."

"That's our plan," said Lang as he shook her hand. "That is most definitely our plan."

CHAPTER 23

LANG DOWNSHIFTED QUICKLY AND ACCELERATED immediately, throwing the rear end of the Porsche hard into the right-hand bank of the turn. Coming out of the hairpin, he shifted back into third and pumped the accelerator. The tires complained angrily over the whine of the engine as the frame shot back into its natural alignment with the car's inertia. Lang felt his head snap back hard into the headrest as he rocketed down the short straight stretch of Benedict Canyon. Again he downshifted as he roared into the next curve, to the left this time, where the road surface was cracked and uneven. The tires chirped loudly as they bounced over the broken pavement. In an instant, he felt them regain their footing and steady his trajectory through the bend and off into another brief straightaway.

Lang wondered if Nigel Daultry had enjoyed driving those Olympian racing machines of his on the grand-prix courses of Europe half as much as he enjoyed nibbling at the margins of his Porsche's repertoire on the confining streets and canyons of Los Angeles.

The phone sounded its shrill, distinctive ring. "Shit," he said, throttling down to accommodate for the fact that his attention was about to be divided. It was Amy.

"What's going on so late in the day?" he asked, glancing at the analog clock on the dash.

"Get serious, Chris. I have seven oh four. Are you on your way back?"

Lang frowned. The meeting with the accountant who would provide expert testimony regarding lost profits to Pegasus Technologies had run past six-thirty and he hadn't wanted to go all the way back to the office tonight. Besides, everything seemed to be under control as the final days of trial preparation wound down and he had hoped to sneak in a good long workout at the gym and a moonlight swim. "The short and best answer to that question is no. I was hoping to lift some weights and get an early night, frankly." He hoped he didn't sound as guilty as he felt.

"Must be nice," said Amy, confirming that at least he hadn't sounded guilty enough to meet her standards. She continued, "Do you think I'll ever develop enough confidence to work half-days a week before the start of a trial this big?"

"Knock it off, Amy. You know as well as I do that we're as ready now as we'll ever be. Anyway, what's up?"

"Did you get your messages from Alex?"

"No, I forgot. But I bet you're going to bring me up to date."

"Not really. But there is this one from a man who called at four-fifteen with—I'm reading Alex's note—'important information about the Pegasus case.' He didn't leave his name but said he would call later and leave you a voice-mail message. My first thought was that he might be a reporter, but then I remembered that guy who called Max, and thought you should know about this right away."

"That guy left a name: 'Curt Wallen.' "

"Well, this one didn't," Amy said.

"Still, it might be the same guy. You didn't check my voice mail yet?"

"Nope," Amy replied breezily. "Don't have your security code and don't want it. Do you want me to transfer you in?"

"If you don't mind."

"No problem. And call me back if it's anything, okay?"

"Okay. G'night, Amy."

"*Mañana,*" she replied and transferred him into the voice-mail system.

Lang had five new messages, each of which he dutifully listened to. The fifth was the one he was looking for.

"I'm trying to reach Christopher Lang about his lawsuit against Russell Lindstrom. I have information that will make your case against him airtight. It is now six forty-nine. I will call again at exactly ten o'clock. I will not leave another message."

Lang waited, but there was nothing more. He punched in Amy's office number and told her about the message.

"Might be Wallen after all. Think so?" she asked.

"Hard to say."

"What do you suppose he wants?"

"Can't really tell, but he obviously wants to talk to me directly, not through a recording. Trouble is that he said he'll call back at ten tonight and I don't really want to sit in my office and wait for a call that late."

"You really think there is something to this?" Her voice did not conceal her incredulity. "Sounds like a crackpot to me."

"I know. But there's a chance it may be something." He did not sound convincing. "His voice sounds pretty businesslike," he added weakly.

"Jesus. You really are obsessed with Lindstrom." Before Lang could give his predictably defensive reply, she let him off the hook. "Anyway, you don't have to come to the office. You can code the voice mail to forward the call directly to your house."

"Really?" he asked, with genuine surprise.

"Welcome to the technology of the eighties," she said wryly.

At ten o'clock, Lang, in his robe, was sitting in his den, watching a high-speed recording of the Cubs losing to the Florida Marlins, when the phone rang.

"Chris Lang," he said, checking his watch as the sweep second hand hit precisely the top of the hour. He punched the pause button on the remote.

"Mr. Lang. Is there a recording device on this telephone?" It was the same voice that had left the voice-mail message.

"Why, no," replied Lang, taken slightly aback by the man's directness.

"You are at home?"

Lang hesitated, feeling more than a little exposed. "Yes, I am. Who is this?"

The man ignored his question. "Do you have an answering machine connected to your line?"

"Yes, I do. What's this all about?"

"Go disconnect it, Mr. Lang. I will call you back in one minute." The line went dead.

Lang went downstairs into the hallway and disconnected the answering machine. Even as he did so, he had no idea why he was doing as he was told. As he stood in the hallway, the phone rang again. It was the same man.

"Who are you and what's this all about?"

"I'll get to that, Mr. Lang. But not over the phone. Did you disconnect the machine?"

"Yeah, I did. What do you want?"

"It's what you want that we need to talk about. Your trial against Russell Lindstrom starts next week, right? And you don't have much of a case against him, do you?"

Lang said nothing, his brain racing to figure out what was going on. He had more than a vague sense that he was being set up. Suddenly, the image of Lindstrom and the Secret Service in his Texas hotel room flashed through his mind.

After a pause, the man continued. "Very well. The point is that I know you're having a tough time building your case against Lindstrom because he made sure that's how it would be. But I can help."

"How?" Lang asked, his curiosity piqued, despite the long odds against this being genuine.

"Do you know Red Rock Canyon?"

Lang searched his mind for a moment. Then he placed it. "The little national park, just off Route 395? North of Mojave?"

"State park," the man corrected him. "Off Route 14. There are three turnoffs to the right once you enter the canyon. Take the second one and follow the road in, exactly a quarter of a mile. I'll meet you there."

"When?"

"Tomorrow morning. Six forty-five."

"Wait a second. Why should I do this, even if I could? How do I know you can help me?"

"I was there, Mr. Lang. At the Hangar. I saw Lindstrom there, dozens of times. I know what happened."

"Hold on," said Lang, intrigued in spite of himself. "Anybody could say what you're saying. There's been a lot of press coverage for this trial. How can I be sure this trip is worth my while?"

"Oh, it is, Mr. Lang. It is. But I'll tell you what. I'll give you a way to check me out before you make the trip. You probably have a reference in your file—an Arrow Dynamics contact report, I believe—to a meeting of all hands on January sixth or seventh. There is a reference in it to an 'MOK.' Right?"

Lang did not reply, furiously ransacking his mind to determine who might have access to that report. The voice continued. "That stands for Molly O'Keefe, Nigel Daultry's girlfriend, the one who always came with him to the field." Lang was stunned. Even with access to the report, it had required a full-fledged investigation— halfway around the world—in order to learn who "MOK" was.

"Molly O'Keefe?" Lang asked feebly.

"Nice try, Mr. Lang. I'll see you at six forty-five. Come alone and don't be late." He hung up. Lang punched in a new number.

Bill Quinn answered the phone sleepily.

"Did I wake you, Bill?" Lang asked, noting that it was 10:09.

"No, Chris. No," Bill replied hesitantly. "We were just, ah, we were . . . It's Chris. Okay. Here's Amy, Chris."

Amy came on the line. "You need a love life, Lang," she said sharply. "Then maybe you wouldn't screw up everybody else's."

"I'm sorry, Amy. It's kind of important or I wouldn't have—"

"It better be," she said coolly.

"Look. I spoke to this guy who left the message. He wants to meet me tomorrow morning in the Mojave Desert. Claims he has information that will cook Lindstrom."

"In the *desert*? Why do I think this is the very crackpot we talked about not three hours ago?"

"He knew about the contact report that described the all-hands meeting on January seventh. The one where we found Molly O'Keefe's initials."

"So?"

"He knew that 'MOK' stood for Molly O'Keefe, who he described as 'Daultry's girlfriend who always came with him.' "

"Whom," she corrected.

"What?"

"Never mind," said Amy curtly. No longer annoyed, she was now working her way along the same mental journey Lang had made during his mysterious phone call. "Since we figured out it was Molly, we've tossed her name around quite a bit."

"But only between us. And with Bill and Seamus, of course. But they're secure."

"And with Ellerby and Andrews. And on transatlantic phone calls. And, jeez, Chris, you just came back from meeting with her in Ireland."

"I know. But he knew the date, too, and the way he laid out

what he knows was very businesslike. Somehow, that goes a long way toward establishing his credibility."

"Is he Curt Wallen?"

"He wouldn't tell me his name."

"Talk about credibility," she replied sarcastically.

"Look, Amy. I'm going to meet him. He insisted that I meet him in Red Rock Canyon up along Route—"

"I know the place. We go through it every year on the way up to Mammoth."

"Right. He's going to be there at six forty-five tomorrow morning and I plan to be there, too. If all goes well, I should be in the office by ten."

"I don't know, Chris," she said. "The whole thing sounds a little shady to me. Maybe even dangerous. Is it really necessary after what Molly O'Keefe told you?"

"Yeah, it's necessary. Molly only gets us as far as the contract with Lindstrom. This guy says he was there during the program. That may mean the testing phase. You know? Where the fraud is?"

"I know," Amy replied, far from persuaded.

"Well, anyway," said Lang, "I'm going. And I don't see any danger here. If he can help, fine. If not, I'm out three hours' sleep and a couple hours of trial prep."

"That's easy for you to say. You weren't followed by a mysterious thug with a phaser set for 'stun.' "

"I know," he said, wondering suddenly whether there *might* be some danger here. "But that was different. We don't even know who that was or who he might have been working for. The two things have nothing to do with each other."

"I hope not," she said dubiously. "You'd better be careful, just the same."

"Don't worry. I will," Lang said, checking the time. "Hey, I've got to get some sleep and you've got to get—"

"Some for myself," Amy said.

Lang laughed. "Right. Good night. And tell Bill I'm sorry for the interruption."

"There's quite a bit I plan to tell Bill but, if it's okay, I don't plan to mention you any more." Lang laughed again. "Be careful," she repeated, very seriously. "And give me a call as soon as you can."

"Call you from the car."

Before he went to bed, he went into the closet and removed a small, heavy bundle from the top shelf. He carefully unwrapped a thirty-eight caliber Smith and Wesson revolver and hefted it in his right hand. There was something very reassuring about the weight and balance of this carefully machined piece of cold steel. He laid it gently on the lower shelf. From a drawer next to it, he took six rounds and loaded it. He put another six in the hip pocket of the suit jacket he planned to wear the next day.

Even if it weren't for the stately brown-and-white sign, it would have been hard not to know you had entered Red Rock Canyon State Park. In any light, the iron-rich, deeply carved, thinly stratified sandstone formations that line the desert canyon range from the darkest ruby to the palest rose, and every shade of red in between. It is a dry and empty place of desolate, forbidding beauty, where rattlesnakes and Gila monsters, scorpions and geckos, slink, dash, and dart among the spare but hearty vegetation. At the first light of dawn, when Lang arrived, the canyon was ablaze in the reddest rays of the new sun, slanting over the sandscape at a stark, severe angle. The desert air, thin and dust-dry, had shed the powerful heat of the previous day and had not yet begun to take on the full burden of another. There was no breeze as Lang pulled off onto the second turnoff to the right after entering the boundaries of the park. He carefully noted the odometer reading. The dust rose in a cloud behind his rear wheels as he crept along the gullied track that passed for a road. He had made good time up from L.A. thanks to the demons harnessed under the deck of the 911 and the absence of the good men and women of the California Highway Patrol. It was 6:18.

He drove slowly for a distance of precisely one-quarter mile along the dusty trail and turned off the engine to wait. He saw no one. He reached behind and under his seat to feel the cold reassurance of the thirty-eight.

The spot seemed a likely place for the type of meeting he was expecting. It was just at a point where the trail curved to the left, around one hill and in front of another, making it the first stretch of the dirt road that was both completely hidden from Route 14 and very nearly hidden from the other direction. In fact, Lang noted as he got out of the car to stretch, he could be seen only from points exactly ahead or behind him or from directly above. He felt a little claustrophobic as he walked a small circle around the car. He checked the readout on his cellular phone. No service. That was not surprising, nestled as he was in a canyon a long way from an urban center, but it added to Lang's vague but growing sense of vulnerability.

He leaned, half-standing, half-sitting, against the front fender, his edginess gradually fading to impatience. Now it was 6:55 and there was no sign of anything. The possibilities marched through Lang's mind in an orderly procession. One: crackpot, no-show. The leading prospect. Two: wrong place. Possible but unlikely. He had carefully noted the first turnoff and chosen the second. Then he had meticulously measured off the prescribed distance on the odometer. Three: The guy was coming but was late. Possible. After all, Lang had no idea where the guy was coming from or what obstacles he might encounter on the way. Four: The guy was already there but was waiting—

Suddenly, the car shook violently, knocking Lang from the fender. He whirled around to see a tall man with a gray crew cut standing next to the rear end on the other side, with his foot resting on the bumper. He smiled an odd and unnerving smile under his mirrored aviator's sunglasses and shook the car again with his foot.

"Okay, okay. I get your point. You got the drop on me." Lang was more annoyed now than alarmed. "Don't scratch the bumper, all right?"

The other man laughed. "You've got bigger things to worry about than the finish on your expensive bumper, Mr. Lang." He removed his foot from the car and came toward Lang. For a second, it occurred to Lang that he might attack him. He realized with a start that the gun he had brought with him to protect against such a possibility was securely tucked away between him and the other man. He tensed involuntarily.

"Take it easy, Mr. Lang," the other man said, stopping in front of him. "Remember, I called you. I'm here to help you, not hurt you."

The man was wiry and appeared to be quite strong, in great shape for his age, which Lang judged to be about sixty. He was dressed in desert fatigues, with the short sleeves rolled up to reveal tattoos on sinewy upper arms, and army boots. There was no sign of where he had come from.

"You're late," Lang said, attempting to seize higher ground.

"Not really," the other man countered. "Trial doesn't start till next week."

"Who are you?" asked Lang.

The man touched his brow the way Lang recalled Lindstrom

had done at Max's funeral. "Will Haverstock, Mr. Lang. And the answer to your prayers."

"How's that?" Lang asked, more than a touch of belligerence to his tone. He did not like being lured to the desert and then kept in the dark.

"I'm going to give you your case against Russell Lindstrom, that's how."

"I already have a case, Mr. Haverstock. And a pretty damned good one at that."

"That's bullshit. Is there a Latin legal term for that? Look, let's get serious, Mr. Lang. For one thing, you're trying to prove that Lindstrom was in on a conspiracy to cover up the aerodynamic defects of the plane Arrow developed for your people. We both know you have no evidence of that. Secondly, you want to prove that Lindstrom personally knew that the prototype would spin without warning, and I happen to know you have no evidence of that. Finally, you came all the way up here just before the trial is supposed to start to meet a man who offered no more than the mere possibility that he had evidence you might use against Lindstrom. It doesn't take a Rhodes scholar to figure that if you had such a world-class fucking case against Lindstrom you wouldn't be chasin' a wild goose like me."

Lang started to reply but Haverstock held up his hand. "Well, lucky for you I'm not a wild goose. I'm going to help you get Lindstrom."

"What's your connection to all this, Mr. Haverstock?"

"I'm an aeronautical engineer, Mr. Lang. I was hired by Lindstrom out of the Air Force. Helped design and develop the U-2, a handful of stealth aircraft, something called Quicksilver technology, some deep-space laser refraction prototypes. Went with him to Arrow Dynamics when he started it. I was there when this project, this StormTree, was being developed."

"You worked on StormTree?" Lang asked, curiosity and enthusiasm rising abruptly against his suspicions about Haverstock.

"That's not what I said. I was involved in another project at the time, but I saw an awful lot that can help you."

"Like what?"

"That Lindstrom was involved in the program from day one. He was there, at the facility, nosing into everything that was going on, from design to dynamic testing right through envelope expansion."

"That's very interesting," observed Lang dryly. "But the

records of the company don't substantiate that claim. There isn't a single reference to Lindstrom in over fifteen thousand pages of records covering every phase of the project."

Haverstock burst into an ugly, disdainful laugh. "Of course there's no reference to him! You're a lot more naive than I thought you'd be, Mr. Lang. You're working with professionally laundered records, records methodically, systematically purged of every reference to the man."

"Fifteen thousand pages over nearly two-and-a-half years' time? Completely purged? Now who's being naive?"

Haverstock smiled that unnerving smile again and shook his head slowly. "You still don't know who you're up against, do you, Mr. Lang? This is not some ordinary company, listed on the New York Stock Exchange, that you can just take to court like any other. These are very dedicated, very careful, very dangerous men. And Lindstrom is the most dangerous of the bunch. Purging fifteen thousand pieces of paper is child's play for these people. Hell, purging fifteen thousand *people* wouldn't require them to break a fucking sweat. And, believe me, they're capable of both."

Lang stood defiantly in the face of the man's words, but said nothing.

"Look," Haverstock said, softening his tone just slightly. "There was something very secret about this project from the start. In a facility where almost everything under development was in a Defense Department black box, this one got handling that went one better. It was military, maybe paramilitary, and it was a pet project of Lindstrom's. He went out and put the hook into the New Zealander, Daultry, the guy with the quiet engine. He flew in the tinhorn military from Nicaragua and Guatemala for the tests. He kept a tight rein on every nut, bolt, and washer in the project. And he closed it down personally when Daultry was killed. Had it boxed up, quick-cooked the engineering report, and shipped the whole sorry mess off."

Much of this, at least according to Molly, was consistent with what Daultry had suspected. Still, Lang was curious about where Haverstock intended to go with it. "I thought Daultry and Lindstrom had a commercial enterprise, for a recreational airplane," he probed.

"That's what Daultry thought he was involved in. That's probably what he was *intended* to think he was involved in. But that's not the way Lindstrom saw it. And, as I see it, it's not the point, is it? You just need to be able to prove that the project was a failure, from an aerodynamic point of view, and that Lindstrom knew it was, right?"

Lang nodded. "And it would help if I could prove that he intentionally covered it up with a false report."

"Piece of cake, Counselor."

Lang eyed him skeptically. Something here was not right, but he couldn't yet put his finger on it. "So? Where's the proof?"

"Let me see if I follow you here. You need proof—evidence you can give the jury—that the StormTree had a tendency to spin and resist recovery, that Arrow Dynamics and, in particular, Lindstrom, knew about the tendency, but that they did nothing to remove it and intentionally concealed it in the final engineering report. Right?"

"That's about right," said Lang, thinking to himself that, if he had proof of all that, the case would exceed his wildest expectations.

"So, what you need is the engineering log."

"Which wasn't maintained on this project."

"Which every one of them, no doubt, swore was not maintained on this project."

"Right."

"But which, in fact, they did maintain with scrupulous accuracy, dutifully recording each flight, by date, time, mission, weather, altitude, and results and pilot impressions. In which they recorded the very envelope-expansion flight intended to begin the run through Mil Spec 92121, the flight on which the pilot encountered a clear tendency to enter a spin, a probable flat spin. A tendency they buried when it came time to write the final report. All with Lindstrom's knowledge and blessing."

As Haverstock spoke, Lang's eyes grew progressively wider. He was nearly unable to grasp what he was hearing. This was vindication of his theory of the case against Lindstrom as if he had scripted it himself. And it was coming from a witness who was there, who knew these things not as a plaintiff's theory but as fact, a witness who was in a position to sit on the stand and fire fatal shots into Lindstrom at powder-burn range. His mind reeled as he reveled in the rare sensation of gratification usually known only to the most fortunate of treasure hunters and diamond miners.

He refocused, trying to catch up to the words Haverstock was still speaking. ". . . a notebook kept in the handwriting of the chief engineer and the pilots themselves."

"Where is the notebook, Mr. Haverstock?" Lang heard himself ask.

"I have it."

"I need it," Lang said unnecessarily.

"I know." Haverstock laughed, this time with something approximating genuine warmth. "Get in and I'll take you to it."

Lang got in his car, all suspicions about the man pushed aside for the moment.

"Keep going down this road for a little ways," directed Haverstock.

Around another bend in the trail, which was now definitely the floor of a secondary canyon, they came to a dusty and slightly beat-up jeep. Not a new-age yuppie Jeep, but an old working jeep from an earlier era.

"Wait here," said Haverstock as Lang pulled alongside and stopped. In a second, he returned and handed Lang a spiral notebook, bent and soiled, with a good-sized grease stain on the cover. In ballpoint pen, someone had written "XRL 22 'The StormTree' " on the cover. "That's it," said Haverstock.

Lang opened it and thumbed through the pages. The book was remarkable for its utter ordinariness. Each page, front and back, contained notes written in several different hands, covering an orderly progression of dated entries. On first glance, there was nothing that Lang could even begin to identify as a smoking-gun entry.

Haverstock watched Lang's face as he skimmed the notebook. "Here," he said, taking the book back. "Look at this entry here. March ninth."

The entry filled the entire page, in a strong and steady hand, different from the writing on the facing page. Lang read it haltingly. " 'Stalling in high AOA.' " To Haverstock, he added, "Angle of attack."

"Right," said Haverstock with an approving smile.

Lang continued, " 'Open to 150 IAS'—indicated airspeed— 'divergent wing rock and aft wing separation . . . full aft stick . . . departure entry conditions: FAS, induce left yaw. Left wing roll-off, full recovery with full forward stick . . . pitch responsiveness good but light at FAS . . . pitch bob had larger amplitude . . . divergent wing rock at full aft stick when induced in nose-high, left yaw.' " Lang stopped and looked at Haverstock.

"Do you know what you're reading?"

"The pilot's report of his subjective impressions in the early stages of departure testing."

Haverstock smiled broadly, like a teacher with a pupil on a

steep learning curve. "Excellent. You've learned something somewhere. Keep going. You're at the good part."

Lang continued, " 'The AOA increased, yaw increased to the
left, nose came up and full forward stick almost would not bring the
AOA down . . . Feeling was that it would depart controlled flight
to the left into a high AOA left-rotation mode with probable flat
spin to ensue . . . Key Q: investigate further or withdraw?' Jesus
H. Christ!"

"Now you know what they knew."

"They knew it would go into a flat spin!"

"Abso-fucking-lutely."

"The lying fucking bastards!" exclaimed Lang, turning the
page to see if there was more. There wasn't; the back of this page
was blank. "They knew all along!"

"At least as early as March ninth they did."

"And they did nothing about it?"

"See for yourself. There are only six pages left in the book at
that point. Look at the last page."

Lang flipped to the back. Less than a quarter of the last page
had writing on it. The final sentence read, "Program complete;
write the report per the contract."

"Son of a bitch!" Lang murmured to himself. The implications
were profound. The case was all but over against Arrow. But, he
thought, that's only part of the objective. "How does this tie in with
Lindstrom?"

"Ah," said Haverstock with a malevolent smile. "I haven't
even told you the best part."

Lang looked at Haverstock expectantly.

"That page was written by the pilot, of course, as you no doubt
assumed. Well, Mr. Lang, I'm here to tell you that this is Russell
Lindstrom's handwriting as sure as I'm sitting here."

"*Lindstrom?* You know that for a fact?"

"I do."

"Are you prepared to take the stand and testify to it?"

"Hell, yes. And I'll take great pleasure in watching that fucker
auger in on this one."

Lang's mind spun. This was too much to hope for! His suspicions about Arrow Dynamics and Russell Lindstrom were not only
right, but he had proof, devastating, irrefutable, smoking-gun
proof, that his entire theory was right! His case was crystallizing in
his mind even as he sat there with Haverstock. Then, suddenly, a
dark thought formed, casting a shadow over his euphoria.

"Hold on, Mr. Haverstock. Why would Lindstrom cover up the spin tendency of the airplane? What difference would it make to him, anyway?"

"That's a good question, Mr. Lang. And one I've thought about over the years as I've carried this"—he gestured to the notebook—"this little insurance policy around. The truth is that I don't know. There's nothing in this notebook that's going to shed any light on the question, either. But I can tell you this—that engine was the whole reason for the program. And the program had all the trappings of a military project."

Lang contemplated him in silence, trying to imagine where this unsettling thread of the story might take him.

Haverstock continued, "I don't think you'll ever prove this, but I believe Lindstrom had a dual-track program on line, one with Daultry for the recreational market—sort of a clean 'front'—and a much more lucrative and demanding one with some third-world military types. I wouldn't be the least bit surprised to find out he has since delivered this little airplane, fully functional and spinproof, to his shadow market by now."

"You're saying that he let this project fail intentionally, knowing the StormTree concept he delivered to Daultry's company would spin uncontrollably, and then finished development of a successful prototype for some shady military purpose?"

"Not particularly shady. But illegal as hell. And completely unprovable."

"Jesus!" exclaimed Lang, his mind furiously processing the new information he was hearing. "But then—"

Haverstock held up his hand and opened the door. "Pure speculation, isn't it, Mr. Lang? But the good thing is it makes no difference to you or your client why he did what he did. All you have to do is prove he did it and you've won your case, right?"

"That's right," admitted Lang as Haverstock got out of the car. "But it'd help—"

"End of the line for me, Mr. Lang. I suspect that down this road there's an even bigger hornet's nest than the one you're already into. If I were you, I would just let it go and take what you need to win your case."

Haverstock got into his jeep and started the engine. "I'll get in touch with you about my testimony," he shouted to Lang. "I know how to reach you."

Before Lang could respond, Haverstock threw the jeep into gear, wheeled around, and roared off into a small, narrow canyon, in the direction opposite the main road. Lang was left sitting in the driver's seat of his dusty Porsche, his mind awash in new information and fascinating possibilities.

CHAPTER 24

IN JUNE THE NATION'S ATTENTION WAS RIVETED ON the state of California. Six days after Russell Lindstrom turned the race for the Republican presidential nomination into a three-way tie with blockbuster victories in the last three state primaries, Pegasus Technologies' lawsuit against Lindstrom and the company he founded, Arrow Dynamics, was scheduled to go to trial in the quaint coastal town of San Sebastian. Fueled by the defendant's high profile in the kindred worlds of politics and business, as well as the nature of the charge—that he intentionally defrauded an equally world-renowned businessman and sportsman—the trial drew astonishing attention from all over the country and around the world. The media, particularly television and radio, descended on the central California coast with the force and impact of a full-scale military invasion, a phenomenon that taxed both the physical assets of the town and the tolerance of its quiet, parochial citizenry.

Every hotel and motel within a radius of seventy miles had long since been booked solid—at premium surcharged rates—for the anticipated six-week trial. A Japanese news organization had actually bought a ranch in nearby San Luis Obispo, on which it constructed a billeting facility out of surplus materials from Operation Desert Storm. By the start of the trial, it had doubled its original capacity and had rented both living quarters and field-office space to news organizations from Denmark, France, and Brazil. Rumors that they had turned down a lucrative proposal from an Israeli group could not be confirmed. Scores of other newspeople had to make do with accommodations as far away as the northern part of Los Angeles County. The traffic on the Pacific Coast Highway was therefore not only heavy, but also virtually nonstop, day and night.

By special arrangement with the city council, a large grassy field about three blocks from the Federal Courthouse became the home of nearly two dozen mobile satellite dishes. From this satellite city, a steady stream of news feeds, including the main feed from CNN and CableStar, both of which would be covering the trial live, poured out through the array of uplinks and into the electronic net that blankets the planet.

For the entire week between the primaries and the start of the trial, the three major networks had originated their evening newscasts from their local remote broadcast facilities. And Milo Rich had ensconced himself in a grand suite in the north wing of the just-opened Santa Ynez Inn for his nightly telecast of *American Idea Net*.

Chris Lang and the rest of the plaintiff's legal team were housed on the top floor of the stately Westgate Hotel in a block of rooms that, ironically enough, included the Presidential Suite. At four o'clock on the afternoon before the trial was to begin, he sat at the conference table in his room, working over his opening statement. He liked to polish his openings just to the point where he left room for extemporizing. Over the years he had learned that, although speaking from notes in an opening statement was a distraction to be avoided at all costs, a "canned" presentation frequently was worse. He had observed that lawyers who spoke to a jury in this fashion not only lost a measure of the jurors' attention, they often lost credibility. He never forgot the insight of a juror he spoke to after winning his first jury trial. "The other fella," said the old gentleman who had managed a John Deere warehouse before retiring, "he talked like a damned used-car salesman. Me, I like a man who has to think before he says something."

The plotting of his opening statement was complicated by some unusual features in his case as it had evolved. He and Amy had made a deliberate decision to withhold any mention of Molly until they actually put her on the stand, in order to blunt Hickman's ability to structure a defense to her testimony. This strategy dovetailed with the decision to "hide" Molly's name on the witness list by designating her under her maiden name. The decision to withhold Haverstock and his notebook, on the other hand, had been forced on Lang, since Haverstock had contacted him so late. Had Lang chosen to designate the notebook as a trial exhibit, the court would either have postponed the trial in order to give Hickman an opportunity to deal with a new witness and a new, highly volatile trial exhibit or, worse, concluded that the designation was late and ordered Haverstock and the log excluded. Neither outcome was acceptable, so he chose to run the risk associated with holding the witness and the exhibit for rebuttal. And risk there was. Simply put, without Haverstock and his prize document, the judge might decide that Lang did not have enough evidence to get his case against Lindstrom to the jury, thus bringing the case to an abrupt and unthinkable conclusion.

From where he sat mulling over the best way to structure his opening statement against these hidden tactical factors, Lang could see across the park to the Santa Ynez, where Lindstrom and his team would be staying. On the roof, he saw several Secret Service agents meticulously scanning every window of every building in the area, each reporting into a microphone concealed in his shirt cuff. Lang knew that on the roof immediately above his own head, the scene was repeated by another team of agents.

Down in the street below, he watched a sudden gathering of reporters—they seemed to coalesce out of nowhere every now and then—scramble toward the entrance of the Santa Ynez. In a moment, the reason for this activity became obvious. Down the main street that ran between the two large hotels came four black limousines. As they pulled smartly up to the front doors, a dozen Secret Service agents poured out of the first two and the fourth cars and scattered through the plaza, pushing back the edges of the growing knot of journalists and onlookers. After a moment, a signal of some kind must have been given, because all four doors of the third car opened simultaneously and Lindstrom, Hickman, Overbrook, and a blond man Lang did not recognize sprang from the car and headed toward the large glass double doors at the front of the hotel.

Lindstrom stopped just short of the doors and, in less than a half minute's time, someone thrust a podium and a dozen microphones in front of him. Once again, the man was instantly engaged in a press conference.

Lang's phone rang. It was Amy, from the next room.

"Check out CNN," she said. "It's on Channel 19."

Lang picked up the remote control from the coffee table and, sure enough, there was Russell Lindstrom, standing before the entrance to the Santa Ynez Inn, looking very presidential in his blue pin-striped suit and red-and-blue tie, answering questions for the press.

"Sweet Jesus," said Lang softly into the mouthpiece of the phone.

"What was it you said about why Lindstrom might not want to delay the trial?" said Amy. "Something about television coverage?"

On the screen, Lindstrom was laughing warmly at a reporter's question. "That's a good question, Bill. No, I certainly do have better things to do with my time these days than sit through a trial of six weeks or so. You may have noticed that we're having a little fun right now with Senator Gordon and Secretary Manetti." The crowd laughed at his understatement. To Hickman, standing at his side, he said, "My goodness, Gentry, I hope you can do *something* to get this thing over in a lot less than six weeks." More laughter. The media love affair with Citizen Lindstrom, Lang noted sourly, was still in full bloom.

"But, and this is important," he continued, "I think the public has a right to know that these irresponsible allegations are entirely baseless. If we had delayed the trial out of deference to the important business of carrying our message to the American people, then I believe there would have been some who'd have concluded that we were being evasive. And I want to be absolutely crystal clear on this: I have nothing to hide, nothing to be concerned about. This trial will be a total vindication of me and, I believe, of the fine men who did their jobs over at Arrow Dynamics."

"What do you think about Chris Lang?" asked a reporter near the front of the crowd. Lang noted wryly that the crowd of reporters, a small group from the vantage point he enjoyed across the street, looked like a veritable throng on the television screen.

"I try not to," Lindstrom quipped, to the predictable reaction of the crowd. "Mr. Lang has a job to do, I guess. And, normally, my view is that a man's got to do the best he can to make a living. After all, that's what I stand for: America's at its best when its people are fully engaged in what *they* do best. But I have to admit, as the complete lack of evidence against me has become clearer and clearer, even to a man of Mr. Lang's tenacity and ambition, I have begun to question his motives. I think it just must be an irresistible temptation to some lawyers to try to keep a case going when the man on the other side draws as much attention as a presidential candidate inevitably does. I am confident, however, that this strategy will backfire in the end, when the simple fact that I have done none of the things alleged is laid out for all to see."

Amy had crossed the hall and entered Lang's room through the unlocked door. She stood next to him as they watched Lindstrom dance with the press in the way that had become nauseatingly familiar over the course of the spring. Lang flicked the remote and killed the picture.

"He's a real piece of work, isn't he?" Amy observed.

"The son of a bitch has made it out to be a personal vendetta between the two of us," said Lang, a touch of genuine disbelief in his tone.

Amy regarded him obliquely. "Well, I don't know how far off the mark he really is."

Lang glared at her for an instant, then turned his thoughts to a different point. "He's awful goddamned smooth, though," he said, sitting down heavily on the sofa. "It's obvious that he's going to go way beyond even what I anticipated in manipulating this trial and its media coverage. He's going to use the trial as the cheapest television blitz campaign in the history of American politics."

Amy shook her head ruefully. "Why do I suddenly feel like we should be paid like workers on his campaign staff?"

But Lang wasn't listening. "Forget whistle-stop tours and bus trips," he said. "This is the ultimate in political campaigning. He'll be on television—not court TV, but the real thing—every day, in prime time on the East Coast, for Christ's sake, looking sharp, being brave and steady under attack from a lawyer whose ambitions have run away with him."

"He'll look indignant, offended, insulted," added Amy. "All the while soaking up the most precious commodity in politics: airtime!"

"It's a two-edged sword, though," said Lang, as much to himself as to Amy. "You'll strut your righteous indignation, all right. But you'll have to get by the minefield we've carefully laid in the rebuttal case, my friend. The partnership of O'Keefe and Haverstock may have a little something to say about all this just when you think you've reached the end of the line."

"Hmmm," said Amy. "Too bad the engineering log got to us too late to designate it as a trial exhibit."

"I know, but I think it's going to work out very nicely in our rebuttal case. Not only will it corroborate Molly O'Keefe, it will

directly rebut the testimony given by Lindstrom and the Arrow
Dynamics witnesses, and it will impeach their credibility up to their
asses. Then Molly, Haverstock, and the notebook explode in that
courtroom, one after the other—boom! boom! boom!—right
there, at the tail end of the trial, and we'll not only have our whole
case, including fraud, in front of the jury, these Arrow guys'll be on
the hook for perjury."

Amy nodded. "I'm glad I have a front-row seat for this one.
Gives me goose bumps."

Lang stole a quick look at Amy to make sure she wasn't being
facetious. The sudden appearance of Haverstock and the notebook,
although arising under doubtful circumstances, had gone a long
way toward erasing Amy's skepticism about their case against Lindstrom. She had seemed particularly impressed with John Carrick's
hurried analysis of the engineering log, which he pronounced not
only authentic, but dispositive in locking down their fraud case
against both Arrow Dynamics and Lindstrom personally. The
months of her doubt—and the enormous respect he had for her
instincts in such things—caused Lang to remain alert to any indication that she might see a pitfall he was missing. Satisfied that her
sentiment was genuine, he got up and went to the window, where
he could see Lindstrom's little charm-fest with the press winding
down.

"I'm still polishing my outline on the motion to exclude Lindstrom's testimony that the Mil Spec was for definitional purposes
only," said Amy as she headed for the door.

"Okay," he replied absently. "How about dinner at six-
thirty?"

"Fine with me," she replied. "Do you want Graham and Clive
to join us?"

He shook his head, still watching the events across the street.
"Just you and me. And John, if he can make it."

"Right," she said. "I'll check with him."

As the door closed behind Amy, Lang drew the blinds and
consigned the balance of Lindstrom's press conference to oblivion.
He returned to the yellow pad before him and tried to focus on
trying a tough case under highly adverse conditions.

June 12 dawned cool and overcast along the central California
coast. By prior arrangement Chris Lang and his trial team of Amy
Quinn, Rachel Cruz, Graham Ellerby, Clive Andrews, and John
Carrick had a continental breakfast delivered to the dining room of

the Presidential Suite that was serving as their home and office. The meal featured nervous conversation and very little eating, the mood of the group dominated by Lang's brooding pretrial introspection. When Lang excused himself at one point to use the bathroom in a rite known to every trial lawyer in the country, Ellerby inquired of Amy, "Is there a problem with our case that we don't know about?"

"No problem at all, Graham," Amy replied agreeably. "This is Chris's game face. Every trial, he's like a boxer or a quarterback, very tightly wound as game time approaches." This explanation didn't seem to reassure Ellerby completely. "The case is good and he's very high on our chances. This is just the way he focuses."

"Every time," added Rachel. She appeared ready to add something else, but decided against it.

Thirty minutes later, they had loaded two minivans in the hotel garage and driven the quarter mile to the courthouse. The old Hotel Sierra Madre had seldom seen as much attention, either as a hotel or as a courthouse, as it did that gray Monday morning. Scores of reporters swarmed all over the grounds as the two minivans pulled up to the driveway. By special arrangement with the U.S. marshal's office, each side had been provided four parking places in the underground garage, a highly unusual privilege that was a direct response to the potential for delays in the proceedings that could result from the crush of media camped out upstairs. Two deputy U.S. marshals met them at the elevator and checked their identification before allowing them to get on. "The courthouse is closed to the public until the trial starts," was the cryptic explanation of the older of the two.

As Lang and his group exited the elevator on the second floor, they encountered an elaborate security installation, far beyond the simple metal-detection station that had been there on their last visit. No fewer than a dozen deputy marshals milled around the lobby where, as soon as the doors were opened to the public, they would be operating a set of six stationary metal detectors, three X-ray cameras, a handbag and briefcase hand-search station, three hand-held metal detectors, and two video security cameras. While they were moving through the gauntlet, Amy noticed a commotion outside on the lawn below. Once again, a spontaneous aggregation of the press swirled and swarmed around the entrance to the building where Lindstrom's entourage was arriving.

"I thought they were supposed to enter through the garage like we did," said Amy. "Not from the street."

The others moved to the window for a look. Once again, Lindstrom was holding court in front of a stand of microphones. One of the deputies moved to the window to join them.

"That's Russell Lindstrom, isn't it?" he asked of no one in particular.

"That's right," replied Graham Ellerby.

"Thought so," said the deputy. "Saw him on the *Today* show this morning. That man's on the tube a lot."

Lang rolled his eyes and led the way down toward the courtroom.

Between eight-thirty and nine o'clock, the courtroom filled to capacity with journalists. Press credentials to the courtroom were strictly regulated and most news organizations were limited to a single pass. However, one of the resident judges was on assignment for the month, so his first-floor courtroom had been converted into an auxiliary press area, where the live feed of the trial was carried on two large-screen televisions. In addition, a number of reporters whose focus was to be the actual trial, not the sideshow it would create, chose to watch on their hotel-room televisions or at other locations around town, including a number of bars and restaurants.

A few minutes before nine, Gentry Hickman led his trial team into the room, causing a marked increase in the decibel level of the buzz coming from the reporters. He was followed by his associate, Randy Overbrook; Arrow Dynamics' in-house counsel, J. D. Royster; Arrow's former chief engineer, now president, Doug Chesney; and Russell Lindstrom. Lindstrom alone looked over at Lang's team, between handshakes and pleasantries with journalists on either side of the aisle. Smiling at Lang, he gave him a touch-to-the-eyebrow salute. They made a formidable-looking team, Chris thought: tall, handsome men, for the most part, well-dressed, and obviously very much at home in the swirl of the adoring media.

Amy leaned over and whispered, "They look so, so *important*!"

Lang whispered back, "Try to imagine them walking in here without their clothes on. That'll help keep it in perspective for you."

Amy laughed involuntarily, and immediately hoped no one would notice. She succeeded in not looking over at the cameras to see if she had been caught. She was surprised by how unobtrusively the two cameras in the room had been placed but, in truth, she had been unable to ignore their presence and suspected that they might have an inhibiting effect as the trial wore on.

At nine o'clock, the judge's clerk, the very proper Mr.

Porterfield, called the case and asked counsel to meet Judge Campbell in his chambers.

Lang and Amy, trailed by Hickman, Overbrook, and Royster, followed the clerk through the heavy oak door. The judge's chambers included two small anterooms, one for his clerk and one shared by his secretary and the court reporter, and a huge office for the judge. It was roughly the size of Lang's office, finished entirely in mahogany. It commanded a view of the north lawn of the courthouse complex, a scene alive with brightly colored flowers and stately palm trees.

Judge Campbell nodded to all counsel and gestured them to the conference table in front of his window. He was even larger and fiercer-looking than Lang and Amy remembered. His girth seemed greater by a perceptible degree and his face appeared to be permanently set in a scowl. He was, in short, thought Amy, the epitome of the bogey man known to every child who ever had a nightmare.

"Gentlemen," he boomed, ignoring Amy's presence. "Let me begin by saying that I have read the pleadings and the motions in this case. And I'm highly skeptical of the plaintiff's case, especially as to Mr. Lindstrom. Therefore, I'm going to invite plaintiff's counsel to dismiss his case against Mr. Lindstrom before we go any further with this matter."

Lang, stunned, fought to conceal his shock. After a brief pause—long enough for every eye at the table to turn to him—he replied, "Your Honor, we have no intention of dismissing any part of our case at this time. We have great confidence that the evidence will show that Mr. Lindstrom was directly, personally responsible for many of the acts of breach by his company and, more to the point, that he knowingly concealed the company's failure to test the prototype properly, as well as its knowledge of defects in the aircraft."

"Come, now, Mr. Lang," coaxed the judge. "Surely you must concede that your allegations are conclusory and the only good reason to keep Mr. Lindstrom in the case is his marquee value."

"Absolutely not," responded Lang, managing to suppress his rising temper in the face of this outrageous attempt by the judge to savage his case before it could get started. "The allegations are merely allegations. The issue will be the quality of the proof, of which I am supremely confident. Proof is, after all, what I assumed this trial would be about."

Campbell scowled threateningly at Lang across the table, his face a poisonous blotch of red and purple. "You will watch your tongue, Mr. Lang!" he warned through clenched teeth. "I'll not tolerate your sarcastic tone in this court. Do you understand me, sir?"

"I do, Your Honor. I meant no disrespect."

"Let's both be clear on something before we go any further," the judge continued. "You will toe the line in this case, Mr. Lang. This is not Los Angeles and I run my courtroom here as I see fit."

"Of course, Your Honor. It's just that your comments were unexpected in light of the fact that the defense has made no motion to dismiss and, frankly, I see absolutely no basis for one."

Hickman took his cue. "Naturally, Your Honor," he drawled, "we agree with the court's assessment of the case and would welcome a decision, *sua sponte,* to dismiss Mr. Lindstrom out of the case. We could certainly put an oral motion to that effect on the record if the court would prefer."

Lang visibly bristled at the suggestion that the court take it upon itself, without so much as a motion, much less briefing and argument, even to consider so drastic a step. "If Your Honor please, this is entirely out of order. Although we can all agree that the court has inherent power to regulate the orderly processes of its own business," he said, carefully diffusing what he anticipated would be the court's response, "I feel that there is no basis on the record before Your Honor, when no one has been given the opportunity to present a shred of evidence yet, to decide what can only be regarded as a motion for a 'nonsuit.' Having reached the first day of trial without a meritorious attack on our case, we are entitled to an opportunity to produce evidence of our allegations. Anything less would amount to a denial of due process."

"Your Honor," started Hickman, obviously attempting to capitalize on the judge's unexpected predisposition towards his client's position.

"Well, Mr. Lang," said the judge, ignoring Hickman. "You'd better have a case against the man or I will throw it right out of this court."

Off the hook for the moment, Lang sat through the remainder of the conference with half his attention on the mundane "housekeeping" proceedings and the balance focused on how much more difficult the judge had just made his chances of getting his case to the jury. The rumble in his stomach was tangible evidence that his adrenal gland, at least, had grasped the depth of his dilemma.

.   .   .

The afternoon of the first day began with the pretrial motions. At precisely 1:30, Judge Campbell stepped from the oaken majesty of the door to his chambers and climbed to his imperial red throne. "All rise," intoned Mr. Porterfield. "The United States District Court for the Eastern District of California, the Honorable Schuyler Campbell presiding, is now in session."

It seemed to Lang that Campbell, once seated, looked at the cameras a long time before he said anything. "Call the calendar, Mr. Porterfield," he said at last.

After the clerk did so, the judge called for argument on the half dozen last-minute motions before him. Throughout the hearing, he continued to look over at the cameras repeatedly, a strange mixture of contempt and curiosity on his gnarled face, unaware or unconcerned that that remarkable face was being beamed to television screens all over the world. The judge's preoccupation with the cameras, thought Lang, at least provided him a welcome reprieve from the old man's acid tongue and churlish temper.

The first several motions went relatively smoothly, involving little debate, no surprises, and only an occasional bark from the judge. Finally, they reached Lang's motion to exclude Lindstrom's testimony that the Military Specification was included in the contract only to define the terms "departure-resistant" and "spin-resistant" and not to require Arrow Dynamics to actually run the Mil Spec test.

"Your Honor," began Lang. "This final motion seeks—"

"It's not the final motion, Counsel," interrupted Campbell. "I've been advised that there will be one further motion by the defense. Is that correct, Mr. Hickman?"

Hickman rose. "Yes, Your Honor, it is. Oral motion, with the court's indulgence."

Lang flushed, an impending sense of ambush sweeping over him. "But, Your Honor, we have had no notice of such a motion—"

"We'll get to that in a minute, Mr. Lang. State your case on your motion, please."

Lang paused to collect himself. It would be a rookie's mistake to allow himself to be drawn into a fight with the judge on this point, worse to let himself be distracted from the important motion he wanted to argue. "Very well, Your Honor," he said evenly. "This

motion seeks to exclude testimony from defense witnesses, specifically Mr. Lindstrom, that would change the clear, unambiguous
terms of the contract. The contract says that Arrow Dynamics
would test the prototype, the airplane that's been referred to here as
the StormTree, for departure resistance and spin resistance 'per Mil
Spec 92121.' The anticipated testimony will attempt to show that
the parties agreed otherwise despite the language of the written
contract—that is, that they agreed to use the definitions in the Mil
Spec for the terms 'departure-resistant' and 'spin-resistant' but not
to test the airplane under the testing provisions of the Mil Spec.
Now, that specification is forty-four pages overall and sets forth, in
great detail, the most comprehensive, thorough departure- and
spin-testing regimen ever devised. Less than five percent of the specification is devoted to definitions. And the definitions in question,
'departure-resistant' and 'spin-resistant,' take up only four and a half
lines *in toto*. If the parties really had intended to adopt only these
two definitions instead of the whole test sequence, Your Honor,
they could have set down these definitions verbatim. Mr. Lindstrom's anticipated testimony conflicts with the clear and unambiguous language of the contract, a contract which is, by its terms, fully
integrated, and under the parol evidence rule and the numerous
cases cited in our written motion, it is inadmissible."

"Let's hear from Mr. Hickman," said the judge, again scowl-
ing at the camera behind the jury box.

"Your Honor," began Hickman, rising to his feet. "The parol
evidence rule in California, if it means anything at all after *Pacific
Gas and Electric*, which I doubt, can't mean that a man who had a
discussion about the terms of the contract, after the time the contract was signed, can't explain what the contract means. That's all
Mr. Lindstrom's testimony will do. If the jury doesn't believe him,
although I'm sure they will, they can just ignore what he says.
Besides, nothin' is stoppin' Mr. Lang from producing another party
to the discussions to dispute what Mr. Lindstrom has to say about
it."

Lang shot to his feet, but wisely held his tongue. Nonetheless,
he was raked by a withering glare from the bench. Hickman had
apparently finished and stood silently observing Lang.

"Counsel?" the judge said, at last.

"But Mr. Hickman's client has insisted, Your Honor, that the
only other party to these alleged discussions was Nigel Daultry and
he is dead."

"Then you will have your work cut out for you, won't you, Mr. Lang?" said the judge, a semblance of a smile tugging at the mass of flesh that was his face.

Titters of laughter swept through the media who made up the gallery. Campbell's smile broadened at his own wit. Lang sat down.

"Motion denied. Mr. Hickman?"

Hickman was on his feet again. "Your Honor, the defense moves for an order excluding plaintiff's Exhibit 127."

Lang's heart stopped. He was talking about the tape of Walt McCluskey's flight! The evidence that proved the StormTree would go into an unrecoverable flat spin!

Hickman continued, "By this motion, the defense moves to exclude horrifying, prejudicial evidence, graphic in nature, of a crash of an airplane that has nothin' whatsoever to do with the testing my clients did under this contract. It is the flight by a pilot hired and paid by the plaintiff specifically to spin the prototype built by Arrow Dynamics, which, as a consequence of his incompetence, he crashed into the ground, losing the aircraft and, more importantly, destroying critical evidence in the case. We don't know who took this videotape or whether or to what extent it has been edited or doctored. We do know that it does not depict a flight made during the testing at Arrow, nor does it depict any flight over which the defendants had any control whatsoever. In every sense, it is irrelevant to this lawsuit. But even if it were relevant, Your Honor, it is highly prejudicial in that it could unfairly sway the jury on a point that has nothin' to do with the case. My clients cannot be held responsible for the stupidity of Pegasus Technologies' hired stunt pilot, but, unless we get this order, that's exactly what may happen. Since it is, at best, only marginally relevant evidence in the first place, it should be excluded under Evidence Rule 403 because its probative value is substantially outweighed by the danger of unfair prejudice and confusion of the issues. Therefore, we ask the court to prevent a miscarriage of justice before it can occur."

Lang leaped to his feet. "If Your Honor please!" he shouted. "That videotape, the manner of production and genuineness of which we intend to prove beyond any question through sworn testimony and carefully maintained records, proves that the final engineering report by Arrow Dynamics is false, a fraud, because the StormTree did enter into unexpected departure and spin and, worse, was unrecoverable despite the enormous skills of a certified, Air Force-trained test pilot of the highest caliber, a man, I might add, who lost his life in the crash shown in the tape."

A buzz swept the huge gallery like a tidal wave as the impact of Lang's words registered.

"Silence!" bellowed Campbell, spraying the vicinity with the output of his prodigious salivary glands. "Another outburst like that and I will clear this courtroom! And I will shut down those blasted cameras, ninth circuit or no ninth circuit!"

The noise level dropped instantly, a hundred pens and pencils flying across notebook pages against the highly unlikely possibility that the tape recorders carried by the press failed to do their job.

Campbell returned his gaze to Lang. Taking this as a signal to renew his argument, Lang spoke. "Your Honor, there is absolutely no basis for the defense motion, even if an oral motion of this kind were permitted under the rules, which it is not. This evidence will show a critical element of the plaintiff's case, supporting a number of related theories. It is relevant in the extreme. And the notion that it is prejudicial is absurd—unless having a tendency to prove that Mr. Lindstrom and his company are frauds and liars is prejudicial."

"You, sir, are out of order!" thundered Campbell, the purple blotches returning to his face. "You are perilously close to finding yourself in contempt! I will not tolerate your condescension toward this court and its processes! Do you understand me, sir?"

Lang was silent for as long as he dared be. Just as Campbell appeared ready to speak, he said simply, "Yes." Then, after a pause, he added, softly, "But I stand by my arguments. To exclude that evidence would be reversible error even before a single witness is sworn."

Amy thought the judge would climb over the bench to get his hands on Lang's neck. The threat of reversal by an appellate court hangs like a sword above every trial but it is the rare trial judge who dares acknowledge its presence, and the rarer trial lawyer who risks taunting the judge with it.

From where he stood, Lang could swear he saw Campbell frothing at the mouth as he spat and sputtered, unable to contain his rage or formulate his words. His first thought was that the man was going to have a heart attack right then and there and, God forgive him, he began to root for it. At last Campbell managed to shout, "One more word like that, Counsel, and I will have you in irons! Mr. Marshal, stand by for my order!"

Irons! Jesus Christ, thought Lang, can this really be happening?

Up on the bench, Campbell was calming himself. Amy wondered if he had ball bearings in his huge paw. He swallowed hard in an obvious show at controlling himself. Lang stood by silently, tee-tering as he was on the brink of disaster.

At last, Campbell spoke. "I have heard the arguments, Coun-sel. Is it true that the tape shows an airplane crash?"

Lang replied quickly, "It is, but—"

"And does the tape show any of the testing that was done by the defendants?"

"No, Your Honor, but it shows—"

"And does the tape show a flight made by a pilot hired by the plaintiff to try to spin the airplane?"

"No, sir," conceded Lang. "He was just supposed to reach spin entry, then pull it out. That's what was wrong with the plane. You can't get it to recover—"

"Under Rule 403, I rule that if the tape is relevant at all, the potential for prejudice and confusion outweighs its probative value. It is excluded. Any further motions?"

Lang stood in stunned silence, his case largely eviscerated in the space of twenty minutes, and all without warning, without a single witness called, without a jury being picked! A fucking *oral* motion, he said to himself, in direct disregard of Campbell's own rules. Hickman rose and said, "I believe that's all, Your Honor."

"Very well. Mr. Porterfield, please call downstairs and tell them to send us a panel of veniremen. We are ready to pick a jury."

Lang sank into his chair and tried to collect himself. It's the top of the first inning, he thought morosely, and we're hopelessly be-hind.

CHAPTER 25

WITHOUT DISCUSSION, AMY HAD TAKEN THE KEYS
from an exhausted Lang and slid in behind the wheel of the van for
the drive back to the Westgate. Lang slumped listlessly, jacket off
and tie undone, in the seat beside her. John Carrick, Graham Ellerby, and Clive Andrews rode with Rachel Cruz in the other van,
following them closely through streets suddenly overrun with ar-
mies of media scurrying to claim seats in the overtaxed bars, restaurants, and hotels of tiny San Sebastian. Neither had said a word
about the trial since Judge Campbell had abruptly announced, at
four-thirty, that jury selection would resume tomorrow at nine
o'clock sharp.

The day had gone poorly but far from catastrophically, Lang
told himself, now free for the first time today from the relentless
pressure of trial. There was no question that his case had taken a big
hit, but it could have been worse, given the judge's obvious inclination. Over the years Lang had come to appreciate that trial was
nothing if not an exercise in perseverance and resiliency, invariably
rewarding the lawyer whose preparation and adaptability best enabled him to ride out whatever unforeseen turns the proceedings

might take. So, thought Lang as he watched the late-afternoon sun wash over San Sebastian, tomorrow we adjust.

But a very different assessment of the day's events was taking place in the other van.

"Just how bad is it, then?" asked Graham Ellerby, his Scottish accent particularly thick from fatigue.

"Not good," was John Carrick's curt appraisal.

"Really?" asked Ellerby, who, like the rest of them, looked as exhausted as he sounded. "Chris was a bit quiet, I thought, after the judge had at him at the start of the afternoon."

"I don't think it's so bad," offered Rachel, moving her eyes back and forth between the scene ahead and the rearview and side-view mirrors. "This was just the start of the trial. A whole lot more's going to happen before we can predict an outcome. Besides, I've seen Chris try a lot of tough cases and you've never seen anyone better."

"Still," said Andrews, "I gather losing Walt McCluskey's video can't help."

"That's putting it mildly," said Carrick from the backseat. He drew an immediate glare in the rearview mirror from Rachel. "But," he continued, perhaps remembering who it was who had hired him, "I suspect if anyone can work around such a ruling, it would be Chris." Rachel returned her eyes to the road.

"I just don't understand the judge's logic," said Ellerby. "If Walt's flight shows anything, it shows what we've been trying to say all along: that the StormTree had a spin susceptibility and an unre-coverable spin mode. What else proves that?"

"Your testimony, I guess," answered Carrick, apparently now committed to looking for a silver lining. "Certainly, my testimony. And the notebook, once we get to it."

"Not nearly as graphic as the bloody video," added Andrews sourly.

"Which is exactly why the judge excluded it," said Rachel, a little testily. She was not pleased with what she considered the in-gratitude of these men, who would have no case at all without Chris Lang. "But, at least you have to like the way the jury's shaping up."

"Actually, I don't think I followed Chris's explanation of how we pick a jury. Are any of the twenty-four people in the box going to stay?"

"Can't tell, yet," answered Rachel, suddenly cast in the unac-customed role of legal expert to laymen. "The process has just begun. Both sides still have three peremptory challenges to go, plus challenges for cause. But what I meant is that the pool of prospective jurors seems more intelligent and better-educated than what we would be seeing down in Los Angeles. And Chris thinks a smart jury will help us here."

"I think a different bloody judge might not hurt, either," added Andrews.

Up ahead, in the lead van, Amy said, "What are you thinking?"

Lang smiled wanly. "Virtually nothing. And that's hitting on all available cylinders."

"I doubt that. It wasn't really all that bad, you know. Now if he'd thrown out your case against Lindstrom, then it would be bad."

"That's true. But he also didn't have that heart attack I was hoping for, so it wasn't all that good, either."

Amy laughed as they pulled into the Westgate's driveway. There was hardly anybody there, in sharp contrast to the driveway of the Santa Ynez, where dozens of reporters milled around, waiting for a glimpse of Lindstrom. She pulled into a spot next to one of the CableStar trucks. Rachel took the next space over. Amy and Rachel quickly determined which files, folders, and binders would be needed for the evening's work and Rachel waited for two bellhops from the concierge's station to meet her and truck them upstairs. She took seriously Lang's injunction that at no time were the trial files to be out of her sight unless he or Amy was working on them.

Upstairs, just as Lang was about to put his card key into the lock on the door to the Presidential Suite, it swung open and he found himself face-to-face with a man he had never seen before.

"Who are you?" he demanded suspiciously.

The man looked flustered. "Security," he replied. Lang could see at least one other man standing behind him in the suite.

"For whom?" Lang demanded again, his tone harsher this time.

A voice from down the hallway behind Lang replied, "For me."

Lang turned to see the tall, gangly figure of Jad Piersall striding toward him. "I'm sorry, Chris. I forgot to tell you about this arrangement," he explained as he approached, his hand outstretched. As Lang shook it, Piersall continued. "In light of the type of people we're dealing with here, I thought a little security to protect the company's investment in the lawsuit would be in order. I certainly had no intention of intruding on your privacy."

"Security, huh?" said Lang, with obvious doubt. "Do you think that's necessary—"

"Absolutely, Chris," Piersall replied firmly. To the man in the doorway, he said, "Are you through?"

"Yes," the man replied.

"You've swept everything, right? Not just the phones?"

"Everything, Mr. Piersall."

"Good. Then you and Charlie can go for now. I'll be in touch." The man nodded and, followed out by his companion, headed down the hall to the elevator. Turning toward Lang, Piersall asked, "Mind if I come in?"

The question seemed a little absurd to Lang under the circumstances, but he shrugged and followed Piersall into the suite. By this time Amy had joined them and Lang introduced her to Piersall. "What's going on?" she asked.

Piersall replied, "Nothing. I just had some private security people in here to do an electronic-surveillance sweep of your place. The company has them on retainer, anyway. No use having your trial strategy broadcast directly to the other side." Before either of them could react or respond, he said, "Helluva show in there today, huh? That judge loves you, Chris."

Lang shrugged again, poorly concealing his annoyance. "Every trial has good days and bad. Ours will come." He headed into the kitchen. Over his shoulder, he called, "Anybody want something to drink?"

"Scotch, if you have it," Piersall replied.

"Diet Coke will do for me, Chris," said Amy.

To Lang's surprise, there was a brand-new bottle of scotch in one of the cabinets above the stove. He grabbed the bottle, a can of soda, and a beer and returned to the living room. "Just what is the story on this security business, Jad?" he asked as he dropped heavily into the deep cushions of the sofa.

"Just a precaution, Chris. There's a lot at stake. Not so much for us—although several million is still worth fighting over these days—but for Lindstrom."

"You were sweeping for electronic bugs? Isn't that a little melodramatic?"

"Hardly," replied Piersall, slugging at his scotch. "I represent a lot of high-technology companies and the incidence of industrial espionage is pretty astounding. We shouldn't assume these people play by the rules. Anyway, as I say, the security folks already work for us so the cost to the company is inconsequential."

There was a knock at the door. Amy went to open it.

"I didn't know you were coming, Jad," said Lang. "If you had given me a little notice, we could have arranged a room for you in this part of the hotel."

Piersall waved him off. "No problem. I made arrangements through another client of mine in the travel business. I'm over in the Santa Ynez."

Lang raised an eyebrow. This guy is full of surprises, he thought. Amy returned with Ellerby and Andrews in tow. They exchanged enthusiastic greetings with Piersall, and had words of encouragement for their chief gladiator, Lang. Not for the first time, Amy wondered at the true nature of the relationship between Piersall and the Pegasus Technologies boys.

Lang and Amy graciously declined Piersall's invitation to dinner at the Santa Ynez, explaining that reviewing the juror profiles they had compiled would take most of the evening. While that was certainly true, the greater truth was that they relished the opportunity to be away from their clients for a few hours. They ordered room service and were treated to a one-hour delay in delivery owing to the unprecedented demand upon the hotel's restaurant.

" 'Sweeping for bugs'?" Lang repeated after they had set up to review the jury information.

Amy shrugged and swigged from her Diet Coke. "It's a little James Bond, I guess, but, after all, I was followed that night by that weird guy. And your Haverstock is sure spooked. Then, there's that business Ro told you—about the guy she's working with. With your kids' flight numbers back east, remember?"

"I remember," Lang replied, obviously mulling all of this over. "The guy—Mark Fassero—checked out okay, though, according to Bill."

"I know. It's all smoke and fog, but, still, there's an element of the unusual to this case that is hard to deny."

"That's for damned sure," he said, getting up to answer a rap at the door. "Whatever happened to straightforward cases with nice clean lines?"

"Clients with those cases hire cheaper lawyers," she called after him.

Lang let the room-service waiter in and signed the tab. The youth, who managed English capably around a strong Latin accent, smiled broadly and thanked Lang profusely. Assured that everything was to the "señor's" liking, he bowed deeply and backed out of the room.

Outside in the hallway, Ernesto Reynoso kept smiling as he rolled his cart down the hallway to the service elevator. And with good reason. From what he had just observed, the job he had been given should not be too difficult at all. And the payoff would be handsome indeed.

Inside the suite, Lang and Amy took a break from their analysis of the jury sheets—a surprising number of the present panel looked very strong on paper—to sit and eat their dinner.

"Television okay with you?" asked Amy. Lang nodded and Amy flicked the remote.

Naturally, CableStar had Milo Rich's program on. She muted the volume while the commercial finished. When Rich came back on-camera, he was seated next to a composed Russell Lindstrom. Lang choked on a cherry tomato in his salad.

"We're back with presidential candidate—and litigant—Russell Lindstrom. Mr. Lindstrom, isn't it a little disheartening to sit through a trial like the one that started today while the machinery of your presidential campaign sits idly by the side of the road?"

Lindstrom smiled disarmingly. "Not at all, Milo. How can you be disheartened when it's becoming clearer every day that Americans by the millions have heard your message and are anxious to pitch in and help discover what's right with the country and retool around it. The dynamics of this race are very exciting, very encouraging."

"Well and good, Mr. Lindstrom. But this can't be good for you. To stand accused of fraud and deceit—and to have to sit through a trial of those charges when you'd rather be working the delegates and mounting your case for the party platform."

"No question, Milo. But, you know, lawsuits are an unfortunate part of American life in this day and age. Something you can't hide from. And I think it's very instructive for the American people to see how easy it is today to find yourself involved in one of these ugly things, where there's more ambition and malice than evidence. But, the lesson will come when the allegations are exposed for what they are and the public sees for itself that the system still works."

"So you think the trial may help your campaign?"

"Not at all. I just think that a confrontation with the truth and justice can't hurt anybody."

"So you're not embarrassed to be on television, in court, every day?"

"I can't help it. But in the end, it will all come out just fine."

Amy punched the power button on the remote. "Give me a break."

"The man's got balls. Translation, 'Embarrassed? Are you kidding, Milo? *Pleeease* keep running those promos for my trial. Keep that wall-to-wall exposure coming.' Just wait, asshole, we've got a few tricks in store for you. Let's get to work, Amy."

Ro whisked through her bathroom, making one final check. She had become quite adept at packing on short notice and this trip would be easier than most. No LAX, no commercial flight. Just a short drive out to the Van Nuys airport and a thirty-minute flight in the company jet up the coast. She swept from the room and fairly flew down the steps. "Hey, guys?" she called up the stairs. "I need a hand with this stuff, please."

The kids appeared from their rooms and grabbed the bags from the top of the stairs. Alma came out of the kitchen as Ro reached the foot of the stairs and headed for the garage. "I'll help you with this, Miss Ro," she said, taking one of her camera cases from her.

"Thanks, Alma," she replied. She had been pleasantly surprised at how quickly the woman had become a member of the household, a steady, reliable support for her with a knack for dealing with the children. "I'll be at the number I wrote on the pad by the kitchen phone. If anything comes up before I call you tonight, Mr. Lang can be reached at the other number you already have. Okay?" Alma nodded. To Jennifer, Ro said, "Speaking of your father . . ."

"No," replied her elder daughter, anticipating the question. "I just tried fifteen minutes ago and got his answering machine."

"That's too bad," Ro replied as she got into the car. "He'll just have to be surprised when I show up, I guess. I should be back here Friday afternoon, guys. And remember, Alma's just here to be on the safe side. I'm counting on you to run things yourselves. You're certainly old enough."

"Don't worry, Mom," assured Jack. "Have a good trip."

She kissed them all and blasted off down the street toward the airport and her next *Beau Rivage* assignment: the emerging media event of the year, the *Pegasus Technologies v. Arrow Dynamics* trial.

As she made the drive to the airport, a sense of well-being settled over Ro. With the surprisingly light evening traffic virtually guaranteeing her timely arrival, she allowed herself to relax and reflect upon why she was feeling so good. A large part of it was quite obvious, of course: She was experiencing a surge of success in a very competitive field and the evidence was mounting that it was not a fluke. David Stingley's faith in her work had been rewarded once again; she had followed up her splashy cover debut in the December *Beau Rivage* with another this month and she was in demand. She had turned down two offers from other publications to cover the trial freelance—her connection with Chris combined with her current hot streak made the assignment a natural—before Stingley had belatedly, and reluctantly, she thought, agreed to let her cover it for *Beau Rivage*. The only explanation he had offered for his hesitation was the one Mark had predicted: that it was "too obvious. And I *hate* to do the obvious."

But she was feeling more than the warm flush of success. It was, she realized, the infinitely more rewarding satisfaction of doing what one was intended to do, of satisfying a larger plan. Simply put, she was at peace with herself and her work in a way that transcended making a good living. And it made her smile a lot lately, a fact each of the kids had noticed. Even now she smiled to think of it.

She checked her watch. Mark would be waiting in San Sebastian, but she would not be late. Yes, there was Mark, too, she thought. A major factor in her life during the past year of discovery. She had been indescribably relieved when the matter of the kids' flight numbers had been resolved so simply, so easily. Hardly the way she had anticipated when she had finally screwed up the courage to broach the subject. They had worked by themselves late into the night polishing a layout and they were both tired and hungry. She had carried around her doubts and suspicions for better than a week by then, and it was wearing on her.

"Mark," she had begun hesitantly. "I need to know something. And I want an honest answer."

He had abruptly stopped what he was doing, and looked at her across the drafting table between them. She recalled vividly that, although the table was awash in the brilliant, concentrated light of the lamp, she could barely make out his features as he stood beyond the cone of light. "What are you talking about, Ro?" The concern in his tone only served to make her that much more uncomfortable.

"Look," she said, plowing ahead before she lost her nerve. "Don't get mad at me, but when you left your calendar in my room in the hotel in New York last December it fell open and I saw that you had written down Alma Garcia's phone number and the flight numbers of my kids' flights between L.A. and Pittsburgh there. I didn't even know what those flight numbers were until a couple of days later."

"My calendar? Alma Garcia? Flight numbers?" he asked, his confusion apparently genuine. "I'm sorry, Ro, but I'm not sure what you're asking me."

"Okay," she said, less sure now that this was a good idea than she had been a moment ago. "I want to know why you wrote my housekeeper's phone number in your calendar and why you kept track of my kids' flight numbers when we went to Gettysburg."

A light seemed to go on in his head. "Wait a minute," he said gently. "There's nothing here to get upset about. Alma Garcia, huh? The housekeeper? Hell, I had forgotten the woman's name. But, as you may recall, you mentioned that David's office gave you her name. I got her number from his secretary, Belle, and I planned to give her a call to check her out. As you may also recall, I had to go to Dallas on short notice and by the time I got around to it, you had already checked her references and hired her. Right?"

Ro listened carefully. It was true that she had hired the woman very quickly, immediately after she talked to her references. "What about the flight numbers?" she asked, her tone revealing a distinct drop in her level of certainty.

"That's when we went to Gettysburg?" he asked, clearly searching his recollection. She nodded tightly. "All right," he said, smiling feebly for the first time since her attack had begun. "I think I know what you're asking me, but I'm not sure I understand your problem with this. I routinely keep track of lots of information in the diary—which you no doubt know since you went through it—including things like flight numbers and times of arrival of people whose whereabouts may become important. When you gave me that information I just wrote it down for future reference since, as you may remember, we were still going to be en route to Gettys—"

"That's not true. I didn't tell you those numbers because I couldn't tell you. I didn't even know—"

"What are you saying, Ro?" he asked, a cold edge to his voice as it rang ominously in the empty conference room.

"First, Mark, I didn't tell you those numbers. And if I had told you flight numbers, I wouldn't have given *those* numbers to you because I didn't know them. The kids were taken off their original flights and put on these flights. I didn't even know about that until late the next day."

"Wait a second," he said. "Wait a second. You *did* tell me the flight numbers and I wrote them down. In fact, you told them to me over the phone about two or three days before we left. I was in the office and you were at home. You were late that day because of a dental appointment. And you called me to go over some details about our trip. Don't you remember?"

She was flustered, suddenly far less sure of herself than she had been. "I remember that time and I remember the dentist, but I didn't tell you—"

"Yes, you did, Ro. You mentioned that you were hoping they could get a direct flight—no, a nonstop flight—but that this flight through—what was it? Cincinnati?—was a direct flight. But that—"

"Stop it, Mark! This is a lie!" There was something condescending in his tone, his studied calm, that heightened her anger, intensified her frustration.

"Jesus, Ro! What are you talking about?"

"This is a lie," she had shouted. "And I don't know why you're lying to me!"

"I really don't know what's going on, Ro," he said, still calmly, chillingly. "But there's something here and you better let me in on it."

"Mark," she said, making an obvious effort to control her raging emotions. "The flights you listed in your book were *not* the ones the kids were booked on. They were the ones they flew on, after their scheduled flights were scratched due to equipment problems."

"You've got to be wrong, Ro," he replied calmly. "I recorded those flight numbers several days before the trip took place. I *couldn't* have recorded the numbers of flights they hadn't been bumped to yet."

"How do you explain this, then? The flight numbers you recorded were the ones that I was billed for on my credit card, the ones they actually flew on."

"Wait a minute," he said. "This is all based on the fact that you were billed for these flights?"

She nodded, her mixture of anger, hurt, and fear balled up in the back of her throat.

To her surprise, he smiled. "Were they bumped to another airline or to another flight on the same carrier?"

"Another airline. What difference does that make?"

His smile broadened. "Well, that explains it. That's all."

"What explains what?" She was exasperated, but her anger was melting to fatigue.

"When you're bumped from a flight to another airline after you've purchased your ticket by credit card, they bill you according to the booked flight and the airlines do the paperwork for the transfer between themselves."

His words swam in her head. "I don't follow you."

"It's okay. What airline were they booked on?"

"USAir."

"And they were moved to which airline?"

"United."

"Okay, I'll show you what I mean." He grabbed the telephone. "Do you remember the flight numbers or the dates?"

She shook her head.

"It's okay," he said, still smiling. He was obviously relieved, thought Ro. He got USAir's number and hit the speakerphone button.

"Good evening and thank you for calling USAir. This is Jackie Polis. How may I help you?"

"Hello, Jackie," answered Mark. "My name is Mark Fassero and I have a billing question. If I book a flight with USAir and bill it to my credit card, and then I get bumped from the flight to a flight on another airline, do I get billed for the flight I booked or the one I actually fly?"

"Well, Mr. Fassero, it is highly unlikely that you would be bumped from—"

"Let's assume I get moved to another airline because of equipment trouble and your flight gets scrubbed. What then?"

"In that case, you would be billed as if you had flown with us and we would work out the accommodating paperwork with the other carrier."

"And why does it work that way, Jackie?"

"Because we guarantee you the fare that you booked through us and this way we avoid the problem of charging you for two flights and crediting your account for the one you don't use. That's really for your benefit, as well, since it can take up to two billing cycles to reflect a credit on some cards."

Mark looked at Ro with a broad smile, gesturing to her as if to ask if she had any further questions. She shook her head. Mark thanked the agent and hung up.

"I don't know what to say, Mark," she said, feeling an odd mixture of embarrassment and relief.

She would never know it, of course, but Mark was equally relieved. "There's no need to say anything, hon," he said. "I can't imagine that there's a mother anywhere who's more devoted to her kids than you are. You thought they were in jeopardy and you reacted the way you should, the way I would expect you to."

"Listen, Mark. About your diary. I didn't read—"

He held up a hand. "No problem." He reached for her and wrapped his arms around her. He gave a little chuckle into her ear.

"What's so funny?" she had asked.

"I'm just trying to recall whether I wrote anything too embarrassingly mushy about you in that book."

"I told you I didn't read it," she had repeated, luxuriating in the swirling rush of relief. A relief she felt still as she pulled into the long-term lot at the Van Nuys airport.

After dinner, capped off with a cigar out on the rear patio of the Santa Ynez, Jad Piersall bade his clients and partners good-night and went upstairs to his room. He had not bothered to rig his door with even the most rudimentary entry-detection device, since the housekeeper would have turned the bed down in any event and it would have been far more trouble than it was worth to arrange with the hotel to keep housekeeping out. Still, he inserted the card key and entered the room with the caution of a man who had spent a good part of his life protecting himself from the unexpected. Inside, the lights were on and the bed turned down. A couple of pricey mints lay on a saucer on the nightstand. And there was a man sitting in the armchair by the window.

"Evening, Captain," said Mark Fassero. He held up a glass. "Scotch?"

"Major Fassero," replied Piersall with a nod. "And, yes, I'd like one."

Fassero rose to hand Piersall the glass. "How's it going up here in Alpha Theater?"

Piersall shrugged. "Pretty much as expected. We got our nose bloodied today but we'll be back tomorrow. Did you bring Mrs. Lang?"

Fassero shook his head and looked at his wristwatch. "Her plane will land in thirty minutes."

"I think this is a bad call, Mark."

Fassero shrugged. "I don't disagree. But I don't think Stingley had a choice. Like it or not, the woman was a natural for this assignment. And she's very good. If we didn't bring her up here, *People* or somebody else would have. It'll be okay, though. At least this way, I get to keep tabs on her around the clock."

Piersall sat down in the other armchair and drank deeply from his glass. "It's not her I'm worried about. If there's a vulnerability here that Lindstrom can exploit, it's Lang's kids."

"I know. But they're covered. Mrs. Garcia is doing her usual fine job."

Piersall shook his head mournfully. "I wonder about the wisdom of our defenses. A small fortune from the Fortress's security funds to keep a fence around Lang and his family so far and we've had what? Two or three hits?"

Fassero held up three fingers on his left hand. "Three: the letter to Ro I intercepted at the magazine, the woman who approached the older girl at school, and that clumsy come-on by Lindstrom himself down in Texas."

"Maybe we overestimated Lindstrom and his reach."

Fassero leaned forward in his seat. "Don't *ever* think that, Captain. It's the last thought you'll have before the bullet hits."

Piersall frowned. "I guess you're right. Up till now has been just the preliminaries. When Lindstrom and Hickman start to see the real artillery in our case, that's when we'll be at maximum risk."

Fassero nodded. "*Semper vigilante.* It's the only formula I know."

Piersall grunted something indecipherable and tossed back the balance of his drink.

Fassero got up, leaving his drink unfinished on the table. "I'm off to the airport. Contact from now on will be indirect."

Piersall rose and offered his hand. "The shame of it is, our best job may do us no damned good if Lang doesn't pull it off."

"Lawyers and politicians, Jad. Without 'em, we could run a pretty tight fucking ship."

Piersall nodded gravely in agreement and walked Fassero to the door, wondering yet again what the odds were that his carefully constructed plan would hold up long enough for them to get the job done.

CHAPTER 26

"LADIES AND GENTLEMEN OF THE JURY," BEGAN
Lang, strong, clear, and fully in command. "This is my first of two
opportunities to talk to you directly. After I have concluded my
opening statement, I will not get another chance to talk to you until
all the evidence is in and the judge has instructed you about the law
you have to apply to the facts as you see them. Now, as you have
heard throughout the process of your selection, that might be as
long as six weeks from now. So I'm going to try to make the most of
our opportunity to talk."

He moved from behind the podium to station himself between
the jury box and the counsel table. This was intended to encourage
familiarity between himself and the jury in a respectful, non-
threatening way. It was also designed to prevent them from continuing to stare at the star of the show, Russell Lindstrom,
something they had seemed intent on doing from the moment they
had first walked into the courtroom.

They were a bright jury, as far as he could tell from *voir dire*,
and he had their full attention for the moment. He knew from

experience, however, that he could count on no more than forty-five minutes, one hour at the outside, of that level of attention. He would, indeed, need to make the most of it.

"The judge has already read you a brief statement describing what this case is about. Sounds simple enough: Two companies entered into a contract to develop and test an experimental airplane; the company that bought the airplane claims it didn't fly as promised and claims that the other company, and its people, knew this and intentionally covered it up. And, do you know what? It really is that simple. It's just going to take a while to tell you the story through the testimony of the people who know what happened. But right now I'm going to tell you, in the next forty minutes, what they're going to say and what the documents people wrote in the course of this case are going to show.

"My client is the plaintiff, Pegasus Technologies. The evidence is going to show that Pegasus Technologies was given a copy of the final engineering report prepared by the defendant company, Arrow Dynamics, for the original customer, Daultry Research PLC. That report laid out the whole design plan, testing plan, test results, and the technical conclusions drawn from those results, of the program to develop the experimental airplane called the StormTree. The Pegasus people were so impressed with the report, especially its conclusions about what a great airplane this was—beautiful, reliable, safe, a 'joy to fly' even for 'low-time,' or very inexperienced, pilots—that they bought the rights to it. Relying on this glowing report of this flawless new aircraft, they decided to build it and market it and sank millions of dollars into the effort.

"But the evidence is going to show that the airplane Pegasus Technologies built from the plans designed by Arrow Dynamics and in reliance on the final engineering report of its testing of the StormTree was not reliable, safe, or a joy to fly. In fact, the evidence will show that this airplane—which is called the Peregrine—built in exacting geometric conformity with the StormTree tested by Arrow Dynamics, did not fly anything like the report said it should. Ladies and gentlemen, the evidence will show that it was dangerous, that it would enter a spin"—he whipped his hand through the air to simulate a spiral—"without the slightest warning, and worse, the evidence will show, the spin it would enter was the most dangerous kind, a flat spin or dead spin—one that is dead level to the earth—a spin the experts will tell you is virtually unrecoverable, even by a pilot of exceptional skill. And since the plane was intended for a recreational market of inexperienced pilots, this was a fatal flaw in the design and testing of the prototype. That's bad enough, but there's more."

"Objection," said Hickman, rising. "That's argument."

"Sustained," said Judge Campbell. "The jury will disregard counsel's last statement. Only statements about the facts of the case are permitted at this time. Mr. Lang, I caution you to avoid characterizing the facts in opening."

Lang paused, doing his best to convey to the jury the impression that he had just been hit with a meaningless, ticky-tack foul—not a big deal. This was, of course, true, but to Lang, they just looked confused.

"The evidence will show," he continued, using the phrase that will almost always convert any argumentative assertion into a factual statement, "that this dangerous tendency—the tendency to go into an unrecoverable spin—was *known* to the people at Arrow Dynamics, Mr. Chesney, Mr. Milinsky, Mr. Castillo, and, yes, Mr. Lindstrom, and they all conspired to hide that fact in the final engineering report."

This last statement hit a chord of some kind with all three men and five women of the jury. Indeed, Jurors Four and Seven sat straight up in their chairs and Three craned her neck to get a look at Lindstrom. Lang took two small, thoughtful steps to his right to give her a direct laser shot at the man himself.

And so it went for the next thirty-eight minutes, as Lang meticulously laid out his proof. He and Amy had developed an approach to the technical areas of the case designed to communicate more effectively so that they would all be speaking the same language. "A flat spin, or a dead spin," he said, the second time he used the latter term, "is a spin that is level to the ground." He held his hand flat to the plane of the floor and rotated it as far as he could to demonstrate the attitude of the spin. The jury looked interested but puzzled. He added, "It's the spin that got Tom Cruise's copilot killed in that great movie *Top Gun*. And, as the experts will tell you when they testify, it's very different from the kind of spin that's a spiral or a cartwheel, like the one that spins Darth Vader off into space at the end of the first *Star Wars* movie." Now, he noted, the lights went on all across the jury box, eight heads nodding in unison. The jury still seemed to be engaged as he neared the end of his statement. And he drew no further objection from Hickman, thus managing to keep Judge Campbell safely locked in his cage.

"And, therefore, ladies and gentlemen, the evidence will show that the man at the controls for this entire operation of deceit and concealment was the man who founded Arrow Dynamics, the man who sought out the original partnership with Nigel Daultry, the man who prepared the contract with its clear and unambiguous promise to perform the rigorous Military Specification test program on the aircraft's spin characteristics, and the man who either prepared or expressly approved the false engineering report—Russell Lindstrom himself."

This was the fourth time he had managed to recite his claim against Lindstrom personally, each time using slightly different phrasing. Each time, he noted, the jury seemed less jarred by the charge, all part of the process of indoctrination necessary to allow the jury to see the famous and illustrious defendant in a darker light.

Amy smiled at him as he finished and headed back to his chair. Andrews nodded slightly and Ellerby winked. All things considered, Lang thought, it had gone very well. Now, thought Lang somewhat darkly, if only I can deliver this package. Meanwhile, Hickman was already in front of the jury box.

"I'm Gentry Hickman, as you may recall from the introductions at the beginning of the selection process. Although you could be forgiven if you had forgotten that over the last week and a half. Like Mr. Lang, I'm not from around here. But my clients are. Arrow Dynamics, the evidence will show, has been here in San Sebastian since the late fifties and has done quite a bit for the community during that time. And you all know Russell Lindstrom, a longtime resident and businessman who may be the first man sued because he had the audacity to run for president."

"Objection!" called Lang, rising.

"Withdraw the remark," said Hickman, preempting a ruling. Campbell said nothing and Hickman continued. "I hope you were listening very carefully to Mr. Lang's opening statement. I really do. He told a good story. Interesting. Highly entertaining. He's real good, too. Good storyteller for a good story. Problem is, his story has nothing to do with *this* case. But you've got to remember, now, as you hear the real facts from the actual witnesses, that this is the story you've been promised by the plaintiff. It's like a contract, ladies and gentlemen, and I want you to remember it so you can hold Mr. Lang to it when he doesn't back it up with the evidence.

"Because the facts are going to show that Arrow Dynamics did design the airplane Nigel Daultry—have I got that right? I'm better with American names, to be honest with you. So, bear with me, please—they did design the airplane that Mr. Daultry asked them to design, to his specifications, as spelled out in a contract. And they did just what they said they would do. Designed it, built it, and tested it. Just exactly as they said they would, agreed to in that contract. And the plane, the StormTree, they called it, was a good one, flew just the way they said it would. The evidence is going to show, however, that although this English company, Pegasus Technologies, the plaintiff, bought the rights to manufacture the airplane designed and tested by Arrow Dynamics, what it built was an entirely *different* airplane, the one it called the Peregrine. And that's the one that didn't fly, that's the one that spun without warning, that's the one that was hard to recover from a spin. All in all, a pretty bad airplane. But not my client's plane. It was these fellahs' plane." He pivoted to point directly at Clive Andrews. "The evidence is going to show that the Peregrine—their plane—was different from the StormTree—our plane, in *nine* separate ways. And the most important way, the absolutely most critical way, was in its weight. Because, ladies and gentlemen, the evidence is going to show that the Peregrine weighed *three hundred and thirty* pounds more than the StormTree.

"Now, that may not be a lot, if you're talking about jumbo jets. But here, where the StormTree weighed eight hundred and seventeen pounds and the Peregrine weighed one thousand one hundred forty-seven pounds, the difference is—I used my handy little calculator for this"—he picked up a yellow tablet on the table and read from it—"*forty percent.* And the testimony you will hear, from Air Force experts, from NASA experts, from FAA experts—we've got a slew of 'em—will prove that the two airplanes are simply not the same in any way that matters in this case. That the one the plaintiffs built was an entirely different airplane, which you could probably figure out for yourselves just from the simple fact that theirs spun and the StormTree did not."

Hickman spoke for just over an hour, his syrupy drawl and colloquial phrasing apparently going down easily with the jury all the way through. Only at the end did he inject drama and emotion into his remarks.

"One final thing, ladies and gentlemen. The evidence—the *evidence,* not some high-priced L.A. lawyer's idea of what he wishes the evidence were—will prove without a doubt that none of this, *none of it,* whatever it was and whatever it means legally for the two companies—none of it had anything whatsoever to do with Mr. Russell Lindstrom. Nothing. He was approached by Mr. Daultry to design an airplane and he sent him over to his old friends at Arrow. Had one call from the Englishman to clear up a paragraph of the contract—which he did—and that was it. Period. He was long gone from this company, by more than a decade, by the time this design-and-testing program ever took place. And by the time you hear all the evidence, you will see that there's no reason on God's green earth for these people to have sued Mr. Lindstrom, except for the obvious fact that he happens to be running for president and is one of the most recognizable men in the world right now."

"Objection!" Lang said, rising. "That's argument."

"Overruled," bellowed the judge. "It sounds like a statement of fact to me, Counsel! Mr. Hickman, have you concluded?"

"I have, Your Honor."

"Very well," said the judge, and he called for the noon recess.

Ro had said a brief good-bye to Lang—he was inundated with pressing matters for the afternoon session and she had no desire to distract him—and left just as the judge had announced the noon recess. The jet proved to be a comfortable alternative to the Friday drive back to Los Angeles, soothing her nerves and relaxing her for the weekend chores ahead. The traffic from the airport was a hopeless snarl, however, and despite her careful planning, she arrived home thoroughly exhausted and in a sour mood. The mood had instantly lightened, though, with the first glimpse of her children. After she got a thorough update of the events that had kept the kids busy during her absence, she sat down wearily with a tall glass of lemonade. The telephone rang.

"Listen carefully, Mrs. Lang," said a man's voice she did not recognize. It was calm, cold, and very disturbing.

"Who is this?" she demanded.

The man ignored the question and continued. "You looked very good up there in San Sebastian this week. Very pretty and stylish."

Suddenly, she realized that she must be dealing with a crank call. Probably some pathetic loner who had caught a glimpse of her on television. "Look, whoever you are, leave me—"

"Listen to me!" he said, a fierce chill in his razorlike voice. "I'm trying to protect you and your family. Your former husband is playing a dangerous game with dangerous people, Mrs. Lang. And the way he's going about it could make you a widow and leave poor little Jennifer, Andrea, and Jack half-orphans by the time the Fourth of July gets here."

She began to shake. This was outrageous, yes, but it was terrifying. "Who is this?" was all she could manage to say.

"Someone who cares about your family. Someone who doesn't want you to spend too much time at funeral homes because your ex-husband's got a personal vendetta against the wrong man. You're a smart woman, Mrs. Lang. You know what to do." The line went dead in her hand.

Jennifer came into the room and immediately saw that the color had drained from her mother's face. "What's wrong, Mom?" she asked.

Ro shook her head, unable to answer. Her hands trembled visibly and her stomach had gone into a tight knot. She felt both threatened and violated. Three times she punched in Lang's hotel phone number before she got it right.

"Hello, this is Chris Lang. We can't answer the phone right now—"

"Dammit!" shouted Ro.

Lang came on the line. "Hello? Who's this?"

"It's me."

"Me?" He paused. "Ro? Is that you?"

"Yeah," she said softly, working to get her emotions back under control.

"Ro, what's the matter? Are you okay? Are the kids okay? Where are you?"

"I'm home and everyone's okay," she replied, her control slowly returning. "I just had a very scary phone call." She reported the call to Lang as best she could recall it.

"Just some crank call, Ro, that's all," Lang responded when she had finished. He found the call disturbing but was inclined to dismiss the threat the caller had made. He was accustomed to dealing with hostile adversaries and the dimensions of his struggle with Lindstrom had grown far beyond anything he had experienced before.

When Ro did not respond, Lang added, "Look, I'm going to call Bill Quinn and see if he or someone else can get over there. You'll feel better."

"Chris," she said, her strength and conviction now fully returned. "Didn't you hear me? The threat was against *you*, not us. It's not us I'm concerned about."

"I'm not worried about it, Ro. This guy Lindstrom is riding a wave of great popularity now, he's developed a real following among the political right. And you know who lives out on the right."

"Yeah," she replied sarcastically. "You do."

"I know, Ro, but the right's got a lot of fringe players, not just working people who believe in less government and lower taxes. He's struck a chord with the survivalists, apparently, and more than his share of skinheads. And an awful lot of people who have nothing better to do than sit in front of the tube all day." His mind was racing to assess whether or not there was a real threat here. He couldn't quite shake the image of Lindstrom and his linebacking corps in the tiny hotel room last winter.

"Look," he continued, trying as best he could from long distance to ease her fears. "I'm sorry this happened. And I'm sorry you're upset. It's crazy that this sort of thing can still reach you years after you moved me out of your life."

"Look, Chris," she said, in a tone as serious as he'd ever heard her use. "I don't scare easily and I don't see phantoms in the dark. This was not a crank call. This was someone close to this case and he made a very deliberate and serious threat against your life. I see no reason to dismiss this."

What she said was true, of course, Lang knew. She was a tough, down-to-earth woman who drew great strength from her working-class upbringing in the solid, no-nonsense environment of the Steel City. To say that she didn't scare easily was an understatement. Still, he was confident that there was nothing to the threat. Besides, Lang knew all too well that Lindstrom and Hickman were convinced that they could beat him in the courtroom. And, he reflected ruefully, nothing had happened thus far in the trial to make them think otherwise.

"I know, Ro. You're right. But, hey, I've got security all around me, at the federal government's expense. I'm safer here than if I were driving on the Ventura Freeway every morning."

She seemed mollified, if only reluctantly. "Chris, these kids need their father a lot more than Pegasus Technologies needs the money."

"But this isn't about money."

"I think that's what worries me. Anyway, I don't want you to take any chances."

"I know. The *kids* need me."

She was not about to be baited. "Kids need a father, Chris. Not a crusader." He remained silent. "This obviously has to do with Lindstrom. Is it really necessary to keep him in the case?"

"Jesus, Ro! Listen to what you're saying! If I back off that son of a bitch now, I've lost everything. Not just in this case but for all time. You can't let these bastards intimidate you. If you do, they've cut your heart out. You know that, Rochelle Deyton."

There was no denying the logic in his words, or the conviction, either, so she didn't try. In an odd way it reminded her of the fiery brawler she had fallen in love with years ago. And didn't want to lose now. For the kids.

"Look, Chris. Just be careful. And don't carry this case against Lindstrom any further than you have to. I think this is a dangerous man and this whole thing scares me."

"Oh, Ro. He's not so dangerous. Just used to getting his own way. And he's not used to dealing with Chris Lang."

She was not fooled by his cockiness, but chose not to pursue it further. Bill Quinn just "happened to drop by" a half an hour later and, though his wife had just returned from a week out of town, he sat and "chatted" for several hours. When the phone rang just before eleven, right after her second call to Lang, Bill advised that she let it ring. He reluctantly got up to leave at fifteen minutes past midnight. At two-thirty Ro saw a sheriff's-department black-and-white cruiser conspicuously parked at the front curb.

Mark Fassero sat at the console in the large closet off his master bedroom, a space he had converted into a nerve center for intelligence gathering—complete with elaborate tape decks, radios, computer screens, and telephone equipment. He was frustrated that Ro hadn't answered his call, but he understood why. His surveillance unit at her house had discreetly backed off with the appearance of Detective Quinn and, from a safe distance, had reported the arrival of the sheriff's cruiser. He knew, then, that she was safe and he was confident that there would be no attempt to make a direct, face-to-face contact for the time being. The plan, at least for the moment, appeared to be limited to intimidation.

He had listened to the tape of the call a dozen times since it had been transmitted to him, trying to assess whether there had been any damage to their plan and the risk that a breach might yet occur. After all, there could be no question now that this was what Lindstrom's people intended, and they had reached a point where an escalation in their effort must be anticipated. Still, judging from the two calls Ro had made to Lang, especially the second, she seemed shaken but unscathed. More significantly, there seemed little chance that Lang was about to lose his nerve. Fassero had frankly had his doubts about Lang, but Piersall, to his credit, had seemed convinced of Lang's determination—and ambition—from the start. Not quite convinced enough to save the money spent to wrap Lang and his family in a security blanket, reflected Fassero ironically, but convinced nonetheless. Lang's tenacity, if anything, seemed greater now than ever before. Challenge him and you only succeeded in making him mad, thought Fassero, mentally filing that piece of information away for another time. Then, he cued up the tape of the mysterious caller for yet another listen.

After hanging up for the second time with Ro, Lang toyed with his outlines for the witnesses to be called during the upcoming weeks, but his concentration was poor. The call Ro had received had upset him far more than he had let on. As he had reviewed the events of this evening he had come to the inescapable conclusion that these guys were, indeed, dangerous bastards and there was little doubt that as he closed the noose—*if* he closed the noose—they would only become more so. The ominous words of Laura Carey came back to him with chilling clarity. "Look at it this way," she had said. "Just imagine you're an intruder in his home, late at night, where his wife and kids are sleeping. And he's got a gun in the nightstand drawer. That's who he is and that's who he thinks you are."

And now, months later and two thousand miles away, swirling a Bailey's around three ice cubes in a glass, he wondered, for the first time since Jad Piersall had ignited the fuse back at the MacNaughton Castle, whether he could really pull this off. He would never have appreciated the significance of the fact that it didn't even occur to him to wonder whether or not he should try.

He rose from the conference table set up in the corner of the living room and went to the window to look down upon the slumbering village of San Sebastian. Under its mask of darkness, he knew, there were unaccustomed currents of emotion here tonight— excitement, danger, hatred, anger—all unleashed by the simple expedient of filing a lawsuit. There was something unholy in that power, he thought, with its awesome potential for abuse. It was a thought that, unbeknownst to Lang, had already occurred to millions of Americans watching the trial on CableStar at one time or another over the course of the past week, whether they could articulate it in that way or not. He rubbed his weary eyes but knew that the events of this day would make falling asleep tonight very difficult. He fixed another drink and stretched out in the recliner in the far corner of the living room.

The intense quiet of the empty suite settled over him like the soothing presence of another person. After court this afternoon the place had resembled a train station or bus depot, with bags, brief-cases, suitcases, dollies, and bellhops appearing and disappearing all around from the four bedrooms that fanned out from the central core of the suite and elsewhere. Clive and Graham, assured that Lang could get along without them over the weekend, had taken off to see Yosemite with Jad Piersall, promising to return by five o'clock on Sunday. Amy had been grateful for Lang's encouragement to go home for the weekend, unaware that she would end up sitting alone waiting for her husband to hand off the safety of Lang's family to another officer of the law. John Carrick had grabbed a flight to Provo for a conference on Defense Industry Downsizing in the New World Order. Rachel Cruz had driven up to Monterey to spend the weekend reconciling with her erstwhile boyfriend, Derek.

Lang, for his part, had decided to remain in San Sebastian, needing time to polish some areas of the case that troubled him. Following this afternoon's lunch break, he had finally called his first witness, Clive Andrews, the man who first relied upon the Storm-Tree test results and engineering report to buy the rights to the project. Clive's testimony had gone well and the jury seemed to like him but, by the time the afternoon recess had come, Lang had only begun to lead him through the long, richly detailed story he would tell. By Lang's reckoning, Clive's testimony alone would consume half of the second week of the trial.

As he lounged here in the dim light of the quiet hotel room, he was more than a little concerned about potential problem areas they expected to encounter over the next seven to eight trial days, espe-cially the admissibility of evidence showing Pegasus's lost profits and rulings that might arise out of the differences between the Storm-Tree and the Peregrine. Although these issues had been fully briefed and he had thoroughly discussed them with Amy, they remained troublesome. And so it went for another hour or more, his mind juggling with more issues than answers, more problems than solu-tions.

It was well after midnight when anxiety began to loosen its grip and Lang headed for bed. Within ten minutes, fatigue and alcohol overcame stress, and he fell into a deep sleep. He heard absolutely nothing ninety minutes later when Ernesto Reynoso quietly entered the Presidential Suite. Nor did he hear a sound as the man moved through the living room to the door of the room Amy was using.

Inside, the young room-service waiter shut the door and turned on the light in the closet, adjusting the closet door so as to allow no more than a sliver of light to fall across the floor of Amy's room. By the small desk near the window he spotted her heavy burgundy litigation bag. Taking care not to move the bag, he opened its unlocked catch and looked inside. Just as he'd been told, there were dozens of manila folders there, each one neatly labeled in the upper right-hand corner. He reached into his shirt pocket and pulled out a small slip of paper. Using a penlight, he reread the word penciled on the paper: "Rebuttal." It was an odd word, one that had never come up in the English-language classes he had taken at the San Sebastian Community Center, one that Banfield had not bothered to explain. "Just look for this word, Ernesto," an impatient Banfield had told him. "It will be in there. In the woman's bag. She's the one who keeps the files for them." Quickly, he moved through the folders one by one, trying to find the word "Rebuttal." At last, right next to a thick one labeled Haverstock's Log, he found one labeled Rebuttal Witnesses.

He opened the folder and found a single sheet of paper on which seven names were written. He didn't bother to try to read them. Instead, he removed the tiny camera Banfield had given him from his pants pocket and laid the page flat on the desk. He flipped on the desk lamp and carefully positioned it over the paper for maximum brightness. Then, he sighted the page through the viewer and snapped three exposures, just as he had been instructed. So intent was he on doing the job he had been given—and doing it precisely the way he was instructed—that he didn't hear Lang's door open outside in the suite.

Lang had awakened parched and uncomfortably warm. He had turned the air conditioner to low before going to bed and it had turned out to be a mistake. The three glasses of Bailey's, of course, were also significant contributors to the cottony dryness growing rapidly in his mouth. He badly needed a glass of ice water. He padded across the suite, first, to the thermostat, which he reset to high and then to the kitchen. He flicked on the overhead light and opened the refrigerator to survey what was in stock. Rachel had volunteered to make the arrangements with the hotel and had laid in nearly a case of bottled water. He took a glass down from the cabinet and loaded it from the ice maker before filling it with water.

He stood before the open refrigerator door as he drank, reveling in the chill escaping from within.

When Ernesto opened the door of Amy's room, he saw a man, facing into the refrigerator, drinking deeply from a tall glass. His heart froze. But his mind was racing. There was no legitimate reason for his being there, so he had no choice but to retreat into the woman's room. He did so, moving as swiftly as he could in total silence. He slid behind the door and stood there, as still as possible, watching what little he could see through the crack between the door and the jamb and listening for any sound that might herald his discovery.

Lang finished his glass of water and poured another. Meanwhile, Ernesto stood perfectly still, large beads of perspiration popping out on his broad bronze forehead. His mind was flooded with the full range of calamitous consequences that would surely follow if he was to get caught. Losing the hotel job that Russell Lindstrom had graciously arranged as a reward for his father's valorous service in Managua would not even be the worst of it. Banfield would be livid, of course. His father and mother would be eternally dishonored. There might be trouble with the law over this; he wasn't really sure. But worst of all would be the disgrace he would bring to the great man himself, disgrace and, quite possibly, he realized with a heightening sense of desperation, disaster in the horrible legal mess he was in with this very man, a mess that Ernesto did not even try to understand. It was, of course, unthinkable that it would come to this. Absolutely out of the question. That's when he made up his mind that he would kill Lang before he would let himself be caught. He sighed heavily, oddly relieved to have found an acceptable, if undesirable, solution. He moved to his right so as to get a better look at Lang. While he watched, he slowly began to clench and unclench his fists, rhythmically flexing the large, powerful hands that had long ago earned him the respect of anyone who had ever seen him spar in the Steel Gloves Gym in downtown San Sebastian.

Meanwhile, Lang finished his second glass and closed the refrigerator door. As he reached to flip off the light, he noticed that the door to Amy's room was slightly ajar. In truth, he did not really remember whether it had been open or closed when he went to bed, but he was reasonably sure it was one or the other. He simply did not recall seeing it partially open all week. From where he stood, he tried to see into the room, tilting his head at an angle, frankly a little reluctant to just go over there and look inside.

Ernesto could now see Lang perfectly from where he stood

behind the door and was certain, from Lang's body language, that Lang could see him. His heart pumped wildly, adrenaline flooding his vital organs as his fists and forearms swelled in anticipation of the inevitable end to this unfortunate turn of events. He began to move ever so slowly from around the door.

As Lang started toward Amy's door, squinting to pierce the dimness there, suddenly the telephones all over the suite rang in unison, sirenlike in the dead quiet of the night. Instinctively, he checked his watch and wondered who would call at two-twenty. Then, he remembered the earlier calls from Ro and, fearing what news this might bring, he fairly flew back into the kitchen to snatch the receiver from the phone on the far wall.

"Hello?"

"Did I wake you?"

"Er, no. Who is this?" asked Lang, now with his back directly toward Amy's door.

"I'm sorry. It's Bill." He sounded reassuringly wide-awake to Lang. "Didn't mean to get you up, Chris, but I figured you might not be able to sleep. I'm home now but Ro and the kids are just fine. I left an around-the-clock, high-profile surveillance team from the sheriff's office out front of their house. They've already checked in with me three times. Everything is fine."

"That's great, Bill," answered Lang, relief flooding through his weary brain. In fact, he was so relieved that for the moment, he forgot all about Amy's door. It was just long enough, however, for Ernesto to steal from her room, across the far wall, and silently out through the double door to the hallway. Moments later, when the brief call had been concluded, Lang remembered the door and went over to it, bravely snapping on the light switch inside. As he suspected, it was empty and completely undisturbed. Smiling at his own fertile imagination, he went back into his room and slept soundly until well past dawn.

CHAPTER 27

LANG TURNED AWAY FROM HIS WITNESS AND CAUGHT the faces of the jurors, all but one or two of whom still appeared alert despite the dryness of Clive Andrews's testimony. The painstaking process of laying the foundation for his client's right to rely on the final engineering report, dull and dreary stuff by any standard, was absolutely critical to his case on both the contract and the fraud claims. Without it, a favorable jury verdict could not withstand appeal. And, besides, the uncontroversial content of this testimony served nicely to buffer the jurors from the bombastic intervention of Judge Campbell, something Lang was sure would eventually erode his own credibility with them. It was time now, however, to run some risks.

"Mr. Andrews, tell me—were any sales of the production aircraft ever made?" asked Lang.

"None."

"Why not?" pressed Lang, already hearing the well-rehearsed answer before it was spoken.

"The Peregrine was not certifiable. It had a clear tendency to enter into a flat spin that was nearly unrecoverable. It would have been financially and morally irresponsible to market the aircraft. It was a death trap."

"Objection," said Hickman, springing to his feet. "This is irrelevant to the issues here. There's no proof that the Peregrine had anything to do with the defendants. Besides, the witness's testimony lacks foundation."

"Sustained," barked the judge.

But the point was made and, for once, Hickman and Campbell unwittingly conspired to underscore it for Lang. He continued to hammer on the connection between the huge investment and the useless, dangerous product his client had gotten as a result. Hickman's objections came in a torrent now, each in turn sustained by Campbell, but Lang persisted and, by dint of his perseverance, got most of what he wanted before the jury. Thus, over the course of that first full week of testimony, Lang slowly, but securely, built the foundation for his case. Graham Ellerby followed his partner, Clive Andrews, to the stand and testified about the actual fabrication of the Peregrine and its dangerous tendency to spin. He finished the week with a harrowing narration of the videotape of Scottish pilot Cam MacNeil's eight-rotation spin. It was hardly the equal of Walt McCluskey's fateful flight of the StormTree, but it was good jury theater nonetheless. And Lang was doubly pleased; he had needed only a little juggling of his interrogation in order to finish that portion of Ellerby's testimony at precisely four thirty-four.

Just as the lights came up, the judge announced the day's recess to a courtroom packed with journalists and jurors still on the edge of their seats. When he finished the jurors' admonition he gave at the end of every day, he hammered once with his gavel, then exited the courtroom as everyone else scrambled to their feet.

"Not too bad," Amy said into Lang's ear as they packed up, watching the jury leave.

"Not bad," repeated Lang. "But we still have to deal with the weight issue head-on."

Amy frowned. "One step at a time, Chris."

"You're right. At least we gave the jury the right evidence to chew on over the weekend."

"Not to mention the weekend news programs."

"Those, too." Lang smiled.

.   .   .

Lindstrom had already left the courthouse and was on his way to a suite at the Santa Ynez to do an interview for the West Coast edition of PBS's *News Hour*. Inside the limousine with him were Hickman, Calabrese, and Banfield.

"Well, Gentry, what do you think?" asked Lindstrom, settling back into the plush rear seat.

"No punches landed yet, Russell. You haven't got a mark on you. Hell, I don't even think the company's been tagged yet."

"Long way to go, though." Lindstrom loosened his tie. He would change clothes at the hotel before going on-camera. He turned to Calabrese. "But will it last long enough to convince those delegates flocking to Kansas City that we're electable, Gina?"

His campaign manager smiled and opened a suede attaché case. "These delegate polls are incredible," she said, fishing out a fistful of computer printouts. "This just came in this afternoon. For starters, seventy-seven percent of the delegates polled agreed with the following statement: 'Mr. Lindstrom is a wrongly accused innocent bystander who is being victimized by an abuse of the legal system.' And, the combination of the trial coverage and your other TV appearances over the last two weeks has clearly boosted your standing. Allen and Associates finds that you have moved into the lead among delegates considered likely to switch candidates after the first ballot." She stopped to let the significance of that statement sink in. "By a wide margin that is growing in every forty-eight-hour sampling."

"Jesus Christ!" whispered Banfield, voicing the sentiments of everyone present. They all knew, of course, that, while the overwhelming majority of delegates elected to the convention in a primary election or state caucus were bound to vote for the candidate to whom they were pledged on the convention's first ballot, these automatic first-ballot votes were split into three virtually equal parts, guaranteeing that the nomination would not be decided on that first ballot. For subsequent ballots, only a handful of delegates were committed to any candidate, meaning the nomination would be decided on the floor of the convention by the delegates who chose to switch candidates.

"I'd say that means you're going to be the Republican presidential nominee," said Calabrese.

Lindstrom was deep in thought. "Thank God for that miserable old judge and Lang's gift for pissing him off," he muttered. "But remember, children, nothing's written in stone, yet. Let's not lose our focus." To Hickman, he said, "The convention is just over five weeks away. We need to wrap this trial up about a week or so before they open in Kansas City. That'll be about the right time to make the most of the outcome. Can that be done, Gentry? Is Lang really going to call one hundred and eighteen witnesses?"

Hickman shook his head. "No. We've run all that stuff down. Of the one eighteen he's designated, we figure he'll call no more than forty or fifty, most of them for very brief, specific testimony. And there are sixty-three he's listed in a group that are former employees of the company. We don't think he's going to call any of them. In fact, we checked with opposing counsel in his last five major trials and found out that, each time, he did exactly the same thing with former employees and never called one of them."

Lindstrom furrowed his brow. "Why would he do that?"

"Couple of reasons. One, it could be a precaution—and a smart one, at that—in case the other side refuses to stipulate to the authenticity of documents. Then you have a pool of witnesses available to call for that purpose. Of course, we already stipulated to authenticity, so that's not an issue here anymore. Another reason could be intimidation. That many names on a list of witnesses scares the shit out of some trial lawyers. Still another reason could be harassment. People whose names get on witness lists in high-profile cases get calls from the press, unwanted publicity. They're your former employees, so they hold you responsible. It can be a tactic to create ill will for your adversary."

Lindstrom's expression indicated that he was not impressed by the answer. "Since we have stipulated to the authenticity of our company documents in this case and since he surely knows *we* will not be intimidated or harassed by this tactic, what do you imagine is the *real* reason for this tactic?"

"I think it's a habit, nothing more. Many trial lawyers develop a way of doing things and they just repeat the pattern each time, without even thinking about it."

"Gentry," Lindstrom said, a patronizing tone in the word, "I assume you have been observing Mr. Lang for the better part of the past year?" Hickman nodded. Lindstrom continued, "And that you have noted that he is an excellent trial lawyer?" Hickman nodded again. "One who rarely, if ever, does anything that he doesn't 'think about'?"

"That's true."

"One who has yet to make a move that was not, in fact, carefully calculated and thoroughly premeditated?"

"That's also accurate," acknowledged Hickman.

Lindstrom paused for a moment. Then, he said, "Has he subpoenaed these former employee witnesses?"

Hickman smiled in spite of himself. Even after all these years, Lindstrom's mind amazed him. It was unheard of to find a layman who knew that putting an adverse witness's name on a designation list meant nothing if you hadn't also had him served with a subpoena to testify. "Yes, he's subpoenaed them all. At least as far as we know. Still doesn't mean anything. The lawyers in those other cases said that Lang subpoenaed all the former employees in each of those cases, too, but still never called any of them."

Lindstrom's ears had pricked up. "What do you mean 'as far as we know'?"

Hickman shifted uncomfortably in his seat. "I mean, we tracked them all down, all but one. All the rest have been subpoenaed but haven't been contacted about what they are expected to testify about. It's a dead issue, Russell. We don't expect any of them to testify."

"Which one haven't you tracked down?"

"I don't know, Russell," replied Hickman, stroking the stubble of his beard with his palm. "Just some former employee we couldn't match up to the records. We figured the records must be incomp—"

"Who?" Lindstrom asked, a razor's edge to the word.

"I don't know. Randy knows. I'll check with him."

Lindstrom snatched the handset of the cellular phone off the console and tossed it to Hickman. "Call him now."

While Hickman punched in Overbrook's number, Lindstrom and Banfield exchanged glances. Gina Calabrese shifted in her seat, trying to focus on something outside her window.

After a brief exchange with Overbrook, Hickman hung up. "M. McKinney," he said. "The one we can't match up to the payroll printouts is M. McKinney. Randy thinks he or she may have been a temp several years back before the company switched over to the new data-processing system and just fell between the cracks."

"Well," said Lindstrom deliberately, his mind furiously processing information, "he's right about one thing. She fell between the cracks. I believe you will find that 'M. McKinney' is Molly McKinney, also known as Molly O'Keefe, former companion and one-time lover of the late Nigel Daultry." Then, more to himself, he added, "Goddammit! Pretty, red-headed Molly O'Keefe! Figured you and your crazy Irish bloodletting had gone to ground for good!"

Hickman felt as though he'd been hit in the stomach. Before he could respond, Lindstrom turned to Banfield, in the seat next to him. "This is definitely another one for you, Dick. Someone's going to have to locate her and talk to her before she testifies."

Banfield nodded. "Right."

Hickman swam up from the depths of his sudden plunge. "I'll have to talk to her, or Randy will, so that—"

Lindstrom waved him off. "It's okay, Gentry. Dick can do it. If one of the lawyers talks to her it will be too official, and it won't look good if she does testify. This way, Dick can pay her an unofficial visit to see if she is really prepared to testify. Maybe she hasn't thought through all of the implications. Perhaps he can help her do that. He won't even have to identify himself, so the fallout if she does testify will be inconsequential."

Hickman was unpersuaded but let it go for the moment. "Well, we should brief him first, before he goes. Wherever he's going."

"Of course," said Lindstrom warmly. "Brief him before he goes. But we'll have to do it soon."

Dick Banfield was delighted with the assignment. He hadn't realized how much he'd missed this sort of work. Now, as he sat in his darkened office before the luminescent screen of his high-powered computer, his mind had achieved that rare, barely remembered state of clarity of purpose fused with the thrill of the hunt. He had no trouble focusing his full attention on the methodical formulation of his plan.

Timing was critical, of course, and what he did had to be coordinated against the backdrop of the unfolding trial. At the top of the list of priorities on his screen was an item termed simply "brush clearance." He punched in a long European phone number.

At the other end of the connection, a dark-skinned man of forty, his blue denim shirtsleeves rolled up tight on bulging forearms, picked up the phone. *"Hola?"* he said.

Banfield replied, "Adolfo! *Cómo estás?*"

The other man's voice brightened immediately. "Señor Dick!" he exclaimed. "It's been a long time, no? Are you coming to Majorca?"

Banfield laughed. "I wish. Unfortunately, I am traveling elsewhere. And so are you."

Now, the other man laughed. "You need some gardening, I think, no?"

"That's right, Adolfo. Brush clearance. Some manual labor."

Well past two in the morning, Mark Fassero was deeply engrossed in preparing his coded report for Colonel Shepard Easley. As always, in addition to his summary of all security measures undertaken and all potential contacts with the subjects under their jurisdiction, he included, at the colonel's direction, his own observations of all other aspects of the operation to which he was privy, including his private assessments of Piersall, Stingley, and the junior-level operatives attached to the mission. He was at the computer, rechecking his own personal encrypting program, when the telephone rang. Still deep in thought, he absently fumbled for the receiver.

"Hello?"

"Mark? This is Piersall. I think we have a problem."

Instantly, years of combat-readiness training locked into place and, despite the hour, the former Major Fassero of Army Intelligence was fully alert and riding a surge of adrenaline. "What's wrong?" he asked.

"We picked up a cellular call from Lindstrom's limo this afternoon."

"Really?" Fassero was clearly incredulous.

"I know. These guys have been awfully damned careful, but they slipped this one time. Hickman placed a call to Overbrook right after court let out. And it sounds significant to me. They're onto the O'Keefe woman. We have to assume that they may send somebody over there to discourage her. With her background, she may be vulnerable to that kind of pressure."

"I agree. But, a slipup? Isn't it more likely a plant?"

"Could be. But we can't take the chance."

"You're right," Fassero agreed, sighing and pinching the weariness from his eyes. "What was the last word from Blades?"

"That's the other thing. Blades took his position right after we found her and reported once, but we haven't had any contact from him for the past twenty-four hours."

Fassero laughed ironically. "Fucking Scarface! Too much sloppy work coming out of this unit lately. You want me to take it?"

"It's a little cumbersome, but, yeah, that's the way the colonel wants to go for now. We're pretty sure the ex is secure for the time being and there's very little likelihood now that they'll get to Lang, anyway. But this O'Keefe angle could be the big threat. Our case shrinks several sizes if she doesn't get into the game."

"Okay. Where am I headed? Ireland?"

"Right. Village of Kilmurry on the cliffs of County Clare."

"Sounds picturesque. I'm assuming this is a 'now' priority?"

"That's our assessment. We don't really know what they're up to. Only that they're aware there's some significance to her name being on the witness list."

"What took them so long?"

"Lang listed her under her maiden name. We're not even sure they know who she really is, yet. Just that they noticed her enough to have a phone call about her."

"Lang used her maiden name?" Fassero laughed. "Sneaky son of a bitch, isn't he?"

"He plays to win."

Bobby Lathrop looked good up on the stand, thought Lang, young and sincere, and handsome in an earnest, All-American way. The women on the jury were riveted.

"And your assignment?" Lang asked.

"I was asked to go to San Sebastian and act as the Pegasus Technologies liaison to Arrow Dynamics while they tried to determine what was wrong with the Peregrine."

Like Andrews and Ellerby before him, Lathrop was thoughtful, respectful, and thoroughly credible as he told his portion of the story Lang was unfolding before the jury like the cards in a cold hand. With the help of the live and computer models of the aircraft, along with charts and graphic enlargements, Lathrop carefully went through each of the nine alleged differences between the two, explaining why each change was made from the StormTree to the Peregrine and, on the basis of his own training at Cal Poly San Luis Obispo—"That's right up the road out here in San Luis, isn't it?" Lang had shamelessly asked him—he explained why none of the changes had any possible effect on the aerodynamics of the aircraft that would be relevant to departure and spin. In doing so, he repeatedly referred to his meticulously maintained journal, the equivalent of an "engineering log," which he carefully described and exhibited to a jury that would need to be familiar with the concept later in the trial. He concluded his testimony with a detailed eyewitness account of the fatal spin of Walt McCluskey, a spin, he testified, so terrifyingly similar to the spins he had seen in the Peregrine that there could be no doubt that the two aircraft were, aerodynamically speaking, father and son.

The entire line of questioning had brought repeated objections from Hickman, nearly all of which were sustained. Nonetheless, Lang managed to get into the record most of what he wanted out of this witness. It was toward the end of Lathrop's testimony, however, that a new and insidious obstacle to Lang's efforts emerged.

After Lathrop had given his opinions regarding the spin characteristics of the two aircraft, Lang started into a new area of interrogation.

"Mr. Lathrop, how many times did you fly—"

"Excuse me," interrupted Judge Campbell. "Mr. Lathrop, you flew the Peregrine, but never the StormTree, correct?"

"That's correct," answered Lathrop, obviously a little thrown by the fact that the question came from the judge.

"But your opinion about the two aircraft and their spin characteristics is based on your personal experience, is that right?"

"And my education and training, Your Honor," replied Lathrop, a shade defensively. "That's right."

"You've never worked for NASA, have you?"

"The National Aeronautics and Space Administration? No, sir."

"Nor for the FAA?"

"That's also right."

The judge looked smugly at Lang. "Thank you, Counsel. You may proceed."

Lang decided against requesting a sidebar conference then and there since that would only serve to draw the jury's attention to the matter, but he was furious. The next morning, before the jury was recalled, he asked the judge's clerk to tell Campbell that he wanted a conference in chambers. A few minutes later, however, when Porterfield emerged from Campbell's chambers, Campbell was right behind him and took his chair.

"I understand that plaintiff's counsel wants to be heard in chambers before we begin today. I don't like chambers conferences during trial but I will hear what you have to say now before we send for the jury."

Lang realized that he was being deliberately put on the spot in front of a courtroom full of journalists so that he could not discreetly raise his beef with Campbell. But he was determined to have his position on the record.

He rose. "Your Honor, the plaintiff recognizes the bench's

right to conduct questioning of witnesses, especially where there is the risk that certain testimony, if not clarified, may mislead the jury. I must, however, take exception to the court's questioning of Mr. Lathrop yesterday at the close of his testimony. There was no need for the court's inquiry, which tended to unfairly and unnecessarily impugn his credibility. The witness, like every other witness in this or any other case, is obliged to withstand cross-examination from opposing counsel. But I respectfully request that the court refrain from further such interrogation. And I want the request noted for the record. Thank you."

Campbell regarded him darkly. "Are you quite finished, Mr. Lang?" he boomed.

"I am," Lang replied, standing motionless at counsel table.

"Well, let me tell you something, Mr. Big City Lawyer. I can ask any question I want of any witness I want any time I want. Do you understand me!" A spray of saliva cascaded over the bench. The judge's color deepened to purple.

Lang stood his ground. "I understand the rules that govern the conduct of trial in the United States District Court and in the Eastern District, Your Honor. I also understand the prejudicial effect that a judge's appearing to take sides can have on the issues being tried."

"Why, you impudent snot!" thundered Campbell. "I hold you in contempt, sir, and assess you a fine of five hundred dollars, payable by the end of today's session. Do you hear me?"

"I do, Your Honor. I mean no disrespect. I have a job to do, as we all do here, and I only want the same chance to do mine well and fairly to which everyone else is entitled."

"If I choose to question your witnesses, Counsel, as well I may, I will do so in order to dispel any false impressions you and they are trying to perpetrate in my courtroom. I will do my utmost to prevent you from doing so. I will not allow you to use my courtroom for your ulterior purposes."

"I have made my record, Your Honor."

"And you have made your bed, my friend. I'll expect your fine paid to the clerk by four-thirty. Bring in the jury, Mr. Porterfield."

In the second-floor dining room of The Roan, *Pegasus Technologies v. Arrow Dynamics* had become the number one spectator sport of the group called the Fortress. When Lang tangled with Judge Campbell at the start of the session, the six men seated before the television set erupted. From downstairs, in the middle of a weekday lunch rush, it sounded as if they had switched to a baseball game upstairs.

"Jesus H. Christ!" boomed General Hendricks. "What the fuck is he trying to do?"

"Well, he's really pissed off that fucking judge," observed Lawrence Crispin.

"There's a news bulletin," added Chris Panotti in a richly sarcastic tone.

"Christ, the way he stands up there and spits those darts, he'd piss off the freaking pope!" bellowed Hendricks.

"He's very good," commented Leon Sikorski. "He is pushing the judge hard but he seems very much under control. This will work out fine."

"Fine!" blasted Crispin. "The jury's not stupid. Eventually they'll catch on that the judge doesn't trust Lang and they'll figure there's a good reason for it."

Sikorski shook his head, his eyes still riveted on the monitor sitting on the huge sideboard. "You're missing the point here. The judge is a small part of the larger equation. For that matter, so is the jury."

Crispin sputtered, missing entirely whatever point the cerebral Pole was making. Hendricks just sat there, arms folded across his massive chest, double chins set in disapproval, watching the drama he had helped set in motion unfold three thousand miles away.

Mark Fassero ran down the corridor of the concourse of the main overseas terminal at the Los Angeles International Airport toward gate 63, wondering why in the hell *his* flights always used the last gate on the concourse. He had computed his timing down to the last minute to catch the final flight of the week from L.A. to Shannon and he had nearly miscalculated. Three jumbo jets had landed within twenty minutes of one another, producing near-gridlock traffic, a factor he ought to have anticipated.

On top of misjudging the traffic, he had taken far too long going over the early proofs of the trial pictures with Ro. There was a limit to how many ways a still photo could portray men in business suits. It should have been a perfunctory task. But since a fair percentage of the photos were of the man his photographer had once been married to, there was a certain awkwardness in the process. He was disappointed, to put it mildly, that Ro had appeared to be so uncomfortable. It strengthened his growing suspicion that she was not entirely over the feelings she had once had for her ex-husband.

Fassero didn't like the man even a little; he was not only a natural rival, but a lawyer as well and, thus, a minister of artificial process and procedure that the soldier personally held in contempt.

Luckily, the plane, though fully loaded, was still parked at the jetway as he raced up to the door. He virtually tossed the boarding pass to the attendant and sped down the ramp to the hulking aircraft. For a man who had always prided himself on thoroughness and preparation, he felt disturbingly unprepared for this spontaneous trip across the ocean to accomplish a vague and ill-defined mission.

As he lurched and snagged his way to his seat in row 43, he passed seat 37-K and its occupant, Richard Banfield, unrecognizable even to Fassero's eye with his blond hair tucked up under a close-cropped curly black wig and his clean-shaven face hidden beneath a short, gray-streaked full beard. Banfield traveled this evening under the passport of Donald Heller, a favorite alias. The old, familiar adrenaline ran hot and quick through his veins tonight and he actually had to remind himself to breathe more slowly and deeply. He flew coach as an accommodation to the need for anonymity, an objective all the more easily achieved since, on the advice of Russell Lindstrom, he had always avoided highly public positions within the organization. Indeed, as the jet rotated off the runway at LAX, he recalled the old man assuaging his feelings when he passed him over in favor of Gina as campaign manager. "You write me the words, Dick," Lindstrom had said. "And you help me chart the course. But I think the bright lights that illuminate the campaign manager may compromise your true talents if and when we decide we need to rely on them." What he hadn't said, noted Banfield, was that there was always a chance that someone who had run into him in Milan might wonder what the hell a Formula 1 grand-prix turbocharger mechanic was doing running a political campaign.

By Banfield's reckoning, they would arrive in Shannon before dawn, local time. This was ideal, really, since he hoped to get to where he was going before daylight. As soon as they were safely out of the climb-out and past the zone of danger to the aircraft's avionics, he pulled out his notebook computer and downloaded the latest encoded intelligence from their small but effective network of information sources. Molly McKinney O'Keefe, former operative of the Irish Republican Army and travel companion to the dean of New Zealand motor racing, Nigel Daultry, lived in a modest but well-maintained farmhouse outside of the coastal village of Kilmurry, in County Clare, about an hour and a half northwest of the airport. He punched in the code that pulled up his international Road Atlas program and located the inset map of Western Ireland. With his finger he traced the main road from Shannon out to Kilmurry. He spent more than a few extra moments tracing along the portion of the road that wound its way through tight switchbacks along the cliffs high above the Atlantic surf. Yes, he thought, if Adolfo has done his job and taken out the interference certain to have been placed around the woman, everything was going to work out fine. Then, he settled back to reflect on his good luck that the former Army Intelligence Major whom he had hoped to find on the ground in Ireland was seated six rows behind him.

CHAPTER 28

COLONEL JOHN W. CARRICK, USAF, RETIRED, WAS everything on the witness stand Lang had hoped he would be when he hired him as his aerodynamics expert. Lang relished walking Carrick through his biography at a deliberate pace, intentionally steeping the jury in the man's remarkable credentials. Respectfully and precisely, Carrick went through each degree he had earned and posting he had drawn in the Air Force. He patiently explained that his doctoral thesis at Georgia Tech had dealt with various aircraft-design techniques for eliminating the most dangerous flight characteristics in military aircraft, and acknowledged, under the gentle pressure of Lang's questioning, that the thesis was now used as a supplementary text in flight-training programs at all three service academies. And, yes, he admitted, "It is now used by the FAA in training its district and general supervisors." Lang stole a quick look at Campbell's craggy purple face as the witness mentioned the FAA. Unfortunately, he could see no indication that the judge was even awake.

The crowning touch of Carrick's biography, however, was deliberately orchestrated by Lang as an "afterthought." After appearing to have wrung out of the modest colonel every conceivable honor and achievement over his lifetime of exemplary accomplishment, Lang said, "Okay, Colonel, let's move on to the work you were asked to do—"

Amy motioned to catch Lang's attention. He bent over while she spoke hurriedly in his ear. Up on the bench, Judge Campbell scowled. At the defense table, Hickman frowned while Lindstrom kept his eyes on the legal pad he had been filling with notes since the trial began.

"Excuse me, Colonel, but I'm reminded that I forgot to ask you about the two and a half years between your M.B.A. at Stanford and your assignment as a professor at the Air Force Academy."

"I was seconded, or assigned, to the National Aeronautics and Space Administration under the auspices of the Air Force."

"And what was your assignment at NASA?" Lang couldn't resist once again looking directly at Campbell, lingering ever so slightly over the acronym "NASA."

"I was assigned to the then-current space program known as Project Apollo."

"You were an astronaut?"

"I was," replied Carrick quietly. The courtroom instantly began to buzz. The jury was in a full lather. Sure, they had had a politician, a presidential candidate, no less, on their "TV show," as several of them referred to it privately, but that had been true for a couple of weeks now and they were just a little blasé about it. But, this, this, for goodness sake, was an honest-to-God astronaut! All pretext at sophistication was gone from their faces. Jurors Four and Eight wore the biggest, goofiest grins Lang had ever seen. No saliva running down their chins, thought Lang, but we're getting there. He felt like resting his case right then and there.

After the judge tapped his gavel and the buzz subsided, Carrick pushed the modesty envelope as far as he could. "But I never drew an actual launch, Mr. Lang. Closest I got was running a two-week extraterrestrial simulation over at White Sands."

The term "extraterrestrial simulation" was a slight modification of the official term used to refer to riding a dune buggy fitted for lunar operation over the desert, but Lang had been able to convince Carrick to make this one concession to theater. From the looks on the faces of the jurors, it was successful.

From there, Carrick escorted the rapt jury through the documents he had examined, the videotapes he had screened, the treatises and scholarly papers he had consulted, and the models, both scale and computer, that he had worked with in the process of reaching his conclusions. By design, he carefully omitted any mention of the engineering-log notebook Lang had acquired from Haverstock, not only to preserve its secrecy but because, in fact, Carrick's opinions had been formed before they heard of the notebook. Then, he listed his conclusions, using the style that Lang always used and had taught him during their many weeks of preparation.

"How many conclusions did you reach?"

"Seven."

"What were they?"

"One, aerodynamically, the Peregrine was the offspring of the StormTree, despite their differing gross weights, since it was constructed in perfect geometric conformity to the earlier aircraft. Two, the aircraft shared virtually identical aerodynamic characteristics in general. Three, they shared a dangerous tendency to depart controlled flight and enter into a flat spin, or dead spin, that was nearly unrecoverable, even by a trained professional test pilot. Four, the aerodynamic concept of the StormTree was not proven as claimed and, in fact, the report falsely described the aircraft's aerodynamics. Five, the aircraft could not have been tested under Military Specification 92121 since any test under that regimen would have detected the dangerous departure and spin characteristics of the StormTree. Six, the aircraft could not have been tested under any competent spin test or the spin characteristics would have been known to the test pilot. Seven, there was never any chance that the Peregrine could have been a successful aircraft from a purely aerodynamic standpoint since the concept upon which it was based was utterly defective."

Lang could see the jury scribbling furiously to copy down these critical and provocative conclusions. He obliged them by moving into evidence Exhibit 427, Carrick's list of conclusions, then provided the court with a full-color enlargement of the page to rest on an easel positioned between Carrick and the jury box.

Carrick continued to be a strong witness for the balance of his two full days under Lang's direct examination. He was consistently clear and cogent, credible and deferential. And he occasionally appeared to be resisting Lang's questions, enhancing his stature as a neutral professional. For his part, Hickman stayed uncharacteristically quiet, seldom objecting to either questions or answers. Lang knew this was the sign of a very savvy opponent; a good expert carries a great deal of weight with the jury, and attacking one by objection invariably alienates the jury. Better to listen and do the damage on cross-examination, if any there is to be done.

The night of Carrick's second and final day of direct testimony, Lang and Amy ordered from the only decent Chinese place in town—and waited an hour and a half for delivery. The two of them, along with Carrick and Ellerby, had just wrapped up an intense strategy session to prepare Carrick for the frontal assault that was expected when Hickman began his cross-examination in the morning. When the food arrived, they were both ready for a break. Lang flicked on the television. A baseball game on ESPN reminded him that he had lost track of the pennant races, a rarity for him. It hardly mattered, however, as the announcer just happened to mention that the Cubs' 6–0 loss to Philadelphia was their ninth in a row. So much for that diversion, thought Lang, clicking over to another station. One of the cable news shows staged a debate between two of the more notorious "talking-head" lawyers in the country. Tonight they provided more humor than insight from where Lang and Amy sat, missing much of what they were trying to accomplish in the trial, while hopelessly overanalyzing the silliest of collateral points.

Amy reached her limit first. "Can we *please* put these guys out of our misery?"

"Okay," agreed Lang, flicking off the television. "I get my daily fill of preening self-importance from the guys on the other side of the case, anyway."

"I've still got to go over my outlines for the Lying Bastards," Amy announced, using the term that she had long since adopted for the group of Arrow Dynamics employees she deposed back in January. "See you later."

Seating himself once again at the conference table, Lang flipped open the three-ring binder containing his working set of trial exhibits, and confronted the infamous final engineering report for the umpteenth time. Here was the fountainhead of his case, the wellspring for both the contract breach and the fraud claims against Arrow Dynamics and, if he could tie Lindstrom to it, against Lindstrom as well. For this document, he was absolutely certain, was an out-and-out fraud, a brazen lie about the aircraft Arrow had designed, tested, and evaluated. Moreover, John Carrick, as careful and considered a man as he'd ever dealt with, agreed. The Storm-Tree had been defectively designed, negligently tested, and fraudulently evaluated. The jury might or might not agree with them, but the real problem was that, even with the testimony of Molly O'Keefe and Will Haverstock, he had nothing to tie Lindstrom directly to that report and, without it, he might never see the jury on his case against Lindstrom.

Innocuous on its face, the report was sixty-five pages in length, consisting largely of charts and graphs detailing climb rate, performance curves, takeoff and landing data and the like, and a twenty-four-page section of text that set out the test data and conclusions in straightforward prose. The document bore no author's name, nor did it credit any individual for any portion of its preparation. The cover read simply, "Final Engineering Report: Experimental Aircraft XRL-22." Then, below, it said, "Prepared for Daultry Research PLC by Arrow Dynamics, Inc."

On the last page, at the bottom, under the date, it said, "Arrow Dynamics, Inc. San Sebastian, California." Too thin, thought Lang, too damned thin for my purposes. He flipped back to the first page. The cover letter that had accompanied the report to Daultry Research didn't help much either. It wasn't even signed by a representative of the company. A curt note, really, addressed to Daultry PLC, it stated quite starkly, "Enclosed herewith please find Arrow Dynamics' final engineering report on Experimental Aircraft XRL-22. With this report, we conclude our efforts under our development contract with you. We trust this will satisfy your needs. Please remit the balance of our final statement at your earliest convenience." Where a signature might have been, it read only "Arrow Dynamics, Inc."

Lang sat staring at the letter designation, XRL-22. There must be something in that designation that he could use. People used designations like this for a reason. For internal reasons, usually, accounting purposes or tracking purposes or general record-keeping purposes. Maybe just for filing purposes. Like the tiny subscript there in the lower left-hand corner of the one-page letter, the computer word-processing code that tells you—what? The file the letter belongs to? The secretary who typed it? "043:PRC:Y001," he read aloud. "What do you mean?"

He flipped the binder open to the section that contained other correspondence written over the course of the project by Arrow Dynamics. There were letters by Steve Castillo, Doug Chesney, Ray Wollersheim, and many others to Daultry PLC, to various suppliers, to the FAA, to dozens of others who touched the project in any small way along the course of its life. Each of them bore such a subscript designation in the lower left-hand corner of the signature page. Lang flipped through the section of the binder. A letter to an epoxy vendor signed by engineer Wollersheim had the code, 127:LSE:135. A requisition letter to a supplier of aviation fuel from Chesney was coded 102:RBS:281. A request from Castillo for experimental-testing clearance directed to the FAA regional office in Van Nuys bore the code 165:SSO:211.

A pattern emerged as Lang examined these word-processing codes. For one thing, the first three numerals in the code were always the same for letters written by a particular individual. Every letter signed by Wollersheim had the number "127" at the beginning of the code. Chesney was always "102," Castillo, "165," and so on. Also, in most cases, the letters in the code were paired up with the same numbers. So, Wollersheim's letters not only all had "127," they also all had "LSE." Chesney's had "RBS," and Castillo's, "SSO." In only four instances did Lang find that this pattern failed. He located two letters written by Chesney that bore the initials "NNC" after the "102," a letter signed by Castillo that had the letters "VRD" after the "165," and one signed by Wollersheim with the letters "PRC" in the code. Lang spent the better part of an hour testing the pattern. It seemed to hold for everyone in the company, all thirty-four employees and former employees who wrote letters that had found their way into the record of the lawsuit.

As Lang studied the documents, a thesis began to take shape in his mind. He needed to test it and he had the perfect tool available for him to do so. As he was penciling out his findings, Amy emerged from her room.

"I need a soda. You want something?" she asked as she moved to the refrigerator.

"No, thanks," he answered. "I want to show you something and see if you agree with my thinking."

Amy slugged hard from the soda can she popped open. "That kung pao was *hot*. What's up?" She sat down on the couch to hear him out.

"I may be onto something here," he began, moving next to her with the exhibit binder open. "Look at the cover letter to the engineering report, here. See this code. I think it's a word-processing code, possibly telling us who wrote it or who typed it."

"If you can read it," said Amy dubiously. She squinted and read, "043:PRC:Y001. Okay, I can read it. But it means nothing to me."

"That's right. Not yet. But I went through the Arrow Dynamics correspondence that's been designated in the case—not all of it, but a big chunk—and I discovered that every letter written by each employee has one of these codes. And, the three-digit numbers at the beginning of the code indicate the author of the letter. See? Chesney is always '102.' Wollersheim is '127.' Castillo is '165.' Merrie Webster, the marketing director, is '232.' And so on."

"Who's '043'?" asked Amy. "Is it Lindstrom?"

Lang smiled. "Exactly the question, Counsel. No indication. No other letter we have in the record bears that number code. But you're getting ahead of me here. So far, what can we safely deduce?"

Amy drank deeply from her soda. "Let's see. That the cover letter wasn't written by Chesney or Wollersheim or Castillo or Webster or anyone else who did write letters that are in the record."

"Exactly!" he exclaimed. "But there's more. These letter combinations—"

"Initials?"

"I think so. But whose?"

Amy looked from letter to letter in the notebook. "They're certainly not the initials of the author of the letters. Raymond T. Wollersheim isn't 'LSE' in any language I know of."

"Nor is Douglas M. Chesney 'RBS,' " noted Lang, watching her as she processed the information. He was anxious to see if she would independently arrive at the same hypothesis he'd reached.

"Secretaries?" suggested Amy. "That would explain why they would usually match up with the author of the letter but not always."

"That's my guess, as well. The odd occasions would represent days when the regular secretary was out and somebody else's secretary or even a temp typed the letter."

"Okay," observed Amy. "But how could we check? We don't know who anybody's secretary was, do we?"

"No, we don't," Lang conceded. "But we do have a long list of past and present employees. It's called the 'plaintiff's witness list.' " He got the binder that contained the case pleading file and flipped to the list. Running his finger down the list, he read the names as he picked them off the list, "Luisa S. Ecchevarria, LSE; Randi B. Smith, RBS; Simone S. Ochoa, SSO; and Nancy N. Chambers, NNC." He paused for her to read the names. "Notice anything about the names on the list?"

Amy continued to study it. "Not really."

"Women," Lang said with a triumphant smile. "Probably secretaries."

Amy looked at him sternly. "What kind of sexist shit is that?"

Lang dropped his smile instantly. "No offense. But, look,
Amy, we're not dealing with the land of enlightenment here. In this
business things are much likelier to be more traditional, certainly in
terms of the roles people play in the workplace. Besides, what else
could the initials mean? They match up too well to be a coincidence."

Amy sat silently for a moment. "I take it you found no one
with the initials 'PRC.' "

"Wrong," he replied with a smile. "Phyllis Rose Covitz," he
read, pointing to the name. "Retired in 1991, currently residing in
nearby Santa Barbara."

"No kidding? So we just have to get in touch with her and we
can find out if she was Lindstrom's secretary. That'd tie him pretty
securely to the final report."

"Not so fast. On two counts. One, I don't think she was his
secretary. Unfortunately, she typed letters for half a dozen other
people in the company."

"That's too bad," Amy said, genuinely disappointed. "What's
two?"

"I don't want to contact her."

"Why not? I'd sure like to know if we're onto something or
just chasing our tails."

"We can ask her on the stand."

Amy regarded him for a moment. "You really want to do
that?" They were both well aware of the risks of asking a question of
a witness in trial to which you don't already know the answer. Like
all generalities, of course, it was a rule frequently broken by good
lawyers where the circumstances warranted.

"I really think so," replied Lang. "I look at it this way. Lindstrom inspires legendary loyalty among his employees, right?"

"Right."

"And who would be more likely to be loyal than an elderly
secretary who stayed around long enough to retire?"

"So?"

"So, if we contact her, the first thing she is going to do is call
Lindstrom and tell him exactly what we asked her and what she said,
thereby giving them time to gather their forces on the issue and,

who knows? Get her to change her mind? Take a trip on the company?"

Amy nodded her agreement.

"Let's just let her respond to the subpoena, show up, and take the stand. We'll go with the hunch."

Gentry Hickman rose and buttoned his jacket as he moved to the podium. "Mr. Carrick," he began in his richest baritone drawl. "Let me ask you, how many times did you actually fly the aircraft known as the StormTree?"

"I never flew it."

"Never?" repeated Hickman, feigning surprise as he peered over his reading glasses.

"That's right," answered Carrick levelly.

"And the Peregrine? How many times did you fly that aircraft?"

"I never flew that one, either."

"I see." Hickman paused for effect. "But you still feel confident in your opinion that"—he picked up and read from a notepad—" 'The Peregrine was the offspring of the StormTree, aerodynamically speakin' '?"

"I do. The data on the two aircraft is virtually identical and test pilots—"

"Thank you, Mr. Carrick. You've answered the question."

Lang rose. "Objection, Your Honor. Counsel is interrupting the witness before he can complete his answer."

"Overruled," said the judge. "The witness had answered the question."

"No, Your Honor," said Carrick, to the surprise of everyone in the room. "I had not." Before the judge could speak, he sped on. "I was going to say that one doesn't need to fly an aircraft to determine the meaning of flight data or to compare aerodynamic configurations. An engineer at a computer screen can do the job quite accurately and, in fact, in my opinion, would have to be incompetent to fail to reach the same conclusion I did here."

Campbell regarded Carrick contemptuously, but said nothing. After a long pause, he nodded to Hickman. "The answer stands. Proceed."

"Now you testified that you were being paid by the plaintiff in this case, is that right?"

"I expect to be paid. That's right."

"You're not being paid by the defendants, though, are you?"

Carrick laughed. "Not that I know of."

"Or by the court."

"No."

"How many hours have you spent on this case so far?"

"About two hundred and twenty."

"That's, what? My math's not too swift, but that's about thirty-three thousand dollars, right?"

"I think that's right."

"How much do you think they'd pay you if you didn't testify exactly the way they wanted you to?"

Lang shot to his feet. "That's argumentative. And it assumes facts not in evidence."

"Sustained," said Campbell, leaving Lang in a momentary state of confusion as he tried in vain to recall the last ruling in his favor.

Carrick replied anyway. "I *know* how much they'd have paid me, Mr. Hickman. The same thirty-three thousand dollars."

Hickman never broke stride. "You testified that, *in your opinion,* the difference of some three hundred and thirty pounds between the two aircraft made no difference aerodynamically. Now, isn't that just a silly, absurd statement, Mr. Carrick, that can only be justified on the basis of the fact that you were paid to say such an outlandish thing?"

"Argumentative," objected Lang.

"Overruled," said Campbell, thereby restoring what Lang had come to regard as the natural order of things. "Answer him."

Carrick kept his poise. "It is not a silly or absurd statement, Mr. Hickman. It is not only true, sir, but it is the only conclusion one can draw from the data, which includes the test results of the two aircraft—the actual test results, not the ones obviously doctored by your clients—and the impressions of the pilots who flew them both."

"What have the pilots' impressions to do with it?" asked Hickman, unwittingly setting up a key point Lang hoped to make in his rebuttal case when Haverstock was on the stand.

Carrick, thorough and well-prepared, was ready for the opening. "In my experience as a test pilot and the supervisor of test-pilot training at Edwards Air Force Base, empirical data only gets you so far in the testing of aircraft, especially experimental aircraft, where the limits of their capabilities and performance envelope are merely suspected and not proven. It is the impressions of the test pilot, senses honed by training and experience, that make the critical difference in teasing out the true characteristics of the aircraft."

So it went with Carrick's cross-examination. A blistering, angry attack on his credentials, his methodology, his conclusions, consistently met with strong, steady, and controlled answers. And yet, Hickman, keenly aware of precisely where the plaintiff's Achilles heel was, doggedly returned to the weight differential. And this was where he inflicted serious damage.

"Let me see if I understand you, Colonel Carrick." His use of the appellation in his heavy Southern drawl made it sound frivolous, ceremonial, and Lang found himself grateful that Hickman had refrained from using it throughout the bulk of his interrogation of his expert. "You believe that the difference of three hundred thirty pounds in the two planes is immaterial aerodynamically. That it makes absolutely no difference. Have I got it right?"

"With these two aircraft, that's right."

"All right, then, sir, let me see if I can figure out what that means. Would a differential of, say, three hundred fifty pounds have made any difference?"

"Objection," said Lang. "That's a hypothetical that calls for speculation." Immediately, he regretted what he said.

The judge ripped off his glasses. "He's *your* expert, Mr. Lang. What's he here for if not to answer hypothetical questions? Overruled."

Carrick answered, less than completely sure of himself. "That's difficult to say. We don't have any data on that differential, no flights were performed in that range, and so on."

"How about five hundred pounds. Would that make a difference?"

"Well, again, there's no data. It would be speculation."

This time Hickman ripped off his glasses. "Come on, Colonel Carrick. Do you really expect this court to believe that there is no weight differential that will change the aerodynamics? And, if there is, can you seriously suggest that three hundred thirty pounds—a *forty*-percent difference—is really irrelevant?"

"I can only tell you, Mr. Hickman, that weight difference or no weight difference, these two aircraft, from all the data that was available to me—and it was very comprehensive data—behaved precisely as if they were as aerodynamic duplicates, in every way. And, on that basis, I concluded that they were identical aerodynamically, which is to say they were both defective and dangerous."

"So says the man who never bothered to put his butt in the cockpit of either aircraft," snapped Hickman disgustedly.

Lang popped up but Hickman preempted him. "Withdraw the remark, Your Honor," he said, with all the contempt he could muster. With that, the cross-examination of John Carrick concluded and the day in court ended with Lang working on his nightly headache.

Richard Banfield, aka Donald Heller, dallied in his seat, making a show of struggling with his carry-on bag and computer case, thereby allowing all the other passengers behind him to exit the airplane before he did. As the last of them moved off down the aisle, he pulled himself together and followed.

Mark Fassero headed for the Budget Car Rental counter. He was exhausted, having had his usual difficulty sleeping on the flight. And, although it was 3:45 in the morning in Shannon and only 7:45 in the evening where he had come from, his body clock was definitely somewhere in between. He had formulated a plan to go straight out to the O'Keefe woman's home and inspect it before she rose for the morning. His objective was to plant a high-powered electronic listening device and locate an observation point from which he could watch her house surreptitiously. He hated assignments where there was insufficient time to work out logistics in advance. He filled out the papers and rented a blue English-drive Ford Escort. Maybe the Fortress would appreciate his frugality on their account, he thought with a wry smile.

Two places behind Fassero in the line was the hirsute Donald Heller. A typical American, it turned out. Not only did he insist on a large American sedan, but he insisted that it be blue.

"Have you ever driven the roads around Shannon?" the lovely young woman behind the counter asked patiently.

"Actually, no," replied the bearded man, doodling on a notepad that had been sitting on the counter. Anyone who had bothered to look at his handiwork would have seen a perfect rendering of the kinks and curves along the coastal stretch of the road he planned to take from Shannon to Kilmurry.

"Well, Mr. Heller," said the girl in her buttery Limerick brogue, "the roads around here are very narrow, with many sharp curves. To be honest, we find that the larger vehicles are not well-suited to our area."

"Do you have one or don't you?" he asked testily.

She checked her computer screen. "I do have one. A Ford

Thunderbird. Left-hand drive. And guess what?" She smiled. "It's dark blue."

"Excellent," he replied triumphantly and he filled out the forms.

Outside in the parking lot, in a thick predawn fog, Banfield could see no sign of Fassero. Out of the gloom stepped a swarthy man, powerfully built, with a thick dark mustache. Banfield recognized him immediately.

"Adolfo!" he said. *"Buenas noches, señor."*

"Señor Dick? I hardly recognize you, my friend!"

"I have to stay nimble, Adolfo. You will recall that better than anyone."

"Sí! I know what you mean."

"How did it go?"

The dark man smiled broadly. "Like always. Sometimes even professionals do not expect surprises. The man with the scar will not be found."

Banfield nodded. "And the woman?"

"I never laid eyes on her."

"Good. Did you see the man take the small Ford?"

"Sí. He is eight minutes, maybe ten ahead of you."

Banfield nodded again. "Then I need to get going." He shook the other man's hand. "I'll be needing a vacation in November, Adolfo. I'd like to fish the warm waters near the harbor."

Adolfo smiled. "You are always welcome at my home, Señor Dick. Just call me when you are ready and I will make all the arrangements."

"Good," said Banfield, climbing into the large, dark blue Thunderbird. Adolfo stepped into the fog and was gone. Banfield's preparations made it unnecessary for him to refer to a map as he roared through the countryside. Years of experience as a road-rally driver and test mechanic on various racing circuits had left him with a highly developed talent for visualizing highways and terrain from the two-dimensional representations of maps. He drove the unfamiliar road as if it were his daily commute.

After about twenty minutes, he dropped his speed perceptibly, calculating that Fassero, unfamiliar with the foggy roads and driving an underpowered vehicle, was probably just beyond the reach of his headlights, and he had no desire to overtake him yet. He drove this way for nearly an hour before he reached the coastal stretch of the highway.

Indeed, about a quarter mile ahead of Banfield, Fassero

hummed along the country road in his tiny Ford, vainly searching for a radio signal that would help him drive off his drowsiness. As it was, he had the windows wide open for maximum air and a high if monotonous noise level. Here along the coast, the fog was gone and he caught sight of the sea off to the west in the dim light of a first quarter moon. He hadn't passed another car since leaving Shannon Airport and was pretty sure he was the only one out on the highway at this ungodly hour. His eyelids were growing heavier. But a couple of unexpectedly sharp curves in the road—with a glimpse of the surf of the Atlantic Ocean pounding the rocks hundreds of feet below the edge of the road—brought him at least a whole level up the alertness scale.

Behind Fassero, Banfield was closing. He had caught a glimpse of taillights up ahead of him on one of the sharper curves and had turned out his headlights. Fortunately, the combination of the faint moonlight and his having studied the road layout in advance allowed him to maintain his speed. He was gaining rapidly now on the smaller car and its unsuspecting driver. Quickly he recalculated the location of the exact point along the road where he intended to catch Fassero. He accelerated.

Fassero, weary eyes on the road ahead and ears totally given to the blast of the wind and the static of an AM radio in search of a signal, had no idea that there was another car behind him. In fact, he hadn't checked any of his mirrors more than twice since he left the airport. Suddenly, he found himself into another one of those damned curves, this one an "S" first to the right, then hard back to the left. He was going too fast and swerved far out to the right, running up on the very narrow berm. But he was trained to deal with adversity and he took this one in stride, braking sharply and pulling the wheel with a strong, steady hand for the curve to the left. But as he did, he felt a massive, monstrous concussion on the left side of the car, an impact so powerful that, even as he struggled to comprehend what force had materialized out of the night to overtake him, the left side—the passenger's side—of the car collapsed into him. He thought he caught the briefest glimpse of the front grille of an automobile looking in through the mangled door at him as he felt his car leave the surface and hang, for what seemed like several seconds, in the heavy air above the booming surf, before plunging more than a hundred feet into the rocks and saltwater spray below.

Banfield, less concerned now with the outcome for Fassero—pretty much a foregone conclusion at this point—than with righting his own vehicle before he followed Fassero into the sea, yanked the automatic transmission into low gear, ripping hard at its moorings but slowing the car effectively enough without leaving the kind of skid marks that might complicate his departure from the country. He swerved as he continued to bleed off speed, then shifted back into drive and headed for his meeting with Mrs. O'Keefe.

CHAPTER 29

UNCHARACTERISTICALLY, LANG'S MIND WAS ELSE-
where as the daily court session was about to begin. He had asked
Amy to arrange through Bill to have his uncle get Molly O'Keefe on
a plane by this afternoon, and she had just told him that Bill had
failed to confirm with her yet. Lang was down to his last half dozen
or so witnesses and it was definitely time to get his best hitter to the
ballpark. He checked his watch. As it inched its way toward nine
o'clock, it was nearing 5:00 P.M. in Shannon. Amy had said the flight
they had booked for her was to leave at noon local time. The situation had the feel of a glitch, and he was growing very uneasy.

"There she is, I'll bet," said Amy softly as they neatened their
notepads and binders on the counsel table in anticipation of the
day's first gavel.

Lang whirled around, thinking in terms of the stunning Irish
redhead, but instead caught sight of a tiny, prim, gray-haired
woman seated in the third row. Realizing that Amy had been referring to Phyllis Covitz, he replied, "I'd say that's a bull's-eye."

"Damned lucky we put all those employees on the witness

list," Amy observed, watching the jury file in from their anteroom under the steady gaze of the U.S. marshal.

"Even the good ones get lucky sometimes," Lang replied. This minimized what he knew had been a true stroke of good fortune: If Phyllis Covitz's name had not been on that list, they could never have called her to testify.

Lang glanced over at the jury and realized that Lindstrom was looking right at him. Damned annoying, thought Lang, how that son of a bitch is always watching me. They locked eyes for the briefest instant, then Lindstrom traced Lang's line of sight and spotted the woman, as well. He rose immediately and, with a bright, cheery smile stretching across his Rushmorean face, went to greet her.

The woman extended a tiny hand that looked incomplete without a white glove over it. Lindstrom swallowed it in his huge paw and, despite the presence of the jury—getting in their first dose of Lindstrom-gawking for the day—embraced her warmly. As they exchanged an animated but quiet greeting, Lang hoped that their intimacy meant that they had once had the close working relationship that he needed in order to have his hunch about the cover letter play out. As they continued to speak in hushed tones, Lang imagined that, somehow, Lindstrom was subliminally planting testimony into her brain. He wondered just what Lindstrom thought of her appearing to testify—or had he already been told?

Mr. Porterfield answered the buzz of the judge's line that meant His Honor was ready to emerge from his cage to try his hand at devouring Lang for yet another day. In a moment, the beefy purple face looming over the huge black robe emerged from behind the heavy door and he swooped down into the massive red chair. Another day had begun.

"Proceed, Counsel," rumbled Campbell, managing to imbue those two words with enough contempt to remind everyone that it was still open season on the plaintiff's lawyer.

Lang rose and moved to the podium. "Plaintiff calls Phyllis Covitz."

The delicate lady ascended the stand gracefully, took the oath from the clerk, and stated her full name for the record.

"Ms. Covitz—is it Miss, Mrs. or Ms.?"

"In my day, young man," she said tightly, "there was only Miss and Mrs. and, thank the Lord, I was and remain a Mrs."

Lang smiled, unsure if her stiffness was nervousness or hostility. "Very well. Then, Mrs. Covitz, I'm Chris Lang, the lawyer for the plaintiff, Pegasus Technologies. How are you today?"

"Fine, thank you," she replied. Lang decided the tightness was more likely to be nerves than animosity, but he would take no chances.

"Did you ever work for the defendant company, Arrow Dynamics?"

"Yes, I did," she replied with a proud thrust of her dainty jaw. "Thirty-three years."

"Congratulations," Lang said, trying to walk the thin line between genuine respect for this elderly, apparently neutral witness and the kind of obsequiousness that can turn a jury off. "What position did you hold there?"

"I held several over that time, Mr. Lang."

"Approximately how many?"

"Well, let's see. I began as a filing clerk in the office—we only needed one in those days—and then I was the steno pool."

"You *were* the steno pool?"

"All by myself," she replied, smiling for the first time. She was warming up, thought Lang with relief.

"Then, as we grew, I became the head steno—that lasted a long time, for most of the sixties, I believe. Then, I supervised the pool. Then, they asked me to read contracts."

"Read contracts?"

"Yes. To summarize them, list the performance benchmarks, deadlines, that sort of thing."

Lang was beginning to feel that he might get lucky. "When did you do that?"

"From 1971 until, oh my, up until 1978 or '79, I should think."

No help there, thought Lang, picking his way through the shadows of untested ground. He decided to step up the pace. "How about during the last five or so years you were with the company? What were your duties then?"

Her face dimmed perceptibly. "Oh," she said, with a sigh. "Then. That's when I was just there to fill in. You know, a little of this and a little of that."

So that was it, thought Lang. They kept her on but moved her out of the way. Her words and her tone conveyed regret, a gentle sadness that spoke volumes about the passage from vitality and relevance into a poignant obsolescence. The image of a career carefully boxed away in a steamer trunk gathering dust in a Santa Barbara attic flashed through Lang's mind.

"Did you do any typing during that time, up until you retired?"

"Oh, sure," she replied, seeming to pull herself back from the gloom of that attic. She raised her tiny hands and typed the air, perhaps a little arthritically. "Still could hit those keys. Most of the time, anyway."

Lang pulled the cover letter from his binder. "Your Honor, I ask that the witness be shown Plaintiff's 34, already in evidence. It's the cover letter that accompanied the final engineering report that Arrow Dynamics sent to Daultry PLC. It is in the Witness Binder Number 1."

"Show the witness, Mr. Clerk," said the judge, disproving the theory that had been growing with reporters and television viewers alike that he was fast asleep. Lang pulled a three- by four-foot enlargement of the letter from one of the several portfolios behind the counsel table and headed for the easel.

"With the court's permission . . ."

"You may approach the witness," responded the judge. "Any objection from the defense to the enlargement?"

"None," replied Hickman, subtly shifting to the edge of his chair. Lang noticed that Lindstrom, the inveterate note-taker, had put his pen down and was almost lounging in his chair, nonchalantly watching the witness.

Lang took the pointer and went for the score. "I show you Plaintiff's Number 34, Mrs. Covitz. Do you recognize it?"

She took her glasses from her handbag. To Lang's dismay, they were thick, massive magnifying glasses. What if she can't even read the fucking code, he thought, with a mild sense of desperation.

"I don't believe so," she said as she studied it closely. Too closely, reflected Lang. "It's from when? Oh, I see. That's four or five years ago." She looked up at Lang. "I'm sorry."

"Well, Mrs. Covitz, let me ask you this. Do you see this set of numbers and letters down here in the lower left-hand corner?"

Again, she pulled the binder up to her face. "I do," she said tentatively.

"How about if I ask you to look at the enlargement?"

She turned to oblige him. Through the lenses of her glasses, her eyes looked to be the size of baseballs to Lang. "Okay, Mr. Lane," she said, mispronouncing his name for the first time. Lang's heart sank. He was going to lose this entire foray. Well, he thought, it won't be for lack of trying.

"These numbers and letters, here."

She studied them for a moment. "I see them. Yes."

"What do they mean?"

"Let's see . . . '043.' I don't recall what that means. 'PRC.' PRC, well, that's me. I typed this letter." She looked up triumphantly and smiled at Lang. Lang smiled back. Behind him, at counsel table, Amy watched Lindstrom as he shifted uncomfortably in his seat. He was not smiling.

"Could the first three numbers indicate the individual who wrote, who authored the letter?"

Hickman objected. "That's leading."

Lang quickly responded. "Your Honor, this is a hostile witness under the rules since she is identified with a party, as a former employee of the defendant company. I'm allowed to lead her." Although Phyllis Covitz was nobody's idea of a hostile witness, he was absolutely right from a technical standpoint and Campbell had no choice but to overrule the objection. Still, it was a relief to Lang when he did so.

"You may answer my question, Mrs. Covitz."

"I believe you're right, Mr. Lang. I believe they do indicate the author."

Lang's heart was pounding as his slow climb up the hill neared the improbable summit. "Who was 043?"

She thought hard for a long, excruciating moment. Finally, she shook her head. "There were so many by that time. I just don't remember."

Lang was crestfallen. Amy thought she saw Lindstrom relax. "Thank you, Mrs. Covitz," Lang said and headed back toward counsel table.

"Don't you want to know what these other numbers are?" she called after him. "I recall what these are," she added proudly.

Lang turned around. "Of course, I do. You anticipated my next question. What are those numbers?"

"They indicate the word processor, the computer that the letter was typed on. Everything was computers by then, you know. That's what the 001 stands for but, again, I wouldn't normally be able to tell you which computer was which, but this one, with the 'Y' there before the number, there was only one of those. The 'Y' means it was off-site, you know, outside the plant, the office, I mean. This one was up at the house."

"The house?"

"Yes. Mr. Lindstrom's ranch up on the hill above the airstrip. This letter was originally typed on the computer in Mr. Lindstrom's study."

As the courtroom erupted, Lang spun on his heel and strode back to the table. Had he looked, as Amy did, he would have seen the vituperative Judge Campbell, very much awake now, casting a dubious eye toward the defendant's table, while several of the jurors actually opened their mouths in shock.

Lunch in the corner of the courthouse cafeteria unofficially reserved for the plaintiff's trial team had never been more cheerful. As the full impact of the surprise testimony of Phyllis Covitz settled over the group, an unprecedented giddiness seized them. The others in the place for lunch, predominantly the media, since Lindstrom's team usually hustled back to its hotel for the ninety-minute noon recess, craned necks and cupped ears to try to snatch something quotable out of the commotion. They had learned early on that Lang, the team's captain, had an inviolable rule against anyone under his direction talking to the press during the trial. Several early attempts to circumvent this order had brought harsh reprimands from Lang and most of the reporters now knew enough to respect the strategy, even if they disagreed with it.

"Well, Chris," said Ellerby, over the din rising from the table he shared with Lang, Andrews, Carrick, Amy, and Rachel. "Does this seal Lindstrom's fate or not?"

Lang instinctively raised a finger to his lips to counsel discretion, although it was likely the comment wouldn't be heard away from the table. "Not at all, Graham," he replied. "The jury can always go either way on a disputed point such as whether or not Lindstrom participated in drafting the report." He saw Ellerby's face fall ever so slightly. "But I do think that the combination of this evidence and the testimony we expect to get from our star witness will be enough to get us past the motion for a nonsuit and give us a crack at the jury." Everyone of the small group at the table was aware of the anticipated testimony from Molly O'Keefe.

"Nonsuit?" asked Andrews.

Amy rose and dabbed her lips with her napkin. "While you're conducting your civil-procedure class, Chris, I'm going to check in for messages." The judge's rule against cellular phones in the courtroom meant that she had to use a pay phone.

Lang nodded and went on. "It's a defense motion that claims, in effect, that even if all the plaintiff's evidence is believed, the plaintiff's case is so thin that the judge—not the jury, mind you—the judge has no choice but to rule in favor of the defendant without even requiring it to put on a defense."

"Well," said Ellerby. "That's a bloody insult."

Lang laughed. "I guess it is, at that. Anyway, if we're going to have any chance to win our case against Lindstrom, we have to get the case to the jury. And the only way to do that is to survive the nonsuit motion. I figure our one-two punch of surprise witnesses should just about do the job."

The group broke up at about one-fifteen, leaving Lang alone to go over his notes on the afternoon's witnesses. Just as he was snapping his briefcase shut, Amy returned. Immediately, Lang knew that something was wrong.

"What's the matter?" he asked.

Amy, ashen and distracted, replied, "I just spoke to Bill. Molly didn't make the flight this afternoon, or morning, or whatever. Seamus drove out to her place again and there's no sign of her. It looks as if there might have been a forced entry at her home but he couldn't find any sign of what might have happened to her."

Lang's heart began to pound. "Forced entry? Was there any sign of a struggle? Any blood or anything?"

"No. Seamus said something about a black shamrock or something or other, I'm not sure what Bill was talking about because I'm not sure *he* knew what Seamus was talking about."

Lang's face lost its color. Aside from the pivotal role Molly O'Keefe's testimony would play in the case, he had felt a surprisingly strong bond develop between them during his brief visit, a connection forged from her passion and his dedication to purpose. The prospect of her being in physical danger made him heartsick.

"That's not all, Chris," said Amy, intruding on Lang's rapidly rising unease. "When Seamus got up there, he found a local police investigation underway along the coastal road about four miles north of Molly's place. Seems there had been an accident on the cliffs up there and a car had gone over the side of the road down into the rocks on the beach. The driver of the car was apparently killed instantly."

Now, Lang's heart froze. "Molly?" he asked.

Amy shook her head. "Mark Fassero."

Lang's head spun, as if he'd lost all sense of equilibrium. The name swam around in his memory, at once terribly familiar and utterly foreign. His mind raced to place it, like a familiar face from one end of your life that suddenly pops up in another.

"You know," said Amy. "From *Beau Rivage*. Ro's friend. Her associate."

Suddenly, recognition crashed in on him, abruptly and violently ending his mental free fall. Mark Fassero? Dead? What was he doing in Ireland? To Amy, he said, "What the hell is going on here?"

"I have no idea. Neither does Bill."

"Does Ro know about this?"

"I don't think anybody does. Bill had just gotten off the phone with Seamus, who was out there when they made the identification. He said the only reason Seamus even bothered to mention the name was that he was an American, and from California. Does he have any family?"

Lang paused, still trying to grasp everything he was hearing. "I don't . . . I don't know. I don't know anything about the guy. What does he have to do with Molly O'Keefe, anyway?"

"Do you think it's related?"

"Four miles apart, halfway across the world? Don't you?"

"Maybe it has something to do with the magazine's piece on the trial. Did you tell Ro about Molly?"

Again, he thought for a moment. "No. Absolutely not. We really haven't talked about the case much at all." He stopped to collect the ideas ricocheting around his mind. "Damned if I know what's going on."

"What's next?" asked Amy.

He snatched his briefcase from the table. "I have four minutes to get back down into Campbell's court and call Leon Kintner to the stand to prove our case for lost profits. At the moment, that's as far ahead as I can think."

Lang moved methodically over the lost-profits material with Professor Leon Kintner, Ph.D. He covered the essential ground with clarity and brevity, having already determined that there was little chance of stretching Kintner's testimony to fill the gap that Molly's delayed appearance had created. He had no choice but to accept the fact that, even if she could still be located, Molly was going to have to testify in his rebuttal case.

Lang finished his direct examination of Dr. Kintner at 4:30 and the judge recessed, leaving Hickman's cross of the witness to begin the following day's session. As Lang packed up his things for the day, he had a sudden impulse. He pulled Amy aside and gave her some brief instructions. Then he hurried from the courtroom, leaving a slightly puzzled associate in his wake.

"Is that lady one of your friends' moms, Andy?" asked Jennifer as she came in through the kitchen door ahead of her sister.

"I don't think so," responded the younger girl, hurrying to slide through the door before it closed behind Jennifer. She didn't make it, snagging her backpack on the knob. "She just came up to me and started talking. I never saw her before."

"I have. Last year."

"What's going on, Jennifer?" asked Ro from the kitchen table, where she was going over the next week's meal plan with Alma.

"You remember that lady who was talking to me one day last year when you picked me up at school? Well, Andy was just talking to her today at the bottom of the driveway."

"What woman?" asked Ro, peering out through the window down the driveway. There was no one in sight. "I don't remember a woman. I'm not sure what you're talking about."

"Mom?" said Jennifer, clearly frustrated. "Remember? You picked me up after school one day and this blond lady was talking to me and you were all 'Who were you talking to, Jennifer?' and 'Don't talk to strangers,' and 'Whose mom is she anyway?' Remember?"

The recollection was forming only dimly in Ro's mind. "I guess. Whose mother was she, anyway?"

"I don't know. I never saw her again. Until just now. Andy was talking to her right out front when I got home."

"Whose mother is she, Andy?" repeated Ro.

"I don't know, Mom."

"Well, let's try this—what was she wearing?"

Jennifer replied. "Suit. Business suit, like one of yours. Green, I think."

"Where was she when you saw her, Andy?"

Her daughter shrugged. "I don't know. She was just there. She got out of a car, I think."

Ro was becoming alarmed now. "What car? What did it look like?"

Another shrug. "Just a car, Mom. A big one, dark."

"Did she try to get you to go with her?" Andrea shook her head. Ro turned to the older daughter. "Did you see anything? Was she parked in front of the house?"

Jennifer replied, "No. When I came along, she was just there, at the bottom of the driveway. I really didn't see the car."

"Did you hear anything she said?" Ro asked.

"Not really. She stopped talking and walked away as soon as I came along."

"Did she say anything to you?"

"No, Mom. Take a pill. She wasn't a criminal or anything."

Ro responded more angrily than she intended. "Don't talk to me that way, young lady. I want to know who's getting out of cars and talking to my kids in front of my house."

"It's okay, Mom," said Andrea. "She was on our side."

"Our side?"

"Well, Dad's side. I remember she said that Mr. Lindstrom isn't a nice man and that we should be sure we help Dad to keep doing a good job."

Ro considered this newest morsel of information. The possibility that the woman was a reporter suggested itself, although that wouldn't fully explain her earlier appearance at Tierra Rejada. "What *exactly* did she say, Andy?"

The girl furrowed her brow. "Okay. Let's see. 'Hi. You're Chris Lang's daughter, aren't you? How did swim practice go? It must be exciting for your dad to be on TV every day. He's doing a great job. You know, that Mr. Lindstrom is not a nice man and your dad is doing the right thing. We should all help him keep up the good work.' Stuff like that."

Despite her concern, Ro allowed herself to be impressed with the child's powers of recall. She asked, "How did she know about swim practice?"

"I don't know."

Jennifer interjected, "Jeez, Mom. Look at her hair. And the backpack is soaked."

Ro nodded. "What did you say to her, Andy?"

"I said Daddy's great. That he always wins his cases. And that the TV part's pretty cool, after all."

Ro smiled. "What did she say then?"

"I don't really remember. Just good-bye, I think."

Ro spoke with a forced airiness that she didn't feel. "We don't talk to strangers around here and both of you know it. Understood?" Strangers talking to her kids was never good, but, since that threatening phone call, everything seemed more ominous.

"Sure, Mom," said Jennifer, opening the refrigerator. Andrea was already on her way up to her room. It occurred to Ro to check with Alma to see if she had seen the woman around before, but the housekeeper had apparently left the kitchen during her conversation with the kids.

It was twilight and Lang was hurtling along the highway, physically detaching himself from the case he had lived for the past several weeks. Each mile he put between San Sebastian and his Porsche felt like a small weight lifted from the great mass piled on his shoulders. He fiddled with the radio. As he approached Los Angeles, he began to pick up the local radio stations. Inevitably, he found the radio equivalent of television's talking heads.

"Why are they out to get this patriot, Russell Lindstrom?" asked a belligerent caller. "This is a great man with great ideas who obviously knows how to get things done. I mean, all we ever do is complain about how the best people stay on the sidelines in politics and we are left with the crooks and the bums to run things. So, what do we get? Sharp-talking, money-grabbing lawyers who try to run him down. When's it going to stop?"

"Hey, look, Curt," replied Roger. "I hear you. But let me be devil's advocate here for a minute. This case has nothing to do with politics. It was filed before Lindstrom started running for president. These allegations don't involve politics, except if you think character is a political issue. You know, whether or not he cheated a business associate."

"That's liberal media crap, Roger, and you know it. If Lindstrom was some big tax and spend lefty pushing a liberal, bleeding heart agenda, you guys in the media would be all over this thing, calling for that smart-ass Lang's head."

Lang hit the scanner on the dial and, two stations later, found the simulcast of *American Idea Net*. "That's where we'll have to leave it for this evening as the drama of the Deadspin Trial unfolds," said Milo Rich. "A drama, I might add, being watched daily by upwards of thirty million Americans on live television. When we come back, we'll have a panel of Convention delegates and an insight into how the men and women who will select their party's presidential nominee are looking at the proceedings out here in California on the eve of the Convention."

Taking a break sounded good to Lang, so he snapped off the radio and drove in silence into the San Fernando Valley.

Andrea answered the door. "Daddy!" she shouted, with typical unbridled excitement. As she leaped across the threshold to hug him she bellowed over her shoulder, "Hey, you guys! Dad's here!"

Lang accepted the embrace and squeezed his younger daughter hard. Jack materialized behind Andrea and waded in for his bear hug. Jennifer came down the steps and hung back demurely. Lang waved her on and she kissed him and hugged him in the reserved way he had long ago come to know as her own.

"Where's your mother?" he asked.

"Upstairs," replied Jennifer.

"I'll get her," said Jack, and he took off, nearly knocking over Andrea in the process.

"Mom's a little upset tonight," said Jennifer.

"Upset?" asked Lang, wondering if she had heard the news. "What's wrong?"

"It's the lady in the street," offered Andrea.

"What lady?" asked Lang, truly puzzled.

"Some woman who has appeared out of the blue twice within the past year to have unsolicited conversations with each of your daughters," said Ro, coming down the stairs. "I think our nerves have been a little jangled since that damned phone call."

"What phone call?" asked Jack.

"Never mind," replied Lang. "I need to talk to your mother, guys." He gestured toward the living room. "And we could use a little privacy."

He noticed Ro's face blanch slightly. "What's wrong, Chris?"

"Come on in here," he said, leading her off into the living room. He sat her down on the couch and took a seat on the chair opposite it. "I have some bad news, Ro."

This time, her face drained completely of its color. Lang struggled to come up with a way to do this gently, yet without needlessly dragging it out. "I learned today that there's been an accident. In Ireland, within the last day or two. Ro, I'm sorry to tell you that your friend Mark's been killed."

"Mark?" Her face revealed that she, too, was having trouble comprehending what she was being told. Her lip quivered. "An accident? In *Ireland*?"

Instinctively, he reached out and took her hands in his. "When's the last time you saw him or spoke to him?"

She was still plainly at sea. Tears welled up in her eyes, but she was obviously inclined toward disbelief. "I, I don't know. Tuesday, I guess. Tuesday night when we worked on the trial layout. He had to rush off to the airport. He was going to Washington to do some advance work on a shoot. Ireland? Chris, are you sure? How can this be?"

Lang slowly told her what little he knew, including the fact that the information had come through Bill Quinn, who had gotten it in turn from his uncle, a constable in County Clare. He tried to step lightly over the details, but Ro dragged out of him all the particulars he knew.

Finally, she rose and shook her head firmly. "This just can't be. There must be some mistake. A man just doesn't get on a plane to Washington, then wind up in *Ireland* and drive off a cliff. It's got to be the wrong man. What could he possibly have been doing in Ireland, for God's sake?" Her tone was almost belligerent. He saw she was shaking. He rose to embrace her but she deftly stepped away.

"It *could* be a mistake, Ro. But the identification was apparently positive."

She shook her head again. "No. Not Ireland. Why?"

"Well, Ro, actually, I was wondering the same thing myself. Are you sure he was going to Washington?"

She shrugged, a tight, stiff shrug. "That's what he told me. Why would he lie about it?"

"I don't know," he answered. It occurred to him that Fassero had lied to her before, but he decided this was definitely not the time to remind her about that episode. "There's something else here that doesn't make sense. Did you know that one of the trial witnesses—one of *my* trial witnesses—is in Ireland?"

She looked at him directly but without comprehension. "No," she replied. "I didn't. How would I? It's not something you told me, is it?"

"No. But I just thought it was a little bit too coincidental. This witness, a secret one for all practical purposes, lives a couple miles from where the accident occurred. I thought maybe, somehow, Mark found out about her and was going to see her, maybe photograph her for your trial piece."

She looked at him with an odd mixture of confusion and contempt. "What are you saying, Chris?"

"Nothing, Ro. I'm not saying anything. Just like you, I'm having a hard time figuring out why Mark was in the vicinity of my witness's home in another country, when I told no one of her identity and you were led to believe he was going to be in Washington, D.C. I don't know what it means, but I think the whole thing is rather odd—suspicious, almost."

Her reaction took Lang completely by surprise. "Why, you son of a bitch! You came all the way down here to tell me this in person so you could watch my reaction! To see if there was a leak in your precious security! You insensitive bastard!"

He was unprepared for this outburst. "What are you talking about, Ro?" he asked. "I came here because I knew this would be terrible news to you, a horrible thing, and I didn't want you to have to deal with it alone."

"You're lying, Chris," she said contemptuously. "You hated him. You were jealous of him. And now you want me to think that he tried to do something underhanded with your precious, almighty case." She bit these last few words off. He could see that her eyes, red and watery, smoldered with unignited rage.

Lang stood his ground. "That's not true, Ro," he said softly. "I did not hate the man. I hardly knew him. Jealous? Yes, I admit to that. Who wouldn't be jealous of another man taking his place with his wife, maybe even his kids? But the reason I came is because, whatever I might have thought of the man, I knew you would be devastated by this news. If you had already heard, I knew you would need someone to lean on, to talk to. If you hadn't, I thought maybe I could tell you in a way that would help you deal with it." He paused to study her face. She stood perfectly still, two heavy tears rolling down her cheeks. He reached for her again. This time she did not resist. As he drew her to him he could feel the rising rhythm of her sobbing. "It's the least I could do. Jesus, it's what you did for me when I lost Max."

She buried her head in his shoulder and wept hard, releasing herself to a great sadness. He squeezed her hard to him and found himself making the little comforting noises he hadn't made since Andrea woke him up with her last nightmare years ago.

CHAPTER 30

AMY TRIED WITHOUT SUCCESS TO KEEP FROM looking back at the door to the huge courtroom. As the great grandfather clock behind Mr. Porterfield labored its way toward nine o'clock, she was becoming increasingly uneasy. Lang had dashed off after yesterday's session with a cryptic word about "something I have to do," leaving the sketchiest of instructions about how to proceed "in the unlikely event" that he did not return by the time court began the next morning. Well, it was about that time now, Amy observed, and the unlikely event seemed likelier by the second. In due course, the clock struck the hour and Judge Campbell, on time for the first time during the month-long trial, shambled out of his cave and the moment was upon her.

As Campbell dropped into his chair, Mr. Porterfield summoned Dr. Kintner to the stand. When the witness was seated, the judge growled, "Proceed with your cross-examination, Mr. Hickman."

And so he did. Amy, having tried a handful of cases involving modest issues and reasonable stakes on her own, was thus unceremoniously thrust onto center stage of a sprawling, media-intensive trial unlike anything most lawyers of twice her age and ten times her experience could imagine. Fortunately, the fact that the trial was being carried live in more than forty countries worldwide was lost on her as she zeroed in on the reality that if the plaintiff's objections and arguments were to be preserved and protected, the full responsibility now was hers. She was oblivious, as well, to the fact that Graham Ellerby and Clive Andrews, seated next to her, were more than a little nervous about their lawyer's unexplained absence.

Gentry Hickman launched into his scathing cross of the lost-profits expert who had testified the day before. It occurred to Amy, in a distant corner of her consciousness, to be amazed at the fact that the trial was proceeding in Lang's absence as if he were nothing more than a mere observer.

While Amy guarded the stronghold in San Sebastian, Lang pushed his Porsche hard to make up time on the way back. As he hopscotched from one public-radio station to the next, trying to keep abreast of the events up in San Sebastian, his mind was not yet in the courtroom; images from the night before kept him preoccupied. Ro's anguish at the news of Mark Fassero's death had confirmed for Lang the closeness that she and Fassero had shared, but he had thrust that unhappy fact to the back of his mind and done his best to comfort her. It had not been easy. They had talked deep into the night, trying vainly to come to grips with things that seem designed to elude them. As he put her to bed with the first light of dawn stirring behind her curtains, he knew there was no reasonable chance of making it back to San Sebastian by the start of the morning's session. Of course, Amy was more than capable of defending Hickman's cross-examination of Dr. Kintner and doing his redirect examination; she was the lost-profits expert, anyway. As long as he was back by the time the afternoon session started, when they would rest their case and Hickman would ask for a nonsuit, he would be fine. When his brain had completed processing that thought, it had gone out and stayed out for several hours.

He had awakened with a start to the sight of the morning sun blazing through the open guest-room drapes. By his watch it was just past eight, plenty of time to shower, eat, and get back to court around noon. He went down the hall to Ro's room, where he found her still asleep. He sat down on the edge of her bed and could not resist gently touching her cheek. Just as she began to open her eyes, Jack appeared in her doorway. Seeing his father there clad only in his shorts, Jack observed, "Hoo, boy, Dad! Way to go!" Then, he disappeared down the hall.

"Jack!" Lang called after him. "Jack! It's not what you think!"

Ro smiled dreamily up at him for the briefest moment before she recalled why he was there. Once again, they embraced, not as lovers but once more as two beleaguered souls, neither together nor entirely apart, stranded in an emotional hailstorm.

Meanwhile, in the courtroom of Judge Schuyler Campbell, Amy defended against Hickman's cross-examination of Dr. Kintner deftly, objecting, with occasional success, to a number of his questions, and did a reasonably good job of rehabilitating the witness through her redirect examination. Redirect and recross of Dr. Kintner had gone so smoothly, in fact, it was finished by midmorning, and still there was no sign of Lang. This put Amy in something of a quandary. She knew that there were no witnesses left in their case until rebuttal, so the appropriate action was to rest her case. But that was a heavy responsibility for a young second-chair lawyer to assume, since resting the case meant that any gaps in it could not be closed, that the case had to be able to stand on its own from an evidentiary standpoint. If something critical to the fabric of the case was missing, the trial could be irretrievably lost here. Nonetheless, Amy drew a deep breath and intoned, "Plaintiff rests, Your Honor."

Judge Campbell's head came up as if he had heard a shot. He seemed to notice for the first time that Lang was not there. He opened his eyes wide and stared at Amy. "Are you quite sure, Ms. Quinn?"

"I am, Your Honor," she lied. Somewhere out on the highway, Christopher Lang laughed aloud.

"Very well, then. Mr. Hickman?"

Hickman rose, a smirk on his face. "May we approach, Your Honor?"

"You may," replied the judge, and Hickman and Amy moved to the judge's right, on the side opposite both the jury box and the witness stand.

"Your Honor," Hickman whispered, to keep from being heard by the jury. "We want to move for a nonsuit at this time. For that reason, we request that the jury be excused."

"I thought you might," replied the judge, using words that would echo ominously in Amy's head for many hours to come.

Hickman, eloquent and dramatic, moved for the nonsuit on behalf of both of his clients, but made the stronger case for a dis-

missal of the claims against Lindstrom. He argued through the balance of the morning and was still not done when the judge
adjourned for the noon recess. As the courtroom emptied out for
lunch, Amy was pale with anxiety, brought on in equal measure by
the power of Hickman's arguments, the apparently sympathetic ear
he was getting from the judge, and the fact that, even if Lang arrived
during lunch, he could not respond effectively to the many specific
points made during his absence. As these and many other equally
unpleasant thoughts swirled in her head, a strong, firm hand
clamped down on her shoulder. She turned to see the smiling face of
Christopher Lang.

"Where have you been?" she blurted through clenched teeth.

"Well, good morning to you, too. Good thing the jury's gone
or they'd see a side of you they might not like."

"Chris! I'm not kidding. Where have you been? And what are
we going to do?" She looked around to make sure the defense team
was gone, which it was. "Hickman made some damned good
points, you know, and—"

"I know," replied Lang softly. "First things first. We need to
go upstairs and get some lunch." To the perplexed pair of English-
men standing nearby, he gestured that it was time to go. "Not to
worry, Amy. You did a great job with Dr. Kintner and you would
surely do a fine job of whipping Hickman's ass on this motion if you
had to, but I'll take over now."

He looped an arm over her shoulders as they walked toward
the door. She turned to look him in the face. "How the hell—"

"Any word from Seamus about Molly yet?"

She shook her head. "Nothing," she said tightly.

Lang frowned, the only outward sign that his darkest fears
might well be realized. On Amy's face, he read a different concern:
honest doubt about his ability to deal with the motion that was in
progress.

"Look, Amy," he said gently, choosing to deal with her issue
rather than his. "I'm sorry I'm late. You've done your part, now,
and I'm prepared to do mine. I heard his argument on the radio and
I'm more than ready to give Mr. Hickman an earful."

After lunch, that's just what he did, reassembling the shards of
evidence that had been strewn on the floor of the trial and building
a case that, Amy had to admit, looked awfully damned bad for
Lindstrom. As the session ended, she found herself genuinely persuaded that they just might get to the jury. But it was Campbell's
vote, not hers, that would decide the issue.

"Thank you, Counsel. Thank you both," Campbell said in a rare display of civility and even-handedness. "The court will take the motion under submission until tomorrow."

Just a week past midsummer, it was cold and blustery under a leaden sky on the bluffs west of Kilmurry. Seamus Callahan stood at the edge of the cliff, wearing a heavy coat against the bitter wind that rose off the Atlantic, gazing out into the ocean as if the answers he was looking for could be found among the whitecaps snapping up from its sullen gray surface. His eyes stung, red and watery against the breeze. Behind him stood Molly O'Keefe's house, precisely as he had found it that evening nearly a week earlier, when he had come out to see why she had missed her flight to Los Angeles. The back door had been open, standing ajar, and the furniture in the cozy main room had been haphazardly rearranged.

In the thickening gloom of the premature dusk, Seamus walked south along the rim of the cliff to the staircase leading down to the beach below. Since he had had the foresight to bring his electric torch, he decided to chance the descent.

Carefully he picked his way down the steps, the sound of the booming waves crashing over the ancient rocks below rising to a deafening crescendo. He found the base of the stairs awash in the swirling surf of high tide. The spray soaked him in a matter of moments and he felt the chill clear down to his bones. It was deep dusk now and the beam of his torch was overwhelmed by the darkness down here. If there were some clue to Molly's whereabouts to be found at the water's edge, it would have to wait for a daylight investigation.

He climbed back up the stairs, using up the final light of the fading western sky in the process. Reaching the top, he stopped to catch his breath and look back down to the roiling sea. He knew he could learn no more here tonight but was nonetheless reluctant to leave. After a long moment, he headed back toward the road where he had left his car. As he turned, his foot caught in a deep rut in the soft, thick grass and he tumbled to the ground. Quickly, he checked his ankle to see if there had been any damage. He was lucky; it was no more than a mild sprain. Using his torch, he searched the ground to find the rut. It was nearly impossible to see through the thick grass, but he knelt in the heavy, damp matting and felt for it with his hand. In a moment he found it, a depression at least two or three inches deep and just about as wide. He crawled along it lengthwise, tracing it with his hand for two or three meters. It appeared to run directly toward Molly's house. On a hunch, he followed it back in the other direction. It ended at the edge of the cliff, on a portion of the promontory that was not protected by the wood railing. He peered over the edge to the water below. Unsure what, if anything, to make of this, he finally yielded to the darkness and headed back to his car.

Along the way, he tried to follow the rut. Just as he had suspected, it ran along a straight line right toward Molly's back door, stopping about thirty feet from the house, where the soil was packed hard from foot and vehicular traffic in the immediate vicinity of the house. There was no evidence of the depression any closer to the house. Using the torch, he walked a wide arc around the house. About forty feet south of the back door, in a small, thick stand of trees, he found what he had been looking for: an old wooden wheelbarrow with a thick, muddy rubber tire.

The next morning, at 9:35, the judge had yet to take the bench. Amy was amazed at how much calmer Lang seemed than she felt. She had been chewing the end of her pen all morning while Lang chatted amiably with Ellerby and Andrews, even smiling occasionally and exchanging greetings with several of the media regulars. His was more the demeanor of a fan waiting for the start of a ball game than that of a lawyer awaiting a decision that could bring a sudden end to one of the most significant cases he had ever tried. It seemed to her as if, having argued against Hickman's motion as eloquently and as precisely as possible, he had willingly surrendered the fate of the motion to the gods, or in this instance to the caprice of Schuyler Campbell. And, in the end, of course, that was all he could have done. For her part, Amy went back to gnawing at her ballpoint.

At precisely 9:40, the bear in the black robe emerged. Amy drew a deep breath and noted that her palms were slick with sweat. When everyone else had sat back down, Campbell took a sheet of yellow paper from his breast pocket and read to the hushed courtroom. "After careful consideration of the defendants' motion for nonsuit, the court has no choice but to deny the motion." A collective gasp swept over the courtroom, yanking Campbell's head up from the page and bringing a sharp rap of his gavel. Lang couldn't refrain from smiling and Amy waited for the blood to return to her brain. After quiet was restored, the judge continued. "A nonsuit motion is a difficult one on which to prevail. It requires that the plaintiff fail utterly to state a sufficient case, even in the absence of a defense, from which a reasonable jury could find for it. Although I am persuaded that the plaintiff has failed to produce a winning case in any respect, that is not the issue at this stage. The law must abide any house at this point, even a house made entirely of cards, if only to allow it to be blown away with the force of the defense's case. Bring out the jury."

Lang leaned over to Amy. "Now, there's a ringing endorsement, if I ever heard one."

Three thousand miles away, a red-faced General Hendricks barked at The Roan's second-floor dining-room television, "Now there's a fucking endorsement of our chances if ever there was one."

And at his desk in his office across town on M Street, NW, Jad Piersall intoned to himself, "That was too close, goddammit."

Hickman's case was a model of precision and, from Lang's point of view, an exercise in orchestrated perjury. One by one Hickman marched his soldiers to the stand and one by one they parroted the party line. Not that Lang didn't do his best to trip up the defense choreography. During his cross-examination of chief engineer Doug Chesney, he asked, "You testified that you were 'virtually certain' that the reason the StormTree was so aerodynamically sound while the Peregrine had a tendency to go into a flat spin was the difference in their weights, is that right?"

"Yes," replied Chesney confidently. "That and the differences in the design configuration."

"You're referring to the items that were slightly different between the two airplanes?"

"That's right. Nine of them."

Lang listed them for Chesney and he confirmed that they were, indeed, the ones to which he referred.

"Now," continued Lang. "You were in charge of the program at Arrow to try to salvage the Peregrine, were you not?"

"Yes, I was," Chesney replied cautiously, sensing a trap but not sure what to look for.

"How did that program come about?"

"We got a call from one of the men at Pegasus Technologies—Mr. Ellerby, I think—and he told us about the spin problem they were having and asked if we could take a look at it. I told him, 'Sure, just send it out.' And that's what they did."

"That's when Mr. Lathrop brought the Peregrine out to San Sebastian and you tried to get it to fly more like the StormTree."

"That's right."

"And you made modifications to the Peregrine to try to achieve that objective?"

"That's right," Chesney repeated.

"One of the differences was the dorsal fin that the StormTree had and the Peregrine didn't."

"That's right."

"Might that have affected spin dynamics?"

"Might have," conceded Chesney.

"But neither you nor anyone else at Arrow ever suggested adding a dorsal fin to the Peregrine to correct the spin problem, did you?"

"No," replied Chesney, a little nervously.

"And the different style of cockpit seats in the Peregrine. That was another difference between the two aircraft, right?"

"That's right," replied Chesney, realizing where this was going but unable to think fast enough to turn it around.

Lang pounced. "But neither you nor any of the other Arrow Dynamics people ever suggested changing the seats as a way to try to isolate the spin tendency, did you?"

"I didn't," answered Chesney, his mind flying. Then he added, "But I don't know what others might have suggested."

Lang brushed aside the feeble attempt to derail his point. "But in any event, Mr. Chesney, that was never done by Arrow in the course of trying to isolate the spin tendency, was it?"

"No," admitted Chesney, realizing that a lie here would be too easy to expose.

And so it went for each and every item that Chesney had cataloged as a difference between the two aircraft: None of the differences had been eliminated in the effort to determine why the two aircraft supposedly had different aerodynamic characteristics.

"One more thing, Mr. Chesney," added Lang in the offhanded manner that he had perfected over the years. "What efforts were made to reduce the weight of the Peregrine?"

"What do you mean?" asked Chesney warily.

"What did you do to shed weight off the Peregrine?"

"You can't do much about weight—"

"But neither you nor anyone else at Arrow Dynamics ever bothered to tell Bobby Lathrop, 'This plane is too heavy. Let's scrap it and build one that weighs the same as the StormTree.' Did you?"

Chesney was clearly befuddled now. His mind raced but he

could come up with no good response. Instead, he feebly answered, "No."

Lang's assault on Hickman's expert witnesses was similarly aggressive. After the former head of NASA's spin-testing facility testified that he had personally tested the StormTree's spin-resistant characteristics and found them consistent with those reported in the engineering report, Lang asked, "Dr. Rubio, have you ever flown the StormTree?"

"No," replied the courtly old gentleman, with a smile.

"The Peregrine?"

"No," he repeated.

"When did you test the StormTree?"

"Last December, Mr. Lang. Just before Christmas, I think it was."

"And you tested its spin susceptibility?"

"That's right."

"And its spin-recovery tendencies and performance, meaning its ability to get out of a spin once it gets in?"

"That's right."

"And you found that it was resistant to spin, hard to spin, right?"

"That's so."

"And that it was easy to get out of a spin once it got in?"

"That's correct," he replied agreeably.

"And these tests were run in the NASA spin tunnel, right?"

"Yes, the one at Langley Air Force Base."

"And these tests confirmed the conclusions of the defendants' engineering report, right?"

"In every respect, sir."

"But these tests were performed on a model of the StormTree, right? Not on the prototype itself, correct?"

"Why, yes," the old man replied, shifting his weight in the chair. "That's how we test all our aircraft."

"You are aware that the StormTree weighed eight hundred seventeen pounds, are you not?"

"Of course I am," Rubio replied indignantly.

"How much did your model weigh?"

"Weigh?" He consulted his notes. "It weighed twenty-seven pounds four ounces."

"So the real StormTree weighed thirty times what the model tested by you weighed?"

"Approximately."

"So, the relative weight of those two planes, the model and the real StormTree, was irrelevant to the aerodynamics since they perform in the identical manner, correct?"

"That's correct. But the model is constructed with scrupulous fidelity to the geometric configuration of the StormTree."

"Just the way the Peregrine was, is that right?"

"That's my understanding, yes," conceded a troubled Dr. Rubio, fully aware that he had just unwittingly validated Lang's own argument.

That Friday evening Lang's spirits were soaring as he presided over an informal celebration in the Presidential Suite. One by one they went over the week's many developments, savoring everything that had followed in the wake of the judge's decision to turn back Hickman's nonsuit motion. Although Hickman's case was well under way, Lang had scored some points while the other side had the ball.

"The best one," interjected a bubbly Graham Ellerby into the raucous cross-talk that filled the room, "was the FAA fellow."

"Radcliffe?" asked Carrick. "Michael Radcliffe?"

Ellerby nodded as he drew deeply from the glass of Chianti he was enjoying with his pasta primavera. "When he tried to undo the damage done by Chris's decimation of Rubio."

"You mean on the weight differential?" suggested Amy, smiling.

"Exactly. 'The weight, sir,' " he intoned, trying to capture the pompousness of the FAA field supervisor called by Hickman, " 'is the reason for the spin susceptibility of the Peregrine. The extra three hundred and thirty pounds make it highly susceptible to spin and difficult to recover.' So bloody pretentious, so perfectly set up for Chris to ask, 'I guess, then, that a jumbo jet is far likelier to spin and crash than a hang glider?' " The room erupted with laughter.

"I thought the interrogation of Milinsky was better still," said Clive Andrews. "The way you led him all the way down that path about how important the pilot's subjective impressions are to a test program. Perfect lead-in for that engineering log."

"After Milinsky's testimony," Carrick said, "it's going to be damned hard for Hickman to argue that the pilot's impression that the StormTree might spin could have been safely ignored."

"I certainly hope so," said Lang.

Clive Andrews called out, "Lindstrom's on the telly!"

The group moved as one to see what was happening. It was Milo Rich's program with his "special guest" Russell Lindstrom.

Rich was talking to his guest. ". . . to say when you take the stand?"

Lindstrom waved him off. "I'd really prefer to talk about the convention, Milo. I realize that a lot of attention has been focused on this trial and that's unfortunate—"

"Lying bastard," cursed Ellerby, adopting his favorite "Amyism." "He wishes he could afford this much publicity."

"—diverted from the issues into this sideshow. The trial is a travesty, but maybe the best possible argument for legal reform in this country. I think the poll figures will back this up."

"There's something to that, of course," acknowledged the host. "Tonight's CableStar/*Sun Times* poll shows that a whopping seventy-seven percent of those asked support legislation to limit or control lawsuits and nearly two-thirds—sixty-five percent—favor limits on lawyers' fees."

"I think you are seeing a real revolution in this country, Milo, and a fundamental change in our way of governing is coming. And it's exciting."

"Speaking of change, and polls, for that matter, just as we went on the air, these poll results were handed to me." Rich adjusted his reading glasses. "Of all the delegates to the Republican National Convention later this month, nearly seventy percent believe that you have been unfairly accused in this lawsuit and more than sixty percent of those delegates who are committed to someone else on the first ballot believe you have improved your image in their eyes during the course of the trial. What do you make of that, Mr. Lindstrom?"

Carrick interjected, "Just the way he planned it."

Lindstrom replied, "It's a sad commentary on our society, isn't it, Milo, when you have to be falsely accused and hauled into court by overly ambitious, unscrupulous lawyers in order to enhance your position within the party? At any rate, I'm still standing and I'll be standing when this is over, ready to answer the call from my country."

"Christ," whispered an exasperated Lang. The telephone rang and Rachel offered to get it. "Chris," she called out, "it's Bill Quinn on a conference call with Ireland."

Lang replied, "Thanks, Rachel." To Amy, he said, "Why don't you grab an extension?"

After an exchange of greetings, Lang moved directly to the matter foremost on his mind. "Bill has filled us in on what you found at Mrs. O'Keefe's house the other night, Seamus. I'm hoping there's better news to report."

"I'm afraid not," Seamus replied. "There's no sign of her. Of course, as you know, this has happened before."

Lang's brow furrowed. "What's your take on it this time?"

"Frankly, I'm quite concerned. The physical evidence around the house definitely suggests the possibility of foul play." He went on to recount, in detail, his observations at Molly's house. On two occasions they had difficulty following him and he apologized, explaining the second time that it was just past two in the morning in Shannon.

"There is a new element, however. The local people up there, a small, country constabulary, have had reports of the Black Shamrock in the area and they think they may have something to do with her disappearance."

"What's the Black Shamrock?" asked Amy, voicing the very question on Lang's and Bill's minds, as well.

"It's a splinter group of the IRA, more militant, more committed to terrorism. Its latest tactic is to go after members and former members of the IRA itself, as a statement about the failure of the more-established revolutionaries in the movement to act more aggressively for independence of the Northern Irish State. There have been two confirmed murders of this kind recorded during the past two months or so."

His words hung heavily on the line. They were all well aware of Molly's past involvement in the revolution, and the possibility that she might have become a victim was horrible to contemplate. Rachel tapped Lang on the shoulder. He waved her off, not wanting to miss what might be the next word from Seamus. She persisted. "Chris," she said, holding out an opened Western Union envelope. "I think you might want to look at this."

He turned to see the envelope in her hand. It was addressed to "Christopher Lang, Personal and Confidential." "Hold on for a second, please," he said into the receiver and removed the telegram from the envelope. It was from Cape Town, South Africa. The message was brief and he read it quickly. Although it left him with mixed emotions, a small smile nevertheless crept over his face.

"Hang on, Seamus, Bill. I think we may have gotten a little ahead of ourselves."

Seamus replied, "What's that?"

"I just got a telegram from Cape Town."

"South Africa?" asked Bill.

"Right," answered Lang. "It is addressed to 'Christopher Lang' care of the hotel here. I'll read it. 'Dear Chris. Some memories are just too painful. You're a very sweet man (who cuts a pretty fair figure on CNN) and I'm sorry about your case. You'll probably find a way to win, anyway. But it really doesn't much matter to Nigel anymore and it occurred to me that no one really cares which crook is your president anyway.' Then it's signed, 'MO'K.' "

"Whew," said Amy. "There's your basic 'good news, bad news.' "

But Seamus was not entirely convinced. "Could you read it again, Chris?" he asked. After Lang did so, Seamus asked, "Would you do me a favor, Chris? It'd help with our investigation over here. Could you send me the original of the telegram?"

"Sure, Seamus," replied Lang. "We'll make a copy and get the original off to you by FedEx or DHL tonight."

"I appreciate that, Chris. One thing more, if you don't mind."

"What's that?"

"Did you speak with Mrs. O'Keefe after we met with her in Kilmurry?"

"Haven't had the chance, Seamus. Why do you ask?"

"No particular reason," the constable replied. "I don't recall that she addressed you by your first name while we were there."

Lang furrowed his brow. "I believe you're right, Seamus," he replied, remembering the lilting way Molly had said "Mr. Lang." "That is a little curious, I guess. What do you make of it?"

"I'm not sure there's anything to be made of it." Seamus sighed. "Just the suspicious nature of an old beat cop. I'll have my people examine the telegram further when it gets here. In any event, it sounds like it's bad news for your case, but good news about Mrs. O'Keefe."

"That's true," replied Lang, distracted by the implications of Seamus's suggestion. "But our case may be all right, after all. And, I suppose it's still possible that Mrs. O'Keefe may change her mind."

"I wish you the best," said Seamus without conviction.

CHAPTER 31

"IF THE COURT PLEASE, THE DEFENSE CALLS RUSSELL Lindstrom," announced Gentry Hickman, successfully infusing the statement with all the drama and promise the media expected of this long-anticipated moment. Lindstrom rose from his place at the counsel table and strode to the witness stand. Lang was struck by the sheer command of the man's physical presence. He was tall and athletic, a powerful figure of regal bearing who somehow managed to dominate the cavernous courtroom. He stood straight and still, a figure down from Mount Olympus, as he solemnly took the oath.

Even Lang was momentarily swept up in the electricity generated by Lindstrom. There was no denying the presidential quality of this man, a fact of life that Lang would have to deal with in very direct terms if he was to prevail in this trial.

Like all trials, this one had exhibited the ebb and flow of a great, lumbering roller coaster. A good day, a successful pounding away, for example, at Hickman's experts on their theories of aerodynamics, had been followed inevitably by a poor one. Somewhere in the deep recesses of his mind, he kept a running tally. If he was ahead at all as the case wound down, it was by a razor-thin margin.

And now Hickman had rolled out the heaviest artillery of all, Lindstrom himself.

Lang watched the jury as Hickman laid his biographical foundation with Lindstrom. This jury was particularly difficult to read. In general, they had seemed uniformly attentive to Lang and the points he made, even extending him an occasional nod or smile of approval. Yet, there was no mistaking the impact of Lindstrom's potent celebrity on this group of common people from what was, in effect, his hometown. Their eyes danced eagerly each day when he swept into the courtroom and they followed his every move. It was not uncommon to catch one of them—Six and Eight were notorious—staring at him unabashedly for minutes on end, regardless of what was happening up on the witness stand. In his darker moments, Lang could imagine the jurors swamping Lindstrom with autograph requests in the rosy glow that would follow the verdict. But up until now he had managed to banish such thoughts, reminding himself that, despite his occasional cynical suggestion to the contrary, juries, however smart or dull they were, took their duties very seriously and were invariably committed to doing the right thing. In this case, however, he could be forgiven if he despaired occasionally that he was fighting a losing battle against an old-fashioned home-field advantage. Listening to the powerful resonance of Lindstrom's familiar baritone and its peculiar way of imparting absolute credibility to his words, Lang realized that he would need Will Haverstock and his magic notebook to hit a home run if he was to win. And, somehow, that was not a comforting thought.

Lindstrom's two full days under direct examination by Hickman passed quickly and with little controversy, Lang having determined in advance to limit objections to what was absolutely necessary to protect the record on appeal. He quite correctly reasoned that there was no sense in needlessly antagonizing the jury. As for the substance of his testimony, it was everything he had expected. Indeed, it was once again so completely consistent with the testimony of Hickman's other witnesses, it took on an unnatural quality. From Lang's point of view, of course, this was because they were all lying. But nothing in the reverent faces of the jurors indicated that any of them would agree.

"Let's clear up just a few things, Mr. Lindstrom," said Hickman, as if to cue up a well-rehearsed tape in the mind of his witness. "After Mr. Daultry dropped in on you at your home and proposed his idea for a new recreational airplane, what exactly did you do?"

"I put him in touch with Mr. Douglas Chesney, the chief engineer over at Arrow Dynamics. I knew from working with Mr. Chesney in the past that, if there was anything to this idea of Mr. Daultry's, Mr. Chesney was the man to get things rolling."

"Did you prepare a contract?"

Lindstrom smiled a very patronizing but courteous smile. "No, sir. You see, I had nothing to do with Arrow Dynamics at that juncture. My time was fairly well committed to the Bloomington-Gate Chemical Corporation—we had a pretty severe challenge to turn around an ecological nightmare down there in Texas—and, of course, we had just acquired Micro Element Information Systems and we were facing a short timetable and heavy red tape to bring our satellite transmission system online for some U.S. government work."

"What sort of work was that?" Hickman asked unnecessarily.

Lindstrom turned to the judge and, ever the deferential schoolboy despite the fact that no one there could have failed to appreciate who it was whose presence truly commanded the room, asked, "Your Honor, if you please, these programs were and are protected under the National Security Act and I would be very reluctant to be placed—"

"Of what relevance are these programs, Mr. Hickman?" asked the judge.

"The programs themselves, Your Honor, are not relevant or material except to the extent that Mr. Lindstrom's commitment to them bears upon the reasons why he had neither time nor opportunity to play any role to speak of in the aircraft-development program that this case involves."

"I think that point has been amply established, Mr. Hickman," observed the judge, thus advancing Lindstrom's case many times farther than anything Hickman might have done. To Lang, the whole colloquy had the feel of a well-orchestrated skit. All the more so, since he would be unable to object without drawing even greater attention to the invaluable points the defense had just so cleverly made. And, of course, with Molly's eleventh-hour withdrawal from the fray she had never really entered, he had precious little with which to impeach Lindstrom. The notebook, Lang thought, the notebook and Haverstock are all I have left.

"I never really understood Mr. Daultry's project," Lindstrom was explaining, apologetically. "You see, I'm afraid that I was unable to give the man or his idea the attention I'm sure they both deserved. And I'm not proud of that, Mr. Hickman, believe me.

This was a brilliant man, a man of great accomplishment in many different fields, and I wish now that I had been able to give him the time to hear a little more about his project. But I did feel that when I handed him and his idea off to Doug and the Arrow people, he would be in good hands and would get a professional treatment of his idea."

"And did that happen?" asked Hickman.

"I have no way of being sure, of course. But, since this case started, I have read the contract and the engineering report and I'd have to say that it sure looks like the Arrow boys did a pretty fine job of turning Mr. Daultry's idea into a terrific little airplane."

"Let's go right to the point, here, Mr. Lindstrom," said Hickman, slipping on the mantle of bare-knuckles investigative reporter for the moment. "There have been suggestions that you may have written the engineering report. That it was prepared on your own computer, in fact. Is that true?"

Lindstrom smiled, carefully according the question the perfect balance of amusement befitting so absurd a notion, tinged with a deep respect for the seriousness of the stakes. This guy should win a frigging Oscar, thought Lang. "I'm glad you asked me that, Mr. Hickman, because I was here, of course, and I heard the testimony and the insinuation you're referring to. I've known Mrs. Covitz for a very long time and she is a wonderful and sweet lady, as fine a person as you'd ever want to work with. And her sense of fairness and justice are second to none. But, for the life of me, I cannot tell you why she said what she did. I don't know much about computer networks and I can't tell you anything at all about what sort of network Arrow Dynamics had in place at the time this report was written. But I can tell you categorically that I did not write that report, I did not read that report, I did not approve that report, I did not edit that report. If it was drafted at a computer in my home—there are maybe a half dozen or so computers up there, where I do use them for a variety of business and personal purposes, none involving Arrow Dynamics—I have no idea how. And, frankly, if I had been involved in any way with this program— and I wasn't, although from what I can tell, I would have been proud to be a part of such an outstanding effort—do you really think that my job would have been to *write a draft* of the engineering report? Don't you think I might have been involved at a somewhat higher level than that? In any event, no, I did not write the report and I have every reason to believe that Mr. Milinsky and Mr.

Chesney did write it, because that's what they said and that was their job at Arrow."

Lang was heartsick. Even he, who *knew* the son of a bitch was lying, found it hard not to believe Lindstrom. What were the odds that a jury would see through the charade? Lang breathed deeply as he felt the knot in his stomach tighten. He glanced over at the jury box to make sure the jurors hadn't caught his moment of despair. He needn't have worried; every eye was trained on Lindstrom and the rapt expressions spoke volumes about the reverence they felt for the witness. From the look on her face, Amy had seen things exactly as Lang had.

By the end of the second day, Lang's nightly headache had achieved stupendous new proportions. As they arrived back at the hotel, once again passing Jad Piersall's departing electronic-security team as they arrived, he headed straight for his bed and some extra-strength Tylenol. He couldn't sleep but he lay perfectly still, a pillow over his eyes, trying to will the tension away. It took a long time. Eventually, he must have drifted off because he found himself back on a warm, sun-drenched afternoon at Dartmouth. He was early for baseball practice and was limbering up in front of the dugout before the other team members arrived.

"Easy day for getting loose," observed Max Devereaux from the dugout in his thick Polish accent.

"You got that right, Coach," answered Lang.

"Then why are you so tight, Chris?"

"I don't know, Max," he replied. "It has the feel of a game I can't win."

"No such thing. Besides, what's so important about winning, anyway?"

"You know that better than I do. It's what we're here for."

"If you think that, son, I haven't done a very good job of coaching you. It's the game itself, the struggle to be your best, to master the rules and to outplay your potential. The rest of it, the wind, the bad hops, the umpire—"

"Don't tell me about the goddamned umpire, Max! Do you believe that bastard?"

Max shrugged. "I've seen worse. Not for a while, but worse." He looked past Lang into the far reaches of center field. "Got to get going now. The others are coming. You're on your own, now, you know."

"I know, Coach. I know that."

A knock at his door brought Lang back to consciousness. The daylight had long gone from behind the blinds, leaving his room in darkness.

"Chris?" called Amy gently. "Chris? Are you okay?"

He gingerly lifted his head, relieved to discover that the brutal throbbing in his temples had gone. He felt wrung-out, nonetheless. "Yeah, Amy. Come on in." He flipped on the light next to the bed.

"Thought you'd died," Amy said softly. "Everything all right?"

"Sure," replied Lang with a mildly sarcastic edge. "Perjury always gives me a hangover."

"The guy's one hell of a witness, isn't he?"

Lang nodded. "He cozies up to that jury like a cat looking for a handout. You know, I still feel like we're going to get him with Haverstock and the engineering log, but I'd feel a lot better if we had Molly O'Keefe on the team."

"It doesn't seem likely, does it? I mean, for her to just take off after she promised you she'd testify."

"I'm afraid I have to agree," said Lang. "She certainly came across to me as someone who keeps her word."

"What are we going to do?"

"What *can* we do?" he shot back testily. "We can't control all the variables. We have to try the case we've got, not the one we wish we had. So, when Hickman rests, I'll start setting up the notebook and, in the meantime, hope I get that call Haverstock promised."

"He's cutting it kind of close, isn't he?"

Lang shrugged again. "He's cagey, too. Our witnesses seem to have a great deal to be afraid of. I'm pretty sure he's going to call, though. I got the distinct impression he wants to get Lindstrom as much as I do."

Amy laughed. "That's hard to believe." Before Lang could reply she turned and headed back into the suite. "I ordered dinner from room service. It's roast turkey and I think it's still hot."

"Thanks," he replied as he rolled off the bed. He stretched and yawned expansively, drowsily contemplating yet another room-service dinner and late-night final preparations for his cross-examination of Russell Lindstrom. Whatever they were eating for dinner, he knew he was going to need some strong, black coffee.

Lindstrom was as composed and confident under cross-examination as he had been on direct. He answered every question with the conspicuous patience of a parent explaining some of life's more obvious truths to a child. Several hours into the process, Lang was painfully aware that he was making little perceptible progress. Not for the first time he wished that, just once, he could have a witness this good.

"Now, you testified earlier that Mr. Daultry called you after the contract was drafted between his company and Arrow Dynamics and asked you about a particular provision in that contract, is that right?"

"Yes. That's right," said Lindstrom. "The paragraph adopting the definitions of the Military Specification for certain terms."

"That's Section G-5. Now, Mr. Daultry called you and asked you what that paragraph meant, correct?"

"That's right."

"And how did you know what it meant if you didn't draft it?"

Lindstrom smiled his is-that-the-best-you-can-do? smile and answered slowly. "Well, Mr. Lang, first, I can read." The court-room erupted into laughter, which the judge allowed to run its course. Lindstrom continued, "Second, that's what this provision was used for in development programs run by the company when I was in charge. I assumed that it was in there for the usual purpose."

"You 'assumed'?"

Lindstrom was still smiling. "That's right. I assumed."

"Isn't it true that, in fact, you yourself prepared this contract and presented it to Nigel Daultry at your home during his visit, which you described earlier?"

Lindstrom shook his head gently and smiled a rueful smile. "No, Mr. Lang, that is not true."

"And didn't you go over the contract on your dining room table with Mr. Daultry during a two-hour meeting?"

"No, Mr. Lang, that's not true either."

"In fact, Mr. Lindstrom, the whole idea for the StormTree was *your idea* and not Mr. Daultry's at all, wasn't it?"

"That's also incorrect."

Too late, Hickman jumped up to object. "Objection, Your Honor. This is outside the scope of direct examination."

Lang countered, "Your Honor, this is inquiry into credibility and trustworthiness of a witness's testimony, which is always a proper area of inquiry. I would also add that it is most certainly within the scope of direct, since the witness testified about 'Mr. Daultry's idea' during his direct testimony."

"I will overrule the objection," said Campbell, with obvious reluctance. "The answer stands."

Lang continued. "Didn't you concoct the whole plan for this airplane yourself and suggest it to Mr. Daultry at The Partridge restaurant in San Francisco as a sham to get your hands on his WhisperIndy engine?"

Lindstrom was losing his good-natured facade. "No, I did not. And, I must say, Mr. Lang, this is precisely what's wrong with our court system. A man like you can sue anybody he wants and simply invent a version of the facts, without any evid—"

"Thank you, Mr. Lindstrom," said Lang. "You've answered the question." He couldn't help but revel in the fact that he had obviously struck a nerve. To him, this tended to validate everything Molly had said. "Although we certainly appreciate the lesson in legal ethics," he added dryly.

"Counsel!" bellowed the judge. "You will show this witness some respect while you are in my courtroom or I'll take you to the state bar! Do you understand me?"

"I do, Your Honor. I was confused. I thought we all owed respect to the truth and the facts, not a man who doesn't know the meaning of either one."

Lang immediately realized that he had pushed too far. Campbell nearly launched himself straight out of his seat. "One more word like that, sir, and I will have you bound over! Now proceed. And I warn you to do so with caution!"

Lang stood for a long moment at the podium, assessing the situation even as it unfolded all around him. He had paid a heavy price but he had a growing sense that he was finally getting under Lindstrom's skin. This was, after all, his primary objective, since he planned to inflict the mortal wound during his rebuttal case. The strategy was risky—he was losing some critical goodwill here with the jury—but he felt that Lindstrom had left him little choice. Just at the moment when he sensed that Campbell was about to speak again, he said, very softly, "You flew the StormTree yourself, Mr. Lindstrom, didn't you?"

"No," Lindstrom replied curtly. His congeniality was definitely gone now, a substantial moral victory for Lang.

"And you knew that the aircraft would spin, didn't you?"

"No." Lindstrom bit the word off.

"And you wrote the engineering report that concealed the dangerous spin tendency you discovered."

"I did not." To the judge, he said, "Your Honor, how much more of this must I tolerate?"

"Very little, Mr. Lindstrom. Mr. Lang, you will confine yourself to the proper scope of cross-examination. And, ladies and gentlemen of the jury, I remind you that the statements and insinuations of the lawyers are *not* evidence and may not be considered evidence by you."

Lang did his best to ignore the judge. "Isn't it true, Mr. Lindstrom, that Nigel Daultry visited your facility here in San Sebastian some six times during the development program and met with you on each occasion?"

"No, Mr. Lang. That is not true."

"One last question, sir. Do you know Molly O'Keefe?"

With the confidence of a man who knows his flank is covered, Lindstrom answered, "I have never heard that name before. No."

"I have nothing further of this witness," said Lang, with undisguised contempt. "But I reserve the right to recall him during rebuttal."

The proceedings in the courtroom flickered away on the small television set high up on the shelf behind the bar in the Flight Line Cafe. It was late afternoon in Cheyenne and the place was less than half full. But a surprising number of the patrons at the only place that served alcohol at the municipal airport were watching the trial that had captured America's imagination. At the bar, two men were finishing the first Miller Genuine Draft of the day—the one that hits the searing dryness in the back of the throat head-on—as they watched.

"So, what do you think, Hank?" asked the large, beefy man in a grease-stained plaid shirt. "Is Lindstrom involved in this scam or not?"

The other man drained his bottle and tapped it to get the bartender's attention. "Shit, Wayne. He's a freakin' politician, ain't he? If he ain't done what he's accused of, then he done somethin' else. What do you think?"

"I think it's just a hoax pulled off by that lawyer, there," observed Wayne in a tone that indicated he'd thought quite a lot about it. "We finally get someone runnin' for president that can do the job and a lawyer, a *lawyer*, yet, comes out of the woodwork makin' all kinds of charges, allegations, and such. How much do you suppose that son of a bitch makes for struttin' around the courtroom and pissin' everybody off?"

"More in a day than you make in a week." Hank laughed.

Meantime, in the back of the small bar, far from the television and farther still from the glass wall that provided a spectacular vista of the airfield and the dun-colored hills beyond it, sat Will Haver-stock. His blood pressure was up. He could sense it. And, though the Budweiser was cold, he was flushed. Lindstrom was a gifted liar and it angered him beyond words to watch the man bob and weave away from the lawyer's feeble efforts to tag him. But, he'll get his, thought Haverstock as he finished off the beer. And I'm going to give it to him. He plunked down the price of the drink and headed out to check on his airplane.

Lang rode back to the hotel in the van driven by Rachel Cruz. While she spoke on the cellular phone with her secretary back in Los Angeles, he slouched in the passenger seat, turning over the events of the day. Although Lindstrom had held up well on the stand, at least Lang had secured a direct statement before the jury that he had never met Molly. The trick would be to capitalize on it with what he had available. As Rachel clicked off the cell phone, a potential solution from an unlikely quarter suddenly presented itself.

"Chris?" she said, intruding as gently as possible into his thoughts.

"Yes?"

"We've just had a hit on the web site. It could actually be something worth pursuing." When they first set up their operation in San Sebastian, Rachel had suggested that they establish a site on the Internet, taking advantage of the trial's notoriety to collect po-tential new evidence. While Lang was not particularly smitten with the idea, it was a no-risk, low-cost proposition and he approved it. When Rachel had managed to secure the services of a small group of undergrads from UCLA to work part-time at minimal cost to moni-tor the site and follow up on prospects, he had been genuinely impressed with her ingenuity, but hadn't given the project much thought since.

"First one?" he asked, his curiosity piqued.

"No," she replied, a bit defensively. "But the first that might pan out. Seems there's a woman named Dee Callison from up in Pleasanton who claims she was there the night that Lindstrom met Daultry in San Francisco."

Lang sat up in his seat. "She can put them together?"

"Yeah," Rachel replied as she skillfully navigated the clogged streets of San Sebastian. "And, she says there was also a red-headed woman with Daultry whose name was Molly something-or-other."

"No shit? When did we get the hit?" He was calculating how he might wedge such a witness into the rebuttal case.

"About fifteen minutes after Lindstrom said he'd never met Molly," Rachel answered, excitement building in her tone. "The UCLA guys are screening it. They had an immediate response by E-mail and somebody is on the phone with her right now. If it still looks good after that, I'll speak to her, probably tonight, if she's available."

"Can't hurt."

They agreed that Rachel would ask the woman to come down to their headquarters to meet with Amy as soon as possible. Lang closed his eyes to contemplate the depths of desperation that had driven them to consider using witnesses from the gallery.

At the eastern edge of the continent, Jad Piersall had watched the day's proceedings with intense interest. Although he knew what Lang was doing, he was well aware that there was no way to be sure it would work. The pundits playing taped highlights deep into the night certainly hadn't been impressed. And, while the courtroom cameras never showed the jury, he had little doubt that Lindstrom was working the same sort of magic on them that he had on that roomful of fat cats at L'Escoffier last year. He polished off another glass of scotch as the phone rang.

"Hello?"

"Jad? This is Shep Easley."

Piersall shook off the effects of the last two scotches. "Hi, Colonel. What's up?"

"Have you been watching?"

"All afternoon," he replied, watching as his wife drifted into the room.

"I'm not sure your boy can handle this guy."

"He's going to be okay, Colonel. He'd be all right now if the goddamned judge would leave him alone. And don't forget, he still has some pretty big artillery to fire in his rebuttal case."

"I know. I just hope the jury's still open to it by then. Anyway, the reason I called is I wanted an update on our security status."

"Still no word from Blades. We haven't been able to confirm whether Major Fassero ever reached the O'Keefe woman's house before the accident. There's been some police activity at the scene and it's too hard to call as to whether this was a genuine middle-of-the-night accident or a professional hit. Looks like the local cop working with Lang's people has been hanging around the house, so we haven't got a good look at the inside yet. Do we have anything more on the source of the telegram?"

"Not yet. We're having trouble lining up a reliable and secure asset down there to run it down."

"Either way, it doesn't look like it's going to matter. It's going to be hard to get her in time to put her on the stand."

"Agreed," Easley said.

"How's the weather back at The Roan, Colonel?" Piersall asked tentatively.

"Not good. They don't think much of our chances. And they don't share your enthusiasm for your man with the log book."

"They will," replied Piersall, more confidently than he felt.

Luther Anderson leaned against the hood of the great black limousine, enjoying the first cool breeze of the evening wafting over him from the sea. It had been an unusually hot day, even for midsummer, and Lindstrom's driver drank in the sea breeze greedily. He checked his watch. The plane was due in less than two minutes. He scanned the western horizon carefully.

Less than half a minute later he spotted the bright headlight of Mr. Lindstrom's Gulfstream winking in the western sky. He dreaded trying to get his passengers into town. The trial had turned sleepy little San Sebastian into a minimetropolis, where there seemed to be a nonstop traffic jam. He personally looked forward to the end of the trial and the return to normalcy here at home, even if the presidential race would mean that normalcy might not return to the rest of his life for quite some time. The possibility of an adverse result in the trial never occurred to him.

As the jet finished its roll-out, the stairway swung open not fifty feet from the car. Dick Banfield bounced down the stairs with surprising energy, considering the amount of travel he had just packed into five days. Behind him, moving slowly after his four hours inside the sleek but cramped aircraft, was Gary Vanderwald, the electronics genius from Micro Element Information Systems, who was notorious for his fear of flying. He looked pretty green to Luther as he wobbled across the tarmac.

"Hello, Luther," bubbled Banfield, more affable than Luther had ever seen him. Vanderwald said nothing, which Luther properly ascribed to his physical and emotional condition rather than to any lack of common courtesy, although he was also famous for his social shortcomings. Luther noted that Vanderwald's eye had an unnatural tic that looked as if he were hooked up to an electric current. He helped the two men with their bags and roared off toward the Santa Ynez Inn.

As they approached town, Banfield lowered the privacy screen between the passenger compartment and the driver.

"Luther," he said, using the driver's name for the second time in fifteen minutes and, maybe, the third time in a year. Man, thought Luther, he is feeling *good* about something. "Can we swing past the satellite installation in the park on the way to the hotel?"

"Sure can, Mr. Banfield," replied Luther, successfully drawing on his many years of gallant service to hide his annoyance that a painfully slow trip was about to get slower. The route he customarily took to the hotel carefully avoided the center of town, using several backstreets into the Santa Ynez. This would just add another thirty minutes or so to the whole process. The screen rolled back up and he turned up the volume on the ball game.

As they crept along the main street of town, flooded as usual by a fleet of out-of-town traffic looking for amusement in this quiet hamlet, Banfield lowered the screen again. Luther automatically turned the radio down again. "Luther," Banfield said. "We're going to have to find a place to stop along here. We need to get out for a minute."

"Good enough," replied Luther, more agreeably than he felt. Now began the difficult task of locating the rarest commodity of all: a parking space for a large limousine.

In the end, Luther decided to drop the two of them off and circle slowly until they were ready to be picked up again. It took them about fifteen minutes, during which time they seemed to be examining several of the large satellite dishes parked and mounted in neat rows on the grass. As he went by the first time, Luther saw Vanderwald, on his knees behind the Micro E truck, apparently sighting something in the sky above its large satellite dish. On the second trip through the square, Banfield and Vanderwald hopped back in and they were finally on their way to the hotel.

In the back of the car, Vanderwald did some calculations—by hand—in a small, grubby notebook he kept in his breast pocket.

"Can you do it?" asked Banfield, tending to hold his breath. It had nothing to do with the drama of the question, of course. It was the faint but persistent body odor that had emanated from the man since he had boarded the plane in Flint for the trip to San Sebastian.

"Yes," replied Vanderwald simply.

Banfield nodded, infinitely relieved that a major hole in his intelligence net—telephone calls in and out of Lang's suite—would soon be repaired. In all candor, he had been taken by surprise by Lang's precaution of using an electronics surveillance sweeping unit, but was certain, now, that the hitch would be overcome. He was annoyed that it had taken so long for the solution to present itself, but he was not particularly knowledgeable about the properties of microwave transmission and the decision to turn to the Micro E experts had been made just as he was leaving for Ireland. Although it was not Banfield's nature to dwell on what could not—or did not—get done, Lindstrom hadn't seen it the same way. Despite his convincingly confident public persona, Lindstrom was plainly irritated by his team's inability to listen to telephone calls and personal conversations that took place in the Presidential Suite of the Westgate Hotel. His annoyance had gotten especially acute after Ernesto had given them the list of rebuttal witnesses.

Banfield decided that whatever the old man was interested in listening to would be heard now. He turned his attention to the logistics of accomplishing the things Vanderwald needed to make the alternative work.

CHAPTER 32

AS EXPECTED, HICKMAN RESTED HIS CASE THE following afternoon. His final witness, called to underscore the overwhelming press of other, unrelated events on Lindstrom at the time when it was alleged that he was testing the StormTree and falsifying reports, would have been anticlimactic had it not been for the fact that he was the former chairman of the Joint Chiefs of Staff, currently serving as head of the Spense Foundation, and a candidate for the U.S. Senate seat in California. In a trial already top-heavy with celebrity and media hype, General Aloysius Yarr was a fitting capstone for the defense. After running through a carefully arranged chronicle of the many charitable and political activities he and Lindstrom had worked on together during the relevant time frame—each of which, Lang was sure, was meticulously chosen for its political correctness—Yarr launched into a freewheeling oration about the general righteousness of all things Lindstrom. He inflicted no real damage on Lang's case and Lang had just about decided to let the war hero off easy by not asking any questions on cross-examination when he realized that an unusual opportunity for a tactical coup had presented itself.

When Hickman told the court he had no more questions, Lang rose. "Just one thing, General Yarr," he began, standing at counsel table. "You mentioned that you are running for the Senate."

Yarr smiled, proving that this warrior was capable of the transition to politico. "That's right."

"And if Mr. Lindstrom is the Republican candidate, that's going to help your campaign, isn't it?"

"Why . . ." responded Yarr, the smile immediately forgotten in a rush of confusion. It occurred to Lang to be grateful that the Soviets hadn't attacked on Yarr's watch. The courtroom buzz began in earnest.

"Objection!" said Hickman. But he was slow to identify the grounds, probably, thought Lang, because "political embarrassment" is not recognized as one.

Judge Campbell waited a beat. Then he said, "Sustained."

"On what ground, Your Honor, if I may ask?" asked Lang, very calmly.

The judge realized his mistake, but apparently had no ready reply. He turned to Hickman. "Counsel?"

"Argumentative," said Hickman at last.

"I see," said Lang with a smile. Half the jury was smiling with him. There was considerable laughter rippling through the gallery. "General Yarr, isn't it true that the consequences to you and your campaign would be catastrophic if your old friend and ally Russell Lindstrom were to be held liable for civil fraud?"

"Objection!" boomed Hickman.

"Sustained!" came Campbell's reply, an echo to Hickman's shout.

Lang was undeterred. "And that you came here to testify to save your own chestnuts as much as his?" The laughter crescendoed behind him.

"Argumentative!" called Hickman over the din.

"Sustained! Mr. Lang, I'm warning you—"

"No further questions, Your Honor," Lang said quietly as he resumed his seat.

Hickman scowled at the realization that he had no choice now but to rise and advise the court that the defense rested its case. Lang leaned over to Amy and whispered in her ear, "I can't remember. What does Overbrook say about resting your case while the courtroom is laughing at your closing witness?"

Amy kept her eyes straight ahead and fought off the impulse to giggle. Under her breath, she murmured, "Don't gloat. We haven't won a thing yet." They both knew, of course, that without Will Haverstock's testimony, all these little "victories" would add up to fond memories of a case lost. And they still hadn't heard a word from Haverstock since his jeep roared away into the wilds of the Mojave Desert.

Lang was taking his time with Doug Chesney. Chesney had been virtually unshakable when Lang had cross-examined him earlier. But there was a vague uneasiness now, as Lang interrogated him in the rebuttal case, and Lang's deliberate pace was calculated to play upon whatever anxiety it was that he had touched within the witness.

"Now, Mr. Chesney, I know you testified earlier about the procedures used by Arrow Dynamics in conducting the StormTree development project—by the way, there was another designation for the StormTree. XRL-22. Is that right?"

"That's right."

"And that designation, the 'RL' part, meant that it was designed by Russell Lindstrom, did it not? That, in fact, it was the twenty-second aircraft designed by him. Isn't that right?"

Chesney smiled. "No, sir. That is not right. It was, however, the twenty-second aircraft we designed with our radial-linkage package. That's the 'RL,' Mr. Lang. It describes the unique system we devised to connect the control surfaces, rudder, aileron, and winglet. The 'X,' of course, meant that it was an experimental aircraft."

I'll bet, thought Lang. "Really?" he said, a small smile on his lips. "If you say so. In any event, let's focus on one aspect of the program now, if I may. You stated that there were flight cards prepared for every flight, correct?"

"Yes," said Chesney.

"And those are cards, note cards like three-by-five cards—"

"Four-by-six."

"Four-by-six cards," Lang continued, nodding to acknowledge the assistance. "And these are kept by the pilot on a clipboard—"

"Knee board," offered Chesney.

"Knee board." Lang smiled. "As he flies the aircraft."

"Right."

"And you also kept an aircraft log, a log of the running time of the engine. Exhibit 27, right?"

"That's right."

"But on other programs, Arrow maintained a different sort of log, didn't it?"

"You mean an engineering log?"

"Yes, Mr. Chesney, an engineering log. That's a log that records flight data, like the date of each flight in the test program and the pilot who flew it, right?"

"Usually," replied Chesney, nodding.

"And the purpose of each flight?"

"Yes."

"And critical flight information, like weather conditions?"

"Right."

"Maneuvers performed, and the results of those maneuvers?"

"Correct."

"What else?"

Hickman got to his feet. "Your Honor, I'm going to object. It has been established through many witnesses that such a log, which was kept on some programs and not on others, was not kept on this program. That makes this entire line of questioning both irrelevant and speculative."

"Your Honor," replied Lang, trying to head off the ruling he was certain was about to come. "May we approach?"

Campbell nodded and the two lawyers huddled with the judge and the court reporter at the sidebar. Lang spoke. "Your Honor, we intend to prove that the defendants' failure to maintain the engineering log was negligence of the sort that invalidates their whole test program, thereby breaching the contract. I need Mr. Chesney's testimony as a foundation for my expert testimony to that effect."

To his surprise, Campbell quietly mulled over his argument. Hickman, too, was silent. Lang hoped it wasn't because he was thinking through why Lang had just been so uncharacteristically candid about what he was doing and where he was going. The judge looked at Hickman. "Counsel, I'm going to allow a limited inquiry here." Turning to Lang, he said, "The emphasis is on *limited*."

Campbell overruled the objection aloud and Lang continued. "The question was, what else does an engineering log reflect?"

"Any number of things," replied Chesney, moving a little uncomfortably in his chair.

"Well, let me see if I can guess," offered Lang. "It's in the handwriting of the pilot, right?"

"Sometimes," replied Chesney, obviously a little surprised by the question. "Usually," he added.

"And it has the date of the flight, the maneuver to be performed, the center of gravity at which the aircraft was flown, the weather conditions, the altitude achieved, the results of the maneuver, the pilot's impressions and observations, safety tips from one flight to the next, recommendations for areas to be further explored or areas considered too dangerous for further evaluation. That sort of thing?"

Hickman was on his feet. "Objection! That's compound."

But Chesney, for some reason, wasn't listening to his lawyer. Ashen-faced, he answered, "Yes, sir. Most of those things, anyway."

"Sustained," bellowed the judge. "The jury will disregard the answer."

"But you didn't keep one on the StormTree, isn't that so?"

"That's right," replied Chesney, regaining a measure of his composure.

"Are you sure you didn't keep one?"

Hickman, from behind Lang, snapped, "Argumentative!"

"Withdraw the question," said Lang, mooting the ruling before it was made. "Still not sure why you didn't keep one in this case?"

"As I said before," replied Chesney, "we didn't always maintain an engineering log. We didn't do it here. No particular reason. We didn't keep one in the Star Cruiser program or the Adelphi Next Generation Jet Fighter, either. We didn't always keep one."

"Thank you, Mr. Chesney," said Lang gently. "Nothing further."

Hickman, observing the rule that sometimes the most effective examination is the one not made, declined the option of conducting cross of Chesney. As he reached counsel table, Lang nodded to Amy. "You're on."

Amy rose. "Plaintiff calls Dee Callison."

Chesney's head snapped up instantly at the mention of the name. By prearrangement, Rachel Cruz escorted the woman into the courtroom. Lang observed that the Arrow executive's eyes never left her as the two passed in the well; Callison, on the other hand, studiously avoided eye contact. Lang did not regard that as a particularly favorable omen. Not for the first time, he wondered if this cyber witness, as he had called her, would do enough good to justify the risk of the unknown. He had not met her beforehand, leaving the briefing and preparation to Amy, and was relying on Amy's assessment. According to her, the woman was credible and presentable, though unable to do more than place Molly and Nigel in the same room as Lindstrom, talking about an experimental airplane. Of course, that was more than anyone else other than Molly could do. Still, Lang was uneasy about the extemporaneous theater they were about to set in motion.

At least it was obvious that Dee Callison had caught the jury's attention. She was well beyond Amy's description of her as "presentable"; a blue-eyed brunette of about thirty-five who carried her curvaceous frame with poise and confidence, she was striking by anyone's reckoning. Amy took her through the basic background material in workmanlike fashion, laying the groundwork for the heart of her testimony.

"Have you ever met Mr. Lindstrom?" Amy asked at last. Lang watched Lindstrom's face and could detect no sign of recognition.

"Yes. Once."

"Please tell us the circumstances," Amy said, mildly frustrated that Callison was proceeding in such short steps, especially since she had been far more expansive during their interview the prior evening.

"I dated Douglas Chesney for about six months several years ago," the woman answered. "I met him down—up, I guess, from here—in San Francisco for dinner one night. We went to a nice place on Russian Hill called The Partridge. Somebody was having a birthday, one of his friends. Ray. Mr. Lindstrom was there. And Ray's date, Yvonne or Yvette something."

"Was Mr. Lindstrom alone?"

"Yes," the woman replied. "He said his wife was in Oklahoma, on business."

"Did anyone else join you for dinner?"

"Not for dinner, but afterward, for dessert. A man and a woman from another table. Nigel and Molly."

A buzz swept through the courtroom like the Wave. Judge Campbell watched the gallery over his glasses, but decided that his gavel wouldn't be necessary. Amy allowed the swell to subside before continuing. "Did you catch their last names?"

"Nigel Daultry and Molly Keefe."

"O'Keefe?" prompted Amy, the butterflies in her stomach growing to the size of bats. Lang watched for some indicator on the faces of the jury but could see none.

"Yes. I'm sorry," replied the woman hurriedly. "O'Keefe."

"Did Mr. Lindstrom speak with Mr. Daultry and Ms. O'Keefe in your presence?"

"Oh, yes. For several hours."

"What about?"

Hickman was out of his chair. "Hearsay."

Amy responded before Campbell could rule. "Your Honor, the statements are not being offered to prove their truth, merely that the conversation took place."

"Sustained," said Campbell, outraging third-year law students all over the country.

Amy proceeded. "What, if anything, did you hear Mr. Lindstrom say?"

"Same objection," intoned Hickman.

Amy turned to the judge. "That would be a statement of a party, Your Honor. A declaration against interest."

"I'll allow it," said Campbell, thus evening the score for the moment with his second erroneous ruling in a row, this one going the other way.

"He talked about politics. War. Technology."

"Did he say anything about an experimental airplane?"

"She's leading the witness, Your Honor," said Hickman.

"Sustained," said Campbell.

"Do you remember anything else Mr. Lindstrom said?" continued Amy, having successfully planted the cue.

"He talked about an airplane that he wanted Mr. Daultry to develop with him."

"Do you recall anything that Mr. Lindstrom said about that airplane?"

"No. I'm sorry. We all talked for hours, about a lot of different things. And went through a couple bottles of wine, I'm afraid. That's all I recall."

Keenly aware of her strategy conference with Lang on this witness—"Let's get no more than we absolutely need from her and keep the scope of cross-examination as narrow as possible"—Amy thanked Dee Callison and turned her over for cross-examination.

"Ms. Callison," began Hickman, "you were upset when Mr. Chesney ended your relationship, weren't you?"

"Why, no. Not at all. In fact, I was the one who ended it."

"Now, Ms. Callison, isn't it true that you called him several times over the course of a year and a half after you broke up and begged him to see you?"

"No, sir," she replied firmly. "That's not true."

Hickman picked up a sheaf of papers from counsel table. "Well, Ms. Callison, perhaps you can explain the twenty-seven calls placed from your home telephone to Mr. Chesney, both to his home and to his office in that time frame, as reflected on your telephone bill."

Amy rose to object. "There's no foundation for that document, Your Honor."

Campbell nodded. "Sustained."

Hickman shrugged. "Your Honor, may I approach the witness for the purpose of refreshing her recollection?"

"Proceed," the judge said. Hickman handed her the papers. "Please look over these phone records to see if they refresh your recollection that you called Mr. Chesney twenty-seven times during that time frame, Ms. Callison."

Lang tried not to wince as the woman on the stand turned paler with each page she reviewed. Obviously someone in Lindstrom's camp must have seen them interview the woman and been prepared for her attack on Lindstrom.

"I don't know what to say. These look like my phone records. I don't really recognize these numbers but I may have called him."

"Hounded him is more like it, isn't it, Ms. Callison?"

"Argumentative," said Amy.

"Withdraw the question," replied Hickman, satisfied that he had made his point. But he was only getting started. From there he went on to suggest that Dee Callison was a bitter, jilted lover who saw her chance at revenge by testifying against her ex-boyfriend's hero on national television. After the telephone records, he assaulted her with a letter from Chesney to her dated two years after what he called the "alleged San Francisco dinner."

"You did receive this letter, didn't you?" Hickman's tone was contemptuous.

Amy started to rise to object, but Lang put his hand on her arm and shook his head slightly. "We might need the precedent here," he whispered. Amy's frown betrayed her confusion but she said nothing.

"I don't recall," the witness replied uncertainly.

"Well, Ms. Callison, you recall Mr. Chesney asking you"—he positioned himself alongside the witness and made a show of reading from the letter—"to 'please stop calling me at home,' don't you?"

"I, I don't know," the woman sputtered. "I don't think so."

Hickman saw no reason to relent. "Then, how about, 'unfortunately, you obviously thought something was going on that wasn't'? You recall him telling you that, don't you?"

"No. Not really," Callison replied, looking over to Amy for help that wasn't available.

"You're precisely the kind of person who would go out of her way to testify in a case like this, to make someone like Mr. Chesney look bad, aren't you?"

"Argumentative," said Amy. "And compound. And irrel—"

"Withdraw the question," said Hickman, with a wave of disgust toward the stand. He headed back to counsel table. Over his shoulder, he said, "You sought out the plaintiff's lawyers, didn't you? Offered to testify, isn't that so?"

"Well," Callison replied, "I told them that I had information to give the court."

"Information?" Hickman repeated disdainfully. "You probably contacted them on their Internet site, didn't you?" He used the term like an obscenity that couldn't be avoided.

"Irrelevant," shot Amy.

"Overruled," intoned Campbell. "You will answer the question."

Dee Callison blushed brightly. "Well, yes, I did. But only because I—"

"You've answered the question," interrupted Hickman. "Nothing further."

On re-direct, Amy limited her efforts to rehabilitate the shaken woman to the area of reestablishing the dinner participants, and chose to leave the matter there. Lang was grateful that John Carrick was his next witness, his hope being that an abrupt return to the technical aspects of the case would be the most effective means of cleansing the effect of Hickman's potent cross-examination from the jury's mind. "Now, Mr. Carrick," he began. "You heard Mr. Chesney testify about an engineering log. Are you also familiar with such a document?"

"I am," said Carrick, with the confidence of a man who had been trained to ride to the moon in a small closet. "It is an essential record in a properly conducted flight-test program."

"Essential?"

"Yes, sir. By that I mean indispensable. Without the engineering log, you have a program that, by definition, is deficient, negligent."

Hickman was up. "Move to strike, Your Honor. This witness is not competent to render that opinion. And, besides, it's irrelevant to the case. This is not a case about negligence. It's about breach of contract. The standard for Arrow Dynamics' performance is not what this witness says a test program normally requires, it's what the contract requires."

"Motion to strike is granted," said the judge. "The jury will disregard the statement."

Lang pressed on. "Have you ever been involved with a flight test that did not involve maintaining such a log?"

"Same objection!" shouted Hickman.

Before Campbell could rule, Carrick answered, "Never."

"Sustained!" said the judge. "Disregard the statement."

"You've read the contract. In your opinion could the test requirements have been met without maintaining an engineering log?"

"Objection!"

Again, Carrick blurted his answer. "Virtually impossible."

"Sustained!" boomed Judge Campbell again. "Disregard the testimony. And, Mr. Carrick, I caution you to wait until the objection can be ruled upon before answering."

"I'm sorry, Your Honor," said a contrite Carrick, although, in truth, by prior arrangement with Lang, he had no intention of doing so.

"Mr. Chesney mentioned pilot impressions as one of the data that would be contained in an engineering log, if one was kept. What role do pilot impressions play in the context of a test-flight program?"

"Absolutely critical. Over the years, I have flown more than fifty flight tests myself, as either the alpha or the beta pilot—that's primary or secondary, sorry—and I supervised nearly a hundred more while in the Air Force. Pilot impressions are very often the most important data that you can derive from the program, especially where the aircraft is new or experimental. The truth is that engineers, even the best ones, simply cannot plot out every event that will occur in the chain of events that unfolds during a test flight. A good pilot can often sense things about the aircraft, its performance, its handling, its tendencies, that the designers couldn't even have guessed at. The test pilot is rightly called the primary instrument in any test program."

"Would it be possible for a test pilot to sense an aircraft's tendency to enter into a spin even if the aircraft doesn't actually spin?"

Hickman objected. "That's irrelevant and lacks a foundation."

To Lang's surprise, the judge replied, "I don't think it's irrelevant and I believe the witness's qualifications are adequate to support the statement. Overruled."

Carrick answered. "Oh, absolutely. It happened to me in the ThunderHawk, an experimental design from a Dutch company I tested for the Air Force in 1982. During departure testing, early in the Military Specification 92121 regime, I had a sense that the aircraft wanted to tuck in a very docile roll maneuver. That means, it wanted to pitch toward one side, very often the early sign of a spin entry."

"What did you do?"

"I did what any trained test pilot would do. I put the aircraft back on the deck and reported my impressions to the test commander. Further testing was suspended until we devised a computer program that teased out the tendency."

Hickman was up again, definitely unhappy. "If the court please. The witness's self-serving statements about what a good test pilot he was have no bearing on the issues involved here."

"Assuming that is a motion to strike and assuming the ground for it is irrelevancy and lack of foundation, I will grant it. The jury will disregard the witness's last answer."

Hickman sat down. "Thank you, Your Honor."

Fat chance, thought Lang. "Did the aircraft have a tendency to spin?" he asked.

"It certainly did."

"Objection! That's irrelevant," shouted Hickman.

"Sustained," said the judge. "Mr. Carrick, you wait until the objection can be ruled on."

"Sorry, Your Honor, but I had already answered before there was an objection."

"Then don't be so fast with your answers, sir!" barked the judge, clearly approaching the limit of his patience.

"Sorry," said Carrick humbly.

During this exchange, Lang had stayed focused on the jury, trying to gauge how Carrick's tenacity was playing with the only audience that counted. Fair to middling, he concluded. Normally, that would suggest that it was time to tone it down. But not this time. Not yet, anyway.

"What do you conclude from the testimony of the defendants to the effect that they failed to maintain an engineering log in connection with the StormTree project?"

Hickman appeared poised to stand for an objection, but something held him back.

Carrick waited. A good ten seconds went by.

"Mr. Carrick, did you hear the question?" asked Campbell.

"Certainly, Your Honor," he replied. "I was just waiting to make sure it was okay to answer."

Campbell burned brightly but said nothing.

After another pause, Carrick responded, "This was a very good, very professional organization, this Arrow Dynamics operation. Their work over the years has been exemplary and they have literally pushed back the frontiers of aviation in the small-aircraft area. Their people are well-trained and capable and their designs are the standard for many the world over. That they would fail to maintain an engineering log on a project of this kind is inconceivable. I conclude that they are lying."

The courtroom erupted as never before. Shouts and whoops actually arose from the great sprawling gallery. Several members of the jury looked as if they had been physically struck. Judge Campbell brought down his gavel violently and repeatedly. "There will be order in my courtroom or I will have it cleared! Do you hear!"

Gentry Hickman was standing at counsel table hollering at the top of his lungs. "I move to strike! Move to strike! Incompetent, irrelevant, speculation, assumes facts not in evidence! Move to strike!"

The pounding of the gavel was finally taking effect. Up on the bench, Campbell stormed, "Motion granted. The jury will disregard the answer. Do you hear me? The jury will disregard the answer."

Lang, who had sat down in the interim, couldn't help smiling at the chaos that this one, unadulterated word of absolute truth had wrought. He had several more questions he had planned to ask but his sense of drama was far too highly developed to ask them now. As the sea of commotion receded slightly, he rose and said simply, "Nothing further of this witness, Your Honor."

Campbell glared down at him. Without consulting the clock, he said, "We will recess for the day. Reconvene tomorrow at nine." He kept his eyes squarely on Lang as he spoke. "And, ladies and gentleman of the jury, remember the admonition." It was only 3:35 in the afternoon.

That evening, the main room in the Lindstrom suite at the Santa Ynez was alive with its customary high-level after-trial activity. Under bright lights and against a constant din, Hickman, Overbrook, and Royster sat around the large conference table in the center of the room and grappled with the strategic and tactical issues presented by the day's testimony. In the far corner, under the huge window, Gina Calabrese and her campaign staff plotted strategy and tactics of an entirely different kind. Assistants and paraprofessionals of various descriptions floated around the suite taking food and drink orders, repacking litigation cases, delivering fresh news copy, updating political polling books, and replenishing the fresh-cut flowers that constantly poured into the suite. Three television sets with VCR's played on, with or without anyone to watch. Computer terminals sat in a row on the far wall, screens up and on-line, waiting for instructions from any number of human commanders. A copy machine flashed and clattered, spewing out a new generation of offspring for the documents that were the lifeblood of both the legal and the political battles being plotted there. Fax machines hummed and delivered a steady stream of fresh input from far-flung outposts. Hotel personnel appeared regularly at the doorway every two or three minutes, discharging every manner of service to the people paying the enormous and growing bill. The overall effect was of a small, terribly intense office, a nerve center, really, staffed by dedicated and talented professionals.

Off that main room, in the two rooms Russell Lindstrom used for his personal quarters, a very different tone predominated. Lindstrom sat motionless in the teal-colored armchair beside the desk, staring out the window at the midsummer dusk. A single desk lamp was lit against the gathering gloom. From behind him, in the deepening shadows away from the window, came a voice. "Well. What do you think?" It was Dick Banfield.

"I think I'm tired."

Banfield nodded his acknowledgment of the fact, although Lindstrom wasn't watching him anyway.

"Beyond that," Lindstrom continued, still staring out the window. His voice was uncharacteristically scratchy from fatigue. "I think it's a lock."

"Then what are you worried about?" asked Banfield. "You've pushed Lang around since day one. The judge thinks it's a bullshit case. The jury is enthralled with you. And we've successfully eliminated a major surprise or two."

"You've done well, Dick," Lindstrom acknowledged, turning his head to pick up Banfield. "But the man who stops worrying is the man who gets taken out in the next assault."

"We're prepared. For anything."

"Are we?" Lindstrom asked. "I wonder."

Banfield, still standing in the shadows, shifted his weight uneasily. He said nothing.

"I want you to know that *I* know we blew it with Ireland," Lindstrom said. His words hung heavily for a moment.

"Ireland's under control, R.L.," said Banfield defensively.

"I don't mean now," said Lindstrom, his gaze boring in on Banfield through the darkness. "I mean we should have known that Lang went to Ireland and certainly should have figured out why." Before the other man could speak, Lindstrom moved seamlessly from old business to new. "Will Haverstock. The fly in the ointment."

Banfield, grateful for the change of subject, laughed mirthlessly. "I never liked that bastard."

Lindstrom laughed too. "I know."

"What damage can he really do?" asked Banfield. "He had nothing to do with the project. He was pretty much out of the way at the time. Gentry would tear him apart as a disgruntled former employee if he had any damaging lies to tell."

"Possibly. But I'd like to get to him first. This time." He paused, allowing the younger man to make the connection he intended him to make. "How are we doing with the microwaves?"

"They were making progress this afternoon—"

Lindstrom's phone rang. Banfield answered. After a few cryptic words, he hung up. "How's that for timing?" he said to Lindstrom. "Vanderwald's got something he wants to show me downstairs."

Lindstrom smiled. "That's good, Dick. I hate loose ends."

Milo Rich sprawled on the plush sofa in his own suite, across the way in the Westgate. This was excitement such as even he had seldom known. The numbers spread out on the coffee table were hard to comprehend. The stack of printouts from Charlotte confirmed that during the early-evening hours in the East, pre-prime time, upward of forty-four million viewers had been tuned in to the coverage. His own show, which he was only too happy to do directly after the trial broke for the day at 6:35 Eastern time, had held on to an astonishing thirty-five million viewers. Forget the bonus clause in his contract and the fact that he couldn't possibly spend all the money he was pulling down if he lived another hundred years. This was live, unfolding American history and he was a major part of it.

His own analysis and commentary on these extraordinary events in the midst of an intense and highly volatile presidential campaign were molding and shaping public opinion as few journalists ever had in recorded history. It was not a responsibility that he took lightly. He, perhaps alone at this moment in time, realized the awesome implications of what was happening here and he welcomed the burden of public service.

And that led him to the other stack of documents, secret polls conducted by network operatives not for publication but to assist them in discharging their own obligations as stewards of the public trust. And these figures were at least as remarkable. The convention delegates, even as they converged on Kansas City for the convention now just a matter of days away, had been moved powerfully by the trial and the media coverage it had unleashed. Russell Lindstrom had been regarded by many party regulars as a remarkable businessman but a political dilettante as recently as four weeks ago, even *after* the entire primary season, with its seven full-fledged debates, had run its course. Now, he was the clear choice of three out of every four delegates, making him a runaway favorite for the nomination on the second ballot.

Rich drank deeply from a huge glass of mineral water—the brand name he endorsed in ubiquitous television and radio spots— and marveled at the power of the media, of television, of Milo Rich. It's a damned good thing I know the real deal from the bullshit, thought Rich, with neither irony nor humility. This kind of power in the hands of someone whose head wasn't on straight could do real damage.

It was just past eleven and Lang was toying with the idea of going to bed when the phone in his bedroom rang. "Hello?" he said, sounding more alert than he really was.

"It's good theater but you still don't have him, do you?" asked a man's voice. It was familiar but Lang couldn't place it right away.

"Who is this?" he asked, shaking the cobwebs from a very tired brain.

"You know who I am, Mr. Lang."

Lang's heart leaped. It was Haverstock! He tried to suppress the mixture of relief and excitement that instantly overtook him. "Mr. Hav—"

"No names, Mr. Lang. Are we still on?"

"You tell me." Lang was furiously timing out his rebuttal examination of Lindstrom, the only part of his case remaining before Haverstock's testimony—and the notebook—would be needed. He could need him as early as tomorrow.

"Absolutely. I'll be enjoying our business even more than I thought."

"Good. I'm going to need you—"

"I know," interrupted Haverstock. "You'll reach the critical point about midafternoon tomorrow. That's why I'm calling now. You can count on me."

Lang was still not comfortable. "Where are you?"

"Close enough to do what you need. You leave it to me."

Lang was catching on to Haverstock's conversational game. "I don't think you have to worry about this call being overheard. We've carefully swept—"

Laughter at the other end of the line cut him off. "Don't tell me you still don't know who you're up against. How do you play them so well in court when you're so overmatched everywhere else?" Lang was furious but, before he could respond, Haverstock continued. "Look. This has got to be brief. I'll be there. We'll cover the things we talked about. Don't worry. He was there. He flew it. He knew. He blessed the report. Relax, Mr. Lang. You're going to be a hero."

Sensing that Haverstock was about to hang up, Lang said, "Wait!" There was still something about this man and his story that bothered Lang and he was beginning to close in on it. "How do I know you're for real? I mean, you're terrified of these guys, taking all sorts of extreme precautions for your safety, and yet you're willing to take the stand on national television and blow these guys away. How do you square that?"

More laughter. "Look, it's the same principle as you. You're too visible now to be eliminated. Can't do that sort of thing where it's too obvious. My testimony will be my insurance policy once it's done. Same as you. And your wife and kids."

Lang's mind raced. What was this guy saying? "Wait!"

"Good night, Mr. Lang." The phone went dead in Lang's hand. For several minutes he sat there, staring at it.

Across the way in the Santa Ynez Inn, in a fourth-floor room on the east side of the hotel, there was an unusual amount of activity at this late hour. Four men, wearing headphones, huddled around a sophisticated array of receivers, recorders, equalizers, and computers, playing and replaying a section of audiotape on a large reel-to-reel tape deck. The small man with the eye tic sat with his eyes shut, rewinding and replaying the tape with the skill and dexterity of an accomplished musician, continuously adjusting the massive equalizer.

"Try that section again," instructed Banfield. Vanderwald complied.

In their headphones, they heard, "I know. You'll reach the critical point about midafternoon tomorrow. That's why I'm calling now. You can count on me."

Then, the other voice. "Where are you?"

"Close enough to do what you need," answered the first voice. "You leave it to me."

"Wait," said Milinsky. "There's something in the background. Can you isolate it?" he asked Vanderwald.

"Let's wash the conversation out and see if that does it," replied Vanderwald, his eyes still closed. He recued the tape and adjusted most of the slide controls on the equalizer board.

This time, Lang's and Haverstock's voices were faint, overwhelmed by the background noise. There was a machine, and voices, faint and scattered, coins dropping in another phone.

"Is that a vacuum cleaner?" asked Banfield.

Vanderwald shook his head. "Too big. Buffer or polisher, I'd say," he replied, still without opening his eyes.

"What was that?" asked Milinsky. "Sounds like a P.A. system or something."

Vanderwald recued and once again adjusted the equalizer. This time they all heard, over Lang's faint voice, another, amplified voice saying, "The management of the Reno Regional Airport thanks you for not smoking in the terminal area."

"That's Reno!" shouted Milinsky. He turned toward Banfield.

Banfield wore a chilling smile. He carefully removed the headset and left the room.

CHAPTER 33

"YOUR HONOR, PLAINTIFF CALLS RUSSELL LIND-strom," said Lang.

Hickman was on his feet in an instant. He put a firm hand on Lindstrom's shoulder to restrain him from responding to the call. "Your Honor, must we?" he said, a calculated note of fatigue and mild disgust in his voice. "Mr. Lindstrom has already sat through better than a day of cross-examination by Mr. Lang. How much more of counsel's fishing expedition must we endure? I urge the court to excuse Mr. Lindstrom from further testimony."

While Judge Campbell considered this extraordinary request and Lang waited to see if he really would take such an outrageous course of action, Lindstrom lifted Hickman's hand from his shoulder and stood. "Your Honor, I have no problem taking the stand again," he said with a weary smile. "Anything to get this trial over and get back to our real lives."

Hickman turned his palms upward in a show of exasperation. "Withdraw the objection," he said, bringing to an end what Lang was sure was a staged tableau of indignation and presidential-caliber martyrdom. You have to admire these guys, Lang thought. They've got balls like bulls.

After Lindstrom was reminded that he was still under oath, Lang moved directly to the point. "You know what an engineering log is, don't you?"

Lindstrom looked at Lang with undisguised contempt. "I am familiar with the concept."

"Did you participate in the preparation of the engineering log in the StormTree program?"

Hickman shot to his feet. "Objection! Assumes facts not in evidence, lacks foundation."

"Sustained," said the judge wearily.

Lang continued on his carefully charted course. "You have seen the log that was kept on the StormTree program, haven't you?"

"Same objection," called Hickman, not bothering to stand this time.

"Sustained."

"You know, Mr. Lindstrom, the one that listed each and every test flight, envelope expansion, design change? That one?"

Lindstrom was growing angry but held his tongue.

"Objection."

"Sustained."

Lang returned to counsel table and, from a briefcase on the floor, deliberately removed an eight-and-a-half by eleven-inch spiral notebook. It was soiled and the wire spiral that held it together was bent. The cover had a splotch across it, possibly oil or grease. Its pages were swollen from heavy and repeated use. Lang moved closer to Lindstrom.

"A notebook like this, Mr. Lindstrom," said Lang, holding the notebook so that it could be plainly seen by both the witness and the jury. "The one that the pilots and the engineers used to record their raw data from the program, in their own hand, the one that shows, in great detail, every relevant fact about every flight in the test program. You remember that, don't you?"

"Objection! Lacks foundation."

Lang turned to Campbell. "I'm allowed to lay a foundation, Your Honor."

The massive purple blotch that was a United States district judge peered down at Lang over his reading glasses. "Overruled. The witness will answer the question."

"I do not remember such a log, Mr. Lang," came Lindstrom's cool reply. "I think I already told you I had nothing to do with the program."

"You may have, at that," said Lang. "You've said quite a bit, in fact. I'm just trying to figure out if any of it is true."

Hickman was on his feet again, but he didn't need to be. Campbell stiffened like a man at the wrong end of a poker. "Counsel!" he cried. "You will refrain from any further argumentative or inflammatory statements. And I have already warned you: You will treat this witness with respect in my courtroom or I will confine you!"

Lang stood silently, looking almost as if he enjoyed being the object of the judge's animosity. As always, of course, he was after bigger game. He deliberately opened the notebook and turned several pages. At length he asked, "You were involved in the high-angle-of-attack testing, weren't you?"

"No, I was not," Lindstrom replied tightly. Subtly, almost imperceptibly, Lang thought, his facade seemed to be cracking.

"You recall the departure testing conducted on the StormTree prototype in the spring of that year, don't you?" Lang managed to put just a touch of incredulity into the question.

"I do not."

"Really? You recall stall testing in early March, don't you?"

"I do not recall any such thing."

Hickman was up again. "Your Honor, if the court please. Is there no end to the fishing we must endure in the absence of evidence in this case?"

"Well, hellfire, Mr. Hickman. I've done a fair amount of fishing in my day and I resent your comparing this display to that fine and wholesome pastime. Let me see you both up here."

When they were assembled in the usual positions at sidebar, the judge spoke. "What's going on, Mr. Lang? What are you doing?"

Lang was surprised by the question but, as usual, succeeded in hiding the fact. "I don't think I have any obligation to answer that question, Judge. I'm within my rights to ask this witness questions that are relevant to my case. I have no control over how he answers."

The judge was plainly exasperated. "Don't give me any crap about what you're obligated to do. I'm telling you to get to the point or I'll pull the plug on you. Do you understand me?"

"I always understand you, Your Honor. I assure you I know

where I am going and it will become abundantly clear to you and everybody else in due course."

"It better be damned soon." The judge looked to Hickman and shrugged. "I'm going to let him go on, but not much further."

When they had resumed their stations, Lang continued. "You designed the StormTree, didn't you, Mr. Lindstrom?"

The question struck a nerve among the gallery and it registered its trademark buzz. Lindstrom was absolutely implacable up on the stand. "No," he said, biting off the word.

Where are your speeches about the ills of civil litigation and the abuse of the court system, I wonder, mused Lang. "All right, then. You flew the test flight on which the spin tendency of the StormTree was discovered, didn't you?"

Again the buzzing of the courtroom spectators washed over the room.

"Argumentative!" called Hickman.

"I want an answer, Your Honor," shouted Lang above the din. "And I want it under oath and on the record."

Campbell did not respond to him with anything beyond a venomous glare. "Sustained!" he said, slamming his gavel down three times in rapid succession. "We will have order or I will close the courtroom."

Order returned quickly. Lang was determined to follow his plan. "You flew that test on March ninth and reported"—here, he appeared to be reading from the notebook—"that you were open to one hundred fifty miles per hour indicated airspeed. That the angle of attack increased and the yaw increased to the left, the nose came up, and even if you applied full forward stick it almost would not bring the angle of attack down. 'Feeling'—that's *your* feeling—'was that it would depart controlled flight to the left into a high angle of attack left-rotation mode with probable flat spin to ensue.' In other words, Mr. Lindstrom, you reported to the program director that you felt the StormTree was about to enter into a flat spin and that either the aircraft had to be grounded or you had to further investigate this tendency, isn't that right?"

The courtroom erupted. The gavel hand of the angry old man in the black robe beat a furious tattoo on the bench. Several marshals materialized out of nowhere at each door and assumed ready positions lest the room dissolve into anarchy. The Secret Service agents, who had sat through the trial, rose in unison and stationed themselves in a ring around Lindstrom. Lang noticed that Amy's jaw had gone slack at this remarkable spectacle. And meanwhile, all across the country and, indeed, around the world, millions stopped in front of television sets and marveled at the events that were unfolding live and in color out in California. But, most importantly, Lang thought he saw something new and jarring in the faces of the jury. It might have been contempt for him—Lord knows, he was trying to savage a national icon and local deity—but he had an odd sense it was something else. A turning, perhaps, of the great crushing tide.

It took several minutes but at last a semblance of order, if not quiet, descended over the scene. Up on the bench, Campbell was giving his gavel a final slug or two. "There will be order or this case will be finished in a sealed courtroom!"

Lang wondered at what point Campbell would act on that frequently made threat. When quiet, more or less, was restored, Lang spoke. "May I have the witness's answer read back, Your Honor?"

Campbell glowered down at Lang but spoke to the reporter. "Please reread the answer, Madam Reporter."

The woman looked up at Campbell, very nearly in tears. "I didn't get it, Your Honor," she said in a whisper barely audible at counsel table.

Lindstrom spoke, with self-assuredness and, it seemed to Lang, more than a touch of arrogance. "I said, 'No, I didn't.' And I would like to add that this is a fantasy, a fiction, a travesty that goes far beyond anything I could have imagined in my wildest nightmares about the judicial system. That a man could be permitted to stand here in front of the court, whose sacred work he is sworn to protect, and spew lie after lie defies all notions of justice and fairness. Not just coloring or shading the truth, but debasing it, mocking it, abusing it callously and repeatedly. I am sickened by this display and I promise to take every appropriate measure to see to it that practitioners of this vile form of character assassination are removed from the system and put where they can do no more harm."

Now true silence really did capture the courtroom. An eerie silence, which rose like a physical presence and towered ominously over every man and woman in the room. For his part, Lang paused to make the most of the effect and to gather for his finish. It was Hickman who shattered the moment.

"May we approach, Your Honor?" Campbell waved him up.

At sidebar, Hickman said, "This is deeply disturbin' to me,

Your Honor. Mr. Lang is obviously tryin' to circumvent the clear rules of evidence by using a document, or should I say, pretendin' to use a document, that has not been placed into evidence and has no more business in this case than my aunt Millie's cookbook. I want an order directing Mr. Lang to cease and desist at once from referring to that notebook, reading from that notebook, or using that notebook in any way whatsoever."

Lang responded, "That's completely unwarranted, Your Honor. There is nothing improper about the notebook. And I have not been reading from it, although I assure you it says very much what I implied in my question."

To Lang's surprise, Campbell was obviously unsure on this point. He looked to Lang, then to Hickman, saying nothing.

Lang spoke up. "Your Honor, I will represent to the court that this notebook is authentic and substantiates the facts that I included in my last several questions to the witness. I plan to place it into evidence through a subsequent witness."

A light went on in Campbell's head. He scowled. "That's not good enough, counsel. I won't wait for a subsequent witness. If you've got a witness you can get it into evidence with, put him on and be done with it."

Lang's mind was working furiously. Unfortunately, by trying to strengthen his hand with the notebook, he had created a new problem. He needed to finish interrogating Lindstrom about the notebook before he put Haverstock on the stand. It was critical to nailing down the abject nature of Lindstrom's fraud. And he knew Campbell would never tolerate his calling Lindstrom to the stand for yet another time. A solution presented itself. "Your Honor, I would like to show Mr. Lindstrom the notebook to try to refresh his recollection."

Hickman was already shaking his head. "No way, Your Honor. Mr. Lang has already conferred far too much credence on this phantom notebook in front of the jury. Allowing him to show it to Mr. Lindstrom would only exacerbate the problem."

"I agree—" began the judge.

"How about this, then, Your Honor?" Lang sensed that his whole plan might unravel here, leaving him precious little to show for it. The possibility was too catastrophic even to consider. "Let me show Your Honor the notebook in chambers and if you are convinced that it may be genuine, then you can let me show it to the witness."

Hickman was shaking his head again but the judge was getting tired of this issue, and Lang's compromise apparently appealed to his sense of fairness. "I'll agree to—"

Hickman interrupted. "I want to examine it first. With my client."

"No way!" said Lang, nearly allowing his voice to be heard by the jury. "If Your Honor decides that the notebook is probably genuine, then Mr. Hickman should be allowed to see it. Until then, it's my attorney work product and cannot be disclosed."

The judge was decisive. "That's what I'm going to do. Go sit down."

When they had, the judge announced a fifteen-minute recess and disappeared into chambers with Lang's engineering log.

Fifteen minutes became thirty and Mr. Porterfield appeared to announce that the court would recess and resume at two-thirty. At three o'clock, court had still not resumed. Not that the talking heads of the broadcast media hadn't found ways to fill the airwaves with off-the-cuff analysis of the most remarkable day yet in this extraordinary trial. Finally, Mr. Porterfield summoned the attorneys into the judge's chambers.

Campbell stood in his shirtsleeves with his back to the door, looking out across the north lawn through the venetian blinds that covered his large window. His robe was on a hanger on a coat tree beside his desk. The lights were off and the late-afternoon gloom hung heavily over the room.

"Sit down, Counsel," he said, turning to face them and gesturing to the conference table. After the lawyers, all five of them, sat down, he continued. "I have reviewed this notebook." He spoke very slowly, deliberately, seeming to choose his words with uncharacteristic care. He paused, then, looking directly at Lang, said, "I am persuaded that it may well be authentic." His gaze bored in on Lang. "I'd like to know why you decided to withhold this crucial piece of evidence until your rebuttal case, young man."

Lang was silent for the moment. He knew he did not have to respond but decided that his stock with this judge was low enough as it was. "I'd prefer not to get into that, Your Honor. I can tell you that it was a strategic decision based upon factors over which I have no control."

Campbell, in a rare contemplative mood, nodded and pursed his lips. "I will allow you to show the document to the witness to attempt to refresh his recollection."

"Thank you, Your Honor," replied Lang.

But Hickman was not about to go down without a fight. "Your Honor," he said, "I must say that this decision leaves me at something of a disadvantage. An enormous one. As you point out, Mr. Lang has withheld what he feels is a critical piece of evidence, thereby shielding it from both the discovery process and the ordinary process of preparation. I would like a recess to examine the document thoroughly."

Campbell nodded but, before he could reply, Lang interjected, "You can't do that, Your Honor. This is impeachment, rebuttal evidence, and I'm entitled to have the witness examine it cold, without preparation."

"Now, Mr. Lang," replied the judge, "I said I would let him see it. I don't think—"

"This is completely unacceptable," shot back Lang. "The entire office of impeachment testimony is to test the credibility of a witness in the cauldron of the trial process, not to let his lawyer concoct an explanation for an exhibit. I'm entitled to have the jury observe how he responds to this document. It is absolute—"

Suddenly, contemplative Campbell was gone and combative, abusive Campbell was back. "That will be enough, Counsel. Mr. Hickman will get his recess and Mr. Lindstrom will have an opportunity to examine the document before we reconvene."

"This is bullshit, Judge, and you know it." Lang did nothing to mask his contempt for the ruling.

"You will treat this court with respect, my friend," fumed the judge, working up a fresh supply of saliva. "Or you will pay the consequences."

"I will treat this court with the respect that it and its rulings command, Your Honor. And this kind of one-sided, incompetent misreading of the rules of evidence commands no respect at all."

"You are out of line, Mr. Lang!" shouted the judge, as he hit the red button every federal judge has in his chambers.

"I'm sorry, Judge, but I'm trying my best to represent my client and you're screwing with the rules at every turn. Just give me a goddamned chance to try my case on a level playing field for once."

From the rear door, two deputy U.S. marshals burst into the room, weapons drawn, and assumed combat firing positions. The first one, a black man with a bodybuilder's physique rippling under his tight-fitting uniform, barked out, "What's the problem, Judge?"

Campbell was beginning to calm down. "Take Mr. Lang out of here right now, Deputy Charles. Tell the clerk that I have found him in contempt and have fined him one thousand dollars, payable to-morrow before the morning session begins." He tossed the note-book across the table to Hickman. "You have thirty minutes with the notebook, Counsel." With that, he rose and everyone was dismissed.

But Amy had a sudden thought. "Your Honor, if the court please. We have a copy of the notebook. Maybe the original shouldn't leave here just right now."

Judge Campbell turned and regarded her with a naked look of disgust. "Are you suggesting that Mr. Hickman is going to destroy or deface potential evidence after this court has already examined it?"

"Of course not, Your Honor," she replied, trying her best to sound smooth, although she was only conjuring up her words in the split second before she spoke them. "I, we, just wouldn't want Mr. Hickman to bear the burden of that responsibility unnecessarily."

Hickman responded, "I have no problem with the responsibility. As an officer of the court I am perfectly prepared to assume all the obligations that attend my taking custody of the document."

"That's good enough for me," said the judge, putting an end to their discussion.

Lang walked back into the courtroom between the two deputies. To Charles, he said, "Would you mind putting your gun away, Deputy? I don't want to look like a criminal on television." Charles eyed him suspiciously. "I have young kids at home," Lang added.

The deputy holstered his weapon. "I thought you guys liked to get cuffed around in these trials," he said.

"I am getting cuffed around, Deputy. Plenty."

Hickman went directly toward the main door of the court-room, gesturing to Lindstrom to join him. They went out, followed closely by Overbrook and Royster, across the hall and into the attorneys' conference room. They were ensconced there for the next forty minutes.

At last, Mr. Porterfield summoned everyone back into the courtroom. As he reached the counsel table, Hickman handed the notebook back to Amy. "All yours, Counsel," he said breezily.

Amy flipped the book open and was relieved beyond words to find that all of the critical pages were there and unmarked, as far as she could tell.

Lindstrom resumed the stand and the jury was brought back in. When they were again seated, the judge said, "Mr. Lang, you may proceed."

Lang approached Lindstrom with the notebook, well aware of what was at stake and how carefully he must proceed at this point. A document used for the limited purpose of refreshing a witness's recollection may not be shown to the jury or read from or quoted with attribution to the document. Quite simply, it does not exist unless and until it is established that the document does, indeed, refresh a witness's memory of something he has forgotten. "Mr. Lindstrom, you have testified at length that you have no recollection of Arrow Dynamics maintaining an engineering log, that you never saw such a log book, that you did not prepare it, that you made no entries into it, that you do not recall piloting the prototype on a flight during which you recognized a tendency of the aircraft to enter a spin, or advising that either the aircraft should be grounded or the tendency should be further investigated. Is that accurate?"

"Not in so many words," Lindstrom said disgustedly. "But, in general terms, that's accurate."

"All right. I'm going to show you a document, a spiral notebook made by the Mead Corporation on the cover of which—"

"Be careful, Counsel," cautioned the judge. "Let him look at it."

Lang nodded and handed the notebook to Lindstrom. "Very well, Your Honor. I hand you the document and ask you to examine it carefully to determine whether or not it refreshes your recollection of these things you have testified that you do not recall."

Lang smiled to himself. The answer, of course, hardly mattered. It was Lindstrom's reaction and the testimony of his final witness that would do what he wanted. He turned and walked slowly away from the witness, taking the time to study the jury. All eyes were riveted on Lindstrom. As he stood with his back to the witness, Rachel Cruz entered the room through the huge double door and he knew immediately that something was wrong. Her normal bronze coloring was completely washed out and she held her mouth in a tight, white line. She plainly had something to tell Lang but both of them knew this was not the time or the place. The drama of the moment vibrated in every cubic inch of the room.

Up on the stand, Lindstrom carefully turned each and every page of the fat notebook. He spent a full fifteen minutes silently reviewing the log. When he had finished, he asked, "What was your question, Mr. Lang?"

"Does the document refresh your recollection," repeated Lang.

"No," replied Lindstrom. "It doesn't. And it doesn't because it cannot. It is a fake, a fraud. An out-and-out phony document that isn't worth the paper you have wasted to fabricate it. It is but another outrageous attempt to bring me down at any cost. How you people can live with yourselves is beyond me."

"Thank you, Mr. Lindstrom," Lang said with a bright smile. "We will all remember your answer. I have nothing further."

As he returned to his chair, Hickman said, "I have no questions."

While the judge dismissed Lindstrom from the stand, Rachel came forward. If anything, she appeared even more upset than when Lang had first noticed her.

"Chris!" she said in a hoarse whisper.

Lang was alarmed. "Calm down, Rachel," he whispered back. "What is it?"

"It's Haverstock."

Lang's heart seized. "What about him?"

"He had some kind of engine trouble on the way down here."

"And?" Lang asked, rapidly losing all patience.

"His plane went down. It exploded just south of Lake Tahoe. The FAA picked it up from his flight plan and his signal."

"His transponder," offered Lang.

"Right, I guess. Anyway, they said he was killed instantly."

Lang was overwhelmed by a plunging, spinning sensation. He was quickly losing his bearings and was growing more light-headed by the moment. This can't be happening, he thought. This can't be real. In the distant background, he heard Campbell's voice looming. "Counsel?" he said. "Call your next witness or you will be deemed to have rested your case. Do you hear me?"

Lang fought to regain himself. This was a mortal wound, he realized, in many ways. The man was dead. Gone. Erased, incredibly, by the crash of a small plane. "I request a recess, Your Honor," he heard himself say, as if in a dream.

"Request denied," boomed Campbell, like cannon fire from a distant front. "Call your next witness, Counsel, or your rebuttal case is over."

Lang was at a complete loss. He had no recourse, but he desperately needed time to gather his thoughts, to determine if there was an escape route somewhere he could take to higher ground. It was not acceptable to have his case cut off now.

"Counsel," came the judge's voice again, like a bludgeon. Then it stopped. Lang swam up out of the chaos that his mind had become. Porterfield was at the judge's side, whispering to him. Now he was pointing to the far wall. Lang looked. It was the clock they were discussing. It was five minutes before five. The judge was speaking again. "The clerk correctly notes that it is past four-thirty so we will adjourn for the day. Reconvene tomorrow at nine o'clock sharp." He slammed his gavel and disappeared into his chambers, leaving a courtroom in disarray and a plaintiff's case in shambles. Lang looked across to the other counsel table and caught sight of Lindstrom and Hickman, conferring leisurely and smiling broadly.

Ro's parents had arrived in Los Angeles the previous weekend. Ruth Deyton, plainly alarmed at her daughter's despondency, had made what she called an executive decision. Ro had argued that the trip was not necessary, that she was fine, but secretly had welcomed their visit. In fact, their arrival three days ago had done a great deal to push back the heavy sadness brought on by Mark's sudden and senseless death. When her mother had come into her room this morning and suggested—or, more precisely, insisted—that Ro get packed and drive up to San Sebastian to see the end of the trial, it suddenly seemed like a perfectly terrific idea.

The traffic hadn't been too bad and she had made good time. She had decided to listen to her country-music CDs on the trip instead of cruising the dial of the radio as the stations' signals waxed and waned along the coast. As a result, she arrived at the Westgate Hotel at just after six o'clock completely unaware of the surprising developments in the trial.

Amy Quinn greeted her with a hug of genuine warmth at the door of the suite. It was immediately obvious to Ro that things were not going well here. For one thing, everyone, while being perfectly polite, seemed even more preoccupied than usual. For another, the papers she knew they all maintained with carefully structured organization seemed to be scattered and strewn about the room. But mostly, she could tell by looking at her ex-husband. He looked haggard and beaten. His eyes were sunken and his shoulders slumped as she had never seen them before.

"Ro!" he said with real feeling. He moved across the room and enclosed her in a powerful, almost desperate, embrace. He held her for several seconds.

"Are you okay?" he asked, finally letting go.

"Yeah," she said softly. "I really think I am." She looked around the room, at Clive and Graham, at Amy and John Carrick. "The question is, are you okay?"

Lang pushed the hair back out of his eyes and scowled. "If you overlook the fact that everything that could possibly go wrong has gone wrong, yeah, sure. We're okay." He briefly brought her up to date on the events of the day.

Ro was stunned. The string of tragic events swirling about her life and Chris's was almost too much to grasp.

"So," he concluded, "the bottom line is that we now have a very critical piece of evidence, a document that changes the face of the case, and we have no witness through whom to get it into evidence."

"That's not entirely fair, Chris," offered Carrick. To Ro, he explained, "We were just exploring several alternatives for putting this notebook into evidence."

Lang had been looking at Amy. "What's wrong, Amy?"

She shrugged. "I don't know. There's something here that isn't right."

Lang laughed ironically. "That's hardly an insight, kiddo. Just pick a topic."

Amy frowned and shook her head. "I don't know," she repeated. "Something's floating around here that we haven't focused on."

Lang shrugged. "I'll plead guilty to that one," he said. He offered Ro a drink, some food, and a seat. She accepted the first and last. "You're welcome to stay and hear this thing out, Ro. And you're more than welcome to jump in with any suggestions that might raise our *Titanic* before it comes to rest on the ocean floor."

The issue was obvious. They needed a witness as a vehicle to place the notebook into evidence. Lindstrom would be of no help, nor would any of the men from Arrow Dynamics. On the other side of the aisle, the only viable candidate appeared to be Carrick.

"I can testify that this is an engineering log. That the events it reflects are consistent, up to a point, with the known findings of the program. That it is consistent with the type of program we know they were performing—"

"It is *not* consistent, John," interrupted Lang. "That's the whole point. The very aspect of the log that makes it material evidence is that it is inconsistent with the final engineering report. Besides, John, this is a waste of effort. You cannot authenticate a document that you did not prepare or receive. I don't mean to sound harsh, but you are not legally competent to testify as to its origin, its mode or manner of preparation, its chain of custody. In short, your testimony would mean nothing."

Silence enveloped the room as they each grappled privately

with the problem. Rachel Cruz came in from her room down the hall to announce that Lindstrom had just denounced Lang on television.

Andrews expressed his disgust. "Unless we can think of a way to get that log book in front of the jury, I think we're going to be hearing a lot of bashing from that bastard."

In the next few hours ideas came slowly. Lang had fallen silent for a long time, virtually withdrawing from the discussion. Ro noticed that he had taken one of the exhibit binders from his litigation bag and was thoughtfully examining a document. "Rachel," he said, "you did all the input yourself when you created our first database, didn't you?"

She thought for a moment. "You mean the one from the documents they produced to us? Sure did. It took a lot of overtime, if you recall."

Ellerby interjected, with a laugh, "*I* recall. I paid for it."

The remark drew tired laughter from the others, all except Lang. He was obviously on the trail of a specific possibility. "This reference here, to the StormTree's acceleration rates, in the final engineering report. I don't recall any reference to those figures in any of the underlying documents, the flight cards and the memos. Do you, John?"

Carrick moved over to look at the document. After examining it, he said, "I don't recall any, either, but I can't swear to it."

Lang frowned. "That's the problem, isn't it?" Before Carrick could answer, Lang opened the notebook. Sure enough, there was a table there, hand-drawn, near the middle of the log book, that set forth the precise acceleration figures that were summarized in the final report. "See that?" Lang asked Carrick. "Where it says in the report, 'Acceleration rates per test data'?"

"I certainly do," Carrick agreed.

"Good. Look, Rachel. We need a search of the database you created. If, as I suspect, there is no reference to these figures anywhere else but in the final report and the engineering log, I believe I can put you on the stand—"

"Me?" came Rachel's surprised reply.

"Yes," said Lang. "You. And you can testify to that fact. That means we can argue, and I think persuasively, that the engineering log, which is the only documentation that can qualify as 'test data,' therefore becomes a part of the final engineering report by reference. That way, we can then get it into evidence as part of a document already identified and admitted into evidence."

"Can you do that?" asked Andrews.

Amy looked dubious. Lang shrugged. "I think so. Anyway, it's worth a try. Let's go to your computer, Rachel, and do the search."

They all trooped off to Rachel's room, where she keyed into her computer the appropriate search. The computer scanned every word and figure in every one of the more than fifteen thousand pages Rachel had loaded into the database looking for those rates. At the end of the search the screen announced, "Not found."

"Good!" exclaimed Lang. "Let's prepare you to take the stand, Rachel."

An hour and a half later, Lang went to his room, reasonably set to make another assault on the defendants in the morning. He had prepared Rachel well and had honed his "inclusion by reference" argument to as fine a point as he felt was possible. He was banking on the fact that the judge, despite his obvious dislike for Lang and his case, had said that the notebook "might well be" authentic. And, in spite of all that he had seen of this judge himself, he clung to the fact that, by reputation, he was a fair man.

As he was undressing, there was a knock at the door. It was Amy. He received her wearing only his pants. "What's up?" he asked.

"There's something you have to see." Lang was beyond exhaustion and her tone of voice put him immediately on edge.

"What?" he asked. She handed the notebook to him. "I've already seen this, Amy," he said, masking less than all of the irritation he was suddenly feeling.

She opened it to the page bearing their serial stamp number 15,767. "Look at this."

He looked not at the log book but at her. "What's your point, Amy?" he asked testily. He was tired and stressed to his physical limits.

"Look, Chris, I know you're tired. I wouldn't do this to you if I didn't think it was important. I want you to read it carefully. Again."

He eyed her for a moment, then looked at the page. "Okay," he said at last, deciding to play along, if only to move this conversation forward. "I see a page of the notebook which, like all the others, is unnumbered except for the control number we Bates-stamped on it when we got it. It is entirely handwritten, in Lindstrom's hand, according to Haverstock."

"A conclusion that our handwriting expert could neither confirm nor deny," she said. Before he could object, she shook her head and continued. "That's not my point, Chris. Just read it."

Disgustedly he obliged, going over the now-familiar technical description of the pilot's impression that he was about to spin the aircraft. "Feeling was that it would depart controlled flight to the left into a high AOA left-rotation mode with probable flat spin to ensue . . . Key Q: investigate further or withdraw?' " He looked up at her again. "So? This page proves our case for fraud against both the company and Lindstrom. What is your point?"

"Turn to the page before."

He was about to say something, but he bit back the words and did as she told him. He sighed heavily to underscore his irritation. She said nothing, although he could sense her own anger rising. "All right," he said. "This page, also handwritten, by a different author, says, 'Stall and Departures, March 8.' It appears to reflect four flights that day, made with the center of gravity, or 'cg,' set respectively at 114, 116, 118, and 120 centimeters." He looked up at her, almost defiantly. "Is there a point to this, Amy?"

"Look, Chris," she said, about to lose patience herself. "I need you to appreciate the full impact of my reasoning. It's important or I wouldn't do this. You know that."

There was a knock at the door.

"Come in," called Lang.

It was John Carrick. "What is it, Amy?" he asked.

"Just follow us through this, John," she replied. "This is the page before the critical one in the log."

Carrick moved to look at the notebook in Lang's hands. After a moment to get his bearings, he said, "Okay. What's the question?"

Lang continued his summary of the page. "Okay, page 15,766 reflects departure testing done the day before, where the Storm-Tree's center of gravity or fulcrum point was calculated to be 114 through 120 centimeters back from the recognized baseline, with all results being very good in terms of departure and spin resistance."

"Now flip to page 15,768," Amy said.

"The one after Lindstrom's flight?" asked Lang. She nodded. "This page is in the handwriting of the guy who wrote page 15,766, that's two pages back, and reads 'Stalls and Departures, March 10.' It describes results of test flights done at 121, 122, and 122.5 centimeters, each with increasingly poor stability."

"Read the last notation," she instructed.

" 'Stability is largely degraded aft of cg 121 . . . Aft cg for this configuration should be 120.5.' Okay." He looked at her expectantly.

"This means that the pilot who flew the plane on the eighth and on the tenth, same guy, moved through a progression of centers of gravity and determined that the aft cg should be no more than 120.5 centimeters, right?" asked Amy.

"That's right," replied Lang, unable to suppress a patronizing tone in his voice. "And that's what the final report says."

Amy turned to Carrick, who, brow furrowed, was still engrossed in the entries on page 15,768. "How do you square this, John?"

"I can't," he replied.

"Square what?" demanded Lang, fatigue and frustration overtaking him now at a gallop. "With what?"

"The sequence," explained Carrick, his eyes still focused on the handwriting before him. "I should have noticed this before. It isn't exactly obvious, of course, but I should have seen it. This isn't right, at all."

"Would you explain it to me?" asked Lang. "Because I'm reading the same thing you are and it makes perfect sense. They found out the plane would spin so they backed up the center of gravity to 120.5 centimeters so that it would mask the spin tendency it had just a couple of centimeters farther back. That's the fraud."

"Look," said Carrick, apparently ignoring Lang. "The flights on page 15,766 progress, as they should have, through forward cg's to aft cg's in order, as do the ones on page 15,768. The results of the flight on page 15,767 are not in the sequence."

Lang responded quickly. "So, Lindstrom forgot to record his cg the way the other guy did. It was probably 120 centimeters. Big deal."

"No," said Carrick. "Because, if Lindstrom had encountered what he reported there, no one in his right mind would have flown the aircraft at cg's aft of 120, certainly never at 122.5. The aircraft becomes dramatically more unstable in terms of departure and spin the farther aft you move the center of gravity. The pilot would have been in grave danger to fly at 120.5, much less 122.5."

"But, John, we're talking about one or two centimeters, here. With test pilots who have ice water in their veins. I don't see it."

"You're forgetting what a thin margin it was that cost Walt McCluskey his life down there in Winter Haven. An aft shift of one or two centimeters, after Lindstrom discovered and recorded the findings about flat spin tendency on page 15,767? No way. And

Arrow's test pilots were well known for their precision where their own safety was at stake."

"So, what are you saying, John? That they acted imprudently, they took a bad risk?"

"No, Chris. I'm saying something a hell of a lot more serious than that. I'm saying that despite a very clever and, I admit, convincing effort, there is reason to believe that this entry dated March ninth may not be genuine at all."

Before Lang could respond to this astounding statement, Amy stepped in. "Chris, I've done some checking here. This is a spiral eight-and-a-half by eleven-inch notebook made by Mead Corporation. It is sold with one hundred sheets of white, lined paper with a wire spiral spine. No more, no less. If you count the pages in this notebook, you'll find there are one hundred one." She flipped to the front. "The Bates number Rachel stamped on the first page is 15,673 and the last page 15,773. Exactly one hundred and one."

Lang looked closely at the first and last pages. Amy's point was beginning to take shape in his mind but he fought its implications with all his strength. "Yeah, and I suppose that Mead Corporation never made a mistake and put out a notebook with a page or two more or less than one hundred."

But Amy was relentless. "If you'll look closely, you'll see that the wire holding the book together has been slightly bent in a number of places."

"For Christ's sake, Amy," said Lang disgustedly. "The goddamned notebook was kicked around an airport hangar for four months. Just what are you two trying to do? Sabotage the whole fucking case? Whose side are you on, anyway?"

Amy looked as if she'd been slapped across the face but before she said anything, there was another knock at the door. This time it was Rachel. She nodded gravely to Amy.

Amy asked simply, "And?"

Rachel replied, "I just logged off with DataScan. On March ninth of that year, San Sebastian, California, reported 2.3 inches of rainfall in twenty-four hours and virtually nonstop thunder and lightning."

Lang felt his chest contract with the realization that the bedrock of his case against Lindstrom had just dissolved into the sea.

CHAPTER 34

"ARE YOU OKAY?" AMY ASKED SOFTLY.

Lang stared off into the dimness of his room, unaware, and apparently unconcerned, that the clock on his desk crept toward one A.M. The thunder of Amy's earlier, devastating words had long since rolled away into the distance, leaving him exhausted, physically, emotionally, and intellectually. A year's tireless effort, taxing his powers and talents to their limits, had disintegrated in a few stunning moments. Although he had fought ferociously against the evidence she had relentlessly laid out, in the end, there could be no doubt. The notebook, at least the part he had counted on, was "a fake, a fraud," as Lindstrom himself had pronounced it from the stand. Haverstock, the enigmatic answer to his prayers, had concocted a clever, diabolical plot that had come within a hair's breadth of success. Lang was still persuaded, of course, that, notebook or no notebook, Lindstrom had masterminded the fraud that had cost his client millions. Indeed, he was likewise convinced to a moral certainty that there was no more coincidence in Haverstock's fatal accident than there had been in Molly O'Keefe's change of heart. But proof of any of this—from Lindstrom's complicity in the original fraud to his involvement in the collapse of Lang's case—was a most elusive commodity, and clearly beyond his reach now, just hours before the case would go to the jury.

Patiently, Amy repeated her question. This time Lang responded as though in a heavy fog. "A little wrung-out," he said, his voice cracking with exhaustion.

"What are you going to do?" she asked, conspicuously studying his red, swollen eyes and the deep lines that framed them.

Lang smiled ironically. "How long have you known me? Six years or so?"

"More like seven plus, I'd guess."

"Ever know me *not* to know what I'm going to do?" he asked.

"Never," Amy replied.

"Well, that string ends tonight. I have no idea what to do or where to turn. And, as the minutes tick by, I find that I'm caring about it a lot less, as well."

Amy didn't like to see her mentor and friend, a master of control and decisiveness, hopelessly at sea. "You're tired. You'll rally in the morning." She tried her best to sound convincing.

"I don't think so. To where? For what?" There was a vaguely pathetic quality to his words and his inflection that was jarringly out of character. Amy's sense of uneasiness was growing.

"Look, Chris. The notebook's a fake. Correction: Page 15,767 is a fake and it contaminates the rest of the notebook as evidence. But that doesn't mean Lindstrom didn't do what you've told the jury he did, or that he's any less a fraud. You've lost the capstone to your case but not the case itself."

He laughed sarcastically. "What trial have you been watching?" he challenged. But the hint of fire in his words evaporated immediately. "For all our effort, we've barely laid a glove on him, in terms of hard evidence. All we've managed—all *I've* managed—to do is lay down the groundwork for the notebook, for Haverstock's testimony. Without that testimony, and without the notebook, we have smoke and shadows, innuendo and suggestion, but not a good case, let alone the airtight, irrefutable juggernaut we would need to get a hometown jury to turn on its favorite son. As if we could ever have put together that much evidence." He added the last with a bitter edge. "What can we do? What can we really say? That there is evidence to suggest that the innocuous cover letter for the engineering report *may* have been prepared on a computer in his home? Jesus, Amy, even if we turned the jury around, I don't think we have enough evidence to hold on to a fraud verdict on appeal." He stopped and thought about what he was saying. Amy waited. After a long pause, he continued, "I wonder if the better tactic at this point might not be to drop the case against Lindstrom and avoid infecting the rest of the case with its deficiencies."

While Amy could hear her own words of many months ago echo now in the tired voice of her colleague, it brought no sense of vindication. The fact was that she too had become convinced of Lindstrom's culpability over the course of the trial. "That would be a mistake, and you know it," she pronounced evenly, sure enough in this judgment, somehow, to counsel her teacher. "When Campbell tells the jury that you've done that, they'll lose all confidence in you and it will color the way they look at the rest of the evidence. It will be the end. And *that* would be the greater disservice to the clients."

Lang was silent. It was the kind of advice he had received in times past from his own mentor. How I wish I could talk to you right now, Max, he thought. Suddenly, he felt alone and disconnected, standing, in his mind, on a lush green hill in that vast, sprawling cemetery where he had said good-bye. He shook himself back to the present, back to the difficult challenge he now faced. "You're right," he said. "I guess we'd do better to soft-pedal the case against Lindstrom in the closing argument, put most of our eggs into the case against the company."

Amy nodded and got up. "I need some sleep and you look pretty tired yourself." She headed for the door.

"Thanks, Amy," he said. "I know you're not happy to be the one who took the air out of the case, but I'm proud of you. You're one smart lawyer. And I admire your integrity."

She turned and looked at him for a moment. "Thanks, Chris. That really means a lot. I didn't think I had any choice once I started to figure that notebook out. I guess I could have just stopped the process at some point."

"No, you couldn't have. Cases will always come and go. But you have to live with yourself tomorrow, no matter what."

She stood there for a long time, full of things to say but unable to select the one worthiest of the moment. Finally, the moment was lost and she said only, "Speaking of tomorrow, it already *is* tomorrow. See you at daylight." With that, she left.

Seamus Callahan was numb. From the cold, from the fog, from the hour, from the news. An icy rain fell, whipped occasionally by the wind gusting off the sea, a fitting complement to the bleakness of his mood. As he pulled up to the front of the farmhouse, the flashing yellow lights atop two of the three constabulary units there winked out a steady, if unsynchronized, signal of distress and danger, amber smudges of despair through the mist. A sergeant standing guard on the front steps, a familiar face, jerked his thumb over his head to the rear, in mute communication of where the constable could locate the investigating officers.

Seamus found them at the rail along the promontory, strung along down the wood stairs and among the rocks below. Another sergeant, also familiar, saw Seamus approaching and went to meet him.

"Seamus," he said in the easy brogue of western Clare. "You knew the woman, eh?"

"Aye, Colm," replied Seamus, mechanically extending his hand to the other. "That I did."

"It's a homicide, Seamus," said the sergeant grimly. "Bleedin' Shamrock, if you ask me."

Seamus nodded, moving past the man to the stairs. He saw other familiar faces as people moved to greet the constable. "Mornin', McGill," he said to the senior man at the top of the steps. "What is it you found?"

"Her neck was broke, Seamus," replied the huge inspector. "She's Molly O'Keefe all right, but she's spent some time in the sea."

Seamus nodded, swallowed hard, and peered down to the rocks below. He drew a deep breath to steel himself for what he would see there and, summoning all the strength that a lifetime in the business of crime and tragedy could impart, picked his way down the steps to where the county medical man knelt over a body bag.

Lang did not sleep. He played with notes from a closing argument that had suddenly lost its drama, its spirit, but put them aside, vaguely confident that the argument would come to him as he made it. On television, overnight news coverage focused on two stories, the trial, of course, and the Republican National Convention that gave it context. It seemed inconceivable to him that nearly the entire summer had slipped away while the trial had plodded along and that the convention delegates were already assembling in Kansas City.

At four o'clock—seven in the East—the law professors of public radio made their first appearance of the day. Lang listened, oddly mesmerized by the absurdity of hearing about his "plan of attack" when he had yet to formulate one. It must be nice, he thought as he listened to these highly respected lawyers turned journalists, to live in a world where you didn't have to meet the rigors of the rules of evidence to make your case.

"The stage is set," Professor Holtzman intoned pompously. "Christopher Lang has left a nation dangling, his anticipated kill shot hidden until this morning. He has a notebook that, he has implied, will blow a hole right through the middle of Russell Lindstrom's stonewall defense. The question, Professor Larkin, is who is he going to put on the stand to drive this stake through the heart of his nemesis?"

"Allen, I sense doubt in your words, as always," replied Larkin amiably. "If there's one thing we have learned from this trial it is that we underestimate Mr. Lang at our own risk."

Right, thought Lang bitterly as he flicked off the radio. The image of an aircraft, spinning like a "bloody seed pod" toward the hard and unforgiving earth, suddenly flashed through his mind. The parallel between the tragically entangled Walt McCluskey, furiously fighting a losing battle to remove the canopy of the StormTree, and now Lang himself, hopelessly unable to crack Lindstrom's well-crafted defenses, was inescapable. But as soon as it occurred to him, he was ashamed to have drawn the unworthy comparison. At least I'll walk away from my disaster, he thought.

His thoughts were interrupted by a knock at the door. It was Amy. She was in her robe and she was crying. "It's Seamus," she said, holding up the cordless phone. "Molly O'Keefe's been murdered."

Just outside of Washington, D.C., in the early-morning light that leaked through his drawn shutters, Jared Piersall finished packing. He was surrounded by tantalizing brochures and pamphlets trumpeting the soaring beauty of the lush mountain villages of the Berner Alps, a vacation destination he had often promised himself but had never had the time to visit. The plan—*his* plan—had unraveled spectacularly and his failure to achieve his sworn objective would soon be absolute. Knowing as he did the inevitable resolution of the entire affair, he had no desire to sit around and watch it happen. At least he had the breeding to know how to manage such a colossal fall from grace. He licked the envelope Susan would find upon her return from British Columbia and took his revolver from the cabinet. He placed it carefully into its specially made lead-lined case, slid in a small box of ammunition, and tossed the package into the suitcase, where it landed next to the gilt-framed picture of Robert Piersall in his uniform. He proceeded to complete the balance of his packing in workmanlike fashion, all the while imagining the overpowering beauty of the Swiss Alps in the late summer.

Ro Lang had slept poorly again. Her life had seen an astonishing increase in stress and sadness lately, and she was feeling the strain. Thus, it was all the more surprising that, as the first light of the new day beckoned beyond the window, she found herself preoccupied with her former husband's professional plight. It was ironic, to put it mildly, that she felt so keenly his sense of impending failure when it was his unbroken and unbreakable string of successes that she blamed for the disintegration of their marriage. But there was something about all of this that made sense to her, in its own strange way. It was as if the double tragedies of Max Devereaux's death and Mark Fassero's accident had exposed in her a need she never suspected existed. A need, it turned out, that was paradoxically being filled consistently by the man she had decided she couldn't live with a few short years ago. Just as a couple can grow apart as a consequence of each developing and evolving, it occurred to her that two people might conceivably realign their lives by evolving and developing separately. She shook her head at so ponderous a thought, so early in the morning, and turned her attention to the more prosaic business of getting dressed. She dreaded her return to the courtroom and its promise of certain defeat for Chris, but knew she had to go there just the same.

Judge Campbell was thirty minutes late taking the bench, a fact that only served to heighten the sense of anticipation among the legion of journalists piled into the courtroom and overflowing into the television viewing room. One of the network anchors, opening his coverage over a pan shot of the large crowd gathering around the federal courthouse, summed up the prevailing mood with only modest exaggeration: "The nation is holding its breath this morning," he intoned, in the reverent tenor usually reserved for truly historic moments. "In the balance hangs the culpability of a man, yes, but the fate of a candidate and maybe the future of a nation, as well." If all that was true, Chris Lang, looking exhausted and well past his age, could at least be counted among those for whom breathing was coming hard. The next move was his and anyone who even casually followed the trial knew that his next move was to put a witness on the stand whose testimony would bring Lindstrom down with the mysterious notebook.

"Proceed," growled Campbell, in Lang's general direction.

Lang rose. The silence in the room was unprecedented. "Plaintiff rests." The words, so simple, so quiet, so clear, and so unexpected, ignited a firestorm in the courtroom. None of the numerous disruptions that had preceded it in the trial could vaguely compare. Journalists leaped over one another to get outside the courtroom where they could talk to their editors on cellular phones. Secret Service agents wheeled into position around the man who suddenly seemed more a presidential candidate than a defendant. U.S. marshals appeared at every door, ready for any form of civil insurrection. Lang, for his part, simply sat down and let the mayhem wash over him. From his chair he had an unrestricted view of Lindstrom. The man was serenity itself. It was as if he were sealed in a protective shell, impervious to all outside forces. And he exuded unabashed confidence. Of course, from where Lang sat, he had every reason to be confident. Just as the thought formed in Lang's head, Lindstrom locked eyes with him and favored him with the most unnerving, penetrating smile Lang had ever seen. It literally raised the hackles on his neck.

Up on the bench, the surly old man in the black robe was beating his gavel arm into exhaustion, bellowing something inaudible as the melee raged unabated. Minutes went by, the noise and confusion far more reminiscent of the floor of a political convention than the halls of justice. At length, the commotion appeared to die down, owing more to spending its own energy than any effect the gavel might have had. The judge eyed Lang contemptuously but Lang was too exhausted to care. Instead, he sat motionless, floating on the last echoes of the chaos he had unleashed. It occurred to him that he hadn't even bothered to watch the jury. He looked their way now, but could see nothing beyond eight hopelessly confused faces.

By now, Campbell had put down the gavel, his malevolent gaze still fixed on Lang. Lang found this oddly disconcerting but, before he could quite figure out why, the judge said, "At this time, the court will entertain a motion by the defense for a directed verdict in favor of the defendant Mr. Lindstrom and against the plaintiff on all counts of the complaint." The bedlam that had died out only moments earlier returned like a tidal wave. Lang had difficulty comprehending what was happening. The spinning sensation he had experienced had him in its grip. A *directed verdict*? A preemptive decision by the judge to take the entire case against Lindstrom away from the jury, to dismiss the case and thus wipe clean the six weeks of testimony and evidence, denying Lang and his client any chance to see if the jury might agree with what Lang had argued day in and day out? And without the defense even making a motion?

Lang, still fighting to regain his bearings, became aware that Hickman was on his feet, trying to shout over the pandemonium that had once again erupted throughout the vast, unruly court-room. ". . . so move, Your Honor," Lang heard him say. "On the grounds and for the reasons previously argued in support of defendant's motion for nonsuit."

Lang was on his feet, shouting, as well. "This is an outrage, Your Honor! An outrage! There has been no motion made by the defense. A directed verdict cannot be entered by the court on its own motion, Your Honor!"

Somehow, still banging the gavel, the judge heard him. "The motion has now been duly made, Counsel," he bellowed back at Lang. "And I'm granting it!" To the jury, he said, shouting now to be heard at all, "The jury will disregard any and all claims against Mr. Lindstrom. They are dismissed and are no longer part of this case."

"You can't do that in front of the jury, for God's sake!" shouted Lang, nearly blinded by the fury sweeping through him. The strain of six weeks of nerve-racking, unrelenting pressure reached an unbearable crescendo, a physical, palpable presence within him. He was nearly insane with rage at the injustice, the arbitrariness of it all. "This is a travesty, goddammit!" he bellowed, easily surpassing the loudest outbursts of the cantankerous old man on the bench. "And you know it, you son of a bitch! You're deciding the case on your own politics, your own agenda, you incompetent bastard!"

Campbell sputtered and spat, equally furious. "I've had enough! You are in contempt of this court, sir, and you are going to jail!" To the confused and nervous marshals, he shouted, "Put this lawyer in irons, Marshal! And take him to the lockup!"

Suddenly, Lang found himself in the powerful grasp of two huge deputies. He recognized Deputy Charles. Before he could speak, Charles said softly into his ear, "Just take it easy, Mr. Lang. I'm not going to cuff you and I'm not going to hurt you, but we're going to take you out the far door right quick. Understand?"

He did, and he didn't, but it made no difference. As he was hustled away, he caught Amy's face, ashen and stunned. I guess she'll have to give the closing argument, Lang thought distantly.

And then, just like that, he was out of the courtroom, through a side door and in a heavily padded elevator. The grip of the two deputies relaxed as the doors slid closed. Lang reached out to touch the padding lightly.

"It's the freight elevator, Mr. Lang," the marshal explained with a smile. "Although I guess it would protect nutcase lawyers, too, if it came to that."

Charles's partner laughed, but Lang was past humor, past irony, and his mind was miles away. Snipers, he thought bitterly. They've picked off my case, my witnesses, like snipers. Somewhere up above, the courtroom was either under control or it wasn't and Amy was about to make her closing argument—with absolutely no preparation—or she wasn't. Lang thought hard but couldn't recall a time when he had had less idea what was going on or how to exert control over it.

The federal government did not maintain a jail at San Sebastian. Instead, in the basement of the courthouse, in what was once a storage cellar from its days as the Hotel Sierra Madre, there was a small, secure room that could be bolted from the outside. The concrete floor of the room had been covered with white asphalt tile. There were two straight-backed chairs, a small table with a black telephone on it, and a cot, all in government-issue pine wood and maroon Naugahyde. Into this room, Deputy Marshal Lincoln Charles led Christopher Lang.

"This is our detention area," Charles explained, gesturing to Lang to sit down. "Believe it or not, we've had to use it on numerous occasions since Judge Campbell was assigned here." He smiled. When Lang failed to return the smile, he shrugged. "You'll be all right in here, Mr. Lang. But I am going to have to secure the door. You can reach me or Deputy Korchek on this phone here."

Lang's mind was slowly coming out of its free fall. "Look, Deputy, I know you're just doing your job but I have to get out of here. I have a trial to—"

Charles waved him off. "No, sir, Mr. Lang. I'm afraid, trial or no trial, you're not going anywhere until the judge gives the order."

Lang's anger flashed again. "Look, goddammit—"

Charles took a step toward him and loomed menacingly in his face. "Knock it off, now, Mr. Lang. You're here until a court order says otherwise." His face softened. "Look, Mr. Lang. Your associate is a sharp lady. She's probably already called the ninth circuit to petition for your release. You'll be out of here anytime now." He turned to Korchek, who had been standing outside the door. "What are we talking about, here, Wally? Two hours?"

The big blond man stepped into the room. He frowned and shook his head. "Forty-five minutes, tops. You gotta figure that Gallagher's watching this trial just like the rest of the country. I figure he's already prepared a ruling and is waiting for the call."

Charles turned back to Lang, smiling. "That's a good point. The way it usually works is that somebody in the lawyer's office calls the ninth circuit and makes a petition, over the phone, for a writ dissolving the judge's contempt order. The circuit has assigned Judge Gallagher to this courthouse for all emergency appeals and writs, so the call gets routed to him. They just tell him what happened—you pretty much just have to say Judge Campbell's name in the same sentence with contempt and he grants the order overturning the judge—and then his clerk calls Mr. Porterfield and Porterfield calls the deputy at the door."

Lang sat quietly, taking in this remarkable picture of federal justice in latter-day America.

"But, I'll tell you what," Charles continued, holding up an index finger and walking out of the room. "You're at the door, Deputy Korchek," he called back over his shoulder, apparently discharging some arcane military protocol. In a minute, he returned with a small television set. He connected its antenna to a cable outlet on the wall and flipped it on. "Your tax dollars at work," he explained breezily, as the tiny black-and-white picture took shape. It was the courtroom and Amy was standing before the jury.

". . . a clear and unambiguous requirement," she was saying in her strongest, clearest voice, "that the very detailed testing regimen known as the Mil Spec be performed and satisfied in order for the contract to be satisfied by Arrow Dynamics. It was not. And the defendants have admitted as much right here on the stand."

Lang smiled wanly. Despite the surreal state of affairs in which he now found himself, he was still able to appreciate the solid professionalism and undeniable courage of his protégé. Here she was, gamely delivering the closing argument of a massive, notorious trial that she herself had not tried, and she was doing one hell of a job. And she kept it up, methodically hitting all of the points that comprised Pegasus's contract case against Arrow Dynamics. Lang had no choice but to surrender himself to the feeling of helplessness that had recently become his constant companion, and watch. Ten minutes later, there was a sharp knock at the door and Deputy Charles returned, smiling broadly.

He read from a fax he held in his hand. " 'By order of the United States Circuit Court of Appeals for the Ninth Circuit, the Honorable Rory Gallagher sitting by designation, the petition for writ of mandate by Oliver Brace dissolving the order of contempt entered this date by District Judge Schuyler Campbell against Christopher S. Lang is granted and the contempt order is dissolved forthwith.' You can go."

Lang grabbed his jacket. "Thanks," he said softly.

From out in the hallway came Deputy Korchek's powerful baritone voice. "Jesus Christ, Linc! Put on Channel 37!"

Charles did so and he and Lang were immediately treated to a bizarre scene. In a small screen inset in the upper right-hand corner of the muted live feed of Amy Quinn's argument in the courtroom was CableStar's best-known face, Milo Rich, standing on the lawn outside the courthouse.

"—an exclusive interview, given to us under conditions specified by Mr. Lang," he was saying. "Those conditions included the following: that we would tape the interview right then and there, in the parking garage of the Westgate Hotel, at five-fifteen this morning; that we would air the interview, if we chose to do so, as it was taped, complete and unedited; that we would broadcast it no earlier than ten o'clock this morning California time; and that we would make it clear that no fee of any kind was paid for the interview. First, then, the videotape provided to me by Mr. Lang, tape that was shot last October in Winter Haven, Florida, which depicts the fatal crash of the prototype aircraft known as the StormTree. We urge viewer discretion since the video, particularly the end, is very graphic."

"I've already seen this, Deputy," Lang said with a smile. He patted the big man on the shoulder and walked through the door, leaving behind two thoroughly puzzled deputies.

Television sets across the country were switching to CableStar and the unprecedented report by Milo Rich. What they saw was a sleek, futuristic airplane, seen from both a chase plane and the ground, being run methodically through the high-angle-of-attack regime. What they heard in the next few minutes literally captured a nation with its drama and its spectacular, tragic conclusion. As Lang walked down the long, sterile corridor, past several small offices in the bowels of the courthouse, he heard bits and pieces of a familiar sound track.

"Pitchbuck is a constant value," he heard Walt McCluskey's voice say. "Uncrossing controls restores dynamic stability. There was no departure from controlled flight, although I have several loose fillings in my mouth.''

By the time Lang reached the elevator, he heard McCluskey's voice, eerily calm and composed, say, "Oh, oh. The son of a bitch is into a flat spin.''

As he exited the elevator, he saw a large cluster of people massed on the lawn in front of the building, every eye turned toward the oversized CableStar monitor on which the video was playing. The crowd was so quiet, Lang could hear McCluskey say, ''Engine's quit. Power's gone.''

The scene was being repeated all across the country, everywhere the trial had captivated a nation on the eve of its political season for the better part of the summer. In Kansas City, in front of an enormous Republican-party hospitality tent across the mall from the Kemper Arena, where the start of the convention was only hours away, an even larger throng had collected to watch the drama unfold. Several thousand delegates and political correspondents stood around in clusters, coffee cups and soda cans clenched in their hands, observing the StormTree as it drifted helplessly toward the earth to the accompaniment of Walt McCluskey's bone-chilling assessment of the moments leading to his own death. "Goddamn! It's jammed all right. The canopy is one hundred percent torqued shut." Then, the desperate grunts of the pilot's efforts to open the canopy echoed out over the stunned crowd. Finally, on the screen, there were the last, silent moments of the StormTree's spin, and then the explosion and fireball of its impact onto the green hills of central Florida. The crowd, shocked and dazed, let out a collective gasp.

Milo Rich reappeared on the screen. "That was the videotape of the spin of the StormTree prototype flown by retired Air Force test pilot Walter McCluskey, who was killed in the crash,'' he reported. "It is the tape that Judge Campbell excluded from the trial because, in his words, its potential for prejudice and confusion outweighed its probative value. Our agreement with attorney Christopher Lang requires us next to show the actual interview with him early this morning. Remember, the stipulation was that the interview was to be aired without editing. As a result, you will note a poorer quality of tape than you would expect from one of our reports.''

The screen switched settings to the parking garage of the Westgate. Rich again was on-camera. "Good morning,'' he said, looking remarkably alert and well-groomed considering the hour and the short notice he had had for the meeting. "It is just after five o'clock in the morning in San Sebastian, California, on July twenty-fifth. Less than an hour ago I was contacted by Christopher Lang, the attorney for Pegasus Technologies in its fraud and breach-of-contract case against presidential candidate Russell Lindstrom, and asked if we wanted the opportunity to talk to him. We have agreed, as you have already been told, subject to specified conditions.

"Later this morning, Mr. Lang will wrap up his case and deliver his closing argument. The case is then expected to go to the jury. Mr. Lang," he continued, turning to face Lang. "Let me begin by asking you why you have decided to break your self-imposed media silence, a silence you have maintained throughout the trial, and grant an interview at this time."

Lang appeared on-camera, standing opposite the reporter, next to one of the vans he had rented for the trial. In the dimness of the Westgate parking garage, the television lighting, harsh and uneven, exaggerated the lines of fatigue undeniably etched across his face. "I have grave doubts about the outcome of the trial, Mr. Rich," he replied. "Although I am convinced that my client's claims are valid and the defendants—each and every one of them—are liable for everything with which we have charged them." He was tired and drawn but spoke in a strong, clear voice. "As important as this case is, however, I have come to believe that there are far larger issues involved here that compel me to disclose things I know but that I have been prevented from putting before the jury. The fact of the matter is that the bulk of the evidence I had against Russell Lindstrom for fraud has been systematically excluded by the calculated actions of the defense, the rulings of the court, and, for want of a better term, acts of God. The tape you have just seen, the tape that I was not permitted to show the jury, proves, in fact, that the Storm-Tree had a dangerous tendency to spin and, worse, a lethal resistance to recovery. But that's only part of the picture."

The men and women in and around the hospitality tent outside the convention hall remained largely quiet, still very much engrossed in the words and pictures coming from the huge television sets before them.

Meanwhile, Rich stepped into the silence created by Lang's pause. "Why are you revealing these things now, Mr. Lang?" Despite the irresistible plum Lang had given him by handing him the exclusive, he remained skeptical. "Aren't you contaminating the trial process while it is still in progress?"

"No, I'm not," he replied evenly. "As you know, the court has strictly enjoined the jury every day of the trial that it may not watch television and, in fact, the jurors are sequestered here under constant observation in an environment where they have no access to media coverage. Besides, I have taken the additional precaution of securing your agreement to withhold this tape from broadcast until ten o'clock this morning, when we know that the jury will be fully occupied in the courtroom."

"But aren't you concerned about what action the court may take against you for disclosing evidence that it excluded from the case?"

"Not at all," Lang answered. "The court's ruling, after all, was limited to what evidence may be used in the trial. It did not purport to dictate how the information might otherwise be used and, as you know, the First Amendment would make such an order unconstitutional if it had."

Rich appeared satisfied for the moment. "But you say there is more to the 'picture'?"

"Yes, there is," he replied, fatigue held at bay for the moment. "There is a woman from Ireland, whose name is Molly O'Keefe, who was Nigel Daultry's companion of several years and who was present when Daultry and Russell Lindstrom met. She was prepared to testify that they met on more than a half dozen occasions, that Lindstrom wrote the contract he has testified under oath he had never read before the lawsuit was filed, and that the whole idea for the plane was Lindstrom's. She was also prepared to testify that Nigel Daultry told Lindstrom he would not sign the contract if Lindstrom hadn't personally assured him that the danger of an unintended spin by an amateur pilot would be eliminated by the requirement that the aircraft be tested under Military Specification 92121. She agreed to come here and testify—she picked up her airline tickets—but she never got here. The local police found her body in the ocean near her home this morning."

A collective gasp rose up from the crowd of politicos and reporters in and around the hospitality tent, a scene that was being repeated in thousands of locations all across the country.

On the videotape, Lang continued. "But there's even more. There was another witness, a man named Will Haverstock, who used to work for Russell Lindstrom at Arrow Dynamics. He had in his possession a notebook that he claims was the engineering log of the StormTree project that the Arrow Dynamics people testified was not maintained. For the most part, it appeared to be authentic.

Some parts were questionable, but most of it was consistent with the fact that the fatal defect of the aircraft was concealed. I can't say if it was authentic, of course, since I wasn't there when it was prepared. But it would have been a close enough call to warrant its being put into evidence and subjected to the defense's efforts to show how or why it was not genuine. But it never came to that. On the way to testify in this trial, Mr. Haverstock's plane mysteriously developed engine trouble and crashed, killing him immediately. Will Haverstock, an aircraft mechanic of unchallenged credentials with thousands of hours of flight time, developed engine problems and crashed.

"And there's one thing more. After I took Russell Lindstrom's deposition in Texas earlier this year, he came to my hotel and first tried to bribe me with an offer of a position with the Justice Department if I dropped the case against him and, when that didn't work, he threatened to damage my career."

He paused again, this time drawing a deep breath. "Yes, I'm reconciled to the fact that Mr. Lindstrom has outmaneuvered me in the trial of this case. Most of the hard, substantial evidence I had against him has turned into vapor just when I needed it. The circumstances are more than suspicious. I confess that I don't *have* all the answers. But I feel strongly that, whatever may be the outcome of the trial, where rigorous rules of evidence quite properly control the deliberations of the jury, there is, in a sense, a larger, more important jury deliberating over larger, more important issues in a forum where those strict rules do not and should not apply. Since I am uniquely situated to have access to information that may be relevant to these other deliberations, I felt an obligation to put them before that jury and let it decide."

But Rich was obviously disturbed with the picture Lang was painting, a picture jarringly out of phase with his own long-held views. "Aren't you concerned that the public will see you as a sore loser striking out in a naked attempt to extract vengeance?"

"I have no control over what people may choose to think or believe. That is certainly a possibility, I grant you. I will, however, make available all the information I have on Molly O'Keefe and her death, on Mr. Lindstrom's meeting with me in Freeport, Texas, on Mr. Haverstock and his engineering log—both that which is credible and that which is questionable—and on his plane crash, and let those who are interested in these matters decide. Whatever they choose to believe at that point will be fine with me. I have already reached my conclusions."

The tape of the interview ended and Milo Rich came back on the screen. The savvy journalist paused for a moment, allowing its impact to settle in while he tried vainly to reconcile Lang's revelations with his own image of the statesman Russell Lindstrom. "Attorney Chris Lang," he intoned at last, suffusing the words with the historic gravity he ordinarily reserved for documentary pieces. "It would now appear that no matter how this trial comes out, Lang has raised grave questions about the character of one of America's latter-day icons, and his fitness to hold national office."

By the time Rich's benediction ended, Lang had slipped into the back row of the courtroom to listen to the conclusion of Amy Quinn's summation, and the delegates in Kansas City had begun to digest the massive dose of doubt just administered to them.

EPILOGUE

THE THIRD-FLOOR ROOM AT THE GRAND MANAN INN was very much as Ro had remembered it: rich floral wallpaper framed with crisp, white woodwork, polished hardwood floors strewn with downy throw rugs, a cozy little fireplace flickering away in the corner, and a cherry canopy bed high enough to require a step stool. Crossing to the window overlooking the broad lawn and the Bay of Fundy beyond, she was filled with a warm sense of well-being. Yes, she thought, this was a special place from a special time and it had been a good idea to come back. No promises were made, of course, when, bruised and battered by the aftermath of the trial, Chris had suggested a return trip to the far side of Grand Manan Island. But she had readily agreed. Naturally, there were a lot of unanswered questions and they were both being very cautious about feeling their way along untested ground. A great deal needed to be sorted out between them. And yet. . . .

Down on the lawn, she spotted Andrea and Jennifer, sitting on a white wooden bench, engrossed in a quiet conversation. Below, she saw Jack, pants rolled up to his knees as he waded in the cold, clear, gently lapping waters of the bay, fully engrossed in filling his clam bucket with the best and biggest ones he could find. A few yards past him was his father, his own pants legs rolled, doing the very same thing.

As she watched Chris and Jack pick their way along the rugged beach, she reflected on what it was that had emerged in her former husband that made her look upon him differently. Certainly, he was older, and apparently wiser. But that wasn't it. It was his vulnerability, she realized, his unexpected susceptibility to the ferocious forces that seemed to attack him from all sides. From the angry criticism of his handling of the trial among many lawyers—including some in his own firm—to the threats of life-long litigation from Gentry Hickman for sabotaging Lindstrom's presidential aspirations, to the scathing invective he had drawn from Judge Campbell in the press, he was a man under siege, a man suddenly, and, she felt, unfairly, broken loose from his moorings. And yet, it was more than simple vulnerability. He was tough and he had remained tough, a trait that seemed to come as easily to him now, under fire, as it had when the world had been his willing ally. The man on the hill at Max's funeral and the man in her room the morning after she learned of Mark's tragic accident was no more or less than a good man, she had decided, and one worth reconsidering.

On the beach below Ro's window, the water was cold. Lang's ankles, visible through the crystal-clear liquid, were turning blue. Although his bucket was less than half-filled, he called out to Jack, "Take a break, Ace. My feet are freezing off."

Jack agreed, thinking better of protesting his father's call. The truth was he had lost feeling in his feet a good ten minutes ago.

Lang was disengaged, if not quite relaxed, for the first time in many months. The fax from Amy confirming her research that California law protected him from Hickman's threatened suit was reassuring but ultimately unnecessary. Despite the risk of retribution from Lindstrom—and Lang had no doubt that the man was capable of far worse than a mere lawsuit—he was at peace with what he had done and past rethinking his judgment. The fact that the jury had given Pegasus Technologies three and a half million dollars more than they had asked for against Arrow Dynamics for the breach of the contract had been rewarding but oddly anticlimactic. He was resigned to the fact that his enduring sense of the trial would not be the verdict but the loss of three lives.

While Lang and his son were drying off at the water's edge, a green Blackhawk helicopter, barely thirty feet off the water, raced across the narrow stretch of the Atlantic Ocean that separated the mainland from the near side of the tiny island. On board, three large men in dark blue suits and dark glasses, sidearms in shoulder harnesses, silently scanned the sea as the green land mass grew larger on the horizon. In a moment, the chopper swung around the north end of the island and rocketed over the stately slate roof of the inn, rattling its windows and bending its pine trees, swooping down directly above Ro's head towards the beach. It set down on the lawn midway between the bench where the girls were sitting and the water line where Lang and Jack stood. Fear seized Ro as she helplessly watched the sleek military helicopter from the third-floor window. She cried out an unnecessary warning but it was lost in the thunder of the helicopter's rotors.

Instantly, the three men bounded out of the Blackhawk and headed for Lang. Suddenly the image of Lindstrom's burly bodyguards down in Texas flashed in his mind. In an instinctive act of defense he stepped forward, positioning himself between Jack and the oncoming men. He was acutely aware that his other two children were helplessly exposed to whatever threat was about to materialize.

One of the men, reaching inside his jacket, said, "Are you Christopher Lang?"

"Yes," Lang replied. "Who wants to know?"

"United States Marshal John Philipides, Mr. Lang," said the man, showing a shield. "By authority of the United States Senate," he continued, handing Lang a thick sheaf of papers, "I hereby serve you with this subpoena ordering you to testify before the Senate Select Committee on National Security on the twenty-seventh of next month."

Lang straightened his tie and ran the tip of his tongue over his upper lip. Like the racehorse he was, he had been ready to speak ever since he had received the subpoena. His fingertips ran absently over the edge of the thick blue binder next to the neat pile of documents on the green felt table in front of him. The television camera situated behind the ranking member in the Caucus Room of the Russell Senate Office Building was rolling, its red light reminding Lang that, once again, his face was on display all across the country.

"And now, Mr. Chairman," intoned Pennsylvania's bright young junior senator, "to you and this honorable committee, charged with the solemn responsibility to investigate allegations of wrongdoing, involving not merely violations of federal law but unlawful acts that may, in fact, have amounted to treason against the

United States of America, I am pleased to introduce the first witness in this public hearing, Christopher Lang."

Savvy politician that he was, the boyish, photogenic Senator Joe Zink was intent on stretching the fabric of Lang's credibility far enough to clothe himself in this highly political season and thus allowed the buzz caused by the mere mention of Lang's name to linger before continuing.

"And let me say by way of further preface, Mr. Chairman, that in executive session, counsel for this committee has already received unprecedented cooperation from witnesses coming forward to provide, for the first time ever, credible, verifiable testimony, on the record, regarding Russell Lindstrom's sale of a radar deflector to the North Vietnamese, his trading with the Iranians in the late '70s, and his illegally supplying armaments to the Contra rebels in Nicaragua."

The room came alive again, much louder this time, as the implications of the senator's words sunk in. The aging chairman tapped his gavel, though not with much conviction, lest the whole point of this exercise be confounded.

The young senator continued. "And I would further note that each and every witness has specifically cited Mr. Lang's unparalleled courage in the face of public opinion and extreme political pressure as their inspiration for coming forward." He paused again to revel in the reflected glory of the hero of the moment. "Without further preamble, then, Mr. Chairman, I believe that Mr. Lang has a prepared statement for the committee that will add new evidence of corruption and criminal activity by Mr. Lindstrom and his associates involving fraud in the defective design of an aircraft, the death of a test pilot, and the disappearance and death of key witnesses against Mr. Lindstrom. Mr. Lang?"

Seamus Callahan, wearing thick rubber fisherman's hip boots, waded in the surf of the eastern Atlantic, below the cliffs of Kilmurry. Seamus had made several trips to this place over the months. The official investigation was still open but there was little doubt that it would conclude that the murder had been the act of the Black Shamrock splinter group. It would be wrong, of course, thought Seamus bitterly, as he worked his way along a now familiar stretch of the Irish coast, but the fact that he couldn't prove anything to the contrary mattered little to him.

The sun was low in the western sky now and Seamus knew it was time to head back home. Maybe he would come again next weekend and maybe he wouldn't. Probably not. Time to let go of this business. His shoulders sagged as he trudged out of the low surf and headed for the wooden stairs back up the cliff. Halfway up, he turned and looked back, captured for the moment by the way the last rays of the afternoon sun cut through the clear water pooling at the surf line, dancing and sparkling in the rocks not twenty yards away. From where he stood, he could not see the light glinting off a metal object lying half-buried in the coarse sand, or read its simple inscription: The cause is just.

ABOUT THE
AUTHOR

GREGORY MICHAEL MACGREGOR IS THE SENIOR partner in MacGregor & Berthel, a boutique law firm in Los Angeles specializing in commercial litigation. A Phi Beta Kappa graduate of Fordham University and the University of Virginia School of Law, he has tried cases and argued appeals for more than twenty years in both state and federal courts. A native of Pittsburgh, he now lives in Southern California where he divides his time among the skiing, ballplaying, rollerblading, music-making, and dancing activities of his four children.